For Dan, thank you for everything

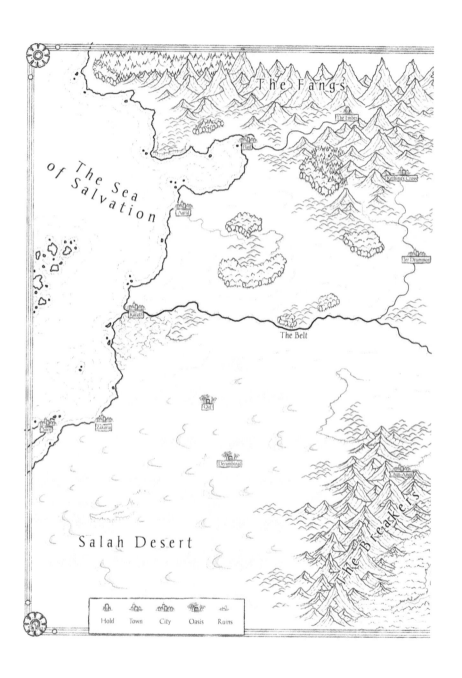

The Fangs

The Ember

Kething's Cross

The Sea
of Salvation

Hall

Aurid

Ier Drummon

Kerath

The Belt

Qar

Derambingi

Sorn

Zakaria

Chan-Anak

The Breakers

Salah Desert

Hold	Town	City	Oasis	Ruins

THE UMBRAL STORM

BOOK ONE OF THE SHARDED FEW

ALEC HUTSON

The Umbral Storm © 2022 by Alec Hutson
Published by Alec Hutson

Cover art by YAM
Cover design by Shawn King

Edited by Taya Latham

ISBN: 978-1-7342574-4-1 (ebook)
978-1-7342574-5-8 (print)

Please visit Alec's website at
www.authoralechutson.com

The Frayed Lands

Gendurdrang
(Ruins)

The Firemounts

The Duskhold

Phane

The Glass Sea

Ashasul

Kezekan Steppes
(The Anvil)

Zeman River

The Tangle

ALBIA

1

DERYN

DERYN SCRAPED the crust of his bread along the inside of his bowl, gathering up the dregs of his barley porridge. As he stuffed this last bite into his mouth his stomach grumbled, already complaining about the paltry meal. He chewed slowly, savoring the sensation of eating, and tried to ignore the pangs that had barely been assuaged after all the climbing he had done this morning.

"Dis all we get?" grumbled Xiv, the hairless Ashasai slave who could scurry up these trees better than any of them. His blade-sharp, copper-colored face was staring down at his empty bowl in disdain.

The fat overseer Jogan shrugged as he finished his own chunk of flatbread – which, Deryn noticed, was at least three times larger than the other pieces that had been distributed.

"I say, is dis all we get?" repeated Xiv, sliding off the root where he'd been perched and dropping to the forest floor.

Jogan did not look up at the Ashasai looming over him. "Bring down more crabs, get more food," he said through wheezing bites.

With a snort, Xiv tossed his bowl into the thick moss. "A few more days like dis, Jog, and none of us will have the strength to go up and get your damn snappers." He waved angrily at a glittering cloud of insects that had suddenly swarmed his head.

Jogan didn't respond to this, and after a moment Xiv turned sharply and stalked off into the underbrush, muttering to himself.

Deryn watched the Ashasai until the coiling serpents of mist closed around him. Even after he lost sight of Xiv, Deryn could still hear the slave cursing as he blundered through the trees, snapping branches and kicking at the forest detritus.

The rest of the men crouched in the clearing with their empty bowls seemed to share Xiv's sentiment, though they all remained quiet, their sullen faces watching the overseer as he noisily slurped the last of his porridge.

"I got one!"

Every face looked up as Chent emerged from among a thick lattice of branches and dark blue leaves. The noseless boy was scrambling down the black trunk of one of the tallest skyspear trees, descending so quickly that for a moment Deryn thought he was going to lose his grip and fall the rest of the way. But he didn't – Chent was skilled with his climbing glove, and he weighed little enough, even carrying the huge dead crab lashed to his back.

A low whistle came from one of the slaves, but Deryn couldn't tell who – like the rest of them, he was goggling at the size of the green-and-black mottled shell and its dangling segmented limbs. The larger of the crab's claws looked big enough to snip a man's head from his neck.

"There's a good lad," Jogan said warmly as the boy reached the ground and dumped his burden among the roots. Chent was breathing hard, his curly black hair plastered to his head. Some of that was certainly sweat, as climbing the trees was exhausting, but Deryn also suspected Chent had gone high enough that he'd passed into the clouds. He felt a little surge of respect for the boy, since the rest of them had avoided entering the cloudbank that had come rolling down the mountain this morning to swaddle the tops of the skyspears. After all, who knew what could be lurking up there?

"Another one," Chent said between gulping breaths. "Way near the top. Bigger even than this fella."

"That so," Jogan said, squinting through the tangle of leaves and branches at where the soaring trunk vanished into the murk.

"Aye," the boy said, picking his way over the roots to the porridge pot suspended above the dying fire. He scooped the last remaining bowl from the sack Deryn had carried here and began filling it with what remained in the pot.

Jogan had lingered at the base of the tree, still looking up. "Indentured," he drawled, and Deryn felt his stomach plummet into his feet. "Go bring me that other crab."

Chent flashed him a gloating smile, then bent over his bowl and began inhaling his food. The respect Deryn had briefly felt for the boy was washed away by the return of his customary dislike. Despite the two of them being nearly the same age, they had never been friends. Deryn suspected that was because Chent was a slave – he'd been sold to Master Ferith after having been caught stealing in Kething's Cross – while Deryn would be free again after the terms of his contract were completed. Which was, of course, also why Jogan wanted *him* to bring down the other crab Chent had discovered. It was dangerous up there, the bark slick from the cloud's condensation, and if Deryn fell to his death then Ferith would lose only two more years of free labor, rather than a lifetime.

Deryn slid from the stump where he'd been sitting and slowly stood. His palms were cold and sweaty, his heart thumping. The thought of going that high filled him with dread. But if he didn't do what the overseer commanded, then he'd be in violation of the contract his mother had signed, and under the law of the Shadow any punishment Master Ferith wished to dispense would be justified . . .

"Hurry up," Jogan growled, his face hardening when he noticed Deryn's hesitation.

"I go."

Deryn glanced over to see Xiv emerge from the underbrush fumbling with the laces of his breeches. The Ashasai frowned, staring upwards. "I be more like to bring down the snapper than dis one, yeah? And dat means more grub tomorrow. Better for all if I do the climb."

"No," Jogan said coldly, and the relief that had suddenly flooded Deryn just as quickly drained away. He knew that tone – there would be no swaying the overseer. "The indentured goes."

"But bosser –"

"It's all right," Deryn said quietly. Arguing was futile and would only annoy Jogan. After all, there were plenty of other ways for the overseer to make their lives miserable. Deryn bent to retrieve the climbing glove he'd tossed down earlier when he'd taken up his bowl. The faded leather was damp, the iron spike protruding from the center of the palm still crusted with bits of bark from the climb he'd done before lunch. He slipped it on, flexing his sore fingers.

Xiv stomped up next to him. His expression didn't suggest anger, but Deryn could see his black eyes blazing like coals in a hearth. "Be careful, boyo," he muttered. "Up dat high it's always damp. Bark gets rotten, as well as slippery. Make sure the spike is sunk deep and true before you pull yourself higher. Understand?"

"I do," Deryn replied, holding the Ashasai's dark gaze. "And thank you for trying to take my place."

"I just want the extra grub, lad," Xiv replied lightly, but Deryn knew that wasn't true. Or at least not entirely true. Among all the slaves, Xiv was the only one he'd consider a friend. The only one who didn't hold it against him that he'd never committed a crime and been sold into slavery, unlike the rest of them.

Steeling himself, Deryn picked his way over the nest of squirming roots and laid his ungloved hand against the skyspear's trunk. When he'd done that before, he'd thought he'd felt a thrumming deep within, as if there was a heart of mulch and vine somewhere pumping sap through the great trees. Not this time, though. That faint vibration might actually be there now, he supposed, but it was subsumed by the blood pounding in his own veins.

Feeling everyone's eyes on him, Deryn did his best to ignore their attention and slapped his climbing glove hard against the tree. The iron spike pierced the bark and lodged in the wood beneath, and, taking a deep breath, he reached with his other hand and grasped a knobby burl, then hauled himself up. With the toes of his boots he found purchase on another small imperfection in the trunk, and once he had his balance he wrenched his climbing glove free and stretched higher.

He quickly settled into the rhythm of the climb, and after he'd ascended past the first layer of large branches he slowed, knowing the others couldn't see him anymore. Some of his tension leaked away, but that only made him more aware of the aching muscles in his shoulders and arms. He'd been indentured to Master Ferith for nearly half a year, had climbed a hundred skyspear trees since the spring rains had finally washed away the snow, yet his body still wasn't as hard and knotted as some of the other slaves who had been crabbing for years.

After he'd ascended maybe a hundred handspan he paused to rest, squatting down on a bough wide enough that a horse could have stood on it without fear of falling. It was clearer up here; he'd climbed above the mist blanketing the forest floor, but had not yet reached where the skyspear passed into the low-lying clouds. Deryn leaned his back against the trunk and closed his eyes. For a moment he caught faint snatches of voices drifting up from below, but then the breeze strengthened and all he could hear was the whispering of the leaves as the wind slithered through the branches. These were the only moments he ever enjoyed now. Alone like this, he could briefly pretend his body didn't belong to someone else. That his mother was still alive, and when he climbed down from the tree he would return to their little hut and she'd be cooking mushrooms or trying to patch the sod on the roof, and then she'd admonish him for going out into the forest where fell cats prowled and kanths hunted. But in the end, she wouldn't be able to stay angry at him.

Deryn forced himself to open his eyes. He couldn't sit here, no matter how pleasant it felt. Jogan and the rest were waiting. If he took too long, the overseer would send up someone else, and Deryn would suffer an inventive punishment for his failure. Jogan was as stupid as an ox by most measures, but in this one way he was surprisingly imaginative. On other days, Deryn could have found a comfortable perch and daydreamed of happier times, but not now. He had to go beyond the middle branches, which he'd been afraid to do ever since he'd first stood at the base of a skyspear and gazed in awe and dread at the towering trees.

Deryn pushed himself to his feet, then nearly lost his balance as something winged fluttered past his face. He watched a huge moth the color of the harvest moon spiral higher through the maze of branches and leaves, towards where the trunk was swallowed by the ghostly fingers creeping down from above. That was where he needed to go, unfortunately. Sighing, he started climbing again.

He found the crab almost as soon as the whiteness enveloped him. It was sunk into the trunk, as if it had been there for years and the bark had slowly grown over the edges of its shell. It was hard to tell where the tree ended and the crab began. Deryn thought it was more likely it had burrowed into the wood, but to be truthful, he knew little about these creatures . . . except that the rich folk of Kething's Cross prized their meat and carapaces.

And this one would command quite a price, he suspected. Its shell was beautifully mottled and massive enough to be worn as a breastplate, and the meat in its larger claw could feed a family. Or a single gluttonous merchant, Deryn supposed, remembering the elaborate meals his mother had helped prepare when she'd worked in the kitchens of a rich house.

It wasn't moving, and Deryn entertained the thought it might be dead. That would certainly make things easier, as the hardest part of crabbing was killing the thrice-cursed things while clinging to the side of a skyspear hundreds of span above the ground. Jogan would be disappointed, since the meat would be spoiled, but he could hardly blame Deryn.

That flicker of hope was extinguished when he noticed the crab's antennae suddenly twitch. Such a movement usually suggested the crab had noticed something strange, and that meant it would soon –

"No, no, no!" he cried, as with a crack the crab's legs and shell lifted from the tree. Bits of bark rained down on Deryn, and he had to shield his face with his ungloved hand. When the cascade stopped, he saw that the crab was scuttling higher with surprising speed.

Deryn followed as fast as he could, praying that in his haste he did not plunge his climbing spike into a rotten bit of wood. Luckily, the branches this high up were much smaller, and he found a few of them easy to grip with his off-hand.

The distance between him and the crab shrank. He lunged, hoping to grab hold of it, but the crab moved just before his fingers closed around one of its legs, and his hand smacked against the trunk. He scrabbled for something to hold on to, but he only tore away a chunk of slimy bark, and for a moment he was unbalanced, his entire weight supported by the single climbing spike. His feet kicked desperately, searching for something to stand on, and he knew that his life spun at the end of a fraying rope.

Then his foot found a knot protruding from the bark, and with a gasp of relief he pressed himself tightly to the damp trunk. He drew in a shuddering breath before looking up again. To his surprise, the crab had not retreated higher. Instead, it had rotated its body so that its head and claws were pointing at Deryn, its antennae waving frantically.

The damn thing wanted to fight.

"All right, then," Deryn muttered, slipping his crabbing knife from his belt. It was a long, thin stiletto that tapered to a wickedly sharp point. Perfect for piercing a crab's head and lodging in what passed for its brain . . . but Deryn had only ever done that after holding one of the things immobilized against the trunk. Not when a crab was trying to *duel* with him.

As if to discourage him from coming any closer, the crab's larger claw opened and then snapped shut. The clacking sound was surprisingly loud, and Deryn had no illusions about what would happen if the claw closed around his arm or hand. The thought of losing fingers or being otherwise mutilated by an angry tree crab was as surreal as it was sobering.

That wasn't going to happen. Gritting his teeth, Deryn pulled himself higher, to where he could stand on a large branch without having to keep his climbing glove attached to the trunk. He felt a surge of confidence having his feet set beneath him, and he smiled grimly. The crab's larger claw was only a few span from his face, but the creature seemed to be wavering now, as if unsure whether it wanted to fight or flee.

Deryn didn't let it decide. Lunging upwards, he grabbed one of the crab's front legs and pulled hard. Its other legs tore free of the bark with a crackle, and it made a rasping chirp that almost sounded like an exclamation of surprise. Deryn leaped back a step and slammed the crab on the branch he stood upon, stunning the creature. Its arms waved sluggishly as he pressed his knee onto its shell, pinning it to the wood as it tried to rise, and then he reached around to jam his knife right between its eyes. The blade slid in with barely any resistance, and immediately the crab sagged in death.

Deryn stayed kneeling on the creature's carapace for quite some time, waiting for his breathing and heart to finally come under control. He'd acted purely on instinct, and now that he could consider what he'd done, it was terrifyingly clear that even a slight misstep would have sent him plummeting to his death. Slowly he stood, pulling his knife from the crab and doing his best to wipe it clean on the skyspear's bark despite his shaking hands. Now he had to make the climb down with this thing slung across his back . . .

"Please."

The voice was a ragged whisper, just loud enough to be heard over the breeze rustling the leaves. With an alarmed cry, Deryn whirled around brandishing his crabber's knife, then nearly dropped it when he saw what was there.

A girl crouched on the same branch, but farther out, near where it was barely large enough to stand. She was perhaps a few years younger than him, with a wild tangle of matted blonde hair and eyes the color and luminescence of dark jade. Her clothing was tattered and much too small for her knobby arms and legs.

"Who . . ." Deryn rasped, staring at this bizarre apparition that had seemingly materialized out of thin air. "Who are you?"

She ignored his question, her brilliant gaze sliding from him to the crab at his feet. "Please give it to me."

Deryn blinked. She wanted the crab? The girl shifted, and he realized he could see her bones moving under the thin fabric of her shift. She looked like she was on the brink of starvation.

"Please, we need to eat," she murmured.

Deryn's thoughts whirled. What was she doing here? There were no girls in the tiny community where the crabbers lived, only a few folk that had been too old or stubborn to leave when the lumber mill closed. Was she lost? But it would take several days to hike to Kething's Cross, with all sorts of dangers lurking in the forest, and there were no other towns or villages anywhere nearby.

"I have to bring the crab back," he said.

"I know," the girl replied softly, her eyes glimmering with unshed tears. "But he'll die if I don't get him food."

Him? So there were others out here in the woods? Deryn glanced around, as if they could be watching from the swirling murk.

She lowered her head until her bangs obscured her face, and he thought he saw a glittering drop fall.

"Wait," Deryn said quickly. "Don't cry." He could sense her desperation. The girl almost reminded him of his mother in her last few days . . .

"Take it," he said, swallowing back the lump in his throat as he stepped away from the crab's carcass. Carefully, he retreated to another branch, trying to seem as unthreatening as possible.

She edged closer, watching him warily. Her balance was incredible, Deryn realized, as if she had lived her whole life in these trees, and she didn't seem remotely concerned about the several hundred-span drop yawning on either side of the narrow branch. Where had she come from?

Suddenly, she darted next to the crab and grabbed it by its smaller claw. Her eyes were wide and fearful, but she appeared to relax slightly when she realized he wasn't about to leap at her. Showing surprising strength, she lifted the dead crab and slung it over her shoulder, then began to back slowly away.

"Goodbye," Deryn said, raising his hand in farewell.

She paused just before she was swallowed by the whiteness. "Thank you," she said solemnly, pressing her hand to her brow in what Deryn assumed was a gesture of gratitude. And then she was gone, the branch shivering slightly as her weight disappeared. Deryn noticed a massive shadow recessed in the mist – another tree, and it must have been close enough that she could cross over to one of its branches.

He stayed there for a long moment watching where she had vanished, his mind churning with questions, until a noise from below made him glance down.

"Oh no," he murmured as he locked gazes with the boy clinging to the trunk. Chent's mouth had dropped open in surprise, and his eyes were wide.

He'd seen. He must have.

"Chent!" he cried out, but the noseless boy had already started to shimmy down the tree.

A coldness formed in the pit of his stomach. Overseer Jogan was not going to be happy about this.

2

DERYN

THE OTHERS IGNORED him as they traipsed back through the forest. Deryn had been expecting a spittle-flecked tirade from Jogan when he finally descended the skyspear, but the overseer had only stared at him coldly for a long moment before turning away and shouting at the other slaves to begin gathering up what they'd brought with them. In some ways, that was even more worrying. It suggested Jogan was going to let Master Ferith decide his punishment, and Deryn truly didn't know what his contract-holder might do. Could he have Deryn flogged? Cut a sigil into his flesh, like the marks carved into the brows of the other slaves? Maybe he'd simply tear up the contract his mother had signed, drive Deryn away from the old logging camp and into the woods. He doubted he'd survive the night if that happened.

As if to punctuate that thought, a raucous chittering erupted from somewhere deeper among the trees. Distracted by the sound, Deryn stumbled over a root, nearly dropping the sack filled with their bowls and climbing gear. Kanths. He'd glimpsed those dog-sized insects a few times as they scurried through the underbrush, black chitin gleaming and serrated jaws spread wide. A single kanth was unnerving, if not truly frightening, but Xiv had told him about seeing a wounded stag swarmed by the insects, how dozens had boiled out of an underground nest to consume every scrap of flesh in moments. Ever since then, Deryn had been hesitant to venture off the old paths the loggers had hacked out of the forest.

Most of the slaves were keeping their distance from Deryn, their mouths thinned and eyes hard. They knew that by failing to return with the crab Deryn had lost them an extra helping of bread and porridge, and it didn't look like they were going to forgive him anytime soon. Even Xiv seemed troubled, and when Deryn managed to meet his gaze the Ashasai quickly glanced away. Only Chent appeared to be in a good mood, whistling cheerfully as he practically skipped his way through the forest, the massive crab he had killed dangling over his shoulder.

Usually Deryn felt relief when the listing bulk of the old lumber mill appeared through the trees, as it meant he would be safe from the forest's dangers until the next day, but this time he felt a tremor of apprehension. He knew some sort of punishment awaited him. Hopefully, he would simply be denied supper, though from the worrying glances Xiv kept casting his way he thought that unlikely.

The sky had darkened on their return hike, and light was already spilling from the mill's windows and doorway. Inside, Old Mim would be chopping vegetables and washing mushrooms and cleaning whatever animals Master Ferith and his son had caught that day. They'd certainly eaten better since the boy and his father had arrived a few months ago, though the slaves would have preferred if their owner had stayed in Kething's Cross, as his presence had resulted in Jogan becoming far more strict.

The shadowy silhouette of the mountain loomed behind the old mill, and Deryn could faintly hear the rumble of the distant waterfall as it crashed into the lake. The rains the night before that had sent the clouds tumbling down the slopes and into the forest must have also swollen the streams higher up the mountain, as the falls sounded louder than most days. He hadn't heard it since the day his mother had died. Thinking of her drew his gaze to the ruins of their small hut. She'd worked so hard to patch the roof and reinforce the sagging walls, but less than a year since it had been abandoned the forest looked to have nearly reclaimed it fully. The pang in his heart he usually felt when staring at what was left of their home was absent – perhaps because he was nervous about what Jogan would do to him tonight for losing the crab.

"Go on, get a fire going," the overseer said, pushing open the lichen-scarred door to the slave barracks. Once it had been a store-house for the felled trees before they were cut into more manageable portions and dispatched to Kething's Cross, but when the crabbers had occupied what remained of the logging camp it had become the communal sleeping area. A dozen pallets lined the walls, and a fire trench was cut through the center of the room, already filled with kindling.

"Get warm," Jogan said gruffly as they filed into the barracks. He snorted and spat out a wad of something vile, then motioned for Chent to hand him the crab the boy had carried back to the camp. "Food bell will ring after I talk with the boss. I'm sure he'll want to hear what happened today." He gave Deryn a long look before turning and vanishing into the gloaming, the door banging shut behind him.

For a long moment, they all stood there staring at each other. "I swears to the deepest black, boy," muttered Samt, a wiry old man with a scar running through one milky eye, "if you bring down some-thin' on all our heads I'll ..."

"You'll do what, chained?" Xiv shot back, taking the sack Deryn had been carrying and tossing it on the floor. "Hurt him without the boss's say and it'll be your hide he stripes. And you know it. So settle down and mind only yourself."

Samt gave Deryn a dark look, but he turned away without saying anything further.

"Dat's what I thought," Xiv muttered, taking Deryn's arm and steering him towards the corner of the barracks they shared.

"Do you think this will truly cause a big problem?" Deryn whispered, unnerved by the venom in the old slave's voice.

Xiv shrugged. "I dunno. If just Jogan was here, maybe you'd

miss a few suppers. But the big boss can be right harsh." He pursed his lips, squinting at Deryn like he was having trouble understanding something. "Why did you do it, boyo? What happened up there?"

Deryn sank down on his pallet. He felt the attention of the rest drift from him, the rising hum of conversations and the clink and clatter as a few of the slaves worked to ignite the fire trench. He put his head in his hands, climbing-sore fingers kneading his scalp.

"A girl. One moment she wasn't there, the next she was. She must have watched me kill the crab, because as soon as I plunged the knife in she appeared, begging for me to give it to her."

"And you did. Dat's what dat little git Chent said when he came down."

Deryn nodded. "She looked so hungry. She said someone would die if she didn't come back with food. She looked like . . ." *My mother.* He swallowed, unable to finish that thought. She hadn't of course. His mother had been tall and fire-haired. But there had been something in the girl's eyes, that same desperation he remembered in the days before the end . . .

"Who was she?"

Xiv sighed, sitting down on his own pallet with his hands on his knees. "Must be the hermit's girl."

"The who?"

"They been here as long as we have, so more den two years, at least. Old man livin' out in the deep woods. And his daughter, we s'possed. Never came to the mill and stayed well away, sometimes one o' us would just catch a glimpse when we were crabbing, dem watching us. Always went away quick, even if we cried out friendly-like. Hadn't seen dem since before you and your mother arrived, so I thought they'd moved on or died. Seem like dis is her, though."

Deryn remembered how her tattered clothes had clung to her thin body, the hollowness of her eyes as she'd begged him to share what he'd just caught.

"They might not live much longer."

"Or maybe you saved dem," Xiv said with a gleaming white grin.

"Crab like dat could feed a man and a girl for a few days, give dem the strength to go out hunting again. Maybe you a hero, boyo."

"Do you think Master Ferith will think that?"

Xiv punched him lightly on the shoulder. "So long as the gutters of Ashasai run red, there is hope."

"What does that mean?"

"Never you mind, boyo." The copper-skinned slave lay back on his pallet, pillowing his head with his hands. "And get some rest."

Xiv's breathing settled into a sleep-grooved rhythm, but even though Deryn's exhaustion was bone-deep he stayed awake staring at the patched ceiling. This was usually when he napped, between returning from a long day of crabbing and the ringing of the dinner bell, but he was still brimming with nervous energy. The other slaves were also anticipating something, as they kept casting him sidelong glances from where they huddled beside the fire trench or were relaxing in their own pallets, but none of them tried to confront him as Samt had earlier.

After a while, rain began to whisper against the roof. It would be another wet day tomorrow, the skyspears slick and dangerous. Deryn turned on his side, facing the wall. How had he ended up here? Why had his mother abandoned him to *this*? Always cold, always hungry. Always scared that the next time he went up a tree a chunk of bark would tear loose and he'd end up a shattered heap among the roots at the bottom. And that no one would care. Maybe Xiv. The other slaves would mutter a prayer to the Broken God before dragging his corpse into the bushes for the fell cats to devour, like they'd done with Rhogan last month. The thought made Deryn's eyes prickle, and he quickly wiped away the gathering tears. He didn't want Chent or any of the rest of them to see him cry.

The door banged open. Deryn sat up, for a moment confused why anyone would be visiting the slaves before dinner, during their daily rest time. Then his heart fell when he saw the huge silhouette of the overseer filling the entranceway. Jogan stepped inside, his piggish little eyes fixed on Deryn. His clothes clung to his body, and he did not look pleased to have just been forced to walk through the cold rain.

"Indentured!" he shouted across the barracks, then beckoned Deryn to come to him. "With me."

The other slaves had all stopped what they'd been doing, watching silently. Deryn swallowed, unnerved by their attention, and stood from his pallet. As he started to make his way towards the glowering overseer, Xiv's hand shot out and grabbed his wrist.

"Take it with your head up, boyo. Don't let dem see you hurt."

Deryn nodded, and Xiv let him go. Taking a deep breath, he held his head higher and squared his shoulders. Whatever punishment Jogan or Master Ferith had dreamed up, it couldn't hurt as much as the tragedies that had brought him here. He'd get through it.

Deryn startled when Chent called out to him as he passed where the noseless boy crouched beside the trench. The slave sigil burned into his forehead shimmered in the glow of the fire. "Pride ain't gonna help you now, indentured."

"What?"

The slave's lip curled as he stared at Deryn through narrowed eyes. "You think you're like one of the Sharded Few, better than others. But you're as worthless as the rest of us. Best you learn that." He turned his back to Deryn and spat, his spittle sizzling in the trench.

I know it, he almost said, but the words caught in his throat. Indentured and abandoned, bastard son of a dead madwoman. Deryn wanted to feel anger towards Chent, take comfort in that swell of hot red rage, but to his surprise he just felt sorry for the boy. Chent was as alone and helpless as he was. Truthfully, it was stupid for them to hate each other.

"I'm sorry," he said to the slave's back. Chent stiffened slightly before he turned away, but the boy didn't say anything more as Deryn trailed Jogan out into the rain.

It was coming down harder than he'd thought, drumming the

ground and hissing upon the leaves of the trees encroaching on their camp. Jogan motioned for him to follow, then set off on a jiggling run towards the old mill. Deryn hunched his shoulders against the rain and jogged after him. The overseer was just a shadow, as the last shreds of twilight were almost completely obscured by the dark clouds that had settled over the camp.

Jogan didn't make for the main entrance of the mill, the large set of double doors that opened onto the communal hall where the slaves ate their meals with the rest of the inhabitants of the old logging camp. Instead, he led Deryn around the building, to where an annex had been grafted onto the side of the structure. This was the place Deryn had been expecting to be taken, as it was where Master Ferith and his son spent much of their time after moving here from Kething's Cross, but still he felt a ripple of fear as they approached. None of the slaves ever wanted to be summoned here.

"In you go," Jogan commanded, pushing open the door and motioning for Deryn to precede him. He ducked under the oddly low lintel, blinking at the brightness within. Lanterns hung from the walls and candles were scattered about on all the flat surfaces, as if in an attempt to banish every possible shadow. An image of kneeling beside his mother in a vast, echoing temple swam up from the depths of his memory, the air spiced with incense as she lit a votive candle in honor of the Broken God.

There was nothing else that evoked the sacred in this room. The chairs and tables scattered about were ornately carved, if a bit worn, but the wood of the floor was rotted and stained with black mold. A faded tapestry on the wall depicted a man thrusting a spear through the chest of a squealing boar, light spilling from a bright point set into his brow. Beside this figure was a servant holding a spare spear, and the resemblance to Master Ferith and his son was unmistakable. Had one of the slaver's ancestors truly been Hollow, in service to the Sharded Few? That would be surprising. A man in hunting leathers with the same color hair as the servant in the tapestry stood in the center of the room, leaning against what looked like a hitching post for a horse. Since this clearly had never been a stable, Deryn wondered uneasily why it had been placed here. Master Ferith's face was flushed, and as he watched Deryn step inside he took a sip from a silver goblet, then seemed to grimace at the taste.

"Hardly the best vintage," he said, but not to Deryn. A boy moved out from behind a wooden screen, smoothing down the tunic he had just donned. His cheeks were also ruddy and his black hair slick, as if he had just recently come inside. Out of the corner of his eye, Deryn noticed a pair of longbows and quivers leaning against the wall, still glistening. It looked like Master Ferith and his son had just returned from the hunt. Given the slaver's sour expression, it didn't appear to have gone well.

Deryn sensed Jogan's bulk join him inside the annex, and then a hand pushed him roughly from behind. He stumbled forward, barely catching himself before he went sprawling on the threadbare carpet.

"Here he is, boss."

"I can see that," Master Ferith murmured, setting down his goblet on a table beside a decanter half full of dark wine. The slaver was slightly shorter than Deryn, but it felt like he was looking down on him from on high.

"Who's this?" the boy asked, adjusting his frilled cuffs as he came up beside his father and began pouring himself a glass.

"This is one of my crabbers," Master Ferith said, crossing his arms. "Though after today, I'm not sure he deserves that description."

The boy drank from his goblet. Along with the midnight-black hair, he also had the same aristocratic features as his father, most notably a hooked nose and sharp chin. "Truly?" he said after he'd swallowed his wine. "Then where is our sigil, Father?" His eyes suddenly widened. "Oh! Is this the one you signed the contract with last fall? The indentured?"

"Aye, it's him," Master Ferith answered, taking up his goblet again and studying Deryn with pursed lips. "You *are* indentured to me, aren't you, boy?"

Deryn hesitated for a moment, surprised to be addressed by the slaver, and Jogan's heavy hand smacked him again between his shoulder blades.

"Yes," he finally managed, eliciting a satisfied grunt from the overseer.

"Then why," Master Ferith continued, swirling his goblet, "are you here before me right now?"

"I . . ." His mind was a scrap of blank parchment. How could he even begin to describe what had happened?

"Jogan," the slaver said simply, and a moment later a heavy blow struck Deryn on the back of his head.

This time, he did fall to his knees, spots of color blooming in his vision as he struggled to focus on the carpet's faded pattern.

"Answer the boss," the overseer growled, and Deryn braced himself for another clouting.

It didn't come, though, and he raised his ringing head to find the slaver and his son regarding him impassively.

"There was a girl," he said quickly. "In the tree. She looked hungry, and she said someone else was starving and needed food. So I let her take the crab I'd killed."

"A girl in the tree?" the boy said in obvious disbelief.

His father held up his hand. "Another slave said the same, Heth."

"But where would she have come from, Father? Kething's Cross is days away, and there's nothing else out here."

"Jogan tells me an old man and a young girl were living in the woods before we even arrived," Master Ferith said. "A recluse, maybe a madman. The crabbers have glimpsed them once or twice, as have the others living here at the camp. They usually stay far away, though. Something must have happened for the girl to approach so brazenly."

"The old man," the boy mused, then took another quick drink. He looked troubled, Deryn thought.

"I suppose so," the slaver replied. "But truthfully, I do not care one whit about some hermit and his daughter. What I want to know is why *you* do." He was staring at Deryn now, his eyes hard.

"She needed help," he replied quietly. "She was starving."

Ferith frowned. "And you are well-fed? Perhaps if that's true, I should reduce the rations of the men. We apparently are doing so splendidly that we can share our bounty with strangers." He let out a deep, long-suffering sigh. "I saved you, boy. Your mother came to me knowing you both would not survive the winter out here. She offered three years of her own life first, but of course you must know why I refused her. And so we settled on you. Three years of food and shelter and transportation back to Kething's Cross when the contract finished, and in return you would work for me like you were one of my own." The slaver shook his head, almost sadly, and reached down for the handle of something lying beside the wine pitcher on the side table. But this only registered for Deryn peripherally, as his mind was whirling at what Ferith had just claimed. His mother had tried to indenture herself first? Why had she not told him that?

The hiss of leather sliding across wood brought his attention back to the slaver. In Ferith's hand was a flail, three wickedly knotted leather cords dangling down to brush the floor. Deryn's stomach tightened at the sight – he'd never suffered under the lash before, but he'd seen the marks on the bodies of the other slaves.

"Jogan," Ferith said, and the overseer seized hold of Deryn roughly and led him over to the wooden post in the center of the room. He wanted to pull away, but he also knew that any resistance would make what was coming even worse. Jogan forced Deryn to his knees and pulled off his ragged tunic, nearly tearing it, then looped a length of rope around his wrists and with practiced movements bound him to the post.

"Perhaps you misunderstand the terms of the contract we signed," Ferith murmured, coming closer. He'd set down his wine glass, and as he approached he was thwacking his palm with the flail rhythmically. "You are mine for three years. When you disobey an order from Jogan, you are betraying me."

Deryn braced himself for what he knew was coming. There would be pain, but he'd felt pain before. At least Master Ferith wasn't driving him away from the camp and into the forest. That would have certainly meant his death.

"Heth," the slaver said, holding out the flail to his son. "You will punish him."

The black-haired boy nearly choked on his wine. "Father?" he managed after recovering from the brief spasm of coughing.

"He stole from you as much as me. A crab that size would be worth a dozen silver valanii in the market of Kething's Cross."

"I'm not sure I –"

"Put down the blasted wine and take the scourge," his father commanded sharply, cutting off his son's stammering.

The boy locked gazes with Deryn. His eyes were wide with surprise.

Ferith stepped closer to his son, taking the cup from him and thrusting out the flail. "Don't feel sorry for him," he growled. "The indentured is a thief. He took what belonged to you. Show him the consequences of such behavior. Surely it outrages you as much as it does me."

"It does," the boy said quietly, his hand closing around the flail's handle. Deryn lost sight of Heth as he approached and moved around behind him. "Such arrogance from a slave."

"Not a slave," Deryn said, surprised by the strength of his voice. "An indentured."

"Quiet," Jogan hissed angrily, raising his hand. Deryn flinched, but the overseer was just holding out a small worn piece of wood. It had strange markings on it, as if it had been chewed. "Bite down on this, boy," he urged, and there was a note in his voice that surprised Deryn. "Unless you want to swallow your tongue."

He hesitated a moment, but then let the overseer shove the length of wood into his mouth. It tasted like blood, stale and coppery.

Would it truly hurt so much he might have bitten off his own tongue? It couldn't be as bad as—

Flame licked Deryn's back.

He gave a muffled cry. Bile rose in his throat and he gagged, nearly spitting out the wood.

"Barely a tickle." Master Ferith sounded annoyed, like his son had disappointed him. "By the Silver Shrike, show the boy who the master is!"

Another burning lash. Warmth trickled down his throbbing back as he squeezed his eyes shut, willing himself to fall into the blackness.

From somewhere far away came a derisive snort. "He will laugh at you with the other slaves! Why should any of them do what we ask if *this* is all they can expect as punishment?"

Pain again, searing this time. It felt like a piece of him had been carved off, leaving him exposed. Before he could fully comprehend this agony, another blow landed. Then another. And another. He was slipping away, hooked claws sinking into his flesh and dragging him beneath the rising waters . . .

"Yes, that's it! Good lad! He won't forget what he's done with the scars you're giving him. Again! Again! Aga—"

3

HETH

HETH LEANED over and watched the line of red unspool in the water. For a moment it was like a ball of twine unraveling, a single plucked thread slipping from his submerged finger, then he plunged his hands fully into the water and the darkness billowed out to fill the basin.

Heth raised his dripping hands, marveling at the starkness of the sudden change. They'd been stained red, warm and slick with the boy's blood. Now they were clean and white again, except for where the rough handle of the flail had abraded his palm. He'd held it too tight. With a shaking thumb he massaged that splotch of redness, willing it to disappear, for if his father happened to see the mark he'd no doubt make some cutting comment. How he shouldn't let the just disciplining of a slave affect him so. How he should neither take pleasure in the act nor dread it. How the lash was a necessary tool of a master.

He needed to make his hands stop shaking.

"Enough," he hissed, hating his weakness. With one hand he clutched the other, forcing an end to the trembling. "It's over," he murmured to himself, breathing in deep and then letting it out slowly.

The boy had deserved his beating. The stupid, scrawny boy who had given one of their valuable crabs away. There were fewer and fewer of the crabs now, he knew. On a good day, the slaves would return with only three or four, most so small that the merchants of Kething's Cross lifted their noses in disdain and would offer only a few valanii. If the catch dwindled any further, his father would be forced to sell most of the men to the mines of the Duskhold, and very few of them would live more than a few more years after that. The boy had suffered tonight, yes, but if it spurred the rest to bring down more crabs and make their operation here profitable again, then it was worth it.

He repeated that thought over and over again as he stared at his hands, willing the tremors to stop. To be fair, he hadn't started shaking until his father had pressed his hands to the flayed back of the unconscious boy and told him he should remember this first bloodying.

"Master Heth."

He turned, cradling his hand to his chest like he had hurt it. One of the old men of this accursed little village stood in the doorway, watery eyes watching him from under a single bristling white brow. Like most of the rest who had been living here when they'd arrived, this ancient creature now served his father for a meager helping of the food he provided to his slaves every night. Heth had never bothered to learn his name. Maybe he didn't even have one – Jogan had told him that when his father's men had first come to the old logging camp, the people still living here had nearly regressed to a more savage state.

"What is it?" he snapped.

"Mam Mim says the stew is near ready. Yer father's already in the hall, and he's asking for ye."

"I'll be there shortly," Heth replied, scowling when he noticed the old man's gaze lingering on his hands. "Go away," he commanded, reaching for a cloth to dry himself.

The old man nodded, ducking his head in a paltry excuse for a bow before turning away. That only annoyed Heth further. He couldn't help but remember when they'd lived in the big house, and how the servants in their gold-trimmed damask uniforms had flourished the most beautiful bows when his father had demanded something. Now here they were, scratching a living from this cold, forsaken forest.

But they'd get it back. They'd get it all back. The blood of the Hollow and the holds ran in their veins, and his father had not yet exhausted all the favors he was owed. Su Canaav was an old and proud name, and it *would* rise again.

Only if he was strong, though. Ruthless and clever, like his father. Not a sniveling coward, weak-kneed at the sight of his slave's blood on his hands. Wait, no. Not a slave – indentured.

Not that it truly mattered.

After the old man left, Heth stayed behind for a moment to finish composing himself. He wondered how the boy was doing – Jogan had dragged him out after his father had finally instructed him to stop the beating, and for a moment before they'd vanished back out into the rain he'd stirred, his eyes fluttering open as he slurred something about his mother. Heth had never met the woman, as he'd arrived months after she'd killed herself, but his father had spoken of her once when telling him the story of his new indentured servant. She'd been a madwoman, apparently, driven out of Kething's Cross after a scandal. For some bizarre reason, she'd come here with her son, to this miserable little hamlet, and tried to survive with an almost complete lack of woodcraft. His father had denied her request to work for him and thus share in the communal food he dispensed every evening – she was prone to strange fits, he had told Heth, screaming at things no one else could see, and her behavior made the other villagers uneasy. But her son did not share the same affliction, and his father had agreed to feed them if she signed away his life for a few years. A reasonable trade, considering they would have certainly starved out here this past winter. But she must have thought otherwise, as soon after she'd gone and thrown herself into the nearby lake. Or maybe her madness had finally overwhelmed her.

Truly, if one was prone to melancholia this village was about the last place Heth would advise coming to. It was cold and damp from the mists rolling off the mountains, surrounded by a dark forest of trees so tall that little sunlight reached the ground. He'd found his own thoughts turning bleak ever since his father had summoned him from Kething's Cross, pulling him away from the taverns and sword-halls he loved so much. Supposedly it was so he could learn this crab-bing business and how to manage the family slaves, but Heth knew his father's finances were precarious. With his mother dead and Heth brought here, the ancestral Su Canaav manse could be shuttered and most of the servants let go, saving a small fortune in upkeep.

Sighing, Heth fiddled with the brass buttons on his waistcoat. His father might be suffering from an avalanche of ill-luck, but still he insisted that Heth keep up appearances. If he did not dress like a master, the slaves would not see him as one. That was one of the first lessons his father had taught him, and it was true even out here, at the ragged edge of civilization.

Finally satisfied, Heth strode from his room in the small house he shared with his father. It was a hundred paces to where the old mill loomed dark and shadowy against the night sky, but thankfully the heavy rain from earlier had slackened into little more than a prick-ling mist. Even still, he hurried towards the huge doors, as he didn't want to have to sit through dinner in wet clothes. As he crossed the clearing, his gaze drifted to the long building that now housed the slaves. The boy would be inside, he knew. It would be several days until he'd be able to rise from his cot without help. Heth forced himself to look away from the muted glow coming from within. The boy had learned a valuable lesson in obedience, and he'd made his father proud. He shook his head, trying to clear it of unwelcome thoughts, then muttered a curse when he realized his hand had started shaking again.

Warmth washed over him as he entered the building. Many years ago when this old mill had processed skyspear saplings, a man had stood in a saw pit in the center of this great room and worked in partnership with another above to cut the massive trees. The saw they'd used was long gone, but the pit had been repurposed into a hearth, and a huge fire was now devouring a great heap of kindling. Stones had been mounded around this firepit to help contain the blaze, and a hole had been cut out of the sod roof to let the smoke escape. The only times Heth felt warm in this cold, wet village were evenings like these in this makeshift hall, with the flames dancing and the wine flowing.

Tonight the mood was a bit more somber than usual, despite the blazing fire. At one long trestle table sat most of the elderly residents of this community, save for the ones involved in the preparation or serving of this evening's meal. They certainly remembered the halcyon days of this mill, when slabs of skyspear hardwood destined for the manses of Kething's Cross and places even more exotic flowed out its doors and along the forest road that wended through the foothills of the Fangs. Perhaps that was what they were thinking about now as they watched the fire with slack faces and empty gazes.

The slaves sat around another table, eight men who represented most of his father's remaining wealth. Two were missing, he noticed – the indentured servant Deryn, unsurprisingly, but also the hairless Ashasai. He must have stayed in the barracks to care for the boy. Heth squirreled away this knowledge for later – his father had told him many times that it was useful for masters to understand the relationships between their slaves. Often, the most powerful pressure point was not the threat of harm to a slave, but harm to someone they cared about deeply.

Most of the slaves looked sullen, which he supposed was to be expected after one of their own had just suffered a lashing. Not all – that noseless boy Chent was grinning like a simpleton, brazenly meeting his eyes as he crossed the room. Heth frowned to show his displeasure at this impudence, and the boy hurriedly lowered his gaze. He kept smiling, though. Apparently, there must be some enmity between the two youngest members of his father's stable. Another tidbit to store away.

His father was seated at another table, closer to the flames. Flanking him were k'Tel and k'Pan, his zemani bodyguards, their scales glowing reddish-gold in the light from the fire. Jogan was there as well, his attention focused completely on the food laid out on the table – a huge iron tureen, from which wisps of steam were rising; several platters of dried sliced meat; an assortment of vegetables and mushrooms; and – of course – a silver decanter of wine that already looked to have been half-emptied. A veritable feast, by the standards of this place.

"Father," Heth said, sliding into his customary chair. The goblet he'd been drinking from in his father's makeshift drawing room had been moved here and refilled.

Ferith nodded at him, then picked up a small bell that had been placed next to his hand and rang it once. Before the chime had faded, the hall was filled with the sounds of two dozen men falling upon their food like ravenous wolves.

"You took your time," his father murmured, then sipped his wine.

"Apologies," Heth replied, though he didn't try to make up a reason for his lateness. His father always seemed to know when he was being less than truthful.

"Meat's gone cold," Jogan grumbled, shoveling a healthy portion onto his plate.

"Doesn't look like that bothers you very much," Heth shot back, not trying to hide his disgust at how much food the fat overseer had already hoarded in front of himself in the moments since his father had announced the start of the meal.

Jogan chuckled as he reached for a gnarled purple fruit. "Not my fault if you lost your appetite after what you did earlier. Some men can't stand the sight of blood, even if it's not their own."

Heth's jaw tightened, and he had the strong desire to throw his wine in the overseer's fat face.

"Jogan," his father said in a calm voice that would have sent chills down the spine of anyone who knew him well. "What are you saying about my son?"

"Nothing," the overseer muttered, ducking his head to avoid

meeting his master's eyes. A flush was creeping up his neck, as if he realized he had overstepped.

One of the zemani croaked a laugh at Jogan's obvious discomfort. K'Tel, Heth guessed, though he always had trouble telling the lizardlings apart. K'Pan was a bit more reserved, his thoughts hidden behind glittering black eyes, while his clutch brother sometimes almost seemed human in how he expressed his emotions. They were both warrior caste and fiercely loyal to his father, bonded for life just after hatching, one of the last tangible traces of his family's former wealth.

"Enough bickering," his father said sternly, stabbing a slice of grey meat with his knife. "Jogan, tell me how the hunt has gone recently. There were two channelers on the same skyspear – do you believe this grove has more crabs of that size to give up? Or should we move on to the southern slopes?"

Heth settled back in his chair and drank deep of his wine as the overseer began to drone on about spawning sites and migration patterns compared to past years. Truly, he couldn't conceive of a more boring topic. Heth's thoughts wandered as the conversation receded, and he idly picked at the food in front of him. Crabs. He should be sparring in a sword-hall or at the Bull flirting with Jessup before she went up on stage to sing, but instead he was here chewing on days-old meat while his father tried to rescue their storied house by catching tree crabs . . .

Heth blinked, coming back to himself. Something had suddenly changed. The din of conversation and the clink of cutlery had vanished. He sat up straight, looking around for what had happened.

Cold surprise shivered through him. Someone was standing at the entrance to the sawmill, clearly having just come in from outside. The man was cloaked, his face hidden by a cowl, and the rest of his threadbare clothes were sodden. For a panicked moment Heth thought it must be the indentured, somehow having dragged himself from his bed, and his hand twitched. But no, this man was taller than the boy, and he did not have the copper skin of the Ashasai.

A stranger. Heth's gaze flicked to his father and found him watching the unexpected arrival with an expression of bemusement.

Heth was feeling a bit more unsettled. Where had this man come from? The wagon that brought supplies and took away their crabs came only once a fortnight, and it would be another four or five days until it returned. There was no reason for travelers to be passing through, nothing beyond this camp except a thousand leagues of haunted forest.

Unless . . . could this be the hermit to whose daughter the indentured had given the crab? He clearly wasn't on the brink of starvation. But who else would be out here? Heth saw his father reach the same conclusion, realization dawning in his face.

The stranger stepped inside, pulling back his cowl. He didn't look like he could have a daughter old enough to be climbing skyspears. Heth would have thought he'd seen around thirty summers, though his face was weather-beaten and seamed by the sun, like the peasants who used to bring their produce to the markets of Kething's Cross.

The man took in the silent crowd staring at him with a disinterested glance, then shrugged off his cloak and left it puddled on the floor as he approached the table of slaves. They all watched him with mouths agape as he settled onto an empty spot on the bench and reached for a bowl, seemingly oblivious to their attention, and filled it from the tureen in front of him. Then he began to slurp the soup loudly, the sound carrying in the otherwise silent hall.

"You there!" Ferith shouted, and to Heth's surprise, there was more bewilderment than anger in his father's voice. "Announce yourself! Who are you?"

The man ignored him, spitting out something onto the table and then continuing to lustily drink the soup. When he'd emptied his bowl, he tossed it down with a clatter and belched loudly.

His father's chair scraped as he pushed back from the table and rose. "Answer me. Are you the hermit who lives in these woods?"

The stranger picked something from his teeth and flicked it away. Then his gaze wandered slowly around the room, finally settling on the decanter of wine on Heth's table. His attention turned to Ferith.

"You," the man rasped, then cleared his throat and spat. It sounded like he hadn't spoken in a long time. "Bring me the wine."

Someone gave a bark of laughter, quickly stifled. Heth glanced at his father, expecting to see his face twisted in anger, but Ferith had only narrowed his eyes and extended his empty hand towards the zemani seated to his left. The lizardling didn't hesitate, reaching for the scabbarded sword slung over the back of his chair, then with the scrape of steel presented his curved blade to Heth's father.

Ferith's hand closed around the hilt, and he stepped away from the table. It was so quiet in the hall Heth could hear every footstep as his father walked towards where the stranger was still sitting. The man was watching him with an empty expression, as if unaware that his death was approaching.

This was a madman. Or someone who had decided to end his life in a very public and bizarre fashion.

"Rise," his father commanded when he'd come within a few span of where the stranger sat. "If you're lucky, I'll just give you something to make you regret your insolence."

The man's lip curled, and with a long-suffering sigh he slowly stood. As if the spell that had frozen them was suddenly broken, the slaves around the table leapt to their feet and stumbled away.

His father lunged, the sword catching the firelight. Splinters dug under Heth's nails as he clutched at the table in horrified anticipation of what he knew was about to happen.

But it did not. The blade descended, passing through empty air where the stranger had been a moment ago. He'd moved so fast Heth could barely follow. One of the man's hands was clamped on Ferith's arm up near his shoulder, the one that held the sword; even from across the room, Heth could see the shock writ clear on his father's face. He struggled to raise his arm, but the man's grip must have been like iron. Then with the ease of a man pulling a leg from a roast capon the stranger wrenched his father's arm from its socket. There was a crack and a fleshy ripping sound and suddenly blood was spurting from the ragged stump, drenching the stranger.

His father screamed, sounding more animal than man.

Grimacing, as if the keening was an unwelcome nuisance, the stranger reached up with his other hand and pressed his open palm against his father's face. Ferith's legs had gone boneless, Heth realized, but the stranger was keeping him upright simply through the pressure he was exerting through his fingertips. Then the ragged screaming ended as Ferith's face crumpled, and the stranger let his father's corpse fall to the floor with a thud.

No one moved or made a noise. They were as stunned as Heth, unable to comprehend what had just happened.

The moment shattered as the zemani exploded from their chairs and vaulted the table, loosing shrill ululations that snapped Heth from his shock. Scimitar and daggers gleamed as the warrior caste lizardlings rushed the man who had murdered his father.

The stranger ignored them, pulling off his blood-soaked shirt and tossing it aside.

Heth moaned. In the middle of the man's chest was a sunken sliver of amber light, the tracery of glowing lines etched beneath his skin radiating out from this central point like cracks in clay. The zemani must have seen this as well, but to their great honor they did not falter as they closed upon the stranger, even though they knew they were rushing towards their deaths.

For this man, impossibly, was one of the Sharded Few.

4

DERYN

HIS MOTHER WAS LEANING over him, limned by the light pouring through the holes in the sod roof. Her face was shadowed, but he knew it was her from the bright red curls that tumbled past her shoulders. And also as she pressed a cool compress to his brow she was humming a song she'd sung to him a thousand times before.

What's broken will be mended
What's lost will now be found
As the children turn their little faces
Towards the swelling sound

Of a thousand burning hoofbeats
Racing from the West
And the mothers weep with tears of joy
That they could be so blessed

For what's broken will be mended
What's lost will now be found
And at last the line of empty kings
Will once again be crowned

"Mama," he whispered, trying to shift his head so he could see her clearly. Every part of his body felt so heavy, as if something he couldn't see was squatting on him, pressing him down. "Mama," he tried again, louder than before. His mother broke off her singing, lifting the wet cloth from his forehead and wringing it out over a bowl. The drops striking the water sounded wrong, like a fierce rain lashing a roof. Deryn's gaze drifted past the silhouette of his mother, to the blue sky blazing through the holes in the sod they'd never finished patching. They'd intended to. But the first time they'd done it poorly, and the grass he'd packed into the gaps had come crashing down in wet clumps during the first big storm. And before they could make another attempt his mother had . . . his mother had . . .

A shadow passed across the sky, and the darkness in their little house thickened. His mother pulled away . . . or maybe it was him who was receding, plummeting into an abyss that had suddenly opened beneath his cot . . .

"Welcome back, boyo."

His eyes fluttered open to find Xiv's angular face hovering beside him. The Ashasai flashed a white-toothed grin, the corners of his eyes crinkling.

"What?" Deryn mumbled. He was lying on his stomach on his cot, the tangled ball of rags he used as a pillow soaked with spittle. His head felt like it was stuffed with feathers, and his back . . . his back . . .

"Ah," he moaned, reaching around with his hand to explore the pulsing lines of fire sunk into his flesh. He felt fingers close around his wrist, keeping him from touching where the agony was radiating outwards to fill the rest of his body.

"Dat's not a wise idea," Xiv said gently. "Your back was churned up pretty good. Best if you don't touch, let it heal a bit."

Deryn swallowed, squeezing back tears. His throat felt like it was coated with sand. The memory of what had happened flooded him, and though he must have passed out after the first few blows, it felt like the beating had continued well after that.

He spent a few long moments gathering himself, exploring the edges of the pain. It was still terrible, but now that the initial shock had worn away he thought he could handle it. "How long?" he asked, his voice thick.

"Almost two days," Xiv replied. "You was in and out for a while, feverish, calling for your mamsie. I found numbroot in the forest and boiled it down, made you drink it. And we slathered some honey on the wounds to help with the healing."

"Honey? Where . . .?"

"Jog," Xiv said, and Deryn noticed he invoked the overseer's name without his customary derision. "He shared some from the larder. Seemed to help."

Jogan had helped him? Deryn's head throbbed, and something vile crept halfway up his throat before subsiding. Maybe he was still dreaming.

"The fat man has something like a heart, even if it's shriveled and black. Maybe he felt bad for what happened, seeing as how he told the master."

He wanted to sit up. He needed to drink something. Steeling himself against the anticipated pain, Deryn slowly raised himself up on his elbows.

"Whoa, boyo, best for you to rest," Xiv said in alarm.

"No," Deryn muttered as he pushed his way through the waves of agony. With a grunt of effort, he finally brought himself upright. Xiv's copper face was now creased with concern, and Deryn offered a weak smile to try and show that he was all right.

"Water."

"Oh, ya." Xiv lifted a clay pitcher that had been placed beside his cot and filled a wooden cup, then handed it to Deryn.

His hands were shaking as he brought the water to his lips and drank deeply, draining the cup. "I . . ." he began, about to ask for more, but his voice trailed away as he caught sight of something over Xiv's shoulder.

Master Ferith's son was sitting on a cot, staring at him from across the barracks. The boy's face was pale, save for the dark bruises under his eyes. A name swam up from Deryn's clouded memories. Heth. The master had called him Heth.

Panic clawed at Deryn, and he heard again the slaver exhorting his son to strike harder, the crack of the flail as it flayed his skin, his own ragged cries.

"What is he doing here?" he hissed, clutching at Xiv's arm to steady himself.

Xiv glanced over his shoulder. Other slaves were moving about the barracks, Deryn realized. But from the light trickling through the slatted windows it seemed to be late morning. Why weren't they out crabbing? What was going on?

"Oh," The Ashasai said when he realized whom Deryn was staring at. "Well, I suppose you could say the boyo is one of us now."

"One of what?"

"Chained. A slave."

Deryn blinked, trying to understand what Xiv was saying. "His father made him a slave?"

"The master is dead, boyo."

Deryn's gaze drifted from the boy's empty face to the Ashasai. He must have misheard. "What do you mean, dead?"

"You know," Xiv said, crossing his eyes and sticking out his tongue. "Dead dead."

"Then we're free?"

Xiv shook his head sharply. "Ain't free. Ain't crabbing though, either. I don't rightly know what we are. Nobody dared ask him yet."

"Him?"

A tremor passed across Xiv's face. "One o' the Sharded Few."

Deryn stared at the Ashasai blankly. The Sharded Few? He must still be dreaming. The Sharded Few were the warriors of the holds, occupying a position somewhere between gods and men. One had passed through Kething's Cross when Deryn was a small boy, and he still remembered the hysteria that had ensued. The heads of the richest families bowing and scraping as the Sharded rode his horse through the streets, the surging crowd of common folk jostling for a glimpse of this legend made flesh. His mother had lifted him up on her shoulders, and what he'd seen was still etched sword-sharp in his mind's eye: a man sitting straight-backed in his saddle, his black doublet unbuttoned to show the point of dusky light embedded in his chest.

"That's impossible."

Xiv shrugged. "I was here caring for you, boyo, but the others were in the hall and dey saw dis Sharded tear the master an' his lizards apart. Den he ate enough for a dozen men and drank himself to sleep right there at the high table. When he woke, he started yelling for more wine and food. Pretty much all he's done over the last two days is eat and sleep. Kicked the master's boy out of the big house, sent him here."

Deryn felt like he had awoken to an entirely different world. There must be some mistake – the Sharded Few dwelled in the holds and contested amongst themselves for power and glory. They didn't appear in the middle of the wilderness and drink themselves into a stupor.

"I know, I know," Xiv said, and Deryn could see his own disbelief echoed in the Ashasai's face. "But it's true."

"Here, boyo," Xiv continued, patting him on the leg. "I'll go find you some food. Wait for a moment and don't try to go anywhere."

Deryn nodded numbly as the Ashasai moved away from their corner of the room and went to talk with Red Vesch, a slave who had once been a woodsman and was known to keep a small store of nuts and roots and mushrooms he gathered from the forest. While Xiv was doing this, Deryn tried to make sense of what he'd just been told.

The man his mother had signed his indentured contract with was dead. Did that mean by law he belonged to his next of kin? The wounds on his back prickled at the thought. No, if Heth tried to lay claim to him, he'd do what he'd considered a hundred times and flee into the forest. Steal what supplies he could and follow the forest road to Kething's Cross. He lacked the Su Canaav brand that all the slaves had burned into their forehead – if he could last a few nights without being eaten by fell cats, then he'd pass right through the Cross and head to another city where he could vanish. Deryn's gaze returned to Heth. The boy was now staring blankly at the wall, his shoulders slumped. He looked broken, like his entire world had come crashing down around him, and he was currently sitting among the ruins unsure what he should do now.

Deryn felt no sympathy.

A commotion by the barrack's entrance tore his attention from the dead master's son. Jogan's familiar bulk filled the doorway, but Deryn had never seen him look like this before. The overseer's face was haggard, and it seemed that he hadn't taken a knife to his whiskers since he'd brought Deryn to face his punishment.

"Listen you lot. Gavin wants you all to come to the mill."

Silence greeted this pronouncement, worried glances passing between the slaves. Deryn saw Heth's face pale.

"Ain't a request," Jogan said with a scowl.

"He ain't our master." It was Chent who had spoken, his arms folded across his narrow chest.

Jogan sighed deeply, rubbing at his face. "That don't matter, lad. He's Sharded. He can do what he wants. You refuse to come, he comes here and maybe he does to you like he did to Ferith. He wouldn't even break a sweat . . . or give a care at all as he kills you. Believe me. We don't mean nothing to him." He gestured for the slaves to get moving. "Now, come on." His gaze suddenly found Deryn. "You're up, then. That's good. Gavin said everyone, so I was gonna have to drag you out of bed anyway."

Jogan waited impatiently as the slaves slowly exited the barracks. Xiv returned to Deryn and helped him to rise. His back ached, but the flail hadn't touched his legs, at least, so it wouldn't hurt too much to walk once he was already standing.

"Any food?" he murmured, but Xiv shook his head curtly.

"Sorry, boyo. Vesch is being stingy, and can't say I blame him. If he's got some eats squirreled away, it's probably for a time jus' like dis. We all might be out in the forest by tomorrow."

Deryn's stomach twisted, and he tried to ignore it. It was clear that the Sharded was now the ruler of the camp. Either he would let them eat or he wouldn't, but Deryn couldn't believe he'd let them starve. He just had to be patient.

"My shirt," he whispered, and Xiv frowned.

"You sure? Won't feel pleasant where he whipped you."

He.

Deryn glanced again at Heth. The slaver's son seemed even more hesitant than the rest, idling near his cot like he thought he might evade attention, but Jogan was having none of it. As Deryn watched, the overseer marched inside the barracks and grabbed Heth by the arm, then practically threw the boy towards the door. The shock on his face at being roughly handled by a man who had groveled before his father not so long ago should have been satisfying to Deryn. Yet instead, it sent a wave of unease washing through him. How dangerous was this new situation for all of them?

"Here, den."

Deryn dragged his eyes from Heth and focused on Xiv, who had found the lightest of his linen shifts and was holding it out for him. With some effort and a bit of help from the Ashasai slave, he pulled it on, hissing in discomfort as the fabric settled on his wounds.

"You two, come on," grumbled Jogan, motioning for them to hurry.

"Yeah, yeah, bosser," Xiv replied, taking hold of Deryn's arm as if he needed help to stay upright.

"I'm all right," Deryn said, shrugging his hand away. "But thank you."

Xiv gave him a measuring look, as if not entirely convinced, then shrugged and made for where Jogan was waiting impatiently.

Deryn followed them outside. It must have rained most of the time he'd been unconscious, as the ground was spongy and the grass and leaves glistened, but right now the azure sky was unblemished, and the sun was so strong he had to lower his eyes as he approached the old mill. For a moment he felt dizzy, overwhelmed by the brightness of the day and the strain of trying to walk after so long abed. He stumbled and might have fallen, but then there was a hand on his shoulder, steadying him. Deryn looked up, expecting to see Xiv next to him, but to his surprise, it was Jogan. The overseer's face was unreadable, and he said nothing as he helped guide Deryn inside the mill.

Blinking, it took him a moment to adjust to the dimness, as the only light was trickling down from the holes in the roof. The slaves who had preceded them into the large hall were huddled together in a clump only a few steps inside, as if afraid to go farther. Past them, Deryn could see the long trestle tables where they usually took their meals, and beyond those the master's table beside the cold firepit.

It was not empty. A man slouched in the high-backed chair that had once belonged to Heth's father, and before him was the remnants of a great feast. A half-dozen of the huge tree crabs had been torn apart, their shells discarded and legs scattered about, their great claws cracked open. There were also empty bottles of dusky glass, more than Deryn could quickly count, both on the table and in glinting shards strewn across the floor, as if some had been hurled away in anger.

For a few moments, the man ignored the muttering and shifting crowd of slaves, intent on sucking the meat from a massive claw. When he finally finished, he belched and threw the remains into the firepit, then lifted one bottle that still held some dark liquid and drained it.

Deryn tried and failed to match this stranger with what he had grown up believing about the Sharded Few. He did not look like he had ever set foot in the holds – he had the weathered face of a man used to toiling in the fields or the mines, and from his time spent serving the well-to-do in Kething's Cross, Deryn knew that these were not the table manners of the rich and cultured. As if to reinforce this observation, the man cleared his throat loudly and then leaned over and spat. After doing this, he finally seemed to notice the rest of them.

"So you all are slaves," he called out loudly. There was a rough-ness to his voice, an edge that came from being scraped along the bottom of the world. He sounded like the stable hands and kitchen boys Deryn had known back in the Cross, not like a nearly mythical warrior of epic story.

"And I killed your master. You must all be thankful."

A heavy silence followed this pronouncement. The man laughed, but without humor. "Suppose that's to be expected. All the slaves I've ever known, they don't know how to stand once the knee is finally lifted from their neck. Common folk, too." His mouth twisted. "Well, if you need a master, I can take the place of the old one."

"I'll say thank you."

All eyes turned to the noseless boy, Chent. For a moment he quailed under the attention, and then he straightened and puffed out his chest. "I wasn't even the one that stuck that old geezer after we grabbed his bag. That was Minik. Shouldn't never have lost my nose or been put in chains. I'm glad you killed that bastard who bought me. I'll take my freedom."

The man pushed himself to his feet, a hint of a smile at the corners of his mouth. "Right, then. You're free to go." He picked up something that had been lying on the table among the mess and studied it. It was short and curved and the color of bone – the head spine of one of Master Ferith's fearsome zemani guards. He held out the spine, pointing it at Chent, who suddenly looked much less sure of himself. "Now get out."

"What?" the boy said, his voice quavering.

"I'm giving you your freedom. But you can't stay here. So it's the forest for you."

"I . . . I . . ." Chent stammered, his eyes going to Jogan, as if begging him to intervene. The overseer stared back blankly.

The man moved out from behind the table, striking his palm with the spine. "I realized something not too long ago. You see, there are just two kinds of people in this world: the strong and the weak. The rulers and the ruled. Your master, he was your ruler. Your king. He could claim he owned you, that the law of the Shadow bound you to do what he said, but really the fact of it is there was someone some-where with a sword who you lot feared." He glanced down at the spine he held. "Maybe it was those lizards. Maybe the magistrate at

Kething's Cross. Doesn't matter. This here was his kingdom. Now it's mine. If you stay here, you do what I say. You want that freedom, you find it in the forest." He stared off into the distance for a moment before he spoke again. "I saw things out there, though. I think your freedom might last a day, if you're lucky, and then you'll be in something's belly."

"I'll stay." The words were barely more than a whisper. Chent's hands were balled into fists, his gaze fixed on the floor.

"As you please," the man said with a smirk. Then he sighed, rolling his neck, and faced the slaves who had been watching this exchange warily. "So it looks like you all belong to me. But no need for 'master' or 'lord'. I ain't got any airs. Call me Gavin. It was good enough before this"—he tapped the center of his chest—"so it's good enough now." He craned his neck, clearly searching for something among the slaves. Deryn felt his gaze touch on him and then slide away. "Looks like it's true. Not a single woman among the lot of you. How did you all stay sane out here with nothing but that old crone cook to stare at?" The man frowned. "Maybe you're all a bunch of eunuchs. Is that true, boy?" he asked, addressing Chent again. "Did they take more than just your nose?" Gavin laughed harshly, then stumbled slightly before finding his balance. He was drunk, Deryn realized. Very drunk. If they rushed him now, could they overwhelm him? Deryn cast a surreptitious glance at Xiv, but the Ashasai shook his head firmly, as if he knew what Deryn was thinking. And given what this man had done to Ferith and his lizardlings, Xiv was probably correct. Deryn tried to push away any idea of rebellion.

Gavin dragged himself back to the high table – none too steadily – and with a wheezing grunt threw himself into the master's old chair. He picked up one of the bottles, but after finding it empty he tossed it away and it shattered on the floor. Deryn and a few of the other slaves had to quickly step back as fragments skittered close to their feet.

"More crabs," he said, gesturing at the remains on the table. "Go catch more crabs. That's what you lot know how to do, yes?" He leaned forward, placing his elbows on the table, and started to knead his forehead. After a moment he looked up again, and Deryn was surprised by the sudden anger he saw in the Sharded's face.

"Go!"

~

The slaves were quiet after returning to the barracks, as if at a loss for words after their audience with the Sharded. Most retired to their cots, staring at nothing as they considered a future that was far less certain than a few days ago. A few gathered in the corner to toss rune bones, but there were none of the excited exclamations that usually accompanied the game. Heth curled up into a ball, facing the wall, and Deryn got the sense he was trying to avoid interacting with any of the other slaves.

Xiv was sitting cross-legged on his cot, his chin on his knuckles, seemingly lost in thought.

"Do you think this Gavin is truly one of the Sharded Few?" Deryn asked him after he'd finally found a position that was somewhat comfortable for his back.

The question roused Xiv from his ruminations. "Aye, boyo. He's one o' the Sharded. No doubts at all."

"But . . . how? That's not how they act. Murdering and drinking until they're nearly falling down."

Xiv's mouth twisted wryly. "And you know how dey act? Been around the Sharded a lot, have you?"

"Have you?" Deryn shot back, harsher than he intended, but Xiv ignored the edge to his words and simply nodded.

"A little. Down south, the holds are often within great cities. The blood-sharded rule Ashasai from atop the Black Steps, but dey do sometimes descend into the city. I seen dem before, throwing bones in the taverns and betting on the fights. Not like your northern Sharded, staying hidden in their mountain fortresses like dey were gods in truth ruling from on high. You ever seen anyone from the Duskhold?"

"Only once," Deryn admitted. "He visited Kething's Cross, though I don't know why. Pretty much the entire town came out to gawk."

"Bet he stayed the whole time in the magistrate's manse," Xiv said, and Deryn had to nod his agreement. "Probably just there to discuss what tribute needed to go up to feed the Shadow."

"But this Sharded doesn't act anything like the one I saw before. That one looked . . . noble. This Gavin . . . he's different. He speaks like a commoner. He sounds like he could be from Kething's Cross, or somewhere else close by."

"Aye, and dat's the mystery I be thinking about," Xiv said. "Somethin' strange here, we all can see dat. But what can we do? Ain't a man alive who can stand against one o' the Sharded Few. Can't leave, either, unless we think we can outrun a hungry fell cat."

Deryn chewed his lip, considering. "What if we did try to do that? I mean, maybe the forest isn't as dangerous as we think. That girl I saw and her father have survived out there for years, yes? A few of us traveling together so we have enough numbers that some can keep watch while the others sleep . . . We could light torches at night, and we'd have our crabbing knives for protection."

"You think the Sharded would jus' let us walk away?" Xiv asked, his skepticism clear.

"He said Chent could have his freedom if he went into the forest."

Xiv shook his head. "Can't be no king without commoners. Enough of us try to leave, and he'll force all to stay. I seen his kind before. He likes being at the top o' the pile, there's no doubt. And, also, you're forgetin' about dis." Xiv tapped the Su Canaav sigil burned into his forehead. "Even if he don't come after us and tear us limb from limb like he did the master, we would be dead men once we got to the Cross or any other city under the Shadow. Unless you can convince dem dat we belong to you. And no disrespect, boyo, but even if dey don't see the marks on your back, you don't look much like a master."

Deryn slumped against the wall. He had to believe that they could slip away while the Sharded was distracted – or drunk – but if a band of slaves emerged from the wilderness without their master . . . well, the worst would be assumed, and the only uncertainty would be the manner of execution. Unless...

He sat up straighter, and Xiv glanced at him quizzically.

"An idea, boyo?"

Deryn hesitated, unsure if he truly wanted to suggest what had just occurred to him. But if it was the only way the slaves would risk an escape...

"I'm not a master... but he is."

Xiv turned, his gaze going to where Deryn was now indicating: the motionless, curled son of Master Ferith. The Ashasai scratched at his face, his expression uncertain.

"You sure, boyo?"

Deryn's jaw tightened, the wounds on his back beginning to prickle. "If it's the only way. Maybe ... maybe for taking him with us he'll agree to give up his family's claim on our lives."

Xiv nodded. "*Hm.* I ain't sure we can trust him, but I know he don't want to be here after what happened to his daddy." He ran his hand over his bald pate as he let out a long breath. "Well, den, I'll ask around. Quiet like, and only ones I trust won't go runnin' to Jogan or dis Sharded. Red Vesch, no doubt. We ain't getting through the forest without his help."

"Good," Deryn said, willing the itching in his back to subside. "Good."

The next morning, Jogan led the slaves out into the forest to hunt for crabs. Deryn stayed in his cot, trying to find the least uncomfortable position after a restless night. Heth went with the crabbers, to the astonishment of Jogan and most of the other slaves, but Deryn wasn't surprised. He'd caught the boy sneaking glances at him when he'd thought Deryn wasn't watching, and the mix of fear and guilt in his face made it very obvious that he did not want to be alone in the barracks all day with someone he had so recently lashed half to death. Not that Deryn had the strength to exact any sort of vengeance – he felt as weak as a newborn pup.

Much later in the day, he was roused from an uneasy slumber by the sound of shouting coming from outside. Wincing, he dragged himself to his feet and limped across the barracks to the entrance. He opened the door, and then stood there, blinking stupidly as he tried to understand what he was looking at.

The slaves had returned, though most of them had halted on the edge of the forest. Jogan and Xiv and a few others had come close to the old mill and were clustered around something on the ground. As he strained to get a better look at what that was, the overseer stepped away, and Deryn could see that it was a body sprawled on the grass. From the tufts of white hair and homespun clothes, he realized it must be one of the old men who had been living in this settlement before the slavers had come. Something was odd about the corpse, though. It was his head – the body was lying face down . . . but the face was staring up at the sky. It had been turned all the way around.

Deryn's gorge rose, and he retreated from the entrance and made his way back to his cot. Only the Sharded could have done something like this. But why? The old loggers who still lived here were harmless, drifting through the camp like ghosts that didn't know they were dead. Deryn had never seen them angry or even heard their raised voices. Master Ferith had yelled at them occasionally during meal-times for under-salting the stew or dropping a plate, but they had just ducked their head in apology and kept on working. What could that old man have done that the Sharded had *murdered* him?

The crabbers filed in silently a little while later, their faces somber. Jogan lingered in the doorway, as if reluctant to return to the mill or his small shack, and Deryn couldn't blame the overseer. There was indeed some comfort in numbers. Xiv made his way back to their corner of the barracks, and it was obvious from his expression that he was deeply troubled.

"The Sharded did that?" Deryn asked in a low voice as the Ashasai sat down heavily on his cot.

"Aye," Xiv replied after a moment's pause. "One o' the other old ones slunk out to tell us while we was lookin' at the body. Dat geezer . . . he brought Gavin his wine. But the Sharded's been drinkin' like a fish for days now, and the wine's finished. Won't be any more until the supply wagon comes in a few days. Sharded was already drunk, and dis made him fly into a rage, twisted the poor fool's head right around and den tossed him outside like he was nothing . . . just a piece o' refuse." The Ashasai leaned back, looking around the barracks. The other slaves had broken into small groups, their heads together, occasionally casting glances at the entrance, as if afraid the Sharded was about to burst in at any moment. "Dis should convince some o' the others dat we gotta think about leaving. And soon."

No one dared venture into the mill in the days following the murder. The slaves kept to the barracks when they weren't crabbing, with pots of stew lugged over in the evening by Mam Mim and another of the elderly loggers-turned-servants. She was the only one in the settlement who seemed unafraid of the Sharded – when Deryn asked her how she was doing, the old woman snorted and squinted at him with her milky eyes. "He gonna kill me? Then who's gonna cook his food? Unless he wants to be roastin' skewered squirrel and eatin' berries, he'll leave me alone. And he likes those crabs you all catch, so he'll ignore you all so long as you don't bother him. Keep your heads down and you'll all be fine . . . sooner or later he'll get bored and move on. Go to find a woman, maybe." She hacked a laugh, shaking her head. "Bastard is hot-blooded, that's for sure. If I was twenty years younger, I'd be worried, but I ain't, so instead he just rots here gettin' more and more antsy wishin' one of you had soft skin and long hair."

Later that same night, Deryn was shaken awake, a hand pressed to his lips to keep him from making any noise. A shadow moved in the darkness, and then he heard Xiv's voice in his ear.

"Come with me, boyo. And be quiet, don't want any tongues wagging tomorrow."

Deryn rose from his cot and followed the Ashasai, trying his best to conjure up a memory of what the room looked like during the day. So long as they avoided stepping into the fire trench their passage should go unnoticed, as a chorus of snores and wheezing filled the barracks. Still, his heart was in his throat as Xiv eased open the door and led him out into the night. No moon or stars were visible, and Deryn wasn't sure if they were headed towards one of the buildings or the forest until brambles plucked at his legs and he felt roots beneath his bare feet.

Cool, wet darkness enfolded him. Leaves rustled, stirred by the wind, and glimmering insects hummed as they bumbled past his head. Deryn felt a stab of fear that they would lose themselves among the trees, but Xiv did not hesitate as he led them deeper.

When he finally stopped, Deryn just caught himself from walking into the Ashasai's back. The trees did not press so close here, so they must have entered a clearing. How Xiv had found this place in the darkness was beyond Deryn.

"Vesch, that you?" Xiv hissed.

A patch of deeper blackness trembled. "Aye." Deryn recognized the gravelly voice of the old forester.

"Wenick?"

"Aye."

"Lessy?"

"I'm here, Ashasai."

"Heth?"

No answer. In the distance, a bird trilled, the cry almost mournful.

"Damn fool must have gotten lost," grumbled Vesch. "He'll be fell cat food before the sun returns."

"No," came a thin voice. "I'm here." The arrogance Deryn remembered when the boy had beaten him was gone. He sounded scared and unsure. Even still, anger swelled in Deryn's chest, and he realized he was trembling, his nails digging into his palms.

"All right, den," Xiv said quietly. "Everyone's come. You all know what I think we should do. Dat Sharded is dangerous. He could kill any of us for lookin' at him wrong, and I've known others like him. It's only a matter of time. I say we got to go."

"Go where?" Deryn recognized the thick Flail accent. Lessy, the Windwrack man. He had been a sailor once, it was said, on the Sea of Salvation. He was one of the most reserved of the slaves, but when he spoke, others listened. His coming tonight probably had convinced several others as well.

"Well, we leave at night, follow the road for a way. But if the Sharded comes after us den we'll be too easy to find. And we know he's faster than us, and won't get tired easy. So when the sky starts to lighten we slip into the forest and make our own way south and east, towards Kething's Cross."

"How do we keep our way? I could barely find this clearing, and ye showed it ta us just today." That was Wenick, the hill-man from the Wild beyond the Duskhold.

"Won't get lost," rumbled Vesch. "So long as there's a sun in the sky and moss on the trees, I'll have us going in the right direction."

No one challenged this claim. They all knew Red Vesch had been a forester and a poacher in his life-before.

"But then what?" Lessy finally asked. "So say we somehow make it through the forest, come to the Cross or Vessal or another of the twelve towns. We go back to being this one's slaves?" Deryn imagined that unseen in the darkness the Windwracker had jabbed a stubby finger towards where he thought Heth was standing. There was shifting and muttering in the wake of Lessy's question.

"No." The word was barely a whisper.

"What's dat, boy?" Xiv asked. "Speak up."

"No," Heth said again, louder than before. "I'll free you all when we stand before a magistrate. I just . . . I just have to get away from here."

The desperation in his voice was palpable. Deryn supposed that was understandable, given that he had watched the brutal murder of his father.

"And how do we trust *you*?" That was Wenick again, his doubt obvious.

"Please," Heth said quickly. "I'll swear on my family. My father's ghost. My mother's. Anything. If I stay here . . . he'll kill me. I know it."

Deryn believed him. Or, at least, he believed him in this moment. But would Heth feel the same when he was safe in Kething's Cross? Then again, if he lied now, he'd have to sleep forever with one eye open, unless he sold them all to other masters in far-away cities. Betraying men enslaved for theft and violence who had nothing left to lose was utter foolishness.

"He'll kill all of us," Xiv said into the silence that followed.

More mutters, and this time they sounded like agreement.

"So we're agreed," Vesch said. "When do we strike out?"

"Tomorrow night," Xiv told them. "Gather what things you need, and we gonna meet back here at the same time. Hopefully the night is just as black."

5

HETH

Escape.

The thought of getting away from this horrible place sent a thrill of anticipation through Heth, making him lightheaded. Every time Jogan darkened the doorway to the barracks, he was sure he would be summoned before that . . . that *thing* that now slept in his father's bed. That monster. The crawling dread was so terrible that he'd honestly do anything to get away . . . even if it meant fleeing into the forest with the indentured. He worried about that, of course, though it paled beside his fear of the Sharded. He'd watched the boy dragging himself stiffly around the barracks, and he'd honestly been half expecting to awaken one of these days with the sharp edge of a crabbing knife to his throat. But so far, the indentured had done nothing, not even muttered a curse in his direction or shot him a threatening look. Heth supposed he was biding his time, and that there would eventually be a reckoning between them. He had to be ready. And for that reason, the crabbing knife he'd convinced Jogan to give him never left his person.

This particular morning, the indentured seemed to still be sleeping soundly as the slaves prepared to go out into the forest. He was probably exhausted from their meeting last night – Heth had remained awake long after creeping back into the barracks, his body thrumming with excitement, and he imagined the others had gotten little rest as well.

"Right, then," Jogan growled from the doorway. "Let's get going. Gavin is down to the last crab, and I don't think I need to tell you lot we don't want him lookin' around for who to blame when he runs out."

That seemed to instill some urgency in the slaves, and Heth hurried to follow them as they spilled from the barracks and into the bright light of morning.

Where they paused, blinking, and stared in surprise at something as it slowly emerged from the forest. Peering around the slaves, Heth saw a flash of white, the gleam of golden hair. And then a girl stepped from the undergrowth, her hands kneading the hem of her ragged shift.

"What in the frozen hells?" muttered one of the slaves, the copper-skinned Ashasai who was organizing their escape.

Jogan seemed the most surprised, his fat face slack with shock. Beside him, the noseless boy pointed at the apparition emphatically.

"That's her! That's the girl who took the crab!"

"'Course it's her," grumbled the old sailor from the Wrack. "There ain't no finishing school for young ladies out in these woods."

The girl hovered at the edge of the trees, as if reluctant to enter the settlement proper. She looked skittish, like a deer ready to bolt at the slightest hint of danger.

The Ashasai glanced at Jogan, but when the overseer said nothing, the slave cleared his throat and called out to her.

"Hey there, girlie. You all right?"

The girl pulled on a matted lock of her golden hair. Heth could sense how unsure she was, how afraid. Still, after taking a deep breath she stepped closer, away from the safety of the forest.

"I'm all right." There was a tremor in her voice, but she said it loudly. "My da isn't, though. He's real sick. He needs a physicker or a wise woman. None of the herbs are helping him. And I'm afraid of letting any more blood. Please. Help me."

"Ain't no one here like dat –"

"What's this?"

For a moment Heth couldn't draw in enough breath. That voice. He turned towards the old mill, already shaking.

The Sharded leaned against the frame of the entrance, his arms folded across his chest. His head was cocked to one side as he stared at the girl, his expression puzzled, as if he couldn't fathom how she had come to be here.

"Now, where have you all been hiding *her*?"

He sounded more bemused than angry, Heth thought, but Jogan had told them all how his moods could shift in an instant, as temperamental as the sea before a storm.

The girl focused on Gavin, recognizing him as the one with authority. "Please," she entreated, taking another tentative step away from the forest. "My da needs help."

The Sharded pushed himself from the door. His face was a mask of concern, but Heth knew it to be an act. "Your da is sick? I'm so sorry." He swept out an arm, inviting her to enter the mill. "Come here and maybe I can help you."

Heth could sense the horror growing in the slaves as the girl slowly approached the mill. He wanted to call out to her, to warn her away, but the words died in his throat. How could she not sense the tension crackling in the air . . . But in her face there was a desperate hope, the kind that ignores all misgivings.

"Stay away from him."

The warning came from behind Heth, and he whirled around in surprise just as the indentured pushed past.

"No, boyo," moaned the Ashasai slave, and in his voice was the knowledge of how this would end.

The indentured strode up to the girl – whatever pain he usually felt from his wounds seemed to have been forgotten – and took her by the wrist. She did not pull away, staring at him with wide eyes, her mouth slightly open. Her eyes were a shade of green Heth had never seen before, dark and verdant.

"Bring her to me," commanded the Sharded coldly.

"No," the indentured said, starting to walk backwards. The girl went with him, stumbling slightly, her confusion clear.

"He said he might be able to help," she said, her gaze flicking between the boy dragging her away and the scowling Sharded.

"He's lying," the indentured replied in a tumbling rush. "He will hurt you. He's already killed."

"Bring her now," the Sharded repeated, and he began to follow them. His pace was unhurried, almost casual, but Heth knew he could cross the distance between them in an instant. The slaves parted silently as he reached them, their eyes downcast, as if ashamed to be forced to witness what was about to happen. "Don't listen to him, girl. He's a –"

The Ashasai lunged. Light glinted off something he held, and then the Sharded was reeling back, a crabbing knife embedded in his shoulder. Gavin's shock was mirrored in the face of the slave who had stabbed him – the man had meant to plunge the knife into his throat, Heth realized, but the Sharded had moved with preternatural speed at the last moment to avoid what would have been a killing strike.

"Run, boyo!" the Ashasai cried as the Sharded reached up slowly to pull the knife free. He stared at its blood-streaked blade as if fascinated, seemingly unconcerned by the dark stain spreading on his tunic.

Heth glanced over his shoulder just as the indentured and the mysterious girl vanished into the depths of the forest. When he turned back, the Sharded still had not moved. The wound in his shoulder seemed not to be bothering him at all.

"Why would you do that?" he asked suddenly, his fingers tightening around the knife's hilt. To Heth's surprise, he sounded honestly confused. "You know I'm going to kill you now. Then I'll find the boy, kill him too. And drag that girl back here. They're not going to get away."

The Ashasai shrugged, pulling out another crabbing knife from somewhere. "Maybe. I reckon you don't know much about dis forest. You're city-born and bred, I can tell."

The Sharded's other hand drifted up to explore where the knife had torn his shirt. "Been a long time since someone hurt me. Before I got this." He tapped his chest with his now bloodstained fingers.

"I always wanted to stab one o' you," the Ashasai said, settling into a knife-fighter's stance. He was grinning, against all reason.

"Well, I hope you enjoyed it," the Sharded said with a sneer as he stepped towards the slave.

Heth knew what was coming, and he couldn't watch it again. He turned, staring out into the forest where the indentured had fled, trying to keep from thinking about what had happened to his father.

But it wasn't the same. This time the screams lasted much longer, and when the Ashasai made his last, strangled cry, Heth found his cheeks were wet with tears.

6

DERYN

DERYN STUMBLED when the first scream rose up behind them.

"Xiv," he murmured hoarsely, barely catching himself from sprawling in the mulch.

"What's that?" asked the girl, her eyes wide with fear.

"My friend," Deryn replied, a hollowness spreading inside him. The pain in that cry . . . He winced as another scream rent the silence, echoing among the trees.

"Someone is hurting him," the girl said. Her wrist had slipped from his slack fingers, and she turned, staring back the way they'd come.

"That man," Deryn said dully. "The one that wanted you to come to him. He's one of the Sharded Few."

Her face creased in confusion, and she brushed a strand of golden hair out of her eyes. She was older than he'd first thought, he realized. Maybe she was even his own age. Her grubby face and snarled hair had made him think at first that she was much younger.

"One of what?" she asked.

This girl had never heard of the Sharded Few? Deryn could only stare at her blankly for a moment, unsure what to say. How could that be possible? Then he shook himself. They had to run, far and fast.

When Gavin was finished with Xiv, he'd be after them. Deryn tried to decide in which direction they should flee. Deeper into the wilderness, towards the tallest skyspears? There was less undergrowth that way, so it'd be easier to see them, but maybe they could hunker behind one of the massive trunks or among the roots. Then again, to the east was the old forest road, and so long as they stayed close to that they wouldn't get lost, which would be a real danger in the forest proper...

Before he could decide, a small hand slipped into his own. He glanced up, startled, and found himself staring into brilliant green eyes.

"Follow me," she said, then set off. Deryn allowed himself to be pulled along, both hoping and dreading that the screams were finished.

They were not.

The ragged cries grew increasingly faint, though the knife-blade twisting in his gut only became more painful. Xiv had saved him. He'd known what would happen, but still he'd sacrificed his life to give Deryn a few more moments to get away.

He felt untethered, like he was floating outside himself, watching them both plunge through the forest. An ache began in his side, indicating that they had run for quite some time, but it felt like it had been only moments. They splashed across a shallow stream speckled with yellow-shelled turtles, then scrambled up a muddy embankment. The skyspears reared around them, draping the forest in twilight. Something ape-like hooted, then receded among the branches when they ignored its challenge.

Finally they stopped, and Deryn doubled over panting. His tunic was soaked with sweat, but the girl didn't even seem winded by their headlong flight.

"What's your name?" he asked her between gulping breaths as she peered into the tangle behind them for any sign of pursuit.

"Alia," she said softly. "But he calls me Leaf."

"Who does?"

"My da."

Deryn straightened, looking around. They'd stopped at the edge of a pond, and the bright sunlight made its surface shimmer like beaten gold. The skyspears rose around them to pierce the cloudless blue. A long, sinuous shape slipped from the grass and into the water, leaving ripples in its wake.

"Where is your father?"

Alia had her head cocked to one side, as if listening intently. After a long moment, she turned to him, seemingly satisfied that no one had tracked them through the forest.

"He is there," she said, pointing to a heap of branches and listing trees that looked to have been brought down during a storm.

No . . . it was a shelter, Deryn realized. A flap of hide covered an entrance, over which hung the skull of some tined animal.

Her bare feet whispered in the grass as she approached the ramshackle structure, and she did not break her stride as she flung back the hide flap and plunged into the dimness. Deryn hurried to keep up, then nearly collided with her just inside the entrance.

"Oh," she whispered.

Only a little light was seeping through the ceiling of woven reeds, and it took a moment for his eyes to adjust. The interior of the hut was cluttered with chairs and a table rough-hewn from scavenged wood, and strange objects he couldn't recognize in the gloom were scattered everywhere. The air smelled like sage or some other herb had been burned, but underneath that medicinal aroma was something rancid.

Alia took two stumbling steps towards the shadowed recesses of the hut, her hands clenched into fists at her sides. "Oh, Da," she murmured again, and then gave a wrenching cry.

A cot was pushed up against the far wall, and though the darkness was thickest there he could still make out the shape of a man laid out under furs. He was tiny, nothing but a husk. There was no movement, and the only sound Deryn could hear was the incessant droning of flies.

The girl approached the cot, her steps slow and measured. Then she sank down, laying her head upon the chest of the unmoving body. She shuddered, wracked by silent sobs.

Suddenly Deryn felt dizzy, the air so clottingly thick he was struggling to breathe. Trying not to knock over anything so he wouldn't disturb the grieving girl, he stumbled away from the cot, flinging aside the hide flap as he emerged again outside. He sucked in a lungful of the blessedly fresh air, moving away from the entrance, as a whiff of the tainted miasma had clung to him as he fled.

Death. There was nothing but death in that little hut. Whatever the girl had hoped to bring back to help her father, she was far too late.

Deryn watched the entrance, unsure what he should do. It couldn't be healthy, breathing in the vapors rising from a corpse, but he couldn't imagine entering the hut to try and drag her away. Just the thought of trying to pry her from that withered body as the flies buzzed in his ears made him shudder.

No. Let her have her grief. Sometimes it was all anyone had.

The day slowly deepened, the bird's egg blue of the sky darkening as the sun climbed higher. Deryn found a mossy rock at the edge of the pond on which to perch and watched tattered clouds spill down the mountains' slopes to tear themselves further upon the sharp peaks of the skyspears. After a while the forest seemed to become resigned to his presence, and sounds that had disappeared as they'd blundered along gradually emerged again: the trilling of birds and the hollow clacking of kanths, while from the fringes of the pond tiny frogs began to cry and dragonflies danced among the reeds.

Deryn felt numb. The events of earlier had happened in a tumbling rush, an avalanche that had deposited him here, shattered and stunned. Now that he could slowly pick his way through his thoughts, the enormity of it all was overwhelming. Xiv was almost certainly dead. He'd thrown himself between Deryn and the Sharded, giving him a few precious moments to flee. Tears prickled his eyes as he remembered the slave caring for him while he recovered from the beating Master Ferith's son had given him, and all the other small kindnesses he'd shown Deryn since he'd become indentured. He'd been raised to think of Ashasai as decadent and cruel, but Xiv hadn't been like that at all. He'd been a good man. Now he was gone, and if Deryn had not stepped forward to try and protect this girl, he'd still be alive.

What a fool he was. Helping this girl had gotten him beaten half to death, and then lost him his only friend in the world.

With a start, he realized he was no longer alone. The girl had appeared beside him, staring out across the lotus-flecked pond. Her eyes were red and her cheeks glistened, but it seemed to Deryn like whatever tears she'd shed had now stopped. The breeze played with the matted snarls of her long hair, and she reached up to brush aside a stray lock. She appeared to be deep in thought, her brow creased as she chewed on her lower lip.

Alia looked as broken as he felt, and Deryn felt a pang of guilt for the blame he had been prepared to heap on her.

"Your father?" he asked softly, squinting up at her.

"Gone," she said simply.

"I'm sorry."

She didn't reply, continuing to stare at the trees crowding the far side of the pond.

"How long had he been sick?"

She blinked, as if returning to herself. "Months. Many months. There was still snow on the ground when he started coughing."

Half a year, then. Deryn brought his legs up to his chest and laced his hands across his knees. Was it harder to lose a parent in one terrible moment, or watch them slowly fade, helpless to do anything?

"Do you . . . do you want me to do something? I can dig a . . . a grave, if you have any tools."

Now she did look at him. The vibrant green eyes he remembered from when he'd first met her up in the tree looked muted now, drained of color.

"He'd want to stay where he is."

"But the fell cats . . ."

She shook her head sharply. "He would want the forest to take him."

Odd, but Deryn decided not to press her further on this. He rolled his shoulders, trying to quiet the itching on his back, which had been slowly growing worse. The flight through the woods must have broken open some of the wounds.

Silence fell between them for a while. All sorts of questions danced on the tip of Deryn's tongue – who she was, why did she live in the forest, how had she never heard of the Sharded Few – but he found himself unable to break the stillness.

In the end, she was the one who spoke first. "Thank you for trying to keep me safe. And for giving me that crab. I'm sorry for whatever happened to that man."

"It's not your fault," he said softly.

Alia crouched down and picked up a small rock, then tossed it into the pond. It skipped a few times before sinking. "What will you do now? Can you go back?"

Deryn watched the slowly spreading ripples. "To the mill? No. That man I warned you about . . . he's very dangerous. He already killed a few people. And he'd certainly kill me if I returned." He reached around to scratch at one of the scars on his shoulder. "I don't know what I'll do. I wish I could leave this place. The forest, the mountains. Go back to Kething's Cross, or some other town. But I can't."

The girl frowned. "Why not?"

"I doubt I'd survive the journey," Deryn admitted. "There are the cats, and the kanths, the bears, wolves, rethwings . . . The woods are deadly. I don't know how you survive out here."

Alia studied his face for a moment, as if searching for something. Or making a decision. "Those things that scare you . . . they don't scare me. If you're with me, they won't hurt you."

"Why?"

"It's hard to explain," she said after another moment of silence. "The forest and I have an understanding. I grew up here. There's a language to this place, and I can speak it . . . though most importantly, I know how to listen to its warnings."

"So you could help me leave this place? Take me to one of the twelve towns?"

Alia nodded slightly, and Deryn felt a little flutter of excitement in his chest. The thought that a young girl could travel without risk through these woods seemed preposterous . . . but she *had* lived out here for years. And she was very evidently not afraid of what lurked in the wilderness.

"Who are you?" she asked him, and he realized with a start that he had never introduced himself.

"Deryn," he told her, pressing his fist to his forehead. "Son of Galenia. I didn't know my father."

"I saw you many times in the forest," Alia told him, picking up another stone. She didn't throw this one, instead turning it over in her hands. "You were different from the others who tried to catch the crabs. You didn't have this." She traced a symbol on her forehead, the brand of Master Ferith.

"I wasn't a slave. I was indentured, and after another few years of service I'd be free again."

"A slave," she said, her distaste clear. "I know that word. Someone owned those men? Their lives did not belong to themselves?"

"Yes."

Her mouth twisted. "My da spoke true. Wickedness lies in the lands beyond the Wild." She hugged herself, and Deryn noticed again how painfully thin she was. "But I will bring you back there, if that is what you truly wish."

"And then what will you do? Return here?"

Alia was quiet again for a long time, and when she finally spoke, her voice trembled. "I don't know."

Deryn was surprised at how quickly they reached the old forest road. Alia moved with practiced ease through the undergrowth, guiding them unerringly despite the sun and sky being obscured completely at times by the dense canopy. She also seemed unafraid of stumbling into a kanth nest or any other danger, and Deryn just had to assume that she was intimately familiar with these woods. It seemed like they'd been traveling for less than a turned glass when they suddenly emerged out onto the road.

It was a wide scar cut into the flesh of the forest, fringed by the stumps of felled trees. Maybe once there had been a concerted attempt to keep the way free of brambles and creepers, back when great wagons laden with skyspear planks rumbled along here regularly, but now that the only traffic was the supply wagon that came fortnightly the forest had begun to slowly but inexorably swallow the road. Small bright flowers spotted the grass growing around where the wagon wheels had carved furrows, and the sight of them gave him a twinge of nostalgia. He remembered riding in the back of the wagon with his mother when they'd first come to the old logging camp, watching the colorful carpet as it flowed below their dangling feet.

Two years and a lifetime ago.

A large swathe of the sky was now visible, and Deryn could tell by the faint purpling that evening was coming. The thought of spending the night out here surrounded by the forest made his stomach clench, but Alia did not seem the least bit worried. She truly believed that the predators he'd listened to howling and shrieking as he lay awake in the slave's barracks would not take them. Deryn hoped her confidence was not misplaced.

"We'll walk until the moon clears the treetops," she said, adjusting the sack slung over her shoulder. "That should let us reach a shelter my father built last summer for hunting the deer that use this path. Tomorrow night, we'll have to stop earlier and build our own."

Deryn nodded, but Alia had already turned away from him and started walking. He hesitated before following, turning to stare behind himself at where the road vanished among the trees. Somewhere back there was the camp where he'd spent the last two years.

The place where he'd lost his mother and his boyhood and his only friend and was now, beyond all belief, ruled by one of the Sharded Few. He shook his head and hurried to catch up with Alia. Good riddance to it all.

"Tell me about that man," Alia asked when he'd come along beside her, as if she could see his thoughts. "You called him something. The Shattered Few?"

"The Sharded Few."

She glanced at him, her brow crinkling in confusion. "What does that mean?"

Deryn hesitated. What did it mean? How could you explain what the Sharded Few were to someone who had never heard of them before?

"They are . . . special. Stronger and faster than other men. And I heard that some have powers, but that one back at the camp didn't show any, to my knowledge."

"Why are they different?"

Deryn stared at her, trying to tell if she was playing some strange game. Everyone grew up hearing stories of the Sundering, of the last days of Segulah Tain, the creation of the Frayed Lands and the holds. She returned his gaze innocently. If she did know more than she was pretending, then she had a remarkable liar's face. He supposed he had to assume she was telling the truth and that her father had never told her any history at all.

Deryn chewed on his lip, wondering where he should begin. "They are different because they are Sharded. A long time ago, there was something called the Heart of the World. You've heard of this, yes?"

She shook her head, and he sighed. "It was from the Heart that the Radiant Emperor Segulah Tain drew the power he used to unite all creation. But there was a rebellion, and it was broken into fragments. The great men who had cast down the emperor each took a piece of the Heart with them when they established their own realms. And they found that more pieces could be broken away from the fragments, and some men and women were granted powers when they bore such slivers. The Sharded Few, they were called. They are the rulers of this land. Of the world, truly."

"And one of them came to the old logging camp?" she asked. Deryn could hear the skepticism in her voice.

"We all thought it unbelievable as well. But he had a shard, and his power was undeniable. Maybe he's an exile from the holds."

A pair of bright yellow butterflies with wings the size of dinner plates fluttered from the depths of the forest. He watched them dance around each other until they'd vanished among the trees on the other side of the road. "How is it you've never heard these stories? Did you always live in the woods?"

Alia kicked at one of the grey and white puffballs poking up from the grass, scattering its spores to the wind. "We've been here for four winters. Before that we lived deeper in the Wild, where there aren't any roads or towns. But there were other people. We stayed with them for a time, in houses built up in the trees. Then my father had some argument with the headwoman, and we had to leave." Her face scrunched up, as if she was reliving an unwelcome memory. "I wish we hadn't come here. There's not much that can be foraged. I think I've picked clean most of the berries and mushrooms."

"But there are crabs. And deer."

Alia shook her head. "My da never taught me how to hunt these things. He said he made a promise to my mother. She served the Treesworn, you see." Deryn didn't, but he let it pass. "After he got sick, I did try and bring down some of those crabs, but I couldn't get through their shells."

"We use these," Deryn said, pulling out his thin-bladed knife.

"Yes, I saw you. Later I tried to do the same with my father's hunting knife, but the blade snapped."

Deryn frowned, just then realizing what she'd said. "A promise to your mother?"

"She would not have wanted me to kill or eat any animal." A blush colored her pale cheeks. "Though in the bad months during this last winter I did partake of the flesh of a deer. It was that or starve."

"Well, I'm sure your mother would forgive you," Deryn assured her. He'd heard of some strange religion where the followers refused to eat meat, and perhaps this girl's mother had belonged to such a sect. It must have been hard to dwell in the Wild with such beliefs – Deryn wondered if this was the reason her mother was missing, but he held his tongue. He didn't want to talk about his own mother right now, and he doubted she did, either.

He opened his mouth to change the topic, but his words died in his throat when he saw that Alia looked to be listening intently, her head cocked to one side.

"What is it?" he asked, but she waved him silent. Then she grabbed him by the arm and pulled him off the road and into the bushes. Deryn hissed in pain as thorns plucked at him, but Alia didn't seem to be bothered at all by the brambles. Her gaze was trained on the road ahead, her brow furrowed.

"Something coming?" Deryn whispered. She didn't respond, though her grip on him tightened.

And then he heard it. A distant rumbling, but as he listened it seemed to be gradually growing louder. It sounded like . . .

"A wagon!" Deryn cried, and Alia flashed him a reproachful look. Not that anyone could possibly hear them, of course. Deryn concentrated, trying to see it approaching through the trees. Now that it was closer, he could hear beneath the turning wheels the clopping of hooves, and he knew he was grinning like a fool. Sweet fortune had turned her golden face towards them.

"We're saved," he said, craning his head to try and glimpse the wagon. Something white flashed between the branches.

"Saved?" Alia whispered back. "You don't know who this is."

"It's the trader that brings goods to the camp every few weeks. It must be. We'll tell him what's happened, and I'm sure he'll turn around and go back to Kething's Cross. The magistrate will want to hear the story from us."

Alia looked uncertain. "But what if . . ."

"Come on!" Deryn cried, finally shaking himself free of her and stumbling back out into the road. The wagon had just come into view, and Deryn saw it was covered with the white fabric he'd seen earlier. It was being pulled by a pair of piebald horses, and on the drover's bench hunched an old man with a bristly grey beard. He was close enough now that the surprise in his face at seeing strangers on the road was evident.

"Ho!" Deryn cried, pressing his fist to his brow as the driver pulled on the reins and brought his horses to a snorting halt. "Greetings and well met, stranger! You must listen to what has happened! The old logging camp is no longer safe."

The ancient driver did not reply, staring down at Deryn with a bemused expression. A moment later, another man pushed through the covered wagon's flap. He was much younger, and his dark clothes were of fine make, like what Master Ferith and his son had once worn. This must be the trader, Deryn guessed. He propped one foot up on the driver's bench and leaned forward, putting his elbow on his knee. The corners of his mouth were lifted slightly, as if he'd heard something that had amused him.

"Not safe, you say? What has happened, boy?"

7

HETH

HETH LAY on his cot in the barracks and stared at the ceiling. It had only been a few days since this madness had started, but he thought he'd spent more time absorbed by the whorls and knots in the rotting wood above him than anything else in his life. He could close his eyes and summon a perfect recollection, but if he tried to remember what his chambers had been like in the Su Canaav manse or the common room of the Bull the images that came to him were hazy, as if the life he'd lived before coming to this terrible forest had been nothing but a dream.

Maybe he'd died, and this was an afterlife, his suffering a punishment for how he'd comported himself. He hadn't been wicked enough to justify this hell, though, surely? He'd been arrogant, harsh to his servants and slaves, and callous with the hearts of a few young women, but he doubted even they would believe he deserved what had befallen him. Heth sighed, a swell of self-pity rising in his chest.

He blinked in surprise as a shape loomed over him, blocking his view of the ceiling. The sun-scored face of the old slave named Red Vesch stared down at him, his mouth twisted into an expression of mild distaste.

"Yes?" Heth said, pushing himself up onto his elbows.

"We go tonight, lad," the forester rumbled in his gravelly voice. "Be ready."

"But . . . but the Ashasai. He's gone." *Dead. Murdered.*

Red Vesch grimaced, running thick fingers through his wild grey beard. From the few remaining russet splotches in that tangled mess, Heth had to assume the slave's nickname must once have come from the color of his hair.

"Xiv's not here anymore, yeah. But his plan was sound enough. And the danger of staying is clear. The Sharded is a madman, and it's only a matter of time until he turns his eyes to the rest o' us."

Heth nodded slowly. "Then I'll be ready."

Red Vesch grunted in reply. He turned away, but then hesitated and faced Heth again. "Lad, you better not double-cross us. Might be tempting to forget the promise you made when we make it to the Cross and the magistrate is standing there with his guards. But let me warn you – if you refuse to break our chains, one of us will put a knife in your back. Might be me, might be someone else. But it will come, I promise you on the corpse of the Broken God."

The old man vanished, his footsteps receding. Heth's gaze returned to the ceiling, and he found his heart had quickened. Tonight. They'd flee tonight. Despite his fear of the forest at night, the idea of leaving the camp still filled him with relief. He thought of Kething's Cross and a roast goat shank at the Bull and all those people going about their lives without the threat of being murdered by a mad Sharded.

Something else began to grow in his mind, and he tentatively felt around its edges. Outrage. How dare that old slave talk of *killing* him if he didn't set them free? He owed them nothing. Did any of them try to save his father? Had they shown him any kindness after being forced to live here with them in this filthy old barracks? There had been no respect, despite that under the Shadow he was still their master. Heth's mouth twisted as he remembered all the slights the slaves had visited upon him. The disdain in those side-eye glances, how they'd ignored him over the last few days. Red Vesch had warned him that if he didn't set them free he'd get a knife in the back. Fine. He'd sell the lot of them to the mines. They had all been chained for a reason – thieving and poaching, among other crimes. He did not have to honor a bargain struck with such men. And he would need money if he was going to rebuild his family name. Heth closed his eyes, concentrating on the darkness. Please, let the night come soon.

Heth drifted up towards consciousness. Something was dragging him from the depths, pulling him along despite his desire to remain sleeping. With a groan, he opened his eyes to find himself still on his cot. He had a bitter taste in his mouth, some residue from his dreams seeping over into the waking world. The day had aged, and the markings on the ceiling were now lost to darkness. There was still some light trickling through the windows, but he knew from its coloration that this was twilight, not the next morning.

He sat up. The barracks were empty, which was surprising given the time of day. This was about when the evening meals would be served in the great hall, but Gavin had stopped that tradition. Now they all hunkered here in the barracks at night and hoped Mam Mim would bring them helpings of the food she still cooked for the Sharded and the older inhabitants of the logging camp.

Noises from outside. Raised voices, but not in anger. Something was happening. Heth slid from the cot and stood, rolling his neck to work out a kink. Given what had transpired earlier, he would have thought the slaves would be cowering in here, terrified to attract the attention of the Sharded.

He made his way to the cracked-open door and pushed it wide. The slaves were gathered not far from the barracks, their attention fixed on where the forest road emptied into the camp. Heth's breath caught in his throat. A covered wagon was slowly trundling closer, an old man hunched in the driver's seat with his switch across his lap and a broad-brimmed straw hat pulled down over his face.

A trader from Kething's Cross, though not the one that had been visiting every few weeks since Heth had arrived. Some merchant who had thought to try his luck at this old camp, unaware that this decision could prove disastrous. Heth spared a glance at the old mill, wondering when the Sharded would realize they had a visitor. If the merchant was lucky and put up no resistance, Gavin would simply seize the goods he desired. Or maybe he would pay with whatever wealth he had confiscated from Heth's father. Surely the Sharded must realize that squatting at this camp was only possible so long as traders from Kething's Cross continued to make regular visits. Although woe be to this fellow if he hadn't brought any wine.

The driver flicked his crop, and the wagon lurched to a halt in the center of the camp. His watery gaze drifted over the gathered slaves, then he leaned over the side and spat. He didn't seem unsettled by the strange sight of a dozen men silently watching him.

Heth started in surprise as the covered wagon's flap was suddenly thrown aside with an almost theatrical flourish, and a dark-haired man emerged. Putting one expensively tooled black leather boot up on the driver's bench, he slowly surveyed the logging camp with a critical eye. Heth frowned, wondering if he should know this man. From his bearing and vestments he certainly looked rich, but given his youth and striking good looks Heth surely would have been familiar with him if he had hailed from Kething's Cross, or any of the twelve towns, really.

"Gods, what an absolute midden heap," the merchant drawled, shaking his head like he was witness to a tragedy. "What would compel a man to live out here, Phinius?"

The old driver shrugged. "I don't know, my lord."

My lord? Heth frowned in confusion. Nobles did not accompany trading expeditions, even if they had bankrolled the venture.

"Crabs!" the foppish young man cried. "Apparently those delectable crabs we had last summerwane came from these woods and not the sea. They climb the *trees* to catch them! Fascinating, eh?"

"Indeed," replied the old man flatly, then turned his head and spat again.

The trader finally seemed to realize there was a crowd staring up at him. His eyes swept the slaves, his mouth crooked into a smile that Heth was familiar with. It was the kind of arrogant smile he himself had once worn when dealing with those from a caste lower than his own.

"Merchant!"

Heth and the rest of the slaves shifted their gaze from the young trader to the Sharded striding from the mill. Gavin did not have the look of someone who had brutally murdered a man earlier in the day with his bare hands after being stabbed in the shoulder – he was smiling broadly as he sauntered closer, his thumbs hooked into his belt.

"Welcome to our little town," he called up, spreading his arms wide. "We've been waiting for you."

The trader hopped down from the wagon, landing lightly in the grass. "Truly? I had no idea we were expected. Phinius, did you know this?"

"Nope," said the old man, chewing on something. He looked and sounded disinterested, as if all he wanted to do was pull his straw hat down over his eyes and go to sleep.

The Sharded frowned, a flicker of uncertainty crossing his face. "But you are the traders who come every fortnight, yes? To take away the crabs and deliver supplies?"

The well-dressed young man waved his hands as he strolled closer to the Sharded. "Oh, no. Never been here before."

Gavin narrowed his eyes, his jaw clenching. "Then you didn't bring any wine? Spirits?"

"Wine?" the trader said, cocking his head like he was listening to something in the distance. "Of course we have wine. How could one suffer the rigors of the road without a glass in the evening?"

Some of the tension leaked from the Sharded. "Good. Bring it out now; I want some."

The young trader laughed. "Ha! It's not for the likes of you, my scruffy friend. This is firewine from the volcanic soil of the Ember. Very rare, very expensive. *You* certainly do not have the palate to appreciate such a vintage."

Gavin had gone very still at the trader's words. "Scruffy, did you say?" he murmured slowly, the menace in his voice making Heth's blood run cold. They were going to witness two deaths today, it seemed. If only this fool could have seen what the Sharded had done to the Ashasai earlier.

The young trader appeared oblivious. He had come within an arm's reach of the Sharded, and to Heth it was like waiting for a serpent to strike. Any moment now, Gavin would lunge forward and start ripping this poor fool's limbs away.

Heth blinked in surprise, glancing up. The sky didn't seem any more clouded than it had been a moment ago, but it certainly felt like the day had suddenly darkened. No, the wash of blue above the mill hadn't been touched by twilight, yet down here it seemed like dusk had fallen, the shadows lengthening. Some of the slaves were muttering, glancing around uneasily.

If the Sharded noticed anything strange, he chose to ignore it. Instead, with a snarl he lunged towards the trader, swinging a blow that Heth knew would crush the man's skull.

And missed.

Unbalanced, Gavin stumbled forward, his expression incredulous. The trader had stepped aside at just the right moment, and he didn't even seem to have noticed that the Sharded's fist had passed a hair's breadth from his head. He turned, presenting his back to Gavin with his hands on his hips, and faced the old man up on the wagon. He breathed in deep and let it out slowly.

"There's something about the forest air, Phinius. A freshness that makes one feel more alive. Wouldn't you agree?"

The old man shrugged. He seemed unconcerned that his master had nearly been bludgeoned, even though he surely had just witnessed it.

Heth felt rooted to the ground, unable to tear his eyes away from what was happening. His surprise was mirrored in the faces of the other slaves.

The Sharded didn't seem to understand either. Rather than flinging himself at the trader he approached slowly with a puzzled expression. When he was standing a span or so behind the young man, he reached out like he was going to choke him, but then paused with his fingers almost brushing the trader's neck.

Heth couldn't see why Gavin had stopped. The stranger was still smiling blithely up at the old man, seemingly oblivious to the death hovering just behind him. The Sharded's fingers were crooked like he was straining hard, yet he appeared unable to reach the trader.

And then Heth saw it.

Tendrils of glistening black were wrapped around the Sharded's wrists, stretching taut back to the long shadow cast by the mill. Fear stabbed at Heth when he saw this patch of darkness writhe like a nest of worms, more of these unnatural limbs slithering across the grass towards the Sharded.

Gavin shrieked, wrenching his arms free with a tremendous effort, and the living shadows that had seized him dissipated like smoke in the sky. He staggered away from the grasping coils, rubbing at his wrists where the darkness had left livid red marks.

The trader turned to regard him in amusement, his crooked smile returning. "Everything all right, Sharded?"

"I didn't know!" Gavin cried, slipping and nearly falling as he scrambled to get away from the shadowy serpents.

"Ignorance is rarely a good excuse for anything," the trader admonished Gavin, finally strolling towards him. "Did you truly think you could hide from us in the shadow of the Shadow?" He clucked his tongue, shaking his head with a look of profound disappointment.

"Apologies," the Sharded said, quickly stepping away from the grasping tendrils.

The merchant – no, Heth corrected himself, this was most certainly not just a simple merchant – was showing no fear as he approached Gavin. "I must admit, I am curious where you found a shard."

"A barrow!" Gavin almost yelled, trying to avoid the creeping darkness. It was herding him towards the smirking young man, Heth realized. "Heard a rumor that miners had broken into some old graves up in the Fangs. Went up there to look for treasure and found the shard lodged in a skeleton. I never even knew I was special!"

His face was gleaming with sweat, his eyes wide and terrified. He gave a little yelp as a tendril curled around his ankle. As he glanced down, the young man – the Sharded, Heth knew – stepped closer. Panicked, Gavin lashed out, but the stranger casually caught his blow with his open palm. A loud crack sounded, but the young man's hand barely trembled.

"I thought you must be Unbound, but it's still good to hear you say it. Uncle would murder me if I offended one of the other holds."

Gavin shrieked as the Sharded's fingers closed around his fist and squeezed. When he released him a moment later, the hand was strangely contorted, the bones clearly broken. Gavin clutched his mangled hand to his chest, sobbing at the pain. The Sharded stepped closer and shoved Gavin hard in his chest, sending him tumbling backwards. His screaming was abruptly cut off as he landed on his back, his breath driven from him, but it commenced again when he realized he couldn't get up. The glistening darkness was flowing over his body, binding him to the ground.

The Sharded loomed over him, watching his struggles. Then he unbuttoned his shirt, revealing the shining point sunk into his own chest. The radiance spilling from his shard differed from what Heth remembered from when his father had been killed – it was duskier, like twilight's gloaming, while Gavin's had evoked memories of a dancing flame. Black veins were etched under his skin, radiating out from the fragment embedded in his flesh.

Gavin's screaming suddenly became stifled as the shadows slipped into his open mouth. His eyes bulged in panic, his struggles becoming more desperate.

"Much better," the Sharded said, then bent over him and grabbed a handful of his shirt, ripping it away. Heth realized Gavin's fragment was smaller than that of the other Sharded, the lines beneath his skin less pronounced. For a moment, the stranger regarded the glimmering point.

"What do you think, Phinius?" he called out over his shoulder. "Flame or storm? Or perhaps blood?"

The old man didn't bother opening his half-lidded eyes. "Flame, most definitely. Must have been one o' those that fought in the Wildfire Rebellion. The Ember won't be pleased to hear they lost another shard to the Shadow."

"Then let's not tell them," the stranger murmured, reaching down.

Gavin's flesh rippled like water as the Sharded's fingers entered his chest. Even through the darkness in his throat, Gavin's screams of agony rang in Heth's ears, and he was thrashing so hard that for a moment it seemed he would break the shadows holding him. The stranger's face was a mask of concentration, his lips pursed, and then with a ripping sound that made Heth shudder he tore the shard away and straightened. He stared at the light spilling through his fingers with the hunger of a starving man sitting down to a feast.

"I wonder what my uncle will say when he learns what his attempt at punishment brought me," said the stranger with a grin.

The old man did not reply. The Sharded spared him a quick glance, then drew in a deep breath and pressed the fragment he had torn from Gavin to the dusky light in his own chest.

Some among the watching slaves cried out in surprise as light flared, washing over the camp. Then just as quickly it subsided, dwindling until it was no brighter than it had been before. The fragment looked larger to Heth, as if the two shards had fused into one.

The stranger was panting, his face exultant. On the ground, the darkness was retreating, slithering back towards the shadows from where it had first emerged. The light that had once spilled from Gavin's chest was gone, replaced by a knotted scar, and the veins that had been incised into his flesh were already fading. He moaned and coughed, the shadows having finally abandoned his throat.

The Sharded ignored the weakly moving man at his feet. He turned back to the driver, who still looked unimpressed by what had just transpired.

"Are there any more Imbued we should take with us?" He waved his hand towards the gawping crowd of slaves. "This has already been a most fruitful journey, but we should make sure to be thorough."

The old man cleared his throat loudly and spat, then raised his hand and pointed directly at Heth. His insides turned to ice as the attention of everyone shifted to him.

"Not Imbued, but that one's Hollow."

The Sharded raised his eyebrows in surprise. "Truly? How incredible." He approached Heth, stepping over the squirming man they had all feared and hated like he was a dog.

Heth shrank away, but the Sharded shook his head quickly. "None of that, my dear fellow. You must come with me, but don't be afraid."

"With you?" whispered Heth as the Sharded gently took his arm and guided him towards the wagon, still stunned by everything he had just witnessed.

"Yes. Your life has changed." He made a show of looking around at the crumbling buildings. "For the better, I'm sure. You are going to the Duskhold."

"The Duskhold?"

"Indeed," replied the Sharded jovially, motioning for Heth to climb onto the wagon.

"What about that one?" the old man said as Heth clambered up, nodding towards where Gavin was still splayed out on the ground, his legs and arms moving feebly.

"Let us leave him to the others," the Sharded said as he followed Heth onto the wagon. "I'm sure they will treat him like he deserves. He seemed like a lovely fellow."

"Am I truly Hollow?" Heth asked the old man, feeling like he was drifting through a dream.

"Aye, lad," he replied, not as gruff as before. He jerked a gnarled thumb towards the wagon's flap. "Now go back with the others. Time to get moving again."

"Others?" Heth murmured as the Sharded drew back the fabric and pushed him inside. He took two stumbling steps and then stopped abruptly.

Seated on a bench in the wagon, staring at him with wide, frightened eyes, were the indentured Heth had beaten half to death and the filthy girl from the forest.

8

DERYN

THE SLAVER'S son looked like he had just come face to face with a pair of ghosts. His startled gaze flicked from Deryn to Alia and back again, his expression a mixture of disbelief and dismay as he hovered in the entrance, and then the Sharded slipped through the flap and pushed him farther inside the wagon.

"Find a seat," the man said, gesturing towards the empty space on the bench beside Deryn. Taking his own advice, the Sharded collapsed into the only chair inside the wagon, a heavily cushioned, gilded monstrosity that seemed incongruous with the otherwise humble décor. His shirt was half-unbuttoned, the fragment sunk into his chest pulsing with murky light, his skin glistening with sweat.

Heth ignored the Sharded and remained standing, his hands balled into fists like he was expecting to have to fight soon.

Deryn was tempted to oblige him, anger churning in his gut. His back ached just looking at the boy who had nearly crippled him.

"Phinius! Let us be off!" the Sharded called out loudly, his hands curled around elaborate brass hand rests shaped like roaring lions. He blinked, suddenly realizing the tension in the wagon. He lifted his arm and waggled a finger between the two boys, arching an eyebrow. "You two aren't friends?"

"We're not," Deryn said tightly.

The crack of a whip sounded outside, and the wagon started to move. Heth staggered, catching himself from falling by putting a hand on the fabric wall behind him, but he made no move to sit.

"Rivalry for this fair maiden?" the Sharded teased, winking at Alia. She replied with a blank look, not a hint of understanding.

"He was my slave," Heth said softly.

"Indentured," Deryn replied through gritted teeth. "Never a slave. Never yours."

"The marks on your back say otherwise."

Deryn half-rose from the bench, but before he could lunge at the boy the Sharded smacked his hand hard against the hand rest.

"Enough!" he shouted, somehow keeping his smile despite the edge to his voice. "We've all had a most fortuitous day and there's no reason to spoil it by *brawling*."

"Fortuitous?" Deryn asked, remembering the sound of his only friend's screams as he fled into the forest.

"Indeed," said the Sharded, his tone light again. "You have been plucked from this disagreeable situation, and I have acquired my seventh shard." His fingertips brushed the fragment in his chest, and for a moment the light seemed to shimmer.

"Now," he continued, looking pointedly at Heth. "I don't care if you don't want to be close to dear Deryn here, you must sit. I don't like you looming over us all, and if we hit a rock you might go flying through the wall. The fabric is really not all that strong."

Deryn saw the boy's jaw harden, as if annoyed at being commanded to do anything, but he still settled himself cross-legged on the wagon's floor.

"Who are you?" Alia asked suddenly.

The Sharded shifted his gaze to regard her. "Did I truly not introduce myself earlier? How remiss of me. My name is Kilian Shen. My father is Joras Shen, and my uncle is Cael Shen –"

"Master of the Duskhold," Heth interrupted in an awed whisper.

Kilian inclined his head in acknowledgement. "So you are not all a bunch of backwoods savages."

"My lord," Heth murmured, bending forward to touch his brow to the wood of the wagon's floor.

Kilian's smile broadened. "And you have some manners. Excellent. That will come in handy as one of the Hollow."

"The Hollow?" Alia asked, her brow creased in confusion. "What is that?"

"The servants of the Sharded Few," Heth said breathlessly, still speaking into the floor. "My great-great-grandfather was Hollow and served in the Ember, and we always wondered if it would return to our family. It has long been our pride that we stood at the side of the Sharded."

The wagon jounced as a wheel struck something large and immovable. Heth's forehead smacked the floor, and Deryn didn't try to hide his smile.

"Sit up, sit up," Kilian said, sounding exasperated. "You can bow and scrape all you like when we get back to the Duskhold. The Shadow knows, my uncle will insist on it. But for now, let us be more . . . informal."

"Are we also . . . Hollow?" Deryn asked, slightly unnerved to see the arrogant boy prostrating himself before this man.

Kilian chuckled, shaking his head. "No, no, no. You two are both Imbued."

Heth gasped, staring at them in shock.

Imbued? The word was vaguely familiar to Deryn, like he had heard it before spoken around him, perhaps when his mother had served in the houses of the rich.

Kilian's eyes crinkled when he saw their confusion. He seemed to be relishing this, Deryn thought, as if he was imparting knowledge of tremendous importance.

"It means," he said, drawing the moment out even longer, "that if the Shadow wills it, you both might become one of the Sharded Few."

"That's impossible," hissed Heth. He looked aghast, like he couldn't believe what he had just heard.

"There is a sweet irony to it, I suppose," Kilian said, drumming his fingers on the brass lion's head. "Once Deryn served you . . . I'm sorry, what is your name?"

"Heth," the slaver's son said, his voice barely audible.

"Heth the Hollow. Rolls off the tongue. Anyway, Deryn once served you, and now you shall serve him. The Fates have a sense of humor!"

Stunned, Deryn could only gape at the chuckling Kilian. The Sharded Few. It was impossible. He was an indentured orphan without a valanii to his name. It took him a moment to realize through his shock that Alia had risen beside him.

"Stop the wagon," she said, her slim arms folded across her chest. "I want to get off."

Kilian gave her a blank look. "Off?"

"I want to go back to the forest." Alia moved towards the flap, but before her hand touched the fabric the darkness inside the wagon seemed to ripple. She froze, hissing in surprise.

"Why would you return there?" Kilian asked, sounding genuinely puzzled.

"It's my home," Alia said tightly, her gaze still fixed on the writhing shadows.

"You have family out there?"

Deryn saw her hands tighten into fists. "No," she finally said quietly.

"Then you live alone in the woods? Like an animal?" Kilian snorted, as if the very idea was ridiculous. "I can promise you, Alia, that I am offering something of incalculable value. You do not know what it is like to wield the power of the shards. If you are lucky enough to be chosen, the world and all its possibilities will open for you."

"Chosen?" Deryn asked, latching on to this word despite his thoughts still spinning from Kilian's claims.

"Yes, well, not all Imbued become Sharded. It merely means you have the *potential* to bear a shard. You must still be found worthy."

Deryn didn't like the sound of that. "By whom?"

Kilian shook his head. "Not who. What. The Duskhold was raised around one piece of the Heart of the World, as were all the other holds. We call it the Shadow, and it is not merely a rock. It has . . . a will, of sorts. When Imbued are to be judged, the Shadow decides if it allows them to claim a fragment of itself and become Sharded. Less than half of the Imbued clear this last hurdle, and those that fail join the Hollow, serving us in the hold."

Alia shook her head vehemently. "I don't want to be one of your Shattered Few. I don't want to live in the holds. I don't want anything to do with *you*." Ignoring the living darkness, Alia grabbed the wagon's flap and pulled it open. Light poured in, sending the shadows scurrying. The old man driving the wagon twisted halfway around, looking at her quizzically.

"Stop!" thundered Kilian, all trace of levity gone from his voice.

Alia paused, still holding the flap. She turned back to stare at the Sharded, her expression defiant. Heth was goggling at the girl like he couldn't believe anyone would dare challenge a man who could command the very darkness. Deryn felt much the same.

"You can't leave," Kilian said simply, his tone softening. "When the Imbued are found, they must go to the holds. It is far too dangerous to let them wander about." He sighed, staring up at the wagon's ceiling like he was searching for something. "That man back in the forest? The one you both so charmingly warned me about when we first met on the road? He was an Imbued never discovered by our searchers. When a shard fell into his lap, he used his newfound strength to take what he wanted and hurt those who denied him. He was Unbound, not sworn to any hold."

"I wouldn't be like him," Alia said quietly.

Kilian waved his hand, as if to dismiss what she'd just said. "That doesn't matter. We cannot take the chance that you will eventually find a shard. If you try to flee this wagon right now, I will be forced to stop you."

"So we are prisoners," Deryn said, finally finding his voice.

Kilian raised his gaze to the ceiling again and let out a deep sigh. "Mother Dark save me. You're not my prisoners. But I must insist you come with me – it is the law of the Shadow, and if I let you go, my uncle would make sure I suffered as punishment." He gazed around the interior of the bouncing wagon. "More so than I already am."

"And if we don't, you'll kill us," Alia said bitterly, finally letting the flap fall.

"But with a heavy heart!" Kilian exclaimed, almost cheerfully. "Come, let us not discuss this anymore. Alia, sit down. Deryn, close your mouth before you eat a fly."

Slowly, the girl slunk back to the bench and returned to her spot next to Deryn. Her shoulders were slumped, and she looked defeated, like she might start crying. Deryn couldn't imagine what was going on inside her – losing her father and being abducted from her life and learning she was one of the Sharded Few. Or Shattered Few, as this was apparently lodged in her mind.

"Very good," Kilian said, friendly once more. "No need to pout, this is the luckiest day of your lives."

They camped that night by the side of the road, everyone save the Sharded huddled around a fire that Phinius had only coaxed into existence after much cursing and many threats directed at the damp wood. Kilian stayed in the wagon, claiming it in its entirety for himself, and he seemed unconcerned that Alia might take this opportunity to vanish back into the forest. To be honest, Deryn was sure that when he awoke she'd be gone, but to his surprise her snarled blonde hair was the first thing he'd seen when his eyes opened the next day. The Sharded and his driver were dismissive of the threats posed by the kanths and fell cats, and since Alia also had shown no fear of the forest's denizens, Deryn allowed himself to trust their confidence and managed the best night of sleep he'd had in many days. They'd wolfed down hard bread and strips of dried meat while the sun slowly dissolved the grey morning, and when the Sharded finally appeared, looking fresh and rested, they'd clambered back up into the wagon, and with a flick of his whip, Phinius had sent them rolling along again.

They'd claimed the same spots as the day prior – Deryn and Alia side by side on the bench, Heth seated on the floor about as far as he could get from his former indentured. Neither spoke nor even looked at the other, but Kilian seemed oblivious to the taut air. He whistled or hummed as he lounged in his throne-like chair, a dreamy smile plastered on his handsome face. The Sharded appeared perfectly content to luxuriate in the triumphs of the day before, and he obviously couldn't care less about the moods of the three sharing the wagon with him.

It was Alia who finally broke the silence. She'd been staring at Heth for quite some time, and finally she turned to Kilian, frowning.

"What does it mean to be Hollow?"

The Sharded had been sitting there with his eyes closed, possibly napping, and Deryn marveled again at her bravery.

"You told us about the Imbued, and how we could get power like you. What about the Hollow?"

A smile quirked Kilian's lips, though he did not open his eyes. "Heth, would you explain?"

The boy shifted, clearing his throat. "The Hollow stand at the right hand of the Sharded."

"Why? What makes them special?"

Heth's gaze flicked to Alia and then to Kilian. "We serve in the holds."

"But why not anyone else?" Alia persisted. "Why does it have to be *you?*"

"The Hollow are almost as rare as the Imbued," Kilian interjected, finally looking at the girl. "Do you remember how I told you about the Shadow, the piece of the Heart of the World that lies deep within the Duskhold? Great power constantly spills forth from this crystal, and the vast majority of people cannot survive long in close proximity. The Imbued are immune, obviously, but so are the Hollow. And so they are coveted by the holds as servants and guards and cooks, for without them the Sharded would have to perform the most menial of tasks."

From his tone, Deryn could tell how ridiculous Kilian considered this.

"Being Hollow or Imbued is often passed down from parent to child, but not always. When the bloodline is pure, such as in my family, nearly every child is born with the potential to one day bear a shard. But . . . accidents happen. Seeds are, uh, sown, and that is why we have searchers like Phinius constantly scouring the lands, looking for newly gifted to bring back to the holds."

A tingle of surprise went through Deryn at Kilian's words. "I didn't know my father. Does that mean he was one of the Sharded Few?"

Kilian shrugged. "Possibly. Or maybe it was your great-great-great grandfather, or some other distant ancestor. When both parents are not Imbued, there is far less chance of the child being born special. Sometimes the gift lurks hidden for generations before emerging again."

Deryn leaned back against the wagon's wall, his thoughts roiling. Surely his mother would have told him if his father had been one of these magical warriors. Or would she have even known? Then again, it's not likely she would have missed a chunk of glowing crystal embedded in his father's flesh.

His gaze wandered as he considered this, alighting on Heth. The slaver's son's brow was furrowed, his lips pursed, as if he'd just realized something concerning. Deryn could guess what that might be. Clearly Heth had been fed a romanticized version of his family's servitude to the Sharded Few. Deryn remembered the man who had looked like Ferith in the tapestry on the wall of the mill, holding a spare spear as his master slew a monstrous boar. Assisting on hunts was a far cry from emptying chamber pots and stirring soups, but Kilian had just made it sound like being Hollow was a lot more of the latter duties.

"Phinius is Hollow," Kilian added, gesturing to where the old man sat on the other side of the wagon's flap. "He is one of our most valuable servants, in truth. A very small number of the Hollow are born with the ability to sense when someone else has an affinity for the shards. We call them hounds. Just by looking at you all he knew that you were Imbued or Hollow. He is one of several hounds we send sniffing everywhere the Shadow spreads, hoping to increase our strength."

"Does someone like you always accompany him on these expeditions?"

A pained expression briefly flitted across Kilian's face at Deryn's question. He sighed deeply, his fingers tightening on the lion's head hand rest.

"Truthfully, no. My presence here is at the command of my uncle. He somehow reached the erroneous conclusion that I was not taking my duties in the Duskhold seriously enough." The Sharded spread his arms wide, encompassing the juddering interior of the wagon. "That I had to – oh, how did he put it – suffer some so that I might appreciate my position more." He snorted, rolling his eyes. "I, of course, do consider my obligations extremely important. Any irreverence I display is simply to prevent the rest of my family – and indeed the whole of the Duskhold – from collapsing under the weight of its own dour self-importance."

A smile suddenly brightened his face. "And yet this punishment has now turned into an unexpected boon. If I were not with Phinius, he would have had to return to the Duskhold for help when he heard rumors of an Unbound Sharded. Then that disagreeable fool back there might have disappeared if the trail had been allowed to go cold. And our little foray off the map has resulted in finding *two* Imbued and a Hollow. That would be a fantastic result for an entire season of hunting, and yet there you all were, hidden away in the forest." He flexed his fingers, chuckling as strands of darkness crept up his wrist to sheathe his hand. "And I have my long-awaited seventh shard. After I merge this fragment fully, I might even gain another talent." Kilian winked at them, looking almost gleeful.

"My cousins are going to be so jealous."

9

HETH

HETH'S FATHER had always told him that their family was special. His ancestors had not tilled fields or sold trinkets or raised pigs. They had served in the holds for generations, standing at the side of men and women touched by the divine. And they had been rewarded for that loyalty. Heth's great-grandfather had been a child of two of the Hollow, yet the unthinkable had happened and he had been born without his parent's immunity to the searing power of the fragment lodged deep within the Ember, the hold of the flame-sharded. And so they had been forced to leave, but before they had departed the grateful Sharded had gifted them with treasures that had become the seeds for the Su Canaav fortune. When Heth's grandfather had been born mundane as well, everyone had thought the gift had passed out of their family forever. They would have to content themselves with being lords among the common people, rather than servants to gods.

In truth, Heth had been very satisfied with this state of affairs. He'd found that hunting and drinking and dicing seemed just about the perfect way to while away his days. Even after his father had lost much of the family fortune, and Heth had been forced to join him in that miserable old logging camp harvesting *crabs* of all things, he'd known that this was but a temporary setback, and in due time he'd

again be in the Bull laughing with his friends and flirting outra-
geously with the daughters of rich merchants.

But now . . . now his father was dead, his family's slaves were
no doubt reveling in their newfound freedom, and he was being
brought to the holds to serve just as his ancestors once had
done. At first he'd been overwhelmed, grateful that he'd been
rescued from that monster Gavin and awed by the presence of a
true Sharded. Now sitting here, watching this Kilian snore away
the day while one of his own slaves brazenly *glowered* at him – a
boy he'd beaten for stealing only days ago – well, Heth was
starting to feel like his situation hadn't improved very much, if
at all.

The disdain in Deryn's flat gaze was making his skin crawl. Heth
wanted to ask him what *should* be done with disobedient slaves, but
he didn't want to start an argument . . . especially with someone who
might one day become Sharded. That was the most galling aspect of
it all – as Kilian had said, he might become a servant to a boy who
had once served him. And if Deryn failed – which Heth found
himself desperately hoping – he'd at least be considered Hollow, the
same as Heth.

Finally, he couldn't stand the tension anymore. Climbing to his
feet, his face carefully composed so the indentured wouldn't know he
was desperate to get away, Heth pulled aside the flap and joined the
old man on the driver's bench. Phinius didn't acknowledge him,
continuing to stare straight ahead.

"Nice to feel the sun again," Heth said. He knew it sounded like
he was grasping for small talk, but it was true. The forest had thinned
around them, the trees much smaller, and the ever-present clouds
that had hung over the camp had vanished as they descended out of
the foothills pressed up against the Fangs. The sunlight felt glorious
after so many months of cold and gloom.

"So you're Hollow as well?" Heth asked, curious if a direct question would draw out the taciturn old man. "Born up in the holds?"

Phinius didn't reply, but Heth thought he might have seen the
slightest shake of his head.

"Like me then, eh? Is it hard, going from the outside to the Duskhold?"

The driver answered with what was most definitely a shrug.

Heth fought back his rising anger. A few days ago, if a man driving a wagon had ignored him so rudely he would have found his master and demanded him punished. But Phinius was Hollow, like him, and according to Kilian he was highly valued even among the servants of the Sharded. So he swallowed the angry words he wanted to say to the old man and instead watched the wilderness.

Sparse woods gave way to rolling meadows, and the rutted road gradually became smoother. Shepherd boys with crooks watched over flocks of sheep, and smoke rose from holes cut in the sod roofs of homely-looking farmhouses. A sea of amber grain rippled in the wind, spotted with scarecrows. A creeping sense of unreality stole over Heth, watching these peasants go about their humble, happy lives, so far removed from the horrors of the deep forest.

He turned in surprise as Phinius grunted and found the old man pointing a gnarled finger at something on the horizon. Heth squinted, and then almost sobbed in happiness when he recognized the red-tiled roofs of Kething's Cross in the far distance.

Home. He was almost home. Oh, he'd give his soul over to the Broken God for a taste of the Bull's suckling pig, or just to sit and listen in the crowd as Jessup's beautiful voice cascaded over him.

A rustle came from behind them as someone else drew back the wagon's flap. "Phinius," the Sharded said, joining them on the driver's bench, "stop here for a moment. I think a new talent might be ready and I want to see if I can manifest it yet."

Phinius did not reply, but he guided the horses off the road and brought the wagon to a halt. Heth stared at the red roofs of Kething's Cross in dismay, so tantalizingly close yet now not growing any closer.

Kilian hopped down into the grass at the edge of a meadow. He settled cross-legged among a profusion of bright yellow flowers, his hands on his knees and his eyes closed. Heth couldn't see anyone else nearby, and he realized suddenly that was probably what the Sharded wanted.

Deryn and Alia also emerged from the wagon. "What's going on?" the forest girl asked, staring down at Kilian.

"Young master thinks he's ready for his next talent," rumbled the old man, waving at an insect bumbling around his head.

"Talent?" Deryn asked, sounding as confused as Heth felt.

"Four talents with only seven shards would be a feat," said Phinius with a note of respect in his voice. "But the Shen blood is strong. His cousin, Lady Rhenna, mastered her fourth talent with only five fragments in her. Ain't never heard of that happening before."

"*What* is a talent?" Deryn asked, his annoyance plain, but rather than answer him the old man put his finger to his lips.

"Give him some quiet, lad. He needs to concentrate."

Alia snorted and muttered something under her breath, but then they all fell silent, waiting. For what, Heth really wasn't sure. The wind strengthened, making the bowed puff balls rising from the meadow around the motionless Kilian release their spores. Heth watched them vanish into the shadow that was crawling out from under the wagon.

The shadow.

A gasp, but Heth wasn't sure if it was from the indentured or the girl. They'd seen the Sharded manipulate the darkness in the confines of the wagon, but there was something more obscene about watching this black puddle creep across the grass while the sun was shining, almost like a living thing.

Kilian kept his eyes shut while the shadow slithered closer, but he seemed to know when it reached him, his mouth crooking a smile as it spread below him like a stain. The darkness trembled, growing solid, the edges of it rounding until he sat in the center of a circle, and then his eyes flew open and he raised his hands from his knees, palms turned to the sky.

The shadow lifted from the ground, bearing Kilian into the air.

He grinned triumphantly, and with a languid wave of his hand the inky circle drifted towards the wagon.

"The Black Disc, Phinius! This was one of the second-tier talents I most coveted!" He threw back his head and laughed. "And one neither Rhenna nor Nishi has attained. They'll grind their teeth to dust when I float into the Duskhold lounging on my new chariot!" Kilian climbed to his feet, his arms held out to help him keep his balance on the disc as it came to hover beside the wagon.

"We'll be hard pressed to keep ourselves unrecognized if you insist on prancing about on your new toy," the old man said, scratching at a mole on his face with a yellowed nail. "Somebody will see you. And then the magistrate of that there town will insist you go to his manse for dinner and sit you next to his fat daughters . . ."

"I understand, Phinius," Kilian said with a sigh, and then stepped back onto the wagon, the black disc dissolving into shreds of darkness behind him. These remnants of his creation lasted only a moment longer, dwindling into nothingness as the Sharded drew back the flap. Before he ventured once more inside the wagon, he paused and turned back to where everyone except Phinius was watching him with wide eyes.

"This calls for a celebration. Come, my astounded friends, I have a few bottles of firewine I've been saving for a very special occasion."

Heth had been drunk many times in the Bull, but never on anything like firewine. The warmth that usually accompanied drinking had been replaced by a tingling heat that skirted the border between pleasure and pain. The sensation had started in his belly back on the wagon, after the Sharded had scrounged up enough cups for them all and poured in a healthy measure to toast his new ability, but now, seated around the skyspear-wood table at the Bull, it was Heth's head that felt like he'd fallen asleep too close to the fire.

"Lovely place!" Kilian cried over the sound of the dueling lutes racing each other up on the raised stage. His face was flushed, his eyes bright, and Heth wasn't sure if that was the firewine coursing through him or the sense of triumph about what he'd accomplished earlier. It could also be the pretty girl with curly red hair that he was dandling on one knee; she had an arm draped over his shoulder and was giggling as he bounced her in time to the swirling music.

They'd exhausted the Sharded's stash of firewine before they'd even passed into Kething's Cross, but to Heth's very great surprise it turned out that Old Jace, the owner of the Bull, had a special reserve of bottles that he only brought out for discriminating – and rich – customers. So far as Heth understood, Kilian had not let it be known that he was from the Duskhold. The gleam of his gold, though, and the ease with which he let it flow through his fingers, marked him as a man of incredible wealth.

Some of that wealth was now represented on the table in the form of the dismembered carcasses of a half-dozen crabs, a whole roast piglet reduced mostly to bones, and an impressive collection of empty bottles. It was a feast the likes of which even Heth had never enjoyed before.

The indentured and the girl had at first seemed reluctant to partake, even though they both looked half-starved. Alia had refused to eat the meat on the table – which might be why she was only skin and bones, Heth guessed – and Old Jace had instead brought her a huge bowl of buttered mushrooms and greens, which she had then fallen upon like a fell cat finding a doe with its leg caught in a trap. Deryn had eyed the food suspiciously, like it was some kind of trick, but eventually the aromas had eroded his doubts and he'd tried a nibble of the piglet's crackling. After that, all his inhibitions vanished, and he'd attacked the meal with a gusto matched only by Phinius. For being an old man, the Hollow could put food and drink away like he was empty in truth.

By the end of the meal, the indentured seemed to find a confidence Heth hadn't seen from him before. He leaned forward, his face flushed with drink, and stared intently at Kilian.

"What happened back there, on the road? You called it a talent. What is that?"

The Sharded swirled his goblet, then met Deryn's gaze over the rim. "Is this so pressing? All will be clear in good time. Let us simply relax tonight, yes?" The red-haired girl on his knee simpered as he ran a finger down her cheek and chucked her under the chin.

"How can you make the darkness move?" Deryn asked, ignoring his request.

A pained expression crossed Kilian's face, his eyes darting to the girl. Then he sighed and brought his lips to her ear, whispering something. She gave him a sultry look, then slid from his knee and swayed her way across the common room, glancing back a few times to make sure he was still watching her.

"You need to be more . . . circumspect. If anyone realizes I come from the Duskhold, we'll have to suffer through all manner of dreadfully boring fetes and feasts." Kilian finally turned his gaze to Deryn, setting down his goblet and steepling his fingers. "And everything will become clear in time. But if you truly need answers now, very well. The Black Disc is one talent of the shadow-sharded. Talents are . . . abilities. Powers. There are roughly forty different talents that have been granted to those under the Shadow, and we have divided them into three tiers. First tier abilities are the most basic and numerous for all Sharded."

"Like how you made the darkness move?" Alia asked, slurring her words slightly. She'd only had a few glasses of wine, but Heth doubted she had ever drank before and it was clearly affecting her. Her eyes had been nearly closed a few moments ago, but Deryn's question had revived her somewhat.

"No. We call that beckoning, and it's something all Sharded can do with a little training. The stronger we grow, however, the more we are capable of doing. A newly Sharded with but a single fragment might only be able to make the shadows tremble. Even that fool back in the logging camp could have eventually discovered how to slightly control fire, since his shard came from the Ember. I am far beyond such simple tricks - you've seen what I can do with seven shards, actually giving the darkness some solidity and controlling it like I would my own limbs. You should know, by the way, that I am particu-

larly gifted at beckoning. Not all Sharded with my number of fragments can do what I can." Kilian sipped from his goblet, looking
smug. "The darkness should come from somewhere, though. It
cannot be pulled from nothing, except with an act of great will. Luckily, wherever there is light, there is shadow."

"You said all Sharded can do this?" Deryn asked. "Even ones in
the Windwrack and the Black Steps of Ashasai?"

"All of them," Kilian insisted.

Heth found that a little disquieting. Some of the other aspects of
the shards he could easily imagine being manipulated, like wind and
waves and stone. But fire? *Blood*?

"Let us return to your question about talents. As we gain more
shards, these abilities arise naturally. We cannot choose them,
although there is some anecdotal evidence that the talents align
somewhat with our personalities, as if who we are has some influence. Sharded who enjoy fighting seem to gain more martial talents,
for example." Kilian lifted one of the bottles on the table to refill his
goblet, but then frowned when he found it empty. "More powerful,
second tier talents usually arise after the eighth shard is attained,
which is already a very impressive feat to achieve. Third-tier talents
are only for the very strongest, both in number of shards and also
natural ability. They also seem more . . . tailored to their Sharded.
Unique. Talents are also used to determine hierarchy within the
holds. A Sharded with no talents is known as an *arzgan*. The
Unbound back at the mill was an *arzgan*, as he only had a single fragment, and talents only appear after the second or third fragment is
merged. Sharded with first-tier talents are called *sardor*. Most
Sharded can attain this level, but go no further. Those with significant ability can reach the rank of *kenang* when they gain a second-tier
talent – such as me." He grinned, looking pleased with himself. "The
last rank is known as *famdhar*, and they have added a third-tier talent
to the rest of their abilities. In the Duskhold, there are only nine
Sharded known to have reached this exalted status."

"Such strange words," Alia muttered.

"They were military ranks during the time of the First Empire.

Several of the leading rebels who overthrew the Radiant Emperor were generals, including my own ancestor, and they appropriated the terms when establishing the holds."

"So what happens if a Sharded tries to add another fragment but discovers he cannot?" Deryn asked.

Kilian nodded at the question. "It happens to almost everyone, eventually. Most Sharded cannot bear more than a handful of fragments. Beyond that they will suffer from what we call shard-sickness and the fragment will eventually fall away from the rest of their shard. Only a vanishingly small number can withstand bearing dozens and reach *famdhar*, and when such prodigies possessed only a few, they were still stronger than others with the same number of shards."

"Is there a limit to how many shards these . . . these *famdhar* can hold?" Alia asked.

"There is for nearly everyone . . . though whispers persist of a few who have become . . . something else. Immortal. But this might be just a rumor – if these godlike Sharded existed, where are they?" Kilian shrugged and looked around, as if they might be hiding in the Bull. "My father and uncle would know the truth, certainly, but those that dwell in the Duskhold cling as tight to their secrets as dear Phinius here does to his mug of ale." He stretched his arms and yawned. "And I've talked enough. The drinks are done, and I don't want to get thirsty again. My bed is calling." His gaze drifted across the room to where the girl he'd been flirting with earlier was leaning up against the bar. She smiled when she noticed his attention and started to make her way back to their table. Before she reached them, Kilian leaped up from his chair and swept her into an impromptu jig in time to the lute playing. She laughed and threw her head back as he spun her around, and then they stumbled towards the stairs that led to the second floor and their rooms.

Deryn watched him go with pursed lips, his brow furrowed like he was trying to understand everything the Sharded had said. Alia had slumped back in her seat, her eyes closed. She looked on the verge of falling asleep right there. Phinius had ignored their conversation, cracking crab legs and sucking out the meat with single-minded determination.

Heth licked his lips. Should he say something to the indentured? Truly, he'd done nothing wrong, but Deryn was clearly still angry about the beating his father had made him inflict on the boy. But perhaps an apology – even if he really didn't mean it – would make the rest of the journey to the Duskhold a bit more bearable. He cleared his throat and sat forward.

"Heth!"

He blinked, his thoughts scattering. A large, florid-faced young man had appeared beside their table, grinning at him. For a moment, Heth couldn't place him, but then he remembered – Wellim, the youngest son of a merchant who owned the rights to one of the silver mines up in the Fangs. He'd hung around the sword-halls and pretended to be a duelist, but he'd been far too clumsy to ever enter the circle for a challenge.

"Wellim," he said just as a beefy hand clapped him on the shoulder.

"Fire and ashes, I thought you were out in the woods chasing crabs?"

Heth looked at Phinius, who had slowed but not completely stopped his eating to watch this exchange.

"I . . . was. Things changed."

"I bet you're glad to be back," Wellim said, thumping him again like they were old friends. "I remember when my father brought me up to the mines so I could start 'learning the business.' By the Broken God was it miserable. Watching these hollow-eyed fools trudge into a hole in the ground every day, and all there was to do was play cards and wager on which of the slaves would die down there."

Heth shifted in his seat, glancing at Deryn. The indentured was staring knives at the fat idiot, his jaw clenched.

"You bet on which man would die that day?"

"Eh?" Wellim shifted his attention to Deryn. "Had to pass the time somehow, and it was great good fun when you were right. Made more than a few valanii that way, enough to pay for a few rounds here at the Bull."

Heth could almost hear the indentured's teeth grinding from across the table.

"Calm, lad," Phinius said quietly.

"Wait," Wellim said, wagging a sausage-thick finger at Deryn. "I know you. You're the scullery boy, used to bring me my pudding before bed. Your mother worked in the kitchens. She was mad as a frothing fox, one day started screaming at nothing and smashing dishes. My father threw you both out – what are you doing here, eating and drinking with your betters?"

"My betters?" Deryn said angrily, rising.

For a moment, Heth thought the indentured was going to tell Wellim that he was traveling to the Duskhold to test for a shard, but before he could, Phinius smacked his hand down hard on the table.

"Lad!" he said sternly. "I think perhaps it's time for you to retire."

Deryn hesitated, clearly wanting to escalate what was happening here. Alia stirred beside him, staring up at the indentured sleepily.

"What's going on?" she asked, and this broke the tension. Deryn shook himself slightly and stomped away from the table without saying anything else, headed for the stairs. Alia blinked in surprise, unsure what had just happened, then hurried to follow him.

"Well, how rude," Wellim sniffed. "He's your servant now? You should have him thrashed for his insolence."

"Go away before I thrash *you*," snapped Heth, then shoved his chair away from the table and stood. Wellim stumbled back a step, his eyes wide. "That boy has more courage than you'll ever have. I saw him stare down certain death to save that girl's life. Do you know what he is, you fool? He's a . . ." Heth's words trailed away as Phinius cleared his throat loudly.

"He's a what?" Wellim asked, confusion writ clear in his fat face.

"Nothing," Heth hissed, then turned and strode away from the table, headed for the door.

～

A cold drizzle had started to fall while they'd been inside the Bull, slicking the cobblestones of the Cross's main thoroughfare. Heth kept his shoulders hunched, his collar turned up against the rain, but still he felt a frozen trickle traveling down his back. It was a black night, the clouds that had rolled in obscuring the moon and stars, and the darkness was made worse because the lamplighters of the town had been rather remiss in their duties – only a handful of the lanterns dangling from their metal holders alongside the street were lit, and most of those flames were guttering weakly. Apparently, no one wanted to be out in this weather tonight.

Why did he? What did he hope to find?

Warm light was spilling from a few windows of the timber and stone houses of the town's well-to-do citizens, and this was partly compensating for the lack of lanterns. Not that Heth needed any more illumination – he had made this walk when he was so drunk that he couldn't focus on anything beyond a dozen steps in front of him. Many times, in truth.

He turned down a side street lined with cherry blossom trees, their boughs forming a familiar arch. He'd climbed these trees as a child, chasing the cook's cat higher and higher, or sometimes gathering flowers to give to his mother. She'd been sick often when he was a child, a small, doll-like woman propped up in her canopied bed, the windows open to let the sweet smell of the trees come to her on the breeze. Heth would pluck as many of the blossoms as he could carry, then leave them scattered on the pillow beside her as she slept.

At the end of the street was a gate of wrought iron, the great house beyond dark and silent. Heth's fingers curled around the cold, wet metal, and he gave an experimental shake. Locked, as he'd expected. After his father had summoned him to the old logging camp, Ferith had shuttered the ancestral Su Canaav manse, letting almost all the servants go and selling most of the treasures his family had accumulated over the decades since his ancestors had left the Ember, with the intention of buying them back after their fortunes recovered. But there were likely some useful items still inside – for one thing, he hadn't emptied his wardrobe before heading off into the forest. Heth eyed the spiked tops of the pickets – if his hand slipped on the slick metal while trying to clamber over he'd impale himself, and wouldn't *that* be an inglorious end to the storied Su Canaav name.

But the house shouldn't be entirely abandoned, as his father had left a skeleton staff of servants to deter robbers and squatters.

"Hello!" Heth cried through the fence at the hunched and shadowed manse. "Barnabas? Lessa? Is anyone there?" He rattled the gate, though even he could barely hear anything over the pattering rain.

He glanced up at the sky, moon and stars hidden by the thick blanket of clouds. What time was it? He'd thought it wasn't far past evemeal, but maybe their feasting had dragged on deeper into the night than he realized. And the servants who had been left here were old, for the most part, many having served all the way back in his grandfather's day. They likely went to bed fairly early.

He was just about to turn away when a hazy light appeared, bobbing through the overgrown gardens. As it neared, he saw it was a lantern held by a shrouded, bent-back shape. Heth would have recognized that stumping gait anywhere, and he felt a twinge of affection.

"Go away!" the figure growled. "This ain't no charity house. Find a different roof to get out o' the rain!"

"Barnabas!" he cried. "A few months away and you don't know me?"

The lantern's light swung wildly as the hunchbacked old man stumbled in surprise. "Young master? Gods above an' below, welcome back! Should've sent word ye were returning, the old house isn't in any state to receive ye."

"It's all right, I'm not staying," Heth said as the ancient steward of House Su Canaav took up the key dangling on a chain around his neck.

"Well, ye'll stay for the night at least," the old man muttered as he unlocked the gate and swung it wide. "Come on, let's get ye out of this damned rain."

"I have a room at the Bull," Heth said as Barnabas shuffled up the path to the manse's elaborate portico. "And I'm traveling with others – we're leaving early on the morrow."

The old servant tilted his head to one side, and Heth could imagine the confusion crinkling his wrinkled face. "Is the master in town? Or did he stay up in the forest hunting those crabs?"

"Barnabas," Heth said, and something in his voice made the steward stop and turn around. "My father is dead."

The old man clutched at his chest like his heart had just skipped a beat. "Truly?" he whispered, blinking rheumy eyes. The light inside the lantern was wobbling in his trembling hand.

Heth could only nod, his throat tight.

Barnabas was quiet for a moment, and then he drew himself up straighter. "Terrible news, young master."

Heth nodded, and the steward turned away. He followed Barnabas as the old man took another key from the chain around his neck and unlocked the great door of polished black skyspear wood. Grunting with the effort, the old man pushed the door open. Hinges squealed in protest, making Heth wince.

"Sorry, young master," Barnabas muttered apologetically as he stepped inside. "Haven't opened the front door in months, must have stiffened up a bit. I usually go in the servant's entrance."

Heth stepped inside as the steward wandered the grand foyer lighting candles with the help of a char cloth and his lantern. White linen covered the entranceway's divans and side tables, and from the wet tracks he had made on the dusty floor no one had been in this room for quite some time. Heth shivered, finally realizing once he was out of the rain how chilled he was.

"Your closets are still full," Barnabas said when he noticed the trembling. "Bit musty, perhaps, but the clothes are dry at least. Why don't ye go up and change, and I'll pour us a drink in the kitchen."

Heth glanced in surprise at the old steward. If his father was here, the thought of sharing a nightcap with the help would have horrified him. But that was just it, wasn't it? Things had changed forever. Barnabas was watching him carefully, as if curious how this rather brazen overture would be received.

Heth ran his fingers through his rain slicked hair, then nodded. "That sounds good, Barnabas. I'll be down in a moment."

Heth hadn't been in the kitchens since he was a small boy. There had been a woman, he vaguely remembered, a cook who would sneak him cakes if he crept in after dinner when his father had retired to his solarium to drink with the old overseer, the one before Jogan. He'd gone to her crying several times when his father had struck him for doing something childish. She'd held him tight and whispered that everything would be all right, and even then he knew it wouldn't be, that his mother would still be upstairs in her bed on the morrow. Still, it had made him feel better. Her apron had been perpetually covered in flour, and the smell of baking bread had clung to her. He still loved that smell.

Barnabas was seated at a long counter with a dusky bottle of green glass and a pair of chipped ceramic tumblers in front of him. Not the fine crystal or glass Heth had always used before, even when he was a boy – these were servant's glasses.

The steward saw where he was looking and shrugged apologetically. "Sorry, lad. Your father locked up the nice tableware, and I don't have the key."

"It's fine," Heth said, sliding onto a high stool. He placed the bag containing what he'd gathered from upstairs – a few changes of clothes and mementoes he didn't want to part with forever – on the counter beside the bottle.

"I see ye've taken down the sword," Barnabas said as he poured a dram into each of the cups.

Heth's hand drifted to the hilt at his side. The grip was worn smooth, and there was little to suggest that this sword was a beloved family heirloom, other than it had hung in a place of high honor over the fireplace in the dinner hall. But this was the blade his ancestor had left the Ember with, gifted to him by one of the Sharded Few.

"I don't think I'm coming back, Barnabas."

The steward raised his cup. "Never say never, lad. We have a saying where I'm from, out in the moors. 'Tomorrow will be misty.' And it was, always. Can't count on very much in this life, but ye can be sure what comes next ain't very clear, even if ye think it is." He looked at Heth expectantly. "My old arm's gettin' tired. Let's drink to something."

Heth lifted his own cup. "To what?"

"To the future?"

"How about my father?"

Barnabas studied him from under heavy brows. Then he nodded. "Aye. Of course, lad. To yer father."

They touched cups, and Heth tossed back the drink. Searing warmth slid down his throat to pool in his stomach. He grimaced, motioning to Barnabas for a refill.

The steward complied, his face newly flushed. "Harsh stuff, that. We grew up on it, but I've gotten weak after so many years here in the Cross."

Heth turned the cup on the table in a slow circle, watching the movement of the sluggish amber liquid. "Barnabas, what was my father like?"

The steward leaned back, letting out a long sigh. "Ye should know, young master. He was yer da."

"Well, that's just it. I knew him as a father. And he was . . ." Heth chewed on his lip, old emotions stirring. "Demanding. Distant. When I was younger and something bad happened . . . I'd run to you, or Lessa. Maybe that cook we had until she returned to Flail. But never him. If I came to him crying, he'd frown and tell me I was foolish. Even when . . ." Heth swallowed away the lump that had suddenly appeared in his throat. "Even when my mother died, he didn't hug me or tell me it would be all right. That was you."

"Aye, I remember, lad," Barnabas said softly.

"He was a hard man."

"Family was everything to him," the old steward said after a long silence. "Everything. His whole life was dedicated to restoring yer name, leaving ye with more than what had been given to him. That should tell ye something. He cared deeply, even if he didn't know how to show it."

Tears prickled Heth's eyes, and he blinked them away. He swallowed another mouthful of the vile spirit, wishing it would dissolve the ache inside him.

"What will you do now, Barnabas?"

The steward sighed deeply, rubbing at his face. "Back to the moor, I s'pose. Lessa too. I have enough saved for a nice cottage up there and enough of Gelly's Wrath"—he indicated the bottle with a gnarled finger—"to keep me warm through the winters. This house . . ." he looked around and then shook his head. "It'll be taken by whichever of the other families yer father owed the most to. Sorry, lad. I wish it could be saved and sitting here for ye if where ye going don't work out. But yer father's debts had debts."

Heth crooked a sad smile, then knocked back the rest of his drink. "I don't care much. Not many good memories for me inside these walls."

Barnabas refilled their cups one last time, draining the bottle. He raised his cup again, holding Heth's gaze. "What came before is finished, dead and buried. Let it have no power over us. To the future, lad. Tomorrow is a new day."

10

DERYN

THEY SET off from Kething's Cross the next morning, every step on the way to the wagon sending a spike of pain through Deryn's head. Phinius and Kilian had drunk more than any of them, but the two men from the Duskhold seemed absolutely unaffected by the huge amount of wine they had quaffed the night before. The Hollow servant was his typical stoic self, barely bothering to grunt a greeting as they clambered up into the wagon, while inside Kilian was already ensconced in his throne, grinning like a cat that had just caught a mouse, one leg flung over an armrest. Alia was suffering the most from their feasting, which made sense – she was a tiny slip of a thing, and Deryn suspected it had been the first time she'd ever drunk wine. He had to help her into the wagon, and as soon as they found their customary spots on the bench, she slumped against him, her head on his shoulder. Of the slaver's son there was no sign – he did not join them in the Bull's common room for breakfast, nor did he appear when Kilian proclaimed it was time to depart. Deryn wondered if he had fled during the night, but almost as soon as this thought crossed his mind the flap was thrown back, and Heth tumbled inside, panting hard.

"Apologies," he said between gulping breaths, tossing a heavy-looking bag on the floor. He was dressed in a grey damask tunic and black breeches, both far nicer than what he'd been wearing the day before, and a sword was belted at his waist. He looked like a spoiled rich brat once again, Deryn thought.

"Accepted," Kilian drawled, drumming his fingers on the brass lion head. "But only this one time. The Sharded never wait for the Hollow, Heth. In the Duskhold, if you disrespected my uncle in this manner, he would drag you up to the highest crenellations and toss you over." Kilian said this lightly, his smile never faltering, but Deryn felt quite sure that he was serious.

The Sharded's attention shifted from Heth, as if dismissing him. "Phinius!" he cried, "Let us be off!"

Moments later the wagon lurched into motion, the jouncing and jolting like hammer blows, with his skull the anvil. Deryn was sorely tempted to lean over and put his head between his knees, but he didn't want to look weak in front of the Sharded or the slaver's son. Alia had no such compunctions, and from how she was leaning against him, Deryn suspected it wouldn't be long until she was sprawled unconscious in his lap.

He blinked in surprise when he realized Heth had approached and was standing next to him. The boy was holding a green bag of some glistening, expensive-looking material – silk, perhaps – drawn tight by a golden drawstring. Deryn waited a moment for him to say something, but the slaver's son seemed at a loss for words.

"Well? What do you want?" he finally asked.

Heth shook himself slightly, as if he was waking from a daydream, and held out the sack. "Here," he said. "I brought this for you."

Deryn stared at the bag, but made no move to take it. "What is it?"

"Clothes."

"I have clothes."

"You have what you're wearing, but that shirt won't last much longer. There are holes already opening in the back."

Oh, can you see where you whipped me? Deryn wanted to say, but he held his tongue.

Apparently emboldened by his silence, Heth undid the drawstring and pulled out a fine blue tunic with mother-of-pearl buttons. "This is a little small for me, but it should fit you fine. There are pants in there as well, and another shirt."

"I don't need your charity," Deryn said through gritted teeth.

Heth shrugged. "It's not charity, because I'm not rich anymore. I have nothing except what I'm carrying right now, and these clothes are useless to me. If you don't want them, I'll give them to Phinius, I suppose."

Deryn's gaze drifted from the shirt to Heth's face. The slaver's son was trying to look indifferent about whether Deryn accepted this gift, but there was something in his expression that suggested otherwise. Almost a desperation, Deryn thought.

Maybe this was the boy trying to make amends. Pushing down his dislike for Heth, he reached out and accepted the shirt and the silken bag. He still couldn't bring himself to say thanks, but he managed a grunt that he supposed sounded vaguely appreciative.

Heth nodded slightly, then returned to the section of the wagon's floor he'd claimed as his own.

"There's space on the bench." Alia's voice was barely more than a whisper. Deryn glanced at her in surprise – he'd thought she was dead to the world, but her jade-green eyes were open and fixed on Heth. She weakly tapped the wood beside her, inviting him to sit.

Anger rose in Deryn, and he struggled to smother it. He'd told her why he hated the slaver's son – she had no right to invite him to sit beside them. He wanted to say something scathing, but he held his tongue, his fingers tightening on the slick fabric of the bag he held.

"Thank you," Heth said, and to Deryn's surprise he couldn't hear the usual arrogance in the boy's voice.

Deryn kept his eyes fixed on the floor as the bench shuddered slightly. He knew if he turned his head he'd see the slaver's son over the top of Alia, only a few handspan away. His back itched, and he wanted to throw the bag Heth had given him against the wagon's wall, then storm out to sit with Phinius.

He started as Kilian suddenly clapped his hands. "Well," the Sharded said, sounding inordinately pleased with what he'd just witnessed, "that's wonderful. I can tell you all will soon be the best of friends."

The day passed mostly in silence, as Kilian spent the morning and early afternoon drowsing in his chair. Alia also slept, a damp patch of drool slowly spreading where her head was pillowed on Deryn's shoulder. When she later awoke and sat up yawning, she realized what she'd done and apologized, but Deryn told her that he didn't care. Truthfully, it had felt rather pleasant, though he couldn't bring himself to tell her that much.

When the Sharded finally roused himself, he looked around blearily, as if surprised to find himself where he was. Understanding dawned on his face when his gaze locked with Deryn, and then he chuckled and shook his head as if amazed by his own foolishness. He stood and stretched, then went to a barrel that had not been in the wagon the day before and pried off the lid. Humming to himself, Kilian fished out a few chunks of flat bread, then tossed one to Deryn, who caught it awkwardly.

"A poor meal after that excellent feast last night, but it will have to do," he said, throwing a piece to Heth and Alia.

Deryn bit down and found it less stale than he'd expected. He chewed slowly, enjoying the taste. Bread had been a rare treat back at the logging camp.

Kilian flopped back into his chair, whistling as he tore his bread into smaller chunks.

"How long until we reach the Duskhold?" Deryn asked after he'd finally swallowed some of the chewy bread.

Kilian narrowed his eyes, as if he was mentally calculating an answer to Deryn's question. "Nine days, give or take. Our journey here was rather meandering, so it's a little difficult to say for sure. We'll stay in Nemansk tonight, and tomorrow start on the old imperial road."

"But that skirts the edge of the Frayed Lands," Heth said, sounding surprised.

"Aye, it does," Kilian agreed. "It's the fastest way. If we took the southern route, that would double the length of the journey."

"My father said the Frayed Lands are dangerous. No merchant dares risk that road."

Kilian waved the hand holding his piece of bread, as if dismissing Heth's concerns. "For one, we are not merchants. Any brigand foolish enough to attack us would barely live long enough to realize the depths of his mistake."

"My father said there were other things in the Lands."

"Your father lived in a small town on the edge of civilization and spent his days hunting tree crabs," Kilian replied testily. "Apologies, Heth the Hollow, but he knew very little about the world."

Deryn waited for the slaver's son to say something more, maybe offer up some cutting reply, but he remained silent. Perhaps the arrogance he'd displayed in the past – which had once burned so bright and hot – truly was just cold ashes now.

Deryn had also heard stories about the Frayed Lands, and the thought of going anywhere near those grasslands made him nervous. Every child was told tales of what had happened long ago, when the Heart of the World had been shattered in the great city of Gendurdrang, the ancient capital of the First Empire. Reality had fractured and torn, and from these rents had spilled creatures from elsewhere, things that still haunted the stories parents told their children a thousand years later. There were rumors that the dead also stalked the Frayed Lands, whatever strange power that still lingered after the fall of the Radiant Emperor Segulah Tain refusing to let their souls rest. In the present age none but the People of the Wind in their itinerant tribes dared brave the grasslands, and Deryn had been told that even those bearers of the wind shards did not risk venturing too deep into the Lands.

"Then we will see this cursed ground?" Alia asked. "A woodswitch once told me about this place. She said it was an infection in the world's flesh, and that even in the far distant Wild the great trees could feel the wrongness seeping into the earth."

Deryn turned to Alia, surprised she had heard of the Frayed Lands. He had assumed from her ignorance about the Sharded Few and the Heart of the World that she knew nothing of the events that had shaped the world beyond the Wild.

"The road we will follow does not venture into the Lands itself," Kilian told her through a mouthful of bread, "but yes, you will be able to gaze upon its fringes. And truly," he continued, his voice now softening, "do not be afraid. The edge of the Frayed Lands is no more dangerous than anywhere else. The wind-sharded help keep the things that dwell deeper in the grasslands very far from its borders. Though at night you may still see the remnants of Gendurdrang, and believe me, that is a sight to behold."

"Surely those ruins are very far away?" Heth asked, finally finding his voice again after Kilian's admonishments.

"Oh, yes," the Sharded agreed, dusting his hands free of crumbs as he finished the last of his bread. "Very far away."

The next night they stayed in an establishment even finer than the Bull and enjoyed a repast that would have been beyond Deryn's imagination just a few days ago: blood pudding, tart eldonberry pies, roast squab, and as the centerpiece, a massive boar's head garnished with pastry, its long, curving tusks threaded with golden apples. After their meager lunch, they'd all fallen on this feast like a pack of starving wolves, and by the time Deryn dragged himself upstairs, his head had been swimming on a lake of ale and his stomach had felt like it might explode. He'd flopped into his great wide bed in a room larger than the entire hut he'd lived in with his mother and slept like the dead until Phinius woke him the next morning by pounding on his door.

They'd enjoyed a sumptuous breakfast, Kilian informing them that the route they'd be taking from here to the Duskhold lacked any inns or guesthouses, so they should stuff themselves silly on the butter-poached quail eggs and crisped capons. Everyone had followed his advice, and for much of the following day, the ride in the wagon passed in a shared stupor brought on by too much rich food and drink. When Kilian did break the silence, he regaled them with tales of his life in the Duskhold, elaborate adventures that always finished with him cast in the most flattering of lights. Deryn wondered if Phinius was listening to these stories from his perch outside on the driver's bench, and if he was, what his facial expressions might look like. Deryn suspected quite a few rolled eyes and exasperated smirks.

Days passed, the way growing less hilly as the Fangs receded behind them. The trees shrank and thinned, and the road they trundled along passed through meadows as often as forests. For a while they clung to the edge of a great silver lake, glassy save for where a lone sampan trawled for fish, its net rippling the water. The lack of other travelers was eerie, and Deryn wondered who had built and now maintained the road.

"The Duskhold," Kilian told him when he asked the Sharded that very question. "This is the fastest way to the hold, though the common folk are too superstitious to travel so close to the Frayed Lands."

The wagon suddenly shuddered to a halt, surprising Deryn. Phinius rarely stopped before nighttime.

Kilian did not seem to share Deryn's confusion as he heaved himself from his chair. "Speak, and it appears," he announced, striding towards the wagon's flap. "Come on. Phinius said he was going to stop for a moment when we arrived at a good vantage so you all could see it."

"See what?" Heth murmured, stirring from his nap.

"The Frayed Lands," Kilian replied, flinging aside the flap and exiting the wagon.

Deryn glanced at Alia and found the girl staring at him in apprehension. "Don't be afraid," he told her, patting her thin arm. "With the Sharded here, there's nothing to fear."

Slowly he stood, stiff from sitting so long, and followed Kilian outside into the brightness of the day.

They'd stopped atop a rise that didn't deserve to be called a hill, though it was still the highest point of anywhere nearby. Its grassy sides were bare of any trees or large rocks, sloping down to merge with the plains below. Deryn drew in his breath at the vastness of the grass sea that spread all the way to the horizon – the color was not uniform, with the grass closest to them burnished gold by the sun. Farther out, it slowly gave way to a deep crimson, and he could also see patches of green and amber and even a purple that reminded him of the sky at twilight. It was beautiful, and the wind rippling the plains made it seem like something huge was slithering through the long grass.

"Look!" Alia cried, having appeared beside him as he drank in the majesty of the great plain. He quickly realized what had drawn her attention in the far distance where the land joined with sky. There were more colors out there, but with a trickling sense of unease, he realized they were not confined to the grasses. The sky just above the horizon glowed, riven by a shifting assortment of hues. It reminded Deryn of something you could occasionally see to the far north during the darkest winter nights, ghostly colors dancing among the distant peaks.

"That's Gendurdrang," Kilian said, staring out at the shimmering with his arms crossed. "The biggest rift is there. The light you're seeing is seeping in from somewhere else, somewhere far away. My father explained to me that the world is like an egg. When my ancestor and the other rebels shattered the Heart, this caused the egg's shell to crack. Not break, thank the Broken God, but enough for some of what presses against the egg to ooze into the Frayed Lands. And occasionally things step through as well. Riftbeasts."

"Demons," Deryn murmured.

"Are they?" Kilian asked, his tone making it clear he didn't expect an answer. "Just because they are from somewhere else does not make them demons. Or evil. But they are dangerous, whatever they are. Not to worry, though, the People of the Wind keep us safe. Long before such creatures reach the border of the Lands, they are dealt with by the wind-sharded."

Phinius cleared his throat noisily, then swallowed whatever had been dislodged.

"Charming," Kilian said with a sigh.

The driver ignored him, pointing with a gnarled finger at the sky to the northeast. Deryn followed where he was indicating and saw dark clouds massing in the distance, the grasslands beneath darkened by shadow.

"Storm coming," the driver grunted.

"How long?"

Phinius shrugged at the Sharded's question. "Tonight, I'd wager. We'll have to hunker down and ride it out. The storms that come off the Frayed Lands are as bad as anything on the Sea of Salvation. No one is sleeping outside tonight."

Kilian scowled when he realized all eyes had turned to him. "Fine, you can come into the wagon. But none of you better snore."

Deryn lay in the darkness with his head pillowed by the rolled-up tunic Heth had given him, listening to the pounding of the rain on the roof and the wagon creaking and groaning as it was battered by the wind. If anyone was snoring, it was impossible to tell with the ferocity of the storm raging outside. Or perhaps, like him, none of the others had fallen asleep yet – the wagon's interior was not that large, and he could feel them shifting. It was not just the noise of the storm, as the bedrolls they used when camping outside were barely padded, and the wagon's wooden floor was far more uncomfortable than the grass.

The fabric of the ceiling was briefly illuminated by a flash of light, and someone gasped, though Deryn couldn't tell who. Moments later, a ferocious crack rent the night, and fear trickled down his spine. There hadn't been many tall trees around where they eventually stopped for the night – were they in danger of being struck by lightning? He started as something brushed his hand, and he almost jerked his arm away before he realized it was Alia. Her small fingers tangled with his and squeezed hard, and though he realized it was ridiculous, he took some comfort knowing she was close to him.

The wagon trembled. Strangely, it felt different from the movement caused by the wind, a shaking that seemed to well up from below. For a moment, Deryn thought he must have imagined it, but then Heth's voice emerged from the darkness.

"What was that?"

"Lightning striking the ground," Kilian replied, his annoyance plain. "Or a tree knocked over by the storm. Now be quiet and sleep."

The wagon shivered again, and this time Deryn heard a rumbling that did not sound like thunder.

"The wind must be tossing the trees around like kindling," Kilian said, though to Deryn he sounded like he was trying to convince himself more than them.

The wooden floor shook harder, making Deryn's teeth chatter.

"Young master . . ." Phinius said nervously, but before he could finish there was a terrific crash, and Deryn was thrown from the wagon's floor, his hand ripped away from Alia. He didn't even have the time to scream before his head smashed against something hard and he tumbled into a deeper blackness.

11

HETH

Mud.

His mouth was filled with cold mud.

Heth raised his throbbing head from the ground and coughed out what he could, also tasting blood and grass. With tremendous effort, he rolled onto his back, drawing in shuddering lungfuls of air.

What?

Had happened?

Rain lashed his face, forcing him to close his mouth to keep from choking on the torrent of water coming down. He was outside, and it was either pitch dark or the knock on his head had left him blind. His limbs and face were quickly growing numb from the wind and freezing rain.

"Kilian?" he croaked, struggling into a sitting position. "Phinius?" Something hard and sharp was digging into his leg, and when he reached down, his fingers found what felt like a length of splintered wood. Not a branch, but a hewn plank.

Had the wagon been tipped over by the wind? But how would it have shattered if this piece of wood had once been part of it?

The sky blazed bright for a moment, and Heth cried out, cowering and covering his head. A sound like the world splitting asunder almost immediately followed, which meant that lightning had struck somewhere close by – he needed to find shelter, get underneath a tree or perhaps whatever remained of their wagon.

Where were the rest of them?

A stuttering series of flashes illuminated the night. Farther away, and not as searingly intense, so Heth was able to assemble a some-what coherent picture of his surroundings before the blackness rushed in again. They were still in the meadow where they'd set up camp, as he'd recognized the copse of stunted trees they're tried to shelter beneath. He'd glimpsed a wheel lying not far from him and what might have been a shred of fabric caught on a length of broken wood . . . it was almost as though the wagon had exploded, scattering debris. Had it been struck by lightning?

Something was confusing about the image burned into his mind's eye. He could have sworn there had been an enormous tree looming over him, nearly the size of a skyspear, but surely he would have noticed earlier when they'd stopped for the night if that was true? Perhaps he'd been flung farther than he thought.

His body certainly felt like he had fallen from a great height. Grit-ting his teeth, Heth struggled to his feet, nearly toppling over again as the wind suddenly gusted. Why was the ground shaking? What was going on? Another sword-stroke of lightning split the sky, staggering him.

The tree. He'd seen it again in the flash . . . Not only that, but it seemed closer than it had been a moment ago. And there had been other trees behind it, like a forest had suddenly sprouted out of nowhere. The ground shuddered again, and he came very close to sprawling face-first in the grass.

Another burst of lightning, longer than the others, and for the first time he realized what he was looking at. Those weren't the trunks of trees . . . they were legs. And swelling above them was a vastness that defied comprehension . . . It looked like a hill that had grown limbs and come to life, but as he struggled to make sense of what he'd seen he realized the shape was bulbous like the thorax and abdomen of a huge insect. There had been a head as well, and in that flash of lightning he'd seen at least four eyes gleaming above mandibles large enough to swallow a horse.

A scream was clawing at Heth's throat, and he fought to keep it from escaping. He didn't want to do anything that could draw the attention of this monster, but his panic was close to overwhelming him ...

"Heth!"

His name, shouted somewhere nearby.

"Heth, please! We need you!"

It was the girl from the forest. Alia. She was calling for him. The ground trembled as the enormous spider-thing took another step. Was it moving towards him?

He could tell where Alia's pleas for help were coming from, and it was in the same direction as the creature. He should turn and run in the opposite direction and not stop until he collapsed. He certainly shouldn't be running towards the girl's cries ... so why was he?

Lightning rent the night, etching the massive creature against the sky. Heth wanted to curl up gibbering in fear, but he forced himself onwards. Thankfully, it looked like it had turned away, its monstrous visage swinging in another direction. And in that flash, he'd also seen something else, a large chunk of what remained of their wagon. It had been tipped on its side, and the girl Alia was hunched beside it, straining as she tried to lift a piece of wood.

It was hard to tell how far away she was in the darkness, so he just kept putting one foot in front of the other in the direction where he'd briefly seen her, trying to keep his balance as the ground continued to shudder.

"Ah!" Alia cried as Heth collided with her, nearly knocking her to the grass. Before he could apologize, she was clutching at him and babbling, her voice almost drowned out by the lashing rain.

"Oh, thank the Treesworn! Heth! Help me! I can't move it on my own and that thing is going to come back soon and we have to get out of here *now*!"

"What?" he barely managed, dazed by the sudden onslaught of words. "We need to run! Let's go!" He pulled on her, but she resisted.

"No!" she cried, and at that moment there was another flash, and Heth saw why she was so frantic. Deryn lay sprawled on the churned ground, his legs trapped beneath a large piece of wood. His head lolled to the side and his eyes were closed, and Heth wondered for a moment if he was dead.

A deafening roar erupted behind them, making Heth's head spin. He could feel every step of the creature now through the shaking earth. They might only have a moment before one of those massive legs came crashing down on them all.

Alia was tugging on him, leading him towards where he'd seen Deryn, and then she was guiding his hands to the length of wood that might once have been part of the undercarriage.

"Lift!" she screamed into his ear, and he did just that, his boots slipping on the slick grass as he put his back into it. He felt her beside him doing the same, and something shifted among the shattered wagon, the piece they were hauling on tumbled to the side. Heth crouched down, running his hands over Deryn's limp body until he found the boy's arms. Then he hooked his fingers under his shoulders and began dragging him away from the wagon. His burden suddenly lightened as Alia ducked under Deryn's other armpit, and he let her take half the weight as they stumbled through the grass.

Another roar, so close that Heth nearly emptied his bladder. There was a great crunching noise from behind them, and Heth glanced over his shoulder just as another blast of lightning lit the night.

The wagon had vanished, and in its place was a pillar of glistening darkness. Looming far above was the creature, and he thought its four massive orb-like eyes were fixed on them as they fled.

Oh by the dead and broken divine how can anything be so big and terrible and oh it's seen us and it's coming what can we do where can we run

"The trees!" Alia screamed, yanking him from the tumbling rush of his panicked thoughts.

Trees. Heth peered into the darkness – and yes, it did look like they were approaching tangled silhouettes of deeper black. He felt a shudder go through Deryn, and Heth nearly dropped the boy as he squirmed, coming awake. He wasn't dead, at least . . . but they would all be soon enough, barring a miracle.

"Don't try to move!" Heth yelled, adjusting his grip on the indentured. "Unless you feel up for running!"

"What's going on?" Deryn slurred, and Heth sensed his head turning as he looked about.

"A monster is chasing us!" cried Alia. Somehow, she sounded more excited than terrified.

"Monster?" Deryn murmured, twisting enough that he could glance over his shoulder. "I can't see anything."

"Oh, it's there," Heth said, but he couldn't manage anything more through his panting. How was that waif of a girl carrying half of Deryn's weight? Heth's legs were burning, and his shoulder felt like it was about to be ripped from its socket.

He was on the verge of collapsing anyway when his foot caught on what felt like a root. He went sprawling, letting go of Deryn as he fell. His head struck the ground hard, and again he tasted dirt and grass. Heth lay there for a moment, dazed, feeling the indentured moving weakly beside him.

He had to get up. He had to keep running. Heth started to push himself back to his feet when a weight suddenly materialized on his back, and he collapsed again. Panic clawed at him as he struggled to rise, but then he froze when he heard a voice in his ear.

"Stop moving."

It was the girl, her words barely a whisper. The sharp point pressing into his spine must be her knee.

"But the monster . . ." he hissed, the trembling of the ground beneath him overwhelming the pounding of his heart.

"Be quiet," she commanded sharply.

"Alia . . ." the indentured lying beside him began, but the girl shushed him as well.

"You too."

Heth finally abandoned any thoughts of climbing back to his feet and instead sagged into the ground. He couldn't get up anyway, with the girl kneeling on his back, but he also wanted nothing more in that moment than to dissolve into the wet grass. The strength that had flooded him when he'd thrown aside the wreckage and carried the indentured from where the monster was rampaging had drained away, leaving him feeling as weak as a babe.

Instead, he pressed his face into the earth, breathing in the loamy smell of the soil, tasting dirt on his lips again. He felt himself growing calmer. Resigned, perhaps, to whatever fate was lurching closer.

But was the monster approaching? The shaking of the ground seemed less pronounced than a moment ago. A bowel-knotting bellow suddenly rent the night, and Heth thought it sounded a little farther away than before.

"We ran into some trees," Alia explained to Deryn, sounding impossibly relaxed about everything that was happening. "It can't see us very well, I think. It's like a spider, or a kanth – it hunts prey by the noise and movement it makes. The vibrations. If we stay very still it won't be able to find us."

"Where's Kilian?" Deryn whispered, and from the strain in his voice Heth suspected she had a knee jammed behind his shoulder blades as well.

"I don't know," Alia murmured back. "I must have blacked out because I woke up in the grass with my head ringing and that *thing* looming over me. You were trapped in the ruin of the wagon."

A pause as Deryn digested this. "You saved me."

"It wasn't just me," she replied. "I couldn't lift the wood on top of you. Heth did that."

The silence this time was longer. "Thank you," he finally said, and Heth wasn't sure if he was speaking to both of them, or just the girl.

"How are your legs?" Heth asked, surprising himself.

"They ache, but nothing is broken, I think." Deryn gave a little grunt, and then Heth felt something bump his own legs. "Yes, I can move."

This was followed by a muffled thwack like a fist hitting the back of a skull, and Deryn grunted in pain.

"Now *stop* moving," warned Alia. "Or I'll break your legs myself."

The night passed with agonizing slowness. Gradually the rain slackened until the only drops falling were from the branches above them. The sky still grumbled, and occasionally light blazed briefly through the canopy, but Heth could tell that the bulk of the storm had moved away. Unfortunately, the monster that had accompanied it showed no desire to follow. He could still feel the juddering of the ground as the beast stalked back and forth; sometimes its steps faded, and his hope swelled that it had finally decided to return to whatever abyss it had emerged from, but always it came back. Hunting for them, he assumed. The thought filled him with dread.

Greyness crept into the sky, the shadowy shapes of the trees slowly emerging from the gloom. They hadn't gotten very far before they'd collapsed, as the edge of the copse was less than a dozen paces from where they now lay. When he twisted his head around, he realized he could see where the trees gave way to scrub in every direction – this pocket of trees truly was tiny. The creature must be incredibly simple if it hadn't been able to work out where they must be hiding.

"I'm going to get a better look," Deryn murmured, the first words any of them had said in half the night.

Heth glanced over at him in surprise. The indentured looked determined as he stared through the tangle.

"We should wait," Alia counseled. She'd removed herself from their backs after they'd agreed to be quiet, but she looked ready to leap once more onto Deryn if he started moving towards the boundary of their little sanctuary.

"It must be gone," Deryn said, and as soon as he spoke Heth realized he hadn't felt the ground shake or heard the beast's unnerving, raspy bellowing in quite some time. Or could it be crouched out there, perfectly still, like a spider in its web, waiting for them to move? Heth shook his head. He had to stop thinking of this thing as a giant spider – yes, there had been many legs, a bulbous body, and those four great eyes, but if that thing had come through the rift in the Frayed Lands, it was from another place entirely, one so foreign and strange he shouldn't be trying to compare it to anything in this world.

Heth swallowed as Deryn crawled towards the tree line. He glanced over at Alia and saw that her lips were pursed disapprovingly, but she wasn't trying to stop him. His own curiosity suddenly swelled – what exactly had happened last night? Were Kilian and Phinius dead, their crushed bodies lying out there in the trampled grass?

Tamping down his misgivings, Heth crept to where Deryn had paused and was now peering through the underbrush.

The grassy meadow had been churned into a muddy mess by the monster, most of the trees reduced to jagged stumps. The remnants of their wagon were scattered about – Heth saw a lonely wheel propped up against a rock, but the rest had been reduced to splinters and torn scraps of fabric. A few staved-in barrels were lying on their sides, provisions spilling out into the grass. Of the great beast there was no sign – Heth could only guess that it had moved on when the storm had passed.

"So . . . what do we do now?" Alia asked, and Heth turned to find her hovering at his shoulder.

"I suppose we should gather what supplies we can," Deryn said, slowly rising to his feet. Heth caught the wince that briefly crossed his face, but the indentured seemed surprisingly hale for someone who had been knocked senseless the night before.

"Look!" Alia cried, and after glancing around the meadow Heth saw what had drawn her attention. The largest piece of fabric from the wagon was moving, as if being pulled by a wind that Heth couldn't feel. Then an arm emerged from beneath the white expanse, and a moment later, a balding head dominated by a bristly grey beard followed.

"Phinius," Heth breathed as the old man struggled to extricate himself from what had been the roof of the wagon. He was pulling on something else that had been hidden – an arm, Heth realized, dangling limp.

The Sharded.

"Is he dead?" Deryn asked, his voice hollow.

"We have to help him," Alia said, stepping forward. She hesitated at the edge of the trees, glancing about as if the monster might come stomping back at any moment, and then stepped out into the open.

"Phinius!" she called, waving her arms to draw his attention.

The old man paused, shading his eyes as he peered across the meadow at her. Even from this distance, Heth thought he saw a smile on the driver's face as he caught sight of Alia. With renewed zeal, he began hauling again at the arm, this time dragging Kilian's body out from under the fabric. For a moment, Heth thought he was dead, but then the Sharded's head lolled to one side, and his hand clutched at Phinius. His leg was twisted unnaturally, though, and it didn't look like he could stand. Broken, Heth guessed.

"Come on!" Alia said, beckoning back towards Deryn and Heth as she started striding through the wet grass. Her tangled blonde hair was shining in the sunlight seeping through the cracks in the slate-grey sky.

Deryn and Heth shared a glance. He thought he saw something in the indentured's eyes, a softening that hadn't been there before, but then he had to hurry as the boy scrambled to his feet and set off after Alia.

They had gone only a dozen paces before the hill rippled.

Heth stumbled to a halt, but Alia and Deryn apparently had not seen what he had, as they continued towards where Phinius was dragging the Sharded through the grass.

He blinked, shaking his head. Surely that had been his imagination. Though now that he thought about it, he couldn't remember seeing a hill covered in reddish dirt and sere grass when they'd set up camp...

The hill lurched.

"Get back!" Heth screamed as the vegetation and earth clinging to the hill shimmered, then melted away, reds and greens and browns running together into a muddy river. Beneath it all was a vast greenish-black carapace gleaming in the sun.

The ground shuddered as the monster raised a massive leg and slammed it into the ground. Heth turned and began sprinting back to the copse of trees, but something made him glance over his shoulder. He moaned in dismay when he saw that Alia and Deryn were running in the opposite direction, towards Phinius and Kilian and the vast creature that loomed above them like an angry god. He hesitated, and then cursing at his foolishness he whirled around and began chasing after the indentured and the girl. What was wrong with him? This was the second time he'd run *towards* the giant monster instead of away.

Heth's stomach dropped into his boots as the spider-creature's bulbous head and its four yellow eyes swiveled to focus on the tiny shapes. It devoured the distance between them with huge steps, and in a few more moments it could pluck them up with its mandibles. And now Deryn and Alia had gone too far – they would never be able to make it back. They were doomed. They were all doomed. Heth slowed and stopped, staring in horrified anticipation of what he knew was coming.

A lone, stunted tree had survived the monster's rampaging the night before. Its bark was the mottled grey of dead wood, its grasping branches skeletal. Heth wasn't sure why he focused on it as the monster swelled larger and larger, except perhaps he didn't want to watch what was about to happen to his companions.

And so it was quite by chance that he saw the figure step out of its shadow.

Heth blinked in surprise.

The man – Heth thought it was a man, but he couldn't be sure from this distance – was cloaked and cowled, leaning upon a black staff.

The beast thundered closer, its unnaturally bent legs pounding the earth, but the figure did not move, seemingly unconcerned by the onrushing abomination. Heth winced, sure he was about to witness this poor fool vanish into the dust cloud stirred up by the monster.

The man moved a heartbeat before he would have been crushed. A darkness swelled beneath him, and then he was being borne aloft atop a glistening Black Disc like what Kilian had summoned on the road to Kething's Cross, except this one was larger and rose much faster, shooting upwards like a loosed arrow.

The giant creature must have noticed the sudden movement, for it arrested its scuttling approach and reared back, mandibles flaring wide.

Meanwhile, as the disc ascended higher the man crouched down on one knee, gathering himself. Then he leaped, his impossibly powerful jump carrying him directly towards the beast's monstrous head.

"Broken God save us," Heth whispered as the man raised his dark staff over his head with both hands. Blue light crackled into existence at one end of the staff, and a shimmering iridescence traveled down its length. The man's cowl had been blown back, and his head looked as black as the shadows he had so recently emerged from. All this Heth saw in a suspended moment, time slowing to a crawl as the man soared higher.

The staff connected with the monster's face, and the blue light flared brighter as a crack like thunder shivered the air. Bellowing, the beast reeled backwards, ichor erupting from the furrow that had suddenly been carved into its chitin. The same yellowish blood trailed from the end of the staff as the stranger plummeted towards the ground, and Heth gasped, certain that the outcome of this mad attack was a body lying broken in the grass. But before he'd fallen very far, the Black Disc reformed beneath his feet, and though he staggered, the man did not even go to his knees. Then he was rising again, brandishing his blazing staff as he surged once more towards the wound he had made in its face. Four yellow orbs locked on him, and massive mandibles large enough to swallow him whole spread wider. From the abyss of the monster's gullet a torrent of green liquid spewed forth, and the hope that had been kindled in Heth was brutally extinguished as the steaming bile washed over the mysterious Sharded.

Heth couldn't imagine what that vileness would do to flesh, but when the vomit subsided the man was still alive, crouched behind a curving black shield he had summoned into existence. The vomit clung to it, smoking and bubbling and even dissolving part of the darkness, but it didn't look like any had gotten through the barrier. With a sharp cutting motion, the stranger dispelled the shadowy shield, then leaped. This time he did not smash his glowing staff against the beast, but landed lightly on the monster's head and began scrambling higher, skirting the madly clacking mandibles and unblinking yellow eyes.

A shudder went through the beast, and it swung itself back and forth, attempting to dislodge the man. Another ear-splitting roar turned Heth's insides to water. The stranger seemed unaffected, though, as he reached the apex of the great head, only slightly unsteadied from the movement of the monster. Blue light flashed again as the Sharded raised his crackling staff and brought it down with crushing force again and again and again, bludgeoning the beast. Lashings of ichor arced from where the blows were landing, and though it was hard for Heth to see exactly what was happening from this distance, it looked to him like much of the staff was disappearing inside the cracked-open carapace.

The riftbeast sagged until its bloated thorax rested on the ground. The legs that had been churning the grass mostly stilled, though a few were still juddering spastically as the life leaked away from the monster.

Heth couldn't believe his eyes. Atop the beast, the man wrenched his staff free where it had been buried in whatever organ or viscera filled its head. Then he stepped off the creature and into empty air, tendrils of darkness coming together in an eyeblink to reform the Black Disc beneath him.

Heth stumbled forward, with some effort tearing his eyes from the descending Sharded as he finally reached the rest of his companions. Alia and Deryn were standing with Phinius, while Kilian lay sprawled in the grass. None of them paid Heth any attention, as they were all watching the stranger as he floated closer. Even Kilian was focused on him, despite his injuries. The Sharded was ghost-pale and glistening with sweat, his dark hair plastered to his face, but still he managed to crook a smile.

"I never thought I'd be so happy to see you, Azil," he called out, propping himself up on his elbows.

Heth gaped in surprise. He'd thought that the man's blackness had been some aspect of being shadow-sharded, but Heth could see now from the color of his skin that he was Salahi. Heth had never encountered anyone from the southern deserts before, though his father had done business with a delegation of merchants that had passed through the twelve towns many years ago. The man Kilian had named Azil had a strong, angular face, and he was as bald as the Ashasai who had sacrificed himself to save Deryn and Alia from the Unbound Sharded. He hardly looked winded from his fight, although wisps of smoke were still rising from his robes where the monster's bile had spattered. The staff that had blazed with blue light was once again just smooth, black wood.

The shadow warrior sighed when he finally stood over Kilian, staring down at the Sharded. He ignored Heth and the rest of them like they weren't even there. "I thought you said the days of me saving your life were over."

Kilian gave an exaggerated shrug, then winced. "I'm afraid I never imagined a riftbeast would escape the Frayed Lands."

Azil frowned, squinting as he stared in the direction of the crimson and gold grasslands. "Hope for the best, prepare for the worst. Your uncle's words."

"Such a positive fellow," muttered Kilian. "But how did this happen? Where were the wind-sharded?"

Azil knelt beside Kilian, his lips pursed as he examined his twisted leg. "The wind-sharded are the only reason you're still alive. When they realized a riftbeast had snuck past their watchers, they sent a whisper on the wind to the Duskhold warning us. And you're lucky I've always wanted to test myself against one of these monsters, otherwise someone slower might have answered the call."

Azil lightly touched Kilian's leg, and the young Sharded hissed in pain. A knife appeared in Azil's hand, and with quick, efficient movements he cut away Kilian's pant leg. He examined the purplish bruise and swollen flesh of his lower leg, then smiled grimly, as if satisfied by what he'd found. "Broken, but no bone is showing. I will splint it, and later a physicker can give you better advice about what needs to be done."

Kilian nodded tightly, seemingly unable to tear his gaze from the lump in his leg.

"Steel yourself, this will hurt," Azil said. The Salahi Sharded gestured, and strands of darkness slithered from elsewhere, knotting together as they wrapped around Kilian's leg. The younger Sharded grunted in pain as the shadows hardened into a gleaming black cast, forcing his leg to straighten.

"That will support your leg somewhat," Azil told Kilian, "but you will still need a crutch when you walk. Which I would advise against doing very much of. Do not fear – I have the strength to carry you on my disc to the Duskhold. Your companions will have to find another way, though."

"I can make my own Black Disc," Kilian said, his voice strained. "I attained that talent just a few days ago, along with a shard."

The Salahi's eyebrows rose. "Truly? Then congratulations are in order, *kenang*. It sounds like you have a tale to tell the rest of the court. A new shard, a new rank, a battle with a riftbeast, and apparently some success on the hunt." He gestured vaguely towards the rest of them. "Is that right, Phinius? Are these three young ones to be tested?"

"Aye, my lord," Phinius answered in his gravelly drawl. "The girl is Alia an' that one is Deryn." He pointed a gnarled finger at the indentured. "An' they're both Imbued. The black-haired fella is Heth the Hollow."

Azil inclined his head slightly. "A rich haul, then. Well done." He shifted his attention to the three of them, and Heth felt a shiver as the Sharded's gaze swept over him. "I am Azil, called by some the Black Sword of the Duskhold."

The Black Sword. Heth had heard outlandish stories of a great Sharded warrior with that title, and now, having watched this man single-handedly slay a massive riftbeast, he suspected they were all true.

Heth bowed as low as he could, and when he straightened he saw that Alia and Deryn had hurried to follow his lead.

"Find something suitable to be used as a crutch," Azil said to them.

This was a command, Heth knew. He'd heard the same note of authority in his father's voice when speaking with his slaves, and some old part of him bristled at being addressed like this.

He crushed that tiny voice without remorse. Even before he'd learned he was Hollow, a man like Azil would have been farther above him in standing than his father had been to his slaves. The Sharded existed outside the traditional boundaries of society, demigods in truth. The most powerful magistrate or lord was still far below any warrior of the holds.

Heth was just turning to start the search for something to use as a crutch when Alia spoke.

"I will go," she said, and then she was off and running, back towards the grove they had sheltered in the night before.

"Wait," Azil called out, bringing her up short. "I am being foolish." He thumped his staff on the ground, and again a shimmering iridescence played along its length. "Kilian may lean on the Darkbringer until we return to the Duskhold."

"Truly?" Kilian said, his surprise banishing the pain from his voice.

"Of course," Azil replied. "It is what staffs are made for, yes?"

"Not that staff," Kilian breathed, and he held out his arms towards Deryn and Phinius. "Help me stand!" he cried, excited as a child being offered a new toy. "I spent my childhood begging you to let me hold the Darkbringer, and now you give it away so freely?"

"You should have shattered your leg long ago," Azil replied as Phinius and Deryn dragged the Sharded upright.

"That almost sounded like a joke," Kilian murmured, his gaze locked hungrily on the length of black wood Azil was holding out for him to take. He reached for it, but the Salahi Sharded drew it back slightly.

"Be careful, Kilian. Do not draw upon its power. You have a long road to travel before you can harness the Darkbringer."

Kilian nodded vigorously, and Azil passed him the staff. As his fingers closed around it, a shudder went through him, like he'd just plunged his hand into an ice-cold stream.

Something caught Heth's eye, the glint of a dusky facet sunk into the wood. "Is that a shard?" he asked before he could stop himself. He winced, expecting a sharp reprimand for speaking out of turn, but Azil only nodded.

"Yes. I believe at least twelve fragments are embedded within. The Darkbringer is one of the most puissant artifacts in all the Duskhold, perhaps eclipsed only by Night, the greatsword of Cael Shen."

Kilian's eyes were closed, and his face had gone slack, as if something flowing through the staff had carried him to a place very far away.

"Adept!" Azil said sharply, and Kilian stirred, blinking like he'd just been woken from a vivid dream.

"Control yourself, or I will take it back."

"I will. I promise." Kilian swallowed like his throat was parched, adjusting his grip on the staff. "I suppose we should return to the Duskhold. I don't think I can carry more than myself on my Black Disc, and Phinius will need to stay to guide whoever is left behind to the Duskhold, but perhaps you could bring one of the Imbued –"

Kilian's words trailed away, his brow furrowing. He was squinting at something in the sky, Heth realized, a black speck soaring on the high winds. A bird, perhaps? But if so, why would the Sharded find it so distracting?

"Azil," Kilian said, and something in his voice made the older Sharded glance at him in concern. "We have company."

The Black Sword of the Duskhold turned to follow where Kilian was looking. "Ah," he murmured, tendrils of shadow writhing around his clenched fists. "I was wondering if they would make an appearance."

12

DERYN

THERE WERE FOUR OF THEM.

All men, Deryn was fairly sure, though it was hard to tell for certain at this distance. They were seated like they rode invisible horses, leaning forward with their hands clutching at nothing he could see. There *was* something there, though – otherwise how could they be soaring through the sky, their long unbound hair streaming in the wind? As Deryn watched with wide eyes, they circled the massive corpse of the riftbeast, their movements strangely synchronized. He realized suddenly that it looked like they were not mounted on four distinct entities, but one long, invisible serpent undulating across the sky.

"What should we do?" Kilian asked, his voice sounding strained. Deryn wasn't sure if this was due to the arrival of these strangers or the pain of his broken leg.

"First you will give me back the Darkbringer," Azil said, holding out his hand.

Kilian sighed, but he handed it over immediately. Phinius stepped closer to Kilian so that the Sharded could lean on him instead.

"And from here on, you will be silent. No jests, no flippant remarks, no . . . observations that might be construed as insulting."

His grip tightened on the staff, and blue light briefly flickered along its length. "The People are proud and demand obedience and respect from those with fewer shards. If you give offense, you will be challenged, and I will not intercede. Do you understand?"

"Yes," Kilian said, and to Deryn's ears he sounded chastened.

Azil continued staring at him for a long moment, then nodded and turned towards where the four strangers were descending. They were indeed all men, none with grey yet in their dark hair, strange blue markings painted on their bodies. They wore what looked to be hide breeches decorated with tassels and vests open to display the glimmering points of grey light sunk into their chests. Two held unnocked bows, quivers visible over their shoulders, and the others clutched long spears of pale wood.

The invisible serpent they rode settled on the ground, and from the way their legs straightened as their feet touched the grass it must have dissolved beneath them.

"Is there any chance they come to claim our shards?" Kilian asked, a note of worry in his voice as the four Sharded waded through the long grass towards them.

"If they meant to attack us, they wouldn't have approached so openly," Azil replied. "The blue markings mean they are from the Falcon clan. The Duskhold has long had cordial relations with them. Now, if they were Crow or Raven, perhaps this meeting would be more dangerous. But I am not worried. Also"—and now he swept out the hand not holding Darkbringer, indicating the mountainous corpse looming over them—"they can see the evidence of my strength."

Azil fell silent as the four wind-sharded reached them. One was very clearly first among them – he was older, but also the most physically powerful, with broad shoulders and a scarred, muscled chest. The light leaking from the shard sunk into his flesh was far greater than what was spilling from his younger companions, and Deryn found his gaze drifting to Azil, wondering if the shard hidden beneath his robes was anywhere near as large. The other three warriors spread out a few steps behind him, their faces grim. One was scowling, and it looked like something had angered him.

With ceremonial slowness, their leader knelt and placed his pale spear in the grass, followed soon after by his companions. Azil did likewise, laying his staff down with great care, as if it was at risk of breaking. Which was impossible, Deryn knew – he had seen it bludgeon the riftbeast to death just a short while ago.

"Greetings to the Duskhold," called out the foremost windsharded. "The Falcon come in peace, long have we been friends. I am Heart's Blood Running, *kahnewak* of the Falcon for twelve summers, slayer of the Tusked Stalker, feared by the dead that still walk."

Azil dipped his head towards the warrior. "Well met, Heart's Blood Running. My name is Azil, and I am the Black Sword of the Duskhold, bearer of the Darkbringer, and the adopted son of Cael Shen."

The older warrior's gaze flicked to the staff lying in the grass, and Deryn heard a sharp intake of breath from one of the other windsharded.

"The Black Sword," Heart's Blood Running said slowly. "That name is known in the Lands. Another time and place, I would ask to test myself against you, *famdhar*." He glanced at the dead riftbeast. Its four great orb-eyes – dulled in death – were almost completely obscured by the ichor leaking from where its head had been partially staved in. "But this is not the time," he finished, turning back to Azil. He spread his arms, indicating the grass. "Come, let us sit. We brought no yurts, as we set off as soon as we realized the riftbeast had evaded our Watchers, so we will have to have this council in the old way, under Father Sky and Mother Sun."

At this, the four warriors sank down cross legged, the three standing behind Heart's Blood Running stepping forward to form a half-circle. Azil mirrored the wind-sharded, resting his hands on his knees with his back sword-straight. The shadow-sharded cleared his throat, looking at the rest of them meaningfully, and they hurriedly joined him in the grass. Phinius helped Kilian to sit, his broken leg encased in shadow extending into the circle they had made, but the wind-sharded did not seem to care about this possible impropriety.

There was silence for a long, measuring moment, and then Azil spoke. "How is it that the riftbeast left the Lands?"

Heart's Blood Running nodded like he had expected this question. Then his gaze slid sideways, to the angry-looking man seated to his right. The younger wind-sharded flushed, his jaw clenching.

"A mistake," Heart's Blood Running said, looking at Azil again. "The riftbeasts radiate an aura that is easily sensed by our Watchers. It is . . . not of this world. I'm sure you also noticed it when you confronted this monster." The wind-sharded paused, and after Azil nodded slightly, he continued. "The storms that lash the Lands share this unique flavor, as they are swollen with the power flowing from the rifts. This riftbeast was hidden because it was moving with the storm, and that was how it passed by our Watchers. It might have reached here completely undetected if a Sharded hunter from my clan hadn't glimpsed it and sent a warning on the wind to my chieftain. I immediately sent my own message to the Duskhold, which you fortuitously received in time, and then set off in pursuit."

Azil leaned forward slightly, and Deryn sensed he was very interested in what the wind-sharded was saying. "Has anything like this ever happened before? A riftbeast using the storms to evade detection?"

Heart's Blood Running shook his head slowly. "The beasts are near-mindless. They have some animal cunning, certainly, a predator's instincts, but not the intelligence needed to stay perfectly obscured by a storm as it moved across the Lands. It must be coincidence . . . and bad luck that the closest Watcher was inexperienced." Again, his eyes went to the man beside him. Deryn thought he could see a vein throbbing in the younger wind-sharded's head, and he was impressed that the warrior was sitting so still even though he was obviously raging inside.

"It wasn't mindless."

Everyone turned to Heth, who swallowed under their sudden attention. Azil frowned, probably annoyed that the boy had ignored his command to keep silent, but the wind-sharded did not appear to be insulted by the interruption.

"What do you mean?" Heart's Blood Running asked.

"I . . . I mean it was s-smart," Heth stammered. He paused for a moment, gathering himself before continuing. "It attacked last night, you see. In the dark while the storm raged. We all hid, some of us in the trees, and some under what remained of our wagon. It couldn't find us. And then the next morning when it grew light, it was gone. Or it seemed to be. But it was waiting – it had somehow taken the form of a hill, with scrub and trees and rocks. Once we had emerged from hiding, that illusion melted away. It knew what to look like so we would let our guard down."

After Heth had fallen silent, the wind-sharded glanced at each other, and Deryn could tell there was some unspoken message being shared.

"This beast is not a kind I have encountered before," Heart's Blood Running finally said slowly. "It is smaller." *Smaller?* Deryn thought, surprised. "Much smaller than the other insectile riftbeasts. Perhaps it is a more intelligent breed. At the very least, word of what this one did will spread among the Watchers. Storms will be carefully investigated, even if the closest Watcher does not want to get wet." This time his gaze did not shift to the wind-sharded beside him, but the younger warrior's face still flushed even further.

"Well, the threat is over with no real harm done," Azil said, and Deryn sensed he was trying to placate the visibly fuming wind-sharded. He must have felt Kilian's flat gaze on him, because he hastily continued: "Except for the injuries to my cousin, but a few months of bed-rest will see him well again."

Heart's Blood Running dipped his head towards Kilian. "We are shamed that our negligence resulted in this, and that the Duskhold was forced to slay a riftbeast outside the Lands. We are indebted to your family and the Shadow for what you did here today. The People do not take such things lightly." He raised his head, squinting up at the hammered blue of the sky. "The least we can do now is help return you to the Duskhold. Your wagon is destroyed, the horses no doubt run off or eaten. It is many days to the next town – my nephew Crimson Grass will escort you to your hold. He also has attained the Wind Dragon talent."

"That is appreciated, but I will take my cousin on my Black Disc," Azil said. "I would keep him close to me so that I can make sure the splint I made with my beckoning does not degrade."

Heart's Blood Running nodded. "Then I will not keep you. I'm certain you wish for him to be brought before the physickers of the Duskhold as soon as possible." He climbed slowly to his feet, and Azil did the same. Then the wind-sharded stepped into the circle, his arm outstretched. Azil met him halfway, and they clasped forearms. "I feared what we would find when we finally caught up with the rift-beast. Never did I think I would meet the legendary Black Sword today. You have an invitation to visit the Lands, shadow-sharded. Tell any of the People my name, and they will treat you like family. Slaying a riftbeast without help is a formidable feat, and I will make sure news of it rings out across the plains."

"Someday I will take up this offer," Azil replied solemnly. "Long have I wished to see the rift and the ruins of Gendurdrang."

Heart's Blood Running chuckled as he finally let go of the shadow-sharded's arm. "We keep well away from that cursed place – it has been years since an expedition dared approach." He paused, his face turning speculative. "Although with a warrior like you alongside a few of our greatest champions . . ." He shook his head. "No. The risk is still too great. The dead do not rest in Gendurdrang, and they remember old grievances. But there are many other wonders to see in the Lands, I promise you."

Azil dipped his head in a respectful gesture. "I look forward to the day when we can meet again."

At this, Heart's Blood Running turned towards his companions. "Silver Fox Leaping. Broken Feather. We return to tell what happened here. Crimson Grass," he said, now addressing the young warrior who was evidently being blamed for letting the riftbeast leave the Lands, "it is your duty to make sure everyone here returns to the Duskhold safely. Do you understand?"

"Yes, *kahnewak*," the boy said, sounding less sullen than Deryn was expecting.

"Then we shall depart. May the empty kings watch over you, children of the Shadow."

Deryn blinked in surprise at the wind-sharded's choice of words. The empty kings were mentioned in a line from the lullaby his mother always used to sing to him when he was a small child. He'd never heard them referenced anywhere else.

Heart's Blood Running and the two warriors departing with him had taken up their weapons again and moved away from the rest of them. Deryn could not see any indication that the wind-sharded champion was using his powers, but suddenly they were rising from the grass on something invisible and sinuous. For a moment the movement of the Wind Dragon was slow, almost languid, but then suddenly it leapt forward, bearing the warriors on its back into the sky. Soon they were nothing more than a dwindling speck over the burnished golden grass of the Frayed Lands, heading north.

When it vanished, everyone turned to look at Azil. "If there was anything you valued in the wagon, try to see if it's salvageable. I can carry a few items on my disc with Kilian and myself, if they are not too heavy."

"I, for one, am glad we already finished my firewine," Kilian said as Phinius helped him to his feet. The old man had found a length of wood somewhere in the grass, and Kilian accepted it as a crutch rather than try and beg Azil for the Darkbringer again. "What a waste *that* would have been."

"You can carry four others, *sardor*?" Azil asked, turning to the wind-sharded that had been left behind.

Crimson Grass's mouth twitched, as if he had to stop himself from sneering at this question. "I've carried a dozen Falcon talons into battle on my Wind Dragon. Four will be simple enough."

Azil stared at the wind-sharded for a long moment without saying anything, and the warrior's arrogance wilted under his flat gaze.

"Forgiveness, Black Sword. I spoke without respect."

Azil finally turned away, motioning for Kilian to join him. "Is there anything you wish to search for, cousin?"

The younger shadow-sharded shook his head as he stumped over to Azil. "I brought nothing of value from the hold."

"Then you are ready to depart?"

"Yes. I'm quite ready to sleep in my own bed again."

"Very well," Azil said as shadowy snakes slithered across the grass to form a Black Disc beneath them. "To the Duskhold."

The wind-sharded had wanted to follow Azil and Kilian immediately into the sky, but Heth had insisted he couldn't leave without the sword he'd taken from his manse in Kething's Cross. So while Crimson Grass waited impatiently, his arms crossed and jaw clenched, the rest of them searched the field and the shattered remnants of the wagon. The riftbeast had churned the ground so much that Deryn thought it highly likely that the sword was now buried under a mound of dirt, but nevertheless he walked his allotted area with his eyes on the grass, hunting for the glint of metal. His head still felt foggy from the blow he had taken last night, and his left leg ached like he had twisted something in his knee, but all in all he was surprised at how quickly he had recovered from his near-brush with death.

Deryn shook his head, still incredulous at what had happened. He had been almost stomped to death by a giant insect. And it had been Heth who had saved him, along with Alia. He pulled his eyes from the ground to stare at the slaver's son across the field. Heth was on his knees sifting through a mound of broken wood and fabric, his expensive-looking damask tunic streaked with mud. He looked almost desperate, Deryn thought. The sword must mean a lot to him – maybe it was his last link to his family and former life. To his surprise, Deryn felt a trickle of empathy for the boy. He knew what it was like to lose a parent and everything else one held dear. Perhaps

Heth wasn't so terrible. The boy had saved his life, after all. Maybe they could even be –

Deryn stumbled as he tripped over something, nearly sprawling in the grass. When he caught himself, he glanced down, and his mouth dropped open in surprise. His foot had kicked a bronze pommel incised with a familiar image of a flame, and there, half-hidden in the mud, was a sheath Deryn had last seen lying next to Heth in the wagon before they'd doused the lamps and made ready for sleep. He bent down and began prying the sword loose – it seemed like it might have been driven into the ground by the monster – and after a moment it came free with a sucking sound. Deryn straightened, staring at the sword in his hand. He suddenly realized where he had seen that stylized image of a dancing flame stamped on the hilt before . . . It was the same as the brand burned into the heads of all the slaves owned by the Su Canaav family.

"My sword!"

Deryn looked up from the flame-sigil to find that Heth had risen and was staring across the meadow at him.

"Looks to be in one piece," Deryn said, holding out the sword as he approached the slaver's son.

"Thank you," Heth said earnestly as he took it, sliding a hand-span of steel from the sheath to make sure the blade was indeed intact. The relief on his face was obvious, and there might even have been tears in his eyes.

Deryn grunted in reply, embarrassed at being a witness to the rawness of the boy's emotions. As he turned away from Heth, he nearly collided with Alia, who had come running up holding a familiar green bag covered in mud.

"I found this," she said, shoving it into his chest. He sighed as he received the silken bag Heth had gifted him back in Kething's Cross – he'd hadn't been sad about losing expensive clothes bought with the labor of slaves, but it didn't feel right rejecting them now.

"Are you ready?" Crimson Grass called from across the meadow, his annoyance plain.

"Yes," Deryn called back, slinging the bag over his shoulder as he started walking towards the wind-sharded. Alia and Heth fell in beside him, the slaver's son fiddling with his belt as he worked to attach his sheathed sword.

"Then we leave now," Crimson Grass told them, unfolding his arms. He was young, but the wind-sharded had an arrogant confidence that made him seem much older. His eyes were the piercing black of a falcon and also contained about as much warmth as a raptor's gaze. As Deryn watched, the glimmering veins radiating out from the shard sunk into his chest flared brighter, and then the wind suddenly gusted, stirring Crimson Grass's long hair and making the tassels tied to his vest and breeches dance.

"Do we need to do anything?" Heth asked nervously, and the wind-sharded's mouth twisted disdainfully.

"Just do not panic, Hollow. If you plummet from the back of my dragon, there will be nothing we can do except perform the last rites and then summon the birds to strip your soul from your body."

Deryn glanced at Alia and found her watching him with wide eyes. The wind had continued to strengthen, making her golden hair writhe. He wanted to reach out and comfort her by taking her hand, but before he could do this he felt something strange. Beneath him, it seemed like the air itself had thickened.

"Silver Shrike!" cried Heth, looking about in alarm as he was lifted from the ground, his legs bowed like he was straddling something none of them could see.

"Deryn . . ." Alia said, her voice strained. Her feet were now dangling over the grass as she rose into the air.

The air finished solidifying, and suddenly he was also borne upwards. In a panic, he slapped his free hand against the invisible thing he was riding – surprisingly, it felt dry and smooth, almost like a serpent's skin. He understood now why they had called it a Wind Dragon.

"Do not throw yourselves about," barked Crimson Grass, sounding exasperated. He had also risen into the air, but while the rest of them looked stiff and ungainly, he was rolling easily with the undulations. "Simply relax and let yourself be carried. It is rare for anyone to plummet from a dragon, but it does happen." He twisted around to glare at Heth, who was leaning forward to try to wrap his arms around the invisible creature beneath him. After noticing the wind-sharded's attention, the boy sat up, though he kept his hands clamped on the Wind Dragon's sides like that would keep him from sliding off. Alia looked like she was doing better than Heth, though she was so still that Deryn suspected she might be frozen in fear. Deryn fought back his own panic as they ascended into the sky, trying not to look down at the ground quickly receding beneath them. He concentrated on the others – Heth and Alia and Phinius and Crimson Grass – and realized that he must be sitting on the tail-end of the creature, as he could see all of them bobbing in front of him.

With a smirk, Crimson Grass turned around again, and as he did this the Wind Dragon leapt forward. The suddenness and speed of the movement startled Deryn, and he cried out, but it was like he was strapped securely to the creature by invisible filaments, and he didn't slide backwards in the slightest. He let out a long, shuddering breath and squeezed his eyes shut, trying to pretend he was anywhere else.

After a while, the gentle movement of the Wind Dragon helped calm his racing heart. He cracked open an eye as he looked down and then had to fight back the bile that rose into his throat. Far below them spread the Frayed Lands, a shimmering sea of red and gold grass.

"Oh, by the Broken God," Deryn moaned. This was even worse than clinging to a skyspear a thousand span above the forest floor.

"Indeed," came a voice that sounded nearby. Deryn looked about in surprise and locked eyes with Crimson Grass, who was again half-turned around. He was two dozen paces away, at least, but it had definitely been him who Deryn had heard.

"The wind obeys me," Crimson Grass said, and this time Deryn saw his mouth move. "It is a kind of beckoning, this carving of channels through the air between us so we can converse freely. Otherwise, the wind would swallow our words." He was quiet for a moment, as if allowing someone else the chance to test this, but no one did.

"You invoked the Broken God," Crimson Grass finally continued, still speaking to Deryn. "And that is fitting, for my people believe the Frayed Lands were in a way his creation."

"What are you talking about?" growled Phinius, and just as Crimson Grass had claimed, the old driver also sounded like he was sitting next to Deryn. His voice was ragged, and Deryn had to revise his assumption that the old man was handling this experience better than the rest of them. He must be paralyzed by fear, as he sounded on the verge of panicking. "The Lands were made when the Heart was shattered. Everybody knows that." He was speaking too quickly, his words a tumbling rush.

"The People of the Wind hold that to be true as well, grandfather," Crimson Grass replied. "But in our stories, it is not called the Heart of the World, but the Heart of God. Segulah Tain found the corpse of the divine and carved away Its heart, and by harnessing the power he made himself the master of the world. When the Heart was shattered, the sharpest fragments sliced open this reality, creating the wonders and terrors of the Lands. And so, Imbued, it is right and proper for you to cry out for the Broken God right now. This place is Its legacy."

"And speaking of the Radiant Emperor," Crimson Grass continued, pointing at something below them, "cast your eyes upon the remnants of his glory."

Deryn followed where the wind-sharded was indicating. A mesa rose from the plains, vertiginous cliffs thrusting up from the grass, and atop its wide, flat expanse was a great ruin, white stone gleaming in the sun. From on high it looked like the scavenger-stripped bones of a vast creature, an unsettling reminder of the dead riftbeast they had just left behind. This one would have been much larger, though – the entirety of Kething's Cross could have easily fit inside the tumbled walls. Deryn had never imagined that men could build such structures, a collection of buildings larger than a town.

"What is it?" he asked as the Wind Dragon swooped lower, offering them a closer look.

"The winter palace of the Radiant Emperor," Crimson Grass

replied. "This was where Segulah Tain and his court retreated in the months when the capital grew too cold. After the Heart was shattered, the last of the imperial loyalists sought sanctuary in this palace. The final battle of the war was fought here, and my tribe still sings songs about it – fighting up the narrow switchback trail, then the bloodletting and looting within its gilded halls. The empress stabbed herself in the heart as the high lords who later became the first masters of the holds watched."

They were low enough now that Deryn could see the collapsed domes and sundered archways, pillars supporting nothing and massive plinths where once statues had stood. He imagined men fighting and dying as flames raged, the empress watching it all with empty eyes and a jeweled dagger in her hand.

"Have you ever explored these ruins?" Heth asked, shouting like he expected the wind to carry away his words.

Crimson Grass barked a laugh, as if the very idea was absurd. "The palace is haunted, Hollow. The First Empire's death-rattle echoed in those halls, and angry spirits wander there still. I would rather brave Gendurdrang than this cursed place. At least the dead there can be ended with sword and arrow."

"Have you seen them?" Alia interjected, interest clear in her voice. "The dead, I mean."

The Wind Dragon banked, leaving the ruins of the palace behind them. Crimson Grass was quiet for a moment, and when he finally spoke, some of the sneering arrogance had left his voice. "Aye. From a distance, but there could be no doubt. They run hunched over in the grass, faster than you would expect. No meat or muscle to weigh them down, I was told. Just bone and withered flesh and whatever dark will drives them forever on. I was mounted so I could not take to the skies without leaving my horse to be torn apart. I rode for the spring encampment and told my uncle and his *kahnetan* swornbrothers, and they rode out to drive the dead away, but when they reached where I had seen them they only found a herd of antelope ripped to pieces, heads missing, and a trail of blood leading deeper into the Frayed Lands. We did not go back to those fields the next year, even though the grazing was good and the hunting plentiful."

Deryn chewed his lip, wondering what could compel men to live out here in these grasslands, threatened by riftbeasts and the living dead and whatever else lurked in the ruins of the First Empire. Heart's Blood Running had been almost apologetic about letting that monster pass beyond the borders of the lands – why had the wind-sharded agreed to become the defenders of the rest of the world from the dangers here? Deryn was tempted to ask Crimson Grass this question, but the young warrior seemed to have retreated within himself after remembering his encounter with the dead. The others must have sensed his mood as well, falling silent as the Wind Dragon climbed higher into the sky.

Deryn was also tired, and trying to concentrate enough to form a coherent line of inquiry seemed daunting. Bruised and battered after the riftbeast's attack, then a sleepless night spent lying in the mud listening to the monster surge and bellow, and finally the heart-pounding excitement of this morning. If he weren't suspended high in the sky on an invisible flying serpent he probably would have already passed out – the feel of the wind rushing over him and the sun on his face was quite comfortable. Deryn shook himself, trying to banish the creeping exhaustion that threatened to steal up and drag him down into unconsciousness. Although he felt securely fastened to the Wind Dragon's back by those invisible bonds, the thought of waking up soaring through the sky was too terrifying to even imagine. Instead, he concentrated on the horizon and the ghostly lights emanating from the lost city of Gendurdrang, deep within the Frayed Lands.

13

DERYN

AFTER A WHILE, the fear of being so high gradually left him, and he passed the time watching the Lands unspool far below. There were no other mesas or hills infringing on the flat monotony of the plains, but there were other things of interest: great herds of bounding animals, their horns glittering in the sun, the occasional tumbled ruin, and of course there was the grass, which gradually changed colors as they traveled. Rich gold gave way to bloody red and then a burnt umber, and there was even a field so pale as to be almost translucent. Deryn didn't see any animals roaming that part of the Frayed Lands, almost as if the spectral grass kept them away, but there were more ruins, including the legs of a mighty statue, the rest reduced to chunks of stone strewn about the plains.

Finally, the Wind Dragon passed beyond the borders of the Lands, and they flew over forests and hills and even a small hamlet of white-stone buildings with tiled roofs beside a swift-rushing river. Deryn peered down as they soared over the town, hoping to glimpse some shocked faces at the sight of them riding the dragon, but although he could see a few figures gesticulating upwards, they were too far away to see their expressions clearly.

"The Firemounts," the voice of Phinius growled in his ear, and

Deryn pulled his gaze from the ground. In the distance, a jagged black line of mountains was now visible, gnawing at the sky.

"Is that where we're going?" Deryn asked, truly hoping it was not. The range looked foreboding, and even the sky seemed darker ahead, like a storm was playing around the peaks.

"Aye," Phinius replied, and his heart fell.

"What's wrong with the sky?" Alia asked, giving voice to the question Deryn wanted to ask. "It looks like twilight has already fallen over the mountains."

"Comes from the Mounts," Phinius replied. "Many of the mountains have fire in their bellies, and the smoke trickles out to stain the sky."

Deryn's mother had told him about such mountains before and how they sometimes exploded, flinging forth ash and burning rock. How could men be so foolish as to live in such a place?

"The Duskhold was built atop one of the dead mountains," Phinius continued, answering Deryn's unspoken question. "Whatever fire once raged inside has gone out, or at least subsided, so don't you worry. If another mountain erupts . . ." Phinius's words trailed away, as if imagining this possibility. "Well, you can bet the shadow-sharded have some plan for keeping themselves safe. Ain't like the Shens to take unnecessary risks."

"It is unnatural," Crimson Grass suddenly interjected, and to Deryn's ears he heard a note of unease. "Living so high, surrounded by stone, with no animals to hunt or grass beneath the feet."

"There are things to hunt," Phinius replied, sounding almost amused by the wind-sharded's tone. "Though I wouldn't try to eat them. Rock spiders, hiding in the crevices. I used to help herd the Duskhold's goats, and we always had to be on the lookout for spiders. They'd lunge out of their hidey-hole and grab the poor beast, drag him back inside and you'd never see the poor bastard again."

"What about balewyrms?" Heth asked.

Phinius cleared his throat and spat over the side of the Wind Dragon. "Fire snakes ain't been seen around the Duskhold for fifty years. Lord Shen's father hunted the last one ever sighted himself, and the skull still hangs in the audience chamber. Big fella. I heard say there might be some still nesting deep in the heart of the mountains where the fire still burns, but I suppose we won't know until one slithers up to the surface. How do you know about balewyrms anyway, boy?"

"My great-great-grandfather," Heth said quietly. "The master of the Ember had tamed one – I was told it was small, stunted, but still more than fifty paces in length. It would curl around his throne and pillow its great skull on his lap."

"I've heard the same," Phinius replied, a hint of respect creeping into his voice. "Old Lord Char. The story was that when the ancient flame-sharded finally died, his pet balewyrm went mad and killed two of his daughters before they finally lopped off its head. Goes to show such beasts can't be trusted."

"One of his daughters," Heth corrected him, his voice sounding distant. "My great-great-grandfather helped pull the other to safety. It's why they rewarded my family when they were forced to leave the Ember, the hold of the flame-sharded. My sword was one of those gifts."

"And that was why you wouldn't leave it behind," Alia said.

"It was given to my family when we left the service of the Sharded Few, and it will be at my side when we return."

"Aye, that is a tale," Phinius said, almost grudgingly. "A Hollow servant saving the life of a Sharded. Rare thing, that."

"You did the same," Alia told him. "When Kilian was hurt, you hid with him, and even stayed beside him after the monster appeared again."

"Wasn't about to leave him behind," Phinius said gruffly. "His uncle would have had me flayed if I came back without the fool lad."

The mention of Kilian made Deryn wonder how the Sharded was faring. The break in his leg had seemed clean, but there were always dangers with such an injury. A stable hand he had once known back in Kething's Cross had been kicked by a horse, breaking a few ribs, and though it hadn't seemed very serious, he'd keeled over and died just a few days later. Something from his fractured bone had leaked out into his blood, the chirurgeon said after examining the body. Deryn hoped nothing similar befell Kilian, as he'd grown to like the young Sharded over the last few days. Despite the vast chasm between their respective stations, he'd never sensed the cold indifference towards those lesser that had been commonplace among the rich and powerful of Kething's Cross, or even back at the logging camp.

The conversation subsided again, and Deryn settled back in his surprisingly comfortable seat. It almost felt like he'd sunk a little into the back of the Wind Dragon, the creature's invisible flesh molding around him. It was far more pleasant than sitting on the wagon's hard wooden bench.

The mountains Phinius had named the Firemounts swelled larger as they continued their approach. Unlike the Fangs and the mountain looming over the old logging camp, no snow or clouds swaddled the peaks, and there seemed to be little in the way of vegetation – a few clumps of hardy trees clung to the slopes, but mostly these mountains looked to be just black rock.

"Home again," Phinius murmured, so quietly that Deryn suspected he hadn't realized that the wind-sharded's control of the air would bring his words to their ears.

Deryn followed where the old Hollow was looking and realized they were soaring towards a mountain that was smaller and squatter than its brethren. Its top was also different – while most of the other Firemounts tapered to jagged peaks, this one was flat, almost like the mesa where the palace of the Radiant Emperor had perched.

As they flew closer, Deryn realized his mistake. The mountain's highest point was not flat, but a great bowl sunk into the stone and filled with water.

"There's a lake atop that mountain!" Heth cried, telling everyone what they could all clearly see.

"Aye," Phinius replied as the Wind Dragon undulated closer. "I was told that long ago the fire grew too hot, deep down in the mountain's belly, and it exploded out through the top. That was many ages in the past. The flames died down, and water collected in the basin left behind. God's Mirror, we call it in the Duskhold."

That was a good name, Deryn decided. From this high up, the water flashed like a pane of unbroken glass.

"And that must be the Duskhold," Alia said, a note of trepidation in her voice.

Deryn looked about in confusion, scanning the lip of the basin for signs of habitation. He couldn't see anything that resembled a building . . . and then he realized he was staring right at it. He'd been expecting a great house, like where the magistrate had dwelled in Kething's Cross, blocks of cut stone piled into walls and towers, maybe a peaked roof of tile or metal.

The fortress clinging to the slope above the lake looked at first glance like nothing more than a natural rock formation, as if it had not been built but hollowed from the stone itself, crudely carved out of the mountain's flesh.

"Are they ants?" Alia murmured, and now that she said it, he couldn't unsee it. The Duskhold did remind him of one of the mounds they'd sometimes stumble across in the forest, honey-combed by tunnels filled with scurrying insects.

Phinius snorted a laugh. "Hah, don't let them hear you say that, lass. Truth be told, they like to think of themselves as gods ruling from the roof o' the world . . . but don't tell them I said that, either." He cleared his throat, then changed the subject. "Wind-sharded! How did you know the way here? I thought your tribes rarely left the Lands."

"It was easy enough," Crimson Grass replied, sounding smug. "Heart's Blood Running told me to fly to these mountains and look for the one with the shattered top, the broken blade among all the swords." He paused for a moment, then continued. "Also, the Black Sword left a trail that's easy enough to sense, a disturbance in the air. It's like following a trail of trampled grass in the plains of an animal too large and fierce to care what might track it."

They were descending now, spiraling towards the brooding fortress. Crooked towers like beckoning fingers rose from the

Duskhold's bulk, some connected by arching ribbons of dark stone. A few of these spires were clustered around a wide, flat expanse of polished black, and Phinius pointed at this courtyard as they swooped lower.

"There, lad. That's where we should land. Looks like they're expecting us."

A few figures were visible, but if this was a welcoming party, it wasn't very well attended.

The Wind Dragon settled on the stone, and Deryn had the strange sensation of the solid entity beneath him melting away. When his feet touched the ground, he nearly stumbled, his legs wobbling. The others seemed to feel the same, and Heth even looked like he might be sick, though Crimson Grass was, of course, unaffected. The wind-sharded stood tall and straight-backed, staring haughtily at those who had come to greet them.

There were three of them, a young woman and a pair of men, though those two could not be more different. One of them was so old he looked like he had been recently exhumed, wisps of white hair clinging to his mottled scalp. He was leaning heavily on a gnarled length of wood, and unlike the Darkbringer, this staff's true purpose was certainly to keep him upright. His robes were simple black cloth, much like what Azil had worn, though the sleeves were frayed, and in places they looked like they'd been patched. Towering over this elder was a mountain of a man with a bristly brown beard, the jerkin straining to contain his great belly stained by what looked to be spilled wine. The young woman with them was standing closer to the old man, and she was dressed in the same style of robes, though not as worn. She was Ashasai, her copper skin a shade darker than Xiv's had been. Thinking of his friend sent a pang of sadness through Deryn. She had a striking, sharp-boned face, and this was accentuated by her lack of hair.

The old man took a step forward, his staff clacking against the stone. "Welcome, Falcon *sardor*, to the Duskhold. You have the gratitude of the Shadow for bringing these four here."

Crimson Grass lowered his head ever so slightly in what Deryn assumed was a gesture of respect. "Long has my tribe considered the Shadow an ally. I did nothing more than what I should."

The old man snapped his fingers, and the girl stepped forward holding a necklace of jagged black stones. "Nevertheless, you have done us a service. Take this, warrior, as a token of our appreciation, and we ask that you give the regards of Cael Shen to your chieftain."

Crimson Grass bowed again, lower this time, as the girl approached him and held out the necklace for him to take. He hesitated before accepting, as if wary of the gift, but then took the necklace and slipped it on, the rough-cut stones around his neck making him look even more like a savage barbarian from the edge of the world.

"Do you require rest or refreshment, wind-sharded?"

Crimson Grass shook his head sharply at the elder's question. "No. I will return at once. This place is not suitable for one of the People."

"Very well," the old man said, then turned away, as if dismissing him. His ancient eyes settled on Deryn and Alia. "Imbued. I am Saelus, and I will be your teacher if the Shadow blesses you with a shard. If it does not, then you will find yourselves in the hands of Torr, second among the Hollow and their leader while our steward recovers from an illness."

At this, the hulking man beside him stepped forward. He cleared his throat and pulled on his beard, looking nervous. "Ah, that's me. I run the kitchens here, but while Elanin is, uh, laid up, it falls on me to welcome the new blood." He shifted his gaze towards Phinius. "Hound, welcome back. Looks like you had some luck this season."

The old Hollow chuckled wryly. "Lost the wagon, my horses, an' nearly my life. Don't sound too lucky to me."

"What it sounds like is a tale to be shared over a cup," the big man rumbled, and at the mention of a drink Phinius's face brightened.

"Aye, if you want to tap a barrel later, it's worth a listen, I promise you."

The crack of the old man's staff against the stone silenced the servants. "You two can gossip like old maids later, after your duties are finished. Torr, take the Hollow and show him to his quarters. Hound, Joras Shen wants to speak with you immediately about what happened to his son."

Phinius's expression instantly became more somber. "Aye, how is the young master?"

"He is safe and resting," the old man replied, a note of impatience creeping into his voice. "Thanks to the Black Sword. If you want to know more, Joras may deign to answer your questions. Right now, though, I am very busy, and this unexpected diversion has already disrupted my day." He turned sharply on his heel and began hobbling towards an arched entrance that led into one of the larger sections of the Duskhold. "Kaliss, bring the Imbued to the novice quarters. Do what is necessary to prepare them for the testing tomorrow, *arzgan*."

"Yes, teacher," the copper-skinned girl called out loudly, but Saelus did not acknowledge her words or look back before he vanished inside the hold.

After the rapping of his staff had faded, Kaliss finally shifted her attention to Deryn and Alia. What little warmth had been in her face while in the presence of her teacher was gone.

"I also have no time to coddle fledglings," she said crisply. "Follow me, Imbued, and try to keep up."

"Wait," Deryn replied, his anger flickering to life. He was very tired of being treated like a slave, and he wasn't about to accept it from a girl who had no claim on him and who couldn't be more than a few years older than he was. "We haven't said our farewells."

Kaliss's coal-black eyes narrowed, but instead of arguing, she gestured impatiently for him to get on with it.

"Goodbye," Deryn said to Crimson Grass. "Thank you for all your help."

The wind-sharded dipped his head slightly. "I wish you both good fortune when you go before the Shadow. Perhaps if we meet again you both will call yourselves the Sharded Few."

The wind gusted, making Crimson Grass's long hair dance. His feet rose from the black stone of the courtyard as the Wind Dragon took form beneath him, and then without another look back at those watching, he ascended into the sky.

Deryn blinked away grit that had been stirred up by Crimson Grass's departure, then turned to Heth, who was still staring upwards at the receding wind-sharded.

"Heth," he said, and the boy's attention shifted to him in surprise. "Thank you for saving my life." Deryn stepped forward, holding out his arm. He was surprising himself more than a little by doing this, but during the long flight he'd realized that the well of anger inside him that had been filled ever since his mother had died had somehow been emptied in the last few days. It felt liberating to unclench the rage that he'd held for so long.

Heth swallowed, hesitating briefly before he reached out and clasped Deryn's forearm. "And thank you for finding my family's sword, Deryn." He might have said more, but suddenly Alia's thin arms were around his neck.

"Take care, Heth," she said. "Good luck being Hollow."

The Ashasai girl snorted loudly. "Where do you think you're all going? None of you are leaving the Duskhold, that I can promise. And if one of you fails the test tomorrow, then you'll be joining this one in the Hollows' quarters. Now come on, or I'll leave you both to find your own way, and that likely would result in a search party needing to be sent out later."

Alia disentangled herself from Heth, leaving the boy looking a little flustered. Torr's huge hand clapped him on the shoulder a moment later, and together with Phinius they turned towards a smaller and less impressive doorway than the one the old man had used.

With a last glance at Heth and Phinius, Deryn hurried to follow Kaliss, who was already striding towards the larger archway. As he caught up with her, his eyes were drawn to a woman standing on a balcony of black stone jutting from one of the crooked towers. She was watching them, the intensity of her attention almost unsettling. She looked like a wraith from the underworld, her skin alabaster white and a waterfall of straight black hair framing her face. She wasn't beautiful, but there was something arresting about her appear-ance, and Deryn found he was having trouble looking away.

"Who is that?" he asked as they neared the shadowed interior of the Duskhold.

Kaliss glanced up at the watching woman, then stumbled slightly, for the first time looking flustered. "Leantha. I don't know why she's here, but the arrival of several Imbued is noteworthy, I suppose, so perhaps Lord Shen sent her. She has his ear these days." Kaliss paused, and when she spoke again she sounded uncertain, like she wasn't sure if she should say what she was about to share. "And not much happens without her notice. Behind her back, a lot of the novices call her the White Spider."

As they passed into the Duskhold's darkness, Deryn briefly locked gazes with the woman. She did not smile or raise a hand in greeting, and to his surprise he found he couldn't hold back a shiver.

14

HETH

"You look like something the dog coughed up," rumbled the big man as he led Heth out of the courtyard and into the Duskhold's cool darkness. Globes of faintly glowing mist were fixed to the black stone walls, illuminating narrow, twisting corridors.

"The lad's been through a lot," Phinius explained, briefly pausing to tap one of the globes. Immediately it brightened, sending the shadows scurrying. "None o' us got any sleep last night. He'll need some rest before you put him to work, Torr, and so will I, before we share that drink. Unless you want me face down in the grog bowl."

"Truth be told, everyone thought you was dead, Phin. The Black Sword came crashing down in the courtyard carrying the young master, who looked to have been through quite the scrap. Melek was out there and saw them hurry him away. Figured you'd all been ambushed by Sharded, and you was lying dead in a ditch somewhere."

Phinius snorted. They were descending on a staircase which spiraled into darkness. "Truth is even stranger, Torr. Riftbeast wandered out o' the Lands and set upon us. It's only a bloody miracle that none o' us or the new Imbued died."

"And the Black Sword killed it? The riftbeast?"

After Phinius nodded, Torr let out a low whistle. "Wish I could have seen that."

"I'll give you it to you by the blows later. Right now, I think you should be telling the boy what will happen. And then I have to go see Joras Shen, the Shadow save me."

"Aye," Torr said, glancing at Heth apologetically. "Sorry, lad. The excitement today has the whole place stirred up."

"It's all right," Heth murmured as they reached the bottom of the staircase. A wide corridor stretched in front of them, light spilling from the many entrances lining its length. A few men and women dressed in simple servant garb were scurrying between the chambers, so intent on their own tasks that they didn't even glance at the new arrivals. One woman was carrying a basket filled to the brim with leafy vegetables, while another had a pair of buckets balanced on a pole slung across her shoulders.

"This here is the kitchens," Torr said with some pride as he led them down the corridor. "My kingdom."

Heth peered through the open doorways and saw that each room was devoted to preparing food: in one, several men were carving away pieces of a half-dismembered boar, while in another a plump matron was rolling out dough, flour coating her arms up to her elbows. A wave of heat rolled over him as he passed a room with brick ovens recessed in the far wall, the smell of baking bread making his stomach twist.

"You wouldn't happen to be a baker's boy, would you lad?" Torr said hopefully when he noticed Heth briefly pausing to breathe in the delicious aromas.

He shook his head, acutely aware once more that *this* was going to be his life from now on. Nothing but drudgery and menial work in the service of the Sharded Few. He glanced at Torr and Phinius, slightly heartened that neither of the men seemed despondent about their lot. But maybe that was because they'd never enjoyed a life of ease, unlike him.

"Ah, well," Torr said, continuing on down the corridor. "Always room in the kitchens, if that's where you're sent."

Heth danced out of the way of a man carrying a huge tureen, then nearly collided with a woman in a blood-spattered apron.

"Careful!" she cried with a scowl, and Heth realized he'd nearly impaled himself on the knife she was holding.

"Sorry," he mumbled, hurrying after Torr and Phinius. Right now, the heat and noise of the kitchens was nearly overwhelming, but surely he'd get used to the chaos if this was where he was sent. There were worse duties in a great house, he knew. Certainly it was better than emptying chamber pots.

They left the clamor behind them as they ascended up a short, broad flight of steps, and then passed through another series of corridors. Heth tried to make a mental map of their path, but he very quickly realized such ambitions were beyond him in his exhausted state.

Torr led them into a corridor lined with doors, then swung one open seemingly at random to reveal a tiny alcove barely large enough for a narrow stone bed covered with rushes. An ancient chest filled most of the rest of the space, its lid clearly broken. Inside was what looked to be a ratty blanket. There was nothing else, not even one of the glowing globes that illuminated the hallway. Once the door was closed, the chamber would be plunged into darkness.

"This is yours," Torr said, sweeping out his arm like he was introducing a grand suite. "It ain't much, but you'll spend most of your time here asleep. Pots under the bed, or you can use the privy down the hall. Just don't fall in the hole, unless you want to end up in the caverns under the Duskhold."

Heth stepped inside his new room, trying not to think of his sleeping chamber in Kething's Cross, with its grand canopied skyspear bed, blankets of dyed wool, and cushions stuffed with goose feathers. The rushes in this little cell looked like they hadn't been changed in a long time.

"I'll leave ya to get some rest," Torr said. "If a bell wakes you, that means the Hollow are being served their supper. Just follow the noise if you're feeling hungry."

"I think I'll sleep until tomorrow," Heth said, already unbuckling his belt and tossing his sheathed sword onto the rushes.

"Aye, you do that, lad," Torr said, clapping him on the shoulder. "And welcome to the Duskhold."

~

"Wake up."

Heth struggled towards consciousness, striving against the black that wanted to drag him back down.

"Wake up, Hollow."

That voice again, more insistent this time. He opened his eyes. He was lying on his stomach, his cheek pressed against dry straw. The stone bed had not been forgiving, and every bone in his body ached. Though the events of the day before – including the long ride on the Wind Dragon – might have shared responsibility for his discomfort.

Heth groaned, pushing himself up into a sitting position. His head felt like he had downed a half-dozen cups of ale, then picked a fight with the biggest fellow in the tavern.

"Look at me when I'm speaking to you."

Blinking away the bleariness, Heth turned to face the doorway to his little cell. A man was standing there, limned by the light of the glow globes hanging in the hallway.

It wasn't Torr or Phinius. This man was small and slope-shouldered, his features soft. He wasn't old enough yet to have gone grey, but his hair was in full retreat from a brow that looked like it was perpetually creased with worry lines. Unlike many of the Hollow he'd seen in this wing of the Duskhold, his clothes looked well made, and a heavy silver chain hung around his neck. Most striking was the pallor of his skin – a shade that was somewhere between the sickly yellow of jaundice and the white of newborn grubs.

"Who are you?" Heth slurred, still feeling like he was mostly asleep.

The man scowled, his plump lips drawing down. "I am Elanin, steward of the Duskhold and first among the Hollow."

Heth yawned. "Oh. Torr said you were sick."

"I have been unwell," Elanin said tartly, "yet I am up about doing my duties. You have slept all night and half the day, and whatever grace you earned because of your trials coming here has been exhausted. It is time to begin your service to the Shadow."

There was someone else standing out in the hall, Heth realized. A much larger man wearing chain mail and a half-helm.

Heth struggled to his feet, wincing. Sleeping on a bed of stone – even with a woven pallet and rushes for cushioning – was going to take a while to get used to.

The steward looked him up and down, apparently unimpressed. He held out his arm and snapped his fingers, and a moment later the man in the hallway handed him a folded set of clothes.

"Change into these . . . I can smell you from here." He tossed the clothes onto the bed.

The garments Heth had taken from Kething's Cross did need a good wash. He'd been wearing them for several days now, including a night spent lying in the mud. Still, they looked far better quality than the roughspun tunic and breeches the steward had just presented him with.

Elanin apparently had no intention of giving him any privacy, so Heth quickly peeled off his sweat-soaked clothes and donned the new garb. It fit him well enough, though the scratchy fabric was a very far cry from the silk-smooth damask he'd been wearing.

"Should I bring these somewhere to be cleaned?" Heth asked, indicating his soiled knot of clothes.

The steward shook his head. "They will be burned."

Heth blinked at him in surprise. "Burned? These are fine clothes, good enough for a nobleman."

Elanin smirked. "Exactly. We cannot have one of the Hollow dressed up in an outfit of finer make than what is worn by the Sharded Few."

"Well, at least let me keep it, then," he argued, trying to tamp down a swell of anger. It would not be wise to make an enemy of the Duskhold's steward on his second day in the hold. "For posterity, to remember my life before."

"That is the other reason you cannot," the steward continued, and he seemed to be deriving satisfaction from what he was telling Heth. "When the Hollow come here, they must divest themselves of their past lives. You were reborn when you entered the service of the Shadow, cleansed of your past. Whether you were a prince or a pickpocket, it matters not. Now you are Hollow, dedicated to the Sharded and the Shadow."

Heth stared at him in stunned silence. His father and grandfather had striven hard to build the Su Canaav name into one worthy of respect and admiration, a legacy that could be passed down for generations. And this arrogant servant was now telling him it had all been for naught, that everything his family had done would vanish in an instant. Something occurred to Heth, and he glanced to where he'd tossed down his blade the night before.

It wasn't there.

"Where is my sword?" he asked, panic overwhelming his anger.

Elanin's smile broadened. "It is gone. As I said, you are not allowed to keep any memento of your time before."

Before he knew what he was doing, Heth took a threatening step towards the steward, his fists clenched. The grub-like little man blanched and stumbled back, but then he mastered himself, his face clouding with fury.

"Gervis," Elanin spat, and the man who had been waiting out in the hall moved into Heth's narrow cell. He was much larger than Heth had realized, and the rage that had been rising inside him suddenly subsided.

"Don't do anything stupid, lad," the man said, resting his hand on the hilt of his own sword. "Ain't our rules, the steward's just doin' what the Sharded tell him to. An' no use gettin' mad at them."

"It was my father's sword," Heth said quietly. "A gift from the Ember when my family left their service."

The swordsman's broad, dull face crinkled in surprise at this, but then he shrugged. "Don't matter. The children of archons and magisters have come here, and they all had to give up their life-before." He paused and then added almost apologetically. "Sorry, lad."

"So you do come from a Hollow family," the steward said, shouldering past the large man. "Then you have no excuse for this insolence. You must understand the duties and obligations we have to the Sharded Few. Did you truly think you could strut around the Duskhold dressed in rich clothes with your family's sword at your side?"

Heth realized that he was trembling, but from anger or sadness or some other emotion he wasn't sure. He remembered his father taking the sword down from its place of honor and holding it out reverently for Heth to touch when he was a young boy, telling him solemnly that it represented the honor of their family. And now, in an eye blink, it was gone.

Heth slumped, feeling defeated. But what could he do? Demand his sword and set out from the Duskhold? There was no way the shadow-sharded would allow him to ever leave their service. After all, if the Hollow vanished, who would cook their food and draw their baths?

He was a slave. As Kilian had said a few days ago, the Fates did certainly have a sense of humor.

"Go with Gervis, Hollow," the steward said, the welter of emotions Heth's insolence had stirred up now replaced with cold disdain. "He will explain to you what your duties will be. And remember – the punishment for disobedience in the Duskhold is death."

Feeling nauseous, Heth nodded mutely. The burly guardsman grunted in what Heth suspected was satisfaction at his sudden change in temperament, then turned and strode from his little chamber. He followed, not looking at the sneering steward as he passed – he didn't trust himself not to wipe that expression from his face with his fist.

"You're lucky," Gervis said as they passed down corridors that from their strange contortions could only have been planned out by a madman.

"Why's that?" he asked when the warrior failed to enlighten him further.

"You're joinin' the barracks," the Hollow explained. "Guard duty.

Easiest job for any of us. Sure, the hounds might have it a bit sweeter, gettin' to roam around dinin' in fancy taverns and sleepin' on soft beds, but here at the Duskhold, there's nothin' better."

They halted outside a door of black wood, and Gervis produced a key from somewhere. Heth realized that this was the first door he'd seen with such precautions, and the reason why was revealed a moment later when the guard swung it open. Inside was a large chamber filled with weapons and armor. Barrels were against the far wall, bristling with sword hilts and polearm handles. A stone table held a haphazard assortment of mail shirts and stacked shields and helms of all shapes and sizes. It looked as much a magpie's nest as an armory, detritus scavenged from a dozen different battlefields.

"This'll do," Gervis said, picking up one of the mail shirts and holding it up in front of Heth. There was a hole in the links just about the right size for a spear-head to fit through and Heth wondered if any blood crusted the shirt's insides.

"Try it," the guard commanded, and Heth slipped it on, attempting not to think about the previous owner. It was heavier than he had expected, and smelled strongly of rust and neglect. Some of the privileged sons of Kething's Cross and the other twelve towns had enjoyed donning suits of metal and cantering about the countryside like the cataphracts of the First Empire, but Heth had preferred the genteel civility of the sword-hall, and the heaviest armor he'd ever worn before this moment was padded leather in the dueling circle.

It was not very comfortable.

"Perfect," Gervis said, showing off his gap-toothed smile. He handed Heth an exotic-looking helm with curving horns that was clearly much too large for him. It looked like it had taken a solid blow from something heavy and blunt.

"Shouldn't our armor and weapons be a bit less . . . broken?"

Gervis shrugged. "I s'pose. Truth is, you'll never have to worry about fighting."

Heth blinked up at him, surprised by this admission. "But you said we are guardsmen."

The Hollow warrior nodded enthusiastically. "Aye. That means we watch the paths to see if anyone is comin' up to the gate, maybe stand around the audience chamber if some important visitor is here. But fight? Anything that would attack a fortress full of the Sharded Few would tear through us like we was cheesecloth. We're, uh, what's the word . . ." His face crinkled as he groped for what he wanted to say. "Decoration. We're just decoration."

Heth quickly revised his estimation of the man's intelligence. He may look like a brainless thug, but he wasn't stupid.

Gervis shoved a long-handled ax into his hand – Heth thought it might have been a halberd, though he'd only heard of such weapons – and then stepped back to look him up and down. After a moment, he nodded, as if satisfied with what he saw.

"You know, I've actually trained with the sword. I was one of the best duelists in Kething's Cross."

Gervis shrugged. "Like I said, don't matter. And you'll prefer this long one given where you're going."

"And where am I going?"

Another gap-toothed grin. "Follow me."

"Silver Shrike," Heth murmured as they emerged from the stairwell onto the roof of the Duskhold. Two other guardsmen in mismatched armor were standing by the battlements leaning on polearms like the one given to Heth, and they briefly turned and nodded. Neither seemed very interested in introducing themselves, and Heth couldn't muster the courage to call out his own greeting. A massive winch and pulley dominated the space, black chains disappearing into holes cut in the stone which were presumably connected to a great door or portcullis below. How anyone could use such a contraption mystified Heth for a moment, but then he remembered the tremendous strength demonstrated by the Sharded Few. Azil could probably turn it one handed, given that the Black Sword's blows had caved in the skull of a riftbeast the size of a small hill.

The wind was stronger up here, and only a few of the Duskhold's crooked towers overtopped them. Heth edged his way to the crude crenellations fringing the roof and looked over the side. His stomach immediately dropped into his boots, and if he hadn't spent much of the previous day clinging to the back of a Wind Dragon he might have felt dizzy. Sheer walls of gleaming black stone plummeted down hundreds of span, to where a narrow switchback trail ended at the blocky barbican that guarded the gate to the Duskhold. Heth swallowed, his eyes following this little path as it meandered through the broken landscape, until finally vanishing into the hazy distance. If this was the only road to the Duskhold, he doubted the Sharded Few received many visitors.

He jumped as Gervis clapped him on the shoulder. "Right here, lad. This is your spot. I want you to stand just where you are and watch the road below."

Heth looked down at the road, empty as far as he could see. "For how long?"

Gervis cleared his throat, then leaned over the battlements and spat. They both watched it fall a long way. "Next changin' of the watch happens around twilight."

Heth glanced up at the sun. It couldn't be very far past midday. "I'm to just . . . stand here for the rest of the day?"

"Aye, lad. As I said, you're one of the luckiest Hollow in the Duskhold."

Heth blinked as the wind gusted, roaring in his ears. Nothing was moving as far he could see – on this side of the Duskhold there was just an endless jumble of black rocks and scree tumbling down the mountainside. It wasn't hot, but the sun was unrelenting, and he already knew that without any shade up here every bit of his exposed skin would soon be burned raw. He should be thankful for the absurd helmet he'd been given, but he was having trouble feeling anything at this moment except a bleak hopelessness.

"Oh, yes," Heth murmured, leaning heavily against his halberd. "Very lucky."

15

DERYN

DERYN'S MOTHER had loved to tell stories. Tales of heroism and tragedy, of the world's bright wonders and shadowed mysteries. When he'd gotten older, Deryn had realized why – they had infused her drab life in the kitchens with color, carrying her away from the dull monotony of being poor and a servant in the houses of the rich. The Labyrinth of Tal Amoch had been one of her favorites, and she'd recounted the story of the young maid wandering in the creation of the Mad Archon so many times that Deryn thought he might be able to find his way out if, like that poor girl, he had awoken in the center of the maze with nothing but his wits and pluck.

He now knew that to be a foolish belief.

The interior of the Duskhold almost perfectly matched his mental conjurations of the labyrinth. Glowing spheres of roiling mist lit narrow corridors as they contorted strangely, sometimes twisting back upon themselves, almost like the ones who had built this place were avoiding something recessed in the rock. Stairs spiraled down into darkness, then a steep ramp climbed upwards again. They passed through empty echoing halls, populated only by twisted, abstract statues shaped from glistening black stone. The ceilings in these great chambers soared so high that they were lost to darkness, but in other cramped corridors, Deryn had to duck his head so he wouldn't brain himself on the low-hanging stone. Occasionally they glimpsed shrouded figures intent on their own duties, but Kaliss did not call out or even acknowledge them. She seemed to want nothing more than to deliver Deryn and Alia to their rooms and discharge herself of this task her teacher had given her.

It was not the most welcoming introduction to their new life.

The silence was the most unsettling aspect of this place, Deryn decided. This was the home of the shadow-sharded, and as such one would expect to hear the sounds of many people living together in close confines. Deryn had grown up in great houses, and there had always been the clatter of dropped plates, the slamming of doors, the chatter of servants or the bellowing of the master. It had only been silent late at night, and even then there had been the creak of the house settling or the wind scraping against the windows. But the Duskhold was as silent as a tomb. A few times Deryn opened his mouth to ask the Ashasai girl about the rooms they were passing through, but each time the question died in his throat, strangled by the stillness of the place.

And it was because of the quiet that he realized something was wrong with Alia.

It was her breathing that he noticed first. Fast and shallow, like she was on the edge of panicking. When he turned to her, he found that her skin looked grey in the sepulchral light of the mist-globes, her eyes glazed and distant. She was also stumbling slightly, like she'd had too much to drink.

"Are you all right?" he asked, putting his hand on her arm to steady her. Her skin was clammy, with a sheen of cold sweat.

She shuddered. "Can't you feel it?" she whispered, as if afraid to draw the attention of the girl leading them through the hold.

"Feel what?" he asked, lowering his voice as well.

She glanced upwards. They were crossing a great hall, but unlike other chambers, the ceiling here was visible, curving above them and inset with glimmering points he suspected were supposed to evoke the stars in the night sky. "The weight of it all pushing down. It's so heavy. I feel like I'm being crushed."

"You don't have to worry about that," he assured her. "The Duskhold has stood for a long, long time. There's no chance that it will collapse."

Alia shivered again. "I know the stone's not going to come crashing down. But still, it's like a great smothering presence . . . aren't you finding it hard to breathe? The air is so stale. And the silence . . ." she cocked her head to one side, listening intently for a moment. "How can there be no noise at all?"

Deryn swallowed, unsure what he should say. She looked terrified, which was unnerving given how she had behaved with an enormous monster hunting for them. He had assumed nothing could frighten her. And while he also found the Duskhold unsettling, it seemed much worse for her. He suspected he understood why. She had grown up in the Wild, surrounded by the unceasing sounds of the forest, the sky never more than a few steps away. Now she was deep in the belly of a windowless fortress carved from a mountain of black stone.

"You'll be fine. I'm here, and I'll protect you."

Alia clutched at his arm and drew in a deep, shuddering breath. She said nothing more, but he knew she was trying to master herself, beat back the fear that was threatening to rise up and drown her. He recognized what she was doing because he'd done it many times while forcing himself to climb a skyspear, especially in his early days of being indentured.

She stared at him with those eyes of flawless jade, and he forced a smile he hoped looked more confident than he truly felt. It must have had some effect, as she appeared to steady herself somewhat. Deryn just caught himself from brushing her matted hair back from where it had fallen across her face.

"So I suppose you only need one bed chamber."

The moment broke, and they both looked at the Ashasai girl. She had stopped at the entrance to another passage and was watching them with her arms folded.

"You should have told me you were lovers."

Deryn felt his cheeks flush. "We're not. Separate rooms, please."

Kaliss snorted and rolled her eyes, then turned and vanished into the black.

They passed from the soaring, shadowy galleries and entered a more welcoming wing of the Duskhold. Here the mist-globes glowed yellow and red, mimicking flames in the way they flickered, instead of the pulsing of the pale corpse-light they'd seen before now. There were signs of habitation as well – through an open doorway Deryn glimpsed a long table, upon which was scattered the remnants of a meal. A girl was gathering up the empty plates and cups, her eyes downcast. Beyond her, a vast patterning of glistening silver threads were sunk into the far wall. There was something compelling about the intricate design, like if he stared at it long enough some secret would be revealed, but as he stood there trying to decipher it, Kaliss's voice jolted him from his reverie.

"You can lose yourself in the Web later," she said, sounding annoyed. "First, let's get you settled."

Deryn murmured agreement, turning away from the shining pattern, and then nearly collided with someone emerging from another side-chamber.

"Careful, friend," the young man said, flashing an easy grin. He was tall and broad, with dark curly hair and startling silver eyes, and was wearing the same style of robes as Kaliss. There was a lilt to his voice that reminded Deryn of the accent that had flavored the speech of Wenick, one of the other slaves in the logging camp. He'd been a hill tribesman from beyond the Firemounts, though he'd lived outside the Wild for many years.

"I'm sorry," Deryn mumbled, ducking his head as he moved out of the way.

The young man studied him appraisingly for a moment, his lips pursed. "Accepted. Would ye happen ta be one of the new Imbued that arrived today?"

"He is," Kaliss said from where she was waiting further down the corridor. "They both are, Menochus."

The boy swung his gaze to the Ashasai. "Ah, Kaliss. What fortune ta meet ye."

The girl scowled, crossing her arms. "This charade is unnecessary. I know you were waiting here to ambush them."

The boy's silver eyes widened, as if he was surprised by this accusation. "Nay, Kaliss. A chance encounter, I promise ye." He turned back to Deryn and thumped his fist against his chest. "I am Menochus, eighth son of Meneloch, and I welcome ye ta the Duskhold."

Deryn almost returned the gesture, but then decided it was wiser to avoid using a greeting he didn't fully understand. "My name is Deryn, and I come from the twelve towns."

"And this maiden?" the boy asked, swiveling to direct the force of his presence at Alia.

She blinked up at him, seemingly overwhelmed by this grinning mountain of a boy.

"Alia," Deryn said.

"She canna talk?" Menochus asked with a frown, and at this Alia shook herself free of the trance she'd fallen into.

"I can," she said quietly. "I come from the Wild, far beyond the Fangs. The deep forests."

The boy's face brightened. "By the Five Peaks! My clan dwells on the fringes of the Wild, but north of here. I'm pleased ta know there's other good, honest blood in the Duskhold now, not just these two-faced city folk."

Alia visibly relaxed. "Are you . . . are you one of the Sharded Few?"

The boy's smile widened, and he tapped his chest through his black robes. "Aye, of course. Just a novice still, but I've only been here for six months. Tell me, fair Alia – are the rumors we've been hearing true? Did Lord Kilian and the Black Sword slay a riftbeast that had wandered out of the Frayed Lands?"

Kaliss sighed deeply. "As I suspected, you were dispatched to gather information. You know Saelus will be upset if he learns you accosted the new Imbued before they've been tested. There are supposed to be kept sequestered until the Shadow has made its decision."

"Accosted?" Menochus cried in mock horror. "Surely not, dour and untrusting Kaliss." Then he turned back to Alia, still clearly hoping for answers.

"Well," she said slowly after glancing at the glowering Ashasai girl. "Azil slew the riftbeast while Kilian was lying in the grass with a broken leg."

"*Lord* Kilian," Kaliss corrected her. "And best you remember *that* while in the Duskhold. He might not act like it, but Lord Kilian is a Shen, and they are the masters of this hold." She stalked back to them and grabbed Deryn around the arm. "I was charged with getting them to their chambers and preparing them for what comes tomorrow. You and the rest of the gossipmongers can interrogate them after their ordeal."

The Ashasai girl pulled him away, and though he tried to resist her – Menochus was the first friendly face they'd met in the Duskhold, and he had his own questions he wanted to ask – he was dragged stumbling after Kaliss. Her grip was like stone, and she didn't even appear to notice his struggles. He had almost forgotten that this slip of a girl was also one of the Sharded Few.

"I hope ta see ye both on the morrow!" the boy cried after them. "And I wish ye luck when ye stand before the Shadow!"

Kaliss released him after they had left Menochus several twisting passageways behind. The bone in his arm ached, but after a moment the pain began to fade.

"That was rude," Deryn muttered, rubbing at the red marks she had imprinted on his skin.

"Imbued are not allowed to mingle with the Sharded until after their testing," Kaliss said tartly, striding away down the hallway.

"But you are Sharded," Deryn said, following her when it became clear she was not going to wait for them.

"I was given a task by our teacher. If you noticed, I haven't engaged you in any idle chit-chat. Nothing about the incident on the road to here, or the wind-sharded who deposited you in the courtyard, or your no doubt tragic upbringings."

"He was kind," Alia said, glancing back the way they'd come.

Kaliss barked a laugh. "Ha! You both have so much to learn. There is no 'kindness' to be found inside these walls. It is a weakness that would prove fatal to anyone bearing a fragment of the Heart. Everyone you meet here – everyone – is striving to acquire as many shards as possible. Power – that is the only goal."

Deryn frowned at the back of the Ashasai girl. "Perhaps that is the only thing *you* care about. But if it was shared by everyone here, why have the stronger Sharded not seized *your* shard?"

"And then what?" Kaliss asked, shaking her head as if amazed by Deryn's naivety. "Cael Shen ruling over an empty Duskhold? How long until one of the other holds attacks and overwhelms him? A single Sharded – no matter how strong – cannot stand against an army. No, the more shadow-sharded that roam these halls, the safer the lords of the Duskhold are. But make no mistake, there will be tests beyond the one tomorrow – and if you show weakness, they will rip the fragment from your chest and give it to someone they deem more worthy . . . and more useful."

Kindness is not a weakness, Deryn thought, but he kept that to himself. He was sure such a sentiment would earn a derisive snort from the Ashasai girl.

"And here you are," Kaliss said, stopping at the end of a long corridor lined with doorways. "The guest quarters. Sleep together, sleep apart, I don't care. But get your rest, as tomorrow will be taxing."

Deryn slept like the dead, and when he awoke, he felt reborn. He lay on a soft woven pallet under a pelt of luxurious silver fur, and as he slowly came back to himself his bed chamber gradually brightened.

The light in the windowless room came from the roiling mist-globe dangling from the ceiling – at first it was a pale pink, like the first blush of dawn in the night sky, and as he watched it slowly brightened to the warm yellow of the morning sun. He wondered briefly what sorcery governed the cycle of these glowing spheres, and then decided that such musings were useless – he was in the Duskhold, a place of legend, spoken of in awed whispers. How could he be so arrogant to think he could understand its mysteries?

Gathering all his willpower, he finally threw aside his furs. The cool air licked his skin, but it was not as cold inside his chambers as he would have expected. Last night he had realized that a faint warmth coursed through the black stone of the hold, rising from the floor. Were there still some embers burning in the mountain's heart? Deryn hoped not, though as Phinius had said, if there truly was any danger the shadow-sharded would not dwell here. This was just another mystery he should simply accept.

He stood and stretched, surprised that he wasn't riddled with aches after everything that had happened over the last few days. The soft bed and deep sleep had apparently done wonders healing his battered body.

To his surprise, someone had entered his chamber during the night. The clothes he had discarded on the floor were missing – as was the green bag Heth had given him – and draped across the back of a beautifully carved chair of dark wood looked to be clothes similar to what he'd seen the denizens of the Duskhold wearing. He padded across the spacious chamber, enjoying the feel of the heated stone beneath his feet, and had his suspicions confirmed when he unfolded the soft black robes. Deryn shrugged into the vestments, realizing he must look like one of the hollow-eyed clerics of the Broken God who had tended to the temple in Kething's Cross. If only his mother could see him now, he thought, shaking his head ruefully.

A sharp rapping on his door made him jump.

"Yes?" he called out, hurriedly tying the black cord at his waist.

"It's time," came the muffled reply through the thick wood. Kaliss, he thought, though he couldn't be sure.

"Coming," he called, then strode across the chamber and pulled open his door. The copper-skinned Ashasai girl was standing outside, looking as annoyed as he'd come to expect. He was slightly surprised to see that Alia had already been summoned from her chambers. It looked like someone had made an attempt at untangling her hair, and her skin had been scrubbed clean. The night before, Deryn had declined the offer of having a bath drawn, and now he wished he'd seized that opportunity. Alia had lost the evidence of a lifetime spent living in the Wild, and she looked fresh-faced and surprisingly beautiful. Deryn realized he was staring and quickly averted his eyes.

His stomach chose that moment to complain loudly, and he seized upon the distraction. "Is there any food? I'm starving." A plate of cold meat and bread had been waiting for them last night in their rooms, but he'd still gone to bed hungry.

"You can't eat before your testing," Kaliss said, and from the amusement in her voice she was very aware of what he'd been thinking a moment ago. "Standing before the Shadow can be . . . uncomfortable. Anything in your belly would end up painting the walls."

"Uncomfortable?" Alia repeated nervously.

"No one has ever died," Kaliss assured her. "But no supplicant has ever claimed they wanted to repeat the experience. Now come." She turned on her heel and began striding away with the same briskness she'd shown the night before. Deryn was starting to suspect this was the way she always behaved.

"What was it like?" he asked as they hurried to follow her.

"I . . . cannot do it justice," Kaliss said, clearly groping for words. "And the lords of the Duskhold have instructed me not to say too much. But rest assured, you will both survive, although it is likely at least one of you will be deemed unworthy of a shard."

"And if that happens, we will join the Hollow?"

Kaliss nodded. "Yes. A poor consolation, but better than being cast out into the world with nothing to your name, I suppose."

Deryn wondered just how much she knew of their pasts. Perhaps serving in the Duskhold was an improvement over hunting crabs or gathering roots and berries in the Wild, but many who came here had family and prospects outside the hold. Would Heth's life be better here, even though his family had owned a manse in Kething's Cross? Thinking of the slaver's son, he was surprised to realize that he hoped the boy wasn't finding his first day serving in the Duskhold too onerous. Heth was not the same boy who had flayed Deryn's back at his father's command.

They descended deeper and deeper into the Duskhold. The steps and passageways sloping downwards seemed to grow narrower until Deryn's shoulders were nearly brushing the walls, and he had to stoop so he wouldn't brain himself on low-hanging lintels. The light globes along this path were more muted, just barely bright enough to illuminate the way forward. From what he could see and feel beneath his boots, the corridors here were more roughhewn, as if far older than the rest of the hold. It truly felt like they were entering the bowels of the mountain, or perhaps the threshold to an underworld.

Unexpectedly, the corridor they were traversing suddenly opened up into a large chamber. It was perfectly round, and in the dim radiance of the roiling mist-globes fixed to the walls Deryn could just see the faint outline of an archway. The darkness beyond was absolute, as if completely bereft of the lights that had been growing progressively dimmer as they pushed onwards. There were no other entrances, but when he started across the chamber, Kaliss held up an arm to stop him.

"Hold," she said, and there was something in her voice that made him glance at her. The Ashasai girl was staring intently at the darkened arch, her other hand having gone to her chest. Deryn felt a crawling unease when he noticed that a ghostly radiance was seeping through the black fabric of her robes.

"It's in there, isn't it?" Alia whispered, edging closer to Deryn.

"Yes," Kaliss murmured, sounding distracted. "The Shadow lies within. You must . . ." She shook her head, as if to clear it. "You must enter."

Deryn glanced at Alia. She was staring back at him, her eyes wide and fearful.

"I don't want to go," she said, her fingers clutching at his robes. "It's so dark. Anything could be inside."

"You must," Kaliss said sharply. She sounded like she was regaining control over herself. "If you balk, they will kill you. Cael Shen will cut off your head and put it on a spike on the Duskhold's walls as a warning for the others. We cannot risk you becoming Unbound, a renegade Sharded." Her voice softened slightly. "It is frightening, but all the shadow-sharded in the hold survived their audience with the Heart's fragment."

"I will go first," Deryn said. He reached out and took Alia's hand for a moment, squeezing it gently.

"Be careful," Alia said, her voice trembling.

Deryn gave her what he hoped was a comforting smile and then strode towards the archway, his eyes fixed on the seamless black.

Heart pounding, he plunged into the darkness.

Deryn came to himself as if waking from a deep, dreamless sleep. For a moment, he didn't know where he was, and then the memories of the past few days washed over him. The riftbeast. The Duskhold. The Shadow.

His jaw ached from clenching it too hard. Deryn raised his arm, passing his hand in front of his face. He saw nothing, and for a moment he feared that he had gone blind.

He was floating, suspended in the blackness. There was a very slight resistance when he moved his limbs, as if there was some substance to the dark. It slid across his skin, raising goosebumps.

He wanted to call out, ask if anyone was there, but the thought of it slipping down his throat made him hesitate. Then again, it was all around him, and he could still breathe, so likely there was little danger of him choking on this stuff.

"Hello?" he asked. His voice returned to him after a few heartbeats, echoing into a great distance until it finally faded away.

He had the strong suspicion that he was no longer in the Duskhold.

"What do I do?" he called out, then shook his head at his foolishness. He was trying to talk to a piece of rock.

The darkness plucked at him. It roiled and eddied like the current of a swift rushing stream, and he felt himself moving. He fought back his rising panic and the urge to thrash and fight and try to swim in the other direction, away from whatever he was being drawn towards.

But this was why he was here. It was why Kilian had rescued him from the forest, why he'd been dragged halfway across the north. To be judged by a fragment of the Heart of the World. Or the heart of a dead god, if what Crimson Grass had said was true.

The back of his neck tingled, hairs lifting. He had the sudden, overwhelming sensation that he was being watched. Like there was something nearby, something vast beyond comprehension. He felt like he was suspended at the bottom of the sea, down where no light could reach, in the presence of some enormous leviathan the size of a mountain floating in the dark. He could feel the water it displaced by its slightest movement washing against him, buffeting him, but he could see nothing. He would see nothing even as it opened its vast maw and swallowed him whole.

He reached out his hand to reassure himself that there was no great swath of scales or pebbled skin hiding in the black and then gasped in fear when his fingers brushed something. It was hard and sharp, an amalgamation of jagged points. To his surprise, he felt a piece of it crumble away under his touch, and reflexively he caught the fragment.

The fragment.

The shard.

A point of absolute coldness pierced his palm, burrowing into his flesh. Tingling numbness raced up his arm, through his veins, as if his blood had been replaced with freezing water. Deryn cried out, trying to open his hand to let the fragment fall, if it was even still there, but he found he couldn't unclench his fingers.

The darkness pulled him down again.

Deryn woke sprawled on the floor, his cheek pressed against stone. He drew in a deep, ragged breath, trying to focus on the hazy lights hovering in the distance.

"Welcome back."

The Ashasai girl's voice. The hem of black robes filled his vision, and then she was squatting down in front of him, her head tilted to one side as she studied him with a wry half-smile.

"And welcome to the Sharded Few."

Oh, by the Broken God. It actually happened. Groaning, Deryn rolled over onto his back. He stared at the ceiling, trying to comprehend what he was feeling. The various aches and pains he'd accumulated over the last few days had now vanished completely. Even the wounds in his back, which had faded into a constant, inescapable annoyance as they traveled, were no longer bothering him.

There was something else. Something new. Could it be? Deryn slipped his hand inside his robes, gently exploring where he sensed a splinter embedded in the flesh of his chest.

His fingertips brushed a sliver of crystal, tiny and hard.

"Oh," he murmured.

"Yes," Kaliss said, coming to loom over him. "Congratulations."

Deryn's thoughts scattered like leaves in the wind. Despite what Kilian had told him, he'd never truly – truly – believed that he would ever become one of the Sharded Few. Phinius must have been mistaken. The Shadow would peer into his soul and see how worthless he was – a boy whose life belonged to someone else, fatherless, the son of a madwoman. How could this be true? Perhaps this was all a fever dream brought on by Heth's lashing, and he would soon awaken back in the slave barracks, Xiv hovering over him.

There *was* an Ashasai looking down on him right now, ironically enough, but not in concern. She looked exultant, dark eyes flashing, her white grin reflected in the dim light.

Seeing her like this, he felt his own excitement stirring in his breast.

Then something occurred to him. "Alia," he rasped, sitting up. His throat was very dry – how long had he been passed out on the floor?

"She entered as soon as you stumbled out and collapsed. I would say she's spent about as much time inside as you did, although each Imbued is different. Sometimes the Shadow makes its choice almost immediately, and other times the judging can last more than a day. You were faster than most, so we should settle in to wait –"

A shuddering gasp came from the direction of the archway. Kaliss and Deryn whirled towards the sound just as Alia staggered out of the Shadow's sanctum, her pale face emerging from the black like the full moon from behind dark clouds.

She looked shaken, her jade eyes vacant.

Deryn struggled to his feet, swaying slightly. He tried to go to her, but a wave of dizziness washed over him, and he just barely kept himself from falling back to the floor.

"Are you all right?" he managed to say.

For a moment, Alia continued staring at nothing, and then slowly her gaze drifted to him. She nodded slightly.

"And the Shadow?" Kaliss asked. The Ashasai girl's fists were clenched, her body rigid with tension. "Were you blessed? Are you one of the Sharded Few?"

Alia swallowed, her hand reaching up to touch where her robes covered her chest. Then her arm fell back to her side, and she gave a slight shake of her head.

"No."

16

DERYN

KALISS HISSED IN DISAPPOINTMENT.

Alia's gaze flicked to her and then back to Deryn, her brow creasing like she was struggling to understand what she had experienced.

"There was . . . something in there," she said. "Something . . . living. I felt . . . I felt like it was watching me. Was it the same for you?"

Deryn nodded mutely. That sense of something vast flensing his flesh, peering into his depths was still there, but it was receding fast, like a dream just after waking. Had he been floating in a dark sea? How could that have been possible?

"I . . ." he began, about to try to describe what he had experienced, when he realized suddenly they were no longer alone. Two figures had appeared in the chamber as if they had stepped from the shadows cast by the roiling mist-globes. Which they very well might have.

It was a man and a woman dressed in the black robes of the Duskhold. They looked so similar Deryn had to assume they were related – both were tall, with midnight-black hair and skin even paler than Alia. So pale, in fact, that Deryn wondered if they had ever stepped out of the hold and seen the sun. But despite these similarities, they could not have comported themselves more differently – the woman's mouth was set in a thin line, her expression cold and haughty, while the man was smiling like he had just met old friends.

For a moment, no one moved, shocked by the unexpected appearance. Then Kaliss ducked her head in their direction, keeping her eyes on the floor when she finally spoke.

"Lord and Lady Shen. We are honored by your presence."

"Please," the man said, waving his hand as if to dismiss her words. "Rhenna and Nishi. Our father is Lord Shen."

Lord Shen. The master of the Duskhold and one of the most powerful men in the world. Deryn felt dizzy, overwhelmed by everything that was happening.

"And you are Kaliss," the man continued, turning his dazzling smile towards the Ashasai girl. She flinched, as if surprised to be the focus of his attention.

"Yes, *kenang.*"

"I've heard quite a bit about you from Saelus. He believes you will soon be joining the adepts, that you have more potential than any of the current crop of novices."

"Teacher Saelus is too kind," Kaliss said softly, her cheeks flushing.

"We are not here to discuss her," the woman interrupted, her voice just as imperious as Deryn had expected. "But rather to formally usher this Sharded and failed Imbued into their new lives in the Duskhold." She turned to Kaliss. "Novice, take the girl and bring her to the steward."

"What will happen to her?" Deryn asked worriedly.

"She will be fine," the man who must be Nishi assured him. "She will be taken care of and given tasks that are suitable for her." He turned his easy smile on Alia, who had been stunned into silence by what was happening. "Do not worry, my dear. There are many who were not chosen by the Shadow now serving alongside the Hollow in this hold."

"Come," Kaliss said, taking Alia by the arm and beginning to gently lead her away. "Deryn must be introduced to the Duskhold's lord. He cannot be kept waiting."

"Deryn!" Alia cried out, and the panic in her voice sent a pang through his chest.

"It's all right," he called out to her. "I'll come to you later! If you need help before then, find Heth!"

She nodded shakily, his words seeming to steady her, and then she allowed the Ashasai girl to lead her into the darkness of the passage from which they'd first entered this chamber.

Deryn continued watching where she'd vanished for a few long heartbeats, his emotions churning. He was worried, yes, but Heth and Phinius were also Hollow. They would take care of her. No, mostly he felt sadness – there had been a connection between them ever since Alia had materialized from the mists, begging for the crab he'd caught. He'd saved her life by helping her flee the Unbound Sharded, and she'd returned the favor after the riftbeast ambush. Something had been growing between them, a bond like he hadn't felt since his mother had died. Well, at the very least, they were both inhabitants of the Duskhold. He could still watch over her, although he suspected that friendships between the servants and the Sharded were frowned upon, if not outright forbidden.

He jumped as a hand clapped his shoulder. "You're thinking deep thoughts, Sharded," said Nishi. "She'll be fine. The servants here are valuable, and the girl will be well taken care of."

He nodded, still staring into the blackness of the corridor.

"What's your name?" the man asked.

"Deryn," he replied quietly. "From the twelve towns."

Nishi stared at him blankly.

"Near the Fangs," his sister added, sweeping past them to stand with her hands on her hips in front of the Shadow's sanctum, peering into its lightless depths.

Nishi's eyebrows lifted. "The Fangs? That's at the very edge of our realm. In truth, you were far closer to the Ember than the Duskhold. Two hundred years ago, you would have been brought before the Flame and not the Shadow."

Deryn shrugged. He had only a vague sense of the geography of these lands. If he were cast out of the Duskhold tomorrow, he would only know to walk in the opposite direction that the sun rose and make damn sure to skirt the edges of the Frayed Lands. Even if he thought it would make the journey faster, there was absolutely no way he would ever purposefully enter those grasslands. Not after he had seen what dwelled within.

Nishi shifted his attention to his sister. "Going back inside, Rhen?"

She did not turn around, continuing to stare into the darkened archway. "Do you ever wonder why it is forbidden?"

"Saelus told me it's dangerous. Sharded have been lost trying to gain a second audience with the Shadow."

"That is the story I heard as well," Rhenna mused. "But I wonder if it is true."

"Another time you can tempt fate by finding out," Nishi said lightly. "Right now, Father is waiting to meet our newest novice."

"Yes," Rhenna said softly, dragging her gaze from the darkness. She paced over to where they waited and took her brother by the hand.

That's . . . odd, Deryn thought, and then he felt Nishi's other hand slide from his shoulder and grip him tightly around the wrist. He looked at the Sharded in alarm, unsure what was happening.

"Are you certain you can do three, brother?"

"I have been practicing, dear sister."

"Practicing what?" Deryn asked. He wanted to pull away from Nishi, but even if he was brave enough to try, he doubted he could break the Sharded's hold.

"Shadow Walking," Rhenna answered. "It is one of my brother's talents."

"I can hear your jealousy," Nishi murmured.

In response, Rhenna turned and regarded her brother coolly. "I have gained more talents than you had at the same age."

Nishi's smile didn't falter, but Deryn thought he saw a slight hardening around his eyes. "And you rarely let me forget it, little sister. Now be quiet – this does require some concentration."

The Sharded lord walked forwards, one hand entwined with Rhenna's and the other still holding onto Deryn firmly.

"What are you doing?" he asked, his apprehension rising. They were not moving towards the Shadow's sanctum or the single passage leading back the way they'd come, but rather a section of the curving wall that appeared entirely unremarkable. Shadows played on the stone, thrown by the churning mists of the light globes. In a few more moments, they'd collide with the wall, and Nishi was showing no sign of slowing.

The shadows shivered and twisted, swelling into a circle of darkness large enough to encompass the three of them. It was like a hole had been cut into the fabric of the world.

They stepped into it. Deryn tried to pull away, but the Sharded's strength was incredible, and he was dragged inexorably forward.

It was like plunging into an icy mountain stream. Deryn gasped, overwhelmed by the sensation of freezing cold rushing over him, numbing his flesh. His eyes ached, and he squeezed them shut, but before he did this, he glimpsed strange shapes recessed in the absolute black, writhing as if dancing to a music he could not hear. His imagination, surely. But was there a faint piping beneath the roaring in his ears? If he concentrated hard enough, he might just be able to hear it clearly . . .

"Ignore what your eyes and ears are telling you," Nishi's voice came, echoing strangely. "For that way lies madness."

Deryn wanted to ask him where they were, what was happening, but his lips felt like they were sewn shut. If it wasn't for Nishi's iron grip on his wrist, he would have given himself over to the gibbering fear clawing in his breast.

A faint light crawled across his shut eyelids. The numbing cold was gone, leaving behind only a faint prickling. Deryn finally managed to work his mouth open, drawing in a shuddering breath.

He opened his eyes. They were back in the Duskhold – though in truth he wasn't sure if they had ever actually left – but now in a room far larger than any other he had so far seen. Instead of mist-globes, several massive braziers taller than a man were scattered about on metal stands. Their ghostly white flames painted the great chamber in shades of charcoal and bone, giving most of the others who had turned towards them at their entrance the pallor of corpses. All except the Salahi Azil, with his ebony-dark skin. The Black Sword was leaning on his great staff at the base of a set of broad steps that climbed up to a high-backed chair carved of some black substance. The man seated in this throne was the only one not looking at them – he was examining an unfurled scroll intently, his face a mask of concentration. Leaning against one of the jagged armrests was a greatsword, its blade a length of glistening darkness and its hilt as white as polished bone.

There were maybe a dozen other black-robed men and women clustered at the bottom of the tiered steps, and most of them bore some resemblance to Nishi and Rhenna. Pale skin and sharp features, their eyes shards of cold darkness. Of all of them, only the Black Sword was showing the hint of a smile. Deryn shivered, though he wasn't sure if it was a lingering chill from the void they had just passed through or rather the welcome they had emerged into.

Deryn recognized two others in the room from when they had arrived yesterday – the ancient teacher Saelus, standing beside an older matron with silver hair, and the striking woman Kaliss had called the White Spider, who was a little apart from the rest leaning against the plinth of an abstract barbed statue of black stone. In the wraith-light of the flames, she looked like she was a statue as well, but carved from unblemished alabaster. An unsettling thought occurred to Deryn as his eyes passed over the black sculpture – was this shape similar to what he'd seen recessed deep in the abyss, frozen here in the act of dancing to unholy pipes? He shuddered, trying to forget what he thought he might have briefly glimpsed in the darkness.

Even more disturbing was the massive skull hanging on the wall behind the throne, its jaws hinged wide like it was poised to swallow the man sitting there. Deryn remembered Phinius's story of an earlier ruler of the Duskhold slaying the last of something he'd called a balewyrm and then mounting its skull in the hold's audience chamber. The remains looked serpent-like, Deryn thought, but the sheer size of the beast beggared belief. If he hadn't encountered a riftbeast so recently, he would have thought these bones might be some clever fabrication to intimidate supplicants in this hall.

The Sharded Few milling around the steps were all staring at Deryn and the two who had brought him here, but the lord looming over them hadn't yet acknowledged their presence, continuing to pore over the scroll with his lips moving as he read.

After an awkward wait, Nishi finally stepped forward and cleared his throat, but still the man did not look at him. Instead, he briskly rolled the scroll and turned towards where the pale-skinned woman was loitering in the shadow of the thorned statue.

"Leantha," the man said, brandishing the scroll in her direction. He did not raise his voice, but it carried clearly across the grand hall. "She is coming."

Murmurs rippled through the gathered Sharded. This was evidently news of some import.

"And does she seem amenable to our proposal?" The woman's reply was even softer, but it carried a sharp edge, like steel wrapped in silk.

"She does not make mention of it," the man responded. "But the very fact that she would make the journey suggests she is interested."

"Father!" Rhenna cried, striding towards the throne. "We have a new Sharded in the Duskhold! I present to you Deryn, once of the twelve towns." She threw out her arm to indicate him, and he wondered if he should approach the steps or sink to his knees. In the end, he remained standing, frozen by his uncertainty.

Slowly, the seated man turned to regard them. His long hair was the purest white, but he otherwise seemed unburdened by his years – there were no lines on his face, and his broad shoulders strained beneath his bulky robes.

The man's black eyes settled on him, and the force of his attention sent a shiver down Deryn's spine.

"Do you know who I am?"

"Cael Shen," Deryn said, then quickly corrected himself. "Lord Shen."

The master of the Duskhold studied him for a long moment, his black eyes glittering. "Welcome," he finally intoned, in a manner that suggested this was a formal initiation. "Today you are reborn in the service of the Shadow. Do you swear to defend the Duskhold and your fellow Sharded unto death? To follow the commands of the obsidian throne and never to betray the sacred trust of your lord?" While he was speaking, Cael Shen had settled his hand on the bone hilt of his greatsword. Kilian had once said Unbound Sharded were ruthlessly dealt with, as Deryn knew he would be if he refused the Duskhold's offer. He doubted very much that Cael Shen would show the same mercy as his nephew had when Kilian had let the Unbound who had slain Xiv live.

He would be a very great fool if he did not swear any oath this man required.

"I do," Deryn said, with as much strength as he could muster. Despite his best effort, his words seemed to be swallowed by the vastness of the hall.

Still, the master of the Duskhold must have heard him because he nodded slightly, his hand slipping from the hilt of his gleaming sword.

"Very well," Cael Shen said, shifting his gaze to the clustered Sharded at the base of his throne. "Saelus, approach."

The old man who had greeted them yesterday stepped forward, leaning heavily on his staff. "Yes, my lord?"

"This cycle is nearly finished, and the Delving is immanent. Do you believe this newly Sharded should join the current novices and participate in their Delve, or should he be the first of next year's *arzgans*?"

The old teacher turned to regard Deryn. Despite his great age, the shrewdness in his gaze was palpable. This was not a mind clouded by the weight of years.

"There is nearly a month until the Delving. In that time, great progress can be made if the student is willing and shows aptitude."

Cael Shen grunted. "Very well, then. I will leave it to your discretion whether he descends into the mines with the others or not. But there is more to being a novice than simply learning how to control the Shadow's gifts. Saelus, I want him educated if he has a chance of spending only a month as a novice. I will not have an adept who does not know the most fundamental truths of this world."

Saelus dipped his withered head. "It will be as you command, my lord."

"Good," Cael Shen said, settling back into his throne as he again took up the scroll he had briefly set aside. "Now, back to more pressing matters. Leantha, come here. I need you to search for any hidden meaning I may have missed. The Mother of Storms can be devilishly clever."

Deryn's head was whirling. He had wanted to ask about Kilian and what would happen to Alia, but he had very obviously been dismissed. A hand touched his arm lightly, and he tore his gaze from the sight of the pale woman gracefully ascending the steps.

Rhenna was beside him, her face impassive. "Come. I will return you to your chamber, Sharded."

17

HETH

HETH'S LEGS HURT.

It had started as a slight ache in his calves around midday, then quickly spread to his feet, and as the sun had crawled across the unblemished blue expanse of the sky, it had migrated back up his leg, and now his hamstrings and lower back were complaining loudly. He was putting as much of his weight as possible on the polearm Gervis had insisted he take from the armory – and thank the Silver Shrike for that – but even so, he wasn't sure if he was going to survive until twilight and the changing of the guard.

The only spot of shade atop the Duskhold was in the shadow of the jagged battlements, and Heth couldn't stop daydreaming about leaning his back against the stone there and sliding down to the ground, maybe closing his eyes and letting the breeze that was the day's only merit carry him to the dream lands.

Which would not be wise, according to the other two guards on duty. The one with the badly broken nose and cleft lip – Heth thought his name was Sandrel, though the fellow had an impediment to his speech that made him difficult to understand – had laboriously described what had happened to the last Hollow who had been caught lounging about by one of the Sharded Few. Heth had no desire to join that unfortunate soul mucking the stables, so instead he tried to ignore how uncomfortable he was and instead concentrate on forcing the sun to descend faster.

Which hadn't worked.

It had been the longest, most mind-numbingly dull day of his life, and he nearly gasped in relief when he finally heard the scrape of footsteps coming up the steps. Gervis was one of the three who finally emerged onto the roof, and he flashed another of his idiotic gap-toothed grins when he saw Heth's expression.

"Even my mum was never so happy to see me," he said, chuckling as he sauntered over to Heth.

The amusement in his eyes was maddening, and Heth could only muster an unintelligible grunt in response.

A meaty hand clapped his shoulder. "Rest up, Hollow. You'll have to be out here at dawn to relieve me."

Heth briefly entertained the fantasy of tossing aside his polearm and leaping over the battlements. At least he'd be off his feet for the plunge down.

"Oh! I almost forgot," Gervis said. "The two Imbued that arrived with you went before the Shadow today. One got their shard; the other failed and was sent to the kitchens."

At once, all his aches and pains were forgotten.

"Who?" he whispered hoarsely.

Gervis's dull face crinkled in confusion. "Who got the shard or who didn't?"

Heth wanted to shake the guard and scream in his face that telling him either would answer both questions, but after a deep breath he brought himself under control.

"Who became Sharded?" he said, as calmly as he could. He didn't even know why he was so nervous – a few days ago the thought of his former indentured elevated so far above him would have been devastating, but things had changed between them. Now . . . he didn't know how he would feel if it was Deryn who had joined the Sharded Few.

"The boy," Gervis said. "He's Sharded. The girl is in the kitchens."

Memories of his father forcing him to press his hands against

Deryn's bloodied back as the boy lay there unconscious rose unbidden. That had been done to teach him how to be a master of other men. And now . . . now it was Deryn who was the master, and not just of a few ragged slaves squatting in the woods. No, he was one of the masters of this world.

It was enough to make Heth feel lightheaded.

And Alia . . . she had failed? Heth wasn't truly surprised, to be honest, as he had never been able to imagine her as one of the Sharded Few. But she still must feel lost and disappointed. He should go to her, let her see a familiar face.

"Thank you for telling me," Heth said as he shouldered past Gervis and made his way to the steps leading down. The other two guardsmen had preceded him, and he didn't want them to get too far ahead. He truly doubted he could make it back to where the Hollow toiled if he lost them in the hold's labyrinthine corridors.

"Meat tonight," a guardsman grunted when he caught up. The one with the lazy eye, he noticed, not the cleft lip. Heth hadn't been sure if this fellow could talk, as he hadn't made a sound all day. He'd just stood there at the battlements, staring in two different directions.

"Wonderful," Heth replied. And it was – he hadn't eaten since an unappetizing bowl of mush for breakfast.

He trailed the two guards to the armory and followed their lead in returning his armor and weapon to the racks. It felt so liberating to not be carrying around that shirt of heavy mail, and he wondered if anyone would care if tomorrow he wore one of the banded leather vests he noticed collecting dust in the corner. Perhaps standing for so long would be easier if he wasn't draped in metal, though that made him wonder why none of the other guardsmen were wearing the lighter armor.

He was about to ask them that very question, but as soon as they'd shrugged out of their chainmail, the guardsmen hurried out of the armory and clattered down the stairs leading to the hall where the Hollow ate their meals. Heth hadn't been given a key yet to lock the room, but he assumed they knew that and didn't care, which in turn made him not care. Honestly, what was the danger of allowing easy access to a bunch of rusted swords when the Duskhold was full of warriors who could catch steel with their bare hands?

Heth made his way to the section of the hold given over to the kitchens. The clamor and commotion was rather refreshing after a day of doing nothing atop the fortress – Gervis might think that the guards were lucky for how little they were called on to actually do, but Heth could see how kitchen work might be far more satisfying. At least you could see what your labor brought about. He stopped a young scullery boy as he dashed from one room to another, but the child only looked at him blankly when he asked about Alia. Another girl carrying a basket of flopping fish shook her head at his question, but an older woman with flour in her hair jerked a chin farther down the long corridor.

"Abattoir," she said, rubbing at her face and leaving a streak of white across her cheek.

Heth frowned, and she must have interpreted his expression to mean he didn't know what that was, because then she added "Meat room. Just follow the smell when ya get to the end of the hall."

In truth, he was familiar with the term . . . but he couldn't imagine Alia working in such a place as he remembered her refusing to eat any animal flesh while staying at the inns near the twelve towns. With a sinking feeling in his stomach, Heth went in the direction the woman had indicated.

This section of the corridor was much quieter, with far less activity – the ovens and kilns and firepits were all down the other end, as well as the long room where the food was prepared to be brought to the feasting hall of the Sharded – and he stood for a moment at the entrances to several passageways listening intently. In the end, it was like the woman had said, and the smell gave away which of these corridors led to the abattoir. It was a sour, fetid aroma, and one Heth had encountered before when hunting with his father, though not so concentrated. It reminded him of offal and voided bowels and the stink of meat left to fester in the sun.

The passageway curved as it descended and then opened up into a vast, dimly lit chamber. He nearly gagged, his eyes watering. All manner of beasts hung from hooks in the ceiling, blood dripping from their flayed carcasses. A few still-living goats were huddled in a pen that took up one corner of the room, and there was a large tunnel carved into the far wall where Heth assumed the animals were herded in from outside the Duskhold.

All the Hollow here were clustered together, their backs to Heth. He couldn't see Alia's golden hair, but whatever was going on had seemed to draw the attention of everyone in the abattoir, so he made his way across the room, careful to avoid slipping on the blood-slicked floor. He shouldered his way between several of the Hollow, then hissed when he saw what they were looking at.

Alia was half-sprawled on the floor, one arm propping herself up from laying completely in the filth. Her head was lowered, her blonde hair veiling her face. Looming over her was a huge Ashasai man wearing an apron that may once have been white but was now pink and splotched with stains of darker red, a cleaver thrust into the belt that was vainly trying to restrain his massive belly. His hairless copper face was flushed scarlet, twisted in rage as he stared down at the girl.

"What's going on?" Heth asked.

The Ashasai jerked his gaze to Heth. "The girl won't work," he snarled. "Won't kill, won't skin, won't cut."

"She was raised not to hurt animals," Heth said, coming to stand beside Alia. "Why, by the Broken God, did she get sent down here?"

"We don't get no choice where we work," the huge Ashasai spat. "You think any o' them wanted to be here?" He gestured angrily at the silent crowd of watching Hollow. "Needs to be done and we do it, or there ain't no meat on the Sharded's table and then someone is gonna get their back striped." He shook his head violently. "Ain't gonna be me, rich boy. Ain't gonna be me."

"Heth."

His name, spoken in barely a whisper. He glanced down at Alia and found that she'd turned her head up to look at him.

White-hot rage filled him when he saw that half of her face was already starting to purple.

"You struck her?" he asked, stepping closer to the fat Ashasai.

The man stumbled back a step in surprise, then seemed to remember that all his fellow butchers were watching and threw out his chest.

"I did. This here's my kingdom, rich boy. Everyone works, no crying and no excuses. Chop and cut and keep quiet. Them's the rules."

The Ashasai overtopped him by about a head and might have weighed twice as much, but Heth's anger had obliterated any qualms he might have had about antagonizing such a large man with such a big knife.

Heth shoved his finger into the center of the Ashasai's stained apron. "She's coming with me, fat man. And if you try to stop us, I'll put you up on one of these hooks where you belong, and your friends here can carve off a piece every time the Sharded want a little bacon with their breakfast."

The color of the Ashasai's face deepened and with a wordless roar he swung his open hand at Heth's head.

He swayed back to avoid the blow, then lunged forward and planted his fist in the man's belly. The Ashasai let out a strangled grunt, clutching at his stomach as he reeled backwards. Heth followed, giving him a two-handed shove that sent the man tumbling into a table covered with pieces of goat. The butcher bounced off the wood and then slid to the floor with a groan.

Someone clubbed Heth across the back of the head, and then arms were around him. He wrenched himself free and turned to find that three of the other butchers had stepped from the gawking crowd.

"That fat pig worth it?" Heth asked, raising his fists and settling onto the balls of his feet. He'd only done a little unarmed combat sparring – and now he inwardly cursed himself for insisting so often on swords when fighting in the circle back in Kething's Cross – but he was also fairly sure these Hollow had never had any training at all. Still, four against one was not good odds. He'd have to strike quick, bloody a few of them, and hope that sapped their desire to continue. Then he could scoop Alia up and get her out of this horrible place.

The three shared a quick glance, as if silently asking what their strategy should be, and Heth didn't give them any time to figure it out. He rushed forward, smashing his shoulder into one of the men and sending him stumbling back, then turned and jabbed his fist into the nose of another. That fellow recoiled, clutching his face, but the last of the three clouted Heth, making his head ring. He grimaced, grabbing that man by his filthy apron, then yanked him off balance as he kicked his legs. The butcher tumbled to the ground with a yelp of surprise, but before Heth could leap on him, someone smashed into him from the side and they went down together in a tangle of flailing limbs.

A boot connected with his ribs. Snarling, Heth seized the leg that had just kicked him and pulled hard, toppling the butcher into a few of his gawping fellows who hadn't yet joined the fray. Heth staggered to his feet just in time to absorb a charge by the man he'd punched first, and so back to the floor he went, the breath driven from his body in a whoosh as blows rained down. He lashed out blindly and felt a satisfying crunch as his fist connected with something that crumpled – the man shrieked in pain as hot droplets rained down on Heth's face. He spat out blood that wasn't his own and tried to surge upwards, but he was driven down by the press of bodies piling on top of him.

Suddenly, hands grabbed Heth by the shoulders and dragged him away from the fight. He struggled briefly, but whoever was holding him had a strong grip, and at least no one was taking this opportunity to beat him further. Across from him, the three young butchers were also being restrained. They were panting heavily in the arms of several large men, including the two guards who had stood watch today atop the Duskhold with Heth.

"Calm yourself, Hollow."

It was a voice he knew, and Heth's heart fell as he turned his head towards Elanin. The grub-white steward was standing beside the fat Ashasai, his plump lips curled disdainfully. The head butcher was still doubled over, glaring at Heth.

"He struck me," wheezed the Ashasai, pointing a sausage-thick finger at Heth.

"He struck her!" Heth shouted back. He tried to shake himself free of the hands holding him, but the blind rage fueling his strength had vanished.

"Silence!" shouted the steward. He turned, looking for something. "Where is the girl? The one who failed her test."

"She ran," one of the butchers who hadn't attacked Heth muttered. "When they were scrappin' she went for the stairs."

"And no one tried to stop her?" bellowed the Ashasai incredulously. "You all just watched her go?"

The butcher picked something from his ear and flicked it away. "This was much more interestin', Pol. The boy was gettin' in some good licks."

"The girl's name is Alia," Heth said, speaking to Elanin and trying to sound as reasonable as possible. "She's been through a lot these last few days. Her father died, she was dragged from her home to come here, and then she wasn't chosen by the Shadow. She's from the Wild, and far as I can tell, she doesn't eat animals. Against her beliefs or something. Getting sent here, to this place, must have been traumatizing." He turned and spat out a wad of blood. "I came down here, and this bastard was standing over her after giving her a thrashing. He deserved everything I did to him, as did these cretins." His arms still restrained, Heth jerked his chin towards the men he'd fought.

"We all got our jobs!" yelled the Ashasai, spraying spittle. "If she don't do hers, she deserves what she gets!"

Elanin held up his hand and the fat man subsided. He narrowed his eyes as he stared at Heth hard. "Hollow, do you truly think it is your duty to dispense justice?" He shook his head slowly. "It is not. It is *mine*."

His hand went to a length of cord coiled at his waist. Heth's heart fell when he realized what it was. With a flick of his wrist, the steward shook out the whip, most of its knotted length coming to rest on the bloodstained floor.

Elanin turned to the cleft-lipped guard who had earlier been so excited about eating meat for dinner tonight. Heth couldn't help but wonder – strangely enough, given the circumstances – if stepping inside the abattoir had affected his appetite at all.

"Sandrel, find the girl and bring her to my quarters. I'll be finished here shortly."

Then his watery gaze drifted to the guardsmen still holding Heth. "Bind his hands. This Hollow has earned himself a dozen lashes."

18

DERYN

DERYN LAY awake and listened to the darkness.

He hadn't noticed the sound before he had climbed into his bed and pulled the blanket of silver fur up to his chin. It was a low susurrus, like a thousand moth wings beating together, or a faint whispering barely heard through a shut door. He'd thrown aside his blanket and made a circuit of his bedchamber, searching for the source, and he'd found that the noise had strengthened when he'd lowered his head to the shadows thrown by the furniture. For a moment, Deryn had even thought he'd heard the faint piping from the dark place Nishi had led them through on the way to the Duskhold's audience chamber, but after listening more carefully he'd decided that this was his imagination and returned to bed.

Still, sleep did not come easy. The itch from the splinter of crystal lodged in his chest had faded, but it was now sending currents of energy coursing through his veins, making his body thrum. It felt incredible, if he was being honest. All the pain and exhaustion that had accumulated over the last few weeks had been instantly effaced when he'd gained his shard, like a teacher wiping a slate clean. After Rhenna had returned Deryn to his chamber, he'd wandered about in a daze, trying to determine the limit of his new strength. He'd easily hefted the massive chair of heavy wood and even broken a knob of rock from the rough-hewn wall. After that, he'd sat on the edge of his bed and tried to sort through all that had happened.

He was one of the Sharded Few.

Deryn couldn't help but remember sitting on his mother's shoulders, straining to see over the crowd at the shadow-sharded riding his horse through Kething's Cross. To think that one day he would be one of those legends, the lords of the world . . .

A stab of pain went through his heart at the thought of his mother. They'd struggled and suffered for so long – she'd worked herself to the bone when he was younger to keep food on their table and clothes on his back. She'd tried so hard to overcome her demons, but the voices would always find her again, no matter how often they'd moved. For a short time in the woods, she'd escaped, but they must have returned for her to throw herself into the lake that cold morning while he'd been off in the woods checking his snares. Surely she hadn't done it just from the guilt of signing his indenture.

With some effort, Deryn pushed aside those memories and slipped beneath the blanket.

But he could not stop himself from thinking about everything that had happened. He had been a slave in all but name, his worth determined by what value could be extracted from his labors. The days had yawned empty and endless, his life not his own. Now he found himself infused with great power . . . yet had his situation changed all that much? He remembered Cael Shen looming over him, his hand on the hilt of his sword, demanding his allegiance. If he had refused, he would have been killed. Kilian and Kaliss had both been very clear on that fact. He thought back to Gavin's rambling speech in the old mill – there were two kinds of people in this world, he had claimed, the rulers and the ruled. Deryn's life may have radically changed, but were his circumstances all that different from when his life had belonged to Master Ferith? He was still one of the ruled.

The fetters he'd worn had not been shattered that day in the forest – his ownership had just been transferred to another.

Something was hardening in his chest, a resolve that surprised him. To be a slave forever was not a fate he could accept. He would learn and grow in strength, devote himself utterly to mastering whatever powers this shard imparted. But there would come a time when he left this place, finally strike the chains from his wrist and seize his own destiny by the throat. Gavin may have been one sort of Unbound, cruel and capricious, but Deryn suspected that was just the man he had always been. He could be someone else, a champion for the weak and helpless.

The kind of man who would have made his mother proud.

But first he would have to become strong, and to do that he would have to conquer the gauntlet of challenges before him.

The whispering from the darkness slowly strengthened as he lay there waiting for sleep to finally claim him. He also noticed the light was changing – the radiance spilling from the mist-globe on the ceiling had been gradually fading ever since he'd returned to his chamber, answering to whatever cycle governed its existence, and now he couldn't sense even a flicker of brightness in its depths . . . And yet unlike the night before, he could still make out the chair on the far side of his room and the outline of the door.

He could see in the dark. Not perfectly, though – it was like a perpetual twilight, the details of everything lost to shadows. Strangely, the realization of this ability frightened him more than his new strength or the thing sunk into the flesh of his chest. Deryn shut his eyes and rolled onto his side, trying to will himself to sleep and ignore the faint whispering of the shadows.

He slept surprisingly well, all things considered, and was startled awake the next morning by a sharp rapping.

"Get up, Sharded! There's no sleeping late in the Duskhold."

Kaliss. Would every morning begin with her dragging him from his dreams? He needed to learn how the rest of the hold woke at a proper time – the lack of windows was disconcerting, and the mist-globes were no substitute for sunlight.

"Coming," he shouted, hurriedly rising and making use of the chamber pot before donning his robes. In his haste, his fingers brushed the fragment buried in the skin of his chest, and a little crackle of energy made him shiver. That was going to take some time to get used to.

More impatient knocking, and Deryn nearly ran across the chamber to fling open his door. Kaliss was standing on the other side, her arms folded and lips pursed.

"Apologies," he said. "Yesterday must have been more tiring than I realized."

"At least you're dressed," she said tartly, her gaze drifting to his waist. "Mostly."

Deryn glanced down and realized he'd forgotten to finish securing his robes. "Ah," he murmured, his face growing hot. "Sorry." With fumbling fingers he cinched the robes closed and quickly tied a knot.

"For you," Kaliss said when he'd finished, holding out a hunk of bread. "I didn't want to waste time waiting for you to eat breakfast in the hall."

As soon as he'd taken the morsel, she turned away and started striding purposefully down the corridor. Deryn hurried after her, relieved that he'd attended to his personal needs before opening his door.

"Is there something important happening?" he asked after he'd caught up with her.

The Ashasai girl did not look at him. "No. But Saelus has given me yet another duty, and that is to dispel your no doubt staggering ignorance about the world. It is a daunting task, and apparently I am the only novice capable enough to be entrusted with it."

"I thought Saelus was our teacher?"

Kaliss snorted. "Saelus helps us to nurture our powers. The hounds return sporadically, bringing new Imbued, some of which are chosen by the Shadow, and Saelus cannot be bothered to instruct each of the newly Sharded. This time, the task has fallen on me."

"Uh, well, thank you."

"Just listen carefully and try to remember everything I say, because if you forget what I tell you today it will reflect badly on me."

"I will," Deryn promised, and Kaliss grunted something unintelligible that sounded skeptical.

She led him deeper into the Duskhold, down corridors he had no memory of walking. Though he supposed it was possible he had been this way before, as the narrow stone corridors all seemed to blend together.

"Where are we going?" he finally ventured after a disorienting number of twists and turns had left him lost.

"Somewhere I go when I want solitude," Kaliss replied. "I don't want to bore any of the other Sharded, since they already know everything I'm about to tell you."

She fell silent again until the passage they were following ended in a soaring archway. "And here we are," she said, and as if responding to her words a pale light kindled in the space beyond. The room was vast, Deryn realized even before he'd passed beneath the arch, far larger than the Duskhold's audience chamber, but the true grandeur still took his breath away. It looked like a cavern, and he wondered if it had been formed naturally long before the shadowsharded had come to inhabit the mountain. The walls closest to him were rough and uneven, curving upwards into a gloom pierced by a forest of jagged stalactites. A lake of black water filled most of the chamber, so perfectly still it resembled a sheet of obsidian. The ghostly light appeared to be seeping directly from a gazebo of white stone perched on a small island in the center of the lake.

"What is this place?" Deryn whispered as Kaliss started on a narrow bridge curving over the water. She didn't answer, and he wondered if she had heard him, but he also didn't want to speak any louder – the silence in this cavern had the same sort of weight and solemnity as the temple of the Broken God in Kething's Cross. Violating the stillness seemed sacrilegious . . . like something might hear and be offended. Instead, he followed Kaliss onto the ribbon of black stone, placing each step with utmost care. He truly did not want to discover just how deep or cold the water was in this underground lake . . . or what might be lurking beneath the placid surface.

He held his breath until he stepped from the bridge onto the edge of the small island. Kaliss had already moved inside the gazebo, sliding onto one of the white-stone benches within. She gestured for him to join her, then turned her gaze to the lake. Deryn sat across from her, folding his arms on the small table between them. He followed where she was looking, but he couldn't tell what exactly had drawn her attention. It was peaceful, he had to admit. The spectral radiance from the gazebo gleamed on the surface of the dark water, reaching with ghostly fingers back the way they'd come.

"I asked Saelus about this place once," she murmured, sounding almost distracted. "He said it is as old as the Duskhold. The first lord of the shadow-sharded built it for his favorite concubine – there is a legend that she was the youngest daughter of Segulah Tain and that her betrayal was crucial to the success of the rebellion." She dragged her eyes from the lake, her gaze settling on Deryn.

He thought of the majestic ruins of the winter palace perched on the mesa at the edge of the Frayed Lands. "Why would a princess of the First Empire give up everything to become a concubine in a place like this?"

Kaliss shrugged. "Perhaps she was a romantic. Or perhaps the story was false – I've realized in my time here that the histories are incomplete. Maybe they were destroyed or never written down in the first place. The Sharded are warriors, not scholars."

"Or perhaps they didn't want the truth to be known," Deryn offered.

Kaliss glanced at him sharply. "You may not be a complete fool. This place . . ." She paused, groping for the right words. "It is darkness made manifest. Everything here is shadowed and hidden, full of secrets."

Deryn attempted a wry grin. "So you brought me out here to tell me it is impossible to know anything about this place?"

Kaliss's mouth twisted, but not into anything that resembled a smile. "If that is all you take away from today, then this lesson will not be entirely wasted. But what Saelus wants me to teach you about is the world outside, at least how the shadow-sharded understand it."

Deryn leaned back, studying the grooves on the table in front of him. There was a gameboard of some kind incised into the white stone, triangles and circles enclosed in a square. He'd never seen its like before. "Such as?"

"Let us start at the most basic," Kaliss replied. "Do you know how many fragments of the Heart persist to this day, and thus how many different orders of Sharded walk these lands?"

Deryn nodded, raising his hands to begin counting them off on his fingers. "Well, there are the northern Sharded. I've lived my whole life under the Shadow, but my town was only a few days' travel from the Ember, the home of the flame-sharded. I've heard that the Flame and Shadow are friendly."

"They were not always," Kaliss interrupted. "The twelve towns were wrested violently from the Flame hundreds of years ago. For the past century, the Flame and Shadow have been allied, and we've fought in several wars together against the other two great powers in the north."

"Storm and Sea."

"Aye, though the latter call themselves the wave-sharded. Their realm is a string of islands in the Sea of Salvation – poor and barren, or so I've heard said, but they draw a great bounty from the depths. Their hold is a fortress of living coral half submerged in the sea. The storm-sharded dwell on the coast, in the great city of Flail. Their hold is a mighty bastion called the Windwrack, constantly battered by the storms that come surging off the sea."

Deryn had heard of all these places, though truthfully he had not known which were real and which were merely fancies spun from traveler's tales. When Flail had been mentioned before, it had been accompanied by shaken heads and curled lips. Those who lived in the city of storms couldn't be trusted, it was said – their moods were as mercurial as the sea before a tempest, and they could change their allegiances depending on which way the wind was blowing.

Then again, they probably had similar stories about those who lived under the Shadow.

"Are they still enemies of the Duskhold?"

Kaliss pursed her lips, as if unsure how to answer this question. "More like rivals," she finally said. "We have not been openly at war since Cael Shen's father ruled the Duskhold. But there is still little love lost between the Shadow and the Storm. They remember the siege of the Windwrack, and some of the older shadow-sharded – such as Saelus – still hold a grudge about the death of Lord Shen's older brother."

"Was he killed in that war?"

Kaliss shook her head. "Before. It was the inciting event. Regas Shen was very different from his brother. A dreamer and an explorer. His ship was dashed to pieces while sailing the Sea of Salvation, and it was discovered that the Windwrack had summoned the storm that drowned him."

Deryn was quiet for a moment. "Then what happens when shadow-sharded encounter storm-sharded? Is it dangerous?"

Kaliss hesitated before answering. "If either hold heard of an ambush by the other, the peace that holds over the north would be shattered. Now, a formal duel witnessed by other Sharded and agreed to by both warriors . . . that happens on occasion. But in truth I would counsel wariness when near the Sharded of every other hold. If they think they can claim another fragment with no chance of being found out, every Sharded will make the attempt." She paused again. "I certainly would."

Deryn swallowed back the protestations he wanted to make here. He couldn't imagine attacking a stranger for no reason, and he truly hoped that Kaliss's sentiments were not as universal among the Sharded as she apparently believed.

"And the south?" she continued, bringing the discussion back. "What do you know about the southern Sharded?"

Deryn shifted. He'd heard a lot, of course. The children of the twelve towns were raised on stories of the dangerous, decadent southlands. Teeming Ashasai, ruled from atop the Black Steps by the blood-sharded. The mysterious canyon-city of Chan-anok, home to the reclusive stone-sharded. The sand-sharded of the merciless Salah desert.

Deryn counted them off on his fingers. "Well, I know of blood, stone, sand . . ."

Kaliss cut him off with a shake of her head. "There is no sand anymore. I've heard rumors of a few Unbound wandering about who were once part of the Shahnate, but I don't know if that's true, as with the shattering of the Sand Shard, they should have lost their power."

"You're speaking of the Conquests."

"The war that began soon after the Copper Crown Accord, yes. When the emir of the great oasis city of Derambinal accepted the title of shah from the other rulers of the Salah, he united the desert under the banner of the copper crown. The sand-sharded had never been as unified as the other holds, with several Sharded families each ruling over a great city or tribe, fighting more often with each other than the powers outside the Salah. Finally forged into one empire, they burst from the desert and attempted to subjugate all before them. Chan-anok fell first, and Ashasai would have followed if the combined strength of Storm, Shadow, and Flame had not defeated the sand-sharded on the plains of Gerendal."

The Conquests may have been nearly thirty years ago, but the reverberations of the war had still been very much in evidence when Deryn was growing up. More than a few folk in Kething's Cross had lost limbs or eyes during the campaign, when the shadow-sharded had levied conscripts and brought them south to oppose the seemingly unstoppable armies of the Salahi.

Something occurred to him. "Azil is Salahi."

"Very perceptive of you."

"No, I mean, was he captured during the war?"

"Rescued," Kaliss corrected him. "The Black Sword was brought as a babe to Cael Shen during the sack of Derambinal, and for reasons I do not know, he was adopted into the Duskhold ruling family. A wise decision, for he is one of the strongest Sharded of his generation."

Kaliss waved her hand, as if to dismiss this line of conversation. "But the Conquests is a history lesson for another day. For now, it is enough that you know of the other Sharded you may encounter. It is easier, perhaps, to consider them as three distinct groups. The first would be the holds that rule realms, either sprawling empires or solitary cities. Those are the Flame, Storm, Wave, Blood, Stone and Shadow. Then there are the fragmented tribes with no hold or ruler – you've encountered the wind-sharded of the Frayed Lands, and in the deep Wild dwell the seed-sharded, though we know little enough of them. And finally there are the lost shards – the Sand Shard, broken apart by the armies of the alliance, and the Ice Shard, lost in the far north when contact with the monastery of Kara Dum was severed."

She frowned, and Deryn thought it looked like she was deciding whether to tell him something else. "There is a legend of another fragment – the Soul Shard – but Saelus told me that if such Sharded ever truly existed, they were hunted to extinction long ago. And who knows, maybe there were others as well, now either lost to time or intentionally excised from the histories. As I said, the Sharded are warriors, not scholars."

Deryn struggled to keep from being overwhelmed by this avalanche of names and places. Some he'd heard mention of before, others she could have been conjuring out of thin air for all he knew. The monastery of Kara Dum? Oasis cities? A Soul Shard?

"This is a lot to remember," Deryn muttered, massaging his temple.

"And it is just our first lesson," Kaliss told him with a humorless smile. "Every morning we will come here, and I will do my best to turn you from a country bumpkin into a worldly warrior of the Duskhold."

Deryn bit down on the inside of his cheek so he didn't respond with a rude remark. "And then what?" he asked. "How do I spend the rest of my days?"

Kaliss rose abruptly, smoothing her robes. "Follow me and find out."

She led him to a section of the Duskhold he hadn't visited before. While much of the hold felt empty and abandoned, these corridors and rooms showed signs of habitation. Still, it was a surprise when he heard the faint echo of voices.

"We're late," Kaliss said, annoyance edging her tone.

"Late for what?" Deryn asked as they approached a large, rounded doorway, runes incised into the stone fringing the entrance.

"Our lesson," Kaliss said, not hesitating as she strode into the chamber beyond.

Deryn followed a step behind, but he paused in surprise when he saw what awaited them beyond the threshold. The room was circular, a sunken bowl with tiered steps marching down to a flat expanse at its center. The first thought he had was that the chamber reminded him of how Xiv had described – with a fondness Deryn had always found strange – Ashasai's fighting pits, where gladiators hacked each other to pieces before a roaring crowd. But instead of blood-soaked sand, this arena's floor was a gleaming silver disc, and it was occupied by a lone, bent-backed figure leaning heavily on a staff.

Saelus lifted his gaze to them. Deryn couldn't see his expression clearly, but he sensed from his posture that the old teacher was less than pleased.

"Novices. Such tardiness is disappointing."

"My fault, master, it won't happen again," Kaliss replied, the contrition in her voice surprising Deryn. He never could have imagined her groveling for forgiveness, even to her teacher.

Saelus lifted his staff and brought it down sharply on the stone – or whatever the silver substance was – the crack ringing throughout the chamber. This was done to draw the attention of the dozen other robed men and women scattered upon the steps, as every face had been turned towards Deryn and Kaliss. Most were young, he thought, maybe around his own age, though a few looked to be older. One heavyset man with a slave-sigil burned into his forehead might have been the same age as his mother.

Saelus didn't acknowledge the Ashasai girl's apology. Instead, he swept out his hand, indicating Deryn with a gnarled finger. "Students!" he cried, his surprisingly powerful voice filling the room. "Meet the newest Sharded of the Duskhold. This is Deryn, your brother under the Shadow."

There was no reaction to this statement, not even muttered greetings or nods of welcome. Expressionless faces watched him silently, as if waiting for him to do something. He felt a cold sweat break out, and it took an act of will not to turn and flee the room. He might have given in to this temptation if he hadn't noticed someone familiar among the students, and he at least seemed happy to see Deryn.

Menochus gave a jaunty wave, so unexpected given the general mood of the chamber that Deryn had to catch himself before his lips twitched into a smile. The hill-tribe boy was sitting on one of the middle-rank tiers, and when he saw he had caught Deryn's gaze, he patted the stone beside him in invitation.

"Sit," Saelus commanded, "and let us return to today's lesson."

Deryn turned towards Kaliss to ask her where he should go, but the Ashasai girl was already descending the steps. He considered following her, but she hadn't waited for him or even glanced backwards, so instead he moved towards the only welcoming face in the chamber.

Menochus's smile broadened as he slipped onto the step beside him. "Welcome ta the Duskhold," he whispered. "And congratulations on yer Shard. I had a feeling ye were blessed."

"Thank you," Deryn replied softly. Down below, a pair of cowled servants were carrying a small metal brazier into the center of the room. Another Hollow was behind them, holding one of the glass spheres filled with roiling white mist. Saelus and the other students had shifted their attention away from the newcomers and to whatever was happening.

"Don't be intimidated by them," Menochus continued, sweeping his hand through the air to indicate the rest of the novices. "Saelus and the rest have filled their heads with talk of how we are all in competition here, that the Duskhold only wants the strongest o' us. So they pretend to be cold iron when most of them are soft as heated copper. Before they got their shard, none o' them could last a month alone in the Wild."

"You don't believe we should be striving against each other?"

Menochus let out a small snort. "Nay. We are all hearthmates here, yes? Likely one day we'll stand shoulder ta shoulder against our enemies – best if we are willing ta lay down our lives for our brothers, yes?"

Before Deryn could offer agreement with what the hulking boy had said, Saelus struck the floor again with the end of his staff.

"Prepare yourselves to reach for the Shadow," the teacher proclaimed, then motioned for the Hollow bearing the globe infused with mist to approach. From the young girl's face, it looked like she wanted to be anywhere else, but still she bravely stepped forwards, holding out the translucent sphere. Seeing her made him think of Alia, and he felt a pang of guilt. He hadn't spared her more than a moment's thought since Kaliss had led her away. He should ask the Ashasai girl if Alia had recovered from her audience with the Shadow and settled in all right with the other servants of the Sharded.

Saelus looked like he was reaching for the globe, but rather than take it from the servant, his hand somehow slipped *inside* the sphere without breaking its exterior.

"Drega's dugs," Menochus murmured, clearly just as surprised as Deryn.

Saelus made a scooping motion, and when he withdrew his hand, a serpent of glowing mist writhed in his open palm. The girl holding the sphere goggled at him, her mouth agape.

Muttering rippled through the novices as their teacher slowly brought the clump of mist over to the black-metal brazier in the center of the silver floor. He walked carefully, his brow knitted as he watched the mist, as if afraid it would squirm from his control and escape if he looked away. Then, when he stood beside the brazier, he tipped his hand, and the coiling tendril tumbled into the center of the curving metal.

A white flame swelled into existence, and it looked just like what had been illuminating the audience chamber of Cael Shen. From his vantage, Deryn could see down into the brazier, and it seemed the fire was feeding on nothing as it climbed higher. Or perhaps it was slowly devouring the black metal itself.

"Observe the shadows cast by the wraithling flame," Saelus said, using his staff to indicate the darkness twisting on the silver floor. Deryn frowned. The white flame seemed to be emitting a pale radiance, so why was it throwing shadows like it was blocking a greater light source? He squinted at the ceiling where several larger mistglobes were sunk into the stone. Finally, he shrugged – he really shouldn't even bother attempting to understand this place.

"Now reach out and beckon the darkness, *arzgan,*" Saelus commanded. "Draw it towards you."

Deryn remembered Kilian speaking of beckoning on the journey to the Duskhold. It was what he had called his manipulation of the shadows.

He glanced at Menochus and saw that the boy was concentrating hard as he stared intently down at the flickering white flame. No . . . he was focused on the dancing shadows it cast. Was he trying to grasp the darkness?

"What are you doing?" Deryn asked, but the boy just gave a curt shake of his head. Even though he had whispered, Deryn worried he had been too loud, as the silence in the room was almost palpable. Every novice was like Menochus, focused on the blackness writhing on the silver floor.

"If you are the one to seize the shadows, you shall be the first into the mines on the day of the Delving," said Saelus. "A great honor."

Clearly, the other novices had already had some practice in beckoning. The shadows no longer seemed to be mirroring the ghostly flame, instead stretching across the floor towards where a knot of the students were sitting close together. Then it shivered, trembling as if being pulled hard in another direction. There were fewer students in that section of the steps, but one of them was Kaliss. She was standing with the hood of her robes thrown back, sweat gleaming on her hairless copper head, her arm extended like she was straining to pull the shadows towards herself.

Deryn didn't know what he should be doing. Surely he wasn't expected to do this beckoning when no one had told him how.

"Grasp it!" Saelus cried. "Feel the Shadow in your breast yearning to be united with the darkness. But do not command! Entreat it. Seduce it. Convince it that it belongs with you, that it is merely an extension of your soul!"

Deryn blinked in surprise, taken aback by the Sharded's impassioned speech. He sounded like the madman who had ranted in the market square of Kething's Cross until the magistrate's guards had dragged him away.

Bewildered, Deryn could only watch as the novices continued their inscrutable battle. The shadow was tugged one way, then another, the movements sharp and sudden, as if someone had jerked hard on whatever was connecting them to the darkness. Inexorably, though, it was being drawn towards Kaliss, whose face was set in a look of grim determination.

Could he do this as well? Feeling foolish, Deryn forced himself to concentrate as he stared hard at the shadows. He frowned – did it seem to have more solidity than usual? Or was it simply his imagination that it had swelled into a writhing black serpent? And could he .. . could he *feel* it, a pocket of utter coldness that almost seemed close enough to touch ... He stretched out, trying to take hold of the darkness, and for a moment he felt it twist in his hand like a snake thrashing to be free. He attempted to close his fingers around its slippery length, and he could swear he felt it lurch towards him before it tore itself from his grasp and wriggled away.

Deryn rocked backwards, nearly sliding from the step. What had just happened? Had he really touched the darkness? He realized Saelus was staring directly at him, his eyes narrowed.

A cry of triumph startled him, and he returned his attention to the shadows just in time to see it dragged squirming to Kaliss. She threw back her head and laughed as the many strands twined, becoming a single serpent of darkness that then wrapped around her body. It indeed was no longer insubstantial, as Deryn could see her robes rippling as it slithered over her. The novices nearest to her had drawn back, envy and surprise in their faces. He guessed they had not been expecting such a display.

"Excellent," Saelus intoned, bringing his staff down once more to signal the end of the exercise. And while Deryn was sure he was addressing Kaliss, the teacher's gaze was still fixed on him. It had never left him since the moment he'd briefly touched the shadow.

"Very well done, novice. You may release the shadow now."

Kaliss ignored her teacher, staring at the looping coils of darkness as if mesmerized by their movements.

Finally, Saelus turned from Deryn, grimacing in annoyance when he saw what the Ashasai girl was doing. Behind the writhing shadows, her face was slack, her eyes distant.

"Enough," Saelus said harshly as he made a cutting motion with his hand. The tendril stretching from Kaliss to the ghostly flame was instantly severed, a gap appearing about halfway along its length.

The Ashasai girl yelped in pain, collapsing awkwardly onto the stone. She blinked as if coming back to herself from somewhere far away.

"You must seduce the darkness, not be seduced by it, *arzgan*," Saelus admonished her sharply.

"I . . . I am sorry, master," Kaliss managed between gulping breaths. "But I felt it, I touched the Shadow . . ."

"That you did," Saelus said, his voice softening. "And you will be the first through the black gate, as I promised. It is rare for one so recently sharded to successfully beckon. You should be proud of what you have accomplished here today, novice."

Saelus's gaze slid from Kaliss, wandering briefly around the room before alighting on Deryn once more. He shivered, wondering if those words were meant for him as well.

19

HETH

HETH SAT on his stone bed in his tiny room, his knees drawn up to his chest. His back hurt too much for him to lie down or prop himself up against the wall, so he had spent the day sitting in this awkward position, slightly hunched and leaning forward with his arms wrapped around his legs. Still, he was lucky that Elanin had no idea how to wield a whip – his father would have snorted in derision at the pathetic blows the steward had delivered. It had only been the final one – when he'd given the length of knotted cord to the butcher Heth had first struck – that had actually lifted some of the skin from his back.

Heth sighed, wishing someone would come to change his poultice. Gervis had brought the bandages when he'd visited to tell Heth that he wouldn't have to join the other guards on top of the Duskhold for a few days. Apparently, punishments like the one administered to Heth were exceedingly rare in the hold, and no one was certain what should happen now. So Gervis had used his authority as captain of the guards to decree that Heth should rest and recover. He was grateful for that, though being trapped in this tiny stone cell staring at the walls was even more boring than standing atop the Duskhold watching clouds crawl across the sky, and he had to keep pulling his thoughts back from the dark paths they wanted to wander down.

The ridiculousness of his situation was not lost on him. Not long ago he had been wielding the whip, punishing Deryn for giving a crab to a starving girl . . . the girl for whom Heth had earned a lashing for trying to protect. He lowered his head between his knees, bewildered by the strands the Fates had woven.

"Heth."

He looked up sharply. Standing in the open doorway was Alia, her arms folded tightly across her chest. She regarded him from lowered eyes, shifting her weight from foot to foot.

"May I come in?"

"Yes," Heth blurted, surprised by how happy he was to see her whole and apparently healthy. He had tried to avoid thinking about what would happen when the steward finally got his pasty little hands on her.

Heth scooted backwards to make room for her on his bed, as it was the only place for her to sit, then winced as his back bumped against the wall.

Alia saw that, and her face crinkled in concern. "Are you all right? Did they hurt you badly?"

Heth forced a smile. "I'm fine, truly," he said, gesturing at the end of his bed. "Please, sit."

Alia nodded and sank down on the edge. She still looked worried, but it had lessened somewhat. Heth did his best to banish all evidence of pain from his expression and posture.

"You seem all right," he said. "I was worried about what they would do to you."

Alia plucked at the cloth of the shift she was wearing. "It wasn't so bad, truly. I ran for a long time in the corridors and got completely lost. Eventually I met an old man – he was kind, and could see that I'd been crying – and he brought me to the kitchens. When that awful steward finally found me there, a few of the older women were taking care of me. I think he was a little afraid of them, as he just yelled for a while and then left in a huff."

"So he didn't strike you?"

She shook her head.

"And have you returned to the abattoir?"

"No." The relief was clear in her voice. "One of the women who gave me soup and helped me to calm down is the head baker. She told Elanin I would work with her to help make the bread. He didn't look too pleased, but she had a roller pin, and he couldn't stop staring at it, like he was afraid she was going to hit him."

Heth didn't have to force his smile now. The thought of the unctuous little steward cowering in front of a gaggle of old women was very satisfying.

Silence fell for a long moment, and Heth noticed Alia was now twisting the piece of her shift that she held. He was just about to ask her what was wrong when she suddenly spoke.

"You whipped Deryn."

Her words felt like a blow. He opened his mouth, ready to offer up all sorts of excuses. *Deryn had violated the contract that had been signed. He belonged to my family. Giving away the crab was the same as stealing.*

My father made me do it.

But after a brief hesitation, he merely nodded.

"Why?" she asked, and to his surprise, she didn't sound accusing.

"Because I was scared," he finally replied softly.

She looked at him with her lips thinned, her eyes measuring. She didn't ask him what he had feared, and for that he was grateful. He wasn't sure what he would have answered.

"You weren't scared in the abattoir, were you?"

He swallowed. "No."

"But there were so many of them."

"I . . . didn't really think about that. I just saw you on the ground and that someone had struck you."

She considered this for a while, her brow furrowed. Then she reached out and laid her hand over his.

"Thank you."

Heth's mouth was suddenly dry. He suspected she meant nothing by the gesture, but he had a sudden, strong desire to lean forward and kiss her. She was so delicate and pale, her wide green eyes deep enough to fall into. She had been starving when he'd first seen her, and covered with layers of forest grime, but now, after weeks of eating well and having been scrubbed clean here in the Duskhold, he realized how pretty she truly was.

"I . . . it was nothing," he said lamely, pulling his hand away from hers. If they kept touching, he thought he might give in to the temptation to pull her closer.

And he was fairly sure that wasn't what she wanted. This was another change, he realized. Before he'd been summoned into the forest by his father, he would have boldly approached any girl he found intriguing and laughed about it with his friends if he'd met rejection.

He didn't want to do that now. He didn't want to risk what he had with Alia.

She rose, still watching him carefully. Had she expected him to do something? He wished he knew, and at the same time he was glad he had not.

"I'm sorry I ran," she said. "I wasn't thinking clearly. I thought . . . I thought if I fled the chamber you would have no reason to fight." Her expression turned faintly embarrassed. "It must sound ridiculous to you, given what we've been through."

"I just assumed you were more frightened of that fat pig butcher than a monster the size of a mountain."

She brushed back a lock of golden hair that had fallen across her face. "I am, though that must sound so strange. An animal I can understand. A man like that . . . I don't know what he's capable of doing." Alia shook her head, as if to clear it of dark thoughts. "I should let you rest." She started to turn away, but then paused. "Oh, would you like me to bring some bread from the kitchens? I can sneak you some fresh-baked rolls."

"It's all right," Heth told her, waving her words away. "I'll go down to the hall later to eat. I've had just about enough of this room."

"Maybe I will see you there," Alia replied, and then with a last quick smile she was gone.

Heth stayed for a while, watching where she had been, thinking about everything she had said. When his stomach grumbled, he slid from his bed and stood, ready to brave the feast hall at last and risk seeing any of the Hollow he'd fought earlier. To his surprise, he realized his back didn't hurt very much anymore.

A dozen long trestle tables filled the cavernous chamber where the Hollow ate, but only a handful were occupied now. Most of the Duskhold's servants dined immediately after the Sharded enjoyed their evening meal, the fires before they were put to bed used to cook porridge and stew, and warm whatever leftovers remained after the lords of the Duskhold had eaten their fill. For the Hollow whose duties occupied them during this time and could only come late, an assortment of bread and congealing meat was left on the tables, along with the cold broth at the bottom of the large tureens.

Heth gathered a handful of stale rolls from a basket and filled a bowl with soup, pleasantly surprised to find that a few chunks of carrot had survived the horde of hungry Hollow. He eased himself onto one of the benches with a sigh, hoping the ache in his belly would help make this meal at least palatable. But after trying a sip of the soup, he suspected he'd have to be truly starving to find this satisfying. He realized, though, that he just didn't care. The smile he'd been wearing since Alia had visited his chamber wasn't about to vanish because of a few cold leftovers.

He'd saved her. The pain from his lashing – already mostly gone – was well worth the knowledge that she had escaped the abattoir and had found a much better situation in the Duskhold's kitchens. Spending her days kneading flour and enjoying the aroma of baking bread was far better for her than smelling stale blood and hacking apart animals. And from what she'd said, there was an older matron in charge of the ovens who had taken her under her skirts and would protect her, unlike those bullies in the butchery . . .

Heth's thoughts scattered as one of those bullies slipped onto the bench across from him. There was no doubt – he remembered this boy's squashed face and pig-thistle hair from the crowd in the abattoir. Not one he'd fought, but the boy also hadn't lifted a hand to help the poor girl being beaten by the head butcher.

Heth glanced about as he started to rise, expecting to see a few more familiar fellows closing on him from different directions.

"Whoa, Whoa," the boy said, holding up his open hands in a calming gesture. "Ain't nobody else here."

Heth slowly lowered himself back onto the bench, eyeing the butcher suspiciously. "What do you want?"

The boy flashed a gap-toothed grin. "Just saw ye come in, thought I'd stop by and see how yer doing."

"Why, so you can roust up your friends to give me another beating?"

The boy's expression crumpled, becoming pained. "Nah, nah. It's not like that. Most of us, we thought ye did a damn fine thing, standing up for that girl."

"Really."

"Aye. Pol, he's a bastard. All of us have tasted the back of his hand before, one time or another."

With some effort, Heth broke apart the rock-hard roll. "And yet none of you helped me." He placed a piece of the bread in his mouth, but rather than risk chipping a tooth, he waited for his spit to soften it somewhat.

The boy ran his fingers through his spiky hair. "Well, we can't just up and leave, can we? And Pol would make our lives miserable if we lifted a finger against him."

"But some of you attacked me after I put him on the ground."

"Yeah, there's a few he favors that like how things are done in the butchery, with them on top. The rest of us, we can't stand them." The grin returned. "Look, I'm Vinish. I just wanted to let ye know we ain't all bad down in the blood pit."

Heth slowly chewed on the now spongy bit of bread, considering what the boy had just said. He supposed he couldn't really blame the other butchers for their inaction – if this was the only life they knew in the Duskhold, how could they risk it for a couple of strangers?

"I'm Heth," he said, reaching across the table. The boy blinked, like he hadn't been expecting this, then hurriedly wiped his hand on his tunic and clasped his forearm.

"Well met," Vinish said. "And I am sorry about Pol. The steward too, Elanin. Both are right asses. I don't understand why they were chosen to boss over the rest of us."

Heth's mouth twisted bitterly. "Oh, I know why."

The boy's brows lifted in surprise. "Truly?"

"It's to give you all someone to hate. So long as you despise your leaders among the Hollow, you won't blame the Sharded for your troubles." This was the exact reason his father had always chosen cruel men as overseers. It was an old slaver's trick to keep the chained from thinking rebellious thoughts. So long as they believed the architect of their troubles was the overseer and not their owner, there was always the chance their lot as slaves could improve.

Vinish nodded slowly. "Never really considered it like that before. Huh."

"They're not all like that, though," Heth said. "I've been placed with the guards. Gervis seems kind enough. I haven't seen him abusing anyone under him, at least."

"I heard you was one of the guards," Vinish said, the words tumbling out. He looked like he was about to say more, but then hesitated.

"What?" Heth asked, taking a spoonful of his soup. Then he grimaced, pushing the bowl away. Far too salty.

Vinish was chewing on his lip. "It's just . . . I don't always want to be chopping up goats in the pit."

Heth filled a cup from the water pitcher on the table and drained it, trying to cleanse his mouth.

Vinish leaned forward with his elbows on the wood, his eyes bright. "Ye were fighting four against one, and most of them ended up on the floor. I can see why they chose ye to guard the Duskhold!"

Heth splashed more water into his cup. "They knew I came in

with a sword, but they never asked to see me swing it before they assigned me to the walls." If what Gervis said was true, then they could honestly care less about his fighting prowess. The Sharded would not expect their Hollow guards to put up any resistance against anything that threatened the hold. But Heth didn't tell Vinish this, as he suspected he knew where the boy was going, and he didn't want to dash his dreams.

"I want to be a guard," Vinish proclaimed, confirming Heth's suspicions. "Get to carry a sword, smell the fresh air and not the stink of offal . . ." His gaze went distant, as if he was imagining life outside the abattoir.

Heth felt a twinge of shame for feeling bad about his own situation. Other Hollow had a much harder life in the Duskhold than him.

Vinish abruptly returned from his thoughts, focusing on Heth again. "Can you teach me?"

"Teach you?"

"How to fight like you did. Then maybe I could convince someone to let me leave the pits and get up on the walls with you."

Heth doubted very much that such a thing was possible. But seeing the hope in the boy's face, and how eager he was for Heth's help, he found himself nodding instead.

"I could do that."

20

DERYN

"You have now learned something of the world beyond these walls, novice, but what do you know of the inner workings of the Duskhold?"

Deryn looked up from the gameboard carved on the tabletop. He'd been idly tracing the pattern incised into the stone, trying to guess the rules and what its pieces might look like. His thoughts had been wandering far afield because Kaliss had been unusually silent this morning. After gathering him from his chambers and leading him to the gazebo in the middle of the underground lake, she'd abandoned him on the benches to stand on the rocky shore of the little island, staring out at the dark, still water with her hands clasped behind her back.

Something was bothering her, but he did not know what, and he had not mustered the courage to ask.

"Not much," he answered, a little too loudly. She was still turned away from him, watching the ghostly light seeping from the gazebo's stone reach with shimmering tendrils across the lake. "I know what everyone under the Shadow is told. Cael Shen is the lord and master of the hold, and his family has ruled for generations."

Kaliss crouched and picked up one of the stones at her feet. With a flick of her wrist, she sent it skipping across the glass-smooth waters. For a moment longer, she watched the ripples expand, and then abruptly she turned on her heel and made her crunching way back across the rock to the gazebo.

"Generations is true," the Ashasai girl said, sliding onto one of the stone benches. "Cael Shen's ancestor raised the Duskhold. He can trace a direct lineage to one of the warriors who led the rebellion against the Radiant Emperor. Only a Shen has ever sat the obsidian throne." She plucked at the hem of her robes, her expression distant. Deryn could sense she was still distracted.

"However, not all the bloodlines have remained so pure," she continued. "Bastards and second cousins and rival branches have usurped the thrones of all the other holds during their long history, except for the shadow and storm-sharded. Indeed, the Khaliva family has been preeminent in the Windwrack for as long as the Shen have ruled the Duskhold. To be honest, that might be part of the reason those two great families have been such fierce rivals. Both can claim a long and proud history." She paused, her lips pursing. "Truthfully, I know nothing of the inner politics of the wind or seed-sharded, or even if they have holds and lords. My knowledge is restricted to the Sharded that rule realms. For example, the Wildfire Rebellion extinguished the original line of rulers in the Ember. The stone-sharded long ago dispensed of kings and queens in favor of their council. The sand-sharded dissolved into warring tribes not long after settling in the Salah desert. The emir of Derambinal claimed to be a direct descendent of the first sand-sharded when he formed the Shahnate, but he and his family were put to the sword when the Conquests failed. And the Ashasai . . ." Her thin lips twisted into a wry smirk. "There has been so much blood and treachery in the city of the Black Steps the citizens rarely know who is ruling them at any given time."

A distant splash carried across the lake. Deryn peered into the darkened recesses uneasily, but Kaliss did not seem worried about what might be sharing the cavern with them. "There have certainly been attempts in the past by factions within the Duskhold to supplant the Shens, but the family has endured. And in the present age, their authority is unchallenged."

"Cael Shen was rather imposing," Deryn admitted, thinking back to the powerful figure looming over the rest of the shadow-sharded, a greatsword of glistening darkness at his side.

"He is the sun around which the rest of the orrery that is the Duskhold revolves. But he is not the only power in the hold. Saelus you've met. He is charged with instructing the novices, those that are newly sharded, and also testing us to determine our potential."

"Saelus seems happy with your progress. Nishi said as much when he came to bring me before his father."

If his words pleased her, Kaliss didn't show it. She merely shrugged, as if dismissing what he'd said. "It is not easy to enter the inner circles of the Duskhold. The strongest shadow-sharded usually are born here, the product of the purest heritages mixing, and there is also . . . a certain prejudice against outsiders. I will need to prove myself worthy to seize a place among them. As will you. Being the first to successfully beckon among the novices will not be sufficient. But enough about Saelus and me," she said, making a dismissive gesture. "We are not truly important. It is the family of Cael Shen that wields power in these halls."

"Rhenna and Nishi."

"Nishi is the heir to the Duskhold, and both are exceptionally powerful Sharded. Their relationship is perhaps what is most gossiped about within the hold."

"They seemed close when they escorted me to see their father."

"And they are," Kaliss admitted. "But they were born less than a year apart, and like many siblings so near in age they have a fierce rivalry. They are constantly in competition for both their father's attention and for pre-eminence among their generation of shadow-sharded."

"Where is their mother?"

"Dead," Kaliss said. "Or so it is rumored. She went mad not long after Rhenna's birth and was confined deep within the Duskhold. The whispers say she perished long ago, but no one knows for certain, and there is not a soul within the Duskhold foolish enough to ask Cael Shen about his wife. It was said that once she was like her son, easily beloved by all, while Rhenna takes after her father. Cold and inscrutable."

Another splash came from somewhere out in the lake. This time the Ashasai girl noticed, half-turning to stare in the direction the sound had come from.

"What about Azil?"

"Ah. Azil. The champion of the Duskhold. There's some discussion about whether even Cael or Joras Shen could stand against him."

"I saw him slay a monster the size of a mountain."

"That story has flown around the Duskhold on swift wings. Lord Kilian has apparently been telling everyone, though he's also been known to be . . . less than reliable."

"It's true," Deryn said quickly. "Whatever he said, it's true. I don't know how he could make the tale any more unbelievable than it already is."

Kaliss's mouth quirked. "Are you sure you truly know Kilian? He's as close to a court jester as the Duskhold has. Which brings a fair amount of consternation to his father."

"Joras Shen."

"Yes. The younger brother of Cael Shen. Not as hard as the Duskhold's master, and far more emotional. His rages are legendary, though so too are his good humors. He is a man of large appetites for many things, and is known to be intensely loyal to his brother."

Deryn had been curious about the Salahi Sharded and how he had come to be adopted into the Shen family, but Kaliss continued on before he could return to Azil.

"Over time many advisors and sycophants have risen and fallen in the Duskhold, powerful shadow-sharded who for a while have had the ear of Cael Shen and his family. The one who is currently ascendant you've seen before."

"Leantha." Deryn remembered the pale woman up on the balcony watching him on the day of their arrival.

"Yes. She is a mystery to most here. Perhaps Cael and his brother know her story, but they have not shared it, to my knowledge."

"She has not lived in the Duskhold long?"

Kaliss frowned "I . . . do not like talking about her. They call her the White Spider for a reason – she sits in the center of her web and seems to know whenever one of the strands is plucked."

"But surely this place is safe," Deryn said, staring out at the vast, empty cavern.

"I would hope so," Kaliss murmured. Then she sighed. "Leantha was once a novice two decades ago. She showed great promise, from what I was told, but soon after being elevated to adept she vanished while on some mission for the Duskhold. Everyone thought she had died, or perhaps was too shamed to return because she'd had her shards ripped out by an Unbound or a warrior from a rival hold. Then, about five years ago, she appeared at the gates of the Duskhold."

"Where had she been?"

Kaliss shrugged. "As I said, perhaps the Shens know. There is some speculation that she had been on some secretive mission for Cael, that her disappearance had been planned. But those are only wild rumors." She leaned in slightly, her voice lowering. "Saelus once told me that the Leantha who returned is different from the one who left. They look the same, but her personality has changed."

"Fifteen years is a long time."

"That is true," Kaliss agreed. "But I would suggest you do not spend too much time considering the mysteries of the Duskhold's elite. You are on a much lower tier of the ziggurat – the lowest, in fact, unless you consider the Hollow as part of the Duskhold's whole. If you are unlucky enough to draw Leantha's attention – or Cael Shen's, or Joras's – speak respectfully and keep your eyes on the floor."

"So we are their servants, like the Hollow?"

Kaliss flashed a humorless half-smile. "It is the way of the world, Sharded. There are only a few true masters – everyone else bows their head to someone. Joras Shen is far above us, but even he defers to his brother."

"And what if I don't want to serve? I've had my fill of being indentured."

"Then you would be Unbound," she replied sharply, "and the Duskhold would dispatch warriors to hunt you down and bring back your head." Her tone softened as she continued. "The best we can do, Deryn, is to rise within the Duskhold. There are layers of authority here, and they are not solely determined by who your parents were. Far more important is how strong you are, how many fragments you bear, and how well you wield the gifts of the Shadow."

"And that's why Saelus favors you, because of your abilities?"

Kaliss's jaw hardened, as if what he'd just said annoyed her. "Yes, but natural ability is only one influence on our strength as a Sharded. I have trained harder than anyone else in our cohort, and Saelus recognizes that." She hesitated briefly. "You were indentured, yes? Well, a hound like that old man Phinius found me on the streets of Phane. I was a guttersnipe, barely surviving on what scraps I could steal. No one would have cared if I curled up in an alley and died, except the barrowman who would have been annoyed because he wouldn't get a valanii for tossing me into his cart and taking my corpse down to the pauper's lichyard. I had no future there. Here . . . here I can rise high by my own merit." She stared into his eyes, as if willing him to understand something important. "You must let go of whatever grievances you still hold tight to. This world is not fair, the Duskhold is not fair, but if we accept that, and learn how to navigate its waters, we can still shape a good life for ourselves. Do you understand?"

Deryn nodded, surprised by the passion Kaliss was showing him, this glimpse behind her high walls.

"Good. Now, we have a lesson to attend. Come with me."

That day, Saelus led them in an exercise he called channeling. For the others, this was something they were familiar with, and they all settled into a similar sitting position with their legs folded underneath themselves and their heads bowed. Menochus had invited Deryn to sit beside him again, and with his whispered instructions and Saelus's commands, Deryn managed to follow along with what the rest of the novices were doing. Channeling was – like beckoning – one of the most important skills for a Sharded to cultivate. It involved slowing your breathing and falling within yourself, concentrating on that sliver of coldness lodged in your chest and the energy – known as *ka* – that the shard was constantly pushing through your body. These rhythmic pulses – almost like a heartbeat, Deryn realized – would dissipate naturally if left unattended, slowly strengthening the flesh and bringing the body more in alignment with the shard it bore. But this process could be markedly refined and quickened if the Sharded concentrated on those bursts of *ka* and guided them through their veins and the other natural pathways that bound the body together. Without channeling, much of the power flowing from the shard was lost, but by performing these exercises regularly, the Sharded would capture more of this energy. It occurred to Deryn that this was what he'd seen Kilian do on the road to Kething's Cross, when he'd sat in the grass silently for some time before demonstrating his newly acquired talent. He had been channeling, fusing the Unbound Gavin's fragment with his own shard, learning to master the heightened energies flowing through him.

During this first lesson, Deryn had surprised himself by successfully sensing his *ka* and even nudging it to be more under control. When he had closed his eyes and concentrated on the shard, he had felt the wildness of its energy, an ocean tempest with buffeting wind and lashing rain. Then it was just a matter of exerting his will over the *ka*, gentling it until the raging seas inside him subsided – it did not become glass-smooth, like the underground lake where Kaliss taught him the history of the Duskhold, but it grew noticeably calmer. From what Saelus had told them in his droning voice as they struggled to channel, once that inner storm completely vanished, it meant that a Sharded had mastered their shard and was ready to try to absorb another fragment.

When the channeling session had finished, Saelus welcomed

another Sharded onto the silver floor. She was lithe and dark skinned, though a few shades lighter than Azil, which suggested that she was only part Salahi. There was a fluidness to the way she moved, and Deryn noticed the other novices straightening and focusing on her as she came to stand before them. He could sense that they were very interested in what she had to say.

"Jaliska," Menochus murmured out of the corner of his mouth as her confident gaze swept the chamber. "Saelus is our primary instructor, but others are brought in ta teach certain topics. She's come a few times, all fairly recently. Before she just watched and listened, but there are rumors that she'll teach us how ta be warriors. Lots o' folks have been disappointed that after all these months we still have learned little about fighting." He glanced sideways, his expression suggesting he was worried Deryn might think he was one of them. "Not me, of course. We hill-folk come inta the world fighting. In fact, first thing I remember is getting clouted by my mama so I would stop attacking the wet nurse –"

"*Arzgan.*" The woman's sharp voice cut through the rustle of whispered conversations like a knife. Silence descended in the chamber, all attention focused on the Sharded.

"I am Jaliska, *kenang* of the Duskhold, and it is my duty to teach you how to be warriors."

She paused, as if expecting to be interrupted by excited murmurings, but the novices remained quiet. Her lips quirked, and then with her hands behind her back she began to pace the arena floor.

"I know you have been yearning to learn how to fight. I was the same. You can feel the strength coursing through your limbs, the power surging in your breast. Some of you have been here nearly a year," she said, her gaze sweeping the novices, "some of you only a few days." The movement of her dark eyes paused, lingering on Deryn. "Saelus forces you to practice channeling and beckoning again and again, then clutters your brain with boring history and knowledge of people and places that you will probably never need. A waste of your time, I'm sure you think. You want to step into this circle and test yourself against your fellows, prove that you should be elevated to adept, stake your place in the future of the Duskhold."

She stopped her pacing and raised her arm, and to Deryn's surprise he saw she now held a curving sword. It had appeared as if summoned from the very air. "And if you do truly believe that, you are a fool, as I was. Our purpose is indeed to be swords for the Shadow, but a blade that is not forged correctly will shatter when it first strikes steel. The ore must be mined and dragged to the smithy before it is hammered and shaped and tempered and allowed to cool, and only when it is ready is it finally sharpened. Now, is it time for you to gain your edge? This we will discover."

Jaliska pointed at a novice sitting on one of the lowest tiers, a heavyset boy with sallow skin and pale blond hair. "You. Come here."

The boy rose and slowly approached her, visibly nervous.

"Ah, Emmon," Menochus whispered. "We'll be lucky if he doesn't pee himself up there."

The Sharded scowled when she noticed the boy's discomfort. "You should not be afraid, novice. If you cannot meet the eyes of your fellow shadow-sharded, how will you contest with those bearing shards of storm or blood?"

Swallowing, the boy raised his head to look Jaliska in the face as he came to stand before her. She smiled, but there was no friendliness in it.

"Better." She reversed the sword smoothly, holding the hilt out to the boy. "Now, take the sword and strike me."

The boy blanched, his expression so comical that there was a titter of laughter from somewhere, quickly stifled.

Jaliska's eyes hardened. "Are you disobeying me, novice?"

"No, Sharded," the boy squeaked, reaching out to receive the sword from her with a trembling hand.

"Good. Now strike."

To Deryn's surprise, Emmon actually drew the sword back and swung at Jaliska's head. He was expecting her to step aside with the unnatural quickness of the Sharded, but instead she casually lifted her arm and caught the blade with her bare hand. A gasp rippled through the watching novices. No blood dripped from where the steel pressed against her palm, nor did she exhibit the slightest hint of pain. Emmon's eyes were agog, his lips moving as he whispered something to himself.

With a flick of her wrist, Jaliska wrenched the sword from the pudgy boy's hand, then tossed it into the air and caught it by the hilt. A moment later, she had the blade laid against Emmon's neck, a single bright red jewel of blood appearing where the metal touched his skin. The boy was absolutely rigid, his face ashen.

"As you can see," Jaliska said to all the novices watching with their hearts in their throat, "this novice and I are not the same. He bears a single shard, while I have nine. With each fragment that I added to that first shard the Shadow chose to bequeath to me, I grew stronger, until steel could no longer cut me, my hand could be thrust into flames without blackening, and I could drink poison like it was water. But with only one shard . . ." She must have suddenly pressed harder, as a line of blood trickled down Emmon's throat. "I was still vulnerable. And even now, a sharded weapon would cut me as easily as this blade does his flesh. Luckily, such artifacts are extremely rare."

Jaliska lifted the sword from Emmon's neck, and the boy sagged in relief. She gestured a dismissal, and with stumbling steps he wobbled back to where he had been sitting and collapsed.

"You may feel like nothing can hurt you now, being freshly Sharded, but let me assure you that this is most certainly not true. Novices die during their Delving. A large enough stone falling from a great enough height will still crush your skull. Stumble into a nest of rock spiders and the swarm can strip the flesh from your bones. But there will come a time, if you are fortunate enough to gain more shards, when mundane dangers no longer truly threaten you." She swung the sword up so that the blade rested on her shoulder as she resumed her pacing. "For that reason, my focus when training you in the art of combat will not be on using a sword or any other piece of sharpened metal. Your body – even now – is a far deadlier weapon, especially when you learn to use it in concert with your beckoning and other talents." She stopped and made a sweeping gesture that encompassed the novices. "All of you, come down here. We begin by learning the proper stances."

Days tumbled past, each blending with the one that came before until Deryn had trouble keeping them distinct in his memory. The routine was the same: wake up, instruction with Kaliss about some aspect of the Duskhold or the wider world, followed by a lesson led by Saelus in the chamber the others called the amphitheater – a reference to a building that had been popular in the cities of the First Empire – during which they usually practiced channeling or beckoning. A midday meal would be served after, bread and cheese or something that was equally filling and could be consumed quickly. During the afternoon classes Saelus stepped aside, watching from the edges of the room as a series of instructors taught various subjects: Jaliska, demonstrating effective fighting techniques for Sharded warriors, or a tall, thin man who called himself the Archivist who gave lectures on obscure topics. Sometimes another random Sharded was brought in to demonstrate their talents, so that the novices might be aware of the breadth of the Shadow's gifts. Nishi Shen even graced them once with his presence to show his mastery of Shadow Walking. Deryn couldn't help but shudder watching the smiling heir to the Duskhold step into a patch of darkness down below and appear a moment later up on the lip of the amphitheater, remembering the cold black void with its faint piping and strange, writhing shapes. He truly hoped that this was not the power the Shadow saw fit to bestow upon him if he managed to attain a second tier talent. Much more appealing was the crafting of simulacrums from the darkness. The novices watched in awe as a pale Sharded woman with sunken eyes molded the darkness into a shape the same size as her, and then with a wave of her hand painted it with her features and clothing. She could even make this copy move and had demonstrated how this could be used in combat by summoning three such duplicates and inviting Menochus to come down and try to strike the one that was truly her. He must not have been paying much attention, as his fists passed through two of the illusions before he guessed correctly and she caught his hand. It was obvious to all watching how such mistakes could be deadly for the warrior who was fooled.

Dinner was always together in the hall he'd briefly entered his first day in the Duskhold, the one with the long table and great, glimmering web of silver sunk into the far wall. Deryn was the first newly Sharded in several months, and the novices had already formed their cliques and factions, and so he found his only warm welcome was with Menochus and another boy from the fringes of the Shadow's realm, a beady-eyed fellow named Gind who might have been part weasel. They sat together on the benches as Menochus regaled them with tales of life in the hills and the adventures of his seven older brothers, all of whom were apparently famous heroes of the Wild. Deryn had considered inviting Kaliss to join them, as she was the only novice to sit alone and apart, but he was almost certain such an overture would be met with a silent stare of flat disdain. The Ashasai girl had made it clear their relationship was purely duty-based – Saelus had given her a task, and she would see it done, but after leaving the cavern where she instructed him each day and entering the amphitheater, she never so much as acknowledged his existence. In the feast hall, she would perch on the edge of a bench, as far as possible from anyone else, and hurriedly wolf down her food before vanishing. When Deryn had asked Menochus where she went, the boy had shrugged indifferently and reached for another mutton rib.

One such supper – perhaps a fortnight after the Shadow had first chosen him – Deryn could no longer contain his curiosity when he saw Kaliss slip away. Menochus questioned where he was going through a mouthful of corned mash, but the hill-tribe boy's interest had apparently ended there, as he hadn't joined Deryn when he'd left the eating hall in pursuit of his tutor.

Wherever Kaliss went every evening, it was not a secret, as she made no attempt to ensure that she was not followed. Still, Deryn lingered far enough behind her as she strode purposefully through the twisting passageways that she wouldn't notice him. He nearly lost her several times when the corridors branched, but he guessed correctly and soon glimpsed the flash of her black robes or heard the slap of her slippers on stone.

Finally, after a twisting descent into the bowels of the Duskhold, Deryn turned a corner and found himself standing at the grand entrance of a chamber he'd never seen before. Statues of robed men brandishing books flanked the open doorway, and runes he did not recognize were carved into the graven lintel. The space beyond was vast, filled by a forest of pillars thrusting up into the gloom and endless rows of bookshelves twice as tall as a man. The entrance he'd come through was raised higher than the rest of the chamber, a short flight of stairs leading down into the stacks, but even from this vantage he couldn't tell how far the library sprawled. Here were far more books than he'd ever seen in his life – in truth, more than he thought must have existed in the entirety of the world.

A flicker of movement caught his eye: Kaliss, disappearing into the depths of this labyrinth. Deryn glanced behind himself, wondering if he could retrace his path back to the novice's quarters. His foray had been successful – he now knew where she went every evening. Surely he shouldn't press his luck any further by wandering around in this maze, especially since it was likely forbidden for him to be here?

And yet . . . he hesitated, chewing his lip as he stared where he'd last seen the Ashasai girl. The curiosity that had compelled him to follow Kaliss hadn't been assuaged; indeed, it had only strengthened as he gazed out over the shelves. Doing his best to ignore the admonishing voice in his head, Deryn descended the steps and entered the stacks, choosing a path that he thought would lead him towards where Kaliss had gone. He knew he should move fast if he wanted to catch up with her before she got too far ahead, but he found his pace slowing as he gazed about in awed wonder. The shelves rose like canyon walls around him, crammed with all manner of books – ancient grimoires of cracked black leather, slim volumes of wooden leaves bound by yellowing twine, even a few works covered in what looked like the copper scales of serpents or lizards. Most of the books had no writing or markings on their spines, so Deryn couldn't fathom how they could be retrieved if the knowledge they contained was ever needed.

Something glimpsed out of the corner of his eye made him turn and with a sharp indrawn breath he froze, his heart turning to ice in his chest. A tall, sword-slender man was drifting silently across the gap at the end of the rows, scrolls piled high in his arms. If he'd turned his head, he certainly would have seen Deryn hunkered within the stacks, but he kept his ageless, unlined face staring straight ahead, intent on bringing his burden somewhere else. It was the Archivist, the sharded scholar who had lectured the novices most recently about the caste structure of the zemani lizardlings dwelling in the vast southern jungle known as the Tangle. He moved in silence, and it must have been a trick of his imagination, but from the way the hem of his robes brushed the floor it truly looked like he was *floating* above the stone.

Then he was gone, as if he had never truly been there at all. After a few steadying breaths, Deryn crept to where the passage between these shelves spilled into a wider avenue, but the Archivist had well and truly vanished. Of course he'd simply turned and gone deeper into the stacks, but the image of him slowly fading into nothing as soon as he was out of sight wouldn't leave Deryn. He shook his head, chiding himself for his foolishness. He knew the Archivist was not a ghost, as the scholar had stood before the novices in the middle of the amphitheater and bored them half to death with his rasping, bone-dry explanations of queens and clutches and castes, but still this strange place made conjuring up such fantasies easy.

Deryn resumed his hunt for Kaliss. He still had a vague map of where he'd last seen her scribed in his head: just down this wider central passage a little way, then a left here, another right . . .

Deryn stopped. Ahead of him, the stacks opened up into a space filled with rows of desks. All were empty, save for one in the very middle piled high with books, and between these teetering towers hunched Kaliss. She was seated on a stool, her back to him, the ghostly radiance seeping from the mist-globes high above playing upon her copper head as she leaned forward, intent on the open tome in front of her.

Deryn chewed on the inside of his cheek, unsure what he should do. It had turned out, unsurprisingly, that she had come to this library to read books, so perhaps he should just leave her to it . . .

"You might as well come here."

Deryn started at the sound of her voice. He glanced around, wondering if she was speaking to someone else and afraid he would see the Archivist staring at him from across this study space with a disapproving frown.

Kaliss sighed deeply as she straightened, leaning back from the book she was reading. She turned around on the stool to stare at him, folding her arms across her chest.

"Deryn, what are you doing?"

A good question, and one he realized he really had no good answer for. "I, uh, I followed you from the eating hall."

Kaliss rolled her eyes. "Yes, obviously. And with a pathetic attempt at being stealthy."

"You knew I was there?" he asked, surprised.

"You don't survive on the streets of Phane if you can't tell when someone is stalking you. And you're as clumsy as a drunken donkey. Now stop hovering and come over here. This isn't the place to shout."

Trying to ignore the flush of embarrassment he felt creeping up his neck, Deryn approached Kaliss's desk.

"I'll ask again," she said in a much quieter voice. "Why are you here?"

"I was curious," he replied, feeling foolish for having disturbed her. "About where you went every evening."

Her black eyes glittered as she studied him. "That's it? You're not trailing me to learn the secret of how I've risen to first among the novices? Perhaps to steal whatever advantage I've found that allows me to beckon and channel better than the rest?"

Deryn blinked, shaking his head. "No . . . no." His gaze traveled over the mounded books and loose scraps of brittle vellum scattered about her desk. "Wait, is that why you're here? Have you found something?"

Kaliss's mouth twisted. "I've found many things, Sharded. Histories and stories and legends, some of which I've shared with you in our morning lessons. But a secret that gives me the power to shape the Shadow's gift better than others . . ." She shook her head. "No. There is but one path we must follow to achieve mastery of our shards, and it is one almost everyone refuses to walk." She made a beckoning gesture to the looming bookshelves, and a serpent of shadow slithered from its depths. "Hard work. Unrelenting effort. Endless evenings spent channeling or staring at the darkness, willing it to tremble."

"Then why . . ."

"Am I here?" she finished, taking the words from his lips.

Kaliss sighed, rubbing at her face. For the first time Deryn realized how exhausted she looked.

"I come to the library when the others are still stuffing their faces and quaffing watered wine because it is the only free time I have. My evenings are spent refining the Shadow's gifts, my afternoons in the amphitheater. Not long ago it was the mornings I haunted this hall . . ." Her gaze slid to him again. "But you know why that is impossible now. So I sneak away when I can to take a few bites from the fruit of knowledge." She made a sweeping gesture at the shelves that ringed them like ancient monoliths. "So much has been forgotten, left to rot and fester down here. Archivist Devenal has confided in me that this most recent generation of Sharded rarely, if ever, step foot inside these archives. The Shens of many centuries ago built this place, filled it with the wisdom of the ages, but now they care little for what their ancestors once esteemed."

Deryn reached out and ran his fingertips across an oddly rucked and seamed red cover. Kaliss hissed at him and slapped his hand away.

"Do not touch. The Archivist has given me leave here, but you have no such permission. If he sees you handling the books, you might get both of us punished and banned."

"If the high shadow-sharded you wish to join do not care about the knowledge in these books, why are you here?" Deryn asked, rubbing at his hand.

Kaliss smirked, like he'd missed something incredibly obvious. "This place *is* my advantage, novice. The shadow-sharded who rule here and their children differ from us – what flows in their veins is purer than our own diluted blood, and they almost certainly have more natural talent at manipulating the darkness. I cannot change that. But by ignoring this place and relying on their gifts, they have given me a chance to close the chasm between us."

"So there *are* secrets here."

Kaliss waved her hand in what seemed like frustration, as if he'd missed the point of what she was saying. "Yes, but as I said, those secrets do not illuminate how to improve one's skill at beckoning or channeling." She indicated the book she'd been reading. "I was searching for any information that might help me during the Delving. This book is almost newborn by the standards of this library, written only a few decades ago. That's because the Delving was started very recently by Cael Shen as a way to test the novices each year and winnow out the weak."

Deryn eyed the book with interest, and he noticed the pages were not yellowed. The Delving was all the novices talked about these days, as it was less than a fortnight away. Saelus had pulled him aside a few days ago and informed him that he would be participating as well. It didn't sound so daunting to Deryn, and from the nervous chattering among his fellows, he sensed they were mostly excited but unafraid. On the day of the Delving, all the novices would be led down into the depths of the Duskhold and brought to the entrance to the long-abandoned mines that honeycombed much of this mountain. Inside would be a few shards, hidden within the tunnels by Saelus. There would be puzzles and traps to test the strength and skill of the novices, and it would be a race to gather the shards first. Whatever they found inside the mines was theirs to keep, a valuable steppingstone as they ascended the Duskhold's steep hierarchy.

"Did you find anything?" Deryn asked hopefully, still staring at the open book.

Realization dawned on Kaliss's face. "*You're* going on the Delve as well? After only a few weeks in the Duskhold?" When he nodded, her face creased in confusion. "That's . . . unexpected. I've been preparing for nine months. But . . ." And now she glanced at him sideways with an odd expression. "Perhaps not entirely surprising."

"Why do you say that?"

Kaliss licked her lips, as if uncertain whether she should continue. "Because . . ." She hesitated, but then seemed to reach a decision. "Because there's something different about you."

Now it was Deryn's turn to be perplexed. "What?"

"The beckoning," Kaliss continued. "I was the first novice to seize control of the darkness during our lessons. Every time, though, I have to fight off the attempts by the strongest of the others. Each of these forays has a . . . a *flavor* that is unique, and I've come to recognize each. Not long ago, I felt a new will trying to grasp the shadow . . . on the very same day I brought you to the amphitheater for the first time."

"You sensed me? I thought I'd touched the darkness, but later I decided it might have been my imagination."

"You did," Kaliss assured him with a slight frown. "And you have every time since. It is getting harder and harder to wrest it away from you." That frown deepened into a scowl. "And this never should have been possible."

Deryn wasn't sure what was upsetting her. "Why? I'm Sharded, like you."

"Because it is far too fast," she snapped. "It took me months before I could feel the darkness, let alone pull it towards me. And *my* progress was swift! Tell me, have you beckoned on your own, outside of the amphitheater?"

Deryn shook his head, and this seemed to soothe her slightly.

"Well, that's something. The wraithling flame makes beckoning far easier. But still, it is only a matter of time before you can." The serpent of darkness that she'd left lying on the floor near her feet suddenly twitched awake, raising its head so she could pet it. As her hand touched it, the entirety of the sinuous shadow evaporated.

A tingling wave of surprise had washed through Deryn as Kaliss was speaking. He hadn't realized that his progress was unusually fast, and to stand before the Duskhold's golden pupil and hear her complain about his accomplishments was more than a little unnerving. Was it possible that the others were not pushing themselves as hard as he was?

Kaliss narrowed her eyes. "So, in reply to your question about whether I have found anything helpful about the Delving here . . . I'm not going to say. Maybe I did, or maybe I didn't. I have worked myself to the bone to be the best channeler and beckoner among the first year Sharded and have spent countless evenings and mornings here in this library searching for anything that will give me an edge. Because this is a competition, Deryn, as I told you on your first day here. We are striving against each other, and now I know that with your inborn talents you are a threat to take what I have earned through blood and sweat."

She turned away from him, bending once more over the book she had been reading, and he couldn't help but feel dismissed. A welter of emotions were rising up from what she'd just said, and none of them felt good.

"Now get out of here, before I call for the Archivist. You must get special permission from Saelus to be allowed in the library as a novice, which I am certain you have not."

Kaliss fell silent, her head moving slightly as she resumed reading. Deryn stayed staring at the back of her hairless copper head for a few long moments, and then with faltering steps and a sickness in his stomach, he began to slowly back away.

Before he re-entered the stacks her voice came again, now stripped of anger and venom.

"I'll see you on the morrow, Deryn."

21

HETH

"Raise your guard before you come towards me. If you approach with your sword that low, I'll stab you through the heart before you even realize the fight has started."

The tow-headed boy with the scar on his cheek dutifully lifted his wooden blade, his face a mask of concentration. He shuffled forward in a somewhat reasonable imitation of what Heth had taught, the tip of his sword wavering.

"You're too stiff," Heth told him, smoothly retreating to the edge of the dueling circle. "You have to loosen up. The whiteness of your knuckles tells me your wrists must be locked tight." He lunged forward without warning, and the boy attempted frantically to meet Heth's sword with his own. As soon as his opponent had committed to the parry, Heth changed the direction of his strike, slipping beneath the boy's defense and tapping him in the belly.

"*Urk*," grunted the boy, dropping his sword as he stumbled back a step, his hands clutching his stomach.

"You're dead, Yennick" Heth said, cutting a quick pattern in the air with his blade. "But there's some improvement."

A snort came from outside the dueling circle, where two other boys were leaning against the wall of the small room. "By improvement, ye mean it'll take him longer to die from that belly wound ye gave him than the stab through the heart yesterday."

The scarred boy scowled and stuck out his tongue at Vinish as he bent to retrieve his sword. "Don't see you doing much better, Vin," he shot back.

"I was serious," Heth insisted, stepping over the chalk-drawn boundary of the circle. "Your footwork was not half-bad there. Like most when they first start their training, you're thinking too much about doing everything correctly. It clutters your mind and keeps you from reacting quick enough. Once the basics are second-nature, you'll see more success in the ring, I promise." He turned to regard the other boys in the room. "And that goes for the rest of you as well. I know in the stories a lad picks up his first sword and suddenly becomes a great warrior, but that never truly happens. It takes years and years of hard practice. Considering we've had less than a dozen sessions, I think you're all coming along well. Certainly better than a lot of the spoiled oafs who used to frequent the sword-halls of my hometown."

Heth could see the effect his praise had on the three butcher's apprentices. They seemed to stand taller, their chests swelling.

"Vinish, Mouser. Let's see you two go against each other. And remember what I told Yannick about his wrists – the looser you hold the sword, the quicker you'll be able to answer what your enemy is doing."

The boys leaped forward, their excitement at getting back in the ring making Heth smile. Only a few steps separated the edge of the fighting circle from the walls, but the space was large enough for their needs and a good choice for a few other reasons. This unused, empty room was relatively close to their sleeping quarters, yet this branch of the sprawling warren was also not well-trafficked early in the morning. They could roll from their beds at first bell – life in the hold was ordered by the daily bells, with most Hollow rising at the second bell, including guards like Heth and the butchers of the abattoir – and come here to train while the kitchen servants were starting the pre-dawn work to prepare the morning meal.

When Heth had first agreed to teach the butcher boys swordcraft, he'd thought he would quickly come to regret his promise. But instead of dragging himself to the top of the Duskhold, exhausted before his duties had even started, he found that these stolen moments at the very beginning of the day made the interminable rest of it somewhat bearable. Now instead of staring out at the rocky black expanse and hating everything about his life, he spent the time remembering the enthusiasm of the boys as they attempted to follow his instruction, their laughter and shared camaraderie. Heth shook his head, bewildered by the twists and turns that had led him here, to a hold of the Sharded Few, teaching the blade to lads he wouldn't even have spoken to a month ago.

And most surprising, that he would become the rebellious slave he once would have punished. These lessons had not gone unnoticed. Yesterday the steward had stopped him in the halls, materializing out of nowhere before Heth could turn away. His dislike had again flared bright and hot, but the man was his overseer, so there was no way he was going to avoid him forever. Heth had wished he could wipe the sneering grin from his face, even more so when Elanin had told him word had reached his ears of a guard training butcher boys in the early morning, and that such actions were strictly forbidden by the Sharded. Heth had stared beyond the grub-like steward as he'd nodded to show he'd heard, and eventually Elanin had pushed past him with a satisfied grunt.

But Heth had no intention of halting these lessons. He could now appreciate the small acts of rebellion that had always infuriated his father. He understood why slaves clung so tenaciously to those moments that demonstrated that they did indeed have agency. They were not slaves in their own minds . . . just like him. And so long as they knew this and kept that flame flickering in their breast, they would be ready when the opportunity for freedom finally came.

The clattering of wood striking wood suddenly stopped, and Heth roused himself from his thoughts. Vinish and Mouser had paused their awkward swings and turned towards the doorway, where the fourth boy who usually took part in these morning sessions had suddenly appeared. Garret was doubled over and breathing hard, as if he had leaped from his bed and run all the way here.

"Sleep late again?" Yennick asked.

Garret shook his head, still gasping for breath. "No," the plump boy finally managed. "I mean, yes. None o' you bastards woke me up when you left." He sounded hurt by this betrayal.

"We heard a little extra sleep can make someone a bit more pretty," Vinish said, grinning. "And the Broken God knows ye need all the help ye can get."

Garret made a face at the boy, massaging what must be a stitch in his side.

"Why did you first say 'no' before 'yes'?" Heth asked, unable to keep the smile from his face.

The wheezing boy straightened. "'Cause I *did* wake up late." His annoyed gaze flashed to his friends before returning to Heth. "But it ain't why I ran here. It's about the girl."

"The girl?" Heth asked, a sinking feeling in his stomach.

"You know, the girl," Garret continued. "The one Pol struck."

"What about her?" Heth asked, all traces of his levity gone.

"She's missing," Garret said. "I ducked down to the kitchens to see if I could grab a roll hot from the ovens, and everyone was in a tizzy. Seems she didn't show up for her morning duties, and they'd checked her room, and she wasn't there, either."

"Maybe she's being sick in the privy," Mouser offered. "You know, woman's day or some such thing."

Garret shrugged. "Could be, but I think they had a look because they sounded concerned. And one o' the other girls in the bakery said she hadn't seen her the night before, an' their rooms are right beside each other." He glanced at Heth, and the look on his face made Heth's blood go cold. "Something else as well. One o' my duties in the blood pit is to make sure the tunnel door is shut tight each evening when the day is done . . . I go back after we eat sometimes to be certain, because Pol would chop me up if I ever left it ajar. And last night . . . it was open, which it's never been before. Thought I might have just forgot, but now . . ."

"You think Alia might have gone through," Heth finished for him.

"Aye," the boy said, looking miserable.

"What tunnel is this?" Heth asked.

"Leads outside the Duskhold," Vinish answered. "To the pig pens and where they let the goats graze."

"Don't mean for certain she went that way," added Garret quickly. "Just seems like a coincidence if she's missing now."

Heth ran a hand through his sweaty hair. Would Alia have tried to escape? The last time he'd seen her, she had seemed relatively happy with her new position in the bakery.

"If she did flee the Duskhold, what will happen to her?"

None of the boys answered, shifting their feet and staring at the floor. Heth gritted his teeth.

"Answer me."

"It ain't good," said Vinish finally. "The Sharded . . . they don't let us Hollow leave. The punishment for trying to get away is . . ." He swallowed, looking like he didn't want to complete this thought.

"It's death," finished Mouser. "I'm sorry."

"She might be all right," Heth said, trying to convince himself. "When I met her, she was living in the deep forest, and before that she came from the Wild. She knows how to take care of herself."

"They won't send other Hollow after her," Vinish said, sounding tired. "It'll be Sharded. This ain't the first time Hollow tried to flee, and it's always the same. They'll want to make an example of her."

Heth felt sick. Someone with the strength of Azil might be hunting her. What if that person had the cruelty of the Unbound Sharded from back in the forest? What would they do to her?

Heth stood there for a long moment, desperately trying to come up with a way he could help. Then it came to him, and he whirled towards the door.

"I have to go," he cried, tossing his practice sword to the stone and shouldering past the surprised Garret as he dashed from the room.

∾

He knew as soon as he'd passed into the part of the Duskhold where the Sharded dwelled. The stonework was finer, intricate friezes carved above doorways leading into shadowy galleries filled with forests of soaring pillars and strangely contorted statues. There was an air of dread solemnity to the echoing silence, in stark contrast to the clamor and bustle of the Hollow quarters. His apprehension kept rising as he pushed deeper into the corridors, but he had to maintain the illusion that he belonged here, that he was just another servant performing his duty for the lords of the Shadow.

It was difficult, though, and the first time he turned a corner and saw a black-robed Sharded coming towards him, he nearly panicked and fled back the way he'd come. It took all his will to instead duck his head and move to the side, his eyes trained on the floor until the silver-haired woman's footsteps had receded into the distance. Then he'd continued on, hoping desperately that despite the vastness of the hold he'd somehow stumble across Deryn.

He passed several other Sharded, his gaze briefly flickering to their faces and then away, trying his best to be as respectful as possible. His greatest fear was encountering another Hollow, one who knew he was not supposed to be here. Heth wasn't sure what the punishment would be for trespassing, but it would almost certainly be worse than the whipping he had already received . . . and any chance of saving Alia would be lost.

When he did finally see a familiar face, he nearly stumbled from the shock. It was the Ashasai girl who had been in the courtyard of the Duskhold when they'd first arrived – or, at least, he was fairly sure it was her. It was always a little difficult to tell those people apart, since all of them were hairless and most had similarly sharp features. But how many Ashasai Sharded could there be in the Duskhold? She also wore the same serious expression he remembered from before, lips thinned in what looked like mild annoyance and her hands clenched at her side. She was striding purposefully down the passage like she was marching off to battle, and he nearly let her pass him by before he found the courage to speak.

"Pardon, Sharded."

She stopped so suddenly it was like she'd walked into an invisible wall. "What is it, Hollow?" she asked crisply, swiveling to face him. Then she blinked, her forehead creasing. "Wait, I know you. You arrived with Deryn."

He swallowed, trying not to wilt under that intense stare. "Yes. Yes, I did. I was actually, uh, I was actually hoping you could tell me where he is."

She was quiet for a moment, studying him. "Why?"

"There's something important he has to know."

She waited expectantly, and after Heth offered nothing else she sighed. "And that is, Hollow? Were you sent by another Sharded?"

"No, I wasn't," he said quickly, trying to avoid having to answer her first question.

She wasn't deterred. "And I don't think your duties should take you here. Which means something has happened that would compel you to risk a very serious punishment. Tell me what it is and why it involves Deryn."

Heth licked his lips, briefly considering trying to bluff his way past her. Her flensing gaze sharpened, and he immediately discarded that idea.

"It's the girl we came with."

"Alia."

He blinked, surprised she knew her name. "Y-yes. She's . . . she's missing."

Now it was the Sharded's turn to look off balance. "Missing?"

He nodded, hoping fervently that he wasn't dooming Alia – or himself – by describing what had happened.

"She's not in the Hollow quarters. And someone unlatched a way to the outside last night – it must have been her."

The Sharded looked confused. "But why? Surely she must know she'll be pursued and that for trying to leave the Duskhold she'll be put to death?"

"I don't know," Heth told her, feeling a swell of relief that this girl hadn't immediately seized him and dragged him in front of someone more senior for punishment.

"What do you think Deryn can do?" the girl asked. "He is only a novice."

Heth felt like he was teetering on the edge of a precipice. "He can find her. Bring her back to the Duskhold before the rest of the Sharded even realize she was gone."

The Ashasai girl frowned. "That's unlikely. If the Hollow quarter is abuzz with this news, then almost certainly someone has been dispatched to tell us."

"Which is why it's important I find him quickly," Heth implored. "Any delay could mean Alia's life." He wanted to fall to his knees and grab the hem of her robe, but he restrained himself. Her face was inscrutable, locked deep in thought. She might be entertaining the idea of letting him continue his search for Deryn, or she could be imagining the most inventive punishment for his brazen behavior.

After a few long, tense moments, she came to a decision, her brow unknitting. "Follow me," she commanded, continuing in the direction she'd been going.

Heth hurried after her, swallowing back the questions he wanted to ask. He didn't want to risk annoying her by pestering her further, and if she *was* taking him to some deep, dark oubliette, he didn't want to know that, anyway.

After passing down a few twisting corridors, she stopped at a door and rapped loudly on the black wood. Almost immediately the door swung open, and standing on the other side was Deryn. He was dressed in the same black robes as the Ashasai girl, but that wasn't the only difference from what Heth remembered from before – he looked taller, his shoulders broader, flushed with a new vitality and strength.

He truly was one of the Sharded Few.

Surprise shivered his face when he saw Heth standing beside the Ashasai girl.

"Heth? What's going on, Kaliss? Why is he here?"

"Apologies, Deryn," the girl said flatly. "I seem to be a little sick this morning. I'm afraid I will have to cancel our lesson for today."

"I . . ." Deryn blinked, his gaze going from Kaliss to Heth and back again. "I hope you feel better tomorrow," he said slowly.

"Thank you," the girl answered. "I would advise you to use this time you now have productively."

"I, uh, I will," Deryn replied, and with a curt nod, the Ashasai girl whirled around and began striding away. Deryn stared after her for a few heartbeats, then shook himself as he turned his attention to Heth. His mouth opened, but Heth spoke before he could give voice to the questions he no doubt wanted to ask.

"Alia's gone."

Deryn rocked back like he'd been struck. "What?"

"She's fled the Duskhold. Something happened, I don't know what."

Deryn's face twisted in concern. "She'll be hunted down when they find out." The worry in his expression deepened to fear. "And then they'll kill her."

"I know," Heth said. "That's why we have to go *now*. We have to find her before they do."

"Yes," Deryn said, his shock at seeing Heth and the fear his news had brought instantly banished by a grim resolve. "How do I get outside to look for her?" he asked.

Heth had been thinking about this same question ever since Gannick had told him the news. He had thought it possible that the Sharded had their own way to leave the hold – though perhaps they simply strolled out through the gate he spent his days watching over – but clearly Deryn hadn't been told about such things. Which left the route Alia had evidently taken.

"She fled through a tunnel in the Hollow quarters where they bring in animals to be slaughtered. We can follow her steps."

Deryn nodded slowly. "Yes, very good. Lead me there." He paused, glancing at Heth sharply. "Wait, 'we'?"

"I'm coming with you," Heth said. "Now, no time to waste. We have to hurry!" Without waiting for Deryn's reply, he turned and began running back the way he'd come, hoping that he remembered the way to the abattoir.

Deryn jogged up beside him a moment later. Heth was pushing himself hard enough that he wouldn't be able to keep up this pace for long, but the newly Sharded boy was not winded in the slightest. When he spoke, it didn't sound like he was even breathing hard.

"If you come, you'll court the same fate as Alia."

"I know that," Heth replied, trying to ignore the cramp growing in his side. "But how will you find her if I'm not there?"

"What do you mean?"

"I'm a hunter. I've spent my whole life tracking animals – it was my father's favorite pastime, and once I joined him in the forest, rarely a day went by when we didn't bring something back for the table."

"Alia isn't a deer."

"No, but she'll leave the same sort of signs that I've been taught to look for."

"Seems risky," Deryn said, sounding dubious.

"Well, I'm coming, like it or not," Heth insisted. He said this with as much force as he could muster, hoping to end the debate here and now, before it truly started. Pretty soon the only sound he'd be able to make would be panting gasps.

Fortune's golden face was turned towards them, and they did not encounter any other Sharded as they ran through the twisting corridors. Most must still be abed, Heth guessed – there was little reason for the masters of the hold to rise early, especially since their days were not governed by the rising and setting of the sun. This thought gave him hope that they might find Alia before hunters were even dispatched, but they still had to move quickly.

And not get lost. There were a few harrowing moments where Heth had to pause at an intersection, but each time he chose correctly, and to his great relief, he soon led Deryn back into the area of the Duskhold given over to the servants. Here they saw several Hollow out and about on their early morning duties, but none dared question them when they realized it was a Sharded racing through the passageways. They caused a bit of a commotion as they passed down the central avenue of the kitchen chambers, but Heth ignored the surprised exclamations and pointed fingers.

His legs felt on the verge of collapse as he bounded down the stairs leading to the abattoir, and the ache in his side now felt like someone had stabbed him with a sword. He just barely kept himself from sprawling on the filthy floor when they reached the bottom by leaning heavily on one of the stained tables.

"Seven bloody hells!" exclaimed a familiar voice.

With some effort, Heth pushed himself from the table and straightened, still struggling to get his breathing under control.

The Ashasai butcher, Pol, was in the middle of the abattoir, his fat face slack with shock and a cleaver dangling limply in his hand. A few of the butcher boys – none who had been training with Heth – were also standing there, wide-eyed and open-mouthed.

"Sharded," Pol breathed, his gaze flickering from Heth to Deryn. His jaw bunched, like he was clenching it to avoid saying anything to the boy who had struck him, then he ducked his head, his cheeks flushing.

"What can we help you with, my lord?" he mumbled, staring at the floor.

Deryn seemed surprised by this show of subservience. He must have had little interaction with the Hollow, as most everyone Heth knew in the Duskhold held the Sharded in abject awe.

"I heard there's a way outside the Duskhold from here."

The Ashasai raised his head, blinking in confusion. "Aye, lord." He gestured at the tunnel set in the far wall. "But nothing on the other side except a few goats and a lot of rocks."

Deryn strode across the abattoir towards the exit. Heth noticed the head butcher staring at him in smoldering rage as he followed the Sharded, and he stuck out his tongue, causing Pol's angry red flush to deepen further into an apoplectic purple. Still, the Ashasai did not dare question Deryn about what he was doing or why he'd brought Heth with him.

The tunnel was low-ceilinged and musty, heaped with dry rushes that crackled beneath Heth's boots. No mist-globes brightened the way, but light was creeping around the bend up ahead, and when they turned the corner they were confronted by a slatted metal gate, through which could be glimpsed a brilliant blue sky.

"Not the most secure fortress, is it?" asked Deryn as he lifted the gate's latch and pushed it wide.

Heth blinked as sunlight flooded the tunnel. "From my experience, the Sharded aren't worried much about invaders," he replied.

In front of them, a jumble of black rocks and dark volcanic soil sloped down to the edge of the lake Phinius had named the God's Mirror. Tufts of vegetation grew here and there, gnawed on by the large number of goats milling about, and pressed up against the smooth exterior wall of the Duskhold was a more crudely built structure of piled stones and thatch. A huge hog was lounging outside this pen, staring at them incuriously.

And the pig wasn't the only one who had noticed their arrival, as a scrawny boy with a piece of straw hanging from his mouth was staring at them with bulging eyes.

Deryn gave the boy a wave, and the straw tumbled from his lips.

"Hello!" Heth cried, making his way carefully over the loose scree to where the boy was sitting. "We're looking for a girl. Blonde hair, very thin. She may have passed this way. Have you seen her?"

The boy didn't respond, his gaze fixed on Deryn. Heth grimaced and snapped his fingers in front of the lad's face to get his attention. The boy startled like he'd been stung by a wasp, then looked at Heth and shook his head.

"N-no. Ain't seen nobody this morning." He swallowed, the apple in his throat bobbing. "Is that . . . is he one o' the Sharded Few?"

"Yes," Heth said, turning away from the shepherd boy to stare out over the glassy surface of the water. Ringing the lake was the lip of the caldera, looming above them like the stands of a vast arena.

"Where do you think she went?" Deryn asked.

"Well, really only one possibility," Heth answered, squinting at the narrow switchback trail that ascended up to the distant ridge. "Unless you think she threw herself into the lake."

Deryn flinched at this, and Heth silently cursed himself. He'd forgotten what the poor boy's mother had done. "Which she wouldn't do," he added hurriedly. "And that means she climbed out of here that way."

"Then let's go," Deryn said, breaking once more into a run. With a sigh and a hand on his aching side, Heth followed.

The climb to the lip of the caldera nearly killed him. It was even steeper than it had looked from the shore of the lake, and when a wave of exhaustion crashed over Heth, he'd swayed and nearly toppled over backwards. Only Deryn's unnaturally quick reflexives had saved him, the Sharded's hand flashing out to grab hold of his shoulder.

At the top, they paused so Heth could catch his breath. While he was doubled over gasping, Deryn showed no signs of fatigue, standing with his hands on his hips as he squinted up at the brilliantly blue sky and the Duskhold, a jagged pile of gleaming black rock. Somewhere up there, Heth knew, his fellow guardsmen were standing watch wondering where he was.

"The sun feels strange," Deryn murmured.

Heth noticed the Sharded wasn't even sweating, despite having done the climb in the black robes of the Duskhold. His own tunic was plastered with sweat and probably smelled as bad as the stables they'd left behind at the bottom.

"It's been weeks since I felt it on my skin. I think some of the other novices might not have seen the sun in months."

"You're not missing much," Heth grunted, finally straightening. "Nearly every waking moment these last weeks, I've been standing on top of the Duskhold with no shade. Much better to spend all your time inside than out, let me tell you."

"How is it, as one of the Hollow?"

Heth shrugged. "It could be worse, I suppose. We're slaves in truth, no doubt about it. They call the overseer 'steward', and he's a right bastard . . . but there are still some good folk."

Deryn's mouth twisted. "Sounds familiar."

Heth ignored this aside, crouching to examine where the trail emptied onto the ridge. It took him only a moment to find what he was looking for.

"There are prints here," he said excitedly. "A small woman's, I would say, or a child's. Leading off in that direction." He pointed away from the hold, along the lip of the caldera. "Alia probably followed the ridge looking for a way down. She could have gone around the Duskhold to reach the road, but I suppose she wanted to put as much distance as possible between herself and the hold. She knew she might have been seen by the watchers on top if she'd gone that way . . . There isn't much to look at up there, and any movement draws the eye."

Deryn nodded, still staring at the hammered blue above like he'd never seen the sky before. "Are you recovered?"

Heth stood. The exhaustion that had been close to overwhelming him had receded with the discovery that Alia had passed this way. They would find her.

"Let's go."

The trail was easy enough to follow, even after Alia abandoned the ridgeline and started descending the scree-strewn slope. A layer of loose black soil covered much of the mountainside and had preserved the evidence of her passage, though in places she had traversed stretches of stone, and it had taken Heth some time to figure out which way she'd gone. Always a straight as path as possible downwards, away from the hold of the shadow-sharded.

"Why would she flee?" Deryn asked when they'd paused for a moment so Heth could look for the traces she'd left behind. "You remember the flight here – it would take at least several days to get out of the mountains. It's suicide. What was she thinking?"

Deryn's words kindled something inside him. He turned his attention from the ground to where the Sharded was staring out over the broken landscape.

"She was thinking she had to escape, even if it killed her," he said bitterly. "This place was a nightmare for her. Trapped within stone, away from the sun and sky, forced to be a slave after a lifetime of living free . . . the first time I saw her in the Duskhold she had just been beaten." Surprise flashed across Deryn's face at this, but Heth pushed on, his tone growing more accusatory. "Did you even wonder for a moment how she was doing in the weeks since you got your shard? And after she'd saved your life?"

"You're not slaves," Deryn said, but his voice was faint.

"We may not have a sigil on our heads," Heth snarled, "but make no mistake, we are slaves. Otherwise, Alia would be free to walk through the gate and leave this place, and we wouldn't be in a race to find her before she's executed as a reminder for the other Hollow that their purpose is to serve the Sharded, nothing more."

He wrenched his gaze from the stricken Deryn and back to the ground. "There," he said, pointing to where the dirt had been disturbed recently. "That way." He rose and began striding in the direction she'd gone.

He could understand Deryn leaving *him* to his fate in the Duskhold. Less than a month ago, the boy had been a slave in his father's stables, and no doubt there was some small part of him that reveled in this reversal of fortune. But to abandon Alia so blithely? Deryn was Sharded, one of the lords of the hold – certainly he could have stepped in to ensure that she was being treated well, even if it wasn't possible for him to set her free. Heth kicked at the loose rocks, sending a few clattering down the slope. He should have done something.

It was then he heard the cries for help. They were faint, welling up from much farther down the slope.

"Deryn!" he yelled, breaking into a run. "Follow me! I hear her!"

The going was rocky, and he had to watch the ground so he didn't break an ankle. It was a surprise, then, when Alia screamed again and it sounded much closer this time. He skidded to a halt, looking around wildly.

And gasped. Alia was perched on a boulder with her legs drawn up, staring in terror at the creatures milling below. They looked like lizards, with russet scales and a row of gleaming spines down their backs, but each was the size of a large dog. Every few moments one beast would lunge for Alia, its long curving claws scrabbling against the stone before it slid back down again. Heth couldn't imagine how she'd climbed atop the great rock given how sheer the sides looked, but he dispatched a quick thanks to the Broken God that she had, as the beasts were clearly intent on feasting on her.

One of the lizards realized they were no longer alone, and it turned to hiss at Heth, its back-spines flaring higher. This drew the attention of the others, and suddenly a half-dozen of these dog lizards were issuing challenges, their legs bunching as they prepared to leap. Cold fear sluiced through him – he had been such a fool to come out here without a weapon. Death was staring out at him from empty black eyes, and as he glanced up at Alia, he saw she was watching him in wordless horror.

"I'm sorry," he said just as the largest of the lizards lunged at him, dagger-claws flashing.

He flinched and closed his eyes, knowing his flesh was about to be torn to bloody ribbons.

But the expected pain never arrived. Instead, the lizard made a strange, croaking gurgle, a mewling noise that almost sounded surprised.

Heth cracked an eye open.

Deryn stood beside him, holding the writhing lizard by its throat. He must have caught the creature when it had jumped at Heth, plucking it from the air. Scaled legs flailed as the lizard desperately tried to free itself, and Deryn grimaced as claws sliced the robes around his belly. Heth was expecting to see blood and viscera spill forth, but whatever wounds he'd just taken only seemed to annoy the Sharded. Deryn reared back, then *threw* the lizard at its brethren like it weighed no more than a puppy. Several of the beasts went down in a tangle of red limbs before quickly scrambling upright. Rather than attempt a joint attack on these newcomers, an unspoken agreement rippled through the pack, and as if of one mind they turned together and fled with their stunted tails between their legs, quickly vanishing among the rocks.

"Deryn!" Alia cried, her voice ragged with relief. She had been injured – she was cradling one of her arms, and her tunic was stained with blood.

"Alia," Deryn said as he approached the boulder. He seemed entirely unaffected by the slashes he'd taken only moments ago. "Thank the Broken God we found you."

"Are you all right?" Heth asked.

Alia managed a shaky nod. "Those things ambushed me. One clawed my arm, but I don't think it's too deep."

"Well, we'll get you stitched up," Deryn said, gesturing for her to come down. "There are physickers in the Duskhold."

Alia's face stilled. "I can't go back there," she said, but she did slide down the side of the boulder into Deryn's waiting arms. The Sharded lifted her as if she weighed nothing and deposited her gently on the ground. Heth felt a brief surge of jealousy, but he tamped it down.

"Then what will you do?" Heth asked.

"Continue down the mountain," Alia said as Deryn tore a strip of cloth from his own robes and started winding it around the bloody wounds on her arm. "Go west, back to the Wild. I know people there, good folk." She brushed back a lock of golden hair, leaving a bloody smear on her brow. "It's different in the deep forests. No kings or lords. No great anthills"—and here she glanced with flashing eyes at the black stone spires of the Duskhold—"full of scurrying insects laboring for the pleasure of their *betters*." The venom with which she infused this last word surprised Heth.

"Is that why you left?" Deryn asked. "Because you don't want to be a servant?"

The anger in Alia's face drained away. She turned to stare down the slope, her expression growing troubled.

"No."

"What happened?" Heth asked, stepping closer to her. The pain in her face was making his own heart hurt. "Did that bastard beat you again?"

She shook her head.

"Then what is it?" Heth pressed.

"He . . . tried to touch me," Alia murmured, her voice faltering.

Heth and Deryn shared a surprised glance.

"Who?" Heth asked, his anger flaring. "The butcher? The fat Ashasai?"

She gave another shake of her head. "No. Not him. It was that steward, the wormy man. He . . . he cornered me last night after the evening meal. He told me he could make my life better in the Duskhold if I . . . would do things for him. And he said he could also make it much worse if I refused. He could have me sent back to the room where they kill the animals. Then he . . . he grabbed me." She swallowed, wiping at her eyes. "I kicked him and scratched him, and he let me go. Then I started running. I had to get out . . . the only way I knew about was the tunnel in the meat room. I . . . I ran as far as I could and found a little cave to sleep in last night. I thought I might be able to make it down the mountain, get to the road, but then those lizard things came." She took in a steadying breath and threw her thin shoulders back, staring at Deryn and Heth defiantly. "I won't return to that place."

Fingernails digging into his palms, Heth tried to fight back the rage that had been building while Alia spoke. That pathetic little grub of a man. He'd wrap his hands around his scrawny throat and squeeze until his head exploded.

"Alia," Deryn murmured. "We're not the only ones who will be looking . . ."

"What in the cold abyss is this?"

Heth turned towards this unfamiliar voice, his heart plummeting into his stomach. Three strangers – two men and a woman – were picking their way over the rocky terrain, all dressed in the black robes of the Duskhold's Sharded. They were young, and Heth doubted any of them had seen thirty winters. One of the men had a shock of fiery hair and a face covered in intricate crimson tattoos, while the other two looked to be brother and sister, as each had the same pale skin and black hair.

The tattooed boy smirked, his brows arching. "What are you doing out here, novice?"

"I was looking for my friend," Deryn replied, moving so that he was between the three newcomers and Alia. He shifted his attention to the other two. "Greetings, Lord and Lady Shen," he said, dipping his head respectfully.

Lord and Lady Shen? Heth's insides twisted. Oh, by the Broken God. They were doomed. Unsure of what he should do, he went down on one knee and lowered his head.

"Up, up," the other man said. He sounded friendly, to Heth's great surprise. "No need to abase yourself, novice. And call us by our names – or '*kenang*' if you must be formal."

Heth risked raising his eyes, emboldened by the Sharded's tone.

"Rhenna," Deryn said, nodding towards the woman with the pursed lips and dagger-sharp eyes. Then he turned to her brother. "Nishi." Finally he faced the red-haired Sharded. "And I'm sorry, I don't think we've met."

"Vertus," the tattooed man said, regarding Deryn coolly. "Eight-sharded, and also an adept like my companions here."

"An honor," Deryn said, bowing to him.

"Yes, yes," Vertus muttered, making a gesture with his hand as if to dismiss such formalities. Heth noticed that his arm was also sheathed in squirming crimson tattoos up to his wrist. "I am curious why *you* have taken it upon yourself to pursue this runaway Hollow, even if she was your friend. Novices are not allowed to leave the Duskhold."

Deryn swallowed, and Heth realized how nervous he was. "I hoped to bring my friend back to the hold before it was realized she had gone."

Heth blinked at this honesty. Then again, what lie could explain away this situation?

"And this one?" Vertus asked, indicating Heth. "So there were *two* Hollows that fled?"

"He is a good tracker," Deryn said quickly. "And also a friend. He wasn't running away, but trying to help me return with Alia."

"Alia," Nishi said, rolling around her name in his mouth. "I remember her now. She was the one who recently failed the Shadow's test. The same day you were granted a shard."

"Yes," Deryn replied, bobbing his head. "Like me, she's new to the Duskhold. She doesn't understand the seriousness of what she did. Please, adepts, have mercy on her." He pressed his hands together pleadingly.

There was no warmth in the woman's face – she truly could have been carved of marble – while her brother's expression had turned sorrowful. Vertus's pale blue eyes had hardened, his jaw clenching.

"How foolish," the tattooed Sharded spat, and to Heth's horror he saw strands of darkness slither forth. "To dare ask for mercy as a novice? You will be lucky if we do not punish you as well for leaving the Duskhold. The Shadow's laws are inviolable. If a servant attempts to flee the Duskhold, the punishment is death."

"That one was not trying to leave," Nishi said, indicating Heth with his chin. "But was brought outside to assist a Sharded. I believe some leniency is warranted." He grimaced, turning to Alia. "Though I do not see how a reprieve is possible here. It is the law of the Duskhold."

"But your father is Cael Shen," Deryn said, and the desperation in his voice chilled Heth. "His command is the law. You could ask him. She only ran away because the steward abused her. You could beg him for leniency!"

Nishi's expression turned quizzical. "Why would I do that? What is this Hollow to me?" He shook his head. "And such a request would only incense my father. To plead for mercy for a servant who has abandoned her sacred duty to the Shadow? If word of such a thing spread, we might have a rebellion on our hands!" This last claim was said jokingly, but neither his sister nor the red-haired Sharded smiled.

They were going to kill Alia. And him, Heth realized, because he would throw himself at them as soon as they went for her. He should be terrified, but he wasn't. Instead, a calm had settled over him. He imagined hefting a rock and slamming it into the face of the sneering tattooed Sharded, the satisfaction he'd feel as the bastard's expression changed from disdain to shock.

Deryn seemed to have come to the same conclusion. One of his hands was clenched, and with the other, he pushed Alia farther behind himself. The obsequious manner in which he had been holding himself had melted away, and now he met the gaze of the Duskhold's heir brazenly. Nishi's faint smile did not waver, but Vertus's scowl deepened further. Rhenna still looked bored, as if what was happening barely warranted her attention.

No one was watching Heth, and he quickly scooped up the sharpest-looking stone by his feet. Maybe he could gouge out an eye if one of them was distracted.

The day darkened, even though there wasn't a cloud in the sky. Around Vertus, the shadows he had summoned began to twist and writhe, forming into a halo of glistening black blades.

"The Crown of Swords, Vertus? Truly?"

The unnatural dusk flickered, the world brightening again. All eyes turned to Rhenna, who had stepped forward to interpose herself between Deryn and the other two Sharded.

"Is that what you think should happen here? An *arzgan* and two new servants of the Duskhold sliced to ribbons?" Her expression had not changed, but contempt dripped from her words.

"Sister," Nishi said, spreading his arms wide as he addressed her, "you know the law –"

"I know the law is what we say it is," she said, cutting him off. "The boy is right. Father does what he wants and cares little for tradition."

"You are not father," Nishi countered, his tone hardening.

"No, but I *am* his daughter," Rhenna snapped. The tension between the siblings was a physical thing, sharpening the air. Even

Vertus seemed taken aback, the blades hovering around him dwindling into scraps of shadow.

"I need a new handmaiden," Rhenna said, gesturing to where Alia was peeking out from behind Deryn. "I have been without one since Gerta sickened last spring."

Nishi snorted, his expression incredulous. "Do you think you can just absolve her –"

"Yes," Rhenna said, cutting him off again. "And if you wish to dispute my claim to this girl, take it up with Father."

For the first time, Nishi's face darkened. "This is foolish, sister."

"I am a scion of the Shadow. I do what I want. I believe I've heard those same words from someone else's lips before . . ."

Nishi's expression changed with jarring suddenness, and he threw back his head and laughed. "Very well, sister," he said, still chuckling. "But you can be sure Father will hear how soft your heart is."

Rhenna narrowed her eyes at her brother but did not reply to this. Instead, she addressed Alia. "Will you return as my handmaiden?"

Fear gripped Heth that Alia would spurn what Rhenna was offering, which he was certain would doom them all. She had said she wouldn't go back to the Duskhold for any reason . . .

Alia's wide eyes flicked from Deryn, to Heth, and then finally to Rhenna.

"I will," she said, and Heth gasped in relief.

22

DERYN

IT LOOKED like a portal to the abyss. The black gate, Kaliss had once called it, and at the time he'd imagined nothing more than dark wood set into stone, perhaps slightly larger than the countless other doors scattered throughout the Duskhold.

He had been wrong.

The entrance to the old mines was three times the height of a man and wide enough that a team of oxen could have been driven through it, fashioned from an iron so black it seemed to drink the spectral light of the mist-globes. It was shaped into a massive, gaping maw, long fangs cut into the metal at the top and bottom of the gate, while above the door two great pits like eyes had been scooped from the stone.

He was not the only one unnerved by the forbidding gate. The rest of the novices milled about eyeing the entrance warily and whispering among themselves, all under the measuring gazes of the Sharded Few. Saelus was there, looking mildly annoyed as always, and their battle master Jaliska. Beside the light-skinned Salahi was her much darker countryman, Azil. Deryn had tried to catch the attention of the Black Sword when they'd all first been led into this great cavern below the Duskhold, but Azil had pointedly ignored him. The Black Sword had spent the entire time speaking in low tones with Jaliska, and he seemed so invested in the conversation that Deryn couldn't help but wonder if there was something between them.

They waited for some time, and Deryn was curious why until two figures suddenly emerged from the shadows. He sucked in his breath when he saw it was the children of Cael Shen. Deryn hadn't seen them since that day on the slopes, and he felt a small trickle of fear at the sight of Nishi's smiling face. He now knew what lurked behind that façade, a man who would have casually murdered all of them that day if his sister had not intervened. Deryn also studied Rhenna carefully as she followed her brother over to where the other Sharded waited. What was truly behind her mask of cold indifference? Had she felt any sympathy for Alia, or did she only want to undermine her brother? He wished he could muster the courage to ask her how Alia was doing. It had been nearly a fortnight since Rhenna had taken her as a handmaiden, and he desperately wanted assurance that the girl was happier.

There would be no chance to do that now, though. After the pair had joined the other Sharded, Saelus nodded towards Azil and the Salahi raised the Darkbringer and brought it down sharply in a ringing strike, sending blue light coruscating along its length. At once, the novices' muttered conversations quieted, all eyes turning to their teachers.

"Novices," Saelus proclaimed into the heavy silence, "the day of your Delve has finally arrived. Some of you have waited a year for this chance; others, less than a month." He turned his age-spotted head to regard the gate looming behind him. "Beyond this door is an opportunity, a chance to prove your worth to the lords of the Duskhold. Five shards have been hidden within the deep tunnels and now await their future masters. Find one, and you will certainly no longer be considered a novice. Two, and you will be foremost among your cohort and formally attain the rank of *sardor* once they are merged. Three, and if you prove capable of channeling such a burden, you cannot be denied an adept's robes." Saelus's gaze drifted to Rhenna and Nishi as he said this, but they gave no sign of agreeing with the old man. To be honest, Deryn thought they both looked rather disinterested in the proceedings.

He, on the other hand, was anything but bored. His whole body was thrumming with a nervous energy, and he could sense a similar excitement bubbling in the other novices. The Delve was a rite of passage, though for a few of the novices this would be their second time descending into the mines. Newly Sharded remained novices until they had completed a Delve after spending a full year under Saelus's tutelage, or returned from this hunt bearing another fragment of the Shadow. Since Deryn had only just been Sharded, he would stay a novice unless he proved himself by gaining a shard . . . which would be hard to do, given his lack of experience compared to the others. He thought it might not be impossible, though – in the various competitions that their teachers had been running over the last few weeks, he'd come close to winning several.

The novice who seemed the calmest had also been the champion of most of those same contests. Kaliss stood apart from her fellows, watching the gate with the look of detached curiosity that Deryn had eventually come to realize was in truth an intense focus. It would be a stunning failure if she did not return with at least a second fragment, and from the mutterings Deryn had heard, half of the novices feared she would gather all the shards that had been hidden before they had a chance to claim even one.

"Kaliss, step forward," intoned Saelus. The old man kept his expression carefully blank, but Deryn thought he might have seen a flicker of pride as the Ashasai girl came to stand in front of him.

"You were the first among your fellows to beckon the Shadow. As such, you will be the first to Delve today. Are you ready?"

"I am, master," Kaliss said, her voice steady.

"Very well," Saelus said, his gaze flickering to Azil. "Go forth, and good fortune."

As the old man finished speaking, the Black Sword of the Duskhold raised the Darkbringer and struck the stone again. No azure light erupted this time; instead, the shriek of metal grinding came from the gate as it slowly opened, the great iron maw parting down the middle. No mist-globes illuminated the space beyond, but Deryn's Shadow-aided vision could still discern a tunnel curving away.

He caught a hint of emotion in Kaliss's sharp features as the gate finished swinging wide, her lips curving slightly in satisfaction. No fear or nervousness, though, and Deryn couldn't help but feel respect for the girl who had worked so long and so hard for this very moment. She glanced at Saelus, and after the ancient teacher's terse nod, she strode forward into the tunnel.

Deryn continued staring where she had vanished until a shiver of movement from Saelus drew his attention. The old man had withdrawn a small hourglass from the folds of his robe, and without any ceremony, he turned it upside down. Grains of sand began to collect at the bottom, and after a moment of confusion Deryn realized that this must be Kaliss's reward for her achievements. A full glass to explore the mines before any of the other novices were allowed inside – Deryn glanced around and saw envy on a few faces, relief in others. At least some of the novices were dreading what they might find inside.

No one spoke while the sand slipped through the glass. When it finally finished, Saelus turned once more to the gathered novices. "Menochus," the teacher said, and the huge boy moved forward eagerly, his silver eyes shining bright. "You were the winner of Battlemaster Jaliska's tournament, proving yourself first among your fellows in strength of arms. Are you ready to begin your Delving?"

"I am," Menochus said, practically bouncing on his heels in excitement. Despite his size, Deryn knew the hill-boy could move with a lethal quickness. He had beaten the rest of the novices when Jaliska had held a contest to discover who was the best fighter among them, easily tossing all his opponents from the ring. He'd even stood a few moments against Jaliska until her far greater power had sent him crashing into the stone steps. Unlike the rest of them, Menochus had clearly spent his youth learning how to wrestle, and this advantage – along with his size and strength – had made the contest against the other novices a foregone conclusion.

"Then enter, and good fortune." Menochus grinned fiercely and fairly sprinted into the mines, eliciting a chuckle and a shake of the head from Nishi. Saelus had no reaction to the boy's enthusiasm except to flip the hourglass once more. Deryn chewed his lip as the pale sand began falling again, hoping that the shards were hidden well. The other novices must have been thinking the same, as they muttered and shift nervously.

Three more novices were allowed entrance to the mines early, though two of them had actually come second in their respective competitions – the Archivist's riddle-contest and Saelus's challenge to channel *ka* without breaking concentration. Both had actually been won by Kaliss, but in this instance the runners-up were allowed to enter the mines early.

When the last grains had fallen once again, Saelus slipped the hourglass back into the pocket of his robes. Deryn could feel the tension in the antechamber, like the novices were dogs straining at their leashes, but the old teacher was apparently in no rush to give the command that would send them rushing into the mines. He seemed to be enjoying this moment, and it was in fact Nishi that finally stepped forward with a sigh and a shake of his head.

"Stop torturing the poor creatures," he said to Saelus, then gestured grandly in the gate's direction. "Good hunting, Sharded. Your Delve begins now."

An explosion of movement followed, with a few of the novices rushing forward into the gloom. Others – including Deryn – were more measured, cautiously approaching the abandoned mines. Saelus and the Archivist had spoken vaguely about what lurked in the bowels of the Duskhold – rock spiders and the scaly little humanoids called xoctl – though, in truth, there was little a mere beast could do to harm one of the Sharded Few. More dangerous were cave-ins and the chasms long ago formed by juvenile balewyrms boring through the rock. Some were large enough to swallow a man and send him plummeting to his doom if he stepped wrong.

Deryn paused at the threshold to the mines and glanced back at Saelus and the other Sharded. Most of them ignored him – Nishi was actually scowling – but Azil smiled faintly as their eyes met. If only Kilian had been here to see them off, because Deryn was certain the irreverent Sharded would have made some quip that would have shattered the tension. As it was, it felt like they were marching into something terrible. Sighing, he finally turned away and plunged through the gate.

The corridor beyond jagged sharply to the left and then opened up into a vast space. It was most certainly a cavern, as the ground was uneven and pocked with stalagmites. A dozen tunnels emptied here, scattered at haphazard intervals along the walls. They all shared the same round shape, but their sizes varied wildly, from a few so small that Deryn would have had to stoop to enter, to one massive entrance that soared several times the height of a man.

The fortunate few who had been allowed to begin their Delve early had already disappeared, but the rest of the novices were drifting among the stone formations peering into the blackness of the tunnels like they could somehow discern where Saelus had hidden the shards. Deryn blew out a slow breath, then made a random choice and started picking his way across the treacherous ground to a middling-sized tunnel wedged between two of the larger ones. One of the other novices – the older man with the faded slave sigil etched into his brow – had the same thought, and they both arrived simultaneously at the tunnel's entrance.

"Ho, Terral," he said, nodding a greeting. They'd only exchanged pleasantries a few times before, but Deryn had been curious about this novice because of his age and the brand on his forehead.

"Deryn," the once-slave grunted. "This one draw you as well, then?"

"Just following my gut," Deryn murmured, squinting into the darkness.

"Aye," Terral said as he moved into the tunnel. "Don't really think there's any way to know which is best. Might as well put ourselves in the hands of the Broken God and trust Its spirit to guide us." The thickset man approached the walls, laying his palm against the stone. "So strange, eh? I spent some time in a mine trying to pull copper from the Fangs, but it was nothing like this place." Frowning, he slid his hand down the wall. "Those tunnels were hacked from the rock by men swinging picks and hammers. But go on, feel this. It's not the same."

Deryn moved closer to the other novice and also placed his palm on the wall. "So smooth," he murmured, surprised.

Terral stepped back, raising his gaze to the arched ceiling. "Perfectly smooth and perfectly round. It ain't natural. Men didn't make these passages, unless they used fire somehow. Melted a path through the rock, though the Broken God only knows how they'd do that."

"There's another possibility," Deryn said, his fingers slipping from the glassy walls. "Jaliska did warn us about holes cut into the floor long ago by fledgling balewyrms..."

Terral coughed nervously. "But surely they can't get that big."

Deryn thought back to the audience chamber of Cael Shen and the massive skull recessed in the gloom. "They did," he said. "Long ago."

They were both quiet for a moment, lost in imaginings of enormous serpents sliding through rock and darkness, and then Terral shook himself and sighed.

"Well, no time for thinking about that. I got to find a shard before that Ashasai witch snags them all."

The witch. Deryn had heard Kaliss called that before. Her intense drive and great success at developing her abilities, coupled with her solitary nature, had not endeared her to the others.

"Don't follow me, lad," Terral said gruffly. "I don't want to fight ya when I find a shard." The big man jogged down the tunnel to where it branched, joining with a much smaller passage. Deryn swallowed, imagining another balewyrm pushing through the stone and finding itself in the wake of its much bigger brethren. Terral paused for a moment at this juncture, then followed the larger tunnel as it curved to the left.

Deryn would have preferred to stay close to Terral, but the once-slave clearly did not want his company. Like most of the novices, he had apparently internalized the notion that they were all in competition with each other. Terral might dislike Kaliss, but it was only because she exemplified this philosophy better than himself. With a sigh and a shake of his head, Deryn quickened his pace as he went down the smaller tunnel. There was another path to greatness; he was sure of it. And maybe he wasn't the only one to believe so . . . He'd considered Rhenna's act of mercy from every angle, and he still couldn't see the one where saving Alia has benefited her.

The tunnel sloped downwards for a time, so smooth in places that he could sit and slide along the floor. Then it leveled off, emptying into another large cavern. His appearance caused some fluttering and shifting among the stalactites dripping down from above, but the shapes he could make out vaguely in the gloom looked small and unthreatening. He investigated the space, unsure just how Saelus would have hidden the shards, but quickly concluded that none were secreted here. When he had finished, he randomly chose another tunnel mouth and continued on.

Deryn searched for what felt like half a day. The mines were a warren of tunnels and caverns, large enough that he rarely encountered his fellow novices. When he did, they grimaced and shied away from him as if expecting conflict, even when he recognized someone who had been friendly in the past and he waved or called out. Occasionally, he saw evidence that other novices had encountered difficulties during their search. In one small cavern with fingers of glowing blue moss climbing the walls, he found the corpses of a dozen segmented, many-legged insects with wickedly curving mandibles. Each was twice as long as a man was tall, their bulbous heads staved in by heavy blows. Lashings of green ichor were everywhere, but that was not the only blood. Red coated the serrated jaws of one of the beasts, and Deryn worried just how seriously his fellow novice had been injured.

As he searched the cavern for more evidence of what had happened, he realized that the centipedes must have been protecting something. A tablet of stone had been placed leaning up against a wall, and in its center was a tiny imperfection from which cracks radiated outwards. Deryn's hand had drifted to the fragment lodged in his own chest, comparing its size with the gap in the fractured slab. There had been a shard here, he was almost certain. Another novice had claimed it, but not without a cost.

His next discovery was entirely unexpected. He had been following an unremarkable tunnel as it twisted and turned, already resigned to the fact that he would fail to secure a shard, when it jagged sharply, and he found his way blocked by a circular iron door. Its hinges were sunk into the stone of the wall, and a looped metal handle had been crudely affixed to its center. For a moment Deryn stood there staring stupidly at the barrier, then he gripped the handle and pulled.

The door did not budge.

He stepped back, examining it more carefully. A ring of runes was etched into the iron around the handle, but they meant nothing to Deryn. No, he realized the circle of runes was not complete, as there was a gap between two of the strange symbols, almost like the carver had been interrupted before finishing. Deryn brushed the smooth metal where the rune was missing, wondering if this absence meant something.

"My lad!"

The friendly bellow rebounded off the tunnel's walls, startling Deryn. He turned, unable to stop his smile from spreading.

"Menochus," Deryn said as the big boy stomped closer. His robes had been torn, and his curly black hair stood up in wild tufts, but he appeared otherwise whole and hearty. "It's good to see you."

"And ye as well," Menochus exclaimed, clapping him on the shoulder. "I've been starved for a friendly face down here. Even the lads I entered the Duskhold with ran away when they caught sight o' me coming."

Deryn nodded. "Aye. Everyone is just so focused on finding those shards." He eyed the hill-tribesman up and down. "Did you have any luck? Looks like you found something."

Menochus chuckled, fingering a flap of his torn robes. "Bumped inta a gaggle of those xoctl things Jaliska told us about. Screechy little monsters. I tried ta talk with them but they rushed me like I looked downright delicious. Had ta throw a few of them against the walls before they all scattered and ran."

Deryn's grin widened as he imagined Menochus tossing around the scaly little imps Jaliska had described.

"Any luck finding a shard?"

Menochus's good cheer faded. "No. I suppose I squandered whatever advantage I got for being let in early. Maybe spent a bit too long poking around in the corners of caverns." He squinted past Deryn at the door filling the tunnel. "This looks promising, though. Any luck getting it open?"

Deryn turned back to the iron barrier. "It's locked. Or stuck, I suppose. Have you seen anything else like it down here?"

"Can't say I have," Menochus mused, brushing past Deryn to run his hands over the smooth metal. He gripped the handle and pulled hard, but the door remained shut. "Must be something behind it. Any ideas?"

Deryn pointed at the runes. "These markings intrigue me. Can you read them?"

The large novice leaned closer, his face crinkling in confusion as he examined the symbols. "Nay. Never seen their like before."

"Do you think they're numbers? Words? Letters?"

Menochus pinched his brow like he felt the first stirrings of a headache. "Truly, Deryn, I've no idea." He sat down heavily with a great exhalation. "Perhaps this door has nothing ta do with the Delve. We are warriors, yes? Not thieves that go around lock-picking strange doors."

"This is a test," Deryn said, scouring the runes for any hint of a pattern. "And we have not only been taught how to fight. The riddles of the Archivist, Saelus's history lessons . . ."

Menochus snorted at this, demonstrating aptly what most of the novices thought about their teacher's interminable lectures.

". . . and they have a library here with more books than one could read in a thousand years. The Sharded Few are not simply warriors." Deryn paused for a moment. "Or at least they used to be more," he finally amended, remembering Kaliss telling him that the shadow-sharded had once been more scholarly than in the present age.

Menochus let out a thunderous sigh. "Ye can keep scratching at that door, if ye like. After I rest for a moment, I'll be on my way."

Deryn blinked, his investigation of the markings suddenly sharpening. "Scratching at the door . . ." he murmured softly, reaching out to trace the symbol at the top of the circle with the tip of his finger. Yes, the same sequence of strokes was hidden in the following rune, but with an added slash. And that new combination could be found in the next one, although with yet another line added. Then at the southernmost point of the circle the runes started to lose bits of themselves, but in an order reversed to how they had gained them. And that meant . . .

"I know what rune is missing," Deryn said slowly.

"And what does that matter?" Menochus replied.

"I don't know," Deryn answered, searching around his feet until he found a jagged piece of rock. "Maybe nothing." With some care, he scratched what he suspected should fill the empty space into the metal, then stepped back to examine his handiwork.

"Congratulations," Menochus said, sounding decidedly unimpressed.

The snap of a heavy tumbler falling into place filled the tunnel, and the novices stared at each other with wide eyes.

"No . . ." Menochus whispered as Deryn laid his hand on the handle and pushed. With the shriek of rusted metal the door swung open.

Menochus hurriedly scrambled to his feet, coming to stand beside Deryn as he gaped at what had been revealed.

The cavern beyond was not large, and it was dominated by a fissure that split the cave in two. They both gasped at the same moment, for on the far wall was a dark slab of stone inset with a glimmering mote of light.

"A shard," Deryn breathed, moving forward until he stood at the edge of the wide chasm. The gap was a dozen span across at least, but he suspected that with a running start he could easily jump it. Still, they would have to be careful, as the abyss yawning below them seemed endless.

"Aye, one shard," Menochus said from behind him, and then he shoved Deryn hard.

23

HETH

HETH WAS asleep on his feet when the first droplet startled him awake. It pinged against his helm, and for a moment he was confused about what could be falling from the endless, unquenchable blue. That was because it had never rained while he'd been atop the Duskhold – rarely did a cloud even mar the great sweep of the sky. He reached up with his hand not clutching the polearm and groped for evidence of what had hit him, belatedly realizing where it had most likely come from and suspecting he would end up with fingers stained with guano. But to his surprise, he found only cool water.

It was then that he saw it, a smear of darkness staining the heavens. Light flickered in its depths, illuminating a roiling storm. Heth pinched himself, wondering if he was dreaming, as the sun was still shining, the rest of the sky clear of even the faintest wisp of white. There was just this one pitch-dark cloud, and it was moving with unnatural speed.

Towards the Duskhold.

"Benni," Heth called out to the other guardsman on duty. "Are you seeing this?"

Benni had long ago mastered the art of which Heth was but a

novice, and it took his name shouted again before he jerked back to awareness with an annoyed grunt.

"Eh?"

"Look," Heth said, pointing at the swelling storm. In the few moments it had taken Benni to rouse from his daydream, the dark clouds had grown noticeably closer.

"By the Broken God," the guard mumbled, his face going slack. "They're here."

"What? Who's here?"

Benni didn't bother answering, striding across the roof of the Duskhold to a great bell of black iron. Heth's unease deepened. The bell was only to be struck when the Sharded needed to be warned of a possible threat approaching the hold. Gervis had told him it hadn't been sounded in years, and he had made it known he didn't expect it to ring out anytime soon.

Benni hefted the great mallet that hadn't been touched in the month since Heth had first stumbled blinking out onto the roof, the guard's ruddy face etched with the effort of holding it.

"Wait! Are you sure you need to –"

A sonorous clang washed over Heth as Benni struck the bell hard, his bones vibrating along with the reverberations. The guardsman immediately dropped the mallet, glancing at Heth with wild eyes.

"It's done," Benni said, as if he'd surprised himself.

"Yes," Heth said, fighting back the urge to scream at the guard. "But why?"

"Gervis said –"

The sound of the door to the roof crashing open made them both jump. One of the shadow-sharded stood there, the rising winds making his robes ripple and dance. He was young, only a little older than Heth, and had a thin face and eyes the same color as the Duskhold's stone. For a moment, those eyes flashed with anger as he stared at Benni and the bell, and then he turned to look towards where the guard was pointing with a trembling finger.

He paled when he saw the black cloud and murmured something Heth couldn't hear clearly, then whirled again to face them.

"You both come with me. We'll need an honor guard, and there's no time to assemble something more . . ." He paused, his lips curling in disdain as his gaze lingered on their piecemeal armor and ridiculous helms. "Something more professional. You'll have to do."

Without another word, he turned and disappeared back inside the Duskhold. Heth and Benni shared a surprised glance – it made sense that a member of the Sharded Few was also on guard duty with them, but they had not known one had been waiting so close by.

Or perhaps their proximity today was because the shadow-sharded were expecting something. After a last lingering look at the approaching cloud, Heth followed the Sharded through the doorway and down the stone steps. Benni came behind him, huffing and grunting. Years of loitering in place day after day had apparently not prepared the Hollow guards of the Duskhold for when they needed to move quickly. Another reason to keep up the early morning training sessions with the boys from the butchery, Heth supposed.

The shadow-sharded was waiting for them at the bottom of the stairs, his lips pursed in annoyance. "We must hurry, Hollow. If there's no one in the courtyard when she arrives, Cael Shen will have my head."

"When who arrives?" Heth asked, but the Sharded had already turned and was striding down the passageway.

They descended more flights of stairs and passed through galleries and corridors. When the Sharded encountered a girl in the servant's garb of the Hollow, he barked orders at her, telling her to find Elanin and inform the steward that runners must be sent to the lords of the Duskhold immediately bearing the message that the Storm had arrived early. She'd blinked in confusion at his commands, but then ducked her head and scurried off.

Heth had a sense of where they were going now, so he was not surprised when they approached an archway emptying into the courtyard where he and Deryn and Alia had first arrived. He remembered the smooth black stone beneath his feet gleaming in the unrelenting sun, but today the entire space had been cast into shadow. When he looked up after passing through the arch, his breath caught.

A great cloud hovered over the courtyard, so low that some of the Duskhold's jagged towers had nearly vanished into the churning darkness. Light pulsed in its depths, followed by a muted growl, and Heth had to fight the urge to run back inside the hold and find somewhere to cower.

"Fire and ashes," Benni breathed in an awed whisper, plucking the words from Heth's mouth.

"Look fierce," the Sharded muttered over his shoulder at them. "The old battleax thought she could catch us off guard. We just need to stall her for a moment until a Shen arrives."

"Stall her . . . how?" Heth asked, but the shadow-sharded ignored him, his face tilted up to watch the cloud as it continued its descent. The towers were the first to fully disappear, then the walls ringing the courtyard were enveloped by the haze. Heth swallowed nervously, his hand clutching the polearm slick with cold sweat. The Sharded standing just a few paces in front of him became a vague shadow as the dark mist rushed in to envelop them. They were inside the cloud now, and it was as clammy and wet as he'd expected. Heth's heart was thumping in his chest, and he wasn't sure if he could keep himself from swinging his polearm wildly if something emerged from the murk.

Just as quickly as it had thickened around them, the cloud began to disperse. Slices of blue expanded as the mist thinned, and Heth squinted from the daylight suddenly trickling down. Within moments it was gone, the last hazy tatters dwindling into nothingness . . . and revealing that they were no longer alone in the courtyard.

"Drega's dugs," Benni whispered hoarsely, again uttering what Heth might have said, if he could find his voice.

A dozen men and women and an assortment of gilt travel chests were arrayed around a palanquin carved of yellow wood. Another indistinct figure was behind the gauzy curtain, reclining on what looked like a mound of cushions. These strangers were an eclectic mix. There were three young, pale-skinned women in robes of pastel colors, nearly indistinguishable in height and appearance save for their starkly different hair – one had golden tresses that reached past her waist, another had a single plaited coil of black, and the last was as hairless as an Ashasai, but without the copper skin of that southern people. Beside this trio was a man in a tabard and breeches of such bright colors that at first glance he appeared to be wearing motley. His chestnut hair looked like it had been cut with a bowl, and he was wearing the sort of arrogant smirk Heth had seen many times before in the manses and sword-halls of Kething's Cross. The rest of the visitors were all men clad in armor – most wore a silvery plate that gleamed in the bright sun and looked more ceremonial than practical, elaborate motifs embossed on their cuirasses and vambraces, but one massive warrior was clad in unadorned grey metal that had clearly seen many battlefields. His scowling face bore nearly as many scars as his armor, including one deep wound that passed through where one of his eyes should have been. The socket was not empty, though, as from its depths a muted yellow light spilled forth. A shard, Heth realized with a nervous swallow.

Strangely, their armor did not glisten, nor did the robes of the girls cling to their slim bodies. Somehow they had avoided getting wet, despite having traveled here on or inside a storm cloud.

The shadow-sharded who had dragged Heth down to the court-yard looked slightly intimidated by the strangers, but after a moment he gathered himself and stepped forward.

"Greetings, from the Shadow to the Storm! We are honored by your presence, warriors of the Windwrack, and welcome you to the Duskhold."

A gnarled hand glittering with jewels drew back the palanquin's curtain. Inside was an older woman in an ornate silver dress that nearly matched the color of her hair. She gazed out at the sparse welcoming party and snorted.

"I've had more impressive announcements after coming down the stairs to breakfast. Where are your lords, little Sharded?"

The shadow-sharded's jaw worked soundlessly for a moment before he found his voice. Heth wasn't sure if the sheen he saw on the man's skin was from the earlier rain or not.

"Ah, apologies Lady Khaliva. The speed of your coming surprised us. We thought you would be another few days traveling."

Lady Khaliva chuckled as she rose from the cushions and stepped down from her palanquin. No one moved to assist her, much to Heth's surprise, though admittedly she seemed like she needed little help despite her age. She was at least a head shorter than everyone else in the courtyard – half as tall as the massive scarred warrior – but in her own way, it was like she towered over all of them.

"So you claim that Cael Shen and his brother could not sense our approach?" She clucked her tongue in what sounded like disappointment. "We should have assaulted these walls years ago, then. We'd have a hundred stormslingers running loose in here before half of you had rolled out of bed."

"And we are grateful you never made such an attempt!"

The voice from behind him was loud and cheerful, and Heth nearly jumped out of his boots. Moments later, a large dark-haired man in the robes of the Duskhold pushed past him, then set his legs in a wide stance and folded his arms as he confronted the strangers.

"Ah, Joras," the old woman murmured. "speak your name, and you appear. It is always the way with your kin, lurking in the shadows." She made a show of peering past him. "Is your brother hiding back there as well, boy?"

Joras threw back his head and laughed. The huge warrior with the dented armor stirred at this, his scowl deepening.

"He is waiting for you, Mother of Storms. Come, follow me."

24

DERYN

THE WHIP CAME DOWN AGAIN, lifting the flesh from his back. Strips of flame ignited, a blinding agony that threatened to scatter what was left of his sanity. Deryn groaned and twisted, trying to avoid the next blow. His hands were free, even though he distinctly remembered Jogan binding him to the hitching post, but still he couldn't move. There was a pressure around his hips and legs, holding him in place, forcing him to suffer the searing lash.

"Heth," he managed through cracked lips. "You don't want to do this."

Deryn tensed, expecting his plea to fall on deaf ears, but the next flaying strike never landed. He swallowed, tasting blood. "This is not you," he gasped.

Deryn felt a presence hovering near his head, just out of sight. He could hear the slow, even breathing of his tormentor.

"It's time to wake up," said a voice he did not know, and Deryn was dragged roughly back to consciousness.

Deryn opened his eyes to blackness, his body aching. He had gotten so used to the darkvision granted by his shard that for a moment he thought he'd been blinded. Panic surged in him, and he felt around his face, terrified that he'd find only gouged, empty sockets.

But no, his eyes were intact.

And that meant . . .

He reached out, and his hand touched something hard. He couldn't see because he was staring at a wall of rock. This realization was accompanied by another: his lower body was wedged firmly in a stone grip. He must have fallen into a crevice. Deryn looked up, peering into the darkness. It was lighter than the rock in front of him, but still he couldn't see very much. How had this happened? He couldn't remember ever seeing a hole in the Duskhold large enough for him to accidentally tumble into . . . Well, maybe the privy, but that would take some impressive contortions, and surely it would smell quite a bit worse.

Memories drifted up from the depths. The black gate, fashioned into a monstrous iron maw. Twisting corridors made glassy smooth by the passage of something huge and scaled and searingly hot. Runes carved into a door with a gap where one was missing . . .

Deryn moaned.

Menochus.

Menochus had shoved him from behind just as he'd laid eyes on a shard. He'd flailed as he'd fallen . . . his shoulder had struck the wall, and he'd tried to grab onto the rock around him, but his fingers had just scrabbled helplessly as he continued sliding down. The last thing he remembered was his head smashing against something hard.

Where was he?

And why would Menochus have done this to him? Deryn felt nauseous, and it wasn't just from his throbbing head. The hill-tribe boy's easy smile swam out of the darkness, his silver eyes crinkling with mirth. They had been friends. Hearthmates, Menochus had claimed. He'd said that was more important than glory and the selfish clawing for personal power that the other novices like Kaliss exemplified.

Deryn leaned his head back until it touched stone. All those kind words, their friendship, tossed away when another shard was finally within reach. If Menochus had just asked, he would have let him claim it. He'd only been in the Duskhold for a month, and he doubted he was even ready to add another fragment to his first. But instead . . .

Instead he'd killed him.

Deryn could sense how tightly he was wedged between stone. And even if he was able to extricate himself without ripping off a leg or grinding his hip-bones to dust, how could he possibly climb out of here? The stone was not as glass-smooth as the balewyrm tunnels above, but there still wasn't much in the way of handholds.

He had to try, though. Trapped down here and dying slowly of thirst was among the worst deaths he could imagine.

"Help!" Deryn screamed. The cry rebounded off the walls, then seemed to dissipate, as if crushed by the immense weight of the stone pushing down. "Can anyone hear me?" he tried again, but only silence answered.

Broken God, please, not like this. With some effort, he pushed down his steadily rising panic and tried to take stock of the situation. His body hurt, and his skin had been scraped raw in several places during his fall, but it didn't seem like anything was broken. That was something, at least. He'd have no chance of extricating himself and climbing out of here with a fractured arm or leg. Squinting above at the distance he'd tumbled, the lack of broken bones was a miracle, and likely it was only because of the shard infusing him with strength that he wasn't already dead or shattered beyond hope.

So now he had just had to pull himself free. This place in the chasm where he'd come to rest narrowed to a width only slightly larger than his body. Below him, he thought it widened again. He frowned, running his fingers along the smooth walls. The lack of handholds would make climbing out extremely difficult.

Gathering himself, he wedged his fingers into one of the few deep cracks in the stone, and then strained to pull himself free. He hissed as the bruised bones in his waist complained, but with the sound of scraping and the tearing of his robes, he was successful in raising himself slightly. Finally the effort proved too much for his trembling fingers, and he subsided again with a pained grunt.

This was not going to be easy.

He tried again, and again, until his fingernails were cracked and bleeding. Each time he was able to shift himself slightly, but without something more substantial to hold onto, he couldn't fully pull himself from the rock squeezing him. He paused to rest, taking deep, steadying breaths to tamp down the panic that was clawing inexorably higher. He could feel that it was only a matter of time before some final reserve of calm snapped inside him. His greatest fear ever since his mother had thrown herself into the frozen waters of the lake near the mill had been dying alone, struggling to breathe, pressed up beneath the ice. This was frighteningly similar, except it was stone instead of water above him, and his death wouldn't take moments, but days of rising thirst and hunger . . .

Deryn hung his head and concentrated harder on his breathing. He must not panic. He must not panic. He had to think of something else while he regained his strength enough to try again. Anything else.

Channeling. He could channel. Deryn reached down into himself, sensing the sliver of coldness lodged in his chest and the tingling energy it was pushing through his body like a second heart. Focusing on these rhythmic pulses, he guided them into his limbs, his spine, and finally up his neck and into his skull, until his head grew light. The ragged bursts of power flowing from his shard became smoother, the storm within him slowly calming.

And he felt his mood growing calmer as well, which he'd found to be a common side effect of channeling. Deryn gritted his teeth and rubbed hard at his face. No good. The detached calmness that accompanied channeling was too close to resignation. If he knew there was no hope and that the end was near, he would indeed fall into himself and try to block out the world. But he couldn't do that now, because he needed to be sword-sharp.

Beckoning, then. Gathering himself, he stretched out towards the darkness. He could feel it as vague, slithery things that slipped through his fingers like a handful of tiny eels. Kaliss had been right that the shadows thrown by the wraithling flame were much easier to sense and seize than the dark anywhere else. Absolute black – like that which filled this chasm – was, in truth, the most difficult. Grabbing shadows when they were thrown by a flame was far simpler than reaching into a lightless abyss and groping around for something to hold on to. But he'd been practicing, and alone in his chamber late at night he'd felt his ability to beckon growing stronger. Recently, he'd even come close to achieving what Kaliss's success had kept him from doing in the amphitheater ...

He felt it. The shock of this sudden and unexpected accomplishment should have jarred the darkness from his grasp, but it did not. And that was because it almost felt like the shadows were reaching towards *him* as much as he was to them. Like there was a will behind the endless black straining to be free ...

With some effort, Deryn separated himself from the darkness. For a few long moments, his mind was empty from the shock of what had just happened. Was this what it was like for the more experienced Sharded to beckon? That it was not so much forcing the darkness to yourself as welcoming it, inviting it? Deryn shuddered. He hadn't enjoyed that at all. It had been like when he'd gone before the Shadow to be judged, the attention of something vast and ancient fixed on him.

He sighed, rubbing at his eyes. So channeling rendered him too calm, and beckoning at this moment was obviously far too stressful. Had he recovered enough to pry himself free? Deryn flexed his fingers, trying to work some of the soreness from them. He bit his lip as a thought occurred to him. The stone here was hard and smooth, but perhaps if he could break a chunk off he could use that to gouge some more handholds from the walls. Maybe ...

The darkness shivered. Deryn blinked, unsure if that had been his imagination. He held his breath as he stared at the patch of black that he thought had trembled for the briefest of moments, hoping he had been mistaken.

Nothing. He couldn't hold back a chuckle at his foolishness. He hadn't been down here for very long, and he was already seeing things.

The darkness moved again, a ripple of deeper black.

The panic he'd managed to push down suddenly surged, and he struggled frantically to free his lower body from the stone's clutch. His hips complained as they scraped against rock, a strength born from this new terror helping to lift him more than he'd previously managed.

What was this thing? Surely it wasn't his beckoning, as he felt no connection to it.

Whatever it was, it didn't look dangerous. The darkness flickered as it slowly moved its limbs. There was a body there, Deryn realized. In fact, the thing had solidified into the shape of a small man perhaps a handspan in height. Featureless, but there was the little head, and the arms even bent as it moved, as if exploring what it could do. The shadow-man was standing on a knob of rock, nearly at head level with Deryn, and he couldn't shake the feeling that it was watching him.

"What are you?" Deryn whispered, the fear he'd felt at seeing this apparition fading as it continued to regard him without showing any hint of aggression.

He couldn't be sure, but it almost looked like it cocked its little head in response, as if confused by what he'd just said. The gesture was so like what a man might do that it shocked him.

Deryn's jaw dropped as he heard a faint chittering. It sounded like the squeaks of some small animal, and if he wasn't staring at a tiny shadow-thing, he would have looked around to see if a mouse had found him down here.

It was trying to talk to him. Or maybe it was doing its best to mimic the sounds he had just made.

"I'm sorry, I don't understand," Deryn said, feeling helpless.

The tiny shadow-man stopped its high-pitched babbling and began to pace back and forth. Again Deryn was taken aback by how much its movements resembled a man of flesh and blood. It truly looked like it was considering a problem while deep in thought.

Was he mad? Had he already tumbled off the edge of sanity, which would mean this was all in his broken mind? Surely he couldn't have already reached such a state. Or had his sense of time been compromised, and he'd in fact spent far longer in this pit than he thought?

Deryn started in surprise as the shadow-man stopped its pacing and whirled to face him. Well, it didn't have a face, but he could sense its attention shifting as it focused once more on him. It chittered something that seemed declarative and raised its little fist in the air, then brought this down sharply into its other hand.

It was like it had made a decision. As he watched in mute astonishment, its body rippled, its limbs merging with a suddenly elongating torso. In moments it had transformed into a serpent of liquid black. Without offering any more of its strange jabbering, it suddenly slithered up the stone walls of the chasm, an undulating line of intense black that within a few heartbeats had vanished from sight.

Deryn could only stare at where he'd last glimpsed the shadow-creature, still unable to fully accept everything that had just happened.

He must be going mad.

25

HETH

To Heth's surprise, he found himself part of the escort tasked with bringing the strangers to the Duskhold's audience chamber. After Joras Shen had invited the old woman inside – he was the second most powerful man under the Shadow, though that was surprising given his demeanor – Heth had hoped he'd be able to slink back to his post up on the battlements. After his encounter with the Duskhold's young lords when they had come close to executing Alia for desertion, he wanted to keep well out of sight until his face might have faded from their memory. But the shadow-sharded who had also been on guard duty atop the Duskhold had seen him and Benni edging for the stairs and had gestured angrily for them to fall in behind the storm-sharded.

Heth had grown up on tales of the Shadow's enemies, stories that described them as treacherous as the sea during a storm. The merchants in Kething's Cross claimed that the caravans from Flail had the most canny and duplicitous traders in the world. Heth had never had much trouble with any of them, and they'd been respectful enough while dining in the Bull. Bad blood still lingered from the old wars between the Storm and Shadow, but it had never turned to blows while Heth was present. In truth, he'd always wanted to visit

Flail, the mighty port on the Sea of Salvation and the greatest city of the north.

These storm-sharded were at first impression jarringly different from the inhabitants of the Duskhold. While the followers of the Shadow all dressed in the same simple black robes and drifted through the cavernous halls in somber silence, these guests from the Windwrack glittered in their silver armor and bejeweled dresses, their loud voices echoing in the hold. Heth noticed the shadow-sharded who had first recruited them to meet the visitors wincing at the sound, but Joras Shen seemed delighted with the noise and even joined in with a booming laugh when one of the storm-sharded said something to him. The Duskhold might be a joyless monastery, but the Windwrack seemed like it could be more akin to the bright court of a merry king or queen.

Finally, they arrived in a vast chamber dominated by a towering set of copper doors inlaid with swirling designs. The stonework here was far more ornate than in the Hollow's quarters, epics carved into the walls of warriors in strangely ornamented armor fighting great monsters while a man hovered above it all, light streaming from his upturned palms. Some of those creatures brought to mind the rift-beast they'd encountered, but others looked even more fantastical, with many leering heads on stalk-like necks, and one monster that resembled the moon if it had been called down and given scuttling legs and jagged teeth.

Joras Shen stepped in front of the great doors as if he expected them to open for him. Heth was waiting for him to knock or push hard on the gleaming metal, but instead the Duskhold's lord made a gesture, and from the recesses of the chamber tendrils of darkness slithered forth. When they reached the doors, they slipped into the deep grooves cut into the copper, flowing like water upward until the twisting design was etched in stark relief against the reddish metal. As the last section near the lintel was filled with black a deep grinding reverberated, and the doors swung inwards.

If this display impressed the storm-sharded, they did not show it.

Heth, on the other hand, was numb with amazement . . . and not a small amount of dread.

Beyond the copper doors was a vast hall illuminated by corpse-pale flames writhing within great iron braziers. A red path stretched from the entrance to a many-tiered dais, where a man with long white hair reclined on a throne of deepest black. Apart from the color of his hair, there was nothing about the man that suggested great age. A greatsword with a blade seemingly fashioned from the same material as the throne leaned against an armrest, and the man's hand gripped its unadorned white hilt.

On the other side of the throne stood a small woman in lighter robes, a color that reminded him of bleached bone. Her hands were thrust into her dagged sleeves, and her cowl was drawn up, but from the slice of her face he could still see her skin looked like marble.

Emerging from the gloom behind the man whom Heth assumed could only be Cael Shen was a massive serpentine skull, its fanged jaws frozen wide in the act of swallowing everything upon the dais. Heth found it nearly impossible to look away from this dead monster as he stepped into the hall, and from the amazed exclamations rising from the storm-sharded, he wasn't the only one impressed. The size of the balewyrm in life must have been horrific, and Heth was sure it would haunt his sleep later. He thought back to his old family stories about how his great-great-grandfather had won the acclaim of the Ember by saving the lord's daughter from such a creature. Nothing nearly this large, though, or Heth certainly wouldn't be here today.

Clustered at the lowest tier was a smattering of robed figures. Surprisingly few, and Heth realized he wasn't the only one disappointed with the size of the reception as the awed muttering about the balewyrm's skull subsided and was replaced by a few grumbled asides.

Most of the procession halted when it neared the dais, though Joras Shen strode over to stand among the gathered shadow-sharded. Heth wondered what he should do, but after glancing at Benni and seeing the same confusion and terror in the other Hollow's face, he decided that remaining quiet and motionless was perhaps the best course of action. Anything to avoid drawing attention to himself.

For a few long moments, the groups of storm and shadow-sharded were silent, as if taking the measure of the other, and then the woman standing at the side of Cael Shen stepped forward.

"Be welcome in the heart of the Shadow, warriors of Storm," she said, and though she did not raise her voice, her words carried clearly. "You are honored guests of the Duskhold and of Cael Shen, master of these halls."

In response to this, the brightly attired young man took a few steps closer to the throne. He raised his head high, as if to show that he was not cowed by the lord looming over them.

"We are honored to accept your invitation, Lord Shen," the man proclaimed, his words echoing in the darkened reaches of the great chamber and returning to them slightly distorted. Heth saw his confidence waver, as if surprised by this, but then he gathered himself and continued. "I present to you the Lady Khaliva, mother of Lord Bailen Khaliva, bringer of storms and master of the Windwrack."

The herald stepped back as the old woman shuffled forward. She did not use a cane despite her great age, though one of the silver-armored warriors accompanied her at her side, as if to lend support if she needed it. The strange white flames made her silver dress glow with an almost spectral radiance, and the jewels at her throat flashed as she tilted her face up to regard the lord of the Duskhold on his throne.

"Quite the paltry welcome, Lord Shen," she said, with no hint of a quaver in her voice. "A more foolish emissary would think you were trying to show insult."

The lord of the Duskhold stirred on his throne, his hand slipping from the hilt of his black-bladed sword. "I apologize," he said, his tone sounding shriven of emotion. No mutterings rose from the gathered shadow-sharded, but Heth could see the surprise writ clear on some of their faces at this admission.

"You have arrived on a day of great importance to our hold. Deep below us, the newly Sharded compete amongst themselves to gather fragments. As is tradition, several members of my court are over-seeing this event as we speak, including my children."

The old woman grunted at this. "*Hm.* So that's why I can't see that old goat Saelus. It would have pleased me to not be the most ancient relic at this audience, but so it goes. In truth, we do something similar in the Windwrack. Every year we hold a tournament that tests the mettle of our novices and rewards the winners with another shard. My late husband and his sons always were madly excited about this, so I know how important it is for some."

Up on the dais, Cael Shen dipped his head. "I appreciate your understanding. Tonight we will have a fete worthy to celebrate your arrival."

A smile quirked the old woman's lips as she turned to regard the silent crowd of shadow-sharded. "Oh. What fun that will be."

Cael ignored her tone, nodding gravely. "Yes. My daughter Rhenna has long wanted to meet the famed Mother of Storms. I hope you will spare a moment for her."

"Of course," Lady Khaliva replied. "I am very interested in meeting the young lady as well."

A brief lull in the conversation followed, and the huge scarred storm-sharded in the dented grey armor took this opportunity to step from the rest of the gleaming cohort. "Lord Shen!" he cried, addressing the lord of the Duskhold boldly. "On the way here, we witnessed something disturbing. A riftbeast, its rotting corpse sprawled in your realm, dead at least a month. Have the People of the Wind failed us? How did this monster leave the Frayed Lands?"

Cael Shen's face tightened briefly at this interruption, but his expression became placid again as his attention shifted to the hulking warrior. He matched gazes with the storm-sharded, apparently unfazed by the sight of the gleaming shard where the man's eye should have been.

"Warden Harath," he said, his words without inflection. "Surely a dead animal does not frighten the legendary Ironheart, *famdhar* of the Windwrack."

From his position behind the storm-sharded, Heth could see a flush creep up the back of the warrior's neck. "Nay, shadow lord, but any strangeness from the Frayed Lands must be brought to the attention of all the holds, as you well know." It sounded like the warrior was speaking through gritted teeth.

"I have already sent shadows bearing this news to all the holds, Warden. Do not fear, your lord has been appraised of what happened, even if he has not relayed it to you. I –"

Heth had let his attention wander around the audience chamber as Cael Shen was speaking, but this unexpected pause returned his attention to the dais.

The Lord of the Duskhold appeared almost . . . perplexed, half-turned around as he looked back at his throne. Heth craned his head, trying to see what had caused this interruption, but all he saw was gleaming black stone – Cael Shen didn't even use a cushion or have a goblet resting on one of the armrests. There was just his sword leaning against one side of the throne and his pale advisor standing on the other, and Heth now realized that she was also staring in shock at something on the great chair.

And then Heth saw it.

Perched on the seat of the throne was a small figure made of shadow, its tiny arms waving frantically.

26

DERYN

DERYN STRAINED with all his strength, and with a crack, the rock broke in half. He heaved it to one side, adding it to the pile he'd already scooped away. Through the gap where the rock had been, he could clearly see that the chasm widened again beyond the narrow section where he'd come to rest. And it seemed to not be straight down – there was enough of an angle to the walls that he thought he could control his descent, even if the stone was as smooth as the walls that now were rising around him and had so far defeated his attempts to climb.

The thought of going deeper into the chasm was terrifying, though. What if the grade of the slope changed and he plummeted into the depths? Could his shard-reinforced body survive another such fall? His situation right now was terrible, but breaking an arm or leg would make it orders of magnitude worse. Then he'd have no hope, instead of the tiny sliver to which he was clinging now . . . the hope that somewhere farther down there a tunnel would intersect with the chasm, and he would have a way to climb back into the warren of passages that honeycombed the rock the Duskhold had been built upon.

Because he wasn't climbing out of this hole. Maybe Xiv could have made it, or one of the others who had been able to scurry up skyspears with an almost ape-like agility, but Deryn had never been one of the better climbers among the slaves. He'd relied on his climbing glove and what he could grip on the trees to ascend, and the stone here had only the tiniest of cracks. He'd ripped a few of his fingernails away already while scrabbling for purchase.

So down it was, unless he wanted to slowly die of thirst. He refused to even entertain the possibility that the Sharded would find him – that would hang his survival on something he couldn't control. He needed to assume he had been abandoned, and that the only way he'd ever see the sun again would be if he saved himself.

With a grunt, Deryn lifted another loose bit of stone and shoved it away from the hole he was making. The volcanic rock down here was brittle, though in places sharp as knives, and his hands had suffered a fair number of shallow lacerations. The blood on his palms was only making it harder for him to get a firm hold, but so long as he –

Deryn's stomach lurched as the ledge of stone he was sitting on suddenly shifted. He held his breath, hoping that the rock was merely settling, then exhaled in relief when after a few heartbeats nothing else happened.

And then the stone beneath him dropped away.

Deryn screamed, his arms flailing wildly as he tried to grab on to something, anything, to arrest his fall. But his fingers slid helplessly across the smooth walls, and along with a small avalanche of the rocks he'd so painstakingly pried loose he tumbled into the darkness.

Deryn smashed into the angled side of the chasm almost immediately. He tried to find something to slow his fall, but his momentum was too great and he kept sliding downwards, and it was all he could do to try to take the brunt of the impacts on his shoulders. Pain flared as sharp protrusions ripped his robes and scraped along his back, opening up the scars that still laced his flesh.

In the sliver of his mind that had somehow remained calm, he became aware that the slope he was sliding down was becoming less steep. Rather than picking up his speed, his awkward descent seemed to be slowing, and then the wind was knocked from him as he slammed into the ground, rolled a few times, and came to a rest.

"Fire and ashes," Deryn murmured, stunned that he had not only survived, but that all his limbs were still attached and nothing seemed broken. He whispered thanks through bloody lips for all the time he'd spent channeling the energy flowing from his fragment and strengthening his body.

Gingerly, he picked himself off the stone, certain some previously unnoticed injury would now reveal itself, but when he finally stood, swaying, he had to admit that somehow he had survived this ordeal nearly unscathed. He could feel blood trickling down his back, his bones ached where he'd struck rock during his fall, and his hands would take a while to heal, but all things considered, he felt tremendously fortunate.

Well, so long as he wasn't currently at the bottom of an even deeper and more difficult-to-escape pit. That didn't look to be the situation, though. His darkvision faltered after only about a hundred paces or so, but it appeared the chasm had emptied into a massive tunnel, one much larger than those he had explored during his Delve. If his theory was true and these passages had once been made by balewyrms, then the size of the monster that had burrowed through the rock here must have been staggering. Luckily, this place looked ancient.

He peered down both ends of the tunnel, trying to decide which way he should go. Deryn thought he could discern great slabs of tumbled stone looming in one direction, suggesting that slightly beyond the limits of his darkvision the passage might be blocked. The other way appeared clear, so that was the route he chose. If either of the directions had sloped upwards, he would have gone that way, but the tunnel here remained level as far as he could see.

He started walking.

His situation was still dire – he was lost far below the Duskhold, and it was extremely likely that this tunnel did not even connect to the warren above where novices searched for shards – but still his heart felt lighter as he pushed into the dark. He was *moving* at least, going *somewhere*. The thought of dying alone trapped in that crevice had been too horrible to truly entertain at the time. He'd stayed sane by assuming he would find a way to free himself . . . or had he? Stayed sane, that is. Deryn remembered the way the darkness had twisted into the shape of a man. He must have imagined that, or created the little avatar of shadow himself subconsciously when he'd been practicing his beckoning. Whatever had happened, he should put it out of his mind for now.

He wasn't sure how long he traveled down the tunnel, but quite a bit of time must have passed, as the muscles in his legs started to burn and the scratchiness of his throat became more insistent. He'd heard that a man could survive only a few days without water, and for all he knew he'd already spent two or three nights down here, as it was very difficult to gauge the passage of time, and he may have been unconscious longer than he thought after Menochus had shoved him into the chasm.

Deryn winced, shying away from that memory. He'd been trying to avoid dwelling on his former friend's betrayal, as it made his situation even more depressing. But if he ever did make his way out of these depths and return to the Duskhold, there would be a reckoning. He couldn't help but wonder what Saelus or the other senior Sharded would do if they knew Menochus had attempted to murder a fellow novice. Would he be punished, cast out of the Duskhold . . . or congratulated for his ruthlessness?

He slowed as he noticed the tunnel ahead vanishing into a deeper blackness. From his experiences during the Delving, this likely meant the passage had broken into a cavern, and this guess proved correct as he drew closer. He could tell that the space beyond was large, but still he stopped in awed wonder when he reached where the tunnel ended.

It was like standing on the threshold of a cave at night, gazing out at the wide world beyond. There were no stars above, only a seamless black that extended past the limit of his darkvision, but Deryn could sense how high the roof of the cavern soared. Mighty stalagmites thrust upwards into the gloom like the fossilized fangs of some long-dead leviathan, and filling the gaps between their broad bases was a forest of waist-high mushrooms, ghostly radiance seeping from their bell-shaped caps. The light was very faint, but Deryn had been so long in the darkness that still he winced in discomfort and averted his eyes. Since something was growing down here, that suggested the existence of water. Deryn licked his cracked lips in anticipation. Perhaps these giant toadstools were even edible, though his months living in the forest had taught him the dangers of consuming strange mushrooms. Or could his shard filter out any poisons he might accidentally ingest? Kaliss or Kilian had once mentioned something about this, but it probably wasn't worth the risk if he wasn't certain.

Great boulders were scattered about the uneven floor, some piled into small hills in a way that almost looked intentional. A few of these mounds had come together to form a barrier that blocked his view of the rest of the huge cavern, like a mountain range splitting a land in half. His eyes traveled the walls as far as he could see, looking for other tunnels emptying into this space. None that he could discern at first glance, but it would take a close-up investigation to be sure.

That could wait, though. First, he wanted to climb to the top of one of those central piles and get a better perspective of what was in the cavern. Perhaps there was a pool of water teeming with cavefish rendered pale and blind by aeons underground. The thought made his stomach twist in hunger, though the Broken God only knew how he would cook a fish, even if he somehow caught one.

Deryn set off across the cavern, keeping himself vigilant for any signs of habitation. If xoctl and rock spiders and those monstrous centipedes had infested the barren tunnels beneath the Duskhold, this area with its carpet of mushrooms must also have its share of denizens. No movement drew his eye, however, as he waded through the waist-high mushrooms, and soon he was clambering up the foothills of the tumbled boulders dividing the cavern. A month ago he would have found the going difficult, but the shard had not only infused his body with strength but also greatly improved his coordination and balance, and he was barely breathing hard when he finally reached the apex and gazed down at what had been hidden on the other side of the cavern.

His thoughts scattered, a numb terror sluicing through him.

It couldn't be.

It couldn't.

It . . .

He let out a tiny gasp, and with that, the paralysis broke. Deryn ducked down behind the rocks he'd been peeking over, still trying to accept what he'd just seen.

Coils. Endless looped coils, and a head pulled from his deepest nightmares. It was more like a lizard than a snake, with horny protrusions surrounding its slitted eyes and a crest of spines flowing all the way down its sinuous red-black length.

A balewyrm. But nothing like the creatures that had carved the tunnels he'd searched during the Delving. This one was massive, dwarfing even the remains Deryn had seen in Cael Shen's audience chamber. A monster of legend from an earlier, vanished age. Even the riftbeast they'd encountered at the edge of the Frayed Lands had not summoned up this sort of primal horror. It was like an ancient part of his brain was responding to seeing this thing, dim race-memories emerging of cowering in fear as leviathans like this slipped through swamps and jungles.

Could creatures like this even exist on land? Surely only in the depths of the sea or earth was it possible for things to grow this large. How could it possibly sustain itself? From Deryn's brief glance, it looked as though a team of horses could have ridden inside if it unhinged its jaws. Surely it didn't subsist down here on *mushrooms*?

With great care not to make any noise, Deryn slowly descended the boulders until he once more stood on the cavern's floor. Maybe it was dead, its flesh preserved by some process he didn't understand. Even if that was true, he didn't think he had the courage to –

I SMELL THEE, LITTLE GODLING.

Deryn fell to his knees, the words echoing in his head, threatening to split his skull asunder. Dazed, he felt a trickling from his nose, tasted blood on his lips. A darkness pressed on the edges of his vision, as if a vast presence was looming over him.

What had that been?

The booming reverberations faded, leaving behind a pulsing headache.

Something had spoken to him. Something had spoken to him *inside his mind*.

LONG HAS IT BEEN SINCE ONE OF THEE DARED TO DISTURB MY DREAMS.

And then he heard it, the rasping hiss of a vast bulk being dragged across stone.

Oh. Mother, save me.

Deryn glanced behind him, at the mouth of the huge tunnel where he'd entered the cavern. To get there, he'd need to cross open ground, totally exposed, while stumbling through the maze of mushrooms. He'd be like a mouse caught in a field by a snake. What should he do? What *could* he do?

The rocks. Deryn staggered to his feet and turned to the heap of boulders he'd just descended. Yes, the way the rocks were piled there was a gap large enough he could squeeze into. A rational little voice in the back of his head was trying to tell him that hiding accomplished *nothing* beyond his immediate survival, but then again, that was all he cared about at this moment. To not be *here* when the balewyrm came looking for him.

The mental image of that monstrous head with its cold black eyes swinging around the rocks spurred Deryn on, and without allowing himself to consider the wisdom of what he was doing, he scrambled into the crevice. He had to turn his body sideways, and even still for a terrifying moment he thought he would not fit, but then with a grunt of effort and the tearing of his already ragged robes he tumbled inside.

Deryn sagged to the ground in relief, but the feeling was short lived. If that voice in his head had indeed been the balewyrm, then it was intelligent, and once it realized where he was hiding, it would pry apart the rocks to get to him. Fire and ashes, all it would take would be a swipe from its tail and the boulders would shift enough to crush him.

HIDING, LITTLE GODLING? THOU ART NOT AS BRAVE AS THY FELLOWS. THEY FOUGHT AND DIED AND THE PIECES OF DREAD ALGEROTH THEY CARRIED NOW ADORN ME.

Deryn clutched at his skull, his head ringing with the force of the creature's presence. What in the black abyss was it talking about? Nothing important enough that he should be distracted right now. Pinching his nose to stop the trickle of blood, Deryn edged his way deeper into the small cave.

The depth of it surprised him. The rocks had fallen in such a way that a small passage had been formed, and he decided to follow it as far as it went. He supposed there was always a tiny chance that he might discover a crevice or tunnel leading down, out of this cavern.

Was that a light up ahead? Perhaps some of those spectral mushrooms had sprouted in here. Deryn pressed on, the path through the rocks jagging left and then opening up into another small space. His heart fell when he saw it was a dead end, but disappointment was replaced with surprise as his eyes fell upon the skeleton.

It was propped splay-legged against a rock, its empty eye sockets staring at Deryn. Whatever clothes it had once worn had rotted away, though a circlet of tarnished metal rested on its skull and in its chest . . . in its chest . . .

Deryn swallowed, his mouth suddenly dry. Embedded in the skeleton's sternum was a shard, and the light he had seen earlier had been its dusky glow. His own fragment was the size of a fingernail, but this shard was nearly palm-sized, and at least as large as the one that had been sunk into the chest of the wind-sharded champion from the edge of the Frayed Lands.

Deryn slowly approached the long-dead warrior. Hesitatingly, he reached out with a trembling hand, unsure how he should attempt to pry the fragment from the bone. But as his fingers brushed the shard a shock lanced through him, answered by a surge from what was lodged in his own chest. The ancient bone seemed to *ripple* slightly, and a spiderweb of cracks appeared, radiating out from the shard. Deryn winced at the sound, hoping the great creature hunting him had not heard.

The shard popped loose from the sternum, and Deryn reflexively caught it. He steeled himself for another crackling burst of energy, but the fragment felt like nothing more than stones chilled by a cold night.

It crumbled into many pieces as soon as it landed in his hand, separating out into a dozen fragments closer in size to the one he already had lodged in his flesh.

Deryn counted again quickly, just to make sure. Yes, twelve. Twelve shards. Nearly twice as many as Kilian had acquired after a lifetime in the Duskhold. This was a treasure of incalculable value, and he had happened upon it in what was likely to be the waning moments of his life. With some effort, he pulled his gaze from the glimmering points of light in his hand. So even if no one would ever know, he had found more shards during his Delve than any novice ever had before. The Fates did have a cruel sense of humor.

With a shaking hand, Deryn slipped the shards into a pocket of his robe. As he did so, he noticed something else in the little cave that he'd overlooked with his attention drawn by the remains of the Sharded. A sword hilt lay near the skeleton's bony fingers, its tarnished grey metal nearly blending with the stone and its blade buried under a layer of grey dust. Deryn reached down to pick it up, then jerked his hand back in surprise. The merest touch of his fingers upon the hilt had sent a vibration through him, and there had been a crackling tingle not unlike when he'd pried the shards from the skeleton a moment ago. Deryn eyed the sword warily, but the sensation hadn't been painful, and as ineffectual as any weapon would be against the monster outside, he would certainly feel better armed. Steeling himself, Deryn gripped the sword's hilt and lifted it. Dust and dirt slid from the blade, revealing not iron or steel but a gleaming white length of what looked like ceramic or perhaps the porcelain from which the richest merchants in Kething's Cross had eaten their meals. But surely such a material would make a terrible sword. Deryn brought the blade close, inspecting it for any chips or cracks, but it looked flawless. And all the while it thrummed in his hand like a thing alive.

COME, LITTLE GODLING. IF THOU ABASES THYSELF BEFORE ME AND TELLS ME TALES OF THE WORLD ABOVE, I MAY YET LET THEE LIVE. THIS TIME I HAVE SLUMBERED LONG, AND MUCH MUST HAVE CHANGED.

The sound of scales sliding along stone came again. Deryn tore his gaze from the strange sword and looked around wildly. The balewyrm was very close.

Moving as quietly as possible, Deryn approached the cave's far side. The way the boulders had fallen, there were several gaps large enough to see out into the cavern beyond, and he lowered his face to one of these holes.

The balewyrm filled his vision. A wall of reddish-black scales rose in front of him, easily three times the height of a man. The monster had unspooled from its curled position and lifted the front section of its body high into the air to better survey the cavern. From his vantage, Deryn could see the paler belly of the great serpent soaring upwards and its wedge-shaped head far above. Something odd drew his attention, tiny points of glimmering light sunk into the flesh of its underside, dozens of them. Could those be . . . shards? And if so, had the fragments increased the balewyrm's strength and granted it the same powers as the Sharded Few? The thought was terrifying.

Something cold touched his hand, and Deryn nearly cried out in surprise. Heart thumping wildly, he looked down to see the small shadow-man he had been certain had been conjured from the depths of his mind standing beside him. Its featureless face was turned upwards, as if watching him.

"What . . ." Deryn whispered, paralyzed by shock, unable to form any of the questions he wanted to ask.

What are you doing here?

What do you want?

*What in the black abyss **are** you?*

The shadow-man curled its hand around one of his fingers and tugged lightly. It was clearly trying to lead him away from the barrier separating him from the balewyrm. Was it afraid that the beast might see him watching from within the rock pile? Deryn would be surprised if that was possible, but then again, he truly did not know the creature's capabilities –

A thump came from outside. The sound was faint, but Deryn suspected – given how far away he thought it had been – that something significant had happened, like a stalagmite toppling over or a tunnel collapsing. He turned back to a chink in the wall to see if he could tell what the noise had been, but the shadow-man pulled him in the other direction with surprising strength, briefly knocking him off balance.

"Why do you not want me to see?" Deryn murmured in annoyance . . . just before a wave of blinding light flooded his sanctuary.

This time he did scream, though it did not matter, as a far louder roar erupted from outside. Spots danced in Deryn's vision, and he knew that if he'd been staring through the gap he likely would have been blinded. Somehow the little shadow-thing had known that was about to happen. But *what* had happened? Sepia light was still trickling through the wall of rocks, but it was far more muted than a moment ago.

Rubbing his eyes and hoping there would not be another flare, Deryn approached the hole, then sucked in his breath when he saw what was happening outside. The great balewyrm's front section was still lifted into the air, but now it was swaying violently back and forth, as if trying to clear its vision from the flash a moment ago. Beyond its head, a roiling ball of yellow energy hovered like a new sun, illuminating the cavern's jagged roof . . . a roof that now had a gaping hole.

As he watched, something dropped through this rent in the stone. It was moving so fast that at first Deryn had trouble understanding what he was seeing, but then it violently arrested its plummeting descent. From his vantage far below, it looked like a perfect dark circle outlined against the radiance spilling from the crackling sphere above.

A Black Disc.

The shadow-sharded had found him.

"Did you bring them here?" Deryn asked, turning to stare wide-eyed at the shadow-man beside him. It ignored his question, seemingly focused on the porcelain sword now dangling limp in Deryn's hand.

"You missed a lot," Deryn informed the creature, and then an enraged hissing drew his attention back outside. Long javelins of gleaming darkness were being hurled by whoever was standing on top of the Black Disc, and several were already embedded in the balewyrm's face. The monster was tossing its head back and forth like a dog trying to dislodge a mouthful of porcupine quills, the Black Disc drifting closer so its master could deliver another blow.

"Be careful," Deryn murmured, just before the balewyrm stopped its thrashing and lunged towards the Disc with startling speed, jaws spread wide.

INSECTS!

Great fangs closed upon the Disc and it shattered like it was made of glass. In the moment before this happened, Deryn saw three figures leap away and go tumbling through the air.

One of them was dark-skinned and had kept his grip on a staff crackling with azure energy. A second, smaller Black Disc coalesced into existence beneath him before he'd fallen very far. Azil.

Another plummeted halfway to the ground before the darkness rushed in to enfold him, and he vanished from sight. Deryn wasn't sure, but he thought that might have been Nishi.

The last Sharded had no tricks to save herself, and she smashed into the stone with terrible force a dozen paces from where Deryn crouched behind the boulders. She lay face down in a puddle of midnight-black hair, unmoving.

Rhenna.

The daughter of Cael Shen. Was she dead?

There was another bone-jarring roar, and Deryn glanced up to see the Black Sword leap from his soaring Disc. Power blazed along the Darkbringer as Azil swung his staff, striking the side of the balewyrm's great head, but unlike the riftbeast he'd slain on the edge of the Frayed Lands, the monster's skull did not crumple under the blow. Its head snapped backwards from the force, but it recovered almost instantly and slammed its snout against the Black Sword, sending him tumbling and tearing the Darkbringer from his grip. The balewyrm made to follow Azil, but then it suddenly reared back, thrashing like something was causing it pain. It was then Deryn noticed the tiny figure clinging to its neck-spines and driving something it held into the monster's scaled flesh over and over again. The balewyrm hissed in rage as it twisted, trying to bring its head around so it could bite the man on its back. Deryn gasped as the monster's coils shifted, nearly crushing Rhenna. What would happen if the weight of the balewyrm came down on her? Could even her sharded body protect her from that?

A flash filled the cavern, followed by a booming crack. The monster jerked its head around, ignoring the Sharded on its back as it turned towards the ragged hole in the cavern's roof. Something else was descending from above, a smoky blackness that reminded Deryn of a cloud, light flickering in its depths. The balewyrm bellowed another challenge, its neck spines flaring.

What was this?

The cloud dissolved into wispy threads, revealing two armored figures hurtling towards the balewyrm. One was encased in gleaming silver and brandished a golden sword, while the other wore tarnished plate and wielded a massive war hammer shimmering with arcane power. They struck the balewyrm at the same time, and Deryn could hear the pain and rage in the great serpent's shriek. Its coils twisted again, coming even closer to Rhenna.

Deryn remembered her facing down her brother on that barren mountainside so that Alia might be spared.

"Oh, bloody black abyss," Deryn muttered. There was another gap farther along the wall of tumbled rocks, down near the floor, and maybe, just maybe, if he pressed himself to the stone he could squeeze his way through . . .

Without stopping to think about what he was doing, Deryn let the sword fall from his hand as he rushed to the hole, then he dropped to his belly and wriggled his way outside. Cold fingers clutched at him, but he ignored the shadow-man.

As he emerged from the rocks into the wider cavern, he made the mistake of glancing up and then froze in awed terror. The balewyrm's head was weaving and bobbing like a hooded serpent as it followed the path of a Black Disc – Azil, Deryn suspected, though he couldn't be sure – while another Sharded, the huge hammer-wielding warrior, soared through the air with his legs sunk into a roiling black cloud. Several others were clinging to the creature's coils, trying to penetrate its scales with their weapons. One had been successful, but it seemed to be bothering the balewyrm about as much as a hornet sting would a full-grown man. Blood was flowing from where the silver-armored Sharded had stabbed with his golden sword, but given the size of the monster, it would take a thousand such wounds before the beast faltered. Who were these armored warriors? They certainly didn't look like shadow-sharded.

Shaking himself, Deryn broke his reverie and lunged for where Rhenna was sprawled. His heart stuttered as the balewyrm lashed at the silver Sharded with his tail, but the warrior leaped clear just before he was swatted into oblivion. The monster's sudden movement brought its coils so close to Deryn that he could see himself reflected in the gleaming scales.

He had to hurry. Hooking his hands beneath Rhenna's slack arms, he started dragging her back towards where he'd found sanctuary. Relief flooded him as she stirred, lifting her head groggily, and she weakly tried to extricate herself from his grip.

"I'm saving you," he told her as the ground shook and a deafening explosion rent the air.

"Who?" she slurred, raising her head. Her eyes were dazed, and blood smeared her pale face. "Oh. It's you."

"There," he said, jerking his head in the direction of the hole he'd crawled through. "There's a space within where we can hide. Can you go in?"

She stared at where he'd indicated for a long moment, and Deryn wondered how much the fall had addled her, but then she nodded shakily.

"Go, then," Deryn said, releasing her and turning back to stare at the raging battle. A jagged spear of lightning flashed from the hammer of the cloud-riding warrior, but it splattered harmlessly against the balewyrm and quickly dissipated, residues of crackling power crawling across its scales. A cyclone of whirling shadows swelled, but the balewyrm scattered it into wisps of darkness by thrusting its horned head inside. Azil shot out of the top of the disintegrating whirlwind atop his Black Disc, just barely avoiding snapping jaws. The balewyrm roared in frustration, and then from its mouth spewed a torrent of liquid fire.

"No," Deryn whispered as the maelstrom engulfed Azil. When the flames subsided, there was no sign of the Black Sword.

Reeling in shock, Deryn turned back to the rocks just in time to see Rhenna's boots disappearing inside. He stumbled after her, feeling numb. He'd seen Azil slay a monster the size of a fortress in a single blow. And now he was . . . he was . . .

A filament of darkness shot from the gap Rhenna had gone through and wrapped itself around his wrist. He stared at it stupidly for a moment and then was nearly jerked off his feet as something on the other end pulled hard.

Rhenna, it must be her. And she was right – he needed to get out of the open. The Sharded were falling, and soon the balewyrm would turn its attention to him again.

Deryn threw himself to the ground and scurried through the hole, then collapsed in a heap on the other side. He lay there panting for a few heartbeats before raising his head to find Rhenna pushed up against a boulder, her eyes wide as she stared at the little shadow man.

Another deafening bellow from outside jolted Rhenna from her astonishment. With some effort, she pulled her gaze from the shadow-thing.

"Is that what I think it is?" she murmured.

Deryn looked from the daughter of Cael Shen to the faceless little man and gave the only answer he could.

"Maybe?"

"Why didn't Saelus say you were an elementalist?" Rhenna hissed. She sounded annoyed, which surprised him. Surely there were more important things to be concerned about right now.

"Azil is dead," he blurted. "I saw it."

Rhenna blinked, her face going slack with shock. Then she pursed her lips and shook her head. "He'll be fine. My brother is very hard to kill."

"I saw –"

"He's not dead," Rhenna said in a tone that brooked no disagreement. She struggled to her feet, swaying slightly. "Now I need to get back out there and help. Nishi will never let me hear the end of it if I spend the first fight against a balewyrm in centuries cowering down here."

"I don't think you understand," Deryn pleaded, interposing himself between Rhenna and the gap they'd crawled through as she moved towards it. "That monster is tearing through the most powerful Sharded in the Duskhold. If Azil cannot slay it, what can you hope to do?" This gave her pause, and Deryn seized on the doubt he saw in her face. "We can escape while the balewyrm is distracted. There's a tunnel on the other side of the cavern –"

Rhenna snorted. "I'll not flee, novice. But if the battle is going as poorly as you say it is . . ." Her gaze drifted to the hole in the wall through which he'd been watching earlier ". . . then my father will enter the fight soon."

Deryn gaped at her. "Cael Shen is here?" he asked as she swept past him to look through the hole.

"Oh, yes. We begged him to let us have the honor of slaying the balewyrm, but it seems we may have underestimated this beast. He will not let us forget this anytime soon, I promise you. Ah, here he comes now."

Deryn joined her at the wall, and his breath caught when he saw what was happening. The rift in the cavern's ceiling where the Sharded had descended was obscured by a churning blackness that was spreading across the stone . . . no, *crawling* would be a more fitting description. And what had looked like a liquid was in truth countless entwined tendrils knotted together to create an incredibly dense lattice. The balewyrm's head was tilted upwards in apparent fascination as it watched these writhing shadows creep across the cavern's ceiling, seemingly unbothered by the weeping wounds pockmarking its scales. Of the other Sharded, there was no sign.

I SENSE THEE, LITTLE GODLING . . . CORPSE-THIEF, GRAVE ROBBER, ABOMINATION . . . YE MAY THINK THOU ART MASTER HERE, BUT I AM OF THE OLD WORLD, AND I DRANK DEEP FROM SORCERY'S WELLSPRING LONG BEFORE ALGEROTH DESCENDED TO STRIDE AND DIE IN THESE LANDS . . .

"It speaks," Rhenna whispered, sounding shaken.

"What is it talking about?" Deryn asked, but Rhenna only shook her head.

"Look!" she hissed, and he turned back to the hole just as vast black tentacles emerged from the roiling darkness. The balewyrm roared a challenge, snapping at the closest arm. It broke apart in its jaws, but now there were a dozen more, all reaching for the beast. It twisted, trying to avoid their grasp, but several fell upon its scales. The balewyrm bellowed again, but it sounded different than before.

The beast was afraid.

It thrashed violently, snapping a few of the glistening black tendrils, but more and more were slipping from the darkness to seize hold of the monster. Soon its movements became more labored, though Deryn could sense how fiercely the balewyrm was straining against these bonds.

And then the lord of the Duskhold arrived.

The crawling darkness covering the ceiling roiled, and from its depths another Black Disc descended into view, trailing wisps of shadows.

"Father," Rhenna murmured, her hands clutching at the stones.

The balewyrm stopped its struggles, then opened its jaws. Molten fire lanced forth, but a barrier of darkness formed in front of the Disc and the flames spattered on it. When the balewyrm's attack subsided, much of the shield had been dissolved, but Cael Shen was untouched.

Before the balewyrm could consider a new stratagem, the shadow-sharded leaped from the hovering black platform, his mane of white hair streaming behind him and his greatsword of glistening darkness upraised. The balewyrm tried to wrench its head free so as to claim him with its jaws, but the tendrils now held it firmly, and it could only roar in frustration as the man swung his sword to meet the beast's neck.

A great gash appeared in its throat, far larger than what should have been opened by the blade. Blood spewed forth in a steaming arc, shimmering in the light of the crackling sphere illuminating the cavern. Another Black Disc materialized beneath Cael Shen before he could fall, but he did not soar away, instead thrusting his sword almost to its hilt in the balewyrm's flesh, then ripped it loose again.

More blood, a flood this time. It washed over the lord of the Duskhold, but he seemed not to care, even though the torrent looked scalding hot.

"He's going to kill it," Deryn said in an awed whisper.

"Of course," Rhenna said, her tone suggesting there could be no other outcome.

But the balewyrm was not finished. The beast had been maddened by the pain, and its struggles grew even more panicked, its coils lashing with such force that the ground shook and the rocks where they were hiding trembled. Fear stabbed at Deryn – if the monster's tail struck the boulders, the whole pile would collapse with them inside. Given he'd seen Rhenna fall from so high and stumble away with no significant injury, he suspected she'd survive being buried, but Deryn wasn't sure what the limits were of his own sharded body.

It never came to that. With a final, desperate shriek, the balewyrm heaved violently against the tentacles binding it, and with a wet tearing sound it broke free. At once the beast threw itself away from the white-haired warrior on his Black Disc, slithering with terrible speed around the end of the heaped rocks and out of Deryn and Rhenna's sight.

Cael Shen's Black Disc shot after it.

"Fire and ashes," Deryn whispered. Rhenna only grunted as a response. She seemed just as stunned as he by what they'd witnessed.

Neither of them said anything more until a few moments later, when a shiver of movement drew their attention. Another Black Disc was rising from behind a stalagmite with two figures on it, and though the distance was great, Deryn thought one of them had dark skin.

"Azil and Nishi," Rhenna said softly, and despite what she'd said earlier, Deryn heard the relief in her voice.

Elsewhere in the cavern, strands of smoke were being drawn towards where two others had just emerged. The armored Sharded – one bright, the other dark – were lifted into the air as the cloud finished forming beneath them. The larger warrior had his massive war hammer slung across his back. His companion gestured with his golden sword, and the cloud surged in the direction Cael Shen and the balewyrm had gone. Azil's Black Disc followed just behind them, the light coruscating along Darkbringer bathing the Black Sword and the heir to the Duskhold in a faint blue radiance.

"Gone to join the chase for the beast," Rhenna said, a bitter edge to her words. "Of course, forgetting about me."

"Who are those armored warriors?" Deryn asked as both the cloud and Disc vanished from sight.

"Storm-sharded," Rhenna said, her voice still sharp. "From the Windwrack. A delegation arrived just before your . . ." She paused and glanced at where the small shadow-man was investigating the skeleton slumped against the wall ". . . your friend appeared in front of my father and communicated your plight."

Deryn blinked in surprise. "It can talk?"

Rhenna shrugged. "I do not know what it did to convince my father. I was with Saelus and Azil and Nishi, keeping watch on how the Delve was going. My father suddenly arrived with those two storm-sharded behind him and said a balewyrm's lair had been discovered by you and that this little shadow-creature was going to lead us to it."

Deryn frowned. "I thought it had abandoned me . . . if it was even real." He glared at the shadow-man reproachfully. "If it could sense the balewyrm, it should have told *me,* and I wouldn't have walked down that tunnel."

Rhenna slowly approached the shadow-man. It ignored her, continuing to poke one of its dark limbs into the ragged hole in the skeleton's sternum.

"This was the corpse of a Sharded," she said slowly, as if noticing the remains for the first time. "And a powerful one, at that. It's too bad someone has already scavenged their shards."

Without thinking, Deryn withdrew the fragments from the pocket of his robes and held them out for her to see. "I did."

Rhenna's face grew even paler when she saw the glimmering points of light piled in Deryn's hand.

"Mother Dark save me," she whispered hoarsely. Her arm seemed to move of its own accord, reaching for the shards, but then she shook herself and forced it to fall back to her side.

She swallowed. "Put those away. Hide them."

"Why?"

Rhenna's jaw tightened. "Because most of the Duskhold would murder you for those shards, if they could get away with it. You've found them on your Delve, and by my father's decree, anything a novice claims down here is theirs by right . . . But those shards – if you can even bear that many – will turn you into one of the most powerful men in the hold. And that will make some people very jealous."

Deryn chewed on his lip, thinking hard. Did he even want so many shards? Maybe if he gave a few to Rhenna she would agree to protect him.

"Perhaps I could give you –" he began, but she shook her head curtly.

"No. It is tempting, of course, but those are yours, Deryn. You found them during your Delve, in the lair of a beast out of legend. And if you are truly an elementalist, then you will be a great asset to the Duskhold. The hold needs you to grow in power."

"Elementalist? I don't know what that is."

Rhenna wiped at a smear of dirt marring her cheek, then turned to stare at the shadow-man as it wandered around the little cave. "To be truthful, I doubt there are many who do. There hasn't been an elementalist in the Duskhold for centuries, long before my father inherited the throne. From what little I know, they were Sharded accompanied by a companion-entity formed of whatever aspect governed their fragment. I've heard rumors that one duke of Ashasai is bonded to a blood-elemental, but I'm not sure if that's true." She shrugged. "Saelus will know more. I'm certain he will be very interested to talk to you about *everything* that happened here today."

Deryn tore his attention from the shadow-man. "Should we . . . follow the other Sharded?"

Rhenna grimaced. "I'm no fool. If that beast can overcome Azil and one of the Wardens of the Windwrack, it's far beyond me. My father will chase it into the tunnels and slay it, or perhaps it will escape. But my part in that battle is finished." Her frown gave way to a wry smile. "Nishi and I did not know what awaited us down here. This has been a humbling experience." She ran a hand through her dust-coated hair. "Come. I'm sure you want to return to the Duskhold."

The thought of escaping these depths was almost surreal. Several times he had been sure he would die down here, in the dark, alone and forgotten. His gaze slid once more to the shadow-man . . . no, the shadow elemental. It was exploring the rest of the cave, apparently as curious as a cat. That thing had saved him. He wasn't sure how he felt about that yet.

Deryn walked over to where he'd dropped the white-bladed sword earlier and picked it up again. Rhenna made a strangled noise, her eyes wide.

"You also found a sharded artifact down here?" She raised her head to stare at the boulders hanging over them. "Maybe I *should* kill you and tell my father the balewyrm ate you."

He tensed, surprised by how serious she sounded.

Then she blew out her cheeks. "I'm jesting. Let's get out of here."

27

ALIA

TWILIGHT HAD RIPPED the sky into bloody tatters and drenched the mountainside in darkness. Alia breathed deep, her hands clenching the wrought metal balustrade of the balcony. Below her, the Duskhold's gleaming black façade plummeted to the scree and rocks littering the distant slopes. She savored the feel of the cool wind on her face, the way it played with her hair and brushed the nape of her neck. The breath of the gods, her mother had once told her. Drawing this essence of the divine within could strengthen soul and body. Alia had found wisdom in that. When she had been in the forest under the boughs of the great trees, or crouched on the edge of a silvery lake, or watching a fell cat flow up the side of a rocky bluff, she had felt the energy that bound everything together.

She had not felt it in the depths of the Duskhold. Buried under rock, far away from the sky and trees and sun. Sequestered away from life itself. It was unnatural to burrow deep into the earth and remove oneself from the web of the world. When Rhenna had ushered Alia into her rooms in this tower and said that she would live here now as her personal handmaiden, she had nearly sobbed in relief. Just having this balcony to retreat to had done so much for her sanity – she still had to spend much of her time in the windowless warren of the hold, but every day she could steal a few moments out here, and that was enough.

This afternoon she had been on the balcony for the passing of several glorious bells, a witness to the fading of the day and the slow creep of night into the sky. She'd finished all her duties long ago, but her mistress had not yet returned. Rhenna had said she might be late, that the Delve could last half a day or even until the next morning. Often the novices found the hidden shards quickly, she had explained, but not always. The teachers of the Duskhold concocted devilishly hard puzzles, and it took time before they were solved. She wondered how Deryn was doing on the Delve. As the newest Sharded in the Duskhold, Rhenna had said that little was expected of him. He wouldn't have the strength or skill yet to be the first to pass the fighting tests – a few fragments were always placed within the nests or lairs of dangerous beasts – nor was he likely to unravel the puzzles that tested knowledge he had not yet learned. Still, Alia was hoping he would do well. He'd risked his life to save hers several times, and in the Wild that kind of debt carried great weight. They were connected now, their life-threads twined.

The sound of the door opening made her turn. Rhenna stood in the entranceway, but Alia hardly recognized her. The Sharded's long black hair was matted and tangled, her usually immaculate robes torn and filthy. Blood on her face had been awkwardly wiped away, leaving a crusted smear. She met Alia's shocked gaze with hollow eyes, then took a limping step into her chambers.

"Mistress, what happened?" Alia gasped.

Rhenna ignored the question. "I need to get clean, Alia," she said as a half-dozen Hollow followed her inside, each carrying a pair of large buckets slopping over with steaming water.

"Of course," Alia replied, her mind whirling as she hurried over to assist her mistress. Had something attacked Rhenna in the tunnels below the Duskhold? She remembered how Deryn had effortlessly plucked that lizard-dog out of the air when it had lunged at him, and she knew Rhenna was far more powerful. What kind of animal could have done this to her?

One after another, the Hollow servants poured their burden into the basin scooped out of the chamber's floor. When the last had finished, they bowed deeply towards the Sharded and retreated outside. As soon as the door clicked shut, a shiver went through Rhenna, and her shoulders slumped, the fist of control she usually kept squeezed tight visibly unclenching.

Her mistress winced as she shrugged out of her robes, and Alia hissed in dismay when she saw the purple blotches marring her skin.

"It's not as bad as it looks," Rhenna assured her. "I bruise easier than most, but they'll fade in a day or two. No broken bones, I think."

Still, Alia could see the pain in her face as she lowered herself into the bath, though the groan that escaped Rhenna's lips was pure pleasure.

"Mother of Dark, that feels good," she murmured.

Alia retrieved a coarse washcloth and a sliver of soap, then crouched down behind her mistress and began to gingerly clean Rhenna's shoulders and neck.

Alia's thoughts wandered as her mistress sank back into her ministrations. If something had happened on the Delve, was Deryn all right? Rhenna was at least as strong as Kilian, which meant she had many shards. Deryn only had one. Alia licked her lips, mustering the courage to ask. Rhenna had shown her kindness, but clearly in this moment she wanted only to relax and forget what had just happened.

"It was a balewyrm," Rhenna said suddenly, startling Alia.

"A balewyrm, mistress?" she responded in confusion, though the name tickled at her memory. Phinius had mentioned something about balewyrms during the flight on the wind-sharded's dragon.

"A creature long thought extinct, at least anywhere near the Duskhold. My grandfather believed he slew the last of the beasts long ago. Yet there one was, sleeping in the tunnels far below us." Rhenna shook her head in disbelief.

Alia wrung out the cloth. The thought of some great serpent coiled in the depths beneath them was more than a little unnerving.

"It was your friend who found it," Rhenna said, and in her surprise Alia fumbled the soap into the water.

"Apologies," she whispered.

Rhenna fished around for the soap and held it out for her to take. "He's fine," she said, then chuckled wryly. "Better than fine, in fact. Stumbling into that monster's lair was the best thing that ever happened to him."

"Why do you say that, mistress?" Alia asked, still a little numb from the fear that had just swept through her.

Rhenna didn't answer, instead sinking below the waters for a moment before emerging again. Alia took this opportunity to reach around her and gently wipe away the blood crusting her brow.

"The beast has fled," Rhenna assured her. "Do not be afraid. And my father has said he will dispatch warriors into the deep tunnels to ensure that there are no other surprises lurking." With a small sound of discomfort, Rhenna rose dripping from the water. She raised her arms so that Alia could begin scrubbing the rest of her body.

Taking up the washcloth again, Alia began doing just that. As always, she was surprised by the hardness of Rhenna's body. Alia had once thought that anyone who lived off the labors of others would be weak and soft, but Rhenna had the lean strength of a Treesworn's spear maiden. Despite being the daughter of the hold's lord, she trained as hard and as long as any warrior in the Duskhold.

Alia had seen Rhenna with the other Sharded, and her mistress was like a different person outside these chambers. She never smiled, except coldly, and every interaction seemed to be a contest for some inscrutable prize. But here, away from the rest of the hold, that mask could be taken off. She was kind to Alia, treating her gently and allowing her small luxuries like spending her free moments out on the balcony or sharing the sweet purple fruit she enjoyed so much. Alia felt sorry for Rhenna that she had to wear the skin of an entirely different person for much of her life. It was her father, Alia suspected. She'd learned enough during her time in the Duskhold to know that he prized strength above all else. Or perhaps he simply hated weakness. Was there a difference?

"Mistress, apologies," Alia ventured softly, hoping she was not overstepping her bounds, "But, Deryn . . . my friend . . . what will happen to him?"

Rhenna raised her dripping arm from the water, filaments of darkness webbing her outspread fingers. "That is for my father to decide now."

28

DERYN

DERYN SAT cross-legged on his blanket of silver fur, his hands resting on his knees. At the other end of the bed, in a position that mirrored his own, was the little shadow-man. The elemental, Rhenna had called him. But what exactly *was* that? Had he summoned this thing, or had it sought him out?

"What are you?" Deryn asked.

The shadow-man cocked its tiny head to one side. Deryn heard a sound, like the fluttering of countless moth wings. Surprised, he realized he'd heard something like it before, as it reminded him of the faint whispers emanating from the shadows when he'd concentrated on the darkness in his room. Had this thing been trying to communicate with him?

He sighed and leaned back against the headboard of his bed, shaking his head in frustration. The elemental did the same, its movements even more exaggerated.

"Did you speak to Cael Shen?" he asked the creature. "How did you tell him where I was?"

The papery beating-wing noises came again, rising at the end with the same intonation as his own question. Was it simply copying the sounds he was making? He felt like he was falling deeper and deeper into madness. If the Hollow servants who had bathed him when he'd returned from the depths hadn't also been able to see the shadow-man, he would have been sure he'd left his sanity in the deep tunnels, perhaps that he'd even imagined the battle between the balewyrm and the Sharded.

An idea came to Deryn, and he scooted forward on the bed. Across from him, the elemental did the same. Shoving aside the voice in his head that kept telling him he should be careful, Deryn extended his arm towards the shadow-man. Like a dark reflection, the elemental did the same, and Deryn could even see a tiny finger just like his own as they slowly moved closer and closer to touching.

Just before that happened, a heavy thump came from the door. Deryn jumped back, and the shadow-man did the same.

"A friend of yours?" Deryn asked the elemental. He could have sworn it gave the tiniest of shrugs, and then the door shivered as something smashed into it with even greater force. Deryn swallowed, looking to where he'd set down the porcelain sword.

"Novice!"

Saelus. Deryn scrambled from the bed and rushed across the room to fling open the door. Outside, his wizened teacher leaned heavily on his staff, looking like a strong wind might knock him over. Deryn glanced at the other side of the door and saw where a fist-sized indentation had crumpled the wood. Apparently, his teacher was not as frail as he appeared.

"Cael Shen summons you, *arzgan*."

"Now?"

"No, at your leisure." Saelus rapped Deryn on the temple with his staff. "Yes, now. Bring the artifact and shards you found and the . . . elemental, if you can command it."

Deryn rubbed where he'd been struck. He turned back to his room and found the shadow-man standing just behind him, its little head tilted up to stare at Saelus.

"Uh . . ." Deryn began, and the elemental swiveled to him with its featureless black face. "Will you come with us?"

The quarters of the Duskhold's master were surprisingly spare. Saelus ushered him inside a room with a low table and three chairs of simple black wood, a brazier in the corner crackling with white fire. The only decorations in the chamber were the weapons on the walls – dozens of swords, maces, axes, flails and staffs, all hanging from hooks driven into the stone. Some were bejeweled, blades gleaming in the pale light like they had been freshly forged and polished, while others were worn and nicked, having seen much use.

Seated in one of the three chairs was Cael Shen. The lord of the Duskhold did not look like he'd recently been drenched in the blood of a monster. He had bathed, his long hair draped glistening across his shoulders, and he regarded Deryn calmly from over steepled fingers. The only sign that it had truly been him who had driven off the balewyrm was a small cut on the cheek beneath his left eye.

"Are you going to strike me down, novice?" he asked softly.

Deryn swallowed nervously, wondering if he should lay down the sword Saelus had instructed him to bring. It might be considered a terrible offense to be holding a weapon in the presence of the hold's lord.

"No, my lord," stammered Deryn, feeling a cold sweat break out. He sensed Saelus moving to take up a position in the corner of the room opposite the wraithling flame. Surely his teacher would tell the Duskhold's master that he had commanded Deryn to present the sword to him?

The corner of Cael Shen's mouth lifted slightly. "Give it to me," he said, holding out his hand.

Deryn stepped forward hurriedly and presented the sword hilt-first. As soon as Cael's fingers closed around the grip, he frowned.

"Interesting. Not a shadow-sharded artifact." He offered the sword to Saelus. "What do you think?"

The old teacher hobbled out of the corner to accept the sword. His face actually showed distaste as he hefted the weapon and examined it. Deryn noticed that the strange white blade did not reflect the light of the wraithling flame.

"Wind-sharded, if I were to guess. How many I can't be sure. I always find determining the exact number of fragments in an artifact that did not come from the Shadow to be difficult. But it is old, and I suspect powerful."

"A great treasure," Cael Shen rumbled. "Especially for an *arzgan*. Tell me, what else did you find in the depths?"

Deryn hastily reached into the pocket of his robes and drew forth his shards. "These, my lord. They were in a skeleton next to where I found the sword."

"*Those* are shadow fragments," Saelus murmured, handing the sword back to the Duskhold's lord. "I can see from here."

"Indeed," Cael Shen said, running a finger along the porcelain blade. "A mighty warrior of Shadow perished in that cavern. I will have Archivist Devenal research who it might have been. Surely there must be records that speak of a *kenang* who wielded a wind-sharded sword."

"The People rarely forge artifacts," Saelus mused. "At least in our present age."

Cael Shen examined the sword for a moment longer, then held it out for Deryn to take.

"As valuable as the treasures are that you discovered, novice, I am more interested in something else."

The shadow-man. Deryn glanced over his shoulder, as it had trailed them through the corridors and he thought it might still be lingering outside the door. But it wasn't there. He looked around wildly, and then his attention returned to Cael Shen when the lord of the Duskhold grunted softly.

"Oh," Deryn whispered. The elemental was in the chair opposite of Cael Shen, his posture a reflection of how the shadow-lord was sitting. The hold's master steepled his fingers again, and the shadow-man did the same. Deryn feared for a moment that Cael would take offense, but he seemed only bemused by the entity's antics.

"Did you summon this thing?" he asked.

"Not intentionally," Deryn replied. "It simply appeared when I . . . when I was in trouble."

"You were trapped in a chasm."

Deryn blinked in surprise. "Yes. But how do you know that?"

Cael Shen tilted his head towards the elemental. It did the same. "It told me," he said, frowning. "No, that is not accurate. It showed me. When it appeared in the audience chamber it did not speak, but when I came close it touched me and in my mind I saw you, lying at the bottom of a well of stone. And then it showed me the balewyrm, and I believe it was trying to tell me you were dangerously close to where this monster laired."

"It went looking for help," Deryn murmured.

"Aye," Cael Shen said, leaning forward to peer into the depths of the shadow-thing. "Which means it is intelligent. Saelus, tell me what you know of elementals."

The old man cleared his throat. "I have to confess little enough, my lord. I am two hundred and seven years old, and during my life there has never been an elementalist in the Duskhold. In the wider world we hear stories of such Sharded. There was an Unbound water-witch of the isles who dwelled in the deep with an elemental that could manifest as a whirlpool. And of course, there is the duke of Ashasai who reportedly keeps an elemental in a great pool of blood large enough to bathe in. None of the tales I've heard ever described the manifested elemental as being so small."

The shadow-man chose that moment to make his moth-wing rustling sounds. Deryn thought he maybe sounded a little aggrieved, as if Saelus had just insulted him.

"Perhaps the diminutive stature of this one is because of its master's lack of shards," Cael Shen mused. "And that means if the Duskhold wishes to avail itself of its true potential, we need Deryn to grow in strength."

"Potential?" Deryn repeated, watching the little shadow-thing swing its feet like a rambunctious child.

"All the stories I've heard about elementals agree on one thing, as I'm sure our lord knows," Saelus said. "They are beings of tremendous power, living manifestations of the shards. Mysterious, yes, but it is known that they can be harnessed for the benefit of their master and the hold he or she is sworn to."

Cael Shen leaned back in his chair, his expression becoming distant. "This could be a stroke of fortune for the Duskhold . . . and just when our hold finds itself on the precipice of greatness." He stroked his chin thoughtfully. "I wonder if this elemental is a gift from the Shadow to show that we are on a path it agrees with." The lord of the Duskhold seemed to reach some decision as his eyes settled on Deryn once more. "You come before me bearing many fragments and a sharded sword. Long ago I decreed that whatever was retrieved on a Delve belonged to its finder, but never did I imagine a novice returning with such a hoard. Nearly all the Sharded here will burn with jealousy when they realize what you have." His mouth twisted. "I care not. You will merge your new shards as quickly as possible. It may take years of channeling, I know, and these things cannot be rushed, but you must try to do it as fast as possible. A fully fledged elementalist could be a great asset in the coming conflicts."

"Conflicts?" Deryn asked in surprise. He hadn't heard that the shadow-sharded were expecting hostilities with any of the other holds.

Cael Shen frowned and shook his head slightly, as if annoyed with himself. "There are always conflicts. Life is a struggle, and only the strong survive and thrive. You are a gift to our hold, and I would use you as soon as you are ready." His gaze turned to Saelus. "Deryn shall be elevated to adept. Let us see how he fares alongside my children and the strongest of the younger Sharded."

Saelus dipped his head. "Some of them will not be happy, but I agree. I will inform Azil he has another student."

"No need," came a new voice as the Black Sword emerged from the flickering shadows cast by the wraithling flame. Traceries of blue light veined the length of the Darkbringer, as if the power within was seeping through the staff.

"Ah, Azil," the lord of the Duskhold murmured. "How did the hunt go?"

The adopted son of Cael Shen shook his head as he collapsed into a chair. "We followed the magma stream you chased it into, but the monster never surfaced, and eventually the way became too difficult to follow. I set wards in the nearby tunnels, and if the balewyrm dares return, I will know." He sighed, running a hand over his hairless head. "A riftbeast and now a balewyrm. It is as if the old world is stirring. What will be next?"

"An elemental," Cael Shen said, gesturing towards the little shadow-man, which seemed to be staring at the Black Sword as if fascinated.

Azil arched an eyebrow at the creature, then shook his head in bewilderment. "What does it mean, Father?"

"That the pulse of history has suddenly quickened," Cael Shen said with confidence. "And we must be ready."

Silence followed this pronouncement, broken by the hissing crackle of the wraithling flame. Finally, Saelus cleared his throat. "My lords, I will return Deryn to his chambers and tell him what he needs to know about being an adept."

Cael Shen seemed lost in thought for a moment, and then he clapped his hands together sharply. "Good. And we have a fete to attend. But before that . . ." He turned to Azil. "Fortune has bequeathed our new elementalist a sharded sword. I would see him trained in its use."

The Salahi stroked his chin. "There are few with enough swordcraft to teach him. Jaliska, yes, but she's already stretched thin. Perhaps one of the Hollow?"

"My lords," Deryn interjected, hoping he wasn't overstepping. "I know someone."

29

ALIA

"LADY SHEN," announced the Hollow guarding the entrance to the great hall, sweeping out his arm to usher them inside. Rhenna did not glance at the man in his ornate ceremonial armor as she passed, though Alia did, peering inside his insect-like helm to make sure it wasn't Heth. The guard's amber eyes widened when he noticed her attention, and he hurriedly averted his gaze. Not Heth. Alia hesitated, tempted to ask whether the guard knew him – and if so, how he was faring but then Rhenna spoke.

"Come. Stay close to me."

"Yes, mistress," Alia murmured, hurrying to catch up with Rhenna as she entered the hall, though she couldn't stop herself from slowing again as she drank in the spectacle of the fete.

She had never been in this chamber before, and the vastness staggered her. Tiered steps ascended to a platform which was empty save for a jagged black throne, and looming behind it, as if emerging from the deeper shadows, was the skeletal head of a great serpent or lizard. Her attention was drawn there first, but after a moment spent staring open-mouthed at these gargantuan remains, she turned to what was happening in the rest of the hall.

It was a swirl of activity. Men and women mingled between long tables groaning under a great feast, many holding silver goblets or fluted golden cups from which wisps of steam were rising. Nowhere could Alia see the dour black robes of the Duskhold – like Rhenna, the Sharded had changed into more formal clothes, the men in smart black doublets with silver buttons and the women in dark glistening dresses, jewels glittering around their necks and fingers. Her mistress's attire was more colorful than most – her gown looked to be woven from spider's silk, and a fist-sized gem the color of fresh blood pulsed at her throat. But still, she was nowhere near as resplendent as their guests. The Windwrack delegation's garb was just as rich, but far brighter, vivid reds and blues and greens, specks of color in a sea of shifting dark. The Sharded of the Duskhold must have outnumbered them ten to one, yet they were very easy to pick out.

Twisting white flames blazed in great braziers, the spectral light sliding over the revelers and the strange barbed statues scattered about. There was music as well – or at least Alia thought that was what it must be. It sounded nothing like the stomping, skittering fiddles that had filled the tavern they'd eaten at in Kething's Cross with joyful noise, or the drums the Wild folk had beaten to ward away what lurked in the night. It was spare and unearthly, summoned by a thin man hunched over a long instrument, his fingers fluttering as he plucked strings with a look of intense concentration.

Rhenna paused while moving through the crowd as a beautiful young woman in a pale blue dress floated past, arm in arm with a handsome, broad-shouldered man with sandy hair. He leaned in closer to her and whispered something in her ear, and she covered her mouth with a gloved hand as she laughed. Rhenna shook her head as they melted back into the swirl of Sharded.

"I never thought I'd see the day," she murmured, turning back to Alia. "When my father's audience chamber would echo with the sound of laughter. *Windwrack* laughter."

"These guests have never come before?" Alia asked, and Rhenna snorted like the very question was ridiculous.

"The storm-sharded have been our enemies for centuries. Countless battles have been fought, lands won and lost. They killed my uncle, my father's brother, and we in turn slew their heir. I would have thought it impossible for our two holds to treat like this, so long as there were those who remembered the past."

Alia nodded. Blood feuds dominated the relationships between the tribes of the Wild, passed down generation after generation. "What changed?"

"The Wars of Conquest," Rhenna replied, taking a silver goblet from the tray of a servant as he passed. "Or as it was known below the Belt, the Ifashan Jihad. The Storm and the Flame and the Shadow united to keep the sand-sharded from dominating the south. It was known that the newly crowned shah would soon after turn his eye to the northern holds, and even with that existential threat, I was told it was difficult to set aside old differences. Most thought things would return to how they had been after our victory at Gerendal, but apparently not."

As if summoned by Rhenna's talk of the Salahi, the crowd shifted and the black-skinned warrior who had slain the riftbeast was suddenly standing beside them.

"Sister," Azil said, nodding a greeting.

"Brother," Rhenna replied, reaching out to clutch at his wrist. "Such a day we've had."

Just from this simple gesture, Alia could sense the bond between these two. There was a warmth here that she'd never noticed between Rhenna and her full-blooded sibling.

The Black Sword flashed a white smile, then sipped from his cup. "Indeed. Years pass in this place with nothing changing, and then an avalanche all at once." He looked her up and down. "You seem relatively hale. I was worried when you fell, but then I saw that boy help you find shelter among the rocks. A good decision, not rejoining the fight. The monster was well beyond you."

Rhenna's mouth twisted bitterly. "That did not stop Nishi. He acquitted himself well while I hid."

Azil laid a comforting hand on her shoulder. "The wisdom of a warrior is about knowing when not to fight. I've told you that before.

Your talents did not lend themselves well to such a battle. Nishi could always Shadow Step away if the balewyrm ever turned its attention to him, as he eventually did."

"And I assume that was how you escaped the beast's fire? Deryn said he saw it consume you utterly."

"Indeed, though it was far closer than I would have liked. Perhaps my defenses would have held even if it had struck me . . . but then again, perhaps not. I have never been tested by such a monster before."

"No one has," Rhenna muttered, taking another drink. "Not in centuries. And then the day the storm-sharded arrive, it wakes." She shook her head, as if still in disbelief. "But I'm grateful than no one was seriously harmed, even the storm-sharded. It would have been difficult explaining to Lord Bailen Khaliva how one of his Wardens perished beneath the Duskhold."

"Or his son."

Rhenna glanced sharply at Azil. "His son?"

"That other warrior, the one with the golden sword . . . that was his heir, Prince Lessian."

Her mistress's face went slack with shock. "Broken God save us. Are you telling me the heirs to both the obsidian and greystone thrones fought side-by-side today?"

Azil nodded, then gestured with his drink at the handsome sandy-haired warrior who was still escorting the beauty in her froth of pastel silks around the chamber. "That's him there. He showed courage, I think."

Rhenna grunted something noncommittal, then very obviously tried to change the subject. "What is this all about, Azil? Why did my father invite the storm-sharded to the Duskhold?"

The Black Sword pursed his lips. "I think it's complicated, Rhen. You see –" He hesitated, his eyes drawn to a massive man shouldering his way through the crowd towards them. "Wait. Another time."

Azil tensed, his hand opening and closing as if he wanted to be holding something. Rhenna had also noticed the approaching man, and Alia heard her suck in her breath.

He was imposing. The warrior – and there was no doubt he was a warrior – was clearly one of the storm-sharded, but he was not dressed in their colorful garb. His tunic and breeches were simple grey cloth, and he wore no jewelry or gold. Something did flash though, and Alia could not keep herself from gasping when she realized it was his eye – a glittering crystal was sunk into the socket, leaking wan light. She was not the only one intimidated by this scarred giant, as the other shadow-sharded nearby drew away from him as he stalked closer.

"Warden Harath," Azil said, inclining his head towards the man as he came to loom over them.

"Salahi," the huge storm-sharded rumbled. "Been a long time since I fought beside one of ye."

It took all of Alia's willpower not to shrink away from this glowering man. An air of barely restrained violence clung to him, and the hand that clutched his massive flagon looked large enough to crush her skull. She thought she saw Azil shift his stance slightly, though his friendly smile did not waver.

"And ye did not disappoint," the warrior continued, a ghastly grin splitting his pocked face. "Ye fought well, Black Sword. We wondered in the Windwrack whether the stories were embellished, and I see they were not. Ye fight like those old demon dervish champions who near swept over the world. The desert blood is strong in ye." He held out his flagon, and with a slightly embarrassed expression, Azil raised his own glass to toast the storm-sharded.

"You honor me," he said softly. "Both you and the young lord fought well. You must have been surprised, called to battle so soon after arriving as honored guests."

Warden Harath's shard flashed, as if in amusement at Azil's words. "How could I let such an opportunity go past? The chance to test myself against an ancient balewyrm? Such monsters have long since been slain or driven out of the Fangs."

"Or so you think," Azil corrected him. "We thought the same."

"Aye," the storm-sharded said, then took such a long drink from his cup he must have nearly drained it. "Perhaps I should lead an expedition into the deep places. I haven't had such a scrap since I was a boy, hunting drakes in the high passes." He seemed to consider this memory for a moment, his expression distant, and then he turned to Rhenna. Her mistress did not wilt under the force of his attention, but Alia could not stop herself from taking a few steps back.

"And ye, lass? Did the Black Sword tell ye of the great battle fought beneath yer hold today?"

Rhenna met his burning gaze without flinching. "I was there, Warden."

The warrior's mangled face creased in confusion. "Eh? I don't remember ye, girl." Then his eyes widened as realization dawned. "Ah! Ye were the *kenang* that fell after going in with the Black Sword." He looked her up and down. "Ye seem recovered. Damn fool thing, a girl thinking she could contest with a wyrm like that."

"The women of the Windwrack do not fight?" Rhenna asked, and even though Alia could not see her face she imagined what her mistress's expression must look like from her tone.

Liquid sloshed from his flagon as the Warden waved it around, as if dismissing the very notion as absurd. "Of course not. Men rule the realm, women the hearth. We fight so they can enjoy untroubled lives."

"But we are all the Sharded Few," Rhenna said, an edge to her voice. "Our strength does not come from our size. Man or woman, what matters is how many fragments we bear."

The great warrior chuckled, as if she'd made a jest. "A shard may make one strong, but it cannot give ye a warrior's heart. Women are not suited to do battle. This is well known."

"Then whenever your hold goes to war, you are fighting with one armed tied behind your back," Rhenna continued, her tone sharpening further. "Half your army stays at home cooking and cleaning when they are needed on the field. I can understand now why the Windwrack has never conquered the Duskhold, despite being so much larger."

"Most of us do not concern ourselves with household duties," someone said from behind Alia, startling her.

Even though this unfamiliar voice was cracked by age, Alia was still expecting to find an imposing figure when she turned, given that all the other storm-sharded she had seen seemed to have stepped from a skald's song. But the woman behind her was even shorter than Alia and so old that in the Wild she might have been expected to walk out into the forest, lest she become a burden on her family. Her dress was shimmering silver, and bright jewels burned on her fingers and in the weave holding up her steel-grey hair.

Rustlings of movement alerted Alia that everyone around her was bowing deeply, and she hurried to do the same, hoping that she was doing it right. Rhenna had shown her the proper way to show respect, but it still felt unnatural. In the Wild, no one abased themselves before even the strongest war chief or wisest Treesworn. Respect was earned in the far north, not given.

"Lady Khaliva," Azil said formally as he straightened. "It is a great honor to finally meet you. I am Azil Shen, son of Cael Shen."

"The Black Sword," rumbled the hulking Warden. "Imaginary sparring partner of half the Windwrack's Sharded."

"I know who you are, boy," the old woman said, ignoring Harath's words. "And I've met you before."

Azil frowned, his brow drawing down in confusion. "Apologies, my lady. I think I would remember such a thing."

She waved an age-spotted hand. "Not likely. You were but a babe, bawling in the ruins of Derambinal. Cael Shen lifted you from where you lay among the shattered stone and you instantly quieted."

Azil looked unsteadied by her words. "I . . . did not know you fought in the Conquests."

One corner of the old woman's mouth lifted. "As my esteemed champion already explained, the women of the Windwrack do not fight on the battlefield. We contest in more subtle arenas, but we are no less valuable to the fortune of our hold. Indeed, what good is the arm without the head to guide it?"

Azil nodded at this, as if recognizing a point well made. "The Mother of Storms has long been respected in the Duskhold. All who have been blessed by the Shadow know how much the Windwrack has been strengthened by your wise counsel."

"Flattery will get you everywhere, my dear boy," the old woman purred, raising her gem-encrusted hand towards Azil. The Black Sword did not hesitate, sweeping down to kiss a star sapphire the size of a robin's egg.

Rhenna was watching this old woman with wide eyes. She looked awed, as if encountering a legend in the flesh for the first time.

Lady Khaliva also noticed Rhenna's expression, turning towards her after Azil had straightened. "And this must be Rhenna Shen, daughter of the Duskhold's lord. You look like your father, child."

For a moment, Rhenna appeared flustered, and then she dipped into a curtsy. "Yes, *famdhar*."

The Mother of Storms regarded her through narrowed eyes. "I have heard much about you, even in the halls of the Wrack. You and your brother are objects of fascination among the storm-sharded. And now Cael Shen tells me you have long wished to meet me."

Rhenna lowered her head in agreement with the old woman. "Your son rules in Flail, but still your word carries the strength of the Storm. I must admit, I have always been intrigued by this."

"Wisdom does not exist in whoever's bottom sits the throne," the old woman muttered, then waved her hand sharply in a gesture of dismissal.

"Harath. Black Sword. I wish to speak with young Rhenna here in private. Go continue your displays of mutual admiration somewhere else, yes?"

Alia couldn't tell if the Warden of the Windwrack grimaced or smiled at the old woman's words, but he did duck his head in acquiescence to her command. Then he clapped a massive hand on Azil's shoulder and began guiding him away from Rhenna and the Lady Khaliva. But before the Black Sword departed, he turned back and spoke once more to the Mother of Storms.

"I would very much like to hear more about the first time we met."

"Seek me out later, *famdhar*," she replied with a faint smile. The

Lady Khaliva looked satisfied with herself, though the reason was beyond Alia.

After a bow even deeper than the one he had offered earlier, Azil followed the Warden of the Windwrack into the swirl of revelers.

"Interesting brother you have," the old woman mused, staring at where the Black Sword had vanished.

"He is the best man I know," Rhenna replied, then blinked as if surprised by the honesty of this admission.

"An echo of what the Sharded Few once were," Lady Khaliva murmured, then turned once more to Rhenna. "But it's you I want to learn more about, my dear. Come, let us wander somewhere more quiet."

"The sculpture hall will be empty. Would you like to see more of my mother's art?"

Now it was the Lady Khaliva's turn to look surprised. She gestured with a jeweled hand at the closest of the writhing statues scattered about the audience chamber. "These were your mother's work?"

"There are far more interesting pieces elsewhere," Rhenna assured her. "And they are best experienced in silence."

The Mother of Storms inclined her head towards her. "Lead on, child."

Alia stepped after her mistress, but the Lady Khaliva froze her with a glance. "I would prefer it was just the pair of us."

"She is only my handmaiden," Rhenna replied.

The old woman patted her arm. "Humor me, child. I have been too long in the Windwrack's halls, where every servant has more than one master."

Rhenna opened her mouth as if to argue, but then reconsidered and simply nodded. "Very well. Alia, return to my chambers and wait for me there. Tell the servants I want another hot bath waiting for me by the eleventh bell – I still feel a bit soiled by everything that happened today."

"Yes, mistress," Alia murmured, stepping back as her mistress and Lady Khaliva moved towards an archway leading into a darkened gallery empty of other Sharded and white-flame braziers.

She stared after them until they disappeared. Her thoughts were whirling from everything she had just witnessed – there were obviously layers here she could not comprehend, but the comradery the Warden had displayed towards Azil and the interest Lady Khaliva had shown in her mistress had not seemed feigned. Yet Rhenna had said that their two holds were ancient enemies, a hatred deepened by blood-feuds that could not so easily be set aside.

Alia shook her head, telling herself to stop assuming that the ways here mirrored the Wild. Perhaps they cared so little for honor and the approval of their ancestors that they could unclench old enmities instead of holding tight to them forever. That was a good thing, surely?

The ethereal notes swirling in the great chamber suddenly quickened, and a ripple of excitement passed through the Sharded. Alia had to move back hurriedly as the crowd shifted to create an open space, and then several men in the somber garb of the Duskhold stepped forward. They beckoned to those watching, twisting filaments of darkness slithering from their shadows to mimic the gestures they were making with their hands. After a moment, answering tendrils slipped from the crowd to twine with these invitations, followed by women with their arms outstretched. Each man took the hand of his newfound partner, and they began a graceful dance in time with the spare music.

Entranced, Alia watched them drift around in circles until she felt a tap on her shoulder. She turned, expecting to be informed that she had no business being here without her mistress present, but then she gasped when she saw who was standing there.

"Kilian!"

Before she could think of what she was doing, she embraced the smiling young man. He staggered slightly, and it was then she realized he was leaning on a cane.

"I'm sorry," she said, blushing as she stepped back. "It's just . . . rare to see a friendly face here." The other Sharded around them were focused on the dancers, and none seemed to have noticed her impropriety.

Kilian winked at her, still grinning. "I will never refuse a hug from a pretty girl."

"But your leg . . ."

"Is almost like new again," Kilian assured her, lifting his cane from the floor and taking a few steps with barely the hint of a limp. He hooked his arm in hers and led her away from the swelling crowd.

"I had feared you were more injured than I thought," Alia said as they wandered towards the shadowed recesses of the great audience chamber. "I hadn't seen you since we came to the hold."

Kilian shook his head. "No, no. My mother has been taking care of me since my return to the Duskhold, and she can be . . . overprotective." He raised his gleaming black cane by its silver orb and gave it a shake. "If she saw me walking around without this, I'd get a tongue lashing to wake the dead."

They approached one of the strange writhing statues Rhenna had claimed were her mother's work. It was like a man, but stretched thin and covered with curling thorns, and the way it was contorted made it seem like it was bending over to examine her as she passed. The back of her neck prickled, as if it really was watching her from its smooth featureless face, and she looked away with a shudder. What kind of mind could have given birth to such things?

Kilian did not seem affected by the looming statue. "I was saddened to hear you were not chosen by the Shadow," he said, his tone light. "But handmaiden to Rhenna Shen is an enviable position for any Hollow."

Alia held her tongue at first, not wanting to talk about her terrible experience in the Duskhold's abattoir or the circumstances that had led her to where she was now. "She is a kind mistress," she eventually said.

Kilian glanced at her with an arched brow, as if surprised by this statement.

"Truly," Alia assured him, and in response he reached out to pat her arm.

"Oh, I am not disagreeing," he answered. "Rather, I am surprised she has lowered her guard around you so quickly. Rhenna is both very much alike and very different from the rest of our family. The image she cultivates is a reflection of her father . . . but I've known her my entire life, and she is not him."

Alia wanted to ask him more about her mistress, but he abruptly turned to her. "Alia, did Rhenna tell you what happened today to Deryn?"

"A little," she replied, unsettled by the sudden intensity of his attention. "She told me he discovered a monster under the Duskhold, and several of the most powerful Sharded had to fight together to drive it off."

"Indeed," Kilian said, his voice rising slightly in excitement as he continued speaking. "That's the story everyone knows, but there are all sorts of outlandish rumors flying around. Some say my uncle was led to the beast by an avatar of Shadow. Others that the balewyrm could speak and told some ancient secrets to Deryn. I even heard that Azil's life was saved by one of the storm-sharded!" He shook his head in disbelief. "Of course, most are untrue, but I have it on good authority at least that Deryn will be raised to adept. He will be trained by the Black Sword alongside me and Nishi and Rhenna and the rest of the Duskhold's most promising. A month in the hold and already elevated so high! It is unprecedented!" He looked at her expectantly, but she could only stare at him blankly.

"I don't know why, I'm sorry," she said.

Kilian shrugged, giving her a lopsided grin. "Ah! I'm sure the truth will come out soon. Still, it is exciting. Nothing changes for so long here in the Duskhold that it seems like the whole place should be embalmed, and then . . ." Alia jumped as he struck the floor sharply with the end of his cane. He chuckled and shook his head, staring back towards the center of the audience chamber where the revelers were gathered. "The storm-sharded feasting in the Duskhold. My grandfather's ghost must be screaming in the abyss."

He touched her arm lightly. "Alia, I believe we can help each other. You want to keep informed about Deryn, yes? And you wish the best for him?"

"Of course."

"Good. As a fellow adept, I will let you know how his training is progressing, and I promise to help him when I can. And in return, perhaps you could answer questions I have about anything . . . interesting that happens to your mistress. Surely, this seems like a fair agreement?"

After a moment's hesitation, Alia nodded slowly.

"Excellent!" Kilian proclaimed, giving her arm an affectionate squeeze. "You know, it truly is wonderful to see you again."

30

DERYN

BACK IN HIS CHAMBERS, Deryn emptied the contents of his pocket onto the small table where he sometimes took his meals. The dozen shards glimmered against the black grain like stars strewn across the night sky, and the roiling mist-globe dangling from the ceiling seemed to dim slightly, as if the fragments drew some of its radiance away. Deryn's mouth was dry, and he felt his heartbeat quickening. Kilian had been overjoyed to obtain his seventh shard, and here he was staring at twice the number of fragments the Duskhold lord had born. What had Rhenna said . . . *Those shards will turn you into one of the most powerful men in the hold . . . most of the Duskhold would murder you for them, if they could get away with doing so.* Frightening words, assuming they were true. And he suspected they were. Deryn remembered the sneering Sharded with the crimson tattoos who had threatened Alia – surely such a man would not hesitate to kill him and take these fragments. Cael Shen said he was to be protected and that Deryn was a valuable asset for the hold . . . but could he really rely on the whims of the Duskhold's master? What if he decided Deryn was not worthy of such power and that these fragments would be better served in the hands of a more ruthless Sharded?

He needed to wield their power as quickly as possible. Then it would not be so simple to take from him what Fate had given. And once he bore such strength . . . he could leave this place, strike out into the world with a chance of evading the hunters who would follow. Menochus's betrayal had served as a needed reminder that the Duskhold was not where he belonged. He could never share the values of those that dwelled here. Never.

Deryn tore his eyes from the scattered shards and looked about for the little shadow-man. He'd been half-expecting the elemental to eventually vanish, returning to whatever abyss it had sprung from, but this had not happened yet. The shadow-man was chasing a large, many-legged insect around the room, and Deryn watched until the undulating little creature disappeared into a crack in the stone wall. The shadow-man did not break stride, dwindling as it squeezed itself into the tiny crevice, but after a moment later it reappeared without its quarry.

"What are you?" Deryn murmured, but the elemental did not reply.

His hope for answers lay in the library. In those endless rows of books, there must be some knowledge about elementals. When he had a free moment, he would seek out the Archivist and ask for help.

But first he had other things to do.

Deryn turned back to the glittering shards. His hand crept inside his robes, and he brushed the cold fragment sunk into his own chest. The memory of how the Shadow had embedded this shard inside him was hazy – he remembered floating in darkness, the feel of something sharp and hard against his hand, and then a sliver of ice had pierced his fingertip and slid through his body's pathways to settle near his heart. But apparently merely touching these fragments would not begin the same process again, as otherwise it would have happened when he'd first pulled the shards from the skeleton.

Perhaps it was simpler than he feared. Keeping his eyes on the shards, Deryn shrugged out of his robes and tossed them aside. He glanced down at his own fragment and the black web radiating out from where it was lodged. Concentrating, Deryn turned within himself, pushing the *ka* flowing from the shard outward through these distended veins. He grasped it easily, and a tingling euphoria flooded him – not long ago, attempting this had been like trying to hold on to a writhing serpent, but now the seas inside him had been gentled by the force of his will.

Which meant he was ready for another shard.

He thought.

He hoped.

What would happen if he was not? Kilian had spoken of shard-sickness, when one of the Sharded Few tried to absorb a fragment before they were ready. Deryn couldn't remember him saying what this entailed. Death? Nausea? Or would his body merely reject the shard, spitting it out like a baby letting its mother know it was full?

Probably nothing that benign. Death, however, was an equally unlikely outcome. Deryn's hand hovered over one of the shards on the table. Why was he hesitating? He was ready. He was sure of it.

His fingers pinched the fragment, and a shock of cold traveled up his arm. He thought he sensed an echoing pulse come from his own shard, but he couldn't be sure. Slowly, he lifted the dusky fragment, examining it from every angle. Outside of the light seeping from its depths, it truly looked just like a tiny chunk of crystal. The heart of a god? Deryn snorted in disbelief.

Then he sighed, knowing he should stop hesitating. Swallowing back his nervousness, Deryn slowly brought the shard closer to his own fragment. The coldness where his flesh bordered the shard in his chest intensified and a prickling numbness spread, making his heart stutter. To be honest, it almost seemed like the shard he held was trying to pull away from his fingers, drawn like iron to the lodestone embedded in his body. As if it wanted to join with him.

The fragments touched, and the sea inside Deryn erupted into a frothing frenzy.

He screamed as he was pulled beneath the churning waves, swallowed by the dark and cold.

Deryn returned to himself with a shuddering gasp. The mist-globe hanging above him blurred, then sharpened once more. He was lying on the floor, cool stone beneath him, his head ringing.

What had happened?

Deryn coughed, his trembling hand gently exploring the ache in his chest. From the pain, he expected the stickiness of dried blood, or maybe even a gaping hole, but his fingers found unbroken flesh sealed around his shard.

A shard that was bigger than he remembered.

It all came rushing back then, and he mewled softly, rolling onto his side. The searing agony after the fragments had touched, the sensation of something alien burrowing its way into his body as it carved a home inside him . . . flooding him with power and strange, stuttering images he couldn't understand.

A skeletal king in ragged finery seated on a throne of amber.

Colors, pulsing in the sky above an endless sweep of grass.

The cries of a babe as it opened golden eyes.

And then they were gone. He reached for them, but they receded, dissipating like smoke in the wind. What had just happened? It had been like he'd glimpsed moments of a life he'd never lived.

Which . . . maybe he had.

The scenes were already gone, yet a vague sadness lingered, something he could not exactly define. His eyes prickled with tears, but it was not from the pain.

Groaning, Deryn sat up. He was naked, sheathed in a cold sweat, and he had a sudden strong urge to wrap himself in the heavy wool of the Duskhold. He reached for where he'd thrown aside his robes, but then froze.

The elemental was crouched an arm-length away, staring at him intently.

And it had grown.

Deryn blinked, trying to decide if this was just his imagination. No – it was definitely larger. Before when it had stood it had been about the height of his hand from his fingertips to his wrist. Now it was bigger than that despite its legs being bent and its body hunched forward. If it straightened, it would be taller than his forearm was long. It had nearly doubled in size. He swallowed, unnerved by these developments.

Had it grown because of him? That would mean they were connected somehow. Which made sense, he supposed . . . But would it get bigger every time he added to his shard? He thought of the eleven other fragments on his table. If the elemental grew twice as large every time . . .

one

A dry whisper, the flutter of moth wings.

"Did you speak?" Deryn asked, hoarse with shock.

The shadow-man did not answer.

"Talk to me, if you can," Deryn commanded. "Tell me what you are. What you want."

The silence lengthened. The shadow-man finally rose from its crouch – and it was much taller now, there was no doubt – and from his sitting position, Deryn leaned towards it, certain it was about to speak again.

A rapping at his door startled both of them. The elemental melted in the blink of an eye into a puddle of darkness, then quickly slid across the room to join with the shadows pooled under his bed. Deryn stared after it, bewildered by this reaction.

The loud knocking grew into an even louder pounding. Shaking his head to clear it, Deryn pushed himself to his feet, swaying as a wave of vertigo hit him. He had to steady himself with his hand on the table, very nearly bringing himself into contact with more of the shards. That thought made his stomach twist and the ache in his chest intensify.

"I'm coming," Deryn mumbled. He took a lurching step towards the door, then realized he was still naked and detoured to scoop his robes from the floor. Hurriedly, he dressed, wincing as the fabric settled over his pulsing shard.

The shards. Whoever this was at the door, he shouldn't let them see his treasures. If knowledge of what had fallen into his lap flew around the Duskhold, he might find himself in danger from the ambitious. With that thought, he swept the glittering fragments into the pocket of his robes, then checked to make sure their glow could not be seen through the dark cloth.

When he finally opened the door, he was not surprised to find Kaliss there, as he had become very familiar with her lack of patience. What did surprise him was her appearance. She looked like she hadn't slept in days, her face drawn and haggard, with dark circles beneath her eyes. One of her arms was in a sling and mostly wrapped with bandages, and a bruise purpled her left temple. Despite all this, her jaw was still set and the gaze focused on Deryn as sharp as always.

"You look terrible," she said.

"You look worse," he replied.

She snorted. "You apparently haven't seen yourself yet."

They stared at each other for a long moment, neither speaking. A silence born of exhaustion, Deryn realized, as if they'd both just experienced a trying ordeal. It struck him like a thunderbolt from the blue that it was the *same* trying ordeal.

"You have a new shard," they both said, then blinked at each other in surprise.

"So it's true," Kaliss murmured. "You did find something other than a monster on your Delve."

"And you claimed a shard that had been hidden."

The edges of her lips lifted in satisfaction. "Shards."

He sucked in his breath. A single novice returning with multiple shards was a rare feat, and assured Kaliss a place among the Duskhold's adepts. "How many?"

"Three," she said, and he heard the pride in her voice.

Three shards, when there had only been five hidden in the tunnels. Menochus certainly had one – a pang of hurt accompanied this thought – and that meant only one other novice had returned from the Delve with a shard.

She had clearly suffered for her prize, though. Deryn gestured at her arm, remembering the corpses of the creatures scattered about the tablet where a shard had been placed. "Did the centipede-things do that?"

She raised her arm slightly, as if to show the injury was not that severe. "Yes. Vicious beasts. I thought nothing short of a sword could pierce our flesh, even though we had only a single shard, but I was wrong. Their mandibles would have shredded armor."

"You earned your reward," Deryn said. "Both during the Delve and in all the work you did to be the best of the novices."

Something in her expression shifted at his words, a softening that he hadn't seen before. After a moment in which she seemed at a loss for words, she blinked and swallowed.

"And you. The Duskhold is buzzing with rumors about what happened. Cael Shen himself driving away a monster *you* woke in the depths. The Shadow and Storm fighting side by side. Someone even said you summoned a shadow elemental to bring a message to the Sharded." She shook her head, the corner of her mouth rising again in wry disbelief. "Though surely the actual story is far less fantastic."

Deryn wondered if he should truly be talking to Kaliss about what had happened. Cael Shen had said he should hide the number of shards he had obtained but hadn't forbidden him from speaking about anything else that had occurred.

"No, you've got the gist of it," he told her and didn't even try to stifle his smile as her jaw fell open.

"What? An *elemental*?"

Deryn jerked a thumb over his shoulder, indicating the chamber behind him. "Yes. It's in there."

Kaliss almost lunged forward, shouldering past him to look wildly around his room. "Where?"

Deryn shrugged. "Under the bed, I think. It seems to be scared of you."

"Scared of *me*?" Kaliss said incredulously.

"I have no idea why. I heard it hopped right up on Cael Shen's throne, and then it had no problem returning to me when I was hiding in a cavern from a hungry balewyrm. But you . . ." The humor in his tone caused her to shoot him a withering stare. "You are apparently far more frightening."

He grunted as she speared his side with her elbow. "You don't know what I am capable of," she muttered.

"To be fair, the thing . . . changed after I merged my second shard. That might be why it's feeling skittish right now."

Kaliss took a few steps into his room, then crouched down to peer under the bed. "Can you get it to come out?"

"I don't know," Deryn replied dubiously. "I don't think so. It seems very . . . independent." He bent down to join Kaliss, concentrating on the darkness. Was the shadow-man still in there, staring back at him?

"Um," he began, then cleared his throat. "Uh, hello? Little fellow, will you come out? This is my friend. She seems scary, I know, but she's really not all that bad." He danced sideways out of the range of another jabbed elbow.

They waited, but nothing crept forth. After a little while, Kaliss straightened, her disappointment evident. "We have to go. I was told to bring you quickly, and we've already wasted quite a bit of time."

"Oh?" Deryn realized he didn't even know what bell it was. How long had he been unconscious after merging his second shard? He didn't feel hungry, but then again, the mere thought of food made his stomach roil. "Are we late for a lesson with Saelus?"

Kaliss glanced at him in surprise. "You didn't know? You're an adept now – we both are. It is a great honor – only *kenang* and the *sardor* with the greatest potential are invited to become adepts. Azil is our new teacher, and today something special is planned. An exhibition. I don't think we'll have to take part, but some adepts of the Duskhold will contest with the storm-sharded. Come, let's talk more on the way. I'd hate to be late for this."

"So, did you merge all three of the shards you found?" Deryn asked as Kaliss led them on a path that ascended through the layers of the Duskhold.

"No," she said as she paused for a moment to catch her breath on the seemingly endless spiraling steps. Deryn slumped against the wall, grateful for the momentary reprieve. Adding fragments to one's shard was far more physically debilitating than Kilian had made it appear on the road to Kething's Cross.

"Just one," Kaliss continued. "It will be some time before I attempt another."

"Because it's so exhausting?" Deryn asked, stooping to rub his aching calves.

She rested her hairless head against the stone of the wall, closing her eyes. "Have you tried to channel since you added to yours?"

"No."

"Do it now."

Deryn complied, concentrating on his shard and the pulses of *ka* it was pushing through his body's pathways.

Kaliss chuckled when she saw his immediate grimace. "Disheartening, yes?"

"I'm back to the beginning," he murmured. The raging tempest he'd gradually quieted over the course of the last month had swelled once more, with much of the increased energy being expelled by his enlarged shard leaking away to dissipate before it could strengthen his body.

"We'll both need to spend some time channeling before we're ready to add any more shards," she said, her lip curling as she shook her head. "Which will be hard. I'm not one to wait when the path to more power is right there in front of me. But I have to be patient and channel my pathways smooth before I do it again. Saelus spoke of what happened to Sharded who tried to merge too many shards too quickly – sickness, madness, even death."

Deryn considered this as they resumed their climb. He should try his best to merge as many of the fragments as possible before word got out about what he'd discovered in the balewyrm's lair, but he also didn't want to risk his sanity or his life. He would have to spend all his free time channeling so he could prepare himself for another shard.

"Ah, here," Kaliss said, and Deryn glanced past her to see that they'd reached the top of the stairs. A low doorway led outside, and the searing blue of the sky made Deryn wince after being within the darkened halls for so long.

They stumbled onto the Duskhold's roof and looked around, blinking. A windowless tower of black stone rose in front of them, flat as a great drum – it wasn't as tall as some of the other slender minarets piercing the sky, but it was by far the broadest. A few figures were climbing the steps clinging to the outside of the tower, and from elsewhere on the roof a Black Disc suddenly lifted into the sky and drifted towards its top.

"Is that where we're going?" Deryn asked, his heart sinking as he quickly estimated the number of steps.

"Yes, unfortunately," Kaliss replied with a heavy sigh.

Deryn decided half-way up that he was very much finished with stairs, and when it came time to descend, he would beg transportation on a Black Disc. He'd even brave the shadow-realm Nishi had pulled him through after the Shadow had granted him his shard if it meant he could arrive back in his chambers without putting his foot on another step.

During the ascent he'd thought of nothing except how miserable he felt, but when he finally arrived at the top that was all instantly forgotten. The crowd gathered on the roof of the tower was not what he had been expecting. More than half were dressed in the black robes of the Duskhold, and Deryn noticed several familiar faces – Azil, blue light playing along the length of the Darkbringer, and beside him was Jaliska, the battlemaster who had instructed the novices in the combat arts. Nishi and Rhenna were there as well, though not standing near each other, the former grinning and the latter glowering, as was usual. The heir to the Duskhold had not escaped his battle with the balewyrm unscathed – one of Nishi's arms was in a sling, though the injury did not seem to be affecting his good cheer. Among the dozen other shadow-sharded was the adept with the crimson tattoos and the cruel smile who had threatened Alia and also a familiar figure leaning on cane, who waved jauntily when he caught sight of Deryn.

"Hello, hello!" Kilian cried. "So good to see you, my friend!"

Heads among the shadow-sharded turned to regard them at this, several with more than passing interest. Deryn wasn't surprised by the flush of affection he felt at seeing Kilian again – the shadow-sharded had shown him more kindness on their journey to the Duskhold than he had experienced over the last month while training in the hold.

"Friend?" Kaliss murmured in disbelief. "You're 'friends' with the son of Joras Shen?"

"We drank firewine together," Deryn muttered out of the corner of his mouth.

Kaliss sighed loudly, and he was sure he could hear her eyes rolling.

He ignored her, mesmerized by the sight of the other group gathered up here. The storm-sharded were resplendent, as colorful as the shadow-sharded were drab, attired in shimmering dresses and bright doublets trimmed with gold and silver brocade. A trio of beautiful maidens – one dark-haired, one fair-haired, and another with no hair at all – were standing together, their delicate hands raised to cover their mouths as they whispered among themselves. The men were mostly young and dashing, broad-shouldered and blue-eyed, hands resting lightly on the hilts of jeweled swords. One was very different, towering over the others with a scowling, scarred visage that would have sent children scurrying for their mother's skirts. Something on his face was gleaming, and Deryn realized in surprise that this warrior's shard was embedded where his left eye should be. It was disquieting to see such a display of power – all the Sharded Few that Deryn had encountered before had kept their fragment hidden, and he supposed this was because they thought concealing their true strength gave them an advantage. But this was the storm-sharded with the crackling warhammer who had fought beside Azil against the balewyrm, and he was evidently not worried about being challenged.

"Look at you, my boy!" Kilian cried.

Deryn dragged his gaze with some effort from the Windwrack's delegation to the Sharded who had rescued him.

"Already up and about after your ordeal! I knew from the moment I laid eyes on you that there was great potential. Great potential!" Kilian clapped Deryn warmly on the shoulder, staggering him. After the climb to get here, he felt like a strong wind might knock him over.

Kilian turned to Kaliss, who had lowered her eyes respectfully. "And this must be the Ashasai girl Saelus is always talking about. Kaliss, is it?"

"Yes, Lord Shen," she murmured, still not looking up.

"Kilian, please," the shadow-sharded said, putting his finger under her chin and then lifting her head so she was forced to meet his gaze. "With your successful Delve, you've been elevated. We are both adepts now, Kaliss, though of course I am *kenang* and you are *sardor*." He frowned slightly, as if something had just occurred to him. "Though that does not mean we are all friends. Only the most powerful and ambitious of the younger Sharded are allowed to train under Azil. Your success among the novices was impressive, but all the adepts achieved similar results in past years."

"I understand," Kaliss replied, and though Deryn heard the same respect in her voice from a moment ago, now she held his gaze.

Kilian noticed this as well. "Good girl," he said, flashing her the smile Deryn had seen many times before, the one both infuriating and charming.

"What's going on here?" Deryn asked as a dark cloud no larger than a small boat crested the top of the tower. It dissolved as soon as it had drifted over stone, a handsome young man with sandy hair hopping down to join his fellows. This was the other storm-sharded who had descended into the cavern alongside the scarred giant, and Deryn guessed that the jeweled scabbard at his side held the golden sword he'd wielded against the balewyrm.

"There is to be a friendly competition between the warriors of

Storm and Shadow," Kilian said, his eyes also fixed on the recent arrival. "No shards may be claimed by the victor, nor will any use of lethal force be countenanced. This is a time-honored ritual to strengthen the bond between holds when treating with each other."

"By fighting?" Deryn said skeptically.

Kilian shrugged. "It is what the holds do best."

"How is the winner determined?"

"The two most senior of the holds in attendance – Azil for the Duskhold and Warden Harath the Windwrack – have already decided on the rules, and they will tell us when we are ready to commence. It might be to first blood, or a spoken surrender. Always the contest will end if one of the Sharded is forced from the ring."

"What ring?" Deryn said, but as soon as he uttered the question he saw it: a white circle perhaps a hundred paces across had been painted onto the dark stone of the tower's roof. The two groups of Sharded had stayed outside its boundaries, milling along its edge.

Kaliss's gaze had been roaming the crowds, a slight frown on her lips. "Excuse my impertinence Lord . . . ah, Kilian, but where is the Mother of Storms? I heard she led this delegation."

"Attending to the reason she's here, I'm sure," Kilian replied. "She has traveled a long way to meet with Cael Shen."

"Why *are* the storm-sharded here?" Deryn asked.

Kilian shrugged. "Believe me, there's been quite a bit of speculation. Of those here, perhaps only Azil and the warden know the true reason for her coming. Most likely it is to sign a treaty between the holds – trade of iron for salt, perhaps, or a formal declaration of peace. Whatever it is, the Ember will not be pleased. The bile between Flame and Storm still flows hot and bitter, and old Lord Char will be incensed when he hears the Mother of Storms visited the Duskhold."

Kilian blew out his cheeks. "I, for one, welcome this new era, if that's what this meeting portends. Lady Khaliva is a relic from an earlier time, when the warriors of our holds shed each other's blood regularly. But that time has passed, and only a few hold tight to those old grievances. The alliance we were forced into when the emir began his wars of conquest set the foundation for what I hope they are building now."

"And we are going to do our part by fighting each other," Deryn murmured as Azil and the hulking Harath strode out into the center of the ring.

"An exhibition only," Kilian assured him. "No prizes will be awarded to the victor, and no lives lost today. For which the warriors of the Duskhold should feel grateful."

"Why is that?" Kaliss whispered as the conversations died around them, the attention of the gathered Sharded settling on the Black Sword and the Windwrack Warden.

Kilian lifted his cane and swept it through the air, squinting into the bright sun. "There is a reason the adepts train on the Drum Tower," he murmured softly. "It is easy to draw upon the darkness down below, but up here there are few shadows. Beckoning and employing our talents is much harder than in the Duskhold, and while it is useful for our training . . . today we will be at a disadvantage facing these storm-sharded."

Azil struck the stone with Darkbringer, sending blue energy crackling the length of the staff. "Fellow Sharded, we are gathered here today for the ritual testing of strength. Our two holds have long been locked in enmity, but a new age is dawning. There is much our realms can offer each other if we exorcise the ghosts of the past. And in that spirit, we have come together for a competition to demonstrate our respect for the martial prowess of the other." He paused for a moment, glancing over at the scarred giant looming over him. "Yesterday I fought side by side with your Warden, and together we defeated a monster of the old world. Never did I imagine I would stand with a hero of the Windwrack, but we showed that we can be mighty allies. Storm and Shadow united will strike fear in the hearts of our enemies and bring a lasting peace to the north!"

A ragged cheer rose from some of the watching Sharded, but Kilian snorted softly.

"But who would those enemies be, if we are friends now?" he

muttered, so softly that Deryn wasn't sure if he was meant to have heard.

The scarred giant beside Azil raised his hand for silence. When the crowd quieted, he motioned towards the storm-sharded. "Warriors of the Wrack! Who will be the first to test their strength and honor in the circle?"

Almost immediately, a young man stepped forward, so quickly that he must have been waiting for this moment.

"I would fight!" the storm-sharded proclaimed loudly, excitement and eagerness writ clear in his face. He had the look of a warrior, Deryn had to admit – tall and broad-shouldered, with hair so fair it was nearly white. Across the forest-green of his doublet pranced a golden stag, and he wasn't the only one among the storm-sharded to wear this sigil.

"Willem Jorel," Warden Harath rumbled. "Second son of Lord Pelinor Jorel. Tell me, lad, how many shards do you bear?"

"Five," the boy said, drawing himself up proudly. "I am *sardor*."

The huge man nodded at this, then turned to the shadow-sharded. "The challenge comes from one with five shards. Is there a *sardor* warrior from the Duskhold who would step into the ring with him?"

The crowd from the Duskhold shifted, and there were some heated whisperings that suggested several of the shadow-sharded wished to face the lord's son. Finally, a thin boy with striking silver eyes seemed to win the argument, striding forward boldly into the ring as several others around his age grimaced in disappointment. Deryn felt a pang of sadness at the sight of the boy's unusual eyes, as they made him think of Menochus.

"Chal En'ok, of the Red River tribe," Azil announced. "From the Wild beyond the Firemounts, and five-sharded as well."

"The challenge is made and accepted," Harath rumbled, then strode across the ring to stand just outside the boundary with his great arms folded. Azil went to a spot opposite him, meeting the Warden's glower with a look of calm equanimity. The two young challengers hesitated for a moment, as if waiting for further instruction, but then, when none were forthcoming, they also took up positions in the circle facing each other.

"This will be a boring match," Kilian whispered. "But it is always the young and foolish who are most eager to throw themselves into the ring."

"How do you know the fight won't be exciting?" Kaliss asked softly.

"Five shards means that almost certainly neither warrior has attained a second tier talent yet," Kilian replied. "And those are always crowd-pleasers. This will be a fight to see whose battlemaster has trained them better."

The two warriors had gone still, and the shadow-sharded boy from the Wild had even closed his eyes, his face going slack as if he was focused completely on something other than what was about to happen.

"What's he doing?" Deryn asked, afraid that the fight would begin and the storm-sharded might land the first blow before his opponent had roused himself.

"They are both channeling," Kilian replied. "Taking a moment to smooth their pathways, tighten their control of the energy that infuses them with strength. Such control will also heighten their reflexes and make what talents they have more formidable."

Azil brought his staff down in another ringing strike, and the Wild boy's eyes snapped open as the storm-sharded shuffled closer in a stance that looked vaguely similar to one Jaliska had taught the novices, knees bent and fists raised. The Duskhold warrior settled back in a defensive crouch, waiting for his opponent to reach him.

The attack when it came was blindingly fast. A half-dozen punches thrown in combinations, all caught and turned away by open palms or raised arms. Deryn could hear the thwack of flesh being struck with vicious strength, but the shadow-sharded's face gave no indication that the blows caused pain. He did give ground, moving backwards smoothly, but rather than press the attack the Windwrack lord hesitated, as if he suspected he was being baited to overextend himself.

Deryn had seen the smaller Jaliska easily handle the largest novices when sparring, but still it was so strange to see a much slighter boy absorbing the strikes of someone bigger without flinching. Muscles and mass were of course irrelevant to the Sharded Few – all that truly mattered was the number of fragments lodged in one's flesh and how well the warrior had learned to wield their power.

After a few moments of consideration, the storm-sharded decided this was no trap, and he again lunged forward. The Duskhold adept brought his hands up to intercept the blow, but this time a crackling white energy flared around the fist of the Windwrack warrior. There was a flash and a crack like thunder, and the shadow-sharded was hurled backwards. He landed hard, and Deryn thought for sure would not rise again, but almost immediately he rolled back to his feet, though he was visibly swaying and wisps of smoke were rising from his blackened palm.

The storm-sharded's lip curled as he stalked forward, his fist still blazing. Rather than retreat, the Duskhold warrior flexed the hand that had caught the blow, and as his fingers spread wide something sprouted from the center of his charred palm. A long, whip-like tendril emerged, writhing in the air like a living thing. The Windwrack boy slowed his approach, his confident sneer vanishing.

"Arm of the Abyss," Kilian murmured. "Very common first-tier talent. So searingly cold, flesh will go numb at the touch."

The tendril began swaying like a hooded serpent preparing to strike, and as the storm-sharded approached it suddenly lashed out. The boy gave a cry of pain and reeled back, clutching at his shoulder where a swatch of the fine green fabric had been torn away, the flesh beneath turned a ghastly white. Emboldened, the shadow-sharded lunged after his opponent, the tendril slithering through the air before him. Just before it struck, the Windwrack warrior's crackling hand flashed out and caught the filament of darkness. Pain shivered his face, but he did not release his grip on the abyssal arm, instead pulling on it hard. The shadow-sharded was sent stumbling forward, clearly surprised, and the Windwrack boy stepped forwards and slammed his hand that was not blazing with power into his opponent's chin.

The Duskhold adept collapsed, the serpentine tendril evaporating. A disappointed groan rose from the watching shadow-sharded, but Azil showed no emotion as he struck the ground again with his staff, sending blue energy crawling across the stone.

"Willem Jorel takes the match," he said in a voice loud enough that it could be heard over the cheering of the Windwrack warriors.

The victor returned in triumph to his fellows, while a few Duskhold adepts rushed into the ring to help the dazed boy to his feet.

"A good start," Kilian murmured. "Quite the feat, catching the Arm of the Abyss with a Blazing Fist. That storm-sharded has promise."

"We won't have to fight today, will we?" Deryn asked, gesturing at Kaliss. The thought of being forced into the circle in his weakened state was more than a little concerning.

"No, no, no," Kilian assured him as a new challenger stepped from the shadow-sharded. It was a young woman with short, blood-red hair teased up into spikes, her silver eyes narrowed in anger.

"Ah, of course," Kilian mused, sounding like he was talking to himself. "Chal's sister Pand. I wonder why Azil is letting her try to avenge her brother's defeat. Never a good idea to allow emotional warriors into the ring . . . unless he wants her to learn a lesson about self-control."

"What if I'm challenged?" Deryn pressed, trying to get some assurance that he wouldn't be called on.

"Do not worry, my boy. There are no newly Sharded among the Windwrack delegation, which means there is no one suitable for you to duel with. They all have four or five shards, at least, and you have only . . ." He stepped back for a moment, looking Deryn up and down. "Mother Dark, did you recently merge another shard?"

Deryn swallowed. He hadn't wanted it common knowledge that he had found a cache of shards in the balewyrm's lair, but he also knew he wouldn't be able to keep the knowledge hidden for very long. He nodded, his hand drifting to where his robes covered his still-aching chest.

"Then you did find something down there," Kilian murmured, studying him with appraising eyes. "And I understand now why you were elevated to adept."

They both jumped as a blinding light washed over them, followed by the rumble of thunder. Kilian shook himself, his easy smile returning as he shifted his attention back to the ring.

"Come, let us watch the fights."

The enraged girl with the spiky hair defeated her opponent with ease, pummeling a doughy Windwrack boy across the ring before shoving him contemptuously outside its border. She had then stood over him, her silver eyes flashing as he mumbled for mercy – which was unnecessary since he had left the circle – yet it had seemed like she was going to strike him again until Azil had commanded her in a harsh tone to return to the other shadow adepts. She had, though not before throwing the Black Sword a rebellious glance. This earned a low whistle from Kilian, as if he couldn't believe she would dare such a thing.

A half dozen more fights followed, with each hold winning three. Deryn saw the Arm of the Abyss and the Blazing Fist several more times – apparently, they were two of the more common first-tier talents – but not all the powers displayed were attacking in nature. One shadow-sharded caused his opponent to become stuck, as if he was sunk to his waist in mud, and after a moment Deryn realized he was being held in place by his own shadow. Another Duskhold warrior had tossed a sphere of darkness that unfolded into a glistening net, and while the surprised storm-sharded had been struggling to free himself, he'd rushed up and knocked him out with a blow to the head.

Excited murmurings rose from the shadow-sharded around Deryn with every Windwrack power displayed. One of the storm-sharded had tossed a javelin of lightning that had caught his opponent flush in the chest and sent him flying outside the ring; another summoned a sphere of crackling energy to keep a shadow-sharded's glistening whip of darkness at bay. One storm talent actually resulted in quite a few guffaws from the watching Duskhold adepts – the Windwrack warrior had conjured up a thick black cloud, then dropped it on the shadow-sharded across from him. He must have thought it would blind his opponent, but moments after rushing into the cloud, he was the one stumbling out clutching at his bleeding nose. Somehow he hadn't realized that the shadow-sharded could see in darkness.

"Have there been any second tier talents?" Kaliss asked as a smug young man from the Windwrack sauntered from the ring, leaving a Shadow adept doubled over gasping behind him. She had watched all the fights with rapt attention, as if memorizing every detail of what was happening.

"No," Kilian answered, sounding somewhat disappointed. "Only the weakest have fought here today. Perhaps the stronger and wiser *kenang* do not want to risk their reputation – oh, what's this?"

A tremor had gone through the crowd of storm-sharded as the latest challenger stepped forward. It was the handsome young man who had arrived late riding his own cloud, the one who had fought the balewyrm. The sigil on his azure doublet was a golden sword, its jagged blade forged from lightning.

"Interesting," Kilian mused.

"Is that him?" asked Kaliss. "The heir? I heard he accompanied his grandmother..."

"Yes," Kilian murmured back. "Lessian Khaliva. Eldest son of Bailen, lord of the Windwrack." He frowned. "But what could he gain by stepping into the circle today?"

"Sharded!" the young man cried, his gaze sweeping all those gathered atop the tower. "These have been a few days to remember. We have feasted and dueled, even fought side by side." He turned to smile at Azil, and the Black Sword dipped his head in reply. "This is the start of a new age in the north. The actions of our ancestors led us to see each other as enemies, but we can choose to release old griev-ances and start anew. What say you, Lord Shen?"

More mutterings rippled through the watchers, but this time mostly among the shadow-sharded. Nishi emerged from that crowd, his smile just as broad as the one worn by the Windwrack lord. Deryn felt a pang of unease seeing it. The heir to the Duskhold had casually discussed murdering Alia for a minor transgression while smiling in just the same manner.

"Lord Khaliva," Nishi replied loudly, "you honor us with your words and your vision of the future. Our elders are meeting now to discuss peace, but it is here, within the circle, that the first real bonds will be forged between our holds."

The sandy-haired young man nodded enthusiastically. "Indeed, Lord Shen. Well said. I only wish you had not been injured during the battle yesterday. I would have dearly loved to test myself against the best under the Shadow."

Nishi raised his arm in its sling, as if to make sure everyone knew Lessian spoke true. "Indeed, Lord Khaliva. Another time. Perhaps soon I will lead a delegation to the Windwrack and we might –"

"I will accept your challenge."

All eyes turned to Rhenna, who had stepped forward to stand beside her brother. Nishi's face went slack with surprise, then for the briefest of moments twisted in anger before his smile returned. He was not the only one upset by his sister's brazenness. Harsh mutterings rose from the crowd of storm-sharded, but Rhenna did not waver. Deryn had noticed a similar reaction whenever another female Sharded from the Duskhold answered Azil's invitation, and the first time it had happened, Kilian had informed him that in Flail women were not allowed to fight. Now the complaints were far louder though, as if this challenge had insulted their young lord.

The Windwrack heir stared at her blankly for a moment, as if trying to place her. Then he blinked, evidently realizing who she must be. "Ah. Lady Shen." He bowed smoothly, and when he straight-ened Deryn noticed a faint crinkling about his eyes, as if he was trying his best not to show his amusement. "I am glad to see you have recovered from your fall."

Scattered laughter followed this. Rhenna's expression did not waver, but Nishi's face colored. He turned to her sharply. "Withdraw your challenge, sister. Lord Khaliva desired a contest between heirs."

"I am also an heir here," Rhenna countered dispassionately. "If anything were to happen to you, stewardship of the Duskhold would fall to me. Our father was also born second, if you remember."

For a long moment, the two children of Cael Shen stared daggers at each other, and then Azil spoke.

"I will allow it. Such a match would be a fitting end to our contest today."

Nishi's jaw tightened, but he did not argue with his teacher. Instead, he turned abruptly away, shouldering his way deeper into the crowd of shadow-sharded.

With his departure, all eyes turned to see what Lessian would do. The heir to the Windwrack looked bewildered by this turn of events, and he glanced over to his scowling Warden for guidance. The scarred warrior's face was flushed, his lone eye smoldering beneath his heavy brow, but he did not voice a protest.

With no help forthcoming, the Windwrack lord shifted his attention to Azil.

"I have never struck a woman."

Azil regarded him impassively. "It is our tradition that women fight alongside the men. Rhenna has trained her entire life as a warrior – I will not insult her or the ways of the Duskhold by forcing her to step back." A shimmer of blue light passed up the Darkbringer. "However, I cannot stop you from withdrawing your challenge."

The easy confidence that Lessian had radiated not so long ago had now completely vanished. He looked shaken, as if events had slipped from his grip, but then something flickered in his face, and he nodded slightly.

"Very well," he said, sounding resigned. "I would be honored to contest with you, Lady Shen." He bowed again, just as deep as before.

Rhenna strode into the ring, and though she said nothing, Deryn saw the ghost of a satisfied smile. She came to stand across from Lessian, adopting a stance with her weight on her back foot and her hands raised.

The indignant murmurings from the storm-sharded subsided, the sudden silence so heavy that Deryn could hear the distant tolling of the great bell within the Duskhold that marked the passage of the day.

Darkbringer cracked against the stone, and the two warriors exploded into motion. Any trace of reluctance in Lessian was now gone as he lunged forward with startling speed, his fist blazing with white-hot energy. He crossed the distance between them in an eyeblink, far faster than any of the other combatants today had moved, but Rhenna was ready, and she raised her arm to block his strike. A black carapace shimmered into existence just before the crackling punch struck her, sheathing her forearm. The sound of Lessian's fist striking the substance was like a hammer crashing down upon an anvil, but while cracks fractured the shadowy vambrace, it did not shatter, and both fighters stepped back from each other. Rhenna's expression was exultant, while Lessian's eyes had widened in surprise.

"Ghost Chitin," Kilian whispered. "One of my own first-tier talents. Useful."

Rhenna made a beckoning gesture, and tendrils of darkness slithered across the stone towards her. Deryn gasped when he felt his own shadow tug free and join the throng. The Windwrack warrior frowned, bringing his hands up in what looked like a defensive posture, but the serpents of darkness ignored him as they rushed to Rhenna. They lifted into the air when they reached the shadow-sharded, forming a sphere that quickly blocked the sight of her. Deryn was expecting some attack to be launched from the depths of this darkness, but almost immediately it began to dissipate. When it cleared, five identical Rhennas were revealed, all having adopted a slightly different fighting stance.

"Mirror Wraiths," Kilian informed Deryn. "One of her two second-tier talents."

Lessian did not seem to be concerned about finding out he was suddenly outnumbered. One corner of his mouth lifted derisively, as if he was unimpressed by the illusion. Then he vanished in a brilliant flash of light.

"Silver Shrike!" Deryn gasped, blinking away the spots in his vision.

The Windwrack warrior was suddenly standing in the middle of the wraith-Rhennas, all of whom recoiled at his re-appearance. Lessian wasted no time, lashing out at the closest copy. His fist disappeared into her with no apparent effect, and even though he must have known this was a possibility, he still lurched forward, unbalanced. Strikes rained down from the other versions, and one certainly was real, as he was driven to a knee by a heavy blow across his back. The mirror wraiths of Rhenna closed around him, but then another blinding burst like a lightning bolt erupted and Lessian was standing outside their circle. He slammed his hand into the back of a Rhenna, and all the images staggered similarly. The one he had struck whirled around, executing a dizzying combination of punches, most of which the Windwrack warrior deflected. One did graze his chin, snapping his head back. Rhenna pressed this advantage by trying to clout the side of his head with a more powerful blow, but Lessian recovered faster than Deryn thought possible, catching her wrist and then yanking her forward. She lost her balance, and the next moment she was tumbling through the air to land flat on her back. Rhenna must have also lost her concentration as the wind was driven out of her, the four other versions winking out of existence.

Lessian was on top of her a moment later, his forearm pressed against her neck. "Yield, Lady Shen," he said, loud enough for everyone watching to hear.

The two Sharded royalty had come close to where Deryn was standing, and he could see Rhenna's lips curl back at this request, revealing blood-stained teeth. She growled something too quiet for Deryn to hear clearly – though it certainly didn't sound like a surrender – and then a monstrous hand shaped of glistening darkness materialized behind the Windwrack warrior. Cries of alarm rose up from the storm-sharded, and Lessian turned as the clawed fingers closed around him. Deryn glimpsed his stunned eyes just before the hand threw him violently towards the circle's edge . . . and right at the crowd of shadow-sharded. Deryn realized that the flailing Windwrack warrior was flying directly at him and raised his arms in what he knew was a useless gesture, but then there was another flash of lightning and Lessian landed hard on the stone in the very center of the ring.

Rhenna had already risen by the time the Windwrack lord had climbed unsteadily to his feet, though she'd made no move towards him. She was breathing hard, her long black hair a tangled mess. She'd bound it back before the match had started, but during the fight it had been jarred loose.

Lessian did not rush over to resume the battle either. He looked exhausted, Deryn thought – he had also acquitted himself well yesterday against the balewyrm, and that must have taken something out of him. A slow smile spread across his face as he shook his head.

"If you will not yield, then I propose a draw, Lady Shen. You fight well."

Deryn could see the tension drain from Rhenna's shoulders as soon as Lessian said this.

"Accepted," she replied, and more mutterings swelled from both crowds of Sharded. Deryn couldn't tell if they were surprised or angry or appreciative of this turn of events – maybe all three.

Lessian bowed once more, even more deeply than before, then after a last glance at Rhenna, he turned and made his way back to the rest of the storm-sharded. She did the same a moment later, her face again arranged into a frozen mask, her head held high. A limp acquired during the match spoiled the effect slightly.

"Congratulations, cousin," Kilian said when she stood among them. She did not answer him, though Deryn thought he saw her nod slightly. None of the other shadow-sharded said anything.

"Warriors of Storm and Shadow!" cried Azil, drawing everyone's attention. The Black Sword and the Warden of the Windwrack had moved to a side of the circle where they could address both crowds of

Sharded. "Today has been well fought by all. We of the Duskhold have a new appreciation for the skill and valor of the Windwrack's finest." He turned, sweeping the Sharded with his gaze. "It is my hope that our centuries of conflict are finally drawing to a close. That we will soon stand side by side as brothers and sisters of the shards." The scarred warrior beside him was nodding in agreement with the Black Sword's words, and when Azil fell silent, he thrust his fist into the air.

"Storm and Shadow!" Warden Harath bellowed, and there were answering cries from both crowds. Though not that many, Deryn noted, and more than a few of the shadow-sharded around him remained silent, their mouths thinned and arms folded across their chests. It would clearly take time to chisel away at the rancor between the holds.

Azil and Harath strode from the circle, and this seemed to signal the end of the competition. As the crowds dispersed, Kilian turned to Deryn and Kaliss.

"So now you've seen some of your fellow adepts in action. What do you think?"

"I think we have a lot to learn," Deryn muttered. "I haven't even manifested a single talent yet."

Kilian smiled. "That I cannot help you with, but what I can do is help lift your fighting skills so that you will not be embarrassed when you are summoned into the circle in the future."

"You would do that?" Kaliss asked, and Deryn thought she sounded more than a little suspicious.

Kilian pressed a hand to his chest. "I have always seen myself first and foremost as a teacher. And also," he continued, thumping his cane against the stone, "I will not be doing any training of my own for a little while yet. Azil usually places an elder adept in charge of instructing the newly elevated, and to be honest, he would likely choose me anyway. By volunteering before he does I hope to get into his good graces."

"Then I accept," Kaliss said quickly, as if she was afraid Kilian might change his mind.

Both of them turned to Deryn, and he returned their stare

blankly for a moment before realizing what they were waiting for. "Oh, yes. Of course. I would be honored to be your student." The sun was blotted for a heartbeat as a Black Disc passed overhead, the first of the shadow-sharded leaving the top of the tower. The ache in Deryn's legs that had never entirely faded seemed to intensify again at the thought of the countless stairs awaiting him. "Perhaps you could tell us more on your Black Disc."

31

DERYN

THREE DAYS LATER, Deryn sat cross-legged in the center of the circle and watched the sun rise from beyond the distant peaks. It had still been dark when he'd ascended the tower, and he'd kept his shoulder pressed against the stone the entire way up, trying not to think of the abyss yawning below. He suspected he'd survive the fall even if he tumbled from the stairs, but he didn't really want to test the limits of his sharded body.

Especially in his current weakened state. He'd spent nearly every waking moment since the competition channeling the power surging from his new fragment, and last night he'd dared to try and add a third shard . . . and while it had seemed to successfully merge, he felt even worse than he had before. He couldn't stop shivering, and his skin was clammy, constantly covered with a cold sweat. If he hadn't promised Kilian that he'd be here for their first training session, he'd have stayed huddled under his fur blanket, willing the Hollow servant who brought him his breakfast to arrive so he could request a pot of hot tea.

But he had told Kilian he'd be here, and he wasn't about to squander the opportunity to be trained by one of the most senior adepts. The raw power of the shards was only useful if it could be harnessed effectively. And thinking of that . . . Deryn concentrated, summoning into existence the talent that had unfolded in his mind not long after the competition between Storm and Shadow had concluded. It had been like suddenly remembering how to tie a knot or speak a language he'd known but then forgotten, as if the ability had been waiting within him to emerge again. He raised his arm, examining it in the dawn light. He could feel something there, like a shell laying gently against his skin, but it was invisible to the eye. With his other hand, he found a jagged piece of rock jarred loose during the contest days ago, and then smashed it hard against his forearm.

Or tried to. Before the stone could touch his flesh, it rebounded against shadowy black armor that flickered into existence and then faded a moment later. It had felt like he'd struck metal, although the sound hadn't been as sharp as if it had really clanged off iron or steel. Ghost Chitin, Kilian had called it. His first talent, and Deryn had to admit he was pleased. He'd been told long ago that the talents each Sharded gained seemed to mirror their personalities, so if he'd been granted an attacking power like the Arm of the Abyss, what would that say about him? Ghost Chitin was about protection, not aggression. Perhaps this insight had little merit, but it did make him feel good. And he was officially *sardor* now, no longer *arzgan*. He truly belonged among the other adepts.

A shiver of movement drew his attention. The shadow elemental curled near him had lifted its head and was staring towards the edge of the tower's roof. When it had finally emerged from under his bed after a day of hiding, it had adopted a new form, that of what he thought was a small dog. After merging his third shard it had grown, but still had stayed dog-like, as if it were a puppy that had aged a few months in a moment.

Coming.

The word whispered in Deryn's mind, dry as bone dust. The creature refused to respond to him, but it occasionally offered cryptic commentary.

"What's coming?" he asked, but as usual it ignored him, its attention focused on the spot where the lip of the roof ended.

He should have expected it, but still he was startled when a Black Disc rose up smoothly and silently from below. Perched on the circle of darkness, Kilian appeared equally surprised, leaning on his cane as he stared down at Deryn. Kaliss was beside him, and the Ashasai girl lifted her arm in greeting. She at least looked like she had expected to find him up here.

"Deryn!" Kilian cried cheerfully, stepping from the Disc with the help of his cane as it dissolved into wisps of darkness. "Good morning. I was ready to be angry at you for not answering my knock on your door."

"Apologies," Deryn replied, climbing to his feet stiffly. "I didn't know you would come to my chamber. I thought it best if I made the trek up here a bit earlier, as I'm moving slowly right now."

Kaliss's slight smile turned down. "You're still feeling the effects of merging your second shard? I've nearly recovered."

Deryn shook his head. "No. I've . . . gone and done my third."

Her eyes widened. "Third? Fire and ashes, Deryn! You need to go slowly, make sure your pathways are calm before you add more fragments!"

Kilian stumped closer, his cane clacking on stone. He was giving Deryn a measuring look, his eyes narrowed thoughtfully. "So you've done two shards in the span of a few days? How remarkable. I've heard that more powerful Sharded like my father can do this, or even two at once, but I never . . . Mother Dark, is that what I think it is?"

The Sharded was frozen, his attention fixed on the shadow-dog that had come to sit at his feet. It was staring up like it expected him to share a morsel of food.

"Ah, yes," Deryn replied. The news of his elemental must have flown around the Duskhold.

"I was there when it appeared in the audience chamber," Kilian mused, peering in unabashed fascination at the little creature. "I'll never forget the expression on Uncle's face when he turned around and saw this fellow waving at him like a long-lost friend." He glanced at Deryn, his eyes bright. "May I pat it?"

"I . . . uh . . . yes?" Deryn said, as much a question as permission. "It's not really a dog, you know. I mean, it can change its shape."

"But look!" Kilian cried excitedly, pointing at the elemental's little tail, which was indeed wagging. He laughed as he lowered his hand and the shadow-dog raised his head to rub against it. "Have you named it?"

"I . . . no."

Kilian gave him a reproachful look. "Why not?"

"Well, I mean, it might already have a name," Deryn stammered. "It just hasn't told me."

"I shall call you Shade," Kilian proclaimed, patting the shadow-dog's head vigorously as it leaned into his hand. "You see? He likes it."

The elemental noticed Kaliss edging closer and turned towards her, its hackles rising. Deryn heard something that he might have believed was a growl if he had never heard a dog growl before.

"He doesn't like you," Kilian said, almost accusingly.

"I did nothing to it!" Kaliss exclaimed, taking a step back.

"Perhaps it knows that in Ashasai they eat dogs," the shadow-sharded mused, to which Deryn let out a deep sigh of exasperation.

"Again, it's not a dog."

Kilian frowned, bending over to examine the elemental more closely. "You think Shade may be a wolf, then?"

Even in the faint morning light, Deryn could see Kaliss's eyes roll. Kilian certainly did not, as he had crouched awkwardly to more easily run his hand down the length of the elemental. "Three shards?" the Ashasai girl asked as she came up to him. "Truly?"

Deryn nodded, fighting back the urge to scratch his aching chest.

"So you found more than one down there. I suspected as much. How many do you have?" Kaliss noticed his hesitation, and smiled grimly. "Good. You're learning. The Sharded Few must guard their strength, even within their own holds."

"I trust you. It's just . . . Cael Shen himself told me I should not speak about what I discovered in the balewyrm's lair."

"The master of the Duskhold knows what we are better than anyone," Kaliss murmured. "Well, just remember you will make yourself sick – or perhaps even permanently damage your pathways – if you try to merge too many shards too quickly."

Deryn nodded. It was true – he felt on the verge of breaking, like a frayed sack carrying too much. He would have to slow down and focus on his channeling until the churning power within him was calm once more. He glanced at Kaliss and found her looking at him strangely.

"I have to admit, I don't understand you, Deryn. When we first met that day in the courtyard and I brought you into the Duskhold, I thought you were soft, like all the other novices. You spoke of kindness and rejected my claims that the life of a Sharded is nothing but a competition. And yet you worked harder than any of them, save me. In a few weeks, you learned how to channel and beckon better than those who had practiced for months. Natural ability surely played a part, but you also must have practiced alone in your room while the rest of the novices slept or frittered away their free time." Her tone had grown more impassioned as she continued. "So, what drives you on? You reject my reasons, but you work harder than almost any. Why?" She sounded almost frustrated. Like this was a question she had spent quite a bit of time contemplating.

Did he dare tell her the truth? No, not yet and maybe not ever. But perhaps he could give her some version of it. Deryn swallowed, unsure exactly what to say. Across from them, Kilian had beckoned the darkness and shaped it into something approximating a stick, then thrown it for the elemental to chase. Which the shadow-dog did and then returned a moment later with it in its mouth, tail wagging.

"We're not so different," he finally said slowly. "You grew up on the streets of Phane, yes? You understood very early that life was not fair, that you would have to take what you needed to survive."

He turned to Kaliss to make sure she wasn't going to argue with him, but she only nodded.

"I also learned early about the world's injustices," he continued. "My mother . . . she was not well. Most of the time she was kind and loving and hardworking, but every once in a while, some spirit went into her, and she could not stop herself from speaking nonsense and making strange sounds. She worked as a servant in the great houses of Kething's Cross until they refused to hire her because of these . . . fits. I don't know if it was true, or some delusion brought on by her condition, but she told me we had to leave the town and go into the woods. A rumor had started that she was possessed by a devil, and it was only a matter of time before they came for her with rope or torches." The old sadness returned, a hollowness spreading in his chest. "Perhaps it *was* madness, because she threw herself into a frozen lake not long after. I was indentured by then. She'd signed my body away so we would not starve." Deryn clenched his fists, nails digging into his palms. The sadness was giving way to anger, as it usually did when he dwelled on his past. A part of that anger was for what his mother had done – not trading him to Master Ferith, as he knew that had been necessary for them to survive – but for killing herself when he still needed her. And part of the anger was for the cruelty of the world that had broken her.

Broken them.

"I could not help her," Deryn said softly. "I was weak. Powerless. That is the lesson I learned when I was younger. If you are not strong, you cannot protect those you care about." Deryn gestured, and strands of shadow slithered to him. Beckoning had become much easier since he had merged his second shard, and with the third pulsing in his chest he almost felt like the darkness was a part of his body. "That is why I strive so hard." He thought of Alia, cowering before the sneering Sharded with the crimson tattoos and cruel eyes. He had been ready to sacrifice himself in that moment, before Rhenna had stepped forward and saved her. Saved them. He knew next time someone like her might not be there. But he would be ready. For his mother and Xiv and all the others he had not been strong enough to protect.

"There will always be someone more powerful," Kaliss said softly, and she sounded almost sad.

"Not if *I* am the most powerful," Deryn replied, and he thought he saw something spark in Kaliss's eyes.

"And that is why you've been hidden away for days," she said. "You missed the storm-sharded's departure, but I'm sure you knew that, and several fetes and feasts."

Deryn shrugged. He'd had more important things to do.

"I thought you must be recuperating from your second shard . . . and yet it turns out you were actually preparing for your third." Kaliss crooked a smile. "I won't be so lax in the future, now that I know I have some competition."

The clump of Kilian's cane approaching made them both turn. The shadow-sharded's face was flushed and his eyes bright. Behind him, the elemental chased a serpent of darkness across the tower's roof.

"Deryn, my boy, if you ever have the chance to acquire another of these things, I would forever be indebted to you if you gave it to me."

"I . . . uh, of course." An easy promise to make when he had absolutely no idea where the elemental had come from in the first place.

"Wonderful!" Kilian cried, grinning like a man who had just struck the best deal of his life. "And now we shall turn to the reason for rising at this ungodly time. Let the training begin!"

Deryn had been expecting Kilian to teach them more stances and strikes and counters, similar to what Jaliska had taught the novices during the fortnight before their Delve. Instead, Kilian focused on a particular technique that he insisted was absolutely crucial for every Sharded warrior to master. Those who struggled to learn it – and there were some – would be at a tremendous disadvantage during combat with another Sharded. It involved channeling while fighting, which initially made little sense to Deryn. The purpose of channeling was to calm the tempest inside oneself and gain control over the power flowing from one's fragment. It was most effective when done in solitude and quiet, not the frenetic chaos of combat. And this was why, as Kilian explained, so many Sharded struggled with the technique. The ability to quiet one's mind and find that inner calmness while facing imminent danger was not easy.

But Kilian claimed it was important, and after following his instructions and experiencing the results, Deryn could understand why. While channeling, the Sharded Few could manipulate the energy pulsing through their body. They could also guide it, so that it collected in their fists or feet while delivering a blow, and doing this magnified the force of the strike significantly. The difference was startling. Kilian had summoned his own Ghost Chitin for this exercise, and Deryn and Kaliss had taken turns trying to strike him. The first dozen punches Deryn had thrown, he could not hold on to that inner calm, and he did nothing against Kilian's dark armor except scrape his knuckles and make his wrist sore. And then something had shifted inside him, the power of the shard surging to follow his command, and the force of his blow had sent a spiderweb of cracks across the surface of the chitin.

For a moment, Kilian had looked surprised, and then he'd grinned. "Excellent! Now you need to keep practicing so that you can do it every time, without fail, even when tired or wounded. Many a Sharded warrior has fallen in battle because they lost concentration at the wrong moment."

Kaliss struggled more than Deryn with this technique, flailing away at Kilian's chitin for far longer without success. Finally she stepped back, panting and sweaty, blood dripping from her hands to patter on the stone. The look of intense frustration on her face did not go unnoticed by Kilian.

"Channeling is impossible when your mind is clouded by anger or exasperation. Take a rest now and bring your thoughts under control. Then we will try again."

Kaliss nodded sharply and stepped back, still visibly fuming. Kilian smiled at her, then turned and wandered away whistling towards where the elemental was lying on the stone as if it were a real dog enjoying the warmth of the morning sun.

Deryn watched the Ashasai girl stalk to the far side of the roof and sit, her legs dangling over the edge. It seemed like she would need a little while to find the calm she needed, so he followed Kilian over to where the Sharded was crouching down to rub the upturned belly of the elemental, his fingers sunk almost to the knuckle in the thing's shadowy substance.

"I have a question," Deryn said as he came to stand beside Kilian.

"Is it about how I managed to ingratiate myself with Shade so fast?"

"Ah, no. I was wondering . . . where do the Sharded *get* their shards? Even the weakest adepts who fought here a few days ago had four or five."

"They certainly didn't find them in a balewyrm's lair," Kilian admitted, leaning on his cane as he straightened again.

"Exactly."

"Well, many of the adepts come from old Duskhold families. The shards they bear once belonged to their ancestors – surely you didn't think the dead were buried with their fragments? That would be a monumental waste of resources. No, they are held until a descendent with promise is ready to merge another shard. The true measure of wealth and power in the Duskhold is how many shards a family controls."

"Then why did you have to get your last fragment in the woods where you found me?"

Kilian sighed deeply, raising his gaze to the sky. "Because my father claimed I was not ready! Oh, I thought I was, but the hard truth of it was that he was right. I would have become shard-sick and it might not even have merged successfully. But several months on the hunt with Phinius, with nothing to do in that wagon except channel . . . by the time I met your Unbound friend I was well prepared. If I hadn't gained that shard, my father certainly would have gifted me one when I returned."

"But what about those the hounds bring back to the hold? The Imbued without storied families to give them treasures?"

Kilian shaded his eyes as he gazed out across the roof at Kaliss. "You mean like her?"

Deryn nodded. "She showed greater promise than any other

novice. But without more shards her progress will be stunted."

"Don't worry about her. Saelus has remarked upon her potential, and even my father has heard her name. I imagine that when she finishes merging all the shards she gained on her Delve and is ready for another, there will be a few powerful patrons who will step forward willing to give her more in exchange for her loyalty. And if she wishes to remain unbeholden to anyone else . . . there are always the Unbound."

"I'm sorry?" For a moment Deryn thought Kilian was suggesting Kaliss might become one of those renegades.

"The outcasts. They are out there, though most are not so stupid as to set up their own little fiefdoms like that fellow in the woods. In olden times, before this most civilized age, warriors would venture out to challenge any Sharded, even the ones still loyal to another hold. Now such actions would lead to swift reprisals once word spread . . . and so instead, ambitious Sharded hunt the Unbound for their fragments."

"Is it dangerous?"

"In the past, not very."

"But now?"

Kilian frowned. "Recently, things have changed. It started a few years ago when one of the many noble houses of Ashasai was violently extinguished. Well, they were thought extinguished. In truth, a prince escaped the bloodletting and fled into the wilderness. Xend an-Azith. Some time later, he emerged again as the leader of a band of Unbound. Usually such developments are violently suppressed, as the holds allow no rivals, but he proved remarkably hard to kill. More and more Unbound flocked to him, and he's become something of a legend. The Unbound King, they call him."

"Does he have his own hold?"

Kilian shrugged. "If he has one, it's hidden. Most believe he dwells in Karath."

The City of the Dead. Deryn had heard Karath spoken about in the same manner as other far-off, legendary places like the oasis cities of the Salah and the canyon-city Chan-anok. It was one of the largest ports on the Sea of Salvation, and the only great city not claimed by the Sharded Few.

"Why haven't the masters of the holds sent their warriors to Karath to root him out?"

Kilian looked at him strangely. "You know why Karath is called the City of the Dead, don't you?" Deryn stared at him blankly, and Kilian shook his head in amazement. "What in the world is Saelus teaching the novices?"

"How to channel and beckon. My learning about the world he put in her hands." Deryn gestured towards where Kaliss was still perched on the edge of the roof, apparently contemplating the jagged peaks rising around the Duskhold.

Kilian grunted. "She teaches geography as well as she fights."

"I learned a lot from her," Deryn said defensively.

"But this is a rather large omission, as it is something you must know. Karath is known as the City of the Dead because it is the only place in the world where our shards have no power."

Deryn blinked in surprise. "No power? You mean . . ."

"We are but common men there. Our strength fails us, we cannot draw upon our talents. A sword thrust by a child will kill us."

"But . . . why would this Unbound King stay there if he cannot use his powers?" As soon as he asked this, Deryn chided himself for being a fool. The answer was obvious, of course. "Because the Sharded Few fear to tread in Karath," he murmured.

"Indeed," Kilian said. "A single warrior of the holds is worth a thousand unsharded outside Karath . . . but not so in the City of the Dead. It is the perfect refuge from the Sharded Few. Aha!" He lifted his cane and gestured with it at Kaliss, who was making her way back to them, her expression less troubled than before. "It seems our dear Ashasai has found her inner peace. Let us continue our lessons."

To Deryn's surprise, they did not stop their training when the sun crested high overhead. He had thought they would break for a midday meal, but Kilian – belying the easygoing attitude he cultivated – proved to be a harsh taskmaster. After Kaliss had finally managed the art of channeling while striking, the shadow-sharded put them in the ring and had them take part in some light sparring. Deryn could sense that Kaliss was going easy on him, for which he was grateful – the exercises this morning had already so exhausted him that he was feeling lightheaded.

But he was not the only one who realized what Kaliss was doing.

"You two look like you're dancing, not fighting!" Kilian shouted, anger edging his words for the first time today. "Do you think your enemies will wait until you are rested and have a full belly before attacking?"

"Apologies," Kaliss said, and she had the good sense to sound chagrined. "I can tell Deryn is unwell, and I believe neither of us had time for breakfast this morning."

"Well, you're not having lunch either, so best ignore your stomachs."

"Wait, truly?" Deryn asked, wondering if Kilian would relent if he collapsed.

"Yes, I've arranged for another to come here in the afternoon and give you instruction on something I've no experience with."

Deryn wiped the back of his hand across his sweaty brow. "What would that be?"

Kilian didn't answer, instead cocking his head, as if listening intently. "I believe he's just arriving," he finally said, turning to where the stairs reached the top of the tower.

It was then Deryn heard a wheezing panting, and a moment later a head of black hair appeared.

"Heth!" Deryn cried as the boy staggered out onto the roof holding a wrapped bundle tightly to his chest.

"So . . . many . . . steps," Heth gasped, laying his burden on the stone as he tried to catch his breath.

Deryn hurried over to him and put a comforting hand on his shoulder. "I nearly collapsed the first time I climbed them all, and I had a shard. Well done for making it to the top."

"Thank you," Heth said as he straightened. His face creased in concern when he finally laid eyes on Deryn. "Are you all right? You look pale."

"I'm fine," Deryn replied with a grin. "Better now that you're here." And it was true – the pangs in his stomach had vanished with the boy's appearance.

"Good to see you once again, Heth the Hollow." Kilian's tone was light, but Deryn heard a note of impatience.

"Lord Shen," Heth said, bowing towards the shadow-sharded.

Kilian waved his hand, as if to dismiss Heth's formal greeting. "I've told you before, no titles. We're all old friends. Though today you are to be a teacher, and I don't want you to be too kind to Deryn. This lesson will be important. Have you been told what you will do?"

Heth nodded, stooping to unwrap the bundle and revealing a pair of wooden practice swords. "I'm to instruct Deryn in swordcraft."

"Indeed. Kaliss and I are bound for the eating hall, and while there, I will dispatch a servant up here with food for you both."

"Much appreciated, master," Deryn said, bowing even more deeply than Heth had a moment ago.

Kilian snorted and rolled his eyes. "Not you too." He turned to Kaliss, who was staring at Heth like she was trying to place where she'd seen him before. "Come. Let us leave these boys to their blades."

"I would stay," Kaliss said slowly, her gaze now lingering on the wooden swords. "If that's all right."

Kilian shrugged. "Very well. Then I will see you both on the morrow." He turned to Heth. "Work them hard. The Sharded Few only grow stronger when they are pushed to their limits." He waited for Heth's nodded agreement, then made a gesture that knit strands of summoned darkness into a Black Disc beneath his feet. As he rose from the tower's roof, his eyes widened as if he'd just remembered something, and he looked to where the elemental was still puddled on the stone like an orphaned shadow.

"Farewell, Shade!"

32

DERYN

DERYN GROANED in dismay when he heard the knock. He'd just flung himself down on his bed, exhausted after the day's training, and he'd hoped to steal a quick nap before the ringing of the evemeal bell. But no such luck. Grumbling, he rose stiffly and hobbled across his chamber to the door.

"Who is it?" he called, hoping it was just some Hollow servant delivering fresh linens or hot water and he could dismiss them and climb back into bed.

The muffled reply that returned through the thick wood was not at all what he wanted to hear.

"It's Nishi Shen."

Deryn lunged for the door and pulled it open, then bowed low. When he straightened, he found the heir to the Duskhold watching him with a slight smile. His arm was already out of the sling he'd been wearing during the duels a few days ago.

"Lord Shen, it's a pleasure to see you again."

The shadow-sharded sauntered into the chamber, peering around as if looking for something. Deryn suspected he knew what that was.

"Ah, it's not here right now, my lord."

Nishi turned to him with a bemused expression. "Really? The elemental comes and goes as it pleases?"

"It does, my lord."

Nishi grunted in surprise. "Interesting. Does it answer your call?"

"I . . . haven't tried, my lord."

Nishi brushed his fingers against the top of the table where the shards had once been scattered, his lips pursed. For a moment Deryn feared that the shadow-sharded could sense a residue left by the fragments, but then he realized that if Nishi was that sensitive he would already know Deryn had ten shards in the pocket of his robes right now.

"Well, give it your best effort, adept."

"Yes, of course," Deryn replied hurriedly, then cleared his throat. "Ah, hello? Can you hear me?" he said loudly into the stillness. "I'd like you to come out."

Nishi and Deryn looked around the room, but nothing had moved.

"My father wants to see you," Nishi said. "And he expects the elemental to be there. Try again."

Deryn wondered if he should get down on his hands and knees and directly address the shadows under his bed, since that was where the elemental seemed to enjoy staying. He knew that would look rather ridiculous, so he decided to exhaust all other options first.

"Uh, please show yourself. Someone very important wants to meet you."

Nishi looked decidedly unimpressed with his entreaties. "Command it, adept."

"Come out!" Deryn cried. "I summon you!"

"It's not a demon," Nishi said with a sigh. "Does it have a name?"

"No." Deryn hesitated. "Well . . ." He licked his lips, already feeling like a fool. "Come to me, Shade."

"Shade?" Nishi said with a snort.

The darkness pooled under the table shivered.

"Oh, hello," Nishi said, stepping back as the dog-shaped shadow emerged into the light.

As always, Deryn felt a frisson of fear staring into the elemental's featureless face. This time, though, the fear was shot through with excitement. It had obeyed him! Or at least answered his call.

Shade. Apparently it had accepted the name Kilian had given it. And Deryn had also decided that he thought of it as male, as ridiculous as that seemed.

"It feels like the darkness, but it does not respond when I beckon," Nishi mused, and Deryn thought he heard a hint of nervousness in his voice. The heir to the Duskhold crouched down, but he did not reach out to try to touch the elemental. "What are you?"

The shadow-dog stared at him without responding.

"Did you say your father wished to see me, Lord Shen?"

Nishi stood, blinking as if waking from a trance. "Indeed. I shall Shadow Walk us to where he waits. Will . . . *Shade* follow?"

Deryn glanced down to the elemental, which had lifted his head to regard him. Shade looked like he was waiting to hear what he had to say, and Deryn supposed this was progress of a sort.

"Shade, come with us. Please. I command you."

"Very assertive," Nishi muttered, then stepped closer to Deryn and took hold of his arm. "But if it does not, we will return here and walk to the audience chamber. Though I hope it comes. I have to admit, I'm curious what will happen if it enters the shadowrealm."

Nishi's brow furrowed, his jaw tensing as he drew upon his talent. Darkness flowed out from under the bed and crept up the wall closest to them, forming a portal. Cold air slipped through from what lay beyond, making Deryn's skin goosepimple.

"Why can't you just bring us there directly?" Deryn asked, shivering. "I saw you vanish and reappear in the balewyrm's cavern."

"Two different talents," Nishi murmured, still concentrating on some aspect of the path he was forging. "Shadow Stepping is a first-tier talent. It is instantaneous, but only possible between two pockets of darkness the Sharded can see. And others cannot be brought along. Shadow Walking is second-tier and can be done over much larger distances, though we must traverse part of the shadowrealm to get where we want to go."

"You have both these talents?"

"I do. As did my mother. It's why Rhenna is so jealous they manifested in me and not her." Nishi's face relaxed. "There. I've found the path. Let us go."

Steeling himself for what he knew lay beyond, Deryn allowed Nishi to guide him into the portal.

It was more terrible than he remembered. A flensing chill worse than the deepest winter night cut through him, making his bones ache and his blood run cold. In the distance he again glimpsed those strangely contorted shapes undulating like they were dancing to a mad piping at the edge of his hearing. He shivered as he recognized where he'd seen those figures before – they were almost certainly the inspiration for the thorned statues scattered about the Duskhold, the ones with the unnaturally thin limbs and eyeless faces.

A sound startled him, and it evidently surprised Nishi as well because he felt the shadow-sharded's grip on his arm suddenly tighten. The harsh noise echoed hollowly in the darkness, reverberating into oblivion, but Deryn thought it had originated right beside him.

He glanced down and saw Shade keeping pace with them, his shadowy form rippling in the deeper black of this place. Another grating sound emerged from the elemental. It almost sounded like ... Deryn shook his head. Surely not.

It had sounded like a bark.

Shade's head was turned, staring off into the distance at those twisting figures. Was he greeting those things? Warning them away? Inviting them to a feast?

Nishi's pull on his arm became more insistent, his speed quickening. A point of crystalline light appeared in the black, then rapidly swelled as if rushing towards them. Deryn just had time to flinch and raise his arms before they were enveloped by the radiance.

They stumbled into the Duskhold's audience chamber. This time it was empty, though the braziers were lit, their ghostly flames clawing at the darkness. Deryn drew in a shuddering breath, trying to calm his heart. Beside him, Nishi also looked troubled, his face pale and drawn. Only the shadow-dog seemed unaffected by the journey, his little tail wagging as he rubbed up against Deryn's legs.

"They saw us," Nishi murmured, brushing his long hair back with a hand that might have been trembling.

"Who?"

"The . . . Others. That's what I call them. What my mother called them."

"What are they?" Deryn asked. The memory of their unnatural forms had already begun to fade, as if his mind could not accept what it had seen.

Nishi shrugged, the concern draining from his face as he mastered himself. "Who knows? Emissaries of the Shadow, perhaps. It seems your little friend drew their attention."

Deryn looked down at the shadow-dog. "Did you know them?" he asked, not expecting an answer.

Shade barked again.

"It has changed."

Deryn and Nishi turned towards this new voice. From the darkness that filled the deeper recesses of the great chamber strode Cael Shen, the bone hilt of Night thrusting up over his shoulder. He was dressed in black leather and chain mail, the first time Deryn had seen the lord of the shadow-sharded wearing anything but robes. His long white hair was tied back in a topknot, and a silver amulet lay upon his breast.

Deryn ducked into a low bow. "Lord Shen," he murmured as the master of the Duskhold approached. A few steps behind Cael, his advisor Leantha drifted like a trailing ghost, her flawless white face expressionless.

"Father," Nishi said. "I have brought him, as you requested."

Cael Shen ignored his son, folding his arms across his broad chest and staring hard at the elemental crouched beside Deryn.

"Does it change its shape often?"

"No, my lord," replied Deryn. "Only when I merge a shard. The first time it was . . . like a puppy. Now it seems to have grown up."

Cael Shen grunted, then turned back to Leantha. "What do you think?"

"I know little of elementals," the pale woman murmured. "I doubt there are many who do."

"What about its behavior?" the lord of the Duskhold asked Deryn.

"It is . . . odd, my lord. It seems to have the mannerisms of a dog. A real dog."

"Interesting," Cael Shen mused, rubbing at his chin. "We need to learn more. I have already asked Archivist Devenal to gather what information he can find about elementals. Can you read?"

"Yes," Deryn said slowly. "Though I'm probably very out of practice. My mother taught me."

He had learned by the stubs of candles late at night, using books secretly borrowed from the collections of the masters they had served. His mother had loved stories, and as a young girl had begged a kindly old scholar to teach her, and when he was old enough she had shared with him this gift.

"Very good. I am most curious to know how the old elementalists used their . . . companions . . . to benefit their holds." Cael Shen suddenly swiveled to face his son. "Leave us."

Nishi blinked in surprise. "Father?"

"I wish to speak with Deryn alone."

Nishi's gaze flitted to Leantha, his mouth drawing down in annoyance, but he held his tongue. "Of course. I shall see you at dinner."

Cael Shen turned from his son, an obvious dismissal. Nishi opened his mouth to say something else, then thought better and instead whirled around and stalked off, the sound of his footsteps vanishing as soon as the darkness closed around him.

"Do you have more questions about the elemental, my lord?"

Cael Shen regarded Deryn with eyes of deepest black, unsettlingly similar to the realm through which he and Nishi had just traveled.

"You fell into a crevice while on your Delve."

"Yes."

"You were pushed."

Something fluttered in his stomach. "Yes." Deryn hesitated, then dared to ask the question on his lips. "But how do you know this, my lord?"

Cael Shen turned and stared off into the dark. "The shadows remember. I asked, and they showed me." He raised his arm and made a beckoning gesture. Movement shivered the black, the coils of something vast and serpentine shifting.

"What did they show you?" Deryn whispered.

Cael Shen did not answer, but a moment later an enormous snake of glistening darkness slithered into the light. In its jaws was Menochus, his silver eyes rolling in terror, a band of black covering his mouth. He was not struggling, though Deryn suspected that was because he realized the futility of such actions.

"This novice betrayed you for a shard. He thought to kill you and claim what you had discovered."

Deryn's mouth was dry. "He did." The flutter in his belly had turned into an ingot of iron, cold and hard.

Menochus stared at Deryn pleadingly. Behind his gag, he was making muffled noises, tears running down his face.

"Please, my lord," Deryn murmured. "Let him speak."

Cael Shen's brow arched. "Very well," he said, and the shadowy binding over the boy's mouth disappeared.

"Deryn!" Menochus cried. "Lord Shen! I beg ye, show mercy!"

The master of the Duskhold stared at the blubbering boy without compassion. "Tell me, what would your punishment be in the Wild, if you so cowardly turned on one from your own tribe?"

"I did not intend ta kill him!" Menochus fairly screeched, his imploring gaze turning to Deryn. "Truly! I knew ye would survive the fall – I only wanted the shard!"

"Knew or hoped?" Deryn asked quietly.

Menochus swallowed hard. "I . . . I hoped, it's true. But I was right, yes? Please, Deryn. Please. We were friends. I made a terrible choice, and I'm sorry. I just . . . it was this place. All the talk of striving against each other! Saelus always said the Duskhold is like the wilderness – ye do what ye must ta survive!"

"You didn't need to push me to survive." The cold lump inside him was growing harder, anger replacing the sickness he'd felt earlier.

"Aye, aye. Ye speak true. I throw myself on yer mercy. I know ye ta be a good man. A kind man." Menochus's words were tumbling over each other he was speaking so quickly. To Deryn's surprise, the fear filling the boy's eyes elicited a pang of pity in him.

Cael Shen was still unmoved. He gestured, and the serpent of shadow melted away, scraps of its great body encircling Menochus's limbs and neck as he collapsed on the stone sobbing. Another twitch of his fingers and these fetters jerked the boy to his knees, his hands bound behind his back. Menochus might have been straining with all his strength, but it mattered not as he was forced to lean forward, offering up the back of his neck.

"Adept," said Cael Shen, and Deryn wrenched his gaze from Menochus to find that the lord of the Duskhold had drawn his greatsword and was holding out the bone hilt for him to take.

Lightheaded, he gawked at the blade of glistening darkness for a long moment, then looked around wildly for help. Cael Shen watched him with eyes of obsidian. Leantha was staring at nothing, as if what was happening was not even worthy of her attention. Beyond the throne, up on its dais, the vast skull of the balewyrm leered down in amusement.

Deryn remembered being in Menochus's position, waiting for the punishment he knew was coming, helpless to resist. Of course this situation was very different – Master Ferith had ordered Deryn whipped because he showed kindness, while Menochus had done what he did for his own gain. But how much of the decision he had made in that moment had been shaped by the poison of the Duskhold seeping into his soul? The relentless message from their teachers that they must contest with each other if they were to rise high in the hold?

Deryn reached for the hilt, then hesitated, his hand falling back to his side. "My lord, I was wronged. But I would rather see Menochus punished with exile, his shard removed. He was my friend."

Cael Shen regarded him for a long moment. Then he reversed his sword, but rather than slide it into the straps across his back he lifted it and with one smooth motion brought it down on the boy's bared neck.

"No," Deryn whispered as Menochus's head bounced once upon the stone and then came to rest staring up at him in shock, eyes blinking frantically and mouth opening and closing without sound. No blood flowed; rather, a thick tarry sludge was seeping from where the sword had cut cleanly through flesh and bone.

Deryn struggled to breathe, the stone beneath his feet tilting. He stumbled back in horror as the blackness that was not blood oozed closer to his boots.

He'd fantasized about revenge, what he would do to Menochus if he ever had the chance, but this . . . this was terrible. His stomach lurched, and he came dangerously close to spewing its contents out onto the floor. Deryn wanted to run from this room – from the Duskhold – but what would the shadow-sharded do if he did that?

"Deryn."

Cael Shen's voice. It was not comforting or angry or sad. It sounded completely shriven of all emotion, like he had just put on his boots instead of cutting off a boy's head. Deryn looked up, trying his best to avoid catching sight of Menochus's corpse.

"Yes, my lord?" he whispered.

Cael Shen stared at him with pursed lips, the point of his greatsword set on the stone, hands resting on the hilt of gleaming bone.

"The boy tried to kill you and failed. This was always the only proper outcome."

"But . . . exile . . ."

"Impossible. He would still be Imbued, even if we ripped away his shard. Likely he would search for another fragment in the hopes of becoming Unbound, and that we cannot allow."

Deryn forced himself to meet the lord of the Duskhold's glittering black eyes, unwilling to look anywhere else and risk seeing what had happened to the boy who had once been his best friend in this place. Was that disappointment he saw in Cael Shen's flat gaze?

"You must be stronger, boy. Shards are not for the weak – if you lack an iron will and resolve, if you trust too easily and turn your back on those who might benefit from your fall . . . you will end up dead in the mud somewhere, your fragments torn out and adorning the body of another. It is the way of the Sharded Few. And you . . ." The lord of the Duskhold's mouth twisted. "For you it is even more important. You have been given a great gift, Deryn. But your elemental will be of no use to the Duskhold if you do not –"

"**CAEL SHEN!**"

Deryn clapped his hands over his ringing ears. He looked around wildly for who or what had just bellowed, then gasped in surprise when he saw that the ghostly white flames in one of the iron braziers had shot higher. They now blazed a bloody red, and recessed in their depths was a great golden face twisted in rage.

The lord of the Duskhold frowned as he turned towards the huge, glowering visage.

"Lord Char," he called out, stepping over Menochus's severed head as he approached the brazier. "To what do we owe the pleasure of your Fire Sending?"

Deryn glanced at Leantha, unsure if he should be here for whatever was about to happen. Kaliss had mentioned Lord Char before, the master of the Ember just as Cael Shen was master of the Duskhold. The Flame and the Shadow were closest among the holds, in both proximity and friendship. But he received no guidance from the pale woman; she ignored him, her attention fixed on the manifestation that had so suddenly and unexpectedly appeared.

"**Do not play coy with me, Shen,**" snarled the face, gobbets of fire like spittle flying from its mouth to hiss and sizzle on the stone. "**I know you treat with the Windwrack, that you have hosted the *Mother of Storms* herself in your dreary little fortress!**"

Cael Shen folded his arms across his chest as he came to stand before the brazier, gazing up at the enraged face of Lord Char. The waves of heat spilling from the flames were making Deryn uncomfortable, and he was at least fifty paces away. Yet the lord of the Duskhold appeared unaffected.

"It is true," Cael said. "A delegation of storm-sharded stayed in the Duskhold for a few days, including the dowager queen of the Windwrack. It is long past time we set aside ancient grievances and looked to unite the north in peace."

The great face gnashed burning teeth. "**That is unacceptable, Shen! You know the wrongs they have committed against my family. They killed my grandfather, crippled my uncle! Such things cannot be forgiven!**" Eyes like blazing coals narrowed. "**And you have suffered from their actions as much as I! If the spirit of your brother haunts your halls, he must have been incensed to see you welcoming the very woman who planned his death!**"

It might have been Deryn's imagination, but he thought he saw a ripple of movement within the naked blade strapped to Cael Shen's back. "I was there when my father sent his own sending to you during the time of the Conquests, over thirty years ago. He was enraged, angrier than I had ever seen him before. The war we had fought against the Storm and Sea had ended, but the blood between our holds was still thick and black. And yet it was you who approached old Hathen Khaliva with the offer of an alliance, you who first extended the open hand of peace to our enemies."

The flames subsided slightly. "**It was done to save our holds, as you well know.**" Some of the anger had drained from the apparition's voice. "**The emir meant to rule us all, and if Ashasai fell, the north would have been next. But this . . .**" The fire swelled again as its anger returned. "**This is a mistake! There is no threat driving us together! The Storm is as ambitious as the Sand ever was, and they *will* plant a dagger in your back when the time is right!**"

"I am not one to be fooled so easily," Cael Shen said, his words like cold-hammered iron. "Long have Flame and Shadow been allies, and I would be saddened if this brought a wedge between us, old friend."

"**Then you shall not be easily swayed from this course,**" the face growled. "**Very well. Remember to guard yourself, *old friend*. The skies are never as blue as they may seem when you treat with the Storm.**"

And with that, the crimson flames collapsed in an explosion of sparks. For a few long moments, Cael Shen remained standing in front of the now-dead brazier, his hands clasped behind his back.

"Leantha," he finally said without turning around. "Your thoughts?"

The pale woman glided closer, moving in utter silence. "He is an old man, and afraid."

"Afraid of what?"

Leantha laid her long white fingers on Cael Shen's arm, but he did not respond to her touch. "He fears being trapped between the Storm and the Shadow. He fears change. He fears looking impotent in front of his family."

"The son?"

"Yes. Tyran Char is hot-headed and rash, even when compared to his kin. We know he already sees his father as weak and feeble. Our peace with the Windwrack might be what finally compels him to challenge his father for mastery of the Ember."

Cael Shen grunted, staring into the ashes mounded in the brazier. Something glimmered in those depths as a wraithling flame kindled and slowly spread. It seemed to take forever for the white fire to grow to what it had been before Lord Char's visitation, but all that time Cael Shen did not move, lost in thought. Deryn badly wanted to escape this chamber, but he didn't want to risk disturbing the lord of the Duskhold. So he remained motionless, waiting. Eventually a tingle of coldness made him look down, and he found that Shade had curled up around his legs.

"Adept," Cael Shen finally said, jolting Deryn from his reverie, "you may leave. Speak nothing of what you heard or saw here today."

"Yes, my lord," Deryn murmured, bowing even though Cael Shen still had not turned from the brazier where the terrifying face had appeared. He glanced at Menochus's corpse as he began to back away, and he knew Cael Shen was not telling him to be silent about the execution he had just witnessed.

To him, that would not even be worth remembering.

33

HETH

IT WAS SAID that the city of Flail boasted the finest swordsmen in the world. Blades they were called, silver rapiers at their sides and bright plumage from across the sea bobbing from their tricornered hats or sown into their shimmering cloaks. By day they lounged like indolent house cats in smoky wine-halls and under the boughs of persimmon trees in the gardens of their patrons, but when the last bloody tear of sunlight trickled from the sky they stood and slipped on their sword belts, brushed their lips across the hands of admirers, and went out into the night in search of glory. Some would never return, their lives leaking away in dingy alleys or pooling on the sawdust-coated floor of half-valanii taverns. They would be forgotten, even by those who had so recently professed undying affection. Others would stir the city with their deeds, and their names would be spoken in excited whispers by street urchins crouched in shadows and around the gilded tables of merchant princes. For the greatest of these duelists, the highest honor was for a Sharded warrior of the Windwrack to seek them out and become their student, and many a swordsman had parlayed such a relationship into the founding of a great house.

For much of his life that had been Heth's dream. To escape the

drear of Kething's Cross and his father's disapproving frown and flee
to the City of Blades on the Sea of Salvation. The culmination of
these fantasies was always the same – ascending the ranks of the city's
bravos, then teaching the sword to one of the Sharded after being
recognized as the finest duelist in Flail. It was somewhat ironic, then,
that he found himself doing exactly that, though his student was not
a bright lord of the Windwrack but rather his own former lowborn
slave whom he had once scourged for disobedience.

All that was ancient history now. The warmth he saw in Deryn's
eyes when Heth appeared could not be feigned, and he had come to
look forward to their lessons even more than his morning sessions
with the butcher boys. The memories of these times sustained him as
he spent those sluggishly creeping afternoons atop the Duskhold. If
he had the choice, he would have taught Deryn every day, but the
Sharded had many other things to learn as an adept. So it was only
every third afternoon he made the long climb up the Drum Tower to
where the shadow-sharded trained. That intense Ashasai girl Kaliss
was usually there as well, and he had discovered she was not a novice
when it came to the blade. Apparently, she had learned something
when she was younger, though her technique was more suited to the
streets than a dueling circle. It had been a good reminder the first
time she'd stabbed him in the belly that there were no rules in real
battles.

Today Heth was feeling gloomy, as his last lesson with the two
adepts had been yesterday, and he knew he had another interminable watch atop the Duskhold ahead of him tomorrow before
he'd see them again. This morning had gone by particularly slowly
and been particularly dull, without even a bird in the sky or those
slight shivers of movements on the shattered slopes below that
suggested the rock spiders were hunting. And it was because of this,
with his thoughts drifting somewhere far away, that he missed the
tiny figure making its way up the torturous switchback approach to
the Duskhold until one of the other guards grunted in surprise.

"Oy! Have a look at that. What are they doin' down there?"

Heth blinked, focusing on what was below. Strangely, it was just the lone visitor, no wagons or pack animals. Supplies from Phane arrived regularly, but these were large caravans filled with all the goods the shadow-sharded could not produce in this unforgiving land. How would a single man even survive to get here? Unless they were one of the Sharded Few, but surely they'd arrive in more spectacular fashion rather than slowly hobbling up the mountainside.

"Can you see who it is?" Heth asked, blinded by the glare reflecting off the gleaming black rock of the barbican.

The reply was a few moments coming, as if Benni was unsure what he was seeing could possibly be real.

"Looks to me like an old woman," he finally said slowly.

"An old woman?" Heth repeated, bewildered. That was impossible. But the longer he stared, the more details he could make out, and he had to admit it did look like a hunched crone shuffling along the trail.

Heth turned to Gervis, who was staring at nothing as he leaned against the far battlements with a foolish smile plastered to his face.

"Hey, Gervis!" Heth cried across the roof. "Come take a look at this."

Gervis's head jerked up, as if he had been sleeping on his feet, and then he yawned and made his way towards them.

"What is it, boys?"

Benni gestured at the distant plodding figure. "Looks like an old woman comin' to us."

Gervis frowned, then ran a hand through his hair. That was his thinking motion, Heth knew. "Huh," he finally murmured, his gaze drifting across the roof to the great iron bell used to alert the Sharded.

"Surely ain't worth bothering them," Benni protested, but Gervis shook his head curtly.

"Rule is that anything strange is worth a bit of concern. An old lady, comin' up the mountain alone in rock spider territory? Something ain't right. Best tell one of the Few, I s'pose."

Gervis strode across the roof to the warning bell and hefted its mallet. He glanced at Heth and Benni, looking far less certain than he had a moment ago, then blew out his cheeks.

All this for an old woman? Heth imagined whoever was about to be summoned would be less than pleased.

Gervis swung the mallet. Heth winced as the bell clanged, expecting one of the Few to burst out onto the roof like had happened when they'd spotted the storm-sharded. But this time the wait was longer, and the three guards watched each other apprehensively. Apparently, the Duskhold was not expecting any visitors right now.

Finally one arrived, the same young Sharded who had led them down to the courtyard to greet the delegation from the Windwrack. He scowled as he stomped out onto the roof, his black robes rippling in the wind.

"What?" he asked testily, his angry gaze sweeping over them.

Gervis cleared his throat, and the Sharded's eyes focused on him. "Ah, m'lord, apologies about bringin' ya up here. Seems there's someone down below on the road walkin' to the gates."

The Sharded looked like he was trying to grind away some of his teeth. "Someone *on the road*? As in, coming here not on a Black Disc or a Wind Dragon or a Blood Spider, but *walking*? On their *feet*?"

Gervis nodded mutely.

The Sharded snorted. "Some idiot wanders up to our gate and you think you need to tell *me*? Why in the black abyss do we even have guards if they can't scare away a . . . a . . . who *is* here, anyway?"

Benni leaned out over the battlements. "Uh, looks like an old woman, m'lord. Real old. Her clothes are all patched, and there's like bags and pouches hangin' off her. I seen beggars that look more well to do than this one, honestly."

The Sharded's expression darkened further. "A beggar. You've brought me up here for an old beggar woman . . ." Uncertainty flickered in the shadow-warrior's face as his voice trailed away, a moment of consternation. His brow knitted, like something half remembered had occurred to him and he was trying to drag it fully out into the light. Then the color drained from his face.

"Mother Dark," he murmured hoarsely.

The guards glanced at each other.

"Open the doors!" shouted the Sharded as he dashed towards the massive winch and pulley that lifted the gates below. "Open them at once!"

34

ALIA

ALIA HAD NEVER ENCOUNTERED hair like Rhenna's before. It slipped between her fingers black and glistening, smooth as the silken dresses her mistress sometimes wore. She twisted and tucked and turned, intricately knotted braids slowly emerging. It had been years since Alia had last done such plaiting, but she found she had no trouble remembering the complicated patterns. It pleased her, sharing the ways of her people with her mistress.

"Do they mean anything?" Rhenna asked, holding up a small silver hand mirror to watch Alia as she worked. "The braids, I mean."

"They do, mistress," Alia murmured, folding a particularly troublesome strand away. "A braid tells a story. Is the woman married? Betrothed? A widow?" She hesitated briefly. "A spear maiden?"

"You've mentioned that title before," Rhenna said, setting down her mirror and taking up a gnarled purple fruit from a bowl on the table in front of them. She peeled it, revealing the speckled white flesh within. "Spear maiden. What is it?"

Alia's fingers stumbled, the delicate pleating unraveling. She frowned and started again.

"They are warriors. The guardians of the Treesworn."

"A mystery answered with another mystery," Rhenna said, scooping out some of the fruit and popping it into her mouth.

"I'm sorry," Alia said. "I forget you know little of the Treesworn. In the Wild, they are legendary."

"And why's that?" Rhenna asked as she chewed.

"They serve the forest, living apart in the deep wilderness. They can speak with the trees and the animals, and the forest even answers to their call."

Rhenna swallowed, then picked up her mirror again. Her eyes found Alia's in the glass. "The forest answers to their call? It sounds like these Treesworn are the mysterious seed-sharded."

Alia ducked her head slightly in agreement. "After learning more about your people, I think that may be true. The legends do not speak of a rock – a shard – buried in their flesh . . . but I remember a poem sung by a skald when I was very young. He claimed the seeds of the Great Tree enter the bodies of the chosen and take root within."

Rhenna grunted, her gaze becoming distant. "Very interesting. Most of the Wild folk who come to the Duskhold dwelled north of here, like those abominable adept siblings Chal and Pand. To my knowledge, none have ever spoken of these Treesworn."

"The Wild is vast," Alia said quietly. "Even where I lived, beyond the mountains you call the Fangs, the Treesworn were a distant rumor to most. No one I knew had ever encountered them, except . . ." Alia stopped herself, wishing she could take back what she'd just said. As much as she liked her mistress, this was a memory she'd rather not exhume.

Rhenna twisted around slightly as the silence lengthened. "Except?"

"Nothing, mistress. I'm sorry."

Rhenna frowned. "If you truly do not wish to speak of it, I won't compel you. But I *am* curious."

Alia bit her lip, so hard she briefly thought she'd drawn blood. This was knowledge that could have gotten her killed in the Wild . . .

But they were very far from those shadowy glens and sweeping valleys.

"My mother," she finally said, surprised how difficult it was to give voice to this long-hidden secret. "My mother served the Treesworn, until she ran away to be with my father. The boy she'd loved as a girl in her tribe, before they had come for her."

"Served them how?"

"As a spear maiden."

Rhenna was quiet for a moment. "Your mother was Hollow."

Alia blinked in surprise. She had never made that connection before.

"Or possibly an Imbued, like you, who was refused a shard. And she ran away."

"Also like me," Alia whispered. Her fingers were trembling, which was making the braiding even more difficult.

"It seems you come from a rebellious lineage," Rhenna said lightly, as if realizing how unsettled Alia had become.

"They killed her," Alia said suddenly. "She fought them when they found us. She was strong, so strong, but they were many. In the end, they broke her limbs and carried her into the forest. I was hiding with my father. If they'd seen me, I would be dead as well. Her crime was marrying my father, for spear maidens are forbidden from giving themselves to any but the Treesworn."

Rhenna had gone still at her words. "Alia, I'm sorry –"

"Sister!"

Alia screamed, scrambling back from Rhenna and looking around wildly. The door was closed, there was no one else in the room . . .

Her mistress's brother stepped from the slice of shadow created by the angle of the mist-globe's light hitting Rhenna's closet. He was wearing the same smug smile as every other time Alia had seen him.

"Nishi," Rhenna said coldly. "You know you are not allowed to Shadow Walk into my room."

"This is important," Nishi said as he came to stand beside the table where Rhenna was seated. He plucked the half-peeled fruit from the bowl and took a bite, juices running down his chin. As he chewed, he seemed to see her for the first time, his brows rising.

"You look like a savage," he said after swallowing, then shifted his gaze to Alia. "Your handmaid did this? Whatever for?"

"Why did you sport a sling for a few days when I know your arm was not truly hurt?" Rhenna asked, clearly changing the topic.

Nishi chuckled. "Because I wanted to see you get thrashed by the Windwrack boy, sweet sister."

Alia imagined she could hear Rhenna's teeth grinding.

"Why are you here?" her mistress snapped.

Nishi tossed the fruit onto the table. "Father has called a formal dinner for tonight. Only a few are coming – Joras, Azil, Camena, perhaps Leantha and Saelus. He wants us looking like sharded lords . . ." He wiggled his finger at her half-braided hair. ". . . not crazed barbarians."

Rhenna shoved away from the table and stood. Alia glimpsed her face and saw that she was furious.

"What is the occasion?" Rhenna asked tightly.

"An unexpected guest," Nishi replied. "I know little else, although I heard a rumor that someone wandered up to the gate this afternoon."

Rhenna's anger faded, her brow drawing down in confusion. "Who could possibly warrant a formal dinner? Only one of the other hold lords, and none would arrive without an entourage."

Nishi shrugged. "We'll find out soon enough. Seventh bell, the inner feast hall." His annoying smile broadened. "Not much time. I'll leave you now so your pretty little girl here can clean up the mess she's made."

"Get out," Rhenna commanded sharply.

Nishi flourished a mocking bow. "See you soon, dear sister!" he exclaimed, then with a wave of his hand the darkness rippled like the surface of a lake at night, before flowing together to form a doorway. A frozen wind slithered into the chamber from whatever lay beyond, making Alia shiver.

"Nishi," Rhenna said, and her brother looked back before passing into the portal. "Next time you enter my chambers unannounced I'll greet you with the Hand of Night and slap you back to the shadowrealm. Do you understand?"

Nishi replied with a wink, then vanished. At once the darkness ceased its writhing, returning once more to simply shadow on stone.

Rhenna stayed staring at where her brother had departed for a long moment, her fists clenched, and then she growled in frustration and threw herself back into her chair.

Alia approached tentatively, afraid that in her current mood Rhenna might lash out at her as well. "Should I . . . unbraid your hair, mistress?"

With a flick of her wrist, Rhenna sent the fruit Nishi had bitten tumbling to the floor. "No," she said. "Finish what you started. My brother will think it a victory if I show up to dinner later having done exactly what he commanded. He's not our father – he doesn't control me."

"Yes, mistress," Alia murmured, taking up the length of hair she had been working on when Nishi had barged into the chamber. It took her a moment to realize where she had been in the pattern, and then after a deep breath she resumed her plaiting.

Rhenna relaxed slightly as Alia settled into the rhythm of the work, the tension leaking from her neck and shoulders.

"Alia," she said, sounding almost tired, "you said that in the Wild a woman's hair tells a story. What about the braid you're making now? What does it say that I am?"

Alia didn't hesitate. "A spear maiden, mistress. For that is what you are."

Rhenna had chosen to make her home in the Duskhold's tallest spire, and Alia had always assumed it was because she enjoyed the view and the fresh air, but as her mistress led her deeper and deeper into the bowels of the hold, she began to wonder if she hadn't in truth been trying to get as far away from her father as possible. Cael Shen's quarters were deep in the mountain, the corridors leading there low-ceilinged and constricting, and what few rooms they passed shadowed and small. As they descended, Alia felt the familiar weight pressing down from above, the crawling dread that roiled her stomach and goosepimpled her skin. It was as if the mountain had its own brooding presence, and it disliked having her trespass in its depths.

She hadn't wanted to come, but Rhenna had commanded. Most of the others would have a personal servant on hand to fetch whatever was needed during the feast. Her father only kept a single valet to attend to him, so at dinners like this everyone in attendance was expected to bring their own servant.

At the bottom of a spiraling stairwell, they arrived at an ancient door of scarred black wood. Before they entered, Rhenna turned back to Alia, her face serious.

"These occasions are vanishingly rare, so I don't know what to expect. We didn't even hold such a feast for the Mother of Storms, yet now we do? Very odd. Just stay quiet and stand with the other servants, and only approach the table if I call or motion to you. Father will take any disturbance personally, and he will insist on punishment, perhaps even returning you to the Hollow quarters. I know you wouldn't like that. Just don't draw any attention to yourself and you'll be fine. Do you understand?"

After Alia nodded, Rhenna turned back to the door. "Good," she said, lifting her chin and squaring her shoulders. Her hands fluttered like birds, smoothing her dress and tugging at her lace sleeves. She was nervous, Alia realized with a growing sense of foreboding. What would happen here tonight?

When she was satisfied with her appearance, Rhenna raised the knocker and brought it down sharply. Before the clang had faded, the door swung open smoothly, pulled wide by a man Alia had hoped to never see again. The grub-like steward's watery eyes widened when he saw her standing behind Rhenna, then he composed himself and gestured for them to enter.

"The Lady Shen," he announced loudly, and Rhenna swept into

the chamber. Alia followed, holding Elanin's gaze as she brushed her cheek where the marks she had made on his face were faded but still noticeable. He flushed with anger, and she smiled sweetly in return.

This feast hall was not large and was dominated by a long table around which sat a dozen Sharded. At the head in a high-backed chair Cael Shen presided over the gathering, his fingers steepled in front of his thin lips, his expression inscrutable. This was the first time Alia had seen him wearing something other than the Duskhold robes, as he'd donned a fine black doublet trimmed with grey. His long white hair was unbound, falling to his shoulders, and a thin silver circlet rested on his brow. He looked wraith-like, a dead king haunting his long-forgotten barrow.

Alia recognized a few others around the table. On Cael Shen's left was his advisor, Leantha, in a gossamer dress. To his right sat his brother, Joras, larger and more jovial, though there was something in his eyes tonight that made him look troubled. The plump, red-haired matron beside Joras must be his wife, Camena, though Alia had never met her before. Then there was Nishi, gesturing with a golden goblet as he explained something with great passion to a stone-faced Azil. The ancient man who had greeted them when they arrived at the Duskhold was present as well, though Alia had forgotten his name. And then there was Kilian, who winked at her when their eyes briefly met before he glanced over at the only person seated at the table that looked decidedly out of place.

At first Alia thought that one of the hermits living alone deep in the Wild had wandered into the Duskhold and for some reason been invited to dine with the lords of the hold. She was hunched and misshapen, like a stunted tree in the forest forced to contort itself strangely to reach the sunlight. Her hair was a snarled grey mess, matted and filthy, and Alia wouldn't have been surprised if there were birds or some small animals nesting within. The patchwork shawl she wore looked pieced together from faded rags and scraps, and from this dangled all manner of threadbare pouches and bags. Some of these were swinging wildly as she drank lustily from a silver bowl, its matching spoon abandoned on the table unused.

As Alia made her way to where the other servants were lined against the far wall, she noticed that although no one was staring directly, the attention of all the Sharded was fixed on this old woman.

Rhenna must have been the last to arrive, as Cael Shen pushed away from the table and stood after she had settled into the empty chair beside Kilian. All conversation ceased, though the old woman continued to loudly slurp her soup. To Alia's surprise, the lord of the Duskhold did not interrupt her, but waited until she finally lowered her bowl and smacked her lips in satisfaction. Then Cael Shen raised his goblet in her direction.

"I welcome you to the Duskhold, Grandmother. We are honored to have you visit our halls."

Grandmother? Surely he didn't mean that literally. Alia glanced at the servants standing stiffly beside her, but they seemed as confused as she was.

The old woman squinted at Cael Shen for a moment like she was trying to figure out who he was, then shifted her attention to her empty bowl. "This was good. Got any more?" Her voice was raspy, as if she hadn't spoken in a very long time.

Cael Shen raised his hand and snapped his fingers. Immediately, a few of the servants hurried towards a different set of doors than the one Rhenna and Alia had come through a moment ago, and as they vanished the clatter of pots could be heard coming from the room beyond.

Everyone around the table was staring at the old woman, but she ignored them, intent on scraping the inside of her bowl with her finger. Alia had a good view of Nishi's face, which was twisted in revulsion as the crone popped her gnarled finger between her gums and noisily sucked it dry. Rhenna's expression was carefully blank, as was her father's. Kilian appeared amused by what was happening, while his parents both looked bewildered.

"Hadn't had a good soup in a while," the woman muttered. "Nothing like a soup to warm the bones." She hacked a cough, then swallowed whatever had been dislodged in her throat.

"You must be weary," the only Sharded at the table who looked as old as her ventured. "We have made up a chamber for you. Anything you desire, only ask one of the servants and it will be provided."

"*Hm*," the woman grunted. "Don't know what I'd need from the Shadow. Maybe a bit of shade to take with me. Sun was blasted harsh going up your mountain."

"It is quite a trek, Grandmother," Cael Shen said slowly. "A long, arduous trek."

The old woman snorted. "Just ask your question. Want to know why I'm here, do you?"

The servants chose that moment to return, pushing through the doors and into the hall carrying platters heaped with all manner of delicacies. A large bird had been roasted, then set atop a pile of stringy mushrooms arranged to resemble a nest. Massive whorled shells larger than a man's fist gleamed iridescent in the light of the wraithling flames. Pale, plump worms with circular fanged mouths coiled on another plate, garnished with lichen glowing a faint blue.

The old woman seemed to forget what she'd been talking about, clapping her hands together excitedly. "Ah! Now there's a feast!" she exhaled, reaching for one of the worms as they were set down. Alia's gorge rose as she noticed it was still moving slightly. With a deft twist, the old woman separated the thing's head from the rest of its body, then jammed that end into her mouth and began sucking.

Alia had to stop herself from shivering in disgust. Her mother had instilled in her the belief that eating the flesh of dead animals was wrong, and drinking the juices of still living creatures went well beyond that. The others around the table seemed to have no qualms about consuming the worms in this way, as they each took one of the wriggling creatures as the servant came around carrying the platter. For a while the only noise in the room was slurping as the worms were drained.

Cael Shen was the first to finish, tossing the husk onto the floor and turning back to the old woman. She had started on her third worm by this time, her lips stained purple.

"Indeed, Grandmother. I do wish to know why you grace our hall."

The old woman dropped her emptied worm onto the table and belched. Then she rose slightly, reaching for the roasted bird on the table and wrenching a leg free.

"Been a while since I was here. Curious to see if the hospitality has improved any." She sat back down with a grunt, her attention fixed hungrily on the glistening piece of meat she'd come away with. "Also . . ." Her eyes slid from the drumstick to Cael Shen. "Heard some whispers on the wind. The sound of little feet skittering on silken strands. You're up to something." As she said this, her gaze moved to the woman on his left and lingered there. Alia couldn't be sure, but she thought she saw a slight twitching in Leantha's cheek under the old woman's scrutiny.

Cael Shen spread his arms wide, drawing the crone's focus back to him. "The web you hear being woven is simple statecraft, Grandmother. Treaties being agreed to, alliances forged. I assure you it is far beneath your concern, or any of the other Elowyn."

This last word elicited a range of reactions around the table – Rhenna and Nishi glanced at each other in confusion, while the old man's eyes widened and Joras almost choked on the creature he'd just drawn from one of the nacreous shells.

The old woman grunted distractedly in reply, intent on cracking open the leg to get at the marrow within. Cael Shen continued watching her for a while still, as if expecting a response, but none was forthcoming, and finally he turned to the food the servants had laid out as she continued to devour whatever was within reach. Uneasy conversations sparked around the table in the wake of this exchange, but the old woman ignored all of them, intent on her food.

Rhenna was speaking in low tones with Kilian, while Joras Shen and his wife had engaged Leantha and Cael Shen in some whispered exchange. Gradually the tension around the table relaxed, and there was even some muted laughter and then even exclamations of delight as the servants brought out a new course.

Now it almost seemed like any of the many dinners Alia had attended as Rhenna's handmaiden. Her thoughts wandered, and she realized that the way Cael Shen had spoken to this old woman reminded Alia of how the headman in one village she and her father had stayed in for a time had treated an old Treesworn who had lived deeper in the forest. Respect touched by a fair bit of deferential awe, since despite being old and half-mad, the hermit could have laid waste to the village with little effort. But this was the lord of the Duskhold, one of the most powerful Sharded in the world. Why would he act this way towards anyone, let alone an old woman who seemed to have not eaten or bathed in days?

Alia pulled herself back to the present when she saw Rhenna make a beckoning gesture. She stepped forward and leaned closer to her mistress.

"Alia, I want you to go to the kitchens and ask the cooks if they've prepared any of those fruit tarts I like, the ones with –"

"What's this?"

The table quieted, all attention turning to the old woman. She had set down the pig trotter she'd been gnawing on and was staring intently at Alia, black eyes glittering.

"I'm sorry, Grandmother?" Rhenna asked slowly.

"This one!" the old woman said, waving a gnarled hand towards them both. "You keep the Blessed as servants now?"

Rhenna and Alia shared a look of confusion.

"My handmaiden, Grandmother? The Shadow did not deign to grant her a shard, so she joined the Duskhold's Hollow."

The old woman snorted loudly. "Of course that hunk of rock refused her! Or, should I say, she refused it! I've never seen someone less suited for this gloomy place. She still has the sun in her eyes and the smell of the forest about her." She shook her head, matted grey locks swaying. "Foolishness, trying to shove a square fencepost into the round hole you've dug . . ."

"What are you saying?" Rhenna asked, taking the question out of Alia's mouth.

"Grandmother!" Cael Shen interjected loudly. "Will you be interested in watching the shadows perform one of the ancient lays later? We have a disciple here trying to resurrect the old art of Shadow

Telling, and she would be very interested to know what you think of her progress."

"Eh?" the old woman grunted, turning to Cael Shen. "Shadow Telling? So I can get annoyed with how wrong you all are about the past? I think not. I'll be leaving after your cooks stop sending out dishes. Somehow I forgot how stuffy it is under here."

"You won't stay the night?" Joras Shen asked, glancing at his brother. "You're going to go down the mountain in the dark?"

"Better than trying to sleep here with that great black heart beating down below," the old woman muttered, plucking what looked like a desiccated moth from a bowl a servant had just set down.

Some unspoken message passed between the Shen brothers, and then Cael leaned forward, regarding the old woman from over steepled fingers. "Of course. Please let us know what we can provide you for the journey."

The old woman seemed not to hear him, utterly engrossed with peeling away the insect's papery wings from its body.

Grimacing in revulsion, Alia lowered her head to Rhenna's. "I'll go ask about those tarts," she murmured, and then hurried towards the kitchens.

The dinner ended not long after this odd exchange, the old woman abruptly rising and informing the others around the table that she would be leaving. Alia had expected Cael Shen to make some protestations, insisting she should stay the night, but if anything, he looked relieved at the announcement. He had only bowed his head and wished her well, and then she had swept a few table scraps into one of the many pockets sown into her shawl and without another word hobbled from the chamber.

As soon as the door shut behind her, Nishi turned to his father and started to speak, but Cael Shen silenced him with a sharp gesture. No one else dared interrupt the lord of the Duskhold as he sat there with his head tilted, listening hard. A lot of questioning glances passed between the younger Sharded around the table, but their elders wore looks of grim resolve.

Finally, Cael Shen relaxed, letting out a deep breath. "She is gone. She has left the Duskhold." He took a long drink, draining his wine goblet.

"Who was that?" hissed Nishi, glancing at the door as if he feared she might be hovering on the other side with her ear pressed to the wood.

Cael Shen had a distant look in his eyes as he swirled his glass. "She has not changed at all," he murmured, ignoring his son's question. "It is true, then." His gaze slid to his brother. "Do you remember her?"

Joras shook his shaggy head. "No. I was too young when last she visited the hold."

"Yes, of course," Cael Shen mused softly. "Mother was dandling you on her knee for most of the dinner because you wouldn't stay in your chair. And you were crying for your favorite pastry."

"That night is etched sharp in my memory," said the old man. "Your tantrum annoyed her. She said something in a language I'd never heard before, and you didn't make another sound for the rest of the meal. I was afraid you had been struck permanently mute."

"Unfortunately, no such luck," muttered Cael Shen, and his brother's wife snorted laughter before quickly controlling herself.

"How long ago was this?" Rhenna asked, interrupting her elders.

"At least a century," the lord of the Duskhold replied distractedly.

More surprised glances passed between the others.

"But she was not Sharded," stated Nishi. "I felt nothing from her."

"I do not know what she is," his father snapped, as if annoyed at having to admit his ignorance. "I do not know if she is Sharded or not. I do not even know her name. She wanders where she will, and no hold is foolish enough to refuse her whatever she wants."

Rhenna looked troubled by the admission. "You called her something. What are these Elowyn? Are there others like her?"

Cael Shen's gaze flicked to the servants in the hall. They all avoided meeting his eyes, instead staring straight ahead.

"These are secrets that are not suitable for all ears." He made a gesture of dismissal towards the servants. "Go, all of you. Return to your quarters. Your duties are finished for tonight."

Rarely did the master of the Duskhold give direct commands, and the servants wasted no time in obeying. Alia found herself being carried along by the sudden rush to leave the chamber, and though her curiosity had been piqued by Cael Shen's words, she also felt no small measure of relief as the door shut behind her.

Whatever knowledge Cael Shen was about to share, it did not concern her at all.

35

DERYN

"AND BEGIN," Vertus commanded in a bored drawl, waving his hand languidly in the direction of the two *sardor* adepts in the sparring circle. One of them – a lanky young woman named Yvrin with dusky skin and a sharp face – bowed towards her opponent, a heavyset boy with a mop of unruly black hair, but he did not return the courtesy. Deryn had forgotten what he was called, probably because he had never introduced himself. He belonged to the large minority of younger adepts who had been born and raised in the Duskhold, and like most of the rest of them, he looked down with sneering disdain on the Imbued brought to the hold by the hounds. They thought themselves superior, though Deryn had not noticed any difference in their abilities, despite growing up in the hold. If anything, they ended up on their backsides during these bouts more often than the outsiders, and Deryn was looking forward to watching this arrogant fellow humbled.

The two Sharded came together and traded a quick flurry of strikes, neither breaking the defenses of the other. The Duskhold-bred boy had height on Yvrin, but she had a significant edge in speed and mitigated his advantage by darting within his reach and then dancing away before one of his heavy blows could land. This was how most of these sparring matches unfolded – the combatants would first close and gauge the fighting prowess of the other, waiting for a good opportunity to unleash their talents. Every Sharded's reservoir of *ka* was limited, and draining oneself too quickly would leave a warrior at a severe disadvantage if the fight dragged on. Also, if they used their abilities too early in the battle it would likely fizzle against whatever defensive strategy their opponent had devised. Better to hold them in reserve until the other Sharded was tired or distracted, when they could be used to devastating effect.

Neither of the adepts seemed interested in showing their hand too early, continuing to trade blows as they shuffled around the sparring circle. Vertus appeared disinterested in the match, staring past the combatants at the jagged peaks rising up around the Duskhold, but Deryn suspected this was not just because of the lack of talents so far in evidence. Several of the older adepts had shared this attitude with Vertus, a bored annoyance at having to oversee the training of those with fewer shards, as if it was simply not worth their time. Deryn wondered what the tattooed Sharded would rather be doing right now. Probably relaxing with his friends in the wing of the fortress given over to his family, drinking wine and playing the knuckle-bone game that was popular among the Duskhold's elite.

When Deryn had first encountered Vertus on the scree-strewn slope outside the hold, he had thought the Sharded's tattoos signified that he had once come from beyond the realms of men, most likely the northern Wild. But he'd learned later that Vertus was the scion of perhaps the second most powerful family in the Duskhold, the Balenchas. Their history stretched back all the way to the rebellion against Segulah Tain, as their ancestor had been the second-in-command to the Imperator Shen who had led the uprising against the Radiant Emperor. The officers in those long-lost legions had been similarly tattooed to show their rank, and while all the other families had dispensed with these ancient traditions, the Balenchas had held fast to demonstrate that their roots trailed all the way to before the Heart's sundering.

Vertus was not the only Sharded who appeared indifferent to the outcome of the fight. Kaliss was seated beside Deryn just beyond the boundary of the circle, her eyes glazed and unfocused. A sheen of sweat covered her copper skin, as if she was sick, but Deryn suspected he knew what had happened to her.

"So you merged your third?" he murmured just as Yvrin connected with a powerful kick to her opponent's side, causing him to stumble away with a pained grunt.

Kaliss glanced at him, her coal-black eyes bloodshot. "Yes," she said, then grimaced. "You know, I was once ambushed by a gang in Phane and beaten half to death in an alley. This feels much the same. Every bone aches and even though I slept like the dead yesterday it's like I've been awake for days."

"But it merged."

"Of course it merged," Kaliss snapped. "If you can bear three fragments, it would be impossible that I could not as well."

Yvrin had by now pressed her advantage, chasing the boy almost to the far edge of the circle, and for a moment Deryn thought he was going to step beyond the white marking and give her the victory then and there. He might have been considering it, but to accept losing without bringing talents into the battle would be shameful, so with a guttural snarl, he whirled around and flung out his hand. His Arm of the Abyss erupted from the center of his palm, the whip of glistening darkness arcing towards Yvrin's head. She did not even break stride, vanishing just before the tendril reached her and reappearing behind the boy. He must have been expecting her to Shadow Step – the adepts were all intimately aware of the talents the others boasted – but even though he smashed his elbow backwards, she was still a step ahead of him, dodging the blow and then kicking him hard in the back of his leg. With a shriek of agony, the Duskhold boy collapsed to his knees. He might have tried to rise again, but long talons now curved from the tips of her fingers, and several of them were pressed to his neck.

"I yield," he hissed.

Yvrin stepped back, the claws evaporating into mist. She looked to

Vertus, but the Sharded was still staring off into the distance. He did make a vague gesture, dismissing the combatants from the circle.

"Vertus does not seem excited to be here," Kaliss said as Yvrin offered her hand to the boy. He slapped it away, scowling, and dragged himself painfully back to his feet.

"He's no different from the rest," Deryn replied quietly.

Over the last few days, the most powerful of the adepts had taken turns overseeing the training of the weaker. Azil was busy, off on some mission for Cael Shen, so the duty had fallen to the *kenang* Sharded who had already attained their second talent. As the most recent of the adepts to achieve this milestone, Kilian Shen had been the first overseer of these bouts, and that had been a lively, raucous affair. The ones that followed had not been nearly as enjoyable, but no one had showed so much casual disdain towards them as Vertus.

Neither Deryn nor Kaliss had been called upon to fight yet. The reason was not entirely clear, but Deryn suspected it was because they both had only recently been elevated from the novices. Likely it was believed they had only managed to merge a second shard – as far as he could tell, the fewest number any of the other adepts bore was four. This would mean they all had at least a talent to draw upon, and their bodies would be significantly stronger. Deryn didn't think that anyone except for Kaliss knew he had merged a third shard, though some might suspect she had just achieved this feat, given her condition this morning. Unfortunately, Deryn had not been granted a second talent to go along with his first. His ability to summon his Ghost Chitin had manifested almost immediately, appearing in his mind like a skill he'd always been able to do. But there had been no such revelation when his third shard had fully merged. He knew that Sharded did not acquire talents with every fragment they added, but still he'd been disappointed. The strangest thing was, it almost felt like something was hovering on the edge of his consciousness. Perhaps it would reveal itself when he merged his fourth . . . which he thought might be soon, given how successfully he'd smoothed his roiled pathways. Deryn smirked, imagining how annoyed Kaliss would be when she discovered he'd gone and merged his fourth shard just when she'd finally managed her third.

And she would also be staring at a plateau in her ascension, as she had only one more shard remaining from the three she had acquired on her Delve. Deryn still had ten fragments in reserve, an almost unimaginable wealth. Kaliss would have to venture out to hunt Unbound Sharded or perhaps risk exploring the ancient tombs and ruins where shards might sometimes be found . . . or she would need a patron, one of the powerful Sharded within the Duskhold who might trade more fragments for an oath of loyalty.

"Boy!"

Deryn blinked, returning from his daydream. Vertus had spoken harshly – apparently someone had seriously annoyed the Sharded. He glanced around, wondering who had drawn down such wrath, and then realized all the other adepts were staring at him.

Oh.

Deryn swallowed, meeting Vertus's smoldering gaze. "Ah, my apologies, Lord Balenchas. My mind was elsewhere."

"Evidently," Vertus said flatly. "After all, why bother paying attention when you are never called upon to fight? Now stand."

Deryn climbed to his feet. "I suppose the others thought I was not ready."

"And is that true?"

Deryn lifted his chin, trying to show confidence even as his heartbeat quickened. "I would be honored to step into the circle. Though I suspect I have fewer shards than any of the others gathered here."

Vertus gestured dismissively at Kaliss. "Not her. At the most, a single shard separates you both. Such discrepancy is common enough in these bouts."

Deryn bit back what he wanted to say. Surely Vertus could see that Kaliss was in a terrible condition today?

Grimacing, the Ashasai girl slowly stood. Her face was pale, and standing next to her Deryn could see a sheen of sweat, but when she spoke her voice was steady.

"I am ready to fight," she said.

"She's not," Deryn said quickly, returning his gaze to Vertus. "Look, she can barely keep herself upright. She has clearly just merged a shard."

"I can step into the ring with *you*," Kaliss said sharply. "I'm not *that* weak."

Vertus arched an eyebrow. "Is this true, adept? Have you just added to your shard?"

A moment of silence. "Yes," she finally admitted, and Deryn sensed her anger. He knew she despised being perceived as weak or unready. Truly, though, this was for her own good.

"Then you should not fight," Vertus agreed. "You need time to recover." He shifted his attention once more to Deryn. "You, however, have no such excuses. There may be no one here as weak as you, but you gain nothing by sitting and watching your betters test themselves. I wish to see you in the circle."

An icy calmness settled over Deryn. He remembered stepping in front of Alia as a glistening crown of blades whirled around Vertus, and he suspected the adept had not forgotten when a novice had challenged him so brazenly. Now he would gain a measure of revenge by having him beaten soundly in front of everyone. Vertus had known Kaliss was too drained to fight, and that Deryn would have to face an opponent far stronger than himself if she was forced to withdraw.

"Pand En'ok," Vertus said dispassionately, and Deryn's heart lurched in his chest. "You have not had a chance to test yourself today. Will you step into the circle with our newest Sharded? You are both *sardor*, I believe."

The Wild girl with the spiky blood-red hair grinned, showing teeth that had been filed to points. "With joy, *kenang*," she replied in a husky voice, her silver eyes fixed on Deryn.

He did his best to hold her unsettling gaze, trying not to think about the last time he'd seen such eyes. Deryn breathed out slowly to calm himself. Pand and her brother Chal were two of the last adepts he wanted to fight. Rumor held that they had been discovered deep in the Wild, the children of cannibals, in a land so dangerous three

Sharded had accompanied the hound that found them. Whatever cruelty they had experienced in those savage lands seemed to have seeped into their souls, and they were known as the most vicious of all the adepts.

They also were both five-sharded, so Pand would have a great advantage over Deryn. If he had one slight edge, it was that he had seen her fight before and knew what talents she boasted – Sphere of Night, the Umbral Blade, and Tarry Grasp. The first summoned a globe of impenetrable darkness that blinded an enemy, but it was useless against another shadow-sharded with darkvision. The Umbral Blade was a rarer first-tier talent that Deryn had seen Pand employ during her short and brutal contest with the Windwrack Sharded, when strands of darkness had coalesced into a curving black blade. During that earlier fight, the scimitar had not drawn blood, instead turning the flesh it touched white from a numbing cold. It was the Wild girl's last talent that worried him the most, though. Tarry Grasp allowed Pand to fix shadows to stone, keeping her enemies from moving. During the fight with the storm-sharded, she had used this to devastating effect, violently arresting her opponent's attack as he lunged at her, then stepping within his guard before he could recover.

Three talents to his one, and his lone power was purely defensive. He knew he had no chance in the circle with her. Deryn wished that second talent he felt hovering at the edge of his perception had manifested itself – he badly needed one attacking ability like the Arm of the Abyss or the Umbral Blade. Not that it really mattered, he supposed. Five shards meant to him her flesh was like plate armor, and her blows would be a grown man striking a child. Deryn had the sinking realization that Vertus might not just be trying to humiliate him but in fact leave him seriously injured. Another adept would only use enough strength to defeat him . . . but he did not trust the Wild girl to show such restraint.

"He canna send his demon after me," Pand suddenly said to Vertus as she went to take her position in the circle.

She meant his elemental. Her fears were unnecessary, because he hadn't even seen Shade since he had woken this morning. Usually the little spirit flitted around him for a while before curling up in a patch of darkness to wait in his chamber for him to return from his lessons, but there had been no sign of it. The elemental seemed completely independent, coming and going as it pleased. Far more like a cat than a dog despite the form it had recently preferred.

And apparently others had noticed this.

"If what I hear is true," Vertus replied to the Wild girl, "he has no power over his elemental."

Pand frowned, but she still nodded. She was afraid of Shade, Deryn realized. Was it some primitive tribal superstition, or did the other adepts also secretly harbor such fears about him?

"Deryn," Vertus said sharply, the first time the Sharded had used his name. He did not say it warmly. "Will you fight or not?"

It was his choice, then. Perhaps Vertus expected him to refuse and be branded a coward in the eyes of the others. That would be embarrassing, but surely it would be preferable to being thrashed by someone with two more shards and – more importantly – two more talents? Pand was staring at him through narrowed eyes, her lip curled slightly in what looked like disdain, as if she knew he might be considering backing down.

Taking a deep breath, Deryn stepped into the circle. The respect he would earn by answering this challenge would surely outweigh the pain she might inflict.

Right?

"Good luck," Kaliss whispered, and he turned to flash her a far more confident smile than he felt. He did notice her hands were kneading the hem of her robe nervously.

"I'll be fine," he replied, then walked over to a spot two dozen paces from Pand. There was nothing marking the stone here, but it was about where he'd seen all the other fighters wait for the word that would begin the match. It felt strange to finally step into the circle after so long. He'd imagined this moment countless times, but in all those scenarios he'd never expected to be this nervous. Then again, he'd never imagined he'd be standing across from a much stronger Sharded feared for her brutality.

He breathed out slowly, pushing his *ka* through his pathways. Pand had never seen him fight, so she would have no idea what talents he might possess. This might make her tentative, and if he had a talent other than the one he actually did, he might have been able to exploit her hesitation. She would realize fairly quickly, though, that he had no attacking talents, and that his only weapons were his *ka*-infused strikes. If only he could meet her summoned Umbral Blade with his porcelain sword – but of course, sharded artifacts were not allowed to be brought into these fights.

Deryn finished his channeling, his body thrumming with power as he settled into a defensive form. Across from him, Pand adopted a more aggressive stance, ready to leap at him as soon as Vertus gave the word. No doubt she knew he knew what she would do, and that only further eroded his confidence. The Wild girl wanted to end this quickly and ruthlessly.

"Fight!" Vertus cried with far more enthusiasm than he'd shown for previous bouts, and before the word had fully escaped his lips, Pand was charging at him. She crossed the circle in a heartbeat, throwing a vicious jab at his face. Deryn blocked the blow, the force of it making him stagger backwards, pain reverberating up his arm. Then she snapped off a quick combination of strikes, and he just managed to ward them away, each one landing like a heavy wooden truncheon. If one had slipped past his defenses and connected with his jaw, he'd have been unconscious before his head hit the stone.

Desperate for a reprieve he threw a wild punch, and as he'd hoped, she skipped back a step. Deryn shuffled backwards, trying to put some space between them, though having seen her speed now firsthand he knew this was largely pointless. He shook his aching forearm, hoping she hadn't cracked the bone.

Her lip curled when she saw this. "You're doomed, fledgling," she hissed. "You don't belong among us. I'm going to send you crying back to Saelus."

Deryn did not answer her, frantically smoothing out his unsettled *ka* and pushing it once more into his limbs. The pain in his arm faded, but he doubted that he'd be able to withstand another such attack.

Pand must not have realized how close she had already come to defeating him with just this initial flurry, as she abandoned her fighting stance and instead stretched out her hand. A gleaming black scimitar materialized, motes of darkness forming a crackling aura around the blade. She slashed the air, wisps of shadow drifting in the sword's wake.

The Umbral Blade. Deryn had seen other Sharded block the worst effects of this talent with Ghost Chitin, but he doubted there had been a several-shard difference in those instances.

Pand stalked towards him, the scimitar upraised. Deryn could tell that she had little formal training with swords – Heth would have groaned at her footwork and the way she was holding it, though since he wielded nothing, there was little reason for her to adopt a duelist's stance.

Deryn concentrated, summoning his Ghost Chitin. He felt it sheathe his flesh, an armor that would remain unseen until called upon to protect him. It gave him some comfort, knowing it was there. Surely it would at least blunt her strikes.

Pand lunged at him with the blade outthrust, and he leaped away, the curving tip of the sword nearly touching his robes. She pursued, slashing wildly, and he backpedaled so fast he came close to tripping over his own feet. That would have been an embarrassing end to his first bout.

"Fight, coward," the Wild girl sneered. "There's nowhere left to run."

Deryn spared a glance over his shoulder and saw that she was right, as the edge of the ring was only a few paces behind him. He tried to circle away from her, but she quickly cut off his escape. Pand grinned, showing her filed teeth as she flourished the blade.

Deryn ran at her. Her eyes widened, and then she swung the crackling black sword. Without slowing, he raised his forearm, desperately hoping this wasn't a terrible mistake. As the edge of the scimitar struck him the Ghost Chitin manifested, a vambrace of smoky crystal, and there was a screeching sound like nails on a slate board. The force of the blow traveled up his arm, accompanied by a wash of numbness, but the Chitin did not shatter. Then he was within her guard, smashing his elbow into her face and channeling as much *ka* as he could into the strike. She shrieked in rage, and when he whirled around after a few steps, she was holding her hand to her nose, blood leaking from between her fingers.

So he could hurt her. And his Ghost Chitin had survived her Umbral Blade, though he could feel the cracks webbing the invisible armor. Another solid strike at the same location would almost certainly shatter the Chitin, and it wouldn't repair until he could take some time to redirect his *ka* to that spot.

Time he did not have.

Silver eyes flashing, Pand rushed at him again. She'd put both hands on the hilt of her Umbral Blade, and the blood dripping down her face made her look even more savage. Deryn raised his other forearm, taking the slash on his other arm. The Ghost Chitin buckled but held, and before she could swing again, he turned and sprinted away. He just needed a moment to reform his Chitin, and then perhaps he could survive long enough to land a lucky counter.

She wasn't running after him. Instead, she was striding across the circle, her face a bloody mask of cold determination. As she drew near, Deryn went to sprint to the far side of the circle . . . but then yelped in surprise.

His feet were fixed to the stone, cemented by his shadow. Tarry Grip. He hissed in dismay, straining with all his might to lift his boot. But it was to no avail, as if deep roots were holding him in place. Pand's ghastly grin was triumphant now, and she drew the Umbral Blade back. He knew he would only last a few blows before she bludgeoned what remained of his Chitin to pieces.

Suddenly something shifted, there was a faint popping sound, and he could move again. Pand's expression went slack with shock, and Deryn seized the moment by lunging forward and punching her hard again in the face. Her head snapped back, a rope of blood exploding from her already damaged nose as the Umbral Blade evaporated into shreds of darkness. He felt something then, a familiar presence brushing against his leg, and he glanced down as his shadow rippled.

Shade. The elemental must have been hiding in his shadow and had severed Pand's Tarry Grip. This all occurred to Deryn in a flash of insight, but he had no time to dwell on it, as he knew he had to press this small advantage before the Wild girl recovered. He followed after her as she stumbled away, throwing a quick combination of strikes to her stomach and head.

It was like hitting stone. Pand clearly felt each time his punches connected, letting out little gasps of pain, but it didn't seem like she was anywhere close to succumbing to his onslaught.

And then she caught his fist.

"Demon kin," she spat through bloodstained teeth, then struck him hard in the chest. Deryn was lifted from his feet from the force of the blow, his breath ripped away as he landed flat on his back. He gasped, desperately trying to draw in air again, but before he could Pand was straddling him. She reared back and struck again, slamming the back of his head against the stone. His vision darkened, and from far away he thought he heard Kaliss screaming at Vertus to end the fight.

Another blow.

Another.

He reached up weakly, but Pand slapped his hands away.

"Abomination!" she cried.

The blackness pressing at the edges of his vision deepened until the Wild girl was just a vague shadow looming over him. Deryn felt himself slipping away, a swimmer trying to keep his head above water as something dragged him into the depths.

And then it unfurled in his mind. Deryn reached for it, felt its contours, embraced the sudden, startling knowledge, and sent it hurtling at the girl hurting him.

A freezing blast of cold wind rushed over him, followed by a surprised yelp. Pand's weight vanished, the unblemished blue sky filling the space above him where she had been a moment ago.

Cries of alarm erupted, many voices. One rose above the rest, Vertus bellowing for calm, commanding someone to see to Pand.

Why not him? He was the one who had been beaten half to death. Deryn rolled onto his side, grimacing at the pain in his ribs, his face feeling like dough on a baker's worktable. A crowd had surged to the edge of the tower's roof, their backs to him. What had happened? He coughed, tasting blood on his lips. A hand was shaking him.

"Deryn! Are you all right?"

Kaliss. He lay flat again so he could see the Ashasai girl. She crouched over him, her face creased with concern.

"Can you hear –"

A blur of movement, and she was shoved violently aside. A new face hovered over him, one with eyes so strikingly silver for a moment fear seized Deryn that he was dead and Menochus had returned to drag him beyond the veil.

"Bastard," snarled Chal, Pand's twin brother, and then his boot struck Deryn's head with terrible force.

36

DERYN

HE SMELLED THE FOREST.

Rich loam soaked by rain, flowers nestled in the lees of skyspears. Heady as temple incense. It smelled like life . . . and death. Growing and wilting, old rot and new births.

Where was he?

Slowly, painfully, he cracked open his eyes. He was lying on a cot, the black stone above him illuminated by the crawling radiance of a wraithling flame.

The Duskhold. He was in the hold, even though somehow he still smelled the forest.

And he *hurt*.

Months ago he'd awakened in a bed in great pain, his back aflame. This time it was other parts of him that felt shattered, his ribs and sternum and oh – fire and ashes – his face. It was agony just to keep his eyes open.

He spent a few long moments gathering his strength, and then with wincing slowness he shifted slightly, sitting up enough that he could see where he was.

It was unlike any chamber in the hold he'd yet seen. Ceramic pots and planters were scattered about, filled with all manner of stunted trees and flowering shrubs. In one, dark-petaled blossoms had unfurled for the light seeping from the mist-globe fixed to the ceiling, and elsewhere pendulous fruit hung from gnarled branches. One wall was veined by a faintly luminescent vine spotted with red flowers like drops of blood, and another wall was taken up by a workbench covered with glass apparatuses. A shelf groaned above, stuffed with ancient tomes, stoppered bottles of cloudy liquid, and the tiny skeletal remains of strange creatures encased in glass.

His was not the only cot in the room, but all the others were unoccupied. Deryn thought he was alone until the sound of leaves rustling made him turn his head slightly, and a hunched old man with a forked white beard moved out from behind one of the largest trees, a basket half-filled with pieces of bark slung over his arm. He blinked rheumy eyes in surprise when their gazes met.

"Ah! You're awake!" he said, setting down his burden and limping towards Deryn's bed.

"Where am I?" Deryn asked, his words slurring slightly. His head felt like it had been hollowed out and then packed with straw. "Who are you?"

He flinched back as the old man thrust his face close enough that their noses nearly bumped.

"Good, good. Reflexes seem normal. Eyes are clear, if a bit bloodshot."

He moved back just as quickly, pulling on one of his beard's forks as he studied Deryn appraisingly. "No serious damage to your brain, I think. Lucky you."

"You're a physicker?"

The old man bobbed his head. "Indeed, indeed. Malachai Gooth, once of Fair Harbor. Trained at the Erudinium of Karath." He extended his arm towards the workbench, and a moment later a tendril of shadow wrapped itself around a bottle filled to the brim with something disturbingly red.

"And you're Sharded," Deryn murmured as the dark serpent slithered through the air to the old man, depositing the phial in his outstretched hand.

The old man sniffed at its contents, wrinkling his nose in mild disgust. "Not everyone is suited to be a warrior," he said, then winked and flashed Deryn a sly grin.

"The other adept had two more shards than me," Deryn grumbled. "And I think I gave her a few things to remember me by as well."

"Oh, you did, you did," Malachai said, swirling the glass gently to stir the silty residue at the bottom. "That Wild girl spent last night in here. She probably should have stayed longer, to be honest. The fall from the Drum Tower is harrowing, even for an adept."

Deryn blinked in surprise. "She fell from the tower?"

"Yes, you threw her off," the physicker said, distracted by the act of pouring some of the ruby-red liquid into a smaller cup that had materialized in his other hand.

He'd thrown her off? How close had they been to the edge? And what had he done? Those last few frantic moments were a fractured mess, but he remembered her pinning him to the ground, striking his face over and over again . . . and then the sudden, blinding revelation of his second talent. He turned inward, searching for this new ability. There it was, coiled in the recesses of his mind, waiting to be unleashed again. He sensed it was an attack, something he could hurl at his enemies. He frowned, wondering if it was a first-tier talent he'd seen before. Was it the javelins of darkness he'd witnessed a few of the adepts wield in other bouts? Kilian had told him the name of that talent – something to do with spears. Winnowing Spears? Threshing Spears?

But no. The talent he'd lashed out with had been like a great rush of wind. He doubted he'd seen its like before . . . nor did he want to summon it again here, without knowing the extent of its destructive power.

"Drink this," Malachai commanded, holding out the cup he had just filled.

"What is it?" Deryn asked, eyeing the dark film that had already formed on its surface distrustfully.

"Medicine. The Shadow's gifts do not include healing, so we in the Duskhold must make do. This is the sap of the heartsblood tree mixed with water, powdered kanth shell, and a dollop of rethwing guano."

"Guano? Isn't that –"

"Drink," Malachai said, more testily than before.

Deryn took the proffered cup with trembling fingers and tossed it back before he could reconsider what he was doing. To his surprise, it went down more easily than he was expecting, with just a faint bitterness.

"Your sharded body is recovering well," Malachai said, taking back the cup. "This will speed up the healing. Another day or so and you'll be up and about, I promise you."

Deryn sagged back into the cot. "Thank you."

"Oh, it is my pleasure, young adept. I was hoping your little shadow would make an appearance, but no such luck. My dear friend Devenal has been simply obsessed of late."

The Archivist. Deryn felt a twinge of shame that he hadn't yet gone to the library to learn what he could about his elemental.

Humming to himself, Malachai turned away and shuffled back to the basket of bark he'd set down earlier. He rummaged in it, pulling out a particularly thick piece, then without looking at Deryn had one of his beckoned shadows deliver it to his lap.

"Chew this if the pain gets worse," he said absently. "Selassian bark has numbing properties."

Deryn fingered the flaky piece of wood as the old man wandered around the chamber intent on various tasks. He poured water from a jug into pots, pruned a rather ragged looking bit of shrubbery, plucked some bright yellow berries from another bush, and shooed away a large red and black spider that had decided to spin its web between some branches.

"How do these all grow down here?" Deryn asked after watching Malachai work for a while.

"*Hmm*?" the old Sharded replied, straightening from where he'd been bent over a bed of flowers the color of old bruises. "The plants down here are all nocturnal. They sup on moonlight, but our wraith-ling flame is a reasonable substitute."

"And they all have ... healing properties?"

"Of one sort or another. Our shards are not the only form of magic in the world, you know. And once the esoteric arts were far more common, if you believe the legends, but only a faint echo of these persist in the natural world. If we were in the Black Steps, I could merely lay hands on you and your flesh would knit back together, but I am not blood-sharded. Nor would I want to be, even if it would make my tasks easier. And so I must find healing in other places –"

The physicker paused, glancing into the recesses of the room like he'd heard something. Deryn followed his gaze, and saw that the shadows there were roiling, and he knew from being witness to Nishi's Shadow Walking that someone was coming. Sure enough, the churning dark soon settled into the shape of a portal, and a moment later the Black Sword of the Duskhold stepped into the infirmary.

"Azil!" cried the old man warmly.

"Malachai," the sharded lord replied, striding to the physicker and laying his hand on his shoulder affectionately. "It's good to see you. I'm sorry I've not visited in so long."

The old man waved this apology away. "It's nothing, lad. I know Lord Shen has you scurrying about on all sorts of important tasks. The curse of the competent, I'm afraid."

Azil quirked a smile at this. "A curse I know you suffer from as well, old friend. Thank you, by the way, for patching up Joras's boy so well. I feared when I saw the break that he might never walk again without a limp, but now, just a few months later, it's barely noticeable."

Malachai stroked his forked beard, obviously pleased by the Black Sword's praise. "It was easy enough to set, and then I began a regimen of distilled Celvin's Wart to strengthen the bone and help things along. But you didn't come to learn my secrets." He nodded towards Deryn in his cot. "You're here for this boy, yes?"

"Indeed," Azil said, giving the old man's shoulder a final friendly squeeze before turning to Deryn.

"He looks worse than he truly is," the old man said as he trailed

Azil over to where Deryn had struggled once more into a seated position. "The bruises will fade in a few more days. No broken bones, at
least."

The dark-skinned Salahi regarded Deryn with pursed lips. There
was anger in his face, and Deryn truly hoped it was not directed
at him.

"How do you feel?" Azil asked.

"Well enough, master," Deryn replied. "Sore. A little confused,
perhaps."

Azil's brow drew down. "Confused?"

"As to why I'm here," Deryn continued. "Why Pand would keep
beating me, even after I was clearly defeated."

"Were you defeated?" Azil asked, his frown turning up into the
ghost of a wry smile. "Pand ended up nearly as bad off as you. And to
your first question . . . I have not asked her, but I did demand answers
from her brother."

"He kicked me," Deryn murmured, remembering the Wild boy
looming over him, silver eyes blazing with hate.

"And for that he has been punished," Azil assured him. "But why
Pand beat a much-weaker Sharded so mercilessly . . . it seems it is
about your elemental."

Deryn was not surprised, remembering what she had snarled at
him during the fight. *Abomination. Demon kin.*

"The tribe Pand and Chal were taken from lives far to the north,
at the edge of the great glaciers. It is a barren, freezing waste, and it
breeds a hard and vicious people. Superstitious, as well. The existence of spirits and demons is as accepted as the knowledge that the
sun will rise in the morning. Apparently there is a legend mothers
whisper to their children about the Eyeless Man, who wanders the
ice accompanied by a demon black as night, his unholy lover. A living
shadow."

"An elemental?"

Azil shrugged. "Who knows? Likely it is just a story. But Pand and
Chal were raised on such tales, that if the Eyeless Man found you he
would have his demon croon you asleep and pluck out your eyes,

then leave you there, blind and helpless as he continued on his way, once more able to see. At least for a little while."

"So they think I am like this Eyeless Man?"

"They do . . . and it gets worse, as when they were children their most beloved uncle was found frozen not a hundred paces from where their tribe had camped, bloody pits where his eyes had been. As was the custom of their tribe, they ate what remained, and both believe that some shred of their uncle's spirit persists inside them, and that he is the source of their anger towards you."

Deryn grunted at this, unsure what to say.

"Exactly," Azil replied. "But clearly you are not a demon, no more than any of us who consort with the Shadow, so I have sternly rebuked both of them. They should not bother you again . . . but I would also try to stay far away, if that's possible."

Deryn nodded. He had absolutely no desire to see either of the cannibal twins anytime soon.

Azil leaned against his gleaming staff, regarding Deryn in silence for a long moment. Behind him, Malachi had resumed his puttering work, though he was very obviously watching them out of the corner of his eye. Deryn wondered if the Black Sword was waiting for him to say something.

"Do you remember what happened?" Azil finally asked, his dark gaze measuring.

"Not really . . ." Deryn began, running his tongue over his dry lips. He should have asked for some water as soon as he'd awakened. "We were fighting. She was much stronger than me. And faster. I was just trying to stay in the circle long enough to give a respectable showing."

"Did she use her talents?"

Deryn nodded, remembering the hissing crackle of her Umbral Blade.

"She said she seized you with her Tarry Grip."

Deryn shivered. He wished he could forget the feeling of helplessness as his own shadow held him fast to the stone.

Azil adjusted his grip on the Darkbringer, sending a shimmer of blue light along its length. "But you broke it somehow."

Deryn swallowed, reliving those frantic moments. "Yes. I thought I was doomed. But then . . . then I felt something sever the Grip."

"Something? You don't know what it was?" Azil was staring at him intently now.

"It was Shade," he admitted.

"Shade?"

"Sorry, the elemental. That's the name he seems to like. Truly, I didn't know he was there, but apparently he had been hiding in my shadow and it was he who broke the Tarry Grip."

"Hiding in your shadow," Azil said slowly. His gaze drifted around the infirmary. "Could it be here now?"

"Maybe?" Deryn said with a shrug.

"You don't know." Azil sounded like he was stating a fact rather than asking Deryn a question.

"No. I haven't figured out yet how to speak with it. Sometimes it seems like it understands, but even if it does, I cannot command it. It does what it wants."

"Interesting," Azil mused, his gaze unfocusing. He seemed to be considering what Deryn had just said. Finally, he grunted and returned his attention to Deryn. "I wonder if this Shade has anything to do with your talent."

"My talent?" Deryn asked, confused by the sudden change of topic.

"Yes. The talent you manifested that ended the fight so spectacularly."

"I . . . don't remember what I did. That was the first time I had used that power. It just leaped into existence while she had me pinned and was pummeling me . . ."

"That does sometimes happen," Azil explained. "Talents can emerge during times of great duress, and getting bludgeoned into the stone certainly qualifies. Tell me, how many fragments have you merged with your shard?"

"Three, including the one the Shadow gifted me."

Azil's eyes widened slightly. "Three. Very interesting."

"Why is that, my lord?"

"Because it is extremely rare for the Sharded to gain a second-tier talent with only that many fragments. The only other I've ever heard of who accomplished this feat and became *kenang* so early was Lady Shen."

"Rhenna?"

"No, her mother," Azil murmured distractedly, his gaze distant. "Before she disappeared."

"She what?"

The Black Sword's focus sharpened on Deryn once more. "Never mind. But Vertus was very clear about what happened upon the tower. A ragged black tear in the world, from which erupted a black, howling wind. It struck Pand when she was completely unprepared, throwing her backwards and off the roof."

Deryn reached within himself, feeling the edges of this new talent. It coiled deep within him like the sleeping balewyrm, waiting to be prodded awake. "So I am *kenang*? What is this talent called?"

"The Breath of the Mother," Azil told him. "Only a handful of shadow-sharded in the Duskhold share this talent. It is powerful, but difficult to wield accurately. A hacksaw, you could say, not a scalpel. It is also very draining – you'll empty most of your reserves of *ka* summoning it, so if it doesn't end whatever battle you are in, likely it will mean your defeat."

"The Breath of the Mother," Deryn whispered, remembering that howling rush of power that had overwhelmed Pand.

"Saelus believes it is similar to Shadow Walking," Azil continued. "The portal you create is like the gateway to the shadowrealm we use to traverse distances . . . but not into the same hospitable part we pass through. No, this section is filled with a tempest of darkness – the breath of Mother Dark, some long ago poet named it – and it erupts with great force when the breach is made." Azil's expression grew more serious. "You must be careful with it, Deryn. If you had accidentally unleashed the Breath in the direction where the other adepts were sitting, you might have swept the whole lot of them off the tower."

"And I would not have been happy about that," interjected the physicker, his back to them as he pruned the vines climbing the walls.

"That does not mean you cannot use it again if called into the circle," Azil continued. "The purpose of these bouts is not to settle scores or earn respect, but to hone our talents, so they might be of use to the hold when needed. And like your elemental, this could be a great asset to the Duskhold. I have pored over the accounts of the great battles during the Conquest, and they spoke of a half-dozen shadow-sharded standing together to summon rifts that hung in the sky and lashed the army of the emir with terrible winds."

Azil must have seen something in Deryn's face, because he patted his legs comfortingly. "I know these last few months have been a whirlwind. They have been for us all, though it's true that you seem to be at the center of the storm. I promise I will keep an eye on you whenever I can. You are not the first prodigy in these halls – the Shadow does occasionally bequeath us strange powers and gifts. I have my share, as do Lord Shen and others." He lifted his hand, giving Deryn a surprisingly warm smile. "Now I must be off. Rest, and when you are ready, return to the other adepts. Be assured there will be no reprisals from Pand or her brother. They would not dare to challenge a *kenang*, even if they still outstrip you in number of shards."

Azil began to turn away, but Deryn stopped him with a word. "Wait. I'm sorry, but what will happen to Vertus? He was supposed to oversee the fight, and he did not stop it despite what Pand was doing."

Azil's smile faded. "I will speak to him, but there is little else I can do. He is not one to trifle with, Deryn. His is perhaps the only family in the Duskhold that could oppose the Shens, and I do not wish to sow discord between them."

With that, he went over to where the physicker was crouched and bent down to murmur something in his ear. The old man nodded, and Azil clapped him on the shoulder, and then with a final glance back at Deryn he gestured at the wall, opening a portal of churning black. Without any sort of farewell, he stepped into it and was gone.

Deryn hovered at the threshold of the library, the stony old men brandishing their open books looming over him. Now that he had spent some months in the Duskhold, he knew how truly unusual they were – the only other statues he had encountered were the barbed figures that resembled the creatures in what Azil had called the shadowrealm. Kaliss had told him long ago that the library was ancient, as old as the Duskhold, so its guardians must have harkened back to the aesthetics of a much earlier age.

"Very serious fellows," Deryn murmured as he passed beneath their grim gazes. The storing and sharing of knowledge once clearly had been an important part of life in the hold. That seemed to have changed, as he wouldn't even have known this vast hall existed if he hadn't followed Kaliss one evening. None of the novices or adepts had ever spoken about coming here on their own accord, save the Ashasai girl. Deryn could only imagine what secrets had been buried and forgotten among these endless stacks.

He breathed out slowly, awed once more by the sight of all the books. From his vantage up on this platform, he had a sweeping view of the library, and again it surprised him how little the layout of the shelves made sense. There was no pattern he could discern, just random, twisted alleys of books branching from the main avenue that cut through the heart of the vast chamber.

One thing was certain: he would never be able to find anything about elementals without the Archivist's help. With a sinking feeling, Deryn wondered if he could even *find* the archivist among the sprawl. He had been lucky last time that Kaliss had not wandered too deep, as the towering shelves would make it very difficult to orient himself. He supposed he could just wait here for the scholar, though for all he knew there were other entrances and exits to the library recessed in the gloom.

Sighing, he descended the stairs. So long as he stayed close to the central artery he wouldn't get lost, and if he was going to encounter the Archivist anywhere, it would be along the library's spine. He began to traverse its length, his footsteps echoing strangely in the heavy silence, peering down the innumerable shadowy passages built with books.

Deryn froze as the faint sound of voices drifted to him. The acoustics of the library were strange, but he thought they were coming from his left, farther into the labyrinth. He had a brief, irrational fear of some fey creature that lured knowledge seekers to their doom by conjuring up imaginary conversations, but then shoved the thought aside as ridiculous.

Especially since he thought he recognized the voices: Rhenna and Archivist Devenal.

Deryn crept closer, unsure whether he should make a noise to announce his presence. What *was* the etiquette in a library? He considered clearing his throat, but then hesitated. Perhaps he'd hang back just out of sight and wait for the Archivist to be alone.

Runes were engraved on the spines of the grimoires filling these shelves, and as he edged down the book-lined corridor they started glowing with a murky light. He feared this would draw the attention of Rhenna or the librarian, but their conversation continued unabated, and when he reached the end of the stack he realized why.

This passage – along with many others – emptied into a large circular space, creating a sort of spoke in the labyrinth. Hunched in the center was a great desk of gleaming black skyspear wood piled high with all manner of books. There was no chair or stool, unless it was buried under the teetering towers, and Deryn couldn't imagine anyone finding the space to read or even open a book on its surface. Archivist Devenal hovered beside the desk, tall and thin and angular, his attention fixed on one of the books he had pulled from the piles. His unnaturally long fingers flicked through the pages as his bloodless lips read silently.

Rhenna stood a few steps away, her back to Deryn. From her posture, she did not look pleased.

"I can't believe you have nothing here. A dragon's hoard of crumbling old parchment, and *none* of it mentions the Elowyn?" She threw out her arms in an exasperated gesture, indicating the library.

The Archivist continued to mouth whatever he was reading, then tapped his finger on his chin before carefully closing the book. Dust sifted down, glittering in the light of the wraithling flame. He made a beckoning gesture, and a tendril of shadow slithered from a passage, deftly plucking the tome from his hand; it quickly vanished once more into the darkness, apparently sure of its destination. The Archivist reached for another book, but then hesitated when Rhenna gave an annoyed grunt. He turned to her with a frown.

"Do you truly believe I am the repository of everything contained in this library? I have spent a century in these stacks, but I am only one man and have become familiar with only a small fraction of these books. Perhaps if your father saw fit to devote more resources to organizing the wealth of knowledge here I could be of more service. My request for an assistant has been languishing for decades."

The Archivist hefted another book from the desk, and almost at once another serpent of darkness took it from his hand and carried it off into the stacks.

"It seems like you have plenty of help," Rhenna said, which elicited a small chuckle from the librarian.

"Just enough to keep this place from deteriorating into utter chaos."

"But surely you've come across *something* in all your years down here," she pressed, returning to whatever the reason was that she had come.

Archivist Devenal sighed. "I recognize the word. Elowyn comes from the Gilded Tongue of the First Empire, the language spoken by the high families. It means 'The Elders' or 'The Old Ones.'"

"That makes sense," Rhenna said slowly. "My father said the old woman who visited us had not aged in the century since she last visited the Duskhold."

"Was she Sharded?" the Archivist asked, now sounding intrigued.

"I don't know," Rhenna said, her frustration evident. "She gave off no resonances, but of course she couldn't come so close to the Shadow if she was not at least Imbued or Hollow."

"There is another possibility."

Rhenna tilted her head in obvious curiosity. "And that is?"

"She is not human."

Rhenna let out a bark of laughter but quickly stifled it when she realized the Archivist was not joking. "Then what could she be?"

The Archivist shrugged. "There are legends of beings with great power that existed long before Segulah Tain claimed ownership of the Heart and raised his empire. Perhaps she is a relic from this bygone age."

"She seemed mad," Rhenna muttered.

The Archivist continued as if he hadn't heard her. "And then, of course, we all have heard stories of Sharded who reached some vast number of fragments and passed into immortality. Like you, I also thought these to be wild fantasies . . . but perhaps they are not."

"If such Sharded existed, we would know of it," Rhenna insisted. "They would rule the holds like gods that have taken flesh."

"Perhaps. Or perhaps with great power came enlightenment, and our petty squabbles no longer interest them."

"She did not look enlightened."

"And you know what that would look like?"

Rhenna's posture shifted, leaning forward like she wanted to argue this point more, but the Archivist held up his hands placatingly. "Very well, Lady Shen. I shall investigate these Elowyn, read through the old histories to see if there is anyone who matches your description of this crone. Now, I believe someone else requires my assistance."

"Who?" Rhenna asked just as a rope of darkness wrapped around Deryn's waist and dragged him stumbling out of the shadows. She whirled around, anger tightening her face when she laid eyes on him.

"Deryn," she said coldly. "Why are you eavesdropping?"

"I'm not," he said hastily as the tendril encircling him dissolved. "Or I didn't mean to. I'm sorry. I thought it best if I let you finish before I approached Archivist Devenal."

Her expression softened, and she shook her head as if disappointed with herself. "I'm sorry. Sometimes all the secrets and subterfuge of this place puts me in a terrible mood."

"It's all right," Deryn replied, surprised that the first daughter of the Duskhold had just apologized to *him*.

"Why are you here?" she asked, then squinted as if seeing Deryn clearly for the first time. "Mother of Dark, what happened to your face?"

"Ah," Deryn murmured, fighting back the urge to turn away and hide his bruises. "A training bout that got a little heated. Now it's much better – you should have seen my face a few days ago."

Rhenna frowned. "That fight should have been stopped well before anything like that happened. This was on top of the Drum Tower? Who was overseeing the match?"

"Vertus."

Her frown deepened into a scowl. "Of course. He often pushes the bouts too far. I have spoken with Azil before about how he oversees the training, and I will do so again."

"He knows," the Archivist murmured. "Your brother is not one to let something slip beneath his notice. I am certain he thinks the way Vertus conducts the fights will prove beneficial to the adepts. After all, in a real fight outside these walls, with your life or your fragments at stake, there are no rules."

"And what do you know about fights?" Rhenna asked, turning back to the Archivist.

"More than you think," he replied blandly, then reached down to raise the hem of his long robes.

Deryn sucked in his breath when a small Black Disc was revealed hovering above the stone, upon which was set a pair of carved wooden feet.

"Not all of us returned from the wars of Storm and Shadow whole," he continued, as he let his robes fall once more. "But sometimes a great loss ends up giving more than what was taken. I found my calling in this hall, so do not pity me."

With some effort, Deryn tore his gaze from the Archivist's lower body. Surely it was rude to stare, though he couldn't help but wonder how much of the man's legs had been replaced. This did explain how the Archivist had always moved so smoothly when Deryn had watched him before – he was literally floating all the time. It must take a tremendous amount of *ka* to keep his Black Disc manifested for such long periods.

Rhenna's expression had changed dramatically since the Archivist had revealed the evidence of his old injuries. "Apologies," she said, bowing her head in a gesture of respect. "I did not know."

"It is nothing," the Archivist murmured, waving away her words with a flutter of his long fingers, "but it is a good lesson, Lady Shen. Youth brings confidence and conviction, but it does not necessarily bestow wisdom." He shifted his pale gaze to Deryn. "Though you display wisdom now by coming here, young Deryn. I have been expecting you."

"You have?"

"Indeed," the Archivist said, gliding behind the desk and beginning to sift through one of the more precarious piles of books. "Saelus came here just after this year's Delve and told me the startling news that one of the novices had bonded with an elemental." He glanced up from his search. "Is it here now?" he asked, and for the first time Deryn heard genuine emotion in the Archivist's papery voice.

"I . . . don't think so," Deryn replied, and the excitement in the Archivist's face faded. In truth, it was likely that Shade was lurking nearby, either in one of the many dark corners of the library or in Deryn's own shadow. But admitting this would probably result in him being asked to summon the elemental, and he would feel embarrassment when it became clear that the creature did not answer to his calls.

The Archivist grunted something unintelligible and returned to the books on the desk. "As I was saying, Saelus informed me about the Duskhold's new visitor and said that Cael Shen himself wanted me to collect all the knowledge I could about elementals. And so I have been doing that. They are not very well understood, but a few elementalists have lived in the Duskhold over the centuries, and some selfless sages recorded their observations. I even unearthed one book that was written not long after the Sundering and described a fire elemental of terrible strength and potency and the great trial it was to slay its master when he slipped into the throes of madness. Erupting volcanos, burning cities, ash falling from the sky for a month . . . The text even suggests that the elementalist tamed or made a pact with a coven of balewyrms and rode one into battle."

"Ah ha," Deryn murmured, not sure what he should say to this. He would have preferred stories of how elementals were employed to better lives, not destroy them. Hopefully, the lord of the Duskhold wouldn't get any ideas about turning Shade into a weapon.

Rhenna's expression had turned skeptical as the Archivist was speaking. "Having met your little shadow-man, I can't say I found him very dangerous."

"He's not," Deryn said quickly, hoping he was in fact speaking the truth. "He seems to spend most of his time hiding under my bed."

"The histories speak of many things," the Archivist mused, stroking his chin thoughtfully, "but not a *cowardly* elemental."

"May I . . . read these histories?" Deryn ventured, eyeing the mounded books with growing excitement.

"You could, if they were still in the library," the Archivist replied.

Deryn blinked in confusion. "Where did they go?"

"Cael Shen requested all the materials I had gathered. He wished to read the accounts first."

Rhenna looked like someone had just informed her that the sun would set for the last time tomorrow. "My father? *Read*?"

The Archivist seemed to be trying to suppress a smile. "Yes, I was surprised as well. But apparently he is very interested in what Deryn might be capable of doing in the future."

Deryn struggled to hide his disappointment. He had been very much looking forward to shedding some light on the nature of his strange new companion.

"Do not fret," the Archivist said, finally pulling a small, battered book from the mess on the desk. "I'm sure Lord Shen will eventually finish with what I have given him and pass them on to you. Until then, I did make a rather interesting discovery recently." He hefted the slim little tome reverently. "This is the journal of the last elementalist of the Duskhold, Gehart Othakis. Lord Shen has enough reading to occupy his time, and I would not be averse to you borrowing this book first. Do you wish to do so?"

"Yes," Deryn said, nearly leaping forward to receive the journal. "Thank you." Beneath his fingers, the rucked and seamed cover was oddly smooth, like it had been lacquered. In its center, something was inset into the material, circular and gnarled. He opened the book carefully, and his heart fell when he saw the strangely shaped characters that filled the yellowing pages.

"I can't read this."

"Nor can I," the Archivist said, lacing his spidery fingers together. "I do not believe it is any language."

Deryn frowned. "Then ... he was mad?"

"That is a possibility. But I find it more likely he had his own cipher. I heard you were the one to solve the pattern-riddle in the Delve this year – perhaps with some effort you can unlock the mysteries of this book."

"I will try," Deryn said softly.

"Good," the Archivist said. "Now I must apply myself to the task Lady Shen has set to me. I trust both of you can find your way out." He inclined his head towards them, then began gathering up a few of the heavy tomes on the desk. When he finished, he drifted towards the stacks. As he was swallowed by the darkness, Rhenna turned to Deryn.

"Walk with me, adept. I'm curious how you first met my new handmaiden. I find her rather fascinating."

37

ALIA

ALIA WINCED at the sound of shattering glass. She glanced at the other servant standing out in the hallway with her, but the scarred Hollow remained staring straight ahead, his expression carefully blank. Apparently, this was not an uncommon occurrence for the manservant of Cael Shen, though Alia could not hear the lord of the Duskhold's voice inside the chamber. Only her mistress's shouting was seeping through the thick wood of the door, muffled and unintelligible, but so angry that it was putting Alia on edge. Not for the first time, she wondered why Cael Shen had called his daughter to his private chambers for an audience and what could possibly be eliciting such a reaction.

The yelling reached a crescendo a moment before the door was flung open hard enough that it smashed against the stone. Rhenna stormed from the chamber, her face filled with such rage that a wave of panic washed through Alia. In the room she'd just left, Alia glimpsed Cael Shen sitting in a simple black chair, weapons gleaming on the wall behind him, a puddle of red and glass shards at his feet. His fingers were steepled in front of a face that could have been carved from stone.

Alia lost sight of the Duskhold's master as her mistress swept past her in a flurry of dark robes.

"With me," Rhenna snarled, not breaking her long strides or glancing back at her handmaiden to make sure she followed.

Alia hurried after her mistress, but she could only just barely keep up if she pushed herself to her very limit, and soon she collapsed panting in a stairwell as Rhenna's footsteps continued their ascent.

Sometimes she could almost forget that the Sharded Few were so much stronger than other men, but moments like this served as a reminder. Her legs were trembling, and the stitch in her side was making her nauseous. She stayed there huddled on the steps until the pain had faded and then shakily stood again. She wasn't anxious about losing her mistress – she knew where Rhenna was going.

Still, Alia was surprised when she reached their chambers. She had expected to walk into a tempest, Rhenna stomping about in a black rage while yelling about whatever injustice her father had laid upon her, with perhaps more shattered glass or destroyed furniture. Instead, the solar where she entertained guests was quiet, though Rhenna had clearly been here, as the necklace of glittering black stones she'd worn to see her father was tossed carelessly on the floor. Had she returned and then gone somewhere else? Alia walked slowly into the room, listening intently.

Out of the corner of her eye she noticed a shape huddled out on the balcony. Night had fallen some time ago, the moon a hazy smear in the clouded sky, and for a moment Alia thought her eyes were playing tricks on her. But as she approached, she saw a ripple of movement — in the darkness, Rhenna's hair looked like water on a lake at night. She was seated with her knees drawn up to her chest, her back to her chambers, staring into the seamless dark.

"Mistress?" Alia ventured, stepping out onto the balcony. She shivered as the cool air licked her skin, raising gooseflesh.

"Why do the rest of them dwell so deep in the mountain?"

Alia hesitated, caught off guard by the question. And the tenor of her mistress's voice – she sounded hollow, like the anger that had been churning in her not so long ago had completely drained away.

"I . . . don't know," she finally answered.

"They could live up here, if they wanted." Rhenna swept out an arm, indicating the jagged silhouettes of the other spires rising around them. "Almost all the towers are empty. Only a few odd ones occupy them. Like me."

"You're not . . ."

"I am," Rhenna said firmly, cutting her off. "I'm different, even though I've striven my whole life to be my father's daughter. To be worthy of his name and our family's legacy. I have eclipsed my brother's accomplishments, merging more shards and manifesting more talents than he did at my age. If we followed the ways of the wind-sharded, I would be favored to rule the Duskhold when the obsidian throne was empty. And if my father had not returned from the south with Azil swaddled in damask, I would be considered the strongest Sharded of my generation."

She paused, and Alia heard her swallow hard. "And yet . . . and yet . . . it is all a mummer's farce. I am not like Nishi. Or my father. Or my mother, except perhaps in shared madness."

"You are not mad, mistress," Alia said, crouching down beside Rhenna. The moon had emerged from the clouds, painting her face a stark white and revealing the glimmering tracks running down her cheeks.

"Then why does he want to get rid of me?" she cried, her voice wrenching. "Is it because I remind him of her?"

"What are you talking about?" Alia whispered.

"I thought I was a warrior of the Duskhold," Rhenna continued, more quietly. "But in truth I was always a brood mare. The prize to be auctioned off when the time was right." She turned to Alia, her face ghostly in the moonlight. "I am to wed Prince Lessian Khaliva, eldest son of Bailen Khaliva, lord of the Windwrack."

Numb surprise washed over Alia, unsteadying her so badly that she nearly lost her balance and collapsed into her mistress. Rhenna had been betrothed? In the Wild, a man who desired a wife would have to prove himself to the girl's family, and she always could refuse his overtures. To be traded away like a pig or a loom . . . it seemed so barbaric. And yet the holds were supposed to be the beating hearts of civilization.

"That is why the Mother of Storms came to the Duskhold," Rhenna finished, her voice miserable, "so she could arrange this union between our two realms."

"The boy," Alia said slowly, just now remembering the sandy-haired young man from the fete, "he came also. That was him, wasn't it?"

"I fought him," Rhenna murmured, a note of bleak humor creeping into her voice. "On the Drum Tower. If I'd known that he was there for me, I would have beaten him so soundly he would be embarrassed to have me at his side, lest his warriors laugh at him behind his back."

"He did not seem so terrible," Alia offered. "He was comely enough. And did he not throw himself into the battle when the balewyrm was discovered? Brave then, as well."

"I do not even know him!" Rhenna cried, her voice echoing among the shadow-sheathed minarets.

Alia flinched away, but this explosion of anger seemed to have drained her mistress again. Rhenna slumped, her head hanging low.

A thought occurred to Alia then, and a chill stole over her. Would she be returned to the Hollow quarters? Put once more under the control of the steward? She was sure he'd find tasks even more horrific than what she had been asked to do in the abattoir. But even worse was the thought of leaving Rhenna's side. They had become something more than servant and mistress. Friends? The thought seemed ludicrous, but Alia could not imagine how else she could describe their relationship.

Rhenna seemed to read her mind. "You will come with me."

"I'm glad," Alia whispered, relief nearly cracking her voice.

"There is to be a procession, from the Duskhold to the Wind-wrack. A public display of this new friendship between the Shadow and the Storm. It will be like how in the smallest of villages the bride is escorted to her new family, except we will travel across half the known world, stopping in every city and village along the way."

"Just you and I?"

"There will be others, a retinue worthy of the occasion. Two dozen servants and an honor guard of fellow Sharded. My father told me their names – apparently I was the last to know about all this. That boy you came to the Duskhold with, Deryn, he will accompany us. I suppose it's to parade him in front of the storm-sharded and let the other holds know the Duskhold has gained an elementalist. A few older Sharded will go as well, though the only two other adepts will be Yvrin and Vertus." Rhenna's mouth twisted at this last name. Alia recognized it as the boy with the red markings who had threatened her on the mountainside. She had caught him looking at her after that as she accompanied her mistress around the Duskhold. His expression had always been inscrutable, but there had been something in his eyes that made her feel uncomfortable. She wasn't excited to travel with him . . . but she wouldn't be frightened if Deryn was there as well. The thought that they would go together to the Windwrack made her heart lighter. Far away from the oppressive dark of the Duskhold, under the sky and sun . . . she'd smell the grass and trees again, hear the call of birds and the trickle of water. Alia realized she was trembling in anticipation, which then made her feel guilty, as her mistress was clearly despondent.

"The other servants . . ."

"Father is letting me choose them. And the guards."

Alia had to stifle a gasp. Heth. They could request him to come along as well.

"Perhaps it is not so bad, mistress," Alia said, laying a comforting hand on Rhenna's arm.

"Not so bad?" she replied bitterly, though she did not pull away from Alia's touch. "My life is over. I have dreamed of nothing else but being a great warrior of the hold, and my blood and sweat and tears have soaked this stone. And yet now it as all for naught. Women are not allowed to fight in the Windwrack. I shall be expected to do nothing except weave and gossip and bring forth babies for my dear husband."

Alia thought back to that first fete, the bright motes of the Wind-wrack floating in a sea of dark. "The Mother of Storms did not seem so meek," she said, trying to chip away at Rhenna's despair. "Perhaps, like her, you can shape the hold to your will. You are a spear maiden, and you always will be. We have a saying in the Wild – the tiger may pretend to be a lamb, but it cannot hide its stripes. I pity the man who tries to take the sword from your hand."

Rhenna did not reply to this, but she sat up a little straighter. Alia felt a little jolt of surprise as her mistress's hand moved to rest on her own.

They stayed like that for a long while, watching the night.

38

HETH

THIS HELMET DID NOT SEEM like it was forged to fit a human head.

The lines were all wrong, sharp and angular, wide at the top and then tapering to a point well below his chin. When he'd first been handed the helm, Heth had thought it looked like the severed head of a mantis, and after the other guards chosen to escort the wedding delegation had reluctantly donned their own formal armor, that impression had only been strengthened. The lot of them looked like a troop of warrior insects, and only the Broken God knew why the masters of the Duskhold had decided this was how they should present themselves when they ventured out into the world.

"Feel like a bloody fool," Benni muttered, shifting uncomfortably like he had an itch he couldn't reach.

"Can you see out of these things?" Heth asked, adjusting his helmet for what felt like the hundredth time.

"Not very bloody well. Whatever smith put these big bloody eye-holes here and couldn't be arsed to check if they actually worked needs to be flogged."

"You won't be doing any fighting," another guard said, one that Heth couldn't recognize helmed. "Just got to put one foot in front of the other for about a thousand leagues and look good for the peasants. Now be quiet before ye bring some attention down on us."

Heth sighed, giving up on keeping the little flange of metal from partially obstructing his view. That fellow was right – they were as ornamental as the skyspear carriage that would transport the daughter of Cael Shen to her nuptials. The sight of the carriage had taken his breath away when they'd first spilled out into the courtyard – the gleaming black wood was intricately carved with blooming flowers knotted together with vines, which in this land apparently symbolized the impending union. In front of the carriage, a team of strikingly white stallions was clearly impatient to be off, their hooves clopping on the stone as they shifted, their breath misting in the chill morning air.

About a dozen other horses had been brought into the courtyard, and Heth assumed these were for the Sharded Few who would accompany them. Fewer than he would have thought, given the importance of the occasion. Heth gazed at them longingly – it had been over a year since he'd ridden a horse, and he had a sinking suspicion that he would spend much of the journey marching in this bulky, uncomfortable armor.

Though maybe not, as he was fairly certain several of the other guards would collapse long before they even reached Phane. He found it likely that the wagons waiting in the courtyard would carry the Hollow guards along with the servants of Lady Shen and their supplies, at least some of the time.

Benni's elbow nudged him, which would have been fine, except that his vambrace was oddly barbed, and Heth could feel the point through his layers of chain and padding.

"Be careful," he hissed, jerking his arm away.

"Somebody wants ta talk with you," Benni said, tilting his insectile head towards one of the smaller passages spilling into the courtyard.

Heth turned, squinting past the metal attempting to block his vision. The morning's brightness also was doing him no favors, but after a moment he saw a plump boy emerge from the shadowed recesses of the hold and make a beckoning gesture.

Garrett.

Heth glanced around the courtyard. Gervis had arranged them into a formation for when the Sharded eventually appeared, but there was still no sign of the hold's masters, and the captain had been pulled to the other side of the courtyard to discuss something about the disposition of the wagons. He bit his lip, wondering if he should risk the older guard's ire. Garrett again motioned him to approach, more frantically than before. Sighing, Heth left his spot and quickly strode towards him, expecting at any moment to hear Gervis's bellowed outrage.

It never came, and as he approached the entranceway, he saw that the other boys he had trained in swordplay were also there, clustered together a little deeper inside the hold. They looked excited, like it was they who would be escorting a princess of Shadow to the Windwrack.

"Shouldn't you all be in the butchery?" Heth hissed, stealing a quick glance over his shoulder to make sure no one of consequence had yet noticed his absence.

"Had to see you off, didn't we?" Vinish said, the unruly tufts sticking up from his pig-thistle hair making it seem like he had rolled straight from his bed to come here.

"I'll be back before the winter," Heth said, not trying to hide his annoyance. "A month to Flail, a month back, and maybe a few weeks in the Wrack to get the Lady Shen settled. You idiots better keep up with your practicing, or there will be a reckoning when I return."

"We'll stay sharp, promise," Yennick said, scratching at his scar. "But we wanted to give you something to show our thanks."

"What's that?" Heth asked, half-expecting one of them to pull forth a bloodstained packet of meat filched from the abattoir.

Mouser stepped forward, bringing out something from where he'd had it hidden behind him.

Heth's jaw dropped. The boy held a sheath of worn black leather, the familiar bronze hilt of the sword it contained incised with a dancing flame.

"Silver Shrike," Heth whispered as he reached out to receive his ancestral sword. "How did you get this?" His throat tightened as he traced the design with a finger.

Vinish jerked a thumb in Mouser's direction. "Turns out this fellow was quite the rogue back in Phane. Spent his childhood learning how to open doors an' move quiet as the mice they named him for."

"Mousers *catch* mice," the buck-toothed boy said with a grin. "I'm more a cat. But yeah, didn't have any trouble with the lock on the steward's door. Old Wormface had all sorts of goodies piled up in there, probably won't even know I nicked it."

"I can't believe it," Heth murmured, clutching the sheathed sword tightly to his chest. He hoped he'd come far enough out of the light that they couldn't see his eyes.

Vinish clapped him on the shoulder. "Just a token to show we appreciate you wasting all those mornings with us when you could have been sleeping."

"They weren't a waste," Heth replied as he unclasped the ill-made hunk of metal they'd tried to pass off as a sword and buckled on his own blade. He handed the armory sword to Vinish, who took it with wide eyes. "And we'll continue when I get –"

The blast of a horn interrupted him, making them all jump. Heth turned to find that a stocky servant in black and silver livery had entered the courtyard through another, grander entrance and was just lowering a curving horn from his lips.

"I have to go," Heth said, but before he did, he glanced at each of the butcher boys in turn, his hand resting on the pommel of his sword. "Thank you," he said earnestly, knuckling his forehead in a gesture of respect. Then he was off, dashing across the courtyard just as the first of the Sharded Few emerged blinking into the morning light. Luckily for him, all attention was fixed on the new arrivals, and he returned to his spot in the ranks without anyone seeming to notice. Except Benni, who jostled him again with his barbed vambrace.

"Cael Shen, Chosen of the Shadow and Lord of the Duskhold!"

Metal clinked and leather rustled as the guards around Heth drew themselves up straighter. He doubted that very many of them had ever even seen Lord Shen, except at a great distance. Heth's only memory of him before now was as a silver-haired apparition looming high up on his throned dais, a terrifyingly huge skull behind him. Somehow, Cael Shen did not seem at all diminished as he strode out into the courtyard, the mantle of authority still heavy on his broad shoulders.

More of the Sharded Few streamed through the entranceway behind their lord. Most were garbed in the simple black robes of the Duskhold, but a few wore breeches and doublets and other more practical clothes for traveling, and Heth assumed that these were the shadow-sharded who would accompany them. He was expecting to see Deryn, but still he felt a little thrill when he caught sight of him. Alia had been the one to inform Heth that he would be part of the honor guard for her mistress, and she'd also told him with an excitement bordering on giddiness that Deryn would be coming as well. His friend was speaking with the Ashasai girl Kaliss as he emerged into the courtyard, a bulging travel pack slung across one shoulder and a thin wrapped bundle poking up over the other. That must be the blade he'd found, the reason Heth had been enlisted to teach him swordcraft. Deryn had been coy about it when pressed, but Heth knew there was something special about the sword, as otherwise he would have brought it to their lessons before.

Heth recognized a few other Sharded. There was the Salahi who had slain the riftbeast, and beside him was the ancient man who had met them when they'd first arrived. Heth was surprised by the disappointment he felt when his gaze fell on Kilian, as he saw that the shadow-sharded was dressed in robes. Despite being considered high nobility in the Duskhold, Kilian was far friendlier and more approachable than any other Sharded Heth had encountered.

Which, he supposed, might have been why he had been forced to accompany Phinius on the hunt for more Imbued and Hollow.

A ripple went through the crowd of Sharded. At first, Heth couldn't tell what was happening, the press of bodies blocking his view, and then he realized someone important had entered the court-yard. The horn-blower announced this new arrival with several more long blasts, and Heth sucked in his breath as streamers of darkness leapt into the air to form a curving trellis of latticed shadows. A tall woman sheathed in a glistening black dress slowly walked beneath the shadow-fashioned archway, her face hidden behind a dark veil. Heth knew this was the Lady Shen, because several steps behind her with her head respectfully lowered was Alia. The Wild girl looked beautiful, even if the attention of everyone else was on her mistress. She wore a dress that matched her jade eyes, and green strands like vines were woven through her golden hair. She resembled the newborn spirit of Spring being escorted by the last host of Winter, one of the old tales the cook had told him as a child. His heart lifted to think that she was finally leaving the Duskhold, though that thought was bittersweet, as he knew this would likely be the last time he'd ever be near her. She would almost certainly stay in the Wind-wrack with her mistress even after the rest of the delegation returned.

He wondered if he could find a way to remain behind. The storm-sharded were known to elevate blades from Flail to teach their warriors swordcraft – perhaps if he proved himself capable enough, one of them would ask for him to be included as a wedding gift.

A boy could dream, couldn't he?

The veiled bride-to-be had nearly arrived at her carriage. Cael Shen and a few of the other most prominent shadow-sharded were waiting for her there to make their final farewells. Rhenna seemed surprised when her brother Nishi stepped forward and put his arms around her, stiffening slightly before she relaxed into the embrace. Her adopted brother was next, and she clasped him with far more warmth than she had shown a moment before. It seemed obvious to Heth which of her siblings she was closest to, but if Nishi cared, he did not show it, watching Rhenna and Azil with his smirking half-smile.

Her father was the last, standing just beside the carriage's open door. Rhenna stopped in front of him, and with ceremonial slowness Cael Shen lifted her black veil and kissed her lightly on both cheeks. Heth had a good view of her from where he was standing – she was staring straight ahead, her face a frozen mask. He hadn't been expecting to see tears, but still he was surprised that she was showing absolutely no emotion about leaving the only home she'd ever known. The rumors that had been flying about the Duskhold since the engagement was announced must have some truth to them – Lady Shen had not wished for this match.

Something unspoken passed between father and daughter, and then Cael Shen let the veil fall again. Without further ceremony, Rhenna lifted her long dress and stepped up into the carriage, followed by Alia. Joras Shen swung the door shut, the horn sounded again, and the driver sent the team of white horses surging ahead with a flick of his whip.

"And here we go," Heth murmured as the carriage passed through the Duskhold's great gate and into the shadowed interior of its barbican. There was no cheering from the Sharded who had come to see their lady off, though Heth thought he saw Kilian dabbing at his eyes.

"Men o' the Duskhold!"

The unexpectedly close bellow made Heth jump, as he hadn't noticed that Gervis had come over to where they were lined up.

"Let's go, quickly now! Don't want the Lady Shen to have to wait too long for us. Time to show her we're not a bunch of laggards!" The captain of the Duskhold's guard wheeled on his heel after delivering this pronouncement and began to march towards the gate, displaying the unnaturally high gait they'd practiced earlier this morning.

Heth glanced at Benni, who shrugged at him. Sighing, Heth hurried to match their captain's awkward-looking strides, trying to ignore the fact that they were being watched by a large crowd, including the Duskhold's lord and – even worse – Deryn.

It was going to be a very long walk to Flail.

39

DERYN

DERYN WONDERED which of the clomping Hollow was Heth as the guardsmen vanished in a cloud of dust through the gate. They all looked the same in their matching insectile armor, although there was one with a different sword hilt, bronze where the rest was black iron, and it did remind Deryn of the sword he had found buried in the mud months ago. Heth had told him during their first training session that the Duskhold's steward had confiscated the sword, but perhaps he'd somehow regained it. Deryn hoped so, at least. It had been very clear how much that sword meant to him.

"Sharded!"

Deryn had never heard Cael Shen raise his voice before, and it jolted him from his thoughts. All eyes turned to the lord of the Duskhold, who seemed unaffected by the awkward exchange they all had just witnessed between him and his daughter.

"This is a momentous day in our history. An alliance has been sealed between the Shadow and the Storm, our ancient holds united again as they were in the time of the Sundering. Together, there is not a power in the world that can stand before us. The Bloodlords of Ashasai, the Scaled Queendom of the zemani, even the dead-that-do-not-rest in shattered Gendurdrang . . . all will feel fear knowing that the north stands as one."

All the north? Deryn couldn't help but remember that blazing visage erupting in the brazier, gobbets of flame falling near the corpse of the boy who had once been his friend.

"I speak now to the honor guard that will accompany my daughter to her new home . . . you must show the strength of our hold to the Windwrack, and remind the storm-sharded that we are equals. If they insult the Shadow, challenge the fool who would dare, but do not bring dishonor to the Duskhold by being the first to break the peace. Vertus, approach." Cael Shen made a beckoning gesture, and the crimson-tattooed boy stepped from the crowd. Deryn had known the adept had been chosen as part of this delegation, but still his heart sank at the sight of the smirking Sharded.

"I place you first among your fellows. They will answer to your commands, and in turn you will ensure that all return safely to the Duskhold. Do you accept this charge?"

"I do, my Lord Shen," Vertus said smoothly, dipping into a low bow.

Beside Deryn, Kaliss huffed quietly. "Someone should have told him how that bastard stood by and watched the Wild girl beat you bloody."

"I'm sure he knows," Deryn replied out of the corner of his mouth. "Cael Shen is aware of everything that happens in the hold."

"Well, if that's true, be careful," Kaliss continued, slightly louder because the hum of conversations was rising around them. "I won't be there to watch your back."

Deryn glanced over at the Ashasai girl. He was expecting a playful expression, but she looked deadly serious.

"I'll be fine," he told her, and she nodded tightly, her lips pursed.

"Good. I need you around, so I have someone to push me. There's little enough competition here."

Deryn grinned at that claim, shaking his head. They both knew her days of dominating the newly Sharded were behind her – there were many among the adepts with potential similar to her own. Then again, he wouldn't bet against her if the difference was who worked the hardest.

Around them the crowd was dispersing, the black-robed Sharded drifting back inside the Duskhold, while Rhenna's honor guard was moving towards where stableboys held the reins of their horses.

"Alia told me we'll pass through Phane tomorrow. Are you jealous?"

Kaliss snorted, rolling her eyes. "The only reason I'd want to go back there is for revenge on a few bakers and fishmongers who beat me for stealing food when they could clearly see my ribs. I don't have many good memories about my life on those streets."

Deryn nodded, his gaze wandering with his thoughts to the milling horses. He wasn't excited about having to climb up onto one of these snorting and stamping beasts – it would be his first time, and he'd heard that it might be uncomfortable, especially if they traveled a great distance.

"Deryn," Kaliss said, and the abrupt change in her tone brought his attention back to her. The levity from a moment ago had vanished, her expression turning serious again. "I want you to promise me something."

"Anything," he replied, slightly concerned by what he saw in her face.

Her dark eyes seemed to be staring at something only she could see. "When you ride through the streets of Phane, do not ignore those who watch from the shadows. The ones pressing close to your procession will be tradespeople and merchants, matrons and shopkeepers. But look past them, to those who have nothing and are not allowed into the light. A smile from one of the Sharded Few would be kept close in a heart that has known little joy."

"Do you speak of your own past?" Deryn asked quietly, but she did not answer and looked away before he could see the answer in her face.

Most of the Sharded who would make the journey to the Wind-wrack were already mounted by now, some clearly struggling to control their horses. It looked like he wouldn't be the only inexperienced rider among Rhenna's honor guard.

"I do not care about the cheers of the comfortable," Deryn assured her. "I was once the serving girl's son watching from the back of the crowd as the Sharded passed by."

Kaliss forced a smile as she returned from whatever dark pit of memories she'd fallen into. "And it is why we share the hunger. We both know what it is to want."

"Adept Deryn!" Vertus shouted across the courtyard, already astride his horse. "Hurry up and claim your horse before Lady Shen tires of waiting!"

"Safe travels," Kaliss said, pulling a slim black volume from the recesses of her robes. "And something for you to read on the journey. I'm afraid I left some holes in your education, so perhaps this will help fill those gaps."

Deryn received the book, straining to decipher the archaic script spidering across its cover. "*Twilight of an Empire and the Sundering of the Heart*, by Imperator Shen, General of the Steel Legion."

"The ancestor of our own lord and the man most responsible for the current age," Kaliss explained. "A history written by the victor may not be entirely trustworthy, but having read it myself, I think you'll find some interesting insights here. Oh, and don't worry – Archivist Devenal knows I'm lending you this book. Just make sure it survives the trip."

"I will," Deryn said, stuffing the book into his travel bag, right next to the coded diary of the shadow elementalist. "And thank you. I'll bring you back something from the Windwrack."

"Adept!"

Sighing, Deryn turned away from Kaliss and jogged across the courtyard to where Vertus was waiting. The tattooed boy grimaced as Deryn approached, fighting to control his suddenly agitated horse.

"When I call to you, adept, you follow my commands at once," he snarled, yanking on his reins hard. His horse whinnied, misting the air with its breath, and Deryn took an instinctive step back when he realized its eyes were rolling in its sockets.

"Your horse looks terrified," he said.

"And I'm certain it's your fault," Vertus snapped. "I've ridden Arrow here for years without a problem. It's your damn elemental, I'm sure. Where is it hiding?"

Deryn shrugged, even though he could feel Shade squirming about in his shadow. He'd realized after his bout with Pand that keeping the whereabouts of the elemental secret could play to his advantage.

"Never mind," Vertus said. "Go find a horse that won't throw you and let's be off, or I'm leaving you behind." He kicked his horse in the ribs viciously, and the poor beast surged forward, thundering towards the open gate.

A horse. With some trepidation, Deryn made his way towards where the grooms were waiting with the few horses that had not yet been chosen. A few dipped their heads respectfully as he neared, and one of the oldest stepped forward, a red-haired boy with a face smeared with freckles.

"Ho, Sharded," he said. "Sorry we ain't got much to choose from, even though we emptied the stables this morning."

"It's all right," Deryn said, hesitatingly reaching out towards the closest stallion's muscled flank. The horse snorted and shied away, clearly unnerved.

"Huh," the head groom muttered, "Never seen Ajaxis do that before."

Deryn tried not to show his disappointment at the horse's reaction. What could he do if there wasn't a steed willing to take him? Walk with the Hollow guardsmen? Ride in the wagons? In truth, neither of these seemed too terrible an option.

"I'm afraid horses don't like me very much."

The boy's sea-green eyes widened. "Ah, you're that fellow, the one with the little shadow-man. Well, don't worry, there have been other Sharded who the horses don't like. Lord Shen's son has had some trouble as well. Seems they get skittish around those who walk in Shadow." His gaze traveled over the horses until settling on a small russet pony with a shaggy mane, then he smiled as he stepped closer to take her by the bit. "Lucky we brought this old princess out," he said, stroking her grey-flecked muzzle affectionately. "Used to belong to Lady Shen – she was the only horse that would let her up on her back. Hardy old mountain girl, nothing scares her." Deryn approached cautiously, but the pony only turned to regard him calmly with eyes of liquid black.

"Ash is her name," the boy said, handing Deryn the reins. "Right now she's tolerating you, but find an apple for her and she's yours for life."

"I don't know when I'll have an – oh". A shiny red apple had appeared in the groom's hand, and Deryn took the fruit and held it out for Ash. A spark flickered to life in the old pony's eyes, and she lunged forward with surprising quickness to pluck the treat from his hand.

"Good girl," Deryn murmured, stroking her head just like he had seen the groom doing a moment before.

"Let's get you seated," the boy said, patting the saddle, and with less awkwardness than he was expecting, Deryn used the stirrup to swing himself up into the seat. Despite his fears, Ash did not buck him off or whinny in outrage, instead continuing to placidly chew the apple he had gifted her, as if that was all that mattered in the world.

A good start, Deryn thought.

"This is your first time on a horse, yes?" asked the groom, and Deryn nodded. "Thought so. Ash will be good for you, then. She'll know where to go better than you, but if you need to get her moving, put some pressure on her sides with your legs or give her a light tap with your heel. That also means you shouldn't keep your legs too tight as you're riding, lest you confuse her. Sit nice and loose, just as you're doing now." He reached up to hand Deryn the reins. "Use these to turn her, but be gentle. She'll understand what you want with only a little tug."

"Thank you," Deryn said earnestly. The nervousness he'd felt since learning he'd have to ride to the Windwrack was quickly draining away.

"You'll do fine," the groom assured him, scratching the pony behind her ear. "Doubt you'll even have to canter – just sit back and try to stay comfortable, and when you stop for the evenings, find someone who knows a bit about horse care. Should be a few among Lady Shen's servants."

"I will," Deryn replied, his gaze going to where the last of the supply wagons was trundling through the Duskhold's great gate. The rest of the Sharded had already ridden on ahead, except for a lanky girl he recognized with curly black hair sitting astride a magnificent bay like she had been born in the saddle. Yvrin, the adept who had won the bout just before he'd stepped into the ring with Pand. Deryn wasn't sure if she was overseeing the departure of the wagons or if she was waiting for him, but she did flash him a smile as he tentatively nudged Ash into a trot towards where she waited.

"You look like a fish trying to fly," she said with a smile.

"My first time on a horse," Deryn explained, pulling back on his reins to bring Ash to a halt.

"Is that why they gave you a little girl's pony?" she said teasingly, leaning forward to stroke the powerful neck of her own steed. Deryn felt himself blush, even though it had clearly been meant as a jest. Of all the other adepts, Yvrin was the one he found the most intriguing. He still remembered how she had offered her hand to her defeated opponent at the end of their fight, and she was the only person he'd met in the Duskhold who was not afraid to laugh loudly and freely when something amused her. There was a joy in her that seemed almost unique among the shadow-sharded, and for that reason Deryn had hoped to get to know her better . . . and why he'd been excited when he'd heard that she would be one of the other adepts accompanying Rhenna to the Windwrack.

Also, she was quite pretty.

"She seems like a good lady," Deryn said, and as if in agreement, Ash *whuffed* loudly. "I'm just worried I'll be sore if I stay in the saddle all day."

Yvrin grinned again, and her dimples started a fluttering in his chest. "Don't be silly, Deryn. You're one of the Sharded Few. You could cling to the back of a galloping stallion for a day and a night and not feel sore when next you woke." She paused to pluck something from her horse's flowing mane. "I miss it, to be honest. It may sound silly, but I found the ache almost pleasant. A reminder of my time on Helius here." She rubbed his neck, eliciting what Deryn was quickly learning was the sound of horse contentment. "Now, let's be on our way. We can bring up the rear and stay behind the wagons until you feel comfortable on your little pony. Because right now, I won't lie, you look as stiff as one of the wooden knights my da carved for me when I was a girl."

"Thank you," Deryn said, nodding gratefully and trying to keep the smile from creeping across his face, as he was sure he'd look like quite the fool. Spending time alone with Yvrin was what he had daydreamed about happening on this journey, and here it was coming true before they'd even left the Duskhold. With a rueful shake of his head, he gently prodded Ash into motion again, following the Sharded adept through the gate.

40

ALIA

RHENNA STAYED silent in the carriage after the door closed, whatever emotions she might have been feeling hidden behind her black veil. Alia curled up on the cushions across from her, watching her mistress worriedly. She'd been expecting defiance, anger, even sadness, but not a numb acceptance of her fate. This was not the behavior of a spear maiden.

The carriage lurched into motion, though not for long, as they soon came to a halt again. Alia suspected they had passed through the Duskhold's great gatehouse, and now were waiting for the rest of the procession before continuing on. She wanted to unlatch the wooden panel that served as a window inside their little compartment and take a look, but she didn't want to bother Rhenna with this request. Soon Alia heard many feet marching past, and she knew the Hollow guardsmen had departed the Duskhold. She wished she could search for Heth among the warriors in their strange armor, but Rhenna showed no interest in what was happening outside.

The footsteps faded, replaced by the clopping of hooves. Alia jumped in surprise as someone rapped on the other side of the sliding panel, yet Rhenna still did not bestir herself.

"Should I see who it is, mistress?" she murmured as she sat up, but Alia subsided again when Rhenna gave a small shake of her head.

"Lady Shen, we will depart momentarily." The voice was muffled by the wood, yet still Alia recognized it, and a chill went through her as she remembered the day she'd fled the Duskhold, a crown of glistening swords whirling around the head of a boy with crimson tattoos and cruel eyes. Alia looked to Rhenna, but she did not answer, and after a moment the Sharded spoke again.

"Rhenna, this is beneath you," he said, his words sharpened by annoyance. "This procession is to make a display of the new accord between Storm and Shadow. Your father will be disappointed if he is told you sulked the entire way to Flail."

Still Rhenna was quiet, and after a moment Alia heard the Sharded mutter something intelligible and move away from the panel. Rhenna's only response was to snort derisively.

The carriage began moving again, jouncing along the rocky path. Alia settled deeper into the cushions, trying to find a comfortable position despite the incessant jarring. Would this continue? It was even worse than Phinius's rickety old wagon.

That memory set her thoughts wandering, and soon she was remembering those days with Deryn and Heth and the grumpy old driver, the bustle of the towns they'd stayed in and the elaborate feasts they'd shared. It had all been so overwhelming after months of caring for her poor father, watching him fade as she struggled desperately to find enough food to keep them both alive. Alia wondered if she had known what was waiting for her at the Duskhold if she would have slipped away in the night while the others slept. Her gaze drifted to Rhenna, whose veiled face was turned to the wall. Alia was surprised to realize that she wasn't sure what she would choose if given the chance to go back.

She returned to herself as Rhenna suddenly sat up and reached for the wooden panel, then slid it open. Alia leaned forward, curious about what had drawn her mistress's interest. The road down the mountain had twisted and turned, and through the window the gnarled bulk of the Duskhold was visible, gleaming black in the morning sun. As they watched, the hold passed behind a huge outcropping of rock, and Alia wondered if this would be their last glimpse of the hold. Rhenna seemed to think so, as she reached up and unhooked her veil, tossing it disdainfully among the piled cushions. Her cheeks were dry, but her eyes were rimmed with red. Then Rhenna slammed the panel shut with enough force to crack the frame, making Alia gasp. Her mistress threw herself back into the seat, her mouth twisted into a scowl, and stayed like that for a few long moments before looking at Alia.

"What do you remember most clearly about your mother?"

Alia blinked at her. With some effort, she gathered her scattered thoughts, wondering where this question had come from.

"Those times I was with her," Alia said slowly. "Just the two of us. We used to forage together, and she'd teach me what mushrooms and berries were safe to eat, the best kind of moss for staunching blood. I'd also watch her practice her battledance in the evenings after we'd eaten, whirling around the nightfire, spear point glittering. Sometimes my father was there as well."

"No, I mean, is there a single moment that comes to mind when you think of her?"

Alia considered this, and then nodded. "I suppose so. There was one night in the depths of winter when she shook me awake with her finger pressed to her lips. Careful not to wake my father, we crept outside the little hut he'd built, and I followed her as she slipped into the forest. The snow was so deep I'd have had trouble on my own, so I had to keep to the path she made." Alia swallowed as the memory crystallized in her mind. It had been many years since she'd remembered this. "The moon was brighter than I'd ever seen before. The birch trees . . . the snow . . . the world was white, but it was the moonlight gilding everything that made it seem like we were wading through a dream. She took me to a ring of rocks in a clearing, and then she sat in the middle of them and lifted her head to the sky and sang a song in a language I'd never heard before. When she finished, it almost seemed like the forest itself was watching her. And then she stood and dusted herself off and led me back to my bed. I didn't realize until she pulled the furs up to my chin that I hadn't felt cold at all, even though I remember some of the trees bursting that winter because their sap froze."

Rhenna's lips were pursed as she considered this. "*Was* it a dream?"

"I . . . don't know. I don't think so."

Her mistress fell silent, and Alia thought the discussion finished. But after a moment Rhenna spoke again, her face turned towards the cracked panel.

"I never knew my mother."

Alia shifted on her cushion, surprised. Rhenna had always skirted around this topic. Alia had assumed she must have died years ago.

"What happened to her?" The question escaped before she could bite her tongue, and Alia silently cursed herself for a fool. She shouldn't indulge her curiosity now, given how difficult this morning had already been for Rhenna.

"She vanished," she said, her voice hollow.

Vanished? "She left the Duskhold?"

Her mistress shrugged. "I don't know. Perhaps."

Alia wanted to ask more about this, but she forced her mouth closed. It wasn't her place to interrogate Rhenna.

Yet her mistress kept talking. "My mother was always different. She was strong, incredibly so, the strongest of her generation. Even my father was not her equal. But there is a . . . sickness that sometimes comes with such strength. A sadness. Especially for those who can slip into the darkness and enter the shadowrealm."

Rhenna brushed away a lock of black hair that had fallen across her face. "At least I have some memory of her. Holding me, singing to me, like your own mother did for you. She wasn't around much, though. The sadness she'd always felt deepened after my birth. She spent most of her time in bed, unable or unwilling to rise. When she did, it was usually to work on her sculptures."

The statues. She was talking about the unnerving figures of black stone that populated the Duskhold. Rhenna had said her mother had carved them, but what kind of mind could conjure up such beings?

"They are real, you know," her mistress continued, giving an answer to Alia's unvoiced question. "You can see them when you Shadow Walk, writhing in the distance."

"What are they?" Alia whispered.

"No one knows. But my mother was obsessed with them. She dreamed of them. By the time she vanished, she was having visions of them in the Duskhold. My brother told me of waking to her screams and finding her curled up in the corner of his bedchamber, pointing at nothing, tears streaming down her face. When my father burst through the door she told him it had been trying to speak with her . . ."

Rhenna sighed. "Perhaps she was simply mad. Traversing the shadowrealm seems to fray the minds of some. It is why my brother tries to ignore them when he walks the darkness."

"Or maybe these things were trying to tell her something."

Her mistress swallowed. "That is . . . a possibility."

"Where did she go? Your mother. You said she vanished."

"One moment she was in the Duskhold, the next she wasn't. She did not pass through the gate. My father had the tunnels below the hold searched, but found nothing. There is really only one other possible explanation." Rhenna finally turned from the panel, meeting Alia's gaze. "She entered the shadowrealm and did not return. She walked away from the Duskhold and our family. She abandoned me."

There was an old pain in Rhenna's eyes. Alia reached out and gently laid her hand on her mistress's arm, expecting her to flinch away, but she did not. "There is another possibility," she said softly.

Rhenna frowned, her brow creasing. "What?"

"Maybe she didn't abandon you. Maybe those things took her."

The faint pealing of trumpets roused Alia from her nap. She grimaced, pushing herself into a sitting position, her fingers kneading an uncomfortable knot that had formed in her neck. Across from her,

Rhenna was also coming slowly awake, wiping away drool that had collected on the shoulder of her dress.

"Where are we?" Alia murmured as the trumpets sounded again, louder this time.

"Phane," Rhenna replied, reaching for the veil she had tossed away earlier. "It's less than a day's ride from the Duskhold. We'll stay in the magistrate's manse tonight." She sounded less than enthusiastic about this.

Phane. Alia had heard that name before, though she knew little about the city. A few of the Hollow servants in the kitchens had hailed from Phane and had spoken wistfully of their home.

"I suppose it's necessary to pass through here on the way to Flail," Rhenna said grudgingly. "It is the largest city under the Shadow. I'm sure it's buzzing with talk of the wedding."

More trumpets, this time sounding like they were just outside. Alia noticed that the way had become much smoother, as the carriage was barely shuddering now. She remembered the carefully fitted stone roads that had bound together the town of Kething's Cross – this city must have the same. Alia wanted to slide open the panel and see what Phane looked like, but Rhenna seemed to have no desire to do this. She just sat there slumped, her veil crumpled in her hand.

Another sound swelled, a muted roaring. It summoned up a disquieting memory for Alia of watching an avalanche gathering strength high up on a mountain, rocks smashing through trees.

Rhenna must have seen something in her face. "It's the people."

"Oh." Now Alia could hear it, many full-throated voices blending together. "They're cheering."

Her mistress nodded, still looking sullen.

"They love you."

The corner of Rhenna's mouth lifted. "They love the Duskhold and the Sharded Few. We protect them, and their closeness to the hold is the reason their city has grown rich."

Still, she sat up straighter and slipped on her veil again. "But I suppose I can give them what they want," she said, and with much more grace than the last time she had touched the panel, she slid the window open.

Alia blinked as light spilled into the carriage. She struggled to focus on the scene outside as the cheering strengthened, the sight of the panel opening inciting the crowd into a frenzy.

There were more people than Alia had ever seen in one place. They lined the streets a dozen deep, with more hanging out from windows or perched on balconies, wearing a panoply of colors instead of just the black robes of the Sharded or the drab servant garb of the Hollow. And there were children, a rare sight in the Duskhold, squalling babies raised towards the carriage as if to receive some blessing and older boys and girls jumping up and down as they clutched the hands of their parents.

Most of the buildings were built from dark stone or pale white timbers. It seemed unnatural, so many living so tightly pressed together, but Alia had to admit that it was better than burrowing deep under the ground like the insect-nest of the Duskhold.

High-pitched shrieking drew her attention to where an alley emptied into the main thoroughfare. A gaggle of children clustered at the mouth, but they were not clean and well-dressed like those watching the procession with their parents beside them. No, these children looked half-feral, with long unkempt hair and dirt-smudged faces, their clothing little more than rags. The shrieks were because a serpent of darkness had slithered from the alley behind them and was wending around their legs, though to Alia's ear they sounded more excited than terrified. The knot of children dissolved, scampering this way and that as more tendrils emerged to chase them, their cheeks flushed and eyes bright with laughter.

Alia shook her head in disbelief, wondering which of the Sharded was responsible. It hardly seemed in character for any of the Duskhold's denizens.

"It's Deryn," her mistress said softly, also watching the children.

Alia had suspected as much, but she was still curious how Rhenna was so certain. "Are you sure?"

"Yes," she replied. "Can't you see the dog?"

Dog? Alia frowned, unsure what Rhenna was talking about, and then she noticed a dark shape that was different from the shadowy serpents. It did look like a dog, she supposed, and its behavior was certainly dog-like as it bounded around the children like a pup thrilled by all the excitement.

"That is his elemental," Rhenna said. "If I wanted to, I could seize control of his beckoning – the shadow-snakes – but I know if I tried to do the same to that creature, my powers would slide right off it."

"What is it?" Alia asked, unnerved by the thought that some sort of intelligence and will inhabited that shred of living darkness.

"I don't know," Rhenna murmured. "I don't think anyone does. Elementals are a mystery . . . and one I can't help but wonder if the secrets of our own shards are connected to. I'm surprised my father dispatched Deryn on this errand. He is of tremendous value to the Duskhold."

"I'm glad he's here," Alia said softly.

"As are those urchins," Rhenna said as the children passed out of their sight. "This is a moment they'll always remember, when one of the Sharded Few stooped to recognize they existed." There was something almost sad in her voice.

"You could do the same," Alia said, laying her hand on her mistress's arm. "I know it. You could make the people of Flail love you if you showed them your true self."

Rhenna shook her head slowly. "They will never love me."

"How do you know that?" Alia asked, surprised by the certainty she heard.

Rhenna turned to Alia, her dark eyes as mesmerizing as the markings on a hooded serpent. "Because I will never set foot in Flail."

Alia drew back in surprise, but Rhenna's hand closed around her wrist.

"Listen to me, Alia," she said with an almost feverish intensity. "I will not be a brood mare or a tool to further my father's ambitions. I will not marry a man I do not know. I will not trade the dueling ring for a sewing circle."

"Then what will you do?" Alia whispered.

"I will flee. And I want you with me. When we come close to where Kilian found you, we can slip away and go north, into the Wild."

"The Wild . . ."

"Yes! You and I, not as mistress and servant, but as . . . as companions. As friends."

Alia realized she wasn't breathing, and she drew in a shuddering gasp. The thought of returning to the deep forests made her eyes prickle with tears. To see the stars blazing on a clear winter night, the meadows sweeping away speckled with wildflowers, silvery fish leaping from rivers as they strove against the current . . . and to show these things to Rhenna. She swallowed, surprised by the vulnerability she saw in Rhenna's eyes, the fear that Alia would refuse her.

"Will you come with me?" her mistress asked, worry fraying her voice.

Alia turned her hand so that she could twine her fingers tightly with Rhenna's. "Of course."

41

DERYN

IT WAS like trying to see something in the clouds, when one stared long enough and dragons, castles, and faces emerged. The mind searched for a pattern, and if it could not find one, it simply conjured something out of nothing, and then it was all one could see.

That was what Deryn felt like he was doing right now, searching for a secret meaning which did not really exist. Sighing in frustration, he looked up from the tiny crabbed markings filling the yellowed page. Was it a different language even though the Archivist had not recognized it? That would mean Deryn had no hope of reading the book, unless he found someone familiar with the script. Or was it a cipher, as the old librarian had suspected, and once the key was found the elementalist's journal would reveal its secrets? Perhaps, but Deryn had spent a frustrating amount of time fruitlessly poring over these runes. Or maybe – and this possibility could not be discounted – the one who had penned this journal had been a madman, and trying to understand it was all an exercise in futility.

At this moment, Deryn was leaning in that last direction.

Carefully, he closed the age-stiffened cover, trying to keep the leather from cracking further. He'd try again tomorrow night, though he felt no real hope that an epiphany was waiting for him. Setting the diary aside, he glanced at the sun, which was still visible above the treetops. The last two nights they hadn't eaten until night had fully fallen, so he likely had a while yet until the servants rang the dinner bell. He could go down to the stream where most of the rest of the Sharded had gone after setting up their tents. The late-summer day hadn't been oppressively hot, but still, by the time they'd stopped to camp, his clothes had been clinging to him, and he was fairly sure he had smelled worse than his pony. But these were the only moments he had to examine the books – soon enough the day would completely fade, and he'd found that trying to read by his darkvision was nearly impossible and gave him a splitting headache.

Deryn set the diary down in the grass and reached back inside his tent for the book Kaliss had given him. With his finger, he traced the looping silvery script of the title, which despite being somewhat archaic was at least refreshingly comprehensible. *The Twilight of an Empire and the Sundering of the Heart*. If it had truly been written by the Imperator Shen who had overthrown Segulah Tain, then it must have been copied many times over, as this book did not look nearly as ancient as the elementalist's diary. Curious why this was what Kaliss had gifted him, Deryn opened the cover and began to read.

This world differs from the one I was born into. The tyranny of an emperor has given way to the tyranny of the many. Blood has soaked the earth, the great cities have been reduced to shattered stone. Brother has slain brother. The stars wheel overhead as the carrion birds feast, bones gleaming in the moonlight. So much has changed, and yet so much is still the same.

Many years ago, I wondered where the past had gone. Why there was no record of the time before. He destroyed it, I now know. Effaced our history to hide the evidence of his crimes. When I was a boy, my old teacher told me that truth is immutable and cannot be destroyed. But what is truth? We make our own truths – the Radiant Emperor fashioned the world into a reflection of his truth, and now here, in these pages, I will do the same.

. . .

"You can read?"

Deryn glanced up from the book to find Heth standing a dozen paces away, a practice sword in each hand.

"My mother taught me."

Heth shook his head in amusement as he strolled closer, tapping a wooden blade against his leg. "You're one of the Sharded Few now. A warrior. No reason to waste your time with books."

"If you can't read, you'll always be a slave to those who can."

Heth snorted. "More like, if you can't swing a sword, you'll always be a slave to those who can."

"Well, I better be able to do both, then."

Heth grinned, tossing one of the practice swords onto the grass in front of Deryn. "Let's go. We've only got a little while before dark."

Deryn heaved himself to his feet and then stooped to retrieve the sword. "I suppose my edification can wait."

"Excellent," Heth said, cutting a quick pattern in the air with his blade. "I'd hate to think all those skills we've been sharpening might go dull. Let's go find a quiet spot to try and kill each other." He started to turn away, but then hesitated, as if something had suddenly occurred to him. "Oh, you must have brought the sword you found. I mean the special one. You should bring it. It's important to practice your forms with the sword you'll use in an actual battle, so you can get used to the weight and feel."

"And you want to see it."

"And I want to see it."

Deryn ducked inside his tent, then reached beneath his bedroll for where he'd hidden the sword. As always, his heart quickened when he grasped the hilt and felt it thrumming in his hand like a thing alive.

"That's it?" Heth asked, sounding disappointed as he emerged again from the tent carrying the sheathed sword. "I thought it would have jewels in the pommel or glow blue, given the fuss."

Deryn drew the sword from its plain black scabbard, and Heth gave a little hiss of surprise. The unblemished porcelain blade looked unnatural, like a slice of moonlight visible in the day.

"Surely that will shatter the first time it strikes something," Heth murmured, reaching out his hand, but then drawing it back just before he touched the strange material.

"I don't think so," Deryn said, shaking his head. "I've tried its edge on a few things in my chamber back at the hold – a tin flagon, my shaving razor, the wood of my bedpost. Lopped the top of it right off. It feels as strong as tempered steel, even though it's as light as ceramic."

Heth eyed the blade warily. "If it weighs so little, you should most certainly practice your forms with it. Otherwise, your balance will be thrown off later."

Deryn glanced around. The other tents were empty, their Sharded owners either cleaning up after the day's ride or taking care of their horses. But he knew they would return eventually.

"I don't want others to see the sword. Someone might get . . . ideas."

Heth jerked his chin towards the trees fringing the meadow. "We can find a clearing in the woods."

"All right," Deryn agreed, the sword chiming like a bell as he sheathed it again.

They set off in the opposite direction to where the wagons had been circled. Deryn's gaze lingered on the gleaming black wood of Rhenna's carriage, wondering if Alia and her mistress would emerge later from their elaborate tent. He'd been hoping to see them last night, but they'd disappeared behind the shimmering cloth-of-gold flaps as soon as the wedding delegation had stopped for the evening, and they had not emerged again until the next morning. The day before that, they'd been hosted at the sprawling manse of Phane's magistrate, and Deryn had only glimpsed Alia from a distance, far down the length of the massive feast table. He'd wanted badly to ask her how she was faring, but he'd had no chance yet.

They entered the forest, though Deryn wasn't sure if it deserved such a name. The trees were thin and yellow-barked, with stunted branches and reddish leaves, and there was little in the way of underbrush or roots. Late afternoon light trickled down through the canopy, scattering golden coins on the mossy ground. The trees here were not clustered too thick, so Deryn thought they might be able to find enough space to practice, but Heth lead them deeper into the little woods.

"Oh, Silver Shrike," his friend suddenly whispered, his steps slowing. In front of them the yellow trunks had thinned, and through the gaps Deryn could see that the trees gave way to a grassy field sloping down.

At the bottom of the hill unraveled the Frayed Lands, an endless sweep of colors rippling into the horizon. This was the same road they'd traveled on with Kilian, so Deryn had known they would come near the Lands, though he hadn't realized that they'd already drawn so close. The grass swayed and bent as the wind moved across the great plains, and as it did so, the shimmering hues shifted from dark amber to bright crimson to tarnished copper. Dark clouds roiled in the far distance, lightning flickering down to lick the earth. He remembered the People of the Wind's champion speaking of how the riftbeast had moved unseen across the Lands by hiding in the depths of a storm, and he felt a little shiver of unease. Though certainly even if a great monster was lurking out there, the dozen Sharded traveling with them would have little trouble dealing with it. After all, Azil had slain a riftbeast on his own.

"I suppose this is the spot," Heth said, still staring out across the grasslands. "Unless you want to go down the hill where it's flatter."

Deryn snorted. "I'll stay up here, thank you very much."

"Ah, truly you are a brave sharded warrior," Heth said, grinning as he slashed the air.

"Let me get as good as you with a sword, and then I'll be ready to hunt monsters in the Lands."

"Best get on with it, then," Heth said, gesturing with the point of his blade at the sheathed sword Deryn was carrying. "Let me see you go through the Mountain and River forms first. Then do the same with the wooden sword – I'm curious how different it feels."

Deryn nodded and took up a position a dozen paces away from Heth. He set in his feet in the grass, wary of roots, and brought his sword up in the first of the defensive stances Heth had taught him. From Deryn's understanding, the Mountain form was so named because it was strong and unyielding, suitable for when a swordsman couldn't retreat and needed to stand his ground. It relied on strong and supple wrists to turn away the blade of an opponent and a swift riposte when the opportunity arose. Deryn began to sweep his sword through the motions, meeting an invisible blade.

"Good," Heth said, watching him closely. "Now faster."

Deryn quickened the speed of his counters. The porcelain sword was incredibly light, and its thrumming seemed to intensify as it moved through the air, as if it was on the verge of tearing itself from his grip and taking flight.

"Faster," Heth repeated, and the sword became a flickering blur.

"Now strike!" he cried, and Deryn lunged forward, thrusting the sword at his imagined opponent.

A great gust of wind struck Heth and sent him tumbling backwards.

Shocked, Deryn couldn't even call out his friend's name. "Oh," he murmured, slowly lowering his sword while Heth scrambled back to his feet, his eyes wide.

"What in the Silver Shrike was that?" the boy cried, looking around wildly. "Did you feel that wind?"

Deryn did not reply, staring at the shard of moonlight in his hand. Saelus had said he thought the sword had been forged by the People of the Wind, that their fragments were embedded within it. He swallowed and raised the blade again, but this time he extended it in the direction they had come from.

"What are you doing?" Heth asked just as Deryn slashed the air.

This time he could see the surge of wind as it rolled over the grass and struck the closest trees, stripping leaves from branches and even tearing away some of the smaller limbs. The hissing crackle that accompanied the wind's passage was like the forest's sharp exclamation of surprise and pain. Birds rose into the sky shrieking, and as a blizzard of red leaves slowly drifted down, Heth and Deryn watched with mouths agape, the gust having vanished just as quickly as it had appeared.

"I suppose I can't be surprised it's magic," Heth said, running a hand through his mussed hair. "Even so, that's incredible. And think of how useful it could be in a fight! Many times, battles are lost because something unexpected happens – a foot slips in the mud, or someone is blinded when sunlight flashes on metal. How could a warrior keep their concentration and stay disciplined when a wind rises out of nowhere and knocks them back a step just before you charge?" His eyes were wide as he envisioned the possibilities. "You could win any duel if you learn how to harness that power. Or how about you let me borrow it and I'll win the Day of Blades in Flail, and we can split the prize money!"

"I wonder if it can do anything else," Deryn asked softly, turning the sword this way and that as he examined how the strange unlight welling up from its depths slid along the nacreous blade.

"Cut, slash, parry, thrust," Heth said excitedly. "Run through all the forms I've taught you. Just promise me you won't swing it in my direction again . . . I don't want to float away over the Lands like a dandelion seed!"

"I won't," Deryn promised him, unable to hold back a chuckle at the image Heth had just conjured.

"Good," Heth said, edging closer to Deryn, his gaze fixed on the sword. "Now let's scare some more birds."

The sword revealed no other powers during their investigations, though Deryn learned how to better control the surge of wind it created, refining his ability to guide the direction in which it gusted. He found that if he channeled his *ka* as he thrust, forcing his shard's energy into the sword, the wind exploded outward with far more force, enough even to topple a few of the smaller trees. He wondered what someone back at the camp might be thinking, listening to the roar of the wind and seeing the tops of the trees shaking as though in a hurricane.

This experimentation was more than a little draining. After a while he set the sword aside, and Heth led him through a new form with the practice blades. This one was called the Marsh, and it involved drawing your opponent close enough to lock their weapon so they couldn't easily strike, then trying to disarm them. Heth explained that it was most effective if one also wielded a shield-breaker or parrying dagger, but even though Deryn did not, it was still useful to be familiar with this style.

By the time the cloak of twilight had fallen over the world, they were both sweating and breathing hard. Deryn could have continued – in this liminal light his darkvision was even more effective – but Heth was risking injury by trying to spar in the gloaming.

"Tomorrow," Deryn said as he handed back the wooden sword to Heth. "Come find me as soon as we stop. They don't trust me to check the hooves of my pony or brush her down, so no need to wait for me to finish caring for her. We can begin our training at once."

"That sounds good," Heth said, running his fingers through his damp hair. "Though perhaps we should bathe first. I can smell both of us right now, and we're … not very fragrant."

Deryn chuckled and clapped him on the shoulder. "Why bother? We're just going to get sweaty again tomorrow."

"Apparently there's no girl who's got your eye," Heth grumbled as they turned and entered the little woods again, the detritus that had been torn from the branches by the wind-sword crunching under their boots.

"And you?" Deryn asked teasingly. "Is there someone on this journey you fancy?"

Heth snorted in response to this, but Deryn noticed he turned his face away, as if trying to hide his expression.

They passed from the trees, returning to the meadow where the wedding delegation had set up camp. A half-dozen fires had been started while they were gone, and as Heth turned to make his way towards the one where the rest of the Hollow guards were clustered, Deryn took hold of his arm and guided him in the direction of his own tent.

"Come eat with us."

Heth glanced at him in surprise. "The Hollow and the Sharded Few don't mingle."

"But friends do," Deryn said, and though Heth frowned, he allowed himself to be led to a small fire on the other side of the meadow. There were actually two bonfires for the Sharded, the other much larger and surrounded by a more raucous crowd. Deryn noticed Vertus among them, his crimson tattoos gleaming in the firelight, and he instinctively shielded Heth from his sight as they passed. He hadn't heard of any formal rule that prohibited the Hollow and the Sharded Few from fraternizing, but Deryn knew if anyone would take issue, it would be Vertus. He obviously disliked even the Sharded who were not scions of the Duskhold's great families, so no doubt the thought of sharing a meal with the servants would appall him.

Deryn's heart skipped a beat when he approached the smaller fire and noticed who was already sitting there. Yvrin was absorbed in a conversation with a sleepy-eyed older Sharded, and she didn't notice Deryn and Heth even after they'd sat down across from her. She threw her head back at something and laughed loudly, then wiped at her eyes and took a sip from the flask lying in the grass beside her. Deryn couldn't keep his lips from twitching into a smile. He'd learned in their few short days traveling together that her good moods were infectious, brightening even the dourest among the Sharded.

Yvrin suddenly noticed them across the flames and raised her flask towards them.

"Deryn!" she cried, showing him those dimples he'd been daydreaming about earlier. "Where have you been? And who's your friend?"

"Sword training," he replied, gesturing to the hilt at his side. "Heth is my teacher."

Yvrin raised her eyebrows, her mouth making a surprised expression. "No rest for the weary, I see. Well, good on you to try to keep up with your lessons while away from the Duskhold." Her gaze shifted to Heth. "And what's your name, bladesman?"

"Heth," he said, still sounding nervous.

"And you're one of the Hollow guards?"

"Yes," he admitted, almost guiltily.

Yvrin ignored his tone, taking a bite of meat from a skewer she'd been holding in her other hand. "Welcome," she said through her chewing, then gestured with the sharpened wooden stick at where a dozen other skewers were cooling on a cloth beside the fire. "Dinner is there. The mutton the magistrate sent with us is delicious. Help yourself."

"Thank you," Heth murmured, casting a sideways glance at Deryn before rising.

Yvrin stripped the last of the meat from the skewer and tossed it away, then leaned back on her elbows to watch Heth as he gathered some of the spitted mutton.

"You must be starving, marching all day and then teaching the sword."

"It's, uh, I'm fine," he mumbled, handing a few of the steaming skewers to Deryn. "We take turns marching. Half the time we're allowed to rest in the wagon. Honestly, I prefer being outside – the pace isn't arduous, and the fresh air is nice."

"It is," Yvrin agreed. "If I stay in the Duskhold too long, it eventually feels like I've been buried alive in a barrow. That's why I asked to come on this journey." She sucked in a deep breath, then released it with a contented sigh.

"I'm Helvin," the other Sharded said, seizing this break in the conversation to introduce himself. His voice was a gravelly drawl, but his seamed and weathered face was friendly enough. "Good to finally meet you, Deryn. Heard quite a bit."

"We all have," added Yvrin. "Only to be disappointed. Where is the demon familiar? I never saw it in any of our lessons on the Drum Tower."

"He's . . . shy."

"Oh, it's a boy, is it?" Yvrin asked, grinning wickedly. "I mean, you've checked? Had a quick look between its legs?" She lifted her pinky finger and wiggled it, then threw back her head and laughed again.

"No, no, of course not," Deryn said, hoping the firelight hid his blush. "I suppose it's ridiculous to think of it as male."

Heth must have sensed his embarrassment, because he came to Deryn's rescue. "Apologies, Sharded, but where are you from that you find living in the Duskhold so oppressive? Is it the Wild?"

"Nay," Yvrin said, her dimples finally disappearing as she got hold of her mirth. "My people live in the south, not the north, on the Kezekan Steppes."

"The Anvil," Deryn said, remembering his geography lessons with Kaliss. "But that's close to Ashasai. How did you end up in the Duskhold?"

Yvrin took another sip from her flask, then grimaced, though Deryn wasn't sure if it was from the taste of the drink or the question. "The Sanguine City's cruelty to its own citizens is legendary – how do you think it treats its neighbors? Many of my people have drained away while chained atop the Black Steps."

"But you fought to save the city at Gerendal, did you not?"

"We fought with the northern alliance, yes. If it was up to us, though, we would have let the Salahi destroy Ashasai before we turned the desert warriors back." She paused for a moment, staring at something only she could see in the flames. "My father was a war chief, and during the battle his life was saved by one of the shadow-sharded. So many years later, when my Imbued nature became clear, he set me on my horse and pointed me north, told me to find the Duskhold and swear myself to the Shadow. His way of paying the life-debt he owed, I suppose. With *my* life. He wasn't a very good father, to be honest."

The ease with which she'd commanded her magnificent stallion had impressed Deryn, but he'd had no idea that she was one of the horse-masters of the southern steppes. He couldn't help but feel self-conscious about how inept he had been while clinging to the back of his own little pony.

"Here," Yvrin said, tightening the lid on her flask before tossing it across the fire to Heth. "A taste of the Kezekan. I couldn't believe it when I found a trader from my people in Phane, and he was willing to part with this."

"What is it?" Heth asked, unscrewing the lid and taking a tentative sniff. "Oh, fire and ashes," he whispered hoarsely, his nose wrinkling.

"We call it kumiss," Yvrin said, her dimples making a triumphant return. "Fermented mare's milk, with a few other ingredients thrown in to make your hair curl. Now take a drink or throw it here again."

With a look of profound resignation, Heth tilted back the flask and let a tiny bit trickle into his throat . . . and then almost immediately coughed it up, keeping it down only by pressing his hand to his mouth.

Yvrin dissolved into a fit of laughter, and when that finally subsided, Heth was still gasping and spluttering. She wiped at her eyes, then pointed at Deryn.

"Give it to him next," she begged, but Deryn waved the proffered flask away.

"No, thank you," he said.

"Go on, try it," Heth rasped. "It's delicious."

"I'll try some."

All heads turned as new arrivals emerged from the gloom.

"Lady Shen," murmured Helvin, ducking his head as Rhenna sank down beside the fire, Alia beside her. The expression of the bride-to-be was similar to what Deryn had seen her wearing before – he would have described it as imperious disdain – but she was also holding out her open hand towards Heth, as if she truly wanted him to pass her the drink.

"It's, uh, it's an acquired taste," Yvrin said, looking slightly concerned that the heir of the Duskhold had decided to grace their fire.

"You wouldn't believe the vile spirits I had to drink at my father's table," Rhenna said. "Now, Heth"—the Hollow had been staring at

Alia, but when she spoke his name, his gaze snapped to her in what looked like terror—"give it to me."

"Yes, m'lady," Heth whispered as he handed the flask to her.

Rhenna didn't even smell the drink before taking a deep swallow. Her brow drew down, like she was thinking about the taste, and then she replaced the lid and tossed it back to Yvrin. "Not bad. A little bitter."

For a moment, the only sound was the hiss and crackle of the flames. Then Yvrin's wry smile returned.

"You would be very popular among my people. Perhaps one day we can travel to the steppes together."

"I would enjoy that very much," Rhenna replied, her voice deadpan, "if my husband allows it."

An uncomfortable silence fell, and to Deryn's surprise, it was Alia who broke it.

"Mistress," the Wild girl said softly.

Rhenna glanced at her, then sighed. "Yes, I know. Please grant me pardon – I came out here tonight to lift my spirits, not wallow even deeper in my ill-humor."

"It's nothing," Yvrin said quickly, sounding faintly embarrassed that the heir to the Duskhold would offer an apology to them. "And I can speak for all here that we would be pleased to try to cheer you. But to do that, we need a drink everyone can enjoy." She turned to Helvin. "Do you know which Hollow is in charge of the stores? Perhaps we can get a cask of whatever they're drinking at the other fire."

"I'll go ask," the older Sharded promised, rising with a grunt and heading off towards where the rest of the shadow-sharded were sitting.

They watched him go, and then Rhenna turned towards Deryn, fixing him with night-black eyes. "It's good to see you again, Deryn. I was pleased when my father said you would be one of the Sharded accompanying me."

He ducked his head to acknowledge her words. "And I as well,

Lady Shen. Especially when I heard who else would be coming." His gaze flicked to Alia and then Heth.

Rhenna raised her hands towards the flame to warm them. "Yes. The threads of Fate are binding you all tightly. I wonder what the future might hold . . . It seems that you are meant to be together."

Deryn caught Alia glance sharply at Rhenna, surprise in her face. If Rhenna noticed the look, she ignored it.

Yvrin unfolded her legs with a sigh, stretching them out in the grass. "My people have a saying about heart-companions –"

"Lady Shen!"

Vertus emerged from the dark, his red markings nearly blending with the flush on his face. He was clutching a goblet, his lips stained by wine, and he swayed slightly as he took in those gathered around the fire.

"Lord Balenchas," Rhenna said – rather formally, Deryn thought.

Vertus waved his goblet, spilling some of his drink on Heth's leg, though luckily the Hollow boy had the sense not to act affronted. "It's good to see you out of your tent tonight, Rhenna. But what are you doing over here? Come join us at the other fire. I've opened one of the choice firewines my father sent with us."

Rhenna regarded him coolly. "I am comfortable here, Vertus. Perhaps you could bring that wine to *us*."

Vertus blinked at the emphasis she had put on this last word. Again his gaze traveled around the fire, and Deryn sensed he was struggling not to sneer. Then his eyes widened slightly when they fell on Deryn.

"Adept," he said airily, taking a sip from his cup. "I forgot to tell you on the day we left the Duskhold, but I see Malachai patched you up well enough. There's hardly any evidence of the beating."

"A beating that happened because of your negligence," Deryn replied, and Vertus froze with the cup still at his lips. A slight intake of breath came from Heth, but Deryn didn't care. He'd had enough of bullies.

"Have a care, adept," Vertus murmured. "I was given command here."

"But this is my procession," Rhenna interrupted. "And until I am wedded, I still sit higher than you in the Duskhold. Now go fetch me what's left of that firewine."

Vertus turned his smoldering gaze from Deryn to Rhenna. For a moment, it seemed like he was on the verge of some biting retort, but instead he bowed stiffly. "As you wish, Lady Shen," he said, then turned on his heel and strode away.

Silence descended again as uncertain glances were traded around the fire. Then Yvrin raised her flask, firelight gleaming on the metal. "More kumiss, anyone?"

42

HETH

"Wake up!"

A hand was on his shoulder, shaking him.

"*Ermph*," Heth mumbled, opening bleary eyes. The shadow looming over him was featureless in the darkness of his tent, but he knew that voice.

"Alia," he murmured, sitting up. "What's wrong?"

The silhouette moved back a step. "Oh, thank the First Seed. You're all right."

The edge of desperate relief in her voice had the same effect as if she'd poured icy water over his head. His thoughts sharpened, the last remnants of sleep vanishing.

"Why wouldn't I be?" he asked, reaching beside his bedroll for where he'd set his clothes for the next day, very glad it was too dark for her to notice his nakedness.

"Please, come quickly!"

The next thing he heard was the flap rustling as she slipped out of his tent, and for a moment he could only sit in dazed bewilderment. What had just happened? Was something wrong with Rhenna? Why had she come to him and not one of the Sharded? He shook his head as he hurriedly dressed, hesitating only a moment before also buckling on his sword belt. Surely any problem that his sword might solve could more effectively be dealt with by one of the Sharded, but given the fear he'd heard in Alia's voice, he'd just rather follow her armed.

He threw back the flap and emerged into the night. Moonlight drenched the camp, making the white tents of the Hollow glow with a pale radiance. How had Alia even known he was here? She must have watched him return to his tent after their time around the campfire had ended.

"Come!" Alia hissed, beckoning for him to follow her. She looked otherworldly, her skin silvery and her normally golden hair white as bone. It crossed Heth's mind that she *was* a ghost, or perhaps one of those mythical cat-woman spirits who changed their shape to lure poor fools to their deaths, but then he pushed those foolish thoughts aside.

He followed her as she picked her way towards where Lady Shen's tent towered over the rest of the camp. Heth slowed as they approached the entrance, glancing around uncertainly.

"I can't go in there!" he whispered, half-expecting a Sharded guard to emerge from the night and cut him down.

Alia paused at the entrance to the tent and turned back to him, and even in the semi-darkness he could see the fear in her face. "Please," she begged, before vanishing inside.

Shaken, Heth steeled himself for whatever he might find and pushed aside the heavy flaps. The interior of the tent was cavernous, and it would have been black as pitch except for a flickering candle that revealed a small desk, a changing screen, and a large and ornate bed, the transportation of which must have required the dedicated use of a wagon.

And in that bed was sprawled Rhenna Shen.

"Is she ... dead?" he asked softly, not willing yet to come closer. If she was only sleeping and woke to find him standing over her, she might kill him before Alia could explain that she'd in fact dragged him here.

And Heth wouldn't have blamed her.

"No!" Alia nearly gasped. "She's not dead. But I don't know what's wrong." She hovered over her mistress, resting her hand on Rhenna's cheek. "I can't wake her. She usually sleeps very light . . . muttering and twitching as she dreams, and that's how I knew something was wrong. She is so still, so silent."

Fighting back his unease, Heth finally approached the lady of the Duskhold. She looked like a beautiful corpse, her white face framed by a halo of intensely black hair. He was tempted to lean closer and see if she was indeed breathing, but he wasn't feeling quite that brave yet.

"Mistress," Alia said loudly, the desperation clear in her voice. "Mistress, you must wake." Then she glanced at Heth with an expression of profound regret, sighed deeply, and slapped her mistress hard.

Heth flinched at the sound, preparing to fling himself towards the tent flap if Rhenna surged awake screaming.

But she did no such thing. Her head barely moved, as if Alia had struck stone.

"We should get the other Sharded," Heth suggested. "Vertus, I suppose."

Alia grimaced. "Truly? What if . . . what if this is *their* fault?"

Heth looked at her sharply. "What do you mean?"

Alia ran a hand through her long hair, her expression pained. "In the Wild, some warriors dip their arrows in poison made from the skin of a grey toad. I've heard that the effects are similar to this. If the arrow doesn't kill outright, once the venom gets into the blood, the victim falls into a stupor, just like this. They can't be roused, and after a few days, they're dead."

Heth swallowed, his gaze flicking to the tent flaps. "You think she's been poisoned?"

"I don't know!" Alia cried. "But what if we tell someone and they were responsible?"

"Well, we know one person who cannot be involved."

Alia sighed again. "I know, I was just worried about going among the Sharded's tents. If anyone saw me, they'd know something was wrong."

"We don't have a choice. We need Deryn's help. He knows a lot more about being Sharded, and he may even have an idea about how to help her."

Alia nodded, wiping at her cheeks. "I'll stay with her. Can you go get him and bring him here?"

"Of course," Heth promised, trying to sound reassuring. "I'll be back soon – keep trying to wake her up." Tearing his eyes from Rhenna's ghost-face, he turned and plunged outside, and almost immediately it was like the fist squeezing his heart had loosened. He didn't know what was going on in there, but he shuddered to think what would happen to Alia if Rhenna succumbed to whatever was afflicting her. Would she be held responsible? Trying not to think of what someone like Vertus might do to her, he hurried through the camp, soon arriving at Deryn's tent. Or he hoped it was his tent – they all looked the same in the darkness.

"Deryn," he whispered, "It's Heth. Alia and I need your help."

No answer. Cursing under his breath, Heth slowly pushed aside the flap. "Deryn, wake up."

Moonlight spilled into the tent, illuminating a dark shape huddled under blankets. Heth reached down and fumbled around until he felt a leg and then shook it hard.

Nothing. A tingling numbness was spreading through Heth, and his palms were cold and sweaty. He swallowed, slipping fully inside the tent. "Fire and ashes, Deryn, you need to wake up right *now*."

Heth ground his teeth in frustration. He wanted to yell at the boy, but that would surely bring the other Sharded running. Unless – and this was a disquieting thought – they were all in a similar state. He placed his hand where he thought Deryn's head must be in the dark and felt hair, ears, the curve of his face. Still the boy didn't move, though he was relieved when he felt Deryn's breath passing through his slightly parted lips.

"All right," Heth murmured, "I'm truly sorry for this." With his thumb and forefinger, he pinched Deryn's cheek as hard as he could.

There was not even the slightest hitch to his breathing. It was like Deryn's mind had abandoned his body. Heth crouched down and hung his head. What was going on?

He froze when he saw the darkness ripple. Even though he had known it was a possibility that the elemental might be lurking, the appearance of the thing was still unsettling. Many afternoons on top of the Drum Tower it had lolled about while they were sparring or run around chasing its tail like it was a dog in truth, but Heth could never really look past the fact that it was just a shadow come to life.

"Shade," he hissed, though he didn't truly expect it to understand him. "Something is wrong."

The darkness flowed closer to Deryn. It slithered onto his chest and curled there like a snake, then extended an arm or a tendril, or what passed for its own head towards the boy's sleeping face. It almost looked like it was examining him, trying to understand why he wouldn't wake.

Heth clenched his hands into fists, his frustration and fear continuing to rise. Very soon he would have to ignore Alia's fears and go tell Yvrin or Gervis what had happened . . .

He hissed in alarm. Shade was changing, the somewhat solid form it had taken when it clambered atop Deryn melting away, and then this black liquid was flowing across his chest, up his neck, and *into* his slightly open mouth.

"No, no, no," Heth moaned, his heart hammering as the last of the elemental disappeared inside Deryn. Was this bad? What was –

Deryn sat up.

"Oh, thank the Broken God," Heth gasped. "Are you all –"

The words died in his throat as Deryn rose to his feet like he was a puppet pulled up by invisible strings. Light seeped into the tent as the blanket fell away, revealing the glimmering shard sunk into his chest. He was naked, but Deryn made no move to dress or cover himself, instead just standing there, motionless, like he was waiting for something.

In the dusky radiance of the shard, Heth saw that Deryn's eyes were pools of darkness.

"No," he whispered, dread closing around his heart.

Deryn turned to regard him, and a chill crept up Heth's spine as he stared into those black pits.

"*What,*" Deryn said. His voice was strangely hollow, like the word had echoed up from the bottom of a deep well.

Heth's thoughts scattered. He didn't know how to answer this thing that had been his friend, even if he wanted to.

Deryn's mouth worked soundlessly, as if he was struggling to form more words. "*What wrong?*" he finally managed, and then the stiffness in his body subsided slightly.

Its body, Heth supposed. Because this was certainly not Deryn anymore.

"I don't know," Heth stammered, the intensity of that black gaze making his skin crawl. "Deryn wouldn't wake up. And Rhenna won't either. Something has happened to them."

"*Take me her,*" the thing that had been Deryn croaked.

Heth gawked, looking him up and down. A fully clothed man moving through the camp late at night would only draw cursory attention if noticed, but who knew what response a naked Sharded might bring?

Heth gestured at a pile of clothes in the tent's corner. "Uh, perhaps . . . you could get dressed first?"

Deryn's attention jerked to where Heth was indicating. With a too-large step, he crossed the tent and bent stiffly to gather the discarded clothes Heth remembered him wearing earlier than evening. Awkwardly, he started dressing himself, and Heth hurried beside him to help after a few moments of watching him try to jam his head through the tunic's sleeves.

"Let me," he said, and the Deryn-elemental relinquished his hold on the shirt, then went still as Heth put it on properly. Breeches were a bit more difficult, but after a few failed attempts, he managed to guide Deryn's legs where they needed to go.

"Good, now follow me –" Heth said, turning away, but then stopped when he realized Deryn wasn't paying attention, too busy trying to buckle on his sword belt.

"I don't think you'll need that," Heth muttered. "I hope not, anyway."

Deryn lifted his head to stare at Heth, holding the two ends of his sword belt like he had absolutely no idea how to make them work.

"Very well," Heth said with a sigh, stepping closer again to assist him.

"*That,*" Deryn or Shade or whatever murmured, lifting his arm to point at something as Heth threaded the belt through the correct notch.

He glanced around to try to see what had drawn its attention, but he didn't notice anything. Then the darkness shivered, and a book floated towards them carried by tendrils of glistening black.

"*Take that,*" the thing inside Deryn said as the book came to hover in front of Heth.

Swallowing away his fear, Heth held out his hand. The strands bearing up the book dissolved, and he leaped forward to catch it before it could fall to the ground. Its great age was evident, the cover stiff and cracked under his fingers, but Heth had no chance to investigate the book further as Deryn suddenly exited the tent with those strange, overly long strides.

"Wait!" he hissed, hurriedly pushing through the flap, then nearly collided with Deryn, who had stopped just outside the tent and was staring up at the moon with a look of awed wonder.

"This way," Heth whispered, pulling on Deryn's arm. For a moment the thing in his friend resisted, but then it gave a deep sigh of what sounded like satisfaction and allowed Heth to lead it – him? – away.

As they neared Rhenna's tent, Heth couldn't help but wonder what in the seven hells he was doing. Deryn clearly was suffering from the same mysterious affliction as Rhenna, and he didn't think the elemental inhabiting his body was actually helping to overcome whatever had happened. It had merely filled the absence that had been created – but what had caused it?

With jerky movements, Deryn flung aside the gleaming cloth-of-gold flap and entered Rhenna's tent. Alia was bent over her motionless mistress, but she straightened with a surprised gasp as they burst inside.

"Deryn!" she cried, and rushed towards him before stopping abruptly and stumbling back a step, her hand flying to her mouth.

"What's wrong with you?" she murmured as Deryn stalked past her to come stand beside the bed and look down on Rhenna. "Your eyes . . ."

"It's not Deryn!" Heth said, coming to stand beside Alia. "Or, it is, but it's also not. I wasn't able to wake him, just like with Rhenna, but then his elemental flowed *into* him. It's controlling him, somehow."

"Can it help?" Alia whispered, clinging to Heth desperately, her wide eyes fixed on Deryn as he stared down at Rhenna in silent contemplation.

"I have absolutely no idea," Heth replied. "I don't know –"

Light flooded the tent, the night outside suddenly bright as day. It immediately faded, though it did not dissipate entirely, and Heth shared a moment of frozen surprise with the Wild girl just before the first explosion rent the silence.

Alia screamed – or Heth thought she was screaming, as her mouth was open and her throat working – but all he could hear was the ringing in his ears. Outside, a stuttering series of smaller flashes illuminated the interior of the tent, bathing them all in lurid red light as the ground trembled. Alia clutched at him, confusion and fear in her face.

"I'll go see," he yelled at her, though he doubted she could hear him, and when he reached the entrance to the tent, he found she was still beside him.

He pulled back the tent flap and gazed out upon a field of fire.

Pillars of flame were converging on the camp from several directions at once, and atop the closest Heth could see a man gesticulating fiercely. A moment later, a roiling ball of fire erupted from his outstretched hand, tumbling down to strike one of the larger tents of the Sharded. The force of the impact blew the tent apart, and in the wreckage a shuddering form writhed in agony, wreathed in flame.

"Broken God, save us," whispered Heth as Alia moaned in dismay.

The flame-sharded were attacking.

Figures were stumbling from the tents that were not already ablaze, the darkness coalescing around them. Heth glimpsed Vertus as he gestured and screamed at the Sharded perched on the closest pillar, and then a torrent of flame enveloped him. Heth sucked in his breath to see the strongest of their warriors struck down so effortlessly, but when the flames subsided, Vertus was still there, a barrier of solid darkness having protected him from the onslaught.

Other shadow-sharded were not so fortunate. The ambush had clearly taken them unawares, and before they could manifest their powers the flame-sharded pressed their advantage, lashing them with whips of flame and hurling globes that sent fire splattering when they struck. More than a few of the shadow-sharded had already been consumed by the hungry flames, rolling on the ground or burning like torches in the night as they staggered about.

It was a massacre.

He realized Alia was pulling frantically on his arm trying to get his attention, and when he finally wrenched his gaze from the chaos and saw what she was staring at he sucked in his breath.

Flames were crawling along the outside of Rhenna's tent, rapidly spreading. It wouldn't be very long until the structure was consumed, or it might simply collapse inward at any moment.

He whirled around, planning on dragging Rhenna from her bed and carrying her to safety, but he found that the entity inside Deryn had already decided on the same course of action. He was coming towards them with his awkward strides, Rhenna in her gossamer nightgown limp in his arms.

"Where are you taking her?" Heth shouted as Deryn passed him, his blank face staring straight ahead.

"Away!" Alia answered for him, dashing back inside the tent. "And that's good enough!"

Heth winced as a massive flower of flame blossomed nearby, heated air washing over him. "Well, what are *you* doing?" he cried, torn between following Alia into the burning tent or chasing after Deryn as he carried Rhenna away through the middle of the raging battle.

Cursing, he made a decision and was just about to go grab Alia when she reappeared again at the tent's entrance holding a sack.

"Her clothes," she said between gulping breaths.

Heth bit back what he wanted to say about priorities and instead grabbed her arm as he began hauling her in the direction Deryn had gone.

The meadow they'd camped in had been transformed into a raging hellscape, living shadows and flames locked in battle. A blazing bird unfurled vast wings, only to be pierced in the breast by a lance of glistening black. With a shriek it faded into glimmering sparks. Elsewhere a half-dozen simulacra of the same shadow-sharded – Vertus, maybe – was dueling with three red-shrouded warriors, each with glimmering shards sunk into the center of their foreheads. Black tendrils wrapped the legs of one of the attackers looming over them and pulled him shrieking from his pillar of flame, which instantly collapsed.

As they traversed the battlefield, Heth's heart was in his throat, but the shadow and flame-sharded were too intent on killing each other to care very much about a few Hollow fleeing the carnage. Still, the likelihood of being accidentally struck by the powers being unleashed was high, so he didn't allow himself to breathe a sigh of relief until they reached the line of trees fringing the field. And then he realized breathing itself had become difficult, as thick smoke clotted the air.

The creature inhabiting Deryn had already entered the woods, plunging into the underbrush without slowing. Alia followed close behind, but Heth paused and looked back, praying that he would see that the tide had turned.

That hope was dashed now that he could take in the battle's entirety. Most of the tents were ablaze, and from these bonfires had been fashioned all manner of monsters. A burning giant with the head of an aurochs lowered its horns to gore a shadow-warrior, while elsewhere a long serpent slithered through the grass leaving a trail of fire in its wake, and a great insect with strangely jointed legs stalked through the field with its barbed tail poised to strike. There were patches of flame everywhere, and it looked to Heth like soon these conflagrations would merge and the entire camp would be consumed by a maelstrom of fire.

Benni. Gervis. They were certainly dead – what could mere men do when caught between warring demigods? He swallowed back the ache in his throat. They had been good men. What about the shadow-sharded? Had Yvrin and Helvin already been struck down, or were they one of the few pockets of writhing darkness still holding out against the flames?

He shook himself from his daze and turned away from the slaughter. They needed to run, far and fast, before the fire spread to the forest or the flame-sharded realized they had fled.

For they had certainly come for Rhenna, and they did not seem to care at all about taking her alive.

Alia and the thing carrying Rhenna had already vanished into the shadowy tangle, and he followed, branches clawing at his face. The darkness here was nearly absolute, with only a trickle of moonlight filtering through the canopy, and Heth kept his arms out as he pressed into the black so he wouldn't run head-on into a tree.

He'd only gone about a hundred paces when the undergrowth thinned, and he stumbled into a clearing gilded by moonlight. Deryn and Alia were already there, the shadow-sharded standing motion-less in the middle of the grove and the Wild girl hovering beside him speaking in low tones to her still-limp mistress.

"We need to keep going," Heth said, casting a quick glance back the way they'd come. The glimmer of flames was visible, and he knew it wouldn't be long before those fires reached these woods.

"I know," Alia said, brushing Rhenna's hair away from where it had fallen across her face. "I don't know why he stopped. I think he hears something."

Heth frowned, coming closer to Deryn. The boy's face was still expressionless, the black wells that had been his eyes staring at noth-ing, but his head was cocked to one side as if listening hard.

Heth reached out to tug on Deryn's arm, hoping that this would get him moving again, but before his fingers brushed his skin a tremendous crash came from the forest and something hurtled into the clearing. Heth stumbled back in shock as it flashed past him and slammed into a trunk, wrenching roots from the ground and nearly sending a good-sized tree toppling over.

"Oh no," Heth whispered as a man in dark red robes crawled out from the shattered remains of the tree, his face contorted in pain. Blood was welling up from where slivers of wood had scratched his hairless head, the wounds illuminated by the red shard embedded in his forehead. For a moment he looked dazed, then he spat out a mouthful of broken teeth and grabbed hold of a branch that had been torn away. His fragment pulsed, and the length of wood burst into flames. Then he suddenly seemed to realize he wasn't alone in the clearing, staring at them with his mouth hanging open.

Another shuddering crash snapped the attention of everyone to where the flame-sharded had first come flying. Trees were ripped asunder by shadowy serpents, and then from the forest stalked Yvrin, her face blackened by ash and her eyes wild with rage.

The flame-sharded screamed something unintelligible and hurled a fireball at her, but she batted it aside contemptuously with a buckler of shadow, sending it smashing into the woods. Several of the trees immediately burst into flame, and Heth's heart sank even further.

Yvrin crossed the clearing in a heartbeat, and when the flame-sharded swept up his fire sword to meet her charge she caught the blade with a hand sheathed in darkness and shattered it effortlessly. He shrieked in fear, glowing motes swirling around his head, but she did not let him finish manifesting this new talent as she slashed with curving black talons and ripped out his throat in a spray of blood. Immediately, the motes vanished as the flame-sharded collapsed in a heap. Before he could take his last gurgling breath, Yvrin crouched down and used her claws to deftly pluck the fragment from his brow. Then she stood, chest heaving, and turned to the rest of them, her smoke-smeared face now also painted crimson.

"Is Lady Shen dead?" Yvrin asked, directing the question at Deryn.

"No," Heth said quickly, stepping into her line of sight.

She blinked, focusing her attention on him. "What is wrong with her ... with them?"

Heth swallowed, casting an uncertain glance at Alia. "We don't know. Alia couldn't wake her, and when I went to Deryn I discovered he was the same. The . . . elemental went into him as I watched – otherwise he'd still have been in his tent when the attack came."

Yvrin approached the motionless Deryn, peering into the black hollows where his eyes had been. "Mother Dark," she whispered as blood dripped from the claws dangling at her side.

"What should we do?" Heth asked, his voice breaking. He'd kept his panic from seizing him by keeping focused only on what was happening in the moment, but he was coming dangerously close to letting it slip from his grip. Especially with the flames spreading among the trees – Yvrin and the other shadow-sharded clearly had some protection from the heat and smoke, but he and Alia would be overwhelmed quickly.

"Flee," Yvrin said, examining Deryn as she slowly circled him. She paused by Rhenna's head, pulling back her eyelid to meet her sightless gaze.

"Do you know what's wrong with her?" Alia asked, her arms wrapped around herself despite the clearing's rising warmth.

"No," Yvrin murmured, letting Rhenna's eye close again. "I don't know what can be done for them now – or even if they'll survive the night."

"The others –?" Heth began, but Yvrin cut him off brusquely.

"Dead, or soon to be. The Flame brought at least twice the number of Sharded we had, and they took us by surprise."

They all jumped as a burning branch broke with a crack and crashed to the forest floor.

"Run as far and fast as you can," Yvrin told them, watching the fire spread. "Luck willing, the flame-sharded will think you all perished in your tents. Leave the forest and don't look back. I'll find you when I can."

"Are you . . . not coming with us?" Heth asked, the thought of being alone again without the protection of a Sharded making his voice catch.

Yvrin raised her hand, the blood on her claws glistening darkly. "I'm going to find my horse."

They kept ahead of the flames as they pushed on through the forest, finally arriving where Heth and Deryn had trained earlier. The Frayed Lands spread below them like the sea at night, a rippling dark expanse. Far in the distance were the spectral lights of Gendurdrang, like a great port glimpsed on the horizon from a ship's deck. Heth had absolutely no desire to enter the lands where riftbeasts stalked and the dead refused to die, but what choice did they have? The insatiable flames would eventually devour these woods and them as well, if they stayed where they were.

The grassy slope leading down to the plains was steep, and Heth couldn't help but worry that Deryn with his unnatural strides would pitch forward carrying Rhenna, but despite its apparent awkwardness, the elemental inhabiting him seemed to have good balance. They reached the bottom of the hill without any stumbles, and Deryn did not even hesitate as he walked into the high grass of the Lands. Heth, on the other hand, couldn't hold back a shiver as the first long blades brushed his thighs. His imagination wanted to conjure up all sorts of creatures lurking unseen in the grass, but he refused to entertain such thoughts as he followed a few paces behind Deryn. He kept his gaze fixed on the sky and the stars dancing attendance around the swollen moon.

Deryn seemed indefatigable. He never stopped to rest – or even slowed his implacable strides – and by the time the horizon began to lighten, a sharp stitch had begun in Heth's side and his legs were aching. Alia also had deep reserves, as her face in the pale dawnlight showed no strain, nor did she voice any complaints. They had encountered no animals during the night in the Frayed Lands – at least that Heth had noticed – but the light revealed a few deer-like creatures watching them motionless from afar, their spiraling horns picked out against the breaking day. They seemed to be little threat, bounding away through the long grass as Deryn neared, disturbing a flock of dark-winged birds that then rose shrieking indignantly into the sky.

Heth had glanced behind many times during the night, and he'd watched the ridge of trees above them first begin to glimmer with the approach of the forest fire, then glow red, and finally be consumed. He'd feared that the flames would creep down the slope and set the grasslands ablaze, but the fire also seemed to fear the Lands, as it remained in the woods above. Now, in the dim pre-dawn, Heth could see the blackened, twisted remains of the trees, smoke rising from the pockets of flame that still smoldered deeper in the tangle. After staring at the ruin of the forest for a long time, his gaze drifted to the way they had traveled during the night, and his breath caught in his throat.

They were being followed.

"Alia," he said warningly, and she stopped wading through the long grass and glanced at him in alarm. "Behind us."

She turned and squinted, and then the worry in her face melted away. "It's her. The Sharded from the Anvil."

Heth let out the breath he'd been holding, then jogged ahead to lay his hand on Deryn's shoulder. The elemental stopped abruptly, turning to stare at Heth with those unsettling black eyes.

"Wait for a while," he said. "A friend is coming."

"And she found her horse," Alia added, coming up alongside them. Heth turned back to the dark smudge and saw that Yvrin had rapidly closed the distance, coming near enough that he could see that she was mounted on a huge bay stallion. Behind her on a rope trailed a much smaller russet pony, and Heth thought this might be the same one he had seen Deryn riding earlier.

When Yvrin reached them, she swung herself fluidly from the saddle, though she did stumble slightly when she dropped to the grass. Heth leaped forward to catch her, but she waved him away as she straightened.

"I'm fine," she said tightly, though she didn't look fine. Yvrin had attempted to wipe the grime and blood from her face, but she still looked like an apparition from the abyss. She had a fresh wound as well, strips of cloth already darkened by blood wound around her midsection.

"Any change?" she asked, gesturing at where Deryn was standing stiffly with Rhenna still in his arms.

"No," Alia replied, "but they're not getting any worse, either. My lady's breathing is slow but steady."

Yvrin grunted at this, pulling on the rope to bring the red pony closer. "Lady Shen will ride with me. Alia, you can make sure Deryn stays upright on his horse. I don't want him sliding off if the elemental abandons his body."

Alia looked dubiously at the pony. "I'd prefer to walk."

Yvrin shook her head. "You can both take turns. Ash will tire more quickly if asked to carry two men all day."

"What happened back there?" Heth blurted, finally unable to contain his curiosity.

Yvrin turned empty eyes to him. "Death," she said, then ran a hand through her matted curls. "Everyone else who traveled with us is dead. The battle was almost over when I returned, and I barely was able to save Helius and the pony."

"But we're safe now, right?" Alia asked hopefully. "They must think we're dead."

Yvrin grimaced. "They know we are still alive."

"How?" Heth asked, looking behind her to see if any pursuit was visible. "Are they chasing you?"

"I didn't see them, but they will come," Yvrin said grimly. "A Blood Spider was picking its way among the charred tents." She sighed when she noticed Heth and Alia's blank looks. "It means they have a blood-sharded. They are the best trackers in the world."

"Ashasai has allied itself with the Ember?" Heth asked, a coldness spreading in him at the mention of the blood-sharded.

Yvrin's mouth twisted. "I doubt it. I hope not. Ashasai is famously reticent to commit itself to one side or another. Even at Gerendal they kept almost all their forces behind their high black walls and let the northern holds fight and die for their freedom. No, I think he must be Unbound, or a refugee from the Black Steps. Sometimes holds employ foreign Sharded when their own talents are lacking in a particular area."

"But why did they attack us?" Alia cried, and Heth heard the fraying edge of her composure. He couldn't blame her – they had all been pushed to the very brink.

"The Ember despises the Windwrack," Yvrin replied tiredly, her exhaustion becoming more obvious to Heth. "We all knew they must be incensed about this marriage, but no one imagined they might declare *war* over it."

"War . . ." Heth said softly, finally realizing the full importance of what had just happened. There hadn't been a war between the holds for decades, ever since the Conquests had united the north against the Salahi. Kething's Cross and the rest of the twelve towns were right on the edge of the Shadow's realm, far closer to the Flame. Those lands would be the first to be invaded if the flame-sharded attacked, and that filled him with dread after having seen firsthand the devastation their powers could inflict. He imagined the Bull and his family's manse engulfed in flames, all his old friends reduced to nothing but ashes in the wind.

"We have to keep going," Yvrin said, the urgency of her tone drawing Heth back to the present. "Deeper into the Lands. If we turn back, they'll only catch us quicker."

"What is ahead of us?" Alia asked, throwing out her arm to indicate the ghostly lights on the far horizon. "Monsters like the one that attacked us before?"

"The wind-sharded," Yvrin answered. "We have to hope we encounter a tribe before the flame-sharded arrive. Riftbeasts are extremely rare, and no doubt the Watchers are taking great care to ensure none slip by them after what happened."

"The wind-sharded," Heth repeated, hope flickering to life in his breast. "They said they are friends with the Duskhold."

"Some are," Yvrin corrected him. "I only pray those are the ones that find us first."

"What is that?"

Heth roused himself at the sound of Yvrin's voice, raising his head and blinking blearily. He didn't remember falling asleep, but the gentle gait of the pony beneath him – coupled with his exhaustion and the availability of Deryn's back to lean against – had carried him away.

He saw immediately what had drawn her attention. Etched against the bloody dawn, a mesa rose from the grasslands in front of them, the remnants of mighty buildings visible on its flat summit.

The perspective differed from the last time he had seen it, but he knew what this place was.

"It's the winter palace of the Radiant Emperor," he said, trying to pick out the path that must lead up to the ruin.

"Truly?" Yvrin asked, frowning. "I remember Saelus mentioned it a long time ago, back when I was a novice. Something about the War of the Sundering's last battle being fought up there."

"That's what I was told as well by the wind-sharded who brought us to the Duskhold," Heth replied.

"It's too bad the Lady Shen won't remember this," Yvrin said, adjusting her grip on the slumped Rhenna. She had her arms around her while she held the reins, keeping her upright on her horse. "I know she has an interest in the old histories."

"Crimson Grass said the palace was haunted," Heth said, eyeing the shattered buildings uneasily. "And that the wind-sharded steer well clear of it."

"Not all of them," Alia said from where she was plodding beside the horses, gesturing at something in the distance. "Look."

Heth followed where she was pointing, and Yvrin must have done the same because she growled what sounded like a curse in a language he did not understand.

"What's the matter?" Heth asked, the excitement he had felt at seeing the strangers dampened by her reaction. "I thought we wanted to meet the wind-sharded?"

"I was hoping we'd find a camp," Yvrin explained. "Or a caravan on the move. A few warriors, out in the Lands . . . there's no telling how they might react to us. If they are Falcon or Hawk, we can call upon the old treaties. Raven, Crow or Eagle . . . we must be prepared for anything."

"Surely they will help us," Alia said, shielding her eyes from the sun as they drew near. "Like the ones that did before."

"Those wind-sharded were Falcon talons, if I remember correctly," Yvrin said, keeping Rhenna steady as she slid from her horse's back. "Each tribe has a different relationship with the Shadow." With her free hand she motioned for Alia to come closer. "Hold on to your mistress, girl. Keep her in the saddle while I treat with them."

Heth was just about to ask why she did not want to do this while astride her horse, but then she answered his unspoken question.

"When the wind-sharded parlay with one another, they dismount. It means we come in peace." She hesitated a moment. "Perhaps it is better if Deryn stands with me. They might get nervous if he remains on Ash. Heth, can you get him down?"

"I'll try," he said, putting his hand on Deryn's shoulder and giving him a gentle shake. "Uh, Shade? Deryn? You have to go to Yvrin." It had been an exercise in frustration getting the elemental to awkwardly clamber up into the saddle in the first place, but the dismount proved far less of an ordeal. Without a sound or any other sign that he had heard Heth's request, Deryn swung one of his legs over the saddle and dropped gracelessly to the grass.

"Should we come down as well?" Heth asked, but Yvrin shook her head.

"They'll sense you're not Sharded. And Rhenna . . . well, she can't stand anyway. It is obvious something is wrong. Just stay quiet – the People of the Wind do not tolerate disrespect from the Hollow or any unsharded." Yvrin beckoned Deryn to join her in front of the horses. "With me, shadow-man."

Heth glanced at Alia uncertainly as the three wind-sharded cantered closer. He hated this feeling of helplessness, of knowing that despite his skill with a sword these men could kill him easily. It was like back in the old lumber mill when he'd watched Gavin casually murder his father.

The wind-sharded reined up a few dozen paces from where Yvrin and Deryn waited and dismounted. Heth studied them uneasily – he had been hoping they would resemble the ones who had chased after the riftbeast and showed such respect to Azil, but these warriors were very obviously different. The markings on their exposed skin were indigo instead of a light blue, and gleaming black feathers were threaded in their dark hair and fringed their leather jerkins. Also, unlike the Falcon delegation, they did not place their weapons in the grass to show their intentions. They held tight to the hafts of their pale spears, taking the measure of them with hooded eyes. They were all very young, Heth realized, boys who had recently become men.

Yvrin broke the silence first. "Greetings from the Duskhold," she cried. "I am Yvrin Gazkinscion, a daughter of the steppes. These are my companions, all under the protection of the Shadow."

"The Shadow is very far away," said one of the wind-sharded, but another raised his hand sharply to quiet him. The leader, apparently, and the arrogance Heth thought he saw in the young warrior's posture made him nervous.

"I am Last Snow Falling of the Crow, a Watcher against all that would threaten the home fires." His dark eyes slid to Deryn, widening when he noticed the black pits in his face. He adjusted his grip on his spear, his sneering confidence flickering. "What deviltry is this, shadow-sharded?"

"He is an elementalist," Yvrin said quickly. "Some sickness has befallen him, and his elemental has gone into his body to help him flee what befell us on the edge of the Lands."

The Crow warrior tore his attention from Deryn, focusing on what lay behind them. "You speak of the fire. We ride to make sure it does not spread. Are you saying it did not begin naturally?"

Yvrin swallowed, and from her hesitation Heth guessed she wasn't sure how much she should reveal. "Flame-sharded ambushed us," she finally said, evidently deciding the truth was the best course.

Surprised glances were traded between the wind-sharded. "The Flame and the Shadow are at war?" Last Snow Falling murmured, suddenly looking more like a boy out of his depth.

"Yes," Yvrin said simply, not offering any elaboration as to why. Heth kept himself from glancing at where Rhenna slumped – if Yvrin thought it wise not to let it be known that the daughter of Cael Shen was here, he didn't want to accidentally draw attention to her.

"Will you escort us back to the Duskhold? I can promise a rich reward for your help."

"A rich reward, you say," Last Snow Falling said slowly, sharing another look with his fellows. Something unspoken passed between them, and then they began to move, spreading out to partially encircle Yvrin. "More rich than a dozen shards?"

"Do not be fools," Yvrin said, her voice low and dangerous. "I am six-sharded, at least twice what any of you bear."

"You are exhausted and wounded," Last Snow Falling snarled back, whirling his spear as he shuffled closer. A shimmer of red light played along its pale length, gathering in its metal tip until it was glowing like it was fresh from the forge. Coldness stole over him – the warrior's weapon was sharded, like Deryn's sword. "And the two Sharded you travel with are unfit to fight. We will rip the shards from your dead body, and then the shards from theirs, and return as men of consequence to our people."

"And enemies of the Duskhold," Yvrin snarled as the shadows stretched upon the grass trembled.

The corner of Last Snow Falling's mouth lifted. "Perhaps it is time for the Crow to become better friends with the Flame."

He lunged, red spear-tip flashing, but Yvrin was no longer there. He twisted around, sweeping the sharded weapon in a wide arc as if expecting her to appear behind him. It was one of the other wind-sharded who cried out, though, stumbling forward as Yvrin raked his back with long claws of curving darkness. A gust of wind erupted from the outstretched hand of the last Crow warrior, slamming into

Yvrin and lifting her from her feet. She landed heavily, swallowed by the long grass, and as she struggled to rise, more winds bludgeoned her, driving her to her knees. The tremendous force of the wind was flattening the surrounding grass, even though outside of that circle the plains remained untouched. All three of the Crow were slowly closing around her, their faces twisted with the strain of holding her. Yvrin screamed in pain and rage as she was pushed to the ground, unable to even lift her head. She vanished, but then reappeared a moment later in the same spot. Last Snow Falling grinned in triumph when he reached where she struggled, lifting his red-flashing spear as he prepared to drive it into her back.

And then he screamed as a blade pushed through his chest. He stared at the blood-streaked length of white in disbelief, then Deryn withdrew the sword violently and he collapsed in a heap. The other two wind-sharded gaped, the howling wind-tunnel that had captured Yvrin evaporating as they shifted to this new threat. Before they could draw upon another of their powers, Yvrin surged from the ground, slamming into the closest of the wind-sharded and driving her hand into his stomach. He shrieked as her flensing claws bit deep, scrabbling weakly at her arm as she scooped his insides out. The other wind-sharded watched this with wide eyes, but rather than beg for mercy or flee, his hands moved like he was shaping something, and then he reared back and hurled an invisible object at Deryn where he stood over the corpse of Last Snow Falling.

It struck him before Heth could shout a warning, but Deryn only rocked back as a strange ghostly armor flickered into existence. The wind-sharded hissed in dismay, and this turned into a wet gurgling when Yvrin plunged her claws into his neck. As he toppled backwards, Yvrin nearly fell with him, her legs visibly trembling. Heth leaped forward, but Deryn was already there to catch her as she lost her balance.

Heth realized suddenly that Deryn's eyes were blue again.

"Deryn!" Heth cried as the boy slowly lowered Yvrin to the grass. She raised blood-stained but declawed fingers and patted his face, leaving a smear of red.

"About time," she murmured weakly.

Deryn's gaze moved from her face, taking in the stained bandage wrapping her midsection. "You're hurt," he said in concern.

She shrugged, her eyes flicking to Heth as he also came to stand over her. "I'll live." As if to prove this claim true, Yvrin held out her arm towards Deryn.

"Perhaps you should rest . . ." he said uncertainly.

"Help me up," she commanded, and with a resigned sigh Deryn grasped her forearm and pulled her to her feet. She swayed for a moment, then steadied herself.

"It's good you're back," she said, putting a hand on his shoulder. "What happened to you?"

Deryn shook his head in bewilderment. "I don't know. I remember lying down in my tent, drifting off to sleep . . . and then waking up standing here with that wind-sharded about to skewer you. I thought I might still be dreaming right until I stabbed him." He turned slowly, taking in the sprawled bodies, the endless sweep of the grasslands, and Alia standing beside Yvrin's horse with her hand on Rhenna to ensure her slumped mistress stayed in the saddle. "Where are we?" he asked, panic clear in his voice. "What is wrong with Lady Shen?"

Heth put his hand on Deryn's other shoulder and gave a comforting squeeze. "We have a lot to tell you."

While Alia helped Yvrin change her bandage, Heth gave Deryn an abbreviated version of everything that had transpired. Rhenna they brought down from the horse and laid out in the grass – at some point during the battle her eyes had opened, but she was still staring sightlessly up at the hammered blue of the sky. If it were not for the slight rise and fall of her chest, it would have looked like there were four corpses, not three.

"These wind-sharded wanted your fragments," Heth said, taking back the water skin he'd given Deryn. The boy was sitting splay-legged in the grass looking nearly as hollow as Rhenna, Shade curled up beside him. "Yvrin tried to reason with them, but they must have thought we presented too good of an opportunity."

Deryn's face was troubled as he stared at the bodies, and Heth suspected he knew why.

"You did the right thing," Heth said, patting him lightly on the knee. "They were going to murder us."

"I stabbed a man in the back," Deryn murmured, squinting as he raised his gaze to the sky. "I never thought I'd kill anyone . . . I just acted without thinking."

"And I'm glad you did," Yvrin interrupted, wincing as Alia wound the fresh strip of cloth around her. "They had me, embarrassing as it is. The wind-sharded are unique in that they can combine their power, so long as they share the same talents. That was a Wind Cage they had me trapped in, and it had the same force as if forged by a Sharded with eight or ten fragments. More than enough to hold me immobile . . . I couldn't even Shadow Step away."

She ran a hand through her curls, her exhaustion clear. "We need to get moving," she said, and from her tone Heth knew that she'd like nothing better than to lie down in the grass and drift away in the warm sun.

Heth squinted back the way they'd come. There was no sign of pursuit, though the distant sky was still stained by smoke. "How will we know if the flame-sharded are chasing us?"

"They are," Yvrin said with a certainty that allowed no room for argument. "But now we have another problem." Her gaze shifted to the corpses.

"We can bury the bodies," Heth suggested. "It will take a while for them to be found."

Yvrin grimaced and shook her head. "That would take too long. And it won't matter – when they don't return, a wind-whisperer will ask the wind what happened. It is similar to how powerful shadow-sharded can draw the memory of what transpired from the nearby darkness. The wind will tell them about us, then they will begin the hunt. And in the Frayed Lands, it will not take them long to find us."

Alia finished binding Yvrin's wounds and turned to her, concern creasing her face. "Flame-sharded behind us and wind-sharded in front. What can we do?"

Yvrin's shoulders slumped. "I . . . don't know," she finally said quietly. "Eventually someone will come for us. When word gets back to the Duskhold about what happened, the wrath of Azil and Cael Shen will be terrible. Between Shadow Walking and their Black Discs, they can get here quickly . . . once they know."

"So we just have to stay alive until then," Heth murmured.

"Easier said than done," Yvrin said, sounding emptied of hope. "There is no place to hide in the Lands."

"There is," Alia said suddenly, and everyone turned to her as she pointed towards the mesa rising from the plains. "I remember what Crimson Grass told us. He said that the wind-sharded dared not go in the ruins, that they thought it haunted by vengeful spirits."

"She's right," Deryn said. "Perhaps we can find refuge from them up there. And they might not be pleased with the flame-sharded entering that place if they also arrive looking for us."

"The Crow are not friends with any hold," Yvrin mused, and Heth could hear a change in her voice. "Bring the Flame and the Wind into conflict while we hide in the old palace to wait for the Shadow . . . it is as good a plan as we could hope for."

"Assuming the ruins are empty," Heth said softly, squinting at the broken towers clawing at the sky. "The wind-sharded's fears might not be unfounded."

With a grunt, Yvrin heaved herself to her feet, then swayed, the wind stirring her lank hair. "If so, we'll find out if ghosts can die a second time."

43

DERYN

DERYN HAD ENCOUNTERED echoes of the First Empire before. There was a road in Kething's Cross of perfectly cut white stone that was still used as one of the town's central avenues, and he'd stumbled across sunken steps carved into the side of a hill while foraging in the forest. And of course there was the shattered remnants of a bridge that had once spanned the River Havilas, which had been the crossing long before Arturos Kething had built his own. Each time he had been impressed with what remained despite suffering the rigors of a thousand winters.

Even though the skill demonstrated by these old builders awed him, he still felt unnerved as they climbed the ancient road clinging to the mesa's steep walls. And cling was right – the road seemed to have been grafted onto the steep cliffs, wide enough for two wagons to go up side by side yet with nothing beneath it except air. He couldn't understand how it had first been constructed, let alone how it still stood in the present age. To distract himself from thinking about what would happen if the road decided that this would be the day it collapsed, Deryn imagined the history that had been witnessed here. Crimson Grass had spoken of how the last empress had sought sanctuary in the palace above after the shattering of the Heart and the death of Segulah Tain. He envisioned exhausted, grim-faced warriors making this ascent, surrounding a woman in golden robes who sat straight-backed on a horse of purest white, her face sunk with lines of sorrow.

"What was it like?"

Deryn surfaced from his daydream to find Heth had dropped back to bring up the rear with him. Heth had been walking alongside Alia and Rhenna for most of the day, holding the reins of the pony while Alia sat with her mistress on Ash's back. He must have finally come to the same realization that Deryn had arrived at days ago, that Ash knew better than any of them what she should do.

"What was what like?"

"When you were unconscious, or asleep, or whatever you were. We were afraid you were going to die."

Deryn chewed his lip, uncertain how he could describe the experience. "I suppose . . . I suppose at first it might have been like being dead. Or a very deep sleep. There was just blackness. Oblivion." He swallowed. "And then . . . I wasn't alone anymore. I could feel something else out there, even if I couldn't cry out or communicate with it."

"Was it frightening?" Heth asked quietly, glancing behind Deryn at the shadow-dog trailing him.

"It wasn't," Deryn replied. "I knew . . . I mean, I could feel that this presence was there to help me. There were . . . emotions swirling around it. If those had been hate or anger, I would have pushed it away. But what I sensed was concern. Curiosity."

"And what woke you down there on the plains?"

"That was Shade," Deryn said confidently. "He knew I had to do something. Maybe he had been waiting to bring me back because he wasn't sure what would happen, and then he had no choice . . . I'm not sure. It was like I was being thrust upwards out of a watery abyss, and then I broke the surface and found myself standing knee-deep in grass, and Yvrin was about to be impaled."

"Well, it chose the right time to bring you back," Heth murmured, turning away from the elemental. "I wonder if it can do the same for Rhenna."

"I was thinking we should try," Deryn agreed, his gaze going to her limp body as she bounced in time with Ash's clopping steps. "When we get to the top, let's see if Shade can help."

They continued on in silence for a while, and Deryn sensed that Heth was gathering the courage to ask him something else.

"What is it?" he finally asked.

Heth glanced at him and then back to the white bricks of the ancient road. "Well, I was just curious about the fragments you took from the Crow warriors. Why didn't you merge them with your shard, like Kilian did when he found us? Don't you want to be stronger?"

Deryn grimaced. He had tried to avoid thinking about what had happened down below. Yvrin had insisted that he claim the shard of the man he'd killed, and the feeling of his fingers entering the dead Sharded's chest was seared into his memory. The flesh had rippled like a liquid, though there had been enough resistance that he'd had to push with some effort, forced to go nearly knuckle-deep before he could pry the shard out. After, it had broken apart into two grey fragments, and both were sitting heavy in his pocket, unsettling reminders of the life he had stolen. It had been much easier to claim the shards of a man he hadn't killed . . . but the hoard of fragments he'd found in the cavern below the Duskhold was now lost to him, as they'd been left in the camp during the ambush. Yvrin was right. He couldn't afford to leave any shards behind now.

"The Sharded must prepare themselves before merging more fragments. Kilian was ready, but I'm not."

Heth nodded, apparently accepting this explanation. In truth, he suspected he was ready to add a fourth fragment to his shard, and would have likely attempted to do so already if the flame-sharded had not attacked. He had been spending the long days on horseback since leaving the Duskhold pushing his *ka* through his pathways, smoothing the turbulence inside him.

But now . . . the thought of merging the fragment of a man he had killed made him feel nauseous. Each time he had added to his shard with what he had found in the balewyrm's lair, he'd been immersed in the scattered, swift-rushing memories of that dead warrior, glimpses into a life that had ended long ago. He didn't know whether a piece of each Sharded lived on in their fragments, or if these moments had merely been imprinted and would fade, like a hand pressed against a window during winter. But what would he feel if he merged this new shard and saw Last Snow Falling as a child playing with his siblings, or being held tight as his mother sang to him?

He shuddered, dreading the thought.

By the time they reached the top of the mesa night had fallen, cold stars glittering in the endless sky. The switchback road ended at the shattered foundations of what must have been a mighty fortification. Beyond this ruin was a vast open space not unlike the courtyard where they had departed the Duskhold, though this one was bounded not by walls but shadowed galleries, pillars in various stages of collapse. Deeper within the palace, broken towers stabbed the sky, looming over the remnants of buildings bleached the color of ancient bone. There was a strange luminescence to the stone, more than what should have come from just the moonlight, and it reminded him of the gazebo in the underground lake. Thinking of Kaliss made him wish she was here right now.

"It feels like a tomb," Heth said, reaching up to help Alia dismount.

"It is a tomb," Yvrin murmured, wincing as she also slid from her horse. Deryn noticed uneasily that the bandages Alia had changed after the battle were already stained black. How much longer could she go on without collapsing?

"The tomb of the First Empire. This was where the last loyalists fled to make their final stand. By that time Segulah Tain was dead, the Heart shattered, and Gendurdrang was already being devoured by the rifts."

"Seems like a foolish place to flee to," Deryn said softly, hesitant to raise his voice in the oppressive stillness. "There's no escape."

"They clearly did not care," Yvrin said, rummaging in her saddle bags before pulling out a blanket. "They knew they would not be spared by the rebels and must have been seeking somewhere they knew they could bleed any attackers dry. I can't imagine what it was like trying to fight up that road with arrows and burning oil falling from above." She carried the blanket over to where Rhenna slumped on Ash and spread it out on the stone, then sighed. "Not the bedding she's used to, I'm afraid, but it'll have to do. Deryn, Heth, help me get her down."

With great care, they pulled Rhenna from the saddle and laid her on the blanket, pillowing her head as best they could. For a long moment they all stood over her, looking down at her empty eyes and barely moving chest, and then Yvrin sighed deeply.

"I suppose it's the only choice," she said, her gaze sliding to where Shade sat on his haunches watching them. "We need her if we want any hope of surviving what is coming."

"Will it hurt her?" Alia asked.

"It didn't hurt me," Deryn assured her. "It was just like waking from a dream."

Alia fell silent at this, but still she grabbed his arm.

"Deryn?" Yvrin said, looking at him expectantly.

"I'll try. But Shade doesn't always listen to me. He very rarely does, in truth."

Deryn swallowed, turning to face the elemental. "Please wake her," he said, and the shadow-creature tilted his head to one side – a very dog-like response to being addressed. "You saved me. Now save her."

"Surely it can't understand –" Heth began, but his words trailed away as the elemental moved towards Rhenna. It circled her prone body, its head lowered like it was trying to catch a scent, and then with startling quickness it began dissipating, tendrils of shadow leaking from its body to slip between Rhenna's parted lips.

Alia gasped, her grip on his arm tightening, but she did not leap forward to try to stop the elemental as it flowed into her mistress. After only a few heartbeats, the shadow-dog had completely unraveled, vanishing completely. The only remnant of the elemental was in her eyes, which were now stained black. Since no one watching seemed particularly surprised by this, Deryn assumed this must have been what had happened to him.

From what he'd been told, though, Shade had been able to move his body from the moment he had entered him, and save for a slight twitch in her cheeks and a fluttering of her eyelashes, Rhenna remained motionless. The slumped shoulders and dejected faces suggested the others had indeed been expecting more.

"Perhaps we waited too long . . ." Heth murmured, and as soon as he said this, Deryn felt Alia's nails dig into his flesh.

"Give Shade some time," Deryn said, directing his words mostly at the nervous girl clinging to him. "I don't think he'd have gone inside her if he didn't think he could help."

"Well, we can't stand around waiting and hoping," Heth said, the impatience in his voice surprising Deryn. "The Sharded Few are chasing us. They could be coming up the road even now. We should hide, not stand around waiting for her to wake up."

"Hide?" Yvrin replied, her eyes never leaving Rhenna. "And what would that do? The Crow can speak with the wind – it will take them moments to find us once they arrive here, unless you can think of a place that the very air cannot reach. And the flame-sharded have a hunter from Ashasai. No one can hide from the blood-sharded."

"Then what should we do?" Heth snapped back. "Beg for mercy?"

"We fight," Yvrin said, her hands clenching at her sides. "We make a stand right here, but if we want any hope of defeating them, we need Rhenna. She is eight-sharded and one of the strongest young warriors in the Duskhold. With her, we have a chance. But if she does not wake . . ." Yvrin raised her head, meeting Deryn's eyes. "Then it is just Deryn and me. I am injured, and he was a novice until recently."

"I can fight," Heth said, putting his hand on the hilt of his sword.

Yvrin snorted. "You are Hollow. Maybe you could distract one of them for a heartbeat before dying. No, you and Alia must hide deeper in the ruins. These Sharded want us, not you. There's no reason for you to die here."

The muscles in Heth's jaw bunched, the knuckles on his hand gripping his sword turning white. He clearly wanted to argue with Yvrin, but what could he say? She was right, and he must know that. He'd seen what the Unbound Sharded in the woods had done to his father, and that was with only a single fragment and no training in a hold. To a true warrior of the Sharded Few, he was as helpless as a babe.

Heth growled something unintelligible, turning sharply on his heel. He sounded angry, but Deryn knew that more than anything else, he felt frustration at his own weakness.

"Wait," Deryn said as something occurred to him, and Heth paused halfway to the edge of the mesa, glancing back at him. "Sharded weapons can pierce the flesh of the Sharded Few as easily as steel does any normal man." He raised his hand, pointing at Last Snow Falling's spear, lashed across the back of Yvrin's horse. "Heth is a good fighter. If you give him that, he could help us."

Yvrin immediately shook her head. "No. Such a weapon can only be wielded by one of the Sharded Few. The fragments embedded within answer to the call of a warrior's shard. It is just metal and wood in the hands of anyone else, even the Hollow."

The hope that had briefly filled Heth's face flickered and died. Scowling, he stalked into the ruined fortification guarding the entrance to the palace.

"He just wants to help," Deryn said quietly.

Yvrin sighed, rubbing at her face. "I know. But I speak the truth. Alia and Heth must retreat into the palace before the hunters find us. This area will be ravaged by flensing wind or raging flames, and while our Sharded bodies will offer some protection against such things, they would be instantly killed. And also . . ." She hesitated, glancing at her stallion, and Deryn glimpsed sorrow in her face before she quickly controlled herself. ". . . I need them to take care of Helius after I'm gone."

The fatalism of her words shook him. Yvrin wasn't worried about dying up here – she expected to. Despite what she'd said, she did not think Azil or Cael Shen would swoop down at the last moment and rescue them. An icy fist closed around Deryn's heart as he realized just how hopeless she thought their situation was.

"Come here and see this!"

Heth's excited shout jolted Deryn from the dark path he was wandering down. He glanced at Yvrin, whose face was again a mask of grim resolve, and then together they jogged through the broken masonry to where Heth stood on the mesa's edge. He turned as they approached and then gestured frantically at what was happening below.

But Deryn had already seen it, and he sucked in his breath.

Flames writhed across the dark grasslands, undulating like fiery serpents. They moved unnaturally, surging forward and then retreating, striving to encircle something Deryn couldn't see before getting thrust backwards violently again and again. The fires seemed to be struggling with an invisible enemy . . . which, Deryn realized after a moment, they were.

"The Wind is fighting with the Flame," Yvrin murmured, and Deryn heard something that hadn't been in her voice a few moments ago. Hope. "It is our great luck they found each other before one could start the ascent. Whichever Sharded reach this place will be battle-weary and wounded." She took hold of Deryn's arm and pulled him away. "Come. We must prepare our ambush. They will be here soon after dawn, I think."

"Deryn!"

Alia's cry was panicked, and Yvrin hissed in surprise as she pulled Heth behind herself, glistening black claws emerging from her fingers.

"What is it?" Yvrin barked, looking past the bedraggled girl who had just run stumbling up to them.

Alia pointed back the way she'd come, her eyes wide. "It's my mistress! Something's happening!"

They dashed back to the courtyard to find Rhenna just as they had left her, the darkness pooling in her eyes as she stared sightlessly at the stars above. Alia's face crinkled in dismay as she crouched beside her.

"I swear by the First Seed, she coughed and started to move." She lowered her head, her shoulders slumping. "Please, mistress –"

A scream wrenched itself from deep within Rhenna, and she spasmed, her back arching. Alia fell backwards in shock, and then a moment later she was cradling Rhenna's head in her hands to keep her from dashing her skull against the stone.

"Hold her!" Yvrin commanded, leaping forward to grab her legs. "She could break herself to pieces!"

Deryn rushed to Rhenna's side and pressed his weight down on one of her arms, trying his best to hold it immobile. Heth did the same to the other, but another great surge went through Rhenna, and while Deryn and Yvrin kept the limbs they held pinned to the stone the Hollow was flung away like he weighed no more than a puppy. The arm he'd been trying to restrain lifted, then smashed itself into the ground, sending chips of stone flying. Alia yelped in pain, and Deryn glanced at her in panic, but although blood was leaking down her cheek, she still held her mistress's thrashing head.

Rhenna's mouth opened wider, and a sound unlike anything Deryn had ever experienced issued forth. It was a moan echoing up from an abyss, and if he had heard such a thing while in the forest he'd have fled without looking back. He held his breath as one last spasm shuddered through her, and then she went limp.

"Look," Alia whispered, and Deryn saw that the blackness was trickling from her eyes like tears, hissing when it fell onto the stone.

"What is it?" Deryn murmured, glancing at Yvrin, but the shadow-sharded looked as lost as he felt.

"It's moving," Alia said, holding back Rhenna's hair so it wouldn't touch the rapidly growing puddles. The tears were coursing down her face now, a flood of blackness staining her pale cheeks.

For a moment Deryn thought the trembling was just from the falling tears, but then both patches began to flow, slipping away from Rhenna and making a wide circle around where Alia still crouched. The girl whimpered when the crawling darkness passed behind her, but she did not stop holding Rhenna's head to turn around and see what was happening. Instead, she brushed back her mistress's lank black hair . . . and then gasped.

Rhenna's eyes were clear, and she was watching Alia.

"Mistress," the Wild girl whispered.

"Alia," Rhenna said hoarsely, looking around as she sat up. "Where are we? What has happened?" Her gaze settled on Yvrin, who had released her legs and taken a step back to give her space. "What is going on, adept?"

"We were ambushed, Lady Shen," Yvrin told her. "Everyone else who traveled with us from the Duskhold is dead, slain by the flame-sharded. They attacked in the night . . . You had fallen into a trance from which we could not wake you."

"The Ember?" Rhenna said, disbelief clear in her voice. "Lord Char has been my father's friend for decades. I can't . . ." she turned her head, taking in the forest of coldly luminous pillars ringing the courtyard. "Am I dreaming?"

"You're not," Alia said, clasping Rhenna's hand fiercely with her own. "Oh, I thought you were gone."

Rhenna stared at their twined fingers for a moment, her brow furrowed as if she was still struggling to understand what was happening, and then her gaze moved to Alia's face, shining in the moonlight. She reached out and brushed a tear from her cheek.

"This place . . . it is a ruin of the First Empire."

"We're in the Frayed Lands," Yvrin explained, her hand pressed to her stained bandage. Rhenna's thrashing must have reopened her wound. "We've taken refuge in the winter palace of Segulah Tain."

Rhenna focused on Yvrin as if truly seeing her for the first time. "You're hurt."

"I'm fine," the steppe girl answered dismissively. "I caught the edge of what I think was a Blood Saber in the initial attack. I'm not sure – it was hurled from afar."

Rhenna frowned. "You said the flame-sharded ambushed us."

"They have a hunter from Ashasai with them," Yvrin said. "Strong enough to summon a Spider. They've tracked us across the Lands, and soon they're going to enter these ruins."

"Unless the wind-sharded get here first," Heth interjected. "They're fighting the flame-sharded right now for the right to kill us."

Rhenna stared at him in blank confusion. Deryn noticed that behind her the blackness that had leaked from her eyes had merged, assuming a familiar shape. Rhenna blinked as Shade padded up beside her and plopped down on his haunches, staring up at her like he was expecting to be petted.

"We have little time, Lady Shen," Yvrin said. "We need to get ready to fight."

44

HETH

"Where are we going?"

Heth sighed, tightening his grip on the reins of Yvrin's horse as he led the stallion through the maze of shattered stone and tumbled walls.

"I don't know," he replied, trying to keep the edge of annoyance from his voice as he glanced back at Alia. She had paused for a moment to coax Ash through a fallen archway – apparently, mountain ponies were more skittish than the steeds of Kezekan warriors.

"You heard Yvrin. She said we had to take shelter deep in the ruins."

Alia finally grew tired of trying to gently pull the pony along and gave the bridle a sharp tug. Ash *whuffed*, but it did spur her into clopping motion again.

"Surely this is far enough? I don't want to get lost here."

Heth grimaced, remembering the vast conflagrations summoned by the flame-sharded. Even with little to burn here in the ruins, he could imagine a sea of fire flooding the old palace, seeking out and devouring them if they were not wise about where they took refuge.

"They will find us after the battle," Heth told her.

If they survive. That unspoken thought was accompanied by

another pang of guilt. Here he was, a trained swordsman, running and hiding while his friends fought and died behind him. It just wasn't *fair*. Strength should come from swinging a sword countless times, deadliness from the endless evenings spent in the dueling circle. Not from a piece of rock lodged in your flesh. Heth realized he was clenching his jaw so hard his teeth were aching.

"Look," Alia said, and he surfaced from his darkening thoughts to see what she'd found. The Wild girl was standing outside the collapsed remains of one of the more impressive structures, a building that in its ancient glory would have been far larger than the old skyspear mill. A pair of stone lions with strangely manlike faces flanked what would have been the entrance before the roof had come crashing down, and the way the rubble was strewn had created a path deeper into the ruin. A few walls of pearlescent stone were still standing, but he wasn't sure if these would afford enough cover that they could survive the wrath of whatever the flame-sharded summoned.

"I don't think we should stop here," he said dubiously. "There are larger and more intact buildings up ahead."

Alia ignored him, leading Ash past the grim-faced lions.

"What are you doing?" he called out, then sighed and tugged on the stallion's reins to follow her.

"You see?" Heth said as he caught up with her. She'd stopped as the path through the rubble had petered out, staring out at the landscape of shattered stone. "There's nothing here."

She didn't reply, instead raising her arm and pointing at something a little farther on. He squinted into the gloom, and after a moment realized what she had already seen: a broad flight of stairs descending into darkness.

"There," she said. "We can find shelter underground. Surely that has to be safer than up here."

"I suppose so," Heth said slowly. The thought of hunkering in total darkness in the bowels of this haunted place was more than a bit unsettling, but he suspected she was right.

A shiver suddenly went through Alia, and she wrapped her thin arms around herself like she was freezing.

"Are you sure you want to go down there?" he asked gently, realizing at once what was the matter.

"No," she replied. "But I don't want to travel too far from Rhenna."

Before Heth could think of a good argument about why they should keep going, Alia began pulling the pony towards the stairs.

"Fire and ashes," he muttered, but he fell in behind her as she approached the pit in the ground. It looked like the building that had once stood here had been knocked over by some great force, as huge chunks of stone were scattered everywhere. It had been pure chance that these stairs were not choked by rubble.

"It seems to open into a larger space," Alia said, peering down into the darkness.

"Large enough for our horses?" Heth asked, and she answered by handing him the reins of the pony and descending in a flurry of quick little steps.

He tried to ignore his cold trickle of concern as she vanished into the black – surely whatever stories the wind-sharded told about this place were founded on superstitions. Still, he remained on edge until her voice echoed back up.

"Come down and bring the horses!"

Shoving aside his misgivings, Heth began to descend the broad steps. Yvrin's stallion had until now shown remarkable bravery, but even he balked at venturing into the underground space. Heth couldn't blame him, honestly, but the horses also needed to be made safe from whatever the Sharded chasing them might unleash. If anything happened to her horse, Heth was fairly sure Yvrin wouldn't hesitate to throw him over the side of the mesa.

"Let's go," he grumbled, pulling harder on the reins, and after a final aggrieved whinny the stallion began to awkwardly clop his way down the stone steps, followed by the pony.

The space below was not as dark as it had appeared from above. The same faint radiance that infused the ruins was seeping from the walls here, and this, combined with the dawnlight slanting down, illuminated most of the large chamber. Alia was crouched at the bottom of the stairs, investigating an ancient mosaic that had remained bright despite centuries of grime. It showed a hooded figure, light creeping from his long, dagged sleeves. The ceiling here was twice the height of a man, and though it was a little difficult to make out, Heth thought it was covered with faded frescos.

"What is this place?" Heth asked, peering into the depths of one of the arched passageways that emptied into this chamber.

Alia traced the outline of the cowled man in the mosaic, her finger lingering on the emptiness where his face should have been. "Can you feel the weight of the air down here? It hangs heavy like in the old groves, where blood is spilled into the roots to feed the spirits sleeping within the trees. This was a sacred place."

"Perhaps a temple," Heth suggested. "Even in Kething's Cross there were catacombs beneath the house of the Broken God. The priests were entombed down there when they died, and I heard they did rituals as well, though my family was not very religious."

Alia rose, squinting as she raised her head to stare at the light spilling into the room from above. "Do you think we're safe here?"

Heth frowned. "I have to think a killing wind will slip right down those stairs. Flames as well. But those corridors look like they twist and turn – if we go down a ways, I bet we'd be able to find sanctuary."

Alia's jaw tightened as she turned to stare into one of the passage-ways. "I don't want to go too far."

"And neither do I," agreed Heth. "Just enough to put a few walls between us and the ruins above. What do you think?"

Alia grunted something that sounded less than enthused, but still she came over to take the reins of the pony from Heth.

"We'll have to go single-file," he said after quickly estimating the width of the largest passage. "And even then, if it narrows any further Yvrin's horse won't be able to continue."

As if he understood what they were saying, the stallion whickered and tossed his head.

Heth patted his muscled neck. "Don't worry, boy, we won't leave you behind."

Alia sighed. "All right. Yvrin said she thought whoever survived the battle on the plains might arrive at the top of the mesa not long after dawn. That means the fight could already have started. I suppose we should try to get as safe as possible."

"I'll go first," Heth said, and after taking a deep breath he strode into the nearest corridor.

And almost immediately slowed. It was darker here, the ghostly light emanating from the stone a bit more subdued, but that was not what had unsettled him.

There were skulls. Dozens – no, *hundreds* – of skulls stared at him with empty eyes and grinning mouths. They had been placed in sockets carved from the stone, its strange radiance sliding over yellowed bone. A few were so ancient they had collapsed, reduced to nothing but piles of shards and dust.

"By the First Seed," Alia whispered as she joined him in the passage.

"A necropolis," Heth told her, trying to keep the fear from his voice. "I've heard lots of cities have places like this. If there's little space to bury the dead, best to press them in tight."

"Who would want their spirit trapped here?" Alia asked, making no attempt to hide her revulsion. "Better to burn them on a hill and let their souls soar into the sky."

Heth shrugged. "Everyone treats their dead different. You'd hear a lot of outraged folk if you suggested burning a body back in Kething's Cross."

"So you shove them into the ground for worms to eat?" Alia scoffed. "Barbarians."

"At least we know why the wind-sharded think this place is haunted. Some of them must have wandered down here long ago." Heth resumed walking forward, though not as briskly as before. The stallion seemed unconcerned by the leering skulls and the close confines, and Heth wondered if he had been stabled inside the Duskhold. Alia was having a little more trouble convincing the pony to go along, but after a brief show of defiance Ash relented.

The corridor jagged and split, and after a moment's deliberation Heth followed the left branching. They passed about a thousand more skulls and then entered a small circular chamber with three more archways spaced evenly around its perimeter. In the center of the room was an ancient well, the rope and pulley system long since rotted into oblivion.

Alia warily approached the hole and glanced down. "Surely we've come far enough," she said. "Not that I want to stay here, but if we keep going deeper into this place we might get lost."

Heth nodded. "I agree. We must be safe –" He paused, cocking his head. "Wait, do you hear that?"

Alia went still, listening intently. After a moment, she slowly shook her head.

Heth swallowed. The noise was at the very edge of his awareness, but there could be no mistaking what it was.

A voice.

A voice that sounded very familiar.

"What is it?" Alia finally whispered, staring at him fearfully. Heth realized she could see something in his face.

"I think it's coming from this way," he murmured, approaching one of the passages in a daze. There was something carved above its lintel, a many-pointed sun. It looked vaguely familiar.

Heth started as Alia's hand closed around his arm. He drew in a shuddering breath, as if coming awake from a nightmare.

"What is wrong?" she asked, staring into his eyes intently.

"It's my father," Heth said hollowly. "He's calling to me."

Alia's eyes widened, and she dug her nails into his flesh. "That's impossible," she hissed. "And you know that. This place . . . this place must truly be haunted. Or you're imagining it."

Heth slowly shook his head. "No. It's him, I'm sure. And even if it's his ghost . . . I want to speak with him."

Alia released his arm and slapped him hard.

Heth's head rocked back, and for a moment the ringing in his ears blotted out the faint cries of his father.

"It's not your father!" she nearly screamed.

"But what if it is?" Heth said, pulling away from her grip. "I'll just go have a quick look. Stay here with the horses."

"Heth!" she yelled, her voice cracking. "Stay here!"

But he was already moving into the passage, his thoughts honey-thick. Why was he doing this? He knew he shouldn't, but it was like something had taken hold of his body and was pushing him on, towards the voice demanding, asking, begging Heth to rescue him from this place . . .

~

Heth returned to himself trapped in smothering darkness. He'd been outside his body, drifting in nothing. For how long? Why were these stones not glowing at all? He'd stumbled into the passage, but when he turned around, he couldn't see the glow from the well-chamber.

"Alia?" he cried, her name echoing back to him. How long had he been wandering?

"Heth!" Relief flooded him as she answered. But it was faint, so faint, as if muffled by layers of stone.

"Where are you?"

"Where are *you*? You walked into the passage, and I ran after, but you weren't there! Like something had swallowed you!" The fear he heard made his heart ache. Why had he left her?

"How . . . how long have I been gone?"

"I don't know. Not too long. Oh, by the Seed, I thought . . . I thought something had taken you."

Heth stretched out his arm into the black. His fingers brushed over crumbling stone . . . and then a pitted surface with a familiar shape . . . yes, there were the nostrils, the eyes, what remained of the teeth . . .

"The skulls are here. I'm still in the passages, the light has just gone out."

"Can you follow my voice?"

"I think so. Keep talking."

"Oh, uh, all right. About what?"

Heth crept along, running his hands along the walls and their gristly ornamentations. "Anything. What was it like as Rhenna's handmaiden?"

"Oh. It was . . . good." Alia sounded surprised that this was the word she chose. "I mean, the Duskhold was still a nightmare. Yet being with my mistress made it much, much better. I think . . . I think she needed me as much I needed her. She was also unhappy, deeply so."

Heth frowned. Alia's voice had faded as he continued on in the direction he'd been going, so he reversed direction. But after a few steps she sounded like she was even *farther* away. Was there a branch in the corridor that he'd missed? But he'd made sure to touch the opposite wall as he went along so he wouldn't miss a turning in the dark.

Alia continued talking, oblivious to his increasing alarm. "There was a sorrow in her, and I think I was the only one who saw it. She was torn – she wanted to please her father, but also she hated the world he had built in the Duskhold. If I was to guess –"

Heth stopped abruptly as Alia's faint voice disappeared entirely. There was no scream, so he didn't think something had surprised or attacked her . . . But why would she just fall silent like that?

"Alia?" he yelled into the black.

Nothing.

The fear he'd been trying his best to keep a tight grip on was now squirming from between his fingers. He felt a cold sweat break out, and his heartbeat quickened.

Heth frowned, realizing the darkness was no longer seamless. Farther ahead, a faint glow was spilling around a bend in the passage. He drew in a shuddering breath. It didn't look like the glow that had been seeping from the ruin's stone – no, it seemed like there was a source up ahead, though it did not flicker or dance like a flame.

Was there someone down here with him?

He closed his hand around the hilt of his sword and crept forward.

As he approached what he had thought was a bend in the passage, he discovered that it was in truth an ornate entrance decorated by elaborate stone scrollwork. He pressed himself against the wall beside the opening and peeked around the corner, his curiosity almost as strong as his fear.

And jerked his head back.

For a moment, he struggled to understand what he'd glimpsed. There was a room with a circular doorway on the far wall, light spilling from whatever lay beyond. And reclining in front of it was a lion.

Slowly – very slowly – Heth glanced again into the room. He let out a sigh of relief when he saw his suspicions were correct and it was just a statue, like the ones above that had flanked the entrance to this building. This lion also had a vaguely mannish face, and it appeared to be carved from the same white stone as elsewhere in the ruins, the mane a brilliant silver that gleamed in the light emanating from whatever was behind it. Unlike the lions above, this one was smooth and unblemished, but that made sense if it had been sequestered down here away from the elements. For a guardian it was rather underwhelming, as the ancient stonemason had carved it with its eyes shut, like it was sleeping.

Heth stepped fully into the chamber, trying to peer past the statue and see where the light in the other room was coming from. Could part of this underground labyrinth have collapsed, and this was sunlight spilling in from the outside? He took a few tentative steps into the chamber and then froze.

The lion's eyes were now open. They were golden, luminous, with a depth Heth had never seen before in an animal. That awareness was probably the only reason he did not turn and flee from the room – that, and the lesson he'd learned while hunting with his father. Showing your back to a predator was the worst thing you could do. No, better to hold its gaze, show no fear, demonstrate that you are not prey . . .

The lion slowly raised itself from sitting and slid its legs forward, then stretched as if it had not moved for a very long time. Claws longer than daggers scratched the stone, leaving visible furrows behind. The man-like jaws opened wide in a yawn, showing very lion-like teeth.

And all the while it held Heth's gaze, as if taking the measure of him.

He considered drawing his sword, but from the intelligence he saw in those golden eyes he felt certain it would know that was a threat . . . and even with his blade in his hand Heth would be quickly torn to pieces. Now that it had stood, he could see that he barely reached the shoulder of this creature, and it could eviscerate him with one swipe of its paws.

The white lion blinked languidly, and then it slowly turned and began ambling towards the light-filled doorway. As soon as the lion looked away from him, a shiver went through Heth and he felt in control again of his own body. He could run now, back into the darkness of the skull-filled corridors . . .

But he did not. He stood there, terror thrumming through him, and then just before the man-lion passed into the room beyond it turned back . . . and he knew exactly what it wanted.

For him to follow.

45

ALIA

"Heth?"

Alia clenched her fists, willing an answer to return from the darkness. She thought he'd been drawing closer, following her voice, but now he'd gone ominously silent.

"Heth?" she tried again, doing her best to tamp down her rising panic. Should she try to find him? The thought of stumbling around in the black was terrifying, but what if he'd bashed his head on something and was right now lying unconscious?

Alia gnawed on her lip, thinking hard. Perhaps she could bring a piece of the glowing white rock with her? Not a terrible idea. After a moment of searching, she found a chunk of stone about the size of her fist that had crumbled away from the well in the center of the room. She hefted it, wondering if it would be enough to let her see anything in the darkened corridors.

The stallion whickered and tossed his head, as if realizing what she was considering and begging her not to go.

"I'll be back for you," she said, stroking his neck. He watched her out of the corner of his eye distrustfully.

"I promise. Heth needs –"

The crack of something striking stone interrupted her. She hissed in surprise, whirling to stare at the entrance to the corridor where she thought the sound had come from. It wasn't where Heth had vanished, nor was it the one where they had entered the well-room.

Perhaps it had been her imagination. Or a piece of stone falling from the ceiling. Maybe –

The crack came again, closer. Then again. Rhythmic. Like something was approaching, one stumping step at a time. She gasped as the stallion flicked its tail, startling her. Was the war horse trembling?

"You better not be scared," she whispered. "I might need you to kick whatever is coming."

The horse snorted in response, as if dismissing the very idea as ridiculous.

"Come on," Alia begged, hefting the rock as she stared into the darkness. "I'll be right beside you."

Another crack, this time so close it made her jump. She moaned fearfully, tangling her fingers in the stallion's mane.

A figure stepped from the blackness, leaning heavily on a staff.

"Oh," Alia murmured, the shard of rock slipping from her suddenly nerveless fingers.

46

DERYN

MORNING when it finally arrived was wan and sickly, the rising sun obscured by a thick blanket of clouds. Deryn hunkered behind a white-stone pedestal that once had been the base for a mighty column, watching Yvrin draw patterns in a patch of bare earth.

"So this is the edge of the mesa," she said, cutting a line in the dirt with a branch snapped from one of the small shrubs growing among the ruins. "And here is the old gatehouse or barbican or whatever used to stand where the road empties onto the plateau." She raised her head, casting a glance across the courtyard to the tumbled walls and chunks of stone. "They'll have to come through there to reach the palace proper."

"A good place for an ambush," Rhenna murmured, her back against the plinth of another broken pillar.

Yvrin frowned. "It is and it isn't, my lady. After we get in the first blow, we'd be forced to fight in close against what is likely superior numbers."

She scooped a handful of pebbles up and started placing them in a square beyond the gatehouse she'd sketched out. "I think among the columns is a better place for us to attack from. Once they pass through the ruins and enter the courtyard, they'll be exposed to our ranged attacks while we can remain in cover."

Rhenna rubbed at her sallow face, blinking as if having trouble visualizing what Yvrin had laid out. "Why don't we want to close as quickly as possible? I have my javelins, but your talents are best used in hand-to-hand combat. I've seen you win many a bout by Shadow Stepping next to your opponent and slashing them with your talons. It seems to me our strengths would be best served by rushing them at once."

Yvrin shook her head fiercely, then seemed to realize who she was contradicting and smiled apologetically. "Ah, Lady Shen. I will, of course, follow your lead in this, but I implore you to take my suggestions into consideration."

Rhenna scowled, waving away her words. "Enough. I'm merely providing another perspective. I realize you're far more knowledgeable in these matters than I – you were at your father's knee listening to him plan his raids on the other steppe tribes when Nishi was chasing me around the Duskhold trying to pull my hair."

"I wasn't aware you knew about my past," Yvrin said quietly.

One corner of Rhenna's mouth lifted. "I may have seemed distant, but I paid more attention to the rest of you than you all thought. Especially the few I respected."

Yvrin ducked her head as she blushed, then tried to bring the focus back to what she had drawn by tapping the branch on the pebbles representing where they crouched.

"You are right that my talents will not be very useful in such an ambush," she conceded, and then raised the branch so it pointed at Deryn. "But his will."

Rhenna frowned. "Him? What first-tier talent would help here? Arm of the Abyss?"

"The Breath of the Mother," Yvrin said, almost triumphantly.

Rhenna's brows arched. "Surely not. A second-tier talent? How many shards do you have, Deryn?"

"Three," he murmured, surprised by the intensity of Rhenna's attention.

"I saw it," Yvrin said quickly. "We all did. He tossed that witch Pand right off the Drum Tower."

"Is it true?" Rhenna asked, directing this question at Deryn.

He nodded jerkily. "Yes . . . apparently. That's what Azil called the talent when he told me what happened."

Rhenna leaned back against the stone, looking at Deryn like she was seeing him in a new light. "You are just full of surprises, *kenang*."

He could only shrug helplessly at this, and then Yvrin coughed gently to bring the attention back to her. "Yes, well, I believe our best chance is if Deryn strikes the first blow. We wait until our enemy is exposed, crossing the courtyard, and then he unleashes the Breath while you send a volley of javelins. Hopefully we'll incapacitate a few of the weaker Sharded, and then I'll Shadow Step in to engage the most powerful that remains. A few Mirror Wraiths dancing among the pillars will confuse them further and make them think there are more of us than there truly are."

Rhenna was quiet for a moment, and then she nodded. "A good plan," she said grudgingly.

"But what if they don't come up the road?" Deryn asked, gesturing at the pebbles strewn beside the line that marked the mesa's edge. "The Crow could fly up here on a Wind Dragon."

Yvrin grimaced. "I know. But we can't prepare for that. I hope that if it's the wind-sharded that have won out below, that they'll be too superstitious to brave the ruins. But if they aren't . . . then we run for the closest roofs and try to avoid getting torn apart by the cyclones they are sure to unleash up here."

"But you don't think it will be them," Rhenna said, watching Yvrin carefully.

"I don't," the steppe girl admitted. "The Crow may be formidable, but they won't be expecting such a force from the Ember, along with a powerful blood-sharded. No, I expect it will be the Flame." Her jaw hardened as her gaze drifted across the courtyard. "I hope it will be the Flame."

~

The day slowly brightened, though the sun never managed to fight through the heavy shroud. Deryn wondered apprehensively if this haze was a precursor to an attack and watched the sky almost as much as the ruined gatehouse, half-expecting screaming warriors to emerge from the clouds. Even though he'd only spent a little time in the Frayed Lands, this weather still seemed unnatural – he was far more accustomed to empty skies and sweeping vistas.

He truly hoped the enemy would arrive from the road, so that they could be the ambushers rather than the ambushed. They needed to strike first and incapacitate as many as possible before the enemy could unleash their powers. The image emblazoned in his memory that he kept returning to was the one from the night before, when he'd gazed down from the edge of the mesa at the struggle raging on the plains between the Flame and Wind. It was why they had sent Heth and Alia away, to find safety deeper in the ruins. This entire area might soon become deadly for anyone not bearing a shard, and as much as Heth had wanted to help, there was absolutely nothing he could do against such enemies. Deryn hoped they had found sanctuary somewhere and would stay hidden until this battle was decided.

His gaze slid to where Yvrin was hunkered behind another pillar, maybe two dozen paces from where he crouched. She was examining the tip of the sharded spear that had once belonged to Last Snow Falling, running her fingertip over the barbed red metal. His own hand drifted to the hilt at his side, and the porcelain sword stirred, thrumming under his touch. He knew he would be able to unleash the Breath of the Mother only once – if it was anything like what had happened during his duel with Pand, the effort would drain most of his *ka* reserves – so he planned on utilizing the sword's powers to batter the enemy immediately after. The wind summoned by his sword might not do much damage, but he thought if he channeled a tiny amount of *ka* through the blade as he swung with all his strength, he might create a gust strong enough to disorient their enemies. It would certainly shock any wind-sharded that reached the top of the mesa that someone was using one of their own artifacts against them.

Deryn focused on Rhenna, who was about an equal distance from Yvrin as he was from the steppe girl. She was leaning against a column that was mostly intact, her eyes closed. She looked exhausted, maybe even asleep on her feet, but Deryn knew she was channeling as much *ka* as she could. Like him, she must have found herself nearly empty after Shade had possessed her, as if the elemental had been forced to use her own *ka* in order to break whatever had seized them. Deryn had replenished his reserves while on the long ascent to the palace, but Rhenna had a much larger well to fill and far less time to do it in.

At the thought of Shade, he glanced around, looking for the elemental. No sign of him, but Deryn knew he was lurking somewhere nearby. He wondered if there was some way the shadow-creature could help them in the coming battle –

"Deryn," Yvrin hissed, and his eyes snapped to her in alarm. She had hunkered down further behind her column so she wouldn't be seen from the courtyard, and when their gazes met, she jerked her head towards the remains of the gatehouse.

"They're coming."

Something huge had reached the top of the mesa. Deryn glimpsed it through the shattered stone, a great red shape, bulbous and gleaming. It reminded him of the riftbeast, though much smaller, and briefly he wondered if another of the Frayed Land monsters had somehow found them.

And then it emerged from the ruins.

It picked its way over the detritus almost daintily, placing legs twice the height of a man carefully on the uneven ground. Its abdomen was huge and pendulous, as if swollen with the blood its body seemed molded from, and eight gleaming red eyes like jewels were set on its monstrous head just above glistening fangs.

This must be a Blood Spider, the thing Yvrin had spoken of seeing in the attack on the camp. And that meant the flame-sharded had overcome whatever Crow warriors had arrived to investigate the death of their brethren.

Sudden movement from on top of the Blood Spider drew Deryn's attention. He hadn't noticed it at first, as he'd been distracted by the almost mesmerizing sight of those vast scissoring legs, but a man was perched atop the spider where the head joined with the abdomen. He was Ashasai, his copper skin only a few shades lighter than the beast he was riding, and wearing a long garment patterned with brilliantly colored geometric shapes. His eyes narrowed as he scanned the forest of broken pillars fringing the courtyard, and Deryn hunched lower to avoid his gaze.

Behind the great spider, a half-dozen men and women followed, all with flashing red shards set into their brows. They wore robes of different colors, though each reminded Deryn of fire – deep crimson like the last embers in a dying hearth, the orange of a well-fed campfire, the yellow flame of a torch. The clothes were tattered, stained in places, and he saw that a few of these flame-sharded were limping. They had not remained unscathed from the violence below. Deryn supposed that was to be expected – they had fought two battles in the last few days, and he doubted they had rested at all since the first ambush. Exhaustion was writ clear in their faces as they came to stand around the legs of the motionless spider, which had halted so the blood-sharded could survey the crumbled palace.

Deryn's gaze was drawn to another figure stumbling in the midst of the flame-sharded. His breath caught in his throat as the shackled man raised his ash-stained face from the ground and stared with empty eyes at the ruins ringing the courtyard.

Vertus.

One half of his head looked to have been scorched, his hair burnt away and the skin blistered with weeping sores. The crimson tattoos that had once covered his face had been obliterated on that side, but elsewhere they were visible beneath a layer of grime.

"Stay quiet," a low whisper came from nearby, and he turned to find that Yvrin had Shadow Stepped to behind the pillar next to him. Her face was grim, her knuckles white around the haft of the sharded spear.

"They've taken Vertus prisoner," Deryn hissed at her.

"I know, I see," she murmured back. "The plan has changed. After you unleash the Breath, you and I will strike at the flame-sharded and try to free him. He must be wearing Karathinite shackles – that's the only metal that could hold one of the Sharded Few. But since he's the one wearing them, they will only inhibit *his* strength. If I can get to him, I can tear them off, and then we'll have another eight-sharded at our side, even if he's weakened."

"Should I still summon the Breath with him there?"

She nodded. "He's strong enough it won't kill him. He won't enjoy it, but he'll forgive us once he's free."

"And Rhenna?"

Yvrin jerked her chin in the spider's direction. "The blood-sharded is hers. He's strong, more than ten-sharded. I do not know what he's doing consorting with the Flame. Rhenna just needs to hold him off until we free Vertus and take care of the others, then we'll join forces and overwhelm him." She peeked around the edge of the pillar. "They're moving again. I've already told Rhenna what I just told you. I'll count down from ten, and then you unleash the Breath. Are you ready?"

Deryn nodded, trying to ignore the pounding of his heart.

Yvrin must have seen something in his face, because suddenly she winked at him as she held up her open hand. "Don't be scared. Just remember your training and strike hard and fast." One finger fell. Then another. Deryn swallowed, turning back to the enemy. The spider was in the middle of the courtyard, and the flame-sharded had spread out on either side of it. Vertus was among the group on its left, and he looked on the verge of collapse as he staggered over the rock-strewn ground.

Reaching deep within himself, Deryn pulled forth the thing that had been sleeping inside him since that day on the Drum Tower. The *ka* coursing through his pathways quickened as he brought the Breath of the Mother to the very edge of becoming reality, holding it back like it was a dog straining at its leash, desperate to be loosed.

"One," Yvrin said in a voice louder than before, and with a gasp, he let the talent burst forth.

It was like a great flower blossoming from nothing. A point of darkness appeared in the air, and then it billowed outwards like reality had suddenly been torn asunder. Deryn gasped, leaning heavily against the pillar to keep from collapsing – he felt hollowed out, like nearly all the *ka* he'd been cultivating over the last day had drained at once from his pathways.

This all happened in the blink of an eye, and their hunters were just raising arms in alarm when something exploded from the rift. It was a wind, if the wind was black and accompanied by a keening like a soul in torment. The Breath of the Mother rushed across the courtyard, first striking the Blood Spider. Glistening red legs shattered like they were made of ice, sending fragments flying in every direction. The man on its back leaped away as the beast toppled forward, but Deryn couldn't dwell on what had happened to the blood-sharded, as the Breath had already reached the others.

A few of the Sharded managed to summon hovering shields of roiling flames, but the black wind tore these barriers easily as it passed through them, scattering gobbets of fire. Then it washed over the enemy – two were blown from their feet like Pand had been, tumbling through the air, while the others staggered, fighting to stay upright. One clawed at his face, which was now blackened and bubbling, and Deryn wondered if something else had erupted from the shadowrealm along with the wind.

He couldn't let them recover. Even though his body felt emptied by bringing the Breath into existence, Deryn pushed himself away from the pillar and charged into the courtyard. With the tiny amount of *ka* he'd held in reserve he summoned his Ghost Chitin armor, hoping it would be enough to provide some protection despite how little power he could devote to forging it. Out of the corner of his eye, he saw a huge lance of squirming red flash past him, and it must have slammed into the ruins because a moment later he heard a crack like stone splitting apart.

Rhenna, drawing the attention of the blood-sharded. The size and power of that attack shocked him, and he hoped she had recovered enough to hold off the Ashasai until they could come to her aid.

He'd crossed half the distance to the flame-sharded, and a few of them had recovered enough to notice his approach. One screamed a warning, flames enveloping his hands as he raised his arms towards Deryn.

Without breaking his stride, Deryn ripped his sword from its sheath, and then as he channeled through the blade some of the last few precious drops of *ka* he hadn't already dedicated to his Ghost Chitin he slashed the air in the direction of the flame-sharded.

Unlike the swirling black air of the Breath, this blast of wind was invisible, and he wasn't even sure if anything had happened until the robes of the flame-sharded rippled and one of them was again knocked to the ground after just having climbed back to his feet. This wind carried with it dirt and small rocks, and the flame-sharded who had stayed standing still had to cover their faces. Despite being unable to see, one of them raised his hand palm-out towards Deryn, and a moment later, a great blast of flame erupted, rushing towards him.

If he could have reacted faster, he probably would have thrown himself to the ground, but the raging torrent of fire enveloped him before he even fully understood what was happening.

I'm dead, he thought as the flames rushed over him, but somehow his Ghost Chitin held, and he only felt a blast of terrible heat without the scorching touch of the fire. The conflagration did not end, though, continuing to wash over him in pummeling waves, and he sensed his Ghost Chitin beginning to blister and crack – in moments it would fail, and then he would find out just how long his Sharded body could survive inside a raging inferno. He struggled forward, but now he'd become disoriented, and all he could see around him was a flood of orange and red.

He gasped, falling to one knee as he struggled to breathe. The

Ghost Chitin was even protecting his hands like he was wearing gauntlets, but as his talent faltered, the metal grip of the porcelain sword was getting uncomfortably hot. It wouldn't be too long until his clothes burst into flame.

He'd failed. He'd never even reached the enemy . . .

The flames disappeared. Deryn drew in a shuddering breath and then coughed, his lungs feeling charred. He blinked, trying to focus through the pulsing white islands in his vision to see why he'd been spared.

Yvrin. The steppe girl had Shadow Stepped into the midst of the enemy and was laying about with her wickedly curved claws. The flame-sharded who had been lashing Deryn with waves of flame was clutching at his neck, blood spurting from between his blackened fingers, and as Deryn rose unsteadily he toppled face-first onto the ground.

He had to help her. He had to. Trying to ignore the burning in his chest Deryn resumed running, though this time he was much slower than before. Three of the six flame-sharded had already fallen – two slain by Yvrin, and the other had finally collapsed after failing to peel away the blackness blasted onto his face by the Breath of the Mother. Yvrin was dancing among the remaining flame-sharded, Shadow-Stepping away from whips of flame and hurled fireballs, then slashing with her claws before quickly teleporting again.

All the red-robed Sharded were so determined to catch up with Yvrin's rapid movements that they did not pay any attention to Deryn until he brought his sword down on the outstretched arm of the woman wielding the blazing whip, severing it at the elbow. He was expecting some resistance, but the blade passed through flesh and bone without the slightest hesitation. The flame-sharded screamed in pain and shock, staring at the blood pumping from the stump of her arm, and then her eyes rolled back in her head and she crumpled.

With no time to dwell on what he'd just done, Deryn pivoted towards another of the flame-sharded, who was turning towards him as a halo of flames sparked into existence over his head, but whatever he was about to unleash remained a mystery as Deryn's blade plunged into him. The swelling flames evaporated as the Sharded reached down to clutch at the length of gleaming porcelain protruding from his belly.

"Bastard," he gurgled through the blood pouring from his mouth, and then Deryn wrenched his sword free, and he tumbled to the ground.

Knowing there was one flame-sharded still fighting, Deryn whirled around with his blood-streaked sword upraised, only to find that Yvrin had already ended the battle. She stood over the corpse of a fat man who looked like he'd been mauled by a bear, her chest heaving and her face spattered with gore.

Their eyes met, and she crooked a grin at him. "Not bad, novice."

"We killed them all," Deryn murmured, turning to take in the sprawled bodies. He felt numb, but then another loud crash from among the forest of pillars startled him back to the present.

"And they very much deserved it," Yvrin said, her claws dissolving into shreds of shadowy mist. "Now come on, let's free Vertus and go help Rhenna."

Deryn nodded, finally allowing his cracked Ghost Chitin to crumble away.

"Lord Balenchas," Yvrin cried, striding over to where Vertus had watched the short but brutal fight in wide-eyed disbelief. Or perhaps he was in shock, Deryn realized – there was little recognition in his face as Yvrin stalked closer, and he was swaying on his feet like he could collapse at any moment. "It's good to see you. Are you all right? Did they torture you?"

"N-no," Vertus stammered, blinking as he focused on her. Then he swallowed, raising one manacled hand to indicate his fire-blackened face. "But my head hurts."

Deryn had the sinking feeling that Vertus was not going to be much help.

"Let's get you out of those," Yvrin said comfortingly, taking hold of the chain connecting the two pieces of reddish metal encircling his wrist. She snapped that with ease, then worked her finger inside the bands and after a strained grunt the manacles broke apart.

While she was doing this, Vertus watched her with a look of dazed wonder.

"We have no time," Yvrin said, turning back to Deryn. "Vertus is clearly in shock, but he needs to go now –"

She suddenly stiffened, her eyes widening. Then she stumbled forward a step, her face twisting into an expression of intense confusion.

"Why?" Yvrin murmured, and then she fell forward with a dagger embedded in her back.

"No!" Deryn screamed. He rushed towards where she had fallen, but a blast of wind battered him to the ground.

He scrambled back to his feet as Vertus ripped the dagger from Yvrin and stood. The look of dazed bewilderment was gone from his face, and he chuckled as he cleaned the curving blade on his sleeve. Light rippled along the metal – this was a sharded weapon.

"What have you done?" Deryn rasped, his arm shaking as he raised his sword. Yvrin was motionless, a dark stain spreading through her tunic.

Vertus sneered, laying the edge of his dagger against his other hand. "What should have been done days ago. It was a foolish mistake not killing her first." With a sharp motion he slashed his palm, then lowered his arm as blood poured from the wound to patter on the ground.

A numbing wave of disbelief washed over Deryn, leaving him frozen. Yvrin. He felt sick, his stomach clenching, then his grip on the hilt of his sword tightened as the trembling abated. His jaw tightened. He knew he would die if he charged Vertus right now – the Duskhold noble was eight-sharded, far beyond Deryn – but he didn't care.

"A swordfight, eh?" Vertus said. "I haven't had one of those in years. But I'm afraid my dagger is much too short." As he was speaking, something was happening to the steady stream of blood falling from his hand. It was slowing as it hardened, twisting into a shape that Deryn recognized almost at once.

When Vertus raised his arm a few moments later he held a saber forged from the blood, the grip fused with his hand.

"How can you do that?" Deryn murmured hoarsely, but Vertus merely grinned and shook his head, then lunged.

The sudden attack took Deryn by surprise, and he just barely got his porcelain sword up to knock the blood-blade aside. Vertus was still holding the curving Sharded dagger in his off-hand, and he slashed with it before Deryn could recover from his parry. The shimmering blade sliced his shoulder as Deryn threw himself backwards – not deep, but it burned like fire, and it nearly caused him to lose his grip on his sword.

Vertus also drew back a step, examining the redness trickling down his dagger's blade. "I wonder if your little pet will bond with me when I take your shard," he mused, then brought the dagger to his mouth and tasted the blood.

Deryn realized that Shade had emerged from his shadow and was hunched beside him, what passed for hackles raised as he stared at Vertus.

"It would be a few more shards before you might scare me," Vertus said, addressing the elemental. "And unfortunately, your master will never have the chance to claim more and see what you might have become. But if you wish to stay in this realm, I would welcome our bond."

The shadow-dog grated a bark that left no illusions about his opinion of Vertus.

"Very well," the tattooed Sharded said with a shrug, "Give my regards to the Shadow when you –"

Vertus whirled around, brandishing his weapons. Deryn looked past him, confused, and then gasped in surprise.

Heth stood there, pointing the sharded spear Yvrin had been carrying at the shadow-sharded noble.

Deryn charged while Vertus was distracted, but then skidded to a halt as the Sharded glanced back, his blood-saber raised.

"Two of you, eh?" he said, keeping his curving dagger trained on Heth. "And one a Hollow. Do you know that spear is useless in your hands, whelp? I have nothing to fear from *you*." He turned to face

Deryn completely, clashing his weapons together as he stalked forward.

Deryn gave ground, trying to remember what Heth had taught him about fighting a swordsman armed with a dagger in his off-hand. He couldn't let Vertus inside his guard or the shorter blade would end up between his ribs. Vertus sneered as Deryn retreated, his sword cutting a pattern in the air while the dagger remained motionless, poised to strike.

The point of the spear exploded out of Vertus's throat.

"Silver Shrike!" Deryn cried as the red-metal tip withdrew, leaving a ragged hole. The blood saber disintegrated, Vertus's hands flying up to clutch at his ravaged neck. He tried to say something, but nothing emerged from his mouth except bloody bubbles, and then he toppled backwards.

Heth loomed over Vertus, the gory head of the spear poised to stab him again if the Sharded warrior somehow tried to rise.

Yvrin.

Deryn rushed past Heth and went down beside the steppe girl. He rolled her over, hoping that she somehow still lived.

Her glazed eyes stared at nothing. He lowered his head, an aching hollowness spreading inside him.

"Deryn," Heth said. Feeling lightheaded, Deryn turned to where the Hollow was crouched over Vertus's corpse.

"What?" he murmured, with some effort climbing to his feet again. He had to ignore this grief, at least for the moment. They had to find Rhenna and make sure she lived, or Yvrin's death would have been in vain.

"Come look at this," Heth said, indicating the sprawled body with his chin.

Wiping away his tears, Deryn staggered closer to Heth . . . and then stopped in shock.

The corpse no longer looked like Vertus. Its crimson tattoos had melted away from skin that was several shades darker than what Deryn remembered. The face had broadened and aged twenty years, the red hair now a grey-threaded black. Even the side of his face that had been burned was healed, the skin unblemished.

"How?" Deryn murmured, trying to make sense of this.

"I don't know," Heth said, leaning on the spear as he rose. Staring at the red-metal tip, something else suddenly occurred to Deryn.

"I thought only the Sharded Few could wield a sharded weapon?" he asked.

Heth met his eyes, then slowly pulled down the front of his tunic.

Deryn's jaw dropped. A point of gleaming white radiance was sunk into his chest, surrounded by a web of golden veins.

"What . . . how . . ." Deryn stammered, but Heth cut him off with a sharp shake of his head.

"Where are Rhenna and Alia?"

"Alia . . . Alia I don't know," Deryn mumbled, still reeling from everything that had just happened. "She went with you. Rhenna . . ." His gaze went to the broken columns ringing the courtyard just as another great crack split the air. One of the taller pillars recessed deeper within the palace shuddered and collapsed, raising a cloud of dust. "She's there."

Heth hefted the spear, his face hardening. "Let's go."

The trail of destruction was easy to follow. A swath of pillars had been knocked down as if a giant had waded through this section of the palace, great chunks of stone scattered about and everything veiled by a haze of dust. Deryn and Heth kept themselves hunched as they dashed from one tumbled column to the next following the sounds of battle. Finally they glimpsed the blood-sharded in the middle of a cleared space, fallen columns radiating out from where he was standing. Heth made to charge the Ashasai, but Deryn grabbed him by his arm and pulled him down beside the remnants of a destroyed statue.

"He will kill us like he was swatting insects," Deryn whispered.

Heth grimaced, his eyes blazing. "The one back there thought he couldn't be hurt as well." He lifted his spear slightly, as if to remind Deryn what he carried. "These Sharded bleed like any other men when stuck by the weapons we carry."

Deryn held up his hand placatingly. "Just wait. If Rhenna attacks, he'll be distracted, and that's when we'll rush at him."

Heth pursed his lips, but he didn't argue further. They returned their attention to the blood-sharded, who had begun to stroll through the devastation, looking strangely relaxed for someone locked in battle with a powerful shadow-sharded warrior.

"Come out, Lady Shen!" he called, his strangely high-pitched voice echoing in the ruins. "You've led me on a merry chase, but you can't escape now. I know the sound of your heart. It's beating fast – you're frightened. And I do not blame you for that or think less of you ... but perhaps I will if you keep hiding. Let us finish this, daughter of Shadow."

A shiver of movement, and Rhenna appeared on top of a heap of rubble. "Here I am, leech," she shouted down.

The blood-sharded whirled, bringing his hand up. From the center of his palm exploded a glistening whip of blood; it slithered through the air in the blink of an eye and struck Rhenna in the chest, passing through her and slamming into a pillar. That column exploded in a shower of stone chips and dust, but Rhenna seemed unhurt, the tendril vanishing into her and emerging out her back. The image of her wavered and vanished, and the blood whip retracted back into the Sharded's palm just as quickly as it had erupted.

The blood-sharded chuckled, turning in a slow circle to survey the surrounding ruins. "I had heard you were a mighty warrior. But it seems I was lied to. Now I can understand why I was hired."

"What do you mean?" another Rhenna asked, stepping out from behind a pillar. "Surely your master in the Ember told you why they wanted me dead."

The whip flashed out again, faster even than before. It passed through her and sliced the column she was standing beside, then returned to its master's hand. Her Mirror Wraith disappeared as the top half of the column toppled over onto it.

The blood-sharded grinned, as if enjoying some private jest. "You're still fooled? I would have thought the ruse would be up by now."

"What ruse?" another Mirror Wraith called out and then was obliterated a heartbeat later by the whip.

The blood-sharded gestured grandly back in the courtyard's direction. "What ruse? That my fellow hunters were true warriors of the Ember. You must have never spent much time in the court of your father's dearest friend if their disguises passed muster."

"They were flame-sharded," another copy of Rhenna said as she appeared on top of one of the few intact pillars, though whatever it had once supported had long since collapsed. The blood-sharded put his hands on his hips as he stared up at her.

"They were," he agreed. "But they served my master, not the lord of the Flame."

"And who is that?" the wraith of Rhenna asked, her fists clenched.

"The Unbound King, of course. Xend an-Azith, may the Blood bless his name. We had to empty our ranks of every Sharded who had once served in the Ember to make this charade succeed, I'll have you know."

The wraith looked shaken, and Deryn assumed that wherever she was among the forest of columns the true Rhenna felt the same.

"Why does your master want me dead?"

The blood-sharded threw his head back and laughed long and hard. When he had finished, he faced her again, wiping his eyes. "Oh, my poor little princess, he doesn't care whether you live or die. But there were promises made and a great amount of wealth given to ensure your charred corpse was found on the road to the Windwrack."

"By whom?" Rhenna asked hollowly.

"Why," the blood-sharded replied, his mouth twisting into a vicious grin, "by your father, of course."

"Liar!"

A pale blur burst from behind a pillar not far from where the blood-sharded stared up at the Mirror Wraith. Deryn saw satisfaction in the Ashasai's face as he turned fluidly to meet Rhenna's charge, the whip of blood already cracking through the air.

"No!" Deryn cried, knowing she would not reach the blood-sharded before the deadly filament plunged into her.

And it did. Rhenna did not break her stride in the slightest as the whip entered her belly. Then the blood-sharded's face went slack with shock, and he whirled around just as a javelin of darkness pierced his shoulder. He staggered, the long spear of shadow lodged just above his collarbone, then snarled and ripped it away, the javelin dissolving into shreds of darkness. The Mirror Wraith on top of the pillar had leaped from its perch – no, Deryn realized, the real Rhenna – and landed about twenty paces from the blood-sharded, chunks of stone flying up from the impact.

Before the Ashasai could summon his blood-whip again, Rhenna raised her arm in his direction and clenched her fist violently. A great floating black hand appeared behind the blood-sharded, then like a trap its fingers closed around him with terrible force. He vanished without a sound, completely enveloped.

"Fire and ashes," Heth murmured, staring with wide eyes at Rhenna as she grimaced, squeezing her own hand with all her strength.

"Come on," Deryn said, rising from where they'd been crouched.

Rhenna caught sight of them out of the corner of her eye and turned, the anger in her face giving way to relief.

"Deryn –" she began, but then gave a sharp cry of pain. Deryn froze, his heart in his throat as a dozen red blades thrust outwards from the black substance of the hand. Then they moved, slashing through the fist until it was nothing more than drifting black ribbons and the blood-sharded was revealed again. Rhenna clutched at her hand, trying to staunch the blood pouring from the wounds that had suddenly opened in her flesh. Around the blood-sharded, the long blades had formed a whirling sphere; his sneering mirth was gone now as he stalked towards Rhenna. She glanced up from her shredded hand, and Deryn could see her desperation.

Heth rushed past him yelling a battle cry. The blood-sharded hesitated for the briefest of moments, then flicked his wrist almost dismissively in Heth's direction. One blade detached from its gleaming orbit and lanced towards him, but Heth must have expected something like this as he threw himself to the side. Not fast enough, though - the sword clipped him as it went whirling past, sending up a spray of blood. Heth stayed down on the stone, and for a terrifying moment, Deryn thought he must be dead. Then he tried to rise, only to collapse again with a pained moan.

Deryn glanced from the weakly moving Heth to the smirking blood-sharded. Rhenna screamed something unintelligible and hurled another javelin of darkness, but it shattered against the whirling barrier of blades.

They were doomed, the blood-sharded was too powerful. Deryn's hand tightened on the hilt of his porcelain sword.

So be it.

He gathered himself, preparing to charge into certain death. Perhaps he could distract this bastard long enough for Rhenna to escape.

He realized that Shade was crouched at his feet, staring up at him.

"Sorry," he murmured to the elemental.

touch

The word entered his mind on the flutter of moth wings. Elsewhere, Rhenna was stumbling away from the blood-sharded as his blades flashed closer and closer.

touch came the request again, and Shade rubbed against his leg like he wanted to be pet.

A final goodbye before he threw himself into those threshing swords? Why not. Deryn leaned over, pressing his hand against the top of Shade's head.

And gasped.

Ka flowed into him in a cold torrent, flooding his pathways. He staggered, nearly overwhelmed by the sudden rush of power swelling inside him – a moment ago he had been so drained he couldn't even summon his Ghost Chitin, and now ... and now ...

Something manifested in his mind. It wasn't like how his previous talents had come to him, welling up from within like they had always been lurking deep inside; rather, this was as if a sudden knowledge was being thrust upon him from somewhere else. It felt much like the Breath of the Mother ... but it was also different. Deryn hurriedly decanted the frozen *ka* that had filled him, using it to shape this new – and yet not new – talent that had suddenly burgeoned into existence.

The air between Rhenna and the blood-sharded twisted and tore. Scowling, the Ashasai halted, the wound in his shoulder suddenly beginning to gush. The blood did not trickle down his brightly colored garment but rippled and squirmed, quickly coursing over his body and hardening into a protective armor. Despite already having a barrier of flashing swords, the blood-sharded was taking no risk with what might appear from the rift that had just opened in front of him.

Was this the Breath of the Mother? Perhaps it had felt different because he had used Shade's *ka* to summon it this time. But if so, where was the black wind? This portal almost looked like those Nishi used for Shadow Walking ...

Something moved on the other side of the hovering doorway. The Sharded bared his teeth as the blood that had been flowing over him finished setting, the movement of the whirling red blades quickening. Deryn glimpsed strange black shapes clustered on the portal's threshold, and something else, something pale and round like the moon in a starless sky, a face that looked almost familiar ...

They emerged from the rift with strange, jerky movements, as if they did not know how to move in this new world. Gangly limbs with too many joints dangled nearly to the ground, featureless heads perched above sunken chests. And everywhere there were thorns of different lengths curling from their ape-like bodies, barbs of glistening darkness.

The way they looked ... and moved ... Deryn had never seen

anything so unnatural. So *wrong*. If he was closer to the portal, would he hear that mad piping again?

The blood-sharded shrieked, sending all his swords hurtling at the creatures that had stepped from the portal. The blades of hardened blood struck the shadow-things, some slicing off limbs, others embedding themselves in blackness that did not bleed.

The creatures did not even slow their pace.

"Back, demons!" roared the blood-sharded, serpents of rippling red writhing around his upraised arms.

They reached him before he could unleash whatever talent he was forming. Knotted limbs bristling with barbs wrapped like thorned branches around the blood-sharded, and he was pulled forward as the creatures suddenly began retreating back the way they'd come. His bellows of rage turned to screams of fear as he realized where they were taking him.

Fingers of blood crawled from his open mouth, scrabbling at his cheeks as if a parasite inside the Ashasai was trying desperately to escape what it knew was coming. But before it could emerge fully the thorned shadow-things passed once more into the dark of the shadowrealm and the rift dwindled and vanished, the final scream of the blood-sharded abruptly sliced short.

Silence.

Deryn collapsed to his knees, his head splitting. Rhenna was dragging herself towards him, cradling her savaged hand to her chest.

Heth. He had to save Heth.

Groaning, Deryn heaved himself back to his feet and staggered towards where Heth lay. Relief flooded Deryn when he saw that Heth was not dead, though his face was ashen, his hands pressed to his belly. There was a frighteningly large stain on his shirt around this wound, and yet more blood pooled on the ground beside him. His breathing was labored, but he managed to focus on Deryn as he came to crouch beside him.

"I can feel my insides," Heth slurred. "They want to come out."

"Just . . . just hold on," Deryn said, looking around frantically for some way to stop the bleeding. Red Vesch had once taught him how to pack a wound with moss, but not anything this large . . .

"It's all right," Heth said, his voice growing calmer. "I've dressed enough kills to know I'm not surviving this." He winced, hissing in pain. "I'm going to need you to finish me. One clean thrust to the heart."

"I can't . . ." Deryn gasped. "I can't do that."

"You can," Heth replied. "You have to. Just promise me you'll find Alia and take care of her . . . I lost her in the ruins. There was a lion, and it showed me . . . it showed me . . ." His eyes moved past Deryn, staring at something beyond him.

"Stay with me!" Deryn cried, ripping off his tunic and balling it into something to staunch the blood. He knew it wouldn't work, but what else could he do?

"Alia," Heth murmured, his voice faint.

"I'll find her," Deryn promised, trying to decide if he should remove Heth's shirt to get to his wound. Or would that only make it worse?

"I'm here."

Deryn turned. Alia stood a few paces away, hugging herself as she stared down at Heth. Beside her hunched a gnarled old woman he'd never seen before. She was dressed in a motley assortment of rags, her face incised with lines so deep she looked carved of the same wood as the ancient staff she was leaning on. Who in the frozen hells was this?

"Do you know anything of healing?" Deryn asked Alia, tearing his gaze from the crone.

"A little," she said, wringing her hands in consternation.

"Oh, out of the way," the old woman commanded, stumping closer. "And put your shirt back on, fool."

"Who –" Deryn began, but then the old woman flicked her wrist in his direction, bone bracelets jangling, and suddenly he was crouching a few paces to the left of where he'd been a moment ago.

He gaped at the stranger as she lowered herself to her knees with a pained groan, scowling down at Heth. Deryn started to rise, but then Alia was beside him, her hand on his shoulder.

"Wait," she said softly. "She might be able to help." Alia turned as Rhenna touched her arm gently, and then embraced her quickly before returning her attention to Heth.

Deryn crept closer, keeping a wary eye on this strange interloper. She was muttering under her breath, and it sounded to Deryn like she was carrying on a rather heated conversation with herself, complete with insults and snorts of derision. He noticed Shade had gone very still beside him, staring at this stranger as if transfixed.

Finally the old woman seemed to reach the end of her argument, nodding her head sharply. "Very well. First this needs to come off." She reached down, placing her long yellowed nail on the collar of Heth's shirt, and then with a quick slashing motion sliced it open. As the two halves fell away, Rhenna gasped in disbelief when she saw what had been revealed, the golden veins radiating out from the fragment etched stark against his pale, sweat-slicked chest.

The old woman's gaze lingered on the shard for a long moment, then her scowl deepened. "Oh, now *this* complicates things."

A shudder went through Heth, and he grimaced, baring bloody teeth.

"Fine," the crone said with a sigh, rummaging in one of the many pouches hanging from her filthy shawl and pulling out a stoppered bottle. She waggled it in front of his unseeing eyes. "Just so you know, I've been carrying this around for a thousand years. A thousand! And now I have to use it because some idiot wasn't smart enough not to get stabbed by a bloody sword." With a grunt of effort, she removed the stopper, then upended the bottle over where Heth's hands were still pressed to his belly. It looked like water as it fell, but when it struck flesh it hissed and bubbled, smoke rising. Heth drew in a sharp breath, his eyes snapping open, but despite Deryn's fears, Heth did not cry out in pain or try to twist away. The old woman waited until the bubbles were thick enough that the wound was entirely hidden, and then she leaned closer and blew away the froth. It dissipated like foam on a mug of ale, and Heth slowly raised his trembling hands from his belly to reveal pink, unbroken skin.

"How?" he rasped, blinking up at her in amazement.

"The Tears of Belandria," the old woman said as she stiffly rose. "Don't go getting yourself disemboweled again, because that was the last of it . . . And since Belandria went and got herself killed, there ain't going to be any more any time soon." She shook her head, squinting up at the grey sky as if annoyed by what she had just been forced to do.

"Thank you," Heth murmured. He reached his hand up towards Deryn, who had to struggle for a moment to push past his own stunned disbelief before he could take hold of Heth and help pull him to his feet. As he swayed upright, the spell that had fallen over the rest of them seemed to break.

"Why do you have a shard?" Rhenna asked, almost accusingly. Then before Heth could answer, she whirled on the old woman. Deryn noticed that she'd found a strip of cloth somewhere and had wrapped it around her hand to stop the bleeding. "And who in the name of Mother Dark are *you*?"

The crone sniffed, as if annoyed at being questioned so brazenly. "Just a dusty old relic, daughter of Shadow." Her gaze moved to the radiance welling from the fragment lodged in Heth's chest. "I knew something was afoot when I wandered my way to your dreary home, and so I decided to keep a close eye on what was going on. And now here we are . . . But the web that someone was spinning is now well and truly shredded." She pointed a gnarled finger at the white-glowing fragment. "*That* will change everything. This may be the birth of a new age . . . or at least the end of the current one."

"There is a shard beneath this ruin," Heth said haltingly, his hand drifting to the crystal sunk in his flesh. "A bigger one than this. And it is made of light . . . beautiful light." His eyes became distant, as if reliving whatever he had experienced.

"The Heart of the Heart, Algeroth's own essence," the old woman said. "Stolen away by the empress in the last days of Gendurdrang. We always wondered if it had been destroyed." She scowled, looking almost cross. "And we searched this place! How in the name of the Twelve did it stay hidden?"

"There was a guardian," Heth added, his brow furrowing like he was having trouble remembering what had happened. "A lion, I think. I don't know, it's muddled. The memories fade like a dream. It spoke to me, I think. It said . . . it said I had the blood of emperors in me. The blood of Segulah Tain."

"Of course you do," the old woman said. "You're what they call Hollow, aren't you?"

Rhenna shook her head fiercely. "But the Hollow can't bear shards. Everyone knows that."

The old woman's bristly grey brows rose, and she snorted loudly. "Well, if everyone knows it, then it must be true. Just disregard the fellow here with the shard in his chest, I suppose. Ah, to have the foolish certainty of youth once again. Life was so much simpler." She sighed deeply, then tapped her chin as if considering something. "Oh, I might as well," she finally said, then beckoned towards Alia. "Come here, dear. Let's finish upending your wise mistress's world. It offends me that you are still bereft."

Alia looked uncertainly at Rhenna, but still she stepped closer to the crone. Grumbling to herself, the old woman rooted around in another of her hanging bags, then withdrew something hidden in her fist. "Here, child. Hold out your hand." Hesitatingly Alia raised her arm, and the old woman tipped whatever she held into the Wild girl's open palm. Deryn caught a flash of green light, and then Alia gasped like she had been stung, holding her hand to her chest as she stumbled back. Deryn leaped forward, catching her just as she swooned and fell.

"Peace, daughter of Shadow," the old woman muttered, and Deryn glanced up from the unconscious Alia to find that Rhenna had summoned a javelin of darkness and had leveled it at the crone. "I did not hurt her. In truth, I gifted her what has always been her birthright."

Deryn's attention returned to Alia as she drew in a shuddering breath, her eyes fluttering open. It must have been his imagination, but he thought they looked to be an even darker shade of jade than a moment ago.

"Oh," Alia whispered, unclenching her hand slowly. In the center of her palm was nestled a green-glowing fragment, earth-colored veins radiating out like roots.

"You were always meant for the Seed," the old woman said with more than a little satisfaction. "Just as the boy was destined to bear the Light." She waved dismissively at Deryn and Rhenna. "While you two were far less discriminating."

Rhenna lowered her arm, the shadow-javelin evaporating. She was staring at the green radiance spilling from Alia's hand in open-mouthed astonishment.

The old woman jerked her head around to look to the north, the sudden movement startling them all. She frowned, her face creasing in concern.

"Eh. I suppose I couldn't pour forth the Tears this deep in the Lands. I can feel Old Boney looking this way now." She turned to stare disapprovingly at Deryn. "Not to mention someone just invited the Others to step into this world for the first time in several centuries, and the reverberations of *that* will be felt by many. Won't be long until *he* dispatches a Horror or two from Gendurdrang to investigate – he hates it when we Elowyn trespass, but even more when the other realms spill into this one. I'll have to be off, and I suggest you all make yourself scarce as well, if you wish to keep your skin attached to your bodies."

"But . . . where should we go?" Deryn asked numbly, his head reeling as he tried to come to grips with everything that had just happened.

"First decent question any of you have asked," the old woman said grudgingly. "If I were you, I'd seek out the House of Last Light in Karath. I am bound only to observe, not interfere . . . but the one who dwells there wears no such shackles. If a new age is truly dawning, he may be willing to give you answers, perhaps even aid. Or not. He is as fickle as the rest of us, and not constrained by the old oaths."

With that strange pronouncement, she turned and hobbled a few steps towards the tumbled ruins, as if she meant to simply walk away from them. Then she paused and turned back, looking directly at Rhenna. "Oh, there is something else, daughter of Shadow. Something that even the dweller in the House might not know . . . and an offer to trade *this* information might just be enough to crack open his door."

"What is that?" Rhenna asked quietly, clearly bewildered.

"The one that sat beside your father that night in the Duskhold, the pale woman. You know of whom I speak?"

Rhenna nodded, the confusion in her face deepening further. "I do."

"Well, I've seen her before. Different face, but I'd recognize her anywhere. I was standing in the great square of Ezarin in the city of Derambinal, watching from among the chanting crowd as she placed a copper crown on the brow of Osmari an-Alams and declared him shah of all the Salah and true heir to the Radiant Emperor."

"What?" Rhenna murmured, frowning. "Leantha? How is that possible?"

The old woman shrugged. "Hells if I know."

A terrific crack sounded from behind Deryn, and he whirled around to see a shudder pass through one of the largest pillars still standing. Cracks spread, becoming fissures, and then it collapsed, raising a huge cloud of dust.

When he turned back to the old woman she was gone.

"Well," Deryn said into the long silence that followed. None of them seemed to be able to summon up a better response to what had just happened.

Rhenna shook herself, as if waking from a dream. She looked troubled and confused and exhausted in equal measures. After a moment of staring at where the old woman had disappeared, she turned her tired eyes to Deryn, still holding her wounded hand to her chest.

"Where is Yvrin?"

"She was a good woman," Deryn said softly, standing a few paces behind Rhenna as she knelt beside Yvrin's body.

"She saved us," Heth said. "She saved us all. We never would have escaped the ambush or survived in the Lands if she hadn't been there. She could have fled after she rescued her horse, ridden back to the Duskhold or her homeland . . . but she returned to us, even though she knew we were being hunted."

Rhenna brushed Yvrin's eyes closed. She glanced up as Alia emerged from the forest of pillars leading the two horses. The Wild girl had left them somewhere she thought they'd be safe, and apparently they hadn't panicked and run off during the very loud and very destructive battle with the blood-sharded.

They were very good horses.

Rhenna sat back on her haunches, the breeze stirring her long black hair as the horses approached. About halfway across the courtyard, the behavior of the stallion suddenly changed. Instead of calmly plodding along behind Alia, he broke into a trot, heading straight for where Yvrin lay.

Rhenna watched him, her face impassive.

When he arrived at the body of his mistress, he lowered his head and gently nudged her shoulder with his nose. He stayed staring down at her after she did not respond, and Deryn could sense an awareness in the depths of his eyes.

Rhenna rose and came to stand beside the horse, laying her hand on his muzzle. The stallion did not turn to look at her, his attention fixed on Yvrin.

After a long moment Rhenna turned to Deryn. Her face was calm, but the anger in her eyes almost made him flinch back.

"How did she die?"

"She was stabbed in the back," Deryn said quietly. "She fought well. We killed the flame-sharded, then she broke Vertus's chains . . . and he struck her down."

"Vertus?" Rhenna said, looking around at the other sprawled bodies. "I thought he must have been killed in the fight since he didn't come find me after. He killed her?" She shook her head, clearly incredulous that such a thing could happen. "I've known him since he was a boy. He was an ass, yes, but you could not find anyone more loyal to the Shadow. He was injured . . . perhaps also tortured. Did some madness come over him?" She peered more closely at the corpses. "Where *is* he?"

Deryn dragged his gaze from the grieving horse and indicated the body of the man Heth had slain. He was lying face-down, but even still, it was obvious that he was not Vertus.

Frowning in confusion, Rhenna left the stallion's side and approached the body. Showing no respect to the dead man, she roughly grabbed him by the shoulder and flipped him over. His head flopped unnaturally, barely still attached to his neck.

"That is not Vertus," she said matter-of-factly.

"It looked like him, I swear," Deryn said, coming to stand beside her. "After he died this is who he turned into."

Rhenna crouched beside the corpse, fingering the hem of the robes it wore. "These clothes look like something from the Duskhold. But there's no talent from any of the Sharded of any hold that can make a man look like someone else." She picked up the dagger the man had dropped when he'd fallen, examining it as light shimmered along its curving blade. "A sharded weapon," she murmured. "But not shadow-sharded. I don't know what is inside it, and I'm certain Vertus never had such a dagger. He would have flaunted it if he did." Rhenna frowned, then hooked the tip of the blade under the robe's collar. "Let's see what's under here."

With a deft motion, she sliced open the front of the robes, revealing the pale skin beneath and the point of radiance sunk into his flesh. Her confusion deepened as she examined the shard, and then she sighed and brought her hand to his chest. The skin rippled like water as her fingers slipped within and closed around the fragment, then with a grunt that might have been distaste she pulled it free with a wet ripping sound.

The shard immediately broke apart into smaller fragments. Her confusion deepened into disbelief as she examined what was in her hand.

"Mother Dark," she whispered, offering up what she held for Deryn to see. "How can this be?"

For a moment Deryn didn't understand what had surprised her. There were only four fragments – he distinctly remembered Vertus claiming to be eight-sharded – but since this was clearly not Vertus, that shouldn't have elicited such a reaction from Rhenna. Was it . . .

Oh.

The radiance seeping from each of the four small fragments was a different hue. He thought back to the shards that he'd claimed from the skeleton . . . yes, they'd all looked the same, very similar to the color of the shadow-shard sunk in his own chest. But here he saw one was reddish-brown, another a cloudy grey, another the gloaming dark of a shadow-shard, and the last looked almost transparent.

"They're all different," Deryn said, and Rhenna nodded as she shook the hand holding the fragments in his direction.

"Yes! When a newly-claimed fragment is merged with a shard, it loses whatever aspect it once had." She plucked the reddish-brown fragment from her palm, holding it up. "This looks like a blood-shard to me. I'm almost certain that one is a wind-shard. And there's no doubt that's a shadow-shard."

Deryn thought back to their battle with the man masquerading as Vertus. "He used blood and wind powers when we were fighting, I'm sure of it."

"That *should* be impossible," Rhenna murmured. She set the umber fragment down and picked up the clear shard. "And what is this? It's like nothing I've ever seen before." She held it higher and it flashed like a crystal refracting light. "A man who could change his face . . . no, his whole body. A shard that does not absorb other fragments, but lets them remain distinct . . . a Sharded able to draw upon powers from those different aspects . . ." She clenched her hand around the crystal shard. "Who killed this man?" she asked after a long moment.

"I did," Heth said, stepping forward.

Rhenna held out the three different-colored fragments towards him. He stared at her arm blankly for a moment before realizing what she was doing, then hurriedly presented to her his open hand. She tipped the glowing shards into his palm as he goggled incredulously at the fragments.

"Those belong to you," she said, and his wide eyes flicked up to her face. He looked about to protest, but then hesitated, his mouth hanging open.

"You're one of the Sharded Few now," she said, and then added after a long pause, "Somehow."

Heth snapped his jaw shut, swallowing hard.

Rhenna pinched the clear fragment between two fingers and raised it again to the light, squinting into its glowing depths. "I wish to keep this one. Not to merge it, but because I want to find someone who can tell me what it is . . ."

"Of course," Heth said quietly. Deryn noticed he hadn't closed his hand over the fragments he held, as if certain this was all a mistake and they would be taken from him soon.

Rhenna nodded at his agreement, then slipped the fragment into a pocket. "Perhaps Saelus will know . . ." she began, then grimaced.

An uncomfortable silence descended. Deryn glanced at Heth and Alia and found that they were both staring at Rhenna, who had lowered her head.

"What do we do now?" Deryn asked, giving voice to the question they were all thinking.

After a few more long moments of contemplation, Rhenna looked up again. "We could return to the Duskhold."

Deryn met Heth's startled eyes. He clearly remembered what the blood-sharded had claimed.

"Do you think it's possible what that man said is true?" he asked, surprised by his own brazenness.

Rhenna's eyes narrowed. "No," she snapped with a note of finality.

"Are you certain?" Deryn dared, trying not to flinch at the anger he saw in her eyes. "Because if you're wrong, we'll all be dead."

He braced himself for her response, but to his surprise, the fury building in her suddenly flickered and died. Her shoulders slumped, almost like in defeat.

"No," she said, her voice barely a whisper. "I'm not sure."

Alia hurried over to Rhenna and gathered her into an embrace. The daughter of Cael Shen nearly collapsed into her handmaiden, burying her face in Alia's shoulder.

Deryn and Heth shared a long, uncomfortable look. With Yvrin gone, the mantle of leadership must fall to Rhenna. But she seemed broken by everything that had just happened; her entire world had been shattered, the pieces ground into oblivion.

"I understand little of what is going on," Alia said, the steadiness of her voice surprising Deryn. "But that old woman is someone special. And she said we could find answers in the city of Karath, in the House of Last Light. I say we go there."

"Yes . . . Karath," Deryn said slowly. "Kilian told me that was where the Unbound King was supposed to reside. He hides there because the shards have no power in that city, and so the holds cannot send hunters after him."

"Hunters like might still be pursuing us," Heth add.

"Oh, you can be sure they will be," Rhenna murmured, pushing away from Alia. Her gaze moved from Deryn to Heth and then finally to Alia, where it stayed. After a long moment, she nodded.

"Karath, then. We find Xend an-Azith and force him to tell us if he was behind this attack . . . and if so, why. Then if the House of Last Light is not the invention of a madwoman, we will see what answers lie there. Because I have many, many questions." The strength had returned to her voice, as if that moment of doubt and weakness had never happened. "We have two shards that should not exist." Rhenna looked at Heth as her wrapped hand drifted to the pocket where she'd put the clear fragment. "Along with a crone who appears and vanishes like a spirit and carries a seed-shard in her pocket. Not to mention a Sharded who could change his face and use powers drawn from different fragments." She shook her head, her expression rueful. "And to think, my greatest concern just a few days ago was how to escape my impending marriage."

With a new purpose in her stride, she went over to the stallion and gathered its reins in her hands, then looked back at them all. "We have little time to waste. Take all the shards of the fallen as quickly as you can. There will be others coming after us, and soon. We must be gone before they get here."

She paused, her hand on the bridle, then turned slowly back to the rest of them. There were emotions in her face that Deryn could not immediately identify – worry, perhaps? Uncertainty?

"You do not have to come with me," she finally said haltingly, keeping her gaze fixed on the ground, as if by meeting their eyes she would be exercising some authority she felt she no longer had the right to wield. "Truthfully, you should not come with me. I am dangerous to you all. You could leave me and be safe from whatever hunters come next – they want me, not you."

"I choose to stay," Alia said, stepping closer. Her fingers gently pried apart Rhenna's clenched fist so she could slip her hand inside. "I do not abandon my friends."

Rhenna raised her face to Alia, and despite everything they had all been through he was still surprised by how vulnerable she looked, the relief that now softened the features he'd once found so imperious and cold.

"I will go with you and lend what help I can," Deryn found himself saying, and although he didn't know what was guiding his arm he raised his porcelain sword as if swearing an oath upon the blood-streaked blade.

Rhenna lowered her eyes gratefully at this, and then they all turned to Heth. The slaver's son who had once flayed his back blinked at their sudden attention, as if incredulous that they would ask him to join this madness.

"What?" he said, shaking his head in what looked like disappointment. "Of course I'm coming."

EPILOGUE

KALISS CROUCHED at the edge of the underground lake, staring out across the glass-smooth waters. From behind her welled the spectral light of the little white-stone gazebo, ghostly serpents shimmering upon the dark surface. She felt numb. Broken. The heavy silence of the cavern echoed inside her.

How could he be dead?

Her hand closed around one of the shards of black stone scattered about the shore and she squeezed, its sharp edges pressing into her skin. Kaliss wished for a moment that she was not Sharded, that she could slice herself open and feel the hot blood sliding down her arm ... that she could feel anything except for this aching emptiness.

With a flick of her wrist, she sent the stone skittering across the lake. She hadn't believed the news at first. When the searchers had returned and breathlessly spoken of finding the missing wedding procession, of a field of charred wagons and burned corpses, she had refused to even entertain the thought that Deryn could be among the dead. Surely he had escaped. Surely his story would not end like that, a victim of the hateful and jealous Flame.

But then Cael Shen had returned from his own investigations, and the rage and grief in his face had destroyed the hope she'd so tenaciously clung to.

They were dead. They were all dead.

The last of the ripples faded. Once again, the lake was still, and if she held her breath it would be like nothing living was here . . .

Kaliss turned her head sharply, a shiver of movement drawing her attention. She hissed when she saw a figure moving across the arching ribbon of black stone that connected this island to the cavern's entrance. Anger flared within her – this place was *her* sanctuary. Her secret. How dare anyone else invade it? She rose, her hands clenched at her sides.

Cold surprise washed over her when she realized who was approaching. The gazebo's pale light slid across alabaster skin, disappearing when it touched a high-necked dress of spun shadows. Leantha's face was as white and serene as the moon as she glided closer, her heavy-lidded eyes fixed on Kaliss. She carried an ornate box, carved black wood set with white stones that burned with their own soft radiance. Kaliss swallowed, shifting her weight from foot to foot, unsure what she should do.

"Mistress Leantha," she said, ducking her head respectfully as this unnerving apparition stepped from the bridge and onto the black stone of the island.

"Kaliss," the pale woman murmured, "I thought I might find you here."

"You did?" she answered without thinking and then chided herself.

The ghost of a smile tugged at the edges of Leantha's mouth. "Yes. Come, let us retire to the pavilion."

Bewildered, Kaliss followed the pale woman as she drifted into the gazebo. Leantha paused for a moment, then placed her burden on the stone table before settling gracefully onto one of the benches.

"Please," she said, indicating that Kaliss should sit.

Which she did, her thoughts racing as she tried and failed to come up with a reasonable explanation for this visit.

Leantha was quiet for a moment, her gaze slowly traveling around the inside of the gazebo.

"It has been a long time," she finally said, placing her hands on the table.

"You've been here before?" Kaliss asked, then closed her mouth with a click. Why was she questioning one of the most powerful Sharded in the Duskhold?

"A long time ago," Leantha said softly, her finger tracing the gameboard incised into the stone. "It has not changed at all . . . like an insect caught in amber." Her piercingly black eyes moved from the table to Kaliss. "But the rest of the world marches on, whether or not we wish it to."

"Yes," whispered Kaliss. She knew about what Leantha was speaking.

"Cael Shen has declared war on the Ember," the pale woman murmured, still holding Kaliss's gaze. "It is expected that the Windwrack will join us shortly."

"Good," Kaliss said, her voice strengthening slightly. "They must pay for what they've done."

Leantha's head dipped slightly in agreement. "Indeed. But this war will not be easy, even with the might of the Shadow and Storm united. The Ember is a great fortress, and the Flame – while lacking in subtlety – is a mighty force for destruction."

"I am ready to fight," Kaliss promised.

"I know," Leantha replied. "And I believe you can be a great weapon in the coming struggle."

"Truly?" asked Kaliss, surprised. While she was nearly ready to merge her fourth fragment, there were a hundred Sharded in the hold stronger than her.

"The Duskhold has many warriors," Leantha said as if she'd glimpsed her thoughts, "but none with your . . . unique skills."

Kaliss went very still. Surely, Leantha was not aware of her past, who she had once been. Only one man had ever known, and he had died with a knife between his ribs.

Kaliss's knife.

"No one else in the Duskhold was ever the apprentice of Mazim Chain, the Black Hood of Phane."

Kaliss's fingers itched. She remembered the feel of the hilt in her hand as she stabbed Mazim once, twice, three times. He had been expecting an embrace, but there had been no surprise in his face as she thrust the blade into his heart, just as he'd taught her. He had smiled.

She would never forget that smile.

Leantha suddenly rose, and Kaliss drew in a shuddering breath as she was pulled from her memories.

"I wish to become your patron, Kaliss. You will never want for shards, and I shall help you reach your full potential as one of the Sharded Few. In return, you will enter my service and aid me as I help our master prosecute his war with the Flame."

Kaliss stared at Leantha, still struggling to understand how the White Spider of the Duskhold had learned these things about her.

"What do you say?" Leantha asked, her voice sharper.

Kaliss slowly stood. She was not much smaller than Leantha, but the pale woman seemed to tower over her. "I will serve you," she said softly.

"Very good," Leantha said with a smile that did not touch her eyes. "And to seal our new arrangement, I have brought a gift for you." She unsnapped the latches of the box on the table, then lifted the lid.

Kaliss sucked in her breath. Nestled in a bed of velvet was a silver-bladed dagger, a leering skull carved into its ebony pommel. It was beautiful . . . and she had seen it before.

"This was my master's," she whispered, numb with surprise. "I couldn't find it after . . . after he died. How do you have it?"

Leantha's blank expression gave nothing away. "This has been in my possession for a long, long time. Any resemblance must be a coincidence."

Kaliss reached her hand out slowly, the sense of wading through a dream nearly overwhelming. It really did look the same. Her fingers closed around the smooth grip, and she lifted the dagger from the box. Light slid along the silvery blade, and she could have sworn she felt something stirring within the hilt where it pressed against her palm, a rhythmic throbbing.

Like a pulse.

"It's beautiful," she murmured, turning the dagger this way and that to catch more of the radiance seeping from the gazebo's stone.

Hello, Kaliss.

The words slithered into her mind, soft and sibilant.

Kaliss gasped, but she did not drop the dagger. Her eyes flew to Leantha, who was watching her carefully. Knowingly.

Together, we will do great things.

Hey readers, thank you so much for finishing the first book of The Sharded Few. I truly hope you enjoyed the tale - it was fun to build a new fantasy epic, and I'm excited to reveal more of the world as our characters search for answers to the mysteries presented in the final chapters. The second book will take them to Karath and Ashasai and Gendurdrang and the Ember, and I'm excited to bring you all on the journey.

If you enjoyed the book, I would be thrilled for a review on Amazon or Goodreads. They are of tremendous importance to authors, and we are always hugely appreciative.

Take care, and happy reading.

Alec

ACKNOWLEDGMENTS

As always I have many thanks to give to those who helped bring this book into existence. First, thank you to Davon Collins and Phil Tucker, who read the first iteration of the book and provided excellent feedback. Thank you to Sundeep Agarwal for the fantastic advice and eagle-eye for spotting mistakes. Thank you also to my wife, Shining, who somehow didn't get sick of me during our month-long lockdown confined together in our apartment in Shanghai. And thank you to Wang Jian, who provided great support during all those morning writing sessions at the Tianping Community Center on Wulumuqi Road.

ABOUT THE AUTHOR

Alec Hutson grew up in a geodesic dome and a bookstore and he currently lives in Shanghai, China. If you would like to keep current with his writing, please sign up for his newsletter at www. authoralechutson.com.

ALSO BY ALEC HUTSON